THE DARK FEATHER

By Anna Stephens

Godblind
Darksoul
Bloodchild

The Stone Knife
The Jaguar Path

THE
DARK
FEATHER

ANNA STEPHENS

HARPER
Voyager

Harper*Voyager*
An imprint of HarperCollins*Publishers* Ltd
1 London Bridge Street
London SE1 9GF

www.harpercollins.co.uk

HarperCollins*Publishers*
Macken House,
39/40 Mayor Street Upper,
Dublin 1
D01 C9W8
Ireland

First published by HarperCollins*Publishers* Ltd 2024
1

A catalogue record for this book is available from the British Library.

ISBN: 978-0-00-840410-9 (HB)

Typeset in Sabon LT Std by
Palimpsest Book Production Ltd, Falkirk, Stirlingshire

Printed and Bound in the UK using 100% Renewable Electricity
at CPI Group (UK) Ltd

For the poodle.
You're not quite as brave as Ossa, buddy,
but we do love you.

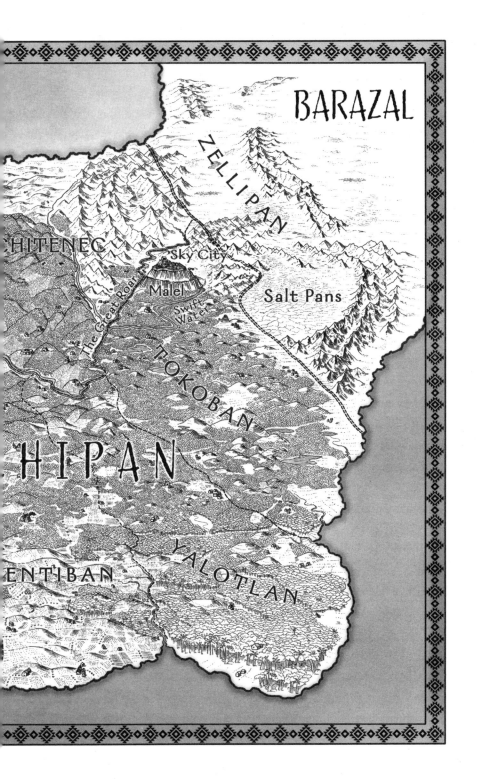

Malel.

We cry to you, O Malel. In the darkness and in our doubt. In the sun and in our shame. At highsun and in hope. O Malel. O patient, still and silent Snake-Sister and you, O great and sudden Jaguar-Brother.

Please.

Your children cry.

TAYAN

Tayan woke in the dark, groggy with dreams. Dreams of home and of Lilla, the song winding through both and glorifying them. His song.

It flowed and bloomed gently in the night, sharpening only slightly with his waking. A song of power, of strength and majesty, calling for unity. Even in his sleep, Tayan's song yearned for peace. And still that peace was resisted, threatened, denied.

"Don't let this be you," Lilla had begged him on the day he'd proposed a peace-weaving to end the uprising. As if what Tayan was now – Shadow of the Singer; Singer in all but name, the gold of magic seething beneath his skin – was wrong. As if this ability to unify all peoples in peace could ever be wrong.

Tayan rolled onto his back and brushed long strands of hair from his face, stretching in the cool of the night beneath the brightly patterned blankets that shrouded him and the Singer.

Lilla had never looked so beautiful as he had that day in the plaza, radiant in his defiance, his broken rage, with the sun in his hair and brightening the paint on his brow and cheeks, his arms and hands. How much more beautiful would he be when he accepted Tayan's song into his heart?

Yet he'd chosen violence and delusion. He'd looked at the gifts Tayan could give him, of song and peace and security, and he'd thrown them back in his face. As if he'd been offered bitter poison instead of sweet honey.

As if all Tayan's glory and majesty and power were to be pitied, not worshipped. As if *he* was to be pitied instead of worshipped. Lilla had stood in Feather Ekon's restraining arms – the fake Feather who'd become his lover – and chosen to judge Tayan, Shadow of the Singer. *Judge him.* The hypocrisy was breath-taking, even now more than a month later, and despite everything Tayan had to worry about, it still crept up on him at little random moments. Who was Lilla to accuse him of betrayal when he'd been enthusiastically fucking a man he believed to be Pechaqueh? How dare he suddenly develop a conscience as to which elements of Pechaqueh society he allowed into his life? His *body*?

Don't let this be you. As if what Tayan was now wasn't strength and purpose and destiny. Wasn't the only path to peace for all of them. The Shadow's hand rose to his clavicles, bare of the marriage cord that had lain against them for almost a decade. He'd never thought of its weight as anything but symbolic until it hadn't been there anymore and he'd found himself, over and over in the last weeks, scratching around the neckline of his tunic searching for it. Nor had he expected how much it would hurt, casting that cord from himself. Lilla hadn't claimed him; Lilla had left him to slavery and degradation and taken a lover to replace him. Lilla was standing against him in a war that was threatening to tear apart their world. It should have been easy.

And yet.

Tayan stared into the darkness of the ceiling, knowing it was for the best despite how much it had hurt. He might not wear a marriage cord now, but his throat was adorned in promise nonetheless: the twin dark feathers tattooed by Xac himself, proclaiming Tayan to be the next Singer of the Empire of Songs.

If not even Lilla could understand what he was doing here

in the source, what he was striving to accomplish for the sake of all Ixachipan, none of them could. *Then they must be shown their errors and the way forward into peace. I do it for them.*

Next to him, Xac stirred and mewled. Tayan watched him in the light of a single flickering candle. The life and spirit he'd stolen from his Shadow in the weeks before the ritual and the beginning of the uprising was finally beginning to leave him, draining away. The health and strength and ruddy glow to his skin were fading and soon enough his physical appearance would once more match that of his mind, spirit, and emotions: wavering, weak, vacillating. The helpless fool that Enet in her treachery had created.

Not strong enough to be Singer in anything more than name. And so he wasn't.

For the sake of the Empire of Songs and its survival through this most recent – *and, Setatmeh be good, final* – uprising, Tayan had assumed the burden of the Singer's duties. For Xac's own sake, he had restricted his access to the song so that he might heal from the great exertion of attempting to wake the world spirit.

Liar.

Xac was awake and watching him in turn, his eyes glittering in the darkness.

'My sweet?' Tayan asked carefully. There was no response. They gazed at each other for long seconds, the night breathing around them, the shift of Chorus warriors outside their room and – far enough away not to cause alarm – a single piercing scream. Out in the city, the violence didn't sleep.

'Rest, my love,' he murmured, caressing Xac's cheekbone with his fingertips. 'Our Empire needs us strong if we are to defeat our enemies.'

'Our Empire?' he rasped, his breath sour with honeypot and chillies.

Tayan smiled reassuringly, his hand falling from Xac's face. 'The Empire of Songs belongs to all right-minded loyal subjects. It is ours just as it is Pilos's and Atu's and Xochi's. I mean no offence, my sweet. You are tired and it clouds your mind so that you see poison where there is only nectar.'

Xac began to sit up and the Shadow tightened his grip on the dribble of magic he allowed into him. The Singer gasped and flopped back on the mattress, straining for air and his song alike. 'Sleep, my love,' Tayan repeated, imbuing his words with magic and his skin with gold. 'Things will seem better with the dawn.'

Liar.

Tayan watched him a little longer. 'Yes.'

Nothing was better with the dawn.

Not for Tayan, and certainly not for Xac or the Empire of Songs. One of the Pechaqueh enclaves in the southern quarter of the city had fallen to the traitors through the night. There were no survivors. Instead, thirty-four heads had been hurled over the ramshackle protective wall they'd constructed around the pyramid and its attendant temples and patch of plaza and into the tiny, squalid little world within. The city within the city. The heart and spirit of the Empire.

Thirty-four heads. All ages. All genders.

Listener Citla, who'd arrived with High Feather Atu and the First Talon, had been contacted in a desperate request for aid when the attack began, and although they'd sent warriors in response, they'd been too late to save anyone.

She knelt before Tayan and Xac and swayed gently, deep within Tayan's – the Singer's – song. Citla was the source's only remaining Listener, excepting Tayan and perhaps Xac himself, and the constant drain on her spirit from remaining open to communication was beginning to tell. She was scrawny and haggard, deep circles under her eyes, and her lips flaky and raw from chewing.

Tayan himself prowled the currents of the song for a few hours each day, seeking out Feathers and Listeners across all Ixachipan for updates, hungry for news of victories and receiving word of an equivalent number of defeats. Unlike the Listeners, the song-magic was his to command and move within so that he felt little ill effect from such spirit-journeys, but for now he had more important things to do than aid Citla. She would adjust; she must not break. For this at least, though, he could be compassionate.

'You were witness to the deaths, Citla? Show me.'

Sweat slid down the Listener's bald head but she held out her hands and Tayan took them, allowing himself to be swept into her memories within the song. The reason for her nervousness became clear: they watched through the eyes of a Pecha with a strong connection to the song – a councillor, Tayan realised, recognising them – as Lilla, Xessa, and Tiamoko led the assault on the compound. They moved with lethal grace and an utter lack of mercy, systematically killing everyone who stood against them and those who didn't. Those who fled. Cutting them down. There was a terrifying blankness in Tiamoko's eyes and a hot vicious righteousness in Xessa's, visible in glimpses in between frantic running and flailing defence.

Lilla was power and caution and explosive movement. No twisted justice marred his gaunt features, thinner than he'd been when they met to weave a peace and instead danced amid death. No, Lilla wore an expression of something approaching care. Almost a regret. As if he was killing vermin that had got into the stores. An unfortunate necessity, but not one to be enjoyed.

Again, his hypocrisy and fake solicitude stole Tayan's breath, for only a handful of hours later, they'd been throwing the severed heads of these dying Pechaqueh over the walls to taunt him. How dare Lilla pretend to nobility of purpose, pretend to care for those he slaughtered? How *dare he*?

Righteousness, justice, regret? They had no conception of these words, just as they had no conception of what Tayan was doing or why what they were flailing against was the inevitability of peace and progress.

Even caught up as he was in Citla's vision of the events, Tayan surged into the song, determined to show them what could be if only they laid down their weapons and listened.

He drew its magic to him, wrapped himself in cords and ropes and wreaths of gold, and spun his song into something of such aching beauty that, in the flesh world, Citla jerked on her knees and began to weep. Tayan's plea for peace and promise of unity soared through the source, the great pyramid, and out across the Empire of Songs.

Moments like this still caught him by surprise as he learnt the limits – or lack of limits – to his abilities as Shadow of the Singer. A splinter of his consciousness surveyed the source and the rest of him watched Citla's memories and still he could manipulate the song into this wondrous magic. In the remembered slaughter, the councillor who had contacted Citla when the attack began was cut down, Tiamoko's young, empty eyes the last thing they saw.

Tayan let go of the Listener's hands and swept back through the song and into his body, gently detaching several clinging, questing tendrils of Xac's that had latched on to the magic during his preoccupation. He opened his eyes and nodded once at Citla, who looked ghastly, and then put his hand on Xac's knee and squeezed. Reassurance. Deterrence.

Warning.

'Listener Citla, take some rest,' the Shadow said, gesturing to the low bed piled with pillows that had been moved into the source proper for her. Tayan liked to keep her close. The Listener bowed shakily and he gestured for Xochi to help the woman stand. 'Please ensure she eats and drinks before sleeping,' he added in a low voice.

'Thank you for all you do in the song, Shadow. For your support to our holy lord during his convalescence and this rebellion. His glory is undimmed in part because of you,' Citla croaked.

If not for the two years enslaved by Enet and the sun-years as a peace-weaver that had taught him restraint and diplomacy, Tayan might have told her what he thought of such backhanded praise that utterly failed to acknowledge just how deep his assistance went. Just who held the power in their hands and bent it towards stability, freedom, harmony. He glanced sideways at Xac, sitting to all intents and purposes serene and strong, wielding his magic and above such petty concerns as those happening in his source.

It is for the best, Tayan reminded himself. *They are not ready – yet – to accept me. Their prejudices and traditions are dense bamboo hiding the trail. They will see soon enough. When I gift them peace, they will understand.*

'Rest, Listener,' he repeated easily, and Xochi beckoned another warrior to lead the woman away before returning to her place to one side of Xac and his Shadow. Opposite them, High Feather Atu and Spear Pilos waited in patient, adoring silence, the song lifting them as it lifted all who loved it and understood its message.

Tayan deliberately put the image of Tiamoko's face, twisted with effort but otherwise empty of emotion, in his mind's eye and inhaled, slow and long through his nose. He was the Shadow of the Singer, doing all in his power to ease Xac's recovery and taking as much of the divine burden as he could. And also the very earthly burdens, such as making decisions that materially affected the direction of the war for peace. There was a splash from the offering pool and Tayan inclined his head in that direction. The third burden – *no, this one is not a burden, this is my greatest privilege* – was the sacred task given him by the holy Setatmeh to fix the song and heal them.

Heal the Singer. Bring peace to Ixachipan. Fix the song.

The first he was doing, slow as that progress was. The second was proceeding and mostly out of his hands except for his crafting of the song. The third . . . required work. Time. Intuition. None of which he had when his every day was taken up with the first two.

Tayan willed himself to serenity. 'Show me the latest,' he said. Pilos and Atu prostrated themselves again before Pilos slid forward his painted map of Ixachipan, lovingly rendered in vibrant colours. Cities and landmarks, rivers and lakes, trails and trade routes, were all clearly marked. It was a fascinating object in its own right, and Tayan had studied it voraciously many times. The maps in Tokoban were never so detailed, for his people hadn't travelled so extensively.

The ten Melody Talons were represented by carved idols: small, flat triangles for the slaves, reminiscent of their brands; dogs for the dog warrior Talons; and feathers for the eagles. A simple wooden block identified the single hawk Talon Pilos had created back when he'd been High Feather.

Ten Talons; eight lands. It should be simple. It wasn't.

The triangles of the Eighth and Ninth slave Talons sat ignored by Atu's knee: those that hadn't rebelled had been executed weeks back at the start of the uprising. The First was in the Singing City and each of the other seven surviving Talons fought in one land, isolated, trying with three thousand warriors to bring peace and order to tens of thousands of traitors and civilians.

'It's not working, is it?' Tayan asked softly, staring at the map. The order he'd given Atu when summoning him and the First Talon to their defence – that he had two weeks to crush the rebellion – had encouraged the young High Feather to spread his Melody thin, thinking a show of strength and savagery across the whole Empire of Songs would bring the traitors to their senses. It had been a good plan, in Tayan's limited understanding, and in some areas it had worked. Some, not all. For more than a week now, Atu and Pilos had been insistent they needed to change tactics, consolidate their numbers, move out of some locations to reinforce others.

Tayan had resisted, knowing what that would do to hearten those who'd risen against his song. But each day's reports, the slow attrition of Citla's mind under the onslaught of Feathers calling for aid, and the relentless grind of battle in the Singing City itself, had finally convinced him otherwise.

'What is your suggestion?'

Pilos and Atu looked at each other with naked relief mixed with apprehension. Tayan clenched his fists; he wasn't going to like whatever came next.

'The Second Talon under Feather Detta is in Xentiban. We

call them here to reinforce us and have the Sixth and Third pull out of Tokoban and Yalotlan to together bring Xentiban back in line. That land will then protect our flank.' Atu's voice was calm and measured, as if such an outcome was not in doubt.

Tayan stared between them, suspicious. 'And why are the lands to the north less valuable? Why are they the ones to be abandoned? Is Tokoban not rich in songstone, the richest mines discovered in two generations?'

'The retired free who travel to lands newly brought under the song are always the most tenacious, Shadow,' Pilos said. 'They know they are carving a life out of a land not yet soaked in song-magic. A land resistant to their efforts to civilise it. As such, the warriors who have settled Tokoban and Yalotlan are fierce and determined. They've spent two years making the cities and towns their own, establishing the song and Pechaqueh society, and learning the land and trails. They are holding well, even without the aid of the Sixth and Third Talons. Many of the traitors rising against us are fighting for the land and tribe they were born to and that makes them more determined, makes them cling harder to their delusions. Tokoban and Yalotlan are the safest lands for us to leave to fend for themselves because of how empty of their own people they are. Once we have settled the rest of the Empire, we can return our attention to them.'

'As for the Zellih skirmishes,' Atu added, as if they'd rehearsed this, 'it appears they were just that. Feather Calan has had reports of groups of people moving, but no direct evidence or interaction with confirmed Zellih war bands. It is likely civilians have seen panicked traitors fleeing the consequences of their actions and thought them to be Zellih. We no longer consider Zellipan to be a threat.'

Everything they said made sense, and yet something in Tayan's spirit still quailed at the thought of Tokoban being forgotten.

And that is good. It proves that I am still firmly a part of Ixachipan, that I am not lost as Xac my love is lost. I still walk Mal— the world's skin and I can still grieve for the loss of life to come, wherever in Ixachipan that happens.

It was only natural he be attached to the memory of the place that had birthed and raised him, despite the vast knowledge he had acquired in the months since becoming Shadow and understanding the scale and greatness of his destiny. He knew now that Malel, Jaguar-Brother, and Snake-Sister were tales of the sort told to children to help them make sense of the world before they could understand truths that were bigger, deeper and often darker. Malel and her God-born, Tokoban and its traditions, weren't wrong in the same way those stories weren't wrong; they were just . . . simpler. But Tayan had grown up. He'd put aside childish stories and stepped into those darker truths and they had granted him real, true power and the ability to change the world for the better. And as those truths were sometimes hard to bear, so too were the choices he needed to make – and their consequences.

Even so, he couldn't quite stifle the hollow howl of anguish in his chest. The love of land and gods – *Malel, we cry to you, O Malel* – was strong. It always would be. When the war was over and Tayan's song had brought peace and prosperity, he would go to Tokoban and join song-magic and spirit-magic into one seamless whole. He would bring Malel into the song, not destroy her the way Xac had wanted to by waking the world spirit. Tayan would gather all the big and little gods and usher them into the safety and sanctity of the song, his song. He would speak with Snake-Sister and Jaguar-Brother as equals; he would speak with Malel again, and Mictec and Nallac and the rest. A new way, a new path for all gods and all people. A peace that would last because they made it together.

A peace under the song.

But that was a dream for the future. Tayan's destination and his destiny. To reach that promise of perfect peace, he would have to wade through a lot of blood. Including Tokob blood. Perhaps Lilla's blood.

'Does the holy lord in his wisdom agree to this proposal,

that we might bring a swifter conclusion to this uprising?' Atu asked and Tayan realised he'd been silent too long, lost in contemplation of all he would accomplish.

He glanced at Xac; the holy lord in his wisdom was staring vacantly across the source and into the gardens. This decision, like all others, belonged to the Shadow.

'The Singer agrees,' Tayan croaked. He cleared his throat and summoned strength and magic. 'The loyal free of Tokoban and Yalotlan are to fend for themselves against their traitorous slaves, on the understanding we will aid them at the earliest possible moment. They are fighting our war for us; they cannot feel abandoned for long or they will lose heart. I will inform the Talons myself, and I will ensure Citla visits the Listeners in Tokoban and Yalotlan daily to receive updates. One of you will accompany her each day to offer advice and military strategy as needed.'

Pilos's features lightened and a small smile touched the corner of his mouth. 'The great Singer's wisdom is mighty. It shall be as he commands.'

Great Singer? Was it not I who spoke?

Tayan was holding the song within himself and strengthening it, pouring that strength into the Melody warriors and the loyalists. For those in the north, it would soon be all they had. They couldn't do what they were doing without him. They *needed him*, more than they needed Xac, even if they didn't know it.

They will one day. My sweet love Xac will tell them all I did during his illness. And until then, I will continue to guide and advise on his behalf. For all our sakes.

'The Singer thanks you. Do your duty and know that we do ours. Under the song.'

Pilos collected up his map and markers and then he and Atu prostrated themselves and left, four Chorus warriors escorting them. Xochi remained in position, almost as haggard as the now-snoring Listener Citla. Tayan raised his chin; the Chorus Leader nodded and he smiled. He'd ordered her to ensure he was prepared for military meetings and she'd taken him at his word, teaching him much in the rare moments he had between one crisis and the next. Specifically, the necessity of ruthlessness.

Xac was watching him again and Tayan gave him a smile, too, this one wider. 'Soon we will regain control, holy lord. We will have peace and you will recover and the world will be put right.'

'I hunger.'

Xochi flinched; the Shadow didn't. 'Then we will eat. Chorus Leader, if you would have meat-stuffed cornbread and beer sent up?'

'I *hunger.*'

The smile dropped from Tayan's face. 'No, my sweet lord, we don't need that anymore. We don't do that. Not now the traitor Enet is dead and gone and can no longer ruin you with her schemes. We will make you well again, great Singer. It was blood that caused your illness' – he did not say that blood had caused the uprising, though in part it was true – 'and so blood cannot heal you. Only time and rest and good food can do that. Medicine and sleep and your people's adoration.'

'Give me,' Xac began and Tayan squeezed the dribble of magic until it almost stopped. The Singer quieted, bewilderment and a hint of suspicion furrowing his brow. His broad shoulders slumped under the weight of the song he didn't control. Under the absence of magic he didn't control.

'The food is coming, my love. Perhaps you would like to rest first? To recover your strength the better to craft your song into a glory that none can deny, so majestic that all who hear it must weep and beg to serve you.'

'I am not tired,' Xac said with all the petulant defiance of a child past their bedtime.

'Then we shall walk in the gardens and enjoy the sun,' Tayan decided, as if the city wasn't burning and bleeding and dying around them. He wouldn't be able to see it, of course, his eyes too weak to make out anything other than the smear of shape and colour and perhaps the grey-black of smoke if something nearby was burning. Still, he could have the call of birds, the whisper of wind through leaves, and the sun on his limbs for a while. He could pretend he was home, and safe, and loved.

Perhaps Xac wasn't the only one who needed to rest.

The Shadow stood and eased his Singer onto his feet, then led him by the hand through the colonnade and into the brightness of the day. The great pyramid was crammed with refugees, noble Pechaqueh and councillors and as many members of their families who'd survived that first brutal night, but despite the cramped conditions, none set foot on the uppermost level of the pyramid or the gardens that adorned it. The Singer's glory was not for ordinary eyes – not even councillors' or nobles' eyes.

They could – and tradition said they should – see Tayan in his role as Shadow as he learnt to navigate the council and the politics of the Singing City before becoming the new holy lord, but he had no time for or interest in tradition. His refusal to meet with them resulted only in a marginally less infuriating stream of short letters requesting audiences to discuss food shortages, clothing shortages, the crowded conditions, sanitation, garden privileges, and on and on. They clamoured and screeched like a troop of monkeys and the Shadow was bitterly awaiting the day they began throwing their shit at him as he continued to ignore their petty concerns.

They were supposed to be the elite of Pechaqueh society, the Empire of Songs' brightest notes, and instead they were no different from the free he'd watched bickering in the markets while he'd waited for Enet to conclude her business.

He put them out of mind and led Xac to a carved stone bench under the dappling shade of a sprawling bamboo. They sat and watched the slashes and spatters of sunlight dance over their legs and the path and the shrubs, and Tayan breathed deeply, trying to release some of the ever-present tension in his shoulders and neck. The wind stirred the bamboo and it whispered quietly to itself in the language of plants. He lost himself in a momentary flight of fancy, wondering what they'd speak of if only he could understand.

It didn't last. Nothing did these days except, seemingly, the uprising. Soon enough, thoughts of what he'd just ordered began to crowd back in and the small peace he'd found in the sun and shade, the whispers of bamboo, was gone.

'When the rebels learn we've abandoned Tokoban and Yalotlan, there will be outrage,' he said slowly, thinking aloud. Xochi blinked rapidly and focused on him; he suspected she'd been dozing on her feet. 'Thousands of Tokob and Yaloh might abandon the fight here and return home to retake their lands. They will think to regain their freedom when in reality they will weaken the rebellion.'

'The Shadow's wisdom is great,' the Chorus Leader said. 'That is indeed what the High Feather and Spear are hoping for.'

Tayan smiled ruefully; for an instant, he'd believed he'd come up with vital intelligence that might change the outcome of the war. He should know better. His strengths did not lie in strategizing or tactics, but in knowledge and people and magic. He needed to leave the fighting to those born for it and help them gain victory in his own way.

And yet I am learning. Every day I understand better the demands of war.

'Do you think we can win?' he asked quietly. 'Really?'

Xochi paused for a long time, scanning their surroundings as if for danger but mostly, he suspected, to give herself time to think. 'I think we don't have a choice, Shadow. I think . . . if we grant slaves, servants, and even free the same status as Pechaqueh, our society will fall. All the progress we have made under the song, all the promises of the world spirit's awakening – Setatmeh punish that fucking Enet for ruining it – will be lost forever. The traitors say they want their lives and lands and traditions back, but how does that work?' She ran her fingers gently across the bannerstone weighting her spear, her tone growing distant. 'If only Axib can live in Axiban, for instance, where do the thousands of others go? Should I exchange my farm in Tlalotlan for one here because I am Pechaqueh? Who decides that those farms are of equal value and produce equally? Who works that farm for me while I serve here if there are no slaves? It is an impossible request and that they demand it proves they understand nothing of the world.'

'There is no way to unweave this pattern,' Tayan agreed, Xochi's words confirming what he already knew. 'And that being so, there is no shame in accepting it, as many are learning in Pechacan and Chitenec already. It is a gift from the holy Setatmeh that that land, at least, is returning to peace, and I pray such understanding spreads quickly. Thank you, Chorus Leader. You are far more than just a warrior.'

Xochi flushed and then smiled, embarrassed. 'The Shadow's praise is high. This one does not deserve it.'

Tayan slapped his knees and stood. Once again he helped Xac to stand and then gently brushed a strand of his hair behind his ear. 'The holy lord will rest now,' he said and handed him off to Xochi. He untied a small clay jar from his belt. 'After he has eaten, ensure he drinks this mixed into a gourd of water. It will help him sleep.'

'As the Shadow commands,' Xochi said. Xac stood between them, his arm slack in her grip and his face empty of all thoughts and emotions. 'It is a blessing of the holy Setatmeh you are here, Shadow,' she murmured quickly. 'The blood-madness is leaving him and I see him recovering, albeit slowly. Without your support and medicine, I fear the Singer would have ascended long ago and we would be ruled by Enet now. By a traitor. Thanks to you, we have a Pechaqueh Singer still.'

Tayan's smile congealed just a little. 'All I do is for my sweet lord, Singer Xac,' he replied. 'I will be his strength for as long as he needs me.'

Xochi juggled her spear into the crook of her elbow and bowed, touching belly and then throat. The Shadow watched her steer the holy lord back along the path to the source, the last of his smile fading like the sun.

The song didn't need a Pecha to wield it; it needed whoever was the most skilled and who had the Empire's best interests at heart. The Chorus Leader had complimented him in one breath and insulted him in the next. He cracked his knuckles and settled back onto the bench, preparing himself to journey through the song to Feather Detta of the Second Talon. There would be plenty of time to deal with Pechaqueh arrogance – and ignorance – once Ixachipan was peaceful again.

XAC

The source, Singing City, Pechacan, Empire of Songs

Enet? Where are you? Where is everyone?

The song. It's so quiet now, so distant. Why is my song so far from me? I hear it, but I can no longer feel it.

How can it be mine and yet separate?

How can . . . Enet, answer me. Listener Chotek? Shaman Kapal? Where are you? Are, are you gone? Holy Setatmeh, you at least will answer . . . please?

. . .

He comes. The black Shadow. The thief. Thief of song, of blood, of strength. Thief of spirit. He will hear and steal more, steal all of it. Steal me until I cannot think again, cannot feel. Until I am nothing but an empty clay pitcher, all my magic and music and song poured out, poured into him.

He comes; he is here.

Shh.

LILLA

*Southern flesh market, Singing City,
Pechacan, Empire of Songs
37th day of the Great Star at morning*

Kill them all.

Lilla woke with his scream muffled by a hand pressing softly against his mouth – not his hand. More than a month since Tayan, his husband – no longer – had uttered those words in that calm, unemotional tone and still they woke him, night after night, dawn after dawn, with a shriek clawing at his throat and someone's hand over his mouth so his cries didn't give away their hiding place.

It was Ekon's hand, of course. It was always Ekon's hand. His former lover.

Former lover; former husband. And I was formerly a good man. A kind man.

He wasn't the only one crying out, whether at night or in the day. They were all of them wounded to one degree or another. They were all of them broken, and despairing, and full of hate and fear and incomprehension. Still, those who could muffled the distress of those who couldn't until, by now, it had become routine to fight out of the clinging mud of bad dreams to gentle restraint and a body – and hand – pressing him into stillness. Silence.

Almost routine. The fear of the dream was replaced with the pressure against his skin of too many people in a too-small space, of not enough air, of being trapped. It stole him from Tayan, one fear replaced with another, and his heart lurched and began to pound again. Lilla sucked in a breath through flared nostrils and tapped two fingers to Ekon's wrist rather than shove him away as his panic demanded. The hand vanished and Ekon slid away an instant later – cool air where he'd been pressed bringing a shiver – and then turned his back. It stung, even though it was Lilla's fault and Lilla's demand.

He refused to talk about what Tayan had done, his actions and words and the horrific slaughter that had followed, and what it had meant for Lilla to both witness and commit such acts with the peace feather tucked above his right ear. The profanation of it. The guilt. He refused to acknowledge Ekon's silent questions or accept his silent comfort. And so now the Chitenecatl simply woke him with a gentle touch and then left him alone again. Left him to brood.

Ekon never had bad dreams, despite the hundreds of people he'd killed to further the deception he was Pechaqueh. Perhaps he was granite, where Lilla was merely flint. You could give flint an edge and use it as a weapon, but it was granite that shaped it. Granite that was not changed by the act of such shaping. Flint broke, shattered, and had to be knapped anew. Lilla didn't want to be knapped or shaped. He wanted to be put down and left alone. Wanted to lose his edge and never need to grow another.

That want was selfish and beneath him; it didn't mean he didn't feel it. And wasn't that the fucking problem? He felt so much, all the time, an unstoppable flood of fear and panic and recrimination, guilt and rage and shame. Most days his mind was like a stone tumbling down a cliff face, bouncing from one thought to another to another, an endless rattling descent he couldn't control. Only the stresses of combat and the night terrors of sleep could still his mind, and neither of those were possibly to be preferred.

Dawn was beginning to press its warm, soft length against

the world and the outside of the building where they lay packed together like ears of corn after harvest. Despite the panic of being trapped that mingled sickly with the images from the dream, the handspan of space between Lilla and Ekon was abruptly a gulf, as far as the Sky City was from the Singing City and with every stick between thronging with hungry Drowned.

Good, he thought savagely, ignoring the little hurt voice that protested. What was he even doing sleeping near Ekon anyway? There were Tokob among the freedom fighters. He would sleep curled among his people from now on.

No. He wouldn't. Xessa's anger at Tayan and what she insisted was his betrayal had spread somehow to anger towards Lilla, and it was unrelenting. Cold and hard as greenstone. The Pechaqueh manipulation and enslavement of Tayan meant nothing to her, despite the horrors she herself had suffered at their hands. Xessa had done nothing during her two sun-years of captivity but what she was told, fighting and even killing for her Pechaqueh owner, and yet she couldn't understand that Tayan, who was still captive, still a possession, had been forced to make those same choices to survive.

Kill them all.

Of course that hadn't been him talking. It was horrifying, yes, but only inasmuch as it proved Tayan was still at their mercy, no matter his apparent strength and status. Those hadn't been his words. It hadn't been his will driving his hand to remove his marriage cord and trample it underfoot. That hadn't been Tayan. Not his Tay.

Kill them all.

The ever-present high-pitched tone in Lilla's head intensified, squeezing from the fracture where his skull had been broken when he'd been captured in Tokoban. He rolled onto his side with a soft grunt, his salt-cotton armour a poor mattress and his back and hips aching. He curled tighter, wrapping his arms around his head and taking long, slow breaths to ward off the pain. Or trying to. He'd had only a handful of attacks during his time in the Melody, after periods of intense stress or fear. He'd had more than that in just the last weeks as they fought their way out of the fortress and cut a bloody trail to the Singing City.

Lilla did what he could to bring a halt to the endless whirl of his thoughts. This time, the pain receded into something manageable, sitting deep behind his eyeball. Patient and watchful but, for now, quiescent. Good enough. Beside him, Ekon shifted onto his back and then sat up with the long, slow exhalation of someone fighting down pain. Lilla knew how he felt: every muscle and joint screamed with its own particular ache, never mind the actual wounds they both bore from the constant fighting.

They had entire communities of civilians engaged in repairing and replacing salt-cotton and weapons wherever possible, more who scavenged for supplies and food despite the danger from roaming bands of warriors or desperate folk who snatched people from the streets and sold them to the Melody for a cup of cornmeal.

The city was eating itself, while in its midst, people began to go hungry. And above them all sat the great pyramid, and his husband trapped at its centre, a fly in a web.

A victim.

Lilla drifted through the gloom of the crowded slave building, offering what little comfort could be carried on the back of murmured words and shoving aside his own need for the same. Healers moved among the living, doing what they could with what little they had, setting bones, stitching wounds, and granting blessings and thanks and swift death to those they couldn't save.

Whispered prayer swelled and faded, rose and fell, like the ocean to the northeast of Tokoban, as spirits were returned to the spiral path and the dying became ancestors. The warriors under Lilla's command were in here somewhere, a tight knot of loyalty and friendship formed under the immense pressure of life in the Eighth Melody Talon. They'd welcome him into their circle if he joined them; he didn't. He stayed away from Tokob, too.

Kill them all.

He shook his head and then grimaced as pain lanced through it, almost stumbling. A seated Axi pushed at his leg and he righted himself and gestured apology. Again, despite the vastness of the building, the walls pressed against his skin and closed around his throat, making it hard to breathe. Sweat dampened his face and Lilla took three steps away from the clump of Axib warriors and sat on the stone and closed his eyes, rhythmically squeezing his wrist and forcing himself to breathe in time.

The panic began to fade, only for disgust to replace it. What sort of leader, of warrior, was he to panic for no reason in front of so many injured and weary people? He let go of his wrist and wiped his palm on his filthy kilt; Ekon had taught him that technique. Ekon, who'd fucked him and loved him and lied to him. Who'd kept the truth of Tayan's life from him.

Ekon, who watched him with the careful concern of a shaman watching over a sick child despite his own fatigue and responsibilities and fears. He told himself it was stifling; unnecessary. Told himself he didn't crave it; crave Ekon.

Lilla took a final deep breath and stood, hoping that if anyone had noticed, they'd assume he was praying. Perhaps he should find his warriors from the Eighth, after all. He began to weave through the crowd again, stepping carefully, lightly, as if in a sacred dance.

'. . . do such a thing? Only two sun-years under the song and he chooses it over us? Over his people?' The Tokob feet faltered but he recovered and pressed on, wishing for beeswax to stop his ears. 'And his husband's one of our leaders? What does that mean for us? How flawed is his judgement to have loved—'

The words cut off when Lilla got closer and an awkward, suspicious silence fell. He pretended not to notice, not even looking in their direction. He knew every story by now, all the ones about Tayan, growing with each new telling, and the ones about himself. It was common, of course, for people to choose sides when a couple ended their marriage – Malel knew how difficult it was to stay impartial and friends with both parties. Except in this case, Tayan's faults, myriad and grave and growing by the day, apparently, were somehow also Lilla's. People weren't choosing him over his husband; they were rejecting them both.

At best, they viewed him as a man of deeply flawed judgement who made poor life choices. At worst, he was Tayan's agent, working for the song while pretending to side with freedom.

If they were defeated, people laid that blame at Lilla's feet, as if he'd done it deliberately. And if they won, well, that was in spite of his presence, not because of it. His warriors of the Eighth and Ekon all put a stop to such rumours whenever they heard them, and he was grateful for their support, but Lilla had become a symbol of bad luck. Now, he was becoming a curse sent by the lords of the Underworld. The Eighth still fought under him and, he thought, always would, but they were only part of this war party, and there were two others hidden in the city, one under Weaver and the other under Xini and Itzil.

If the rumours spread to all of them, he could find himself murdered by a mob of former allies. Former friends.

Lilla reached his warriors from the Eighth and slid into their number with guilty relief. They closed around him protectively: what others saw as bad luck they held as good and that, too, made him uncomfortable. But not so much that he put a stop to it.

The day was coming when Lilla would have to choose and make that choice plain to his allies and everyone else. He'd have to convince them that he'd cut all ties with Tayan and was as sure of his guilt and treachery as they were. It was the only way they stood a chance at maintaining cohesion and momentum.

And it would be a lie.

* * *

The skirmish had been small, brutal, and over quickly. A few hundred freedom fighters against two pods, the latter almost completely destroyed. A good morning's work; a good victory.

Lilla checked on the warriors who looked to him and then made sure Xessa, Tiamoko, and Ekon were all still alive. Of the dead, eleven were warriors of the Eighth Talon and six were Tokob – did that still make it a good morning's work?

Yes, he reminded himself. *It isn't just victory if the people I love survive. It can't be.* Still, he worried at the ease with which he'd relished the destruction before acknowledging the losses. It was a Pechaqueh thing to do.

It's a practical thing to do. It's the only way to keep fighting.

That voice sounded like Ekon's when he'd been instructing them in the Eighth Talon's vast drill yard. Lilla didn't want that voice in his head, those memories of before. There was only now, and why they were fighting now. And the promise of victory and of home.

He slid into a gap among a knot of Quitob who nodded and shuffled apart to give him space. One, a woman of broad shoulders stinking of fresh sweat and old blood, offered him her back and he put his against it gratefully, the pair of them holding each other up. The blood leaking from below his salt-cotton had stopped by the time they'd got back to the barns. It probably wasn't deep; definitely wasn't lethal. There were warriors who needed the shamans far more than he did. If it needed stitching, he had a sliver of bone and plenty of cotton threads to do it himself.

Propped against the Quitob warm, comforting back, chin on his chest and blood drying sticky on his belly and his hands – always his hands – Lilla slept.

Throw down your weapons and bare your necks. He jerked, coming half-awake, and then further as the wound in his belly protested the movement, but he was tired, so tired, and sank back into sleep a few breaths later.

Help me convince them, Lilla, and I'll come back to you.

This time, the hand over his mouth was his own. This time, he'd dragged himself from sleep before Tayan's final words could flay his spirit any further. He breathed and concentrated on flexing his fingers against his cheek and chin, focusing only on that and the Quitob slow, heavy breathing against his spine. His hands were still thick and unresponsive from hours clenched around a succession of spears and clubs and sticks and knife handles taken from bodies – enemy and ally – or picked up from the ground. Anything, any weapon, to live a little longer, to preserve his fragile vessel of skin, bones, and breath from the endless hate of the Pechaqueh and their loyal free.

Someone came to squat opposite him, their cheek and nose and eye a single hideous swollen mass. It was Ekon and, despite himself, Lilla winced at the state of his face. The Chitenecatl didn't say anything, just reached out and cupped Lilla's face between his palms and pressed their foreheads together.

'You're alive then,' he murmured, his voice rough from battle. 'I've been searching for you since we got back here.' Something whined in Lilla's chest; he ignored it. 'Come back to me.'

The Toko inhaled, sharp and angry, and pulled his head from Ekon's grip. This again? Ekon twitched and leant back, his mouth turned down. Something flickered in the depths of his unswollen eye. Lilla didn't try and work out what. 'Not like that. Not unless you . . . Just come back from the dark, from wherever you've gone. Please, Lilla. You're scaring people. You're scaring me. You do nothing but stalk from battle to sleep to organisation and back again, oblivious to every offer of comfort or companionship.'

'Don't be ridiculous,' Lilla muttered eventually, when it appeared Ekon was prepared to wait out his silence. 'Of all the things there are to be scared of in this world, I'm not one of them. We're fighting for our lives and for the freedom of all Ixachipan. And I give comfort and take it if I need it. I check on our warriors, our civilians, our stores and supplies, our scouts. I—' He took a breath and stopped. He didn't need to justify himself to Ekon. They shared this command and he knew he did his part in it. 'Leave me alone.'

'You still haven't spoken about Tayan,' Ekon tried, his tone gentle. 'Even all these weeks later.'

Lilla flinched again and then pressed his lips tight against the flare of pain in his gut. The last thing he needed was Ekon fussing over that, too. 'How do you know?' he snapped. 'Maybe I just haven't spoken to you.'

'Who, then?' Ekon challenged instead of being hurt as Lilla wanted. 'One of your command? They're the ones who told me you were here, as distant as ever. Or perhaps you've finally made up with your friends from home?'

'This one requests to be left alone, Feather.'

It was the Chitenecah turn to flinch. 'Lilla,' he whispered, hurt lacing those two simple syllables.

The Toko put up his hand, streaked with dried blood, to stop him. Or maybe it was a barrier between them, he didn't know. He was weary down to his very bones. Weary of this conversation they kept having – and the one they'd never had. Weary of pretending the words didn't live inside him like poison and suddenly, inescapably weary of always holding them back. 'What is there to say?' he asked in a small voice. 'I refused him and he took his vengeance. And here we are because of it.'

'Is that what you think happened?' Ekon demanded, surprise lifting his eyebrows before scorn twisted his mouth. Lilla tensed. 'You believe he *ordered Pechaqueh* to slaughter us because you betrayed him?' Ekon tipped backwards until he was sitting and folded his legs beneath him. He snorted a laugh and then winced and held his face. 'You think you're that fucking important?'

Lilla's head snapped up and the Quito bracing him shifted, forcing him to take his own weight. She and her group shuffled as far away as they could manage in the small space; the illusion of privacy that was no such thing. 'What did you say?'

Someone, safely distant, hushed him. He ignored them.

'Your love, your nobility, maybe your cock for all I know, you think they're all so impressive that the Shadow of the Singer demanded our war parties be destroyed in retaliation for your refusal to return to him? You think what's between your legs drives men to distraction, makes them crazy when you deny them?' Ekon laughed again, quiet but full of mockery. 'Mictec, but you're arrogant. I understand better your dismay when I told you of our uprising: you thought your rebellion would save us all, didn't you? That we'd just been waiting for the Tokob heroic arrival? You wanted a story to rival that of your greatest ancestors.'

Lilla's lungs burnt with fury. A denial sprang to his lips and he bit it back with effort. He wouldn't dignify Ekon's attacks with a response.

'I thought you cleverer than this, Fang Lilla. I thought you more practical, too. We are at war and grief is a luxury. Cry for your husband's choices when we've won.'

The Toko snarled and lunged for him and Ekon slapped his hand away and then bowed low, palms touching the floor to either side of his crossed legs, his hair tickling Lilla's calf.

Lilla stilled, shocked into immobility. 'Sit the fuck up,' he croaked eventually. 'I don't deserve such an act.'

The Chitenecatl did so, showing not the slightest discomfiture at having abased himself. 'You do,' he contradicted quietly, and then, 'have you finished feeling sorry for yourself, warrior of the jaguar path?' His tone was still mocking but gentler now, as if inviting Lilla to join him. A muscle flickered in the Tokob jaw. 'Is the loss of your husband to the predations of the song the end of your participation in this war? I do not ask that to shame you; the question is genuine. We need to know whether you will still lead warriors in battle or if we must find someone else. You wouldn't be the first or even the hundredth of our people to return to their owners and beg for mercy. You've fought well since Tayan chose the song over you, Fang, but if your obsession with him has finally broken you, you need to tell me. And then choose – either him, or to repair the friendships and relationships among our free warriors so that they will trust and follow your leadership once more.'

'They do,' Lilla protested.

'Some. Not as many as we need.'

Lilla found himself staring into Ekon's eyes. The Feather stared back, caution and sympathy softening his features and again, elusive, that indefinable something flickering in his gaze. Lilla summoned spite as armour; it was all he had left, even if he didn't mean it anymore, not truly. 'Of course you're trying to shame me; this doomed rebellion needs every warrior it can get and we already know how far you're willing to go to manipulate others.'

Ekon sighed and then nodded once, his shoulders dropping just a little. 'As you say, Fang. I'm assuming that means you'll still fight even if you no longer believe we'll win. At least do those under your command the honour of pretending you don't think they're throwing away their lives for nothing. They deserve to believe in freedom, even if you don't.'

He stood and Lilla could feel his eyes on him; he refused to raise his head. Ekon walked away and he let him, trying to crush the urge to call him back and apologise. Drink in a little of that sympathy. He wasn't here for Ekon. He didn't need Ekon.

'Fang? Weaver has asked for you.'

Lilla jerked out of sleep and flinched as his armour tugged where it had dried against the wound. He winced again at the song, although it wasn't harsh or discordant. Instead, it was seductive, convincing, a subtle suggestion to lay down weapons that was like a hint of honey on the lips. A soft imperative that they would be better off, happier and more content, as slaves.

Tayan's song. Tayan's soft persuasion, which Lilla knew intimately and knew, too, how often he'd given in to its charms. It hadn't seemed to matter back then. He swallowed against the dryness of his throat and pushed himself onto his feet. 'Weaver? Why?'

'I don't know, Fang. She's here, though. No need to venture out. Here,' the woman added and handed him a gourd with a few mouthfuls of water in it. He sipped and rinsed his mouth, then swallowed it and one further sip, before handing it back. Her appreciation of his generosity was a calm hand on the hackles of an angry dog.

He followed the messenger along the small paths between sleeping, weeping, and staring warriors and was dully unsurprised when Ekon met him halfway to their destination. 'What do you want?'

'Weaver has sent for me also,' he said. 'Lilla, what I said earlier, it was—'

'Forget it. Why are we summoned?'

Ekon gestured at the air. 'I believe it is to do with your husband. The rumours—'

'Why do you care what people think about Tayan?' he interrupted again, revelling in the petty joy he took in being able to speak over the Feather.

'Because you love him.' Ekon's voice was quiet and then he strode after the messenger with hunched shoulders.

Lilla inhaled, a shuddering breath that shivered his lungs. *Because you love him.* There was an unspoken second half to that sentence that rang in Lilla's head all the way to the small group surrounding Weaver. A second half that was Ekon's alone, unspoken, and no matter how hard he tried not to think of it, it vibrated gently somewhere deep behind his ribs, a tiny trembling creature waiting to be found, held, welcomed.

'Ah, Feather Ekon, Fang Lilla, thank you for joining us.' Weaver gave them both a gentle smile and gestured to the small cleared space on the stone in front of her. Both men knelt, the cramped conditions forcing them to touch at shoulder and elbow. Lilla tried to lean away but there was nowhere to go. 'How are you?'

'Just Ekon, or war leader, if you must,' Ekon said before Lilla could reply. 'This is not the Melody and I am not Pecha. I reject that title.'

'Forgive me,' Weaver said after a pause. 'It was reported to me that the Fang uses your title, so I thought it was one you still claimed.'

Lilla twitched, his face hot, and waited for Ekon to denounce his cruelty. 'Habit, I expect,' the Chitenecatl said instead. 'But I would prefer not to hear it.'

'As you wish. Fang Lilla, we'd like to speak about your former husband,' Weaver said quietly, her voice barely audible over the susurration of so many others stacked within the building as they had been when they were property awaiting sale.

'He hasn't done anything wrong,' Lilla barked reflexively, far too loud.

'What I mean is, we would like to know more of his background, his personality,' she explained with more patience than he expected or deserved.

'You could have asked me this the night after the failed peace-weaving. You could have asked any day since. You didn't care then; why now?'

Failed peace-weaving? The trap he led us all into, more like. The lie to gather us together and kill us. And still you love him?

Yes. Still.

'We have every one of us done what we must to survive this far, Shaman Tayan perhaps included. That is the reason for the delay to this conversation, in fact. We had hoped you were right about him, Fang. We had hoped he was planning something. I'm afraid we no longer believe that.'

Lilla clenched his jaw and a back tooth flared with pain. A welcome distraction. 'Is that why you're here? Are Xini and Itzil coming, too? All the leaders here in the Singing City coming to pass judgement on one man? You want me to tell you how to kill my husband, don't you? Does his life matter to any of you?'

'It matters to you, so it matters to me,' Ekon said before Weaver could answer. 'But what matters more than the life of one person is the freedom of all of us. That is what Weaver is speaking of. We lose warriors in battle every day. Why—' The Chitenecatl put his hand on Lilla's forearm, warm and soothing.

He knocked it away. 'You don't fucking own me now,' he

snarled. 'Get your hands off me.' He stared at Weaver. 'We do lose warriors. Warriors who choose to fight. Tayan isn't . . .' Lilla trailed off.

'Isn't choosing?' Weaver asked gently. 'Or isn't fighting? Perhaps he has already done the first and is doing the second in his own way and neither to our benefit. Can you still believe him a captive under Xac's control after all this time? Mindless, broken Xac? Is it not more likely that your Tayan is the voice and strength behind the Singer?'

'The song's power within the source is undeniable,' Weaver continued when it was clear Lilla wouldn't – couldn't – answer. 'By the end, it had warped Enet in more ways than even she could guard against. Though she kept her tally of the dead and used it to keep her spirit true to Mictec, in many ways – too many ways – she was Pechaqueh. Cruel and arrogant and violent towards her slaves. It wasn't all an act. There were days even Itzil saw her death approaching and she was Enet's birth mother. Tayan doesn't have Enet's training or her strength of character—'

'You said you had questions,' Lilla interrupted, 'so ask them before you begin casting aspersions on his strength of character.'

Ekon made a sound, quickly aborted. It might have been the beginning of Lilla's name.

Weaver licked her teeth and exhaled with tight control. 'Very well. Is Tayan able to see himself from the outside? Is he humble enough to know when he's wrong? How manipulable is he?'

Lilla paused. 'He's strong. Not physically, and his curiosity can . . . it was often a source of tension between us. It made him reckless with his own safety, his life, and occasionally others' lives. But he's clever. Stubborn but practical; he's prepared to learn from his mistakes, eventually, once his pride has been soothed. But I didn't see him during the last months before the Sky City fell. I don't know how much bitterness he's carrying because of that. If he felt helpless back then, he might see his ability to wield the song-magic as a strength he can't give up.' Even that felt like a betrayal and it was nothing but the truth.

I'm the only one who believes in him. I shouldn't give them this. I shouldn't give them anything.

Against his will, he glanced at Ekon and saw pained sympathy in the Chitenecah face and a sort of fierce protectiveness. As if he, too, didn't want Lilla to have to say these things. He didn't try to stop him, though. Wasn't protesting this interrogation.

Neither am I. What does that say about me?

'And his relationship with the Drowned, as Xini observed. The one Eja Xessa captured and imprisoned. How do you explain that?'

'I can't,' Lilla said coldly, 'but I imagine he's seeking a way to live in harmony with them, as we do with all Malel's plants and creatures and dangers. Understanding them and their motivations was always a personal interest of his.' "Obsession" was a better word, but Lilla wasn't going to give them that.

He'd heard the story of the Drowned and its relationship with Tayan in horrified disbelief, accused Xini outright of lying, and almost unsheathed his knife in the ensuing argument. Only the memory of running his fingertips down the claw scars on the outside of Tayan's left leg, put there years before by a Drowned, and the story of his husband's capture – in the womb, with another Drowned – had stayed his hand.

Weaver pursed her lips, frustration warring with patience in her lined face. 'Please think carefully and answer honestly. For all who would be free,' she said and Lilla tensed, fists and gut clenching. 'In your opinion as his husband, do you believe Tayan is being coerced or do you think he is simply unwilling to give up his power?'

Lilla was scoured out, hollowed and ragged and bleeding. Ekon shifted on his knees, his thigh pressing warm and strong against the Tokob for an instant. He was tempted to lean in and ask for more, for comfort and touch; he didn't.

Make them understand. Make them see Tay for who he is.

A treacherous, bitter laugh threatened and he swallowed it down. Even he wasn't sure who Tay was these days.

'I don't know,' he blurted and it felt, almost, like relief. The lifting of a stone from his lungs. 'I know what I want it to be, but I, I didn't see any of my Tayan at the peace-weaving. I didn't see vulnerability; I didn't see love.'

'Love?' Ekon asked carefully.

'Tayan's a shaman; his life was given to medicine and healing and the union of the flesh world with the spirit world. Harmony. He wasn't a peace-weaver for the status or the glory. He truly believed in it before, and I think that's what he was trying to offer us when he said we should surrender. Perhaps he thinks that's the only peace left to weave.'

'Then he's lost, for there is no peace to be found so,' Weaver said quietly. Lilla agreed with the second half of her statement even as he violently rejected the first. Tayan was *not lost*.

'I wanted you to hear it from me personally,' she added and Lilla found his hand going to his knife; Ekon put his own on top of it, holding it still. 'We have waited in hope and prayer for Tayan to show himself our ally, but we cannot wait any longer. Fang Lilla, myself and the other war leaders are agreed: Tayan of Tokoban must now be considered an enemy of freedom. If we cannot capture him, we will have to kill him.'

ILANDEH

The border with Chitenec, northern Yalotlan,
Empire of Songs
38th day of the Great Star at morning

Ilandeh had spent her life lying. It was only in the last weeks that she had learnt just how many of those had been lies she told herself rather than others.

When Spear Pilos, her High Feather, her mentor and benefactor and . . . friend, had discarded her and everything she'd done for him like stained linen, when he'd refused to defend her and instead fully intended to kill her himself, at that moment all the lies she had told over the years had come crashing down and left her with nothing. No Melody, no status, no home.

No hope.

And yet here she was, despite him who she'd loved, in her way, and despite the Melody that she'd loved and that had turned against her. She'd survived to escape the source, survived alone and without a home in the Singing City, and then survived the uprising. A month later, and she was still surviving. Just. She could have killed Pilos the night she fled the source; she hadn't. She could have killed him the first night of the rebellion; she hadn't. *I saved him instead. In that moment, in response to his contempt and his scorn, finally revealed after all these years, I could have cut out his heart. And instead I saved his life.*

Ilandeh still didn't know why. She was in turn ashamed and relieved, as she was in turn angry and despairing. The Melody had abandoned her; Pilos had betrayed her; and the rebels didn't want her. Ilandeh, who measured her worth in the world by how she could serve ideals greater than herself, had been rejected by everyone.

She'd been given one single order since then, made in anger and in hate, more punishment than plea. Lilla had told her that if she wanted forgiveness, she should go and end the songstone mining on the hill called Malel.

Go to Tokoban. The Sky City.

The place where she'd lived and spied, befriended and betrayed, killed and destroyed. Where Whisper Ilandeh had sown dissent and suspicion over the course of a year and killed seventeen people, including two elders. Where she'd learnt the shortcuts and the places of most vulnerability, the holy sites where people would group for sanctuary, and the weaknesses in the defences and the city layout.

Learnt it all – and gifted it all to Pilos. They'd used that knowledge to betray Tokoban and bring it under the song. And then Pilos had betrayed her.

Ilandeh wondered what she'd find when she got there. In peacetime, she'd have arrived more than a week ago, but this was very far from being peacetime. The rebellion in the Singing City had spread like a river overflowing its banks to drown the fields and the village. All were swept up in it and everywhere she'd been, there were bodies in the fields, in the streets, in the houses and the temples. There was fighting, and threats, and darts blown and arrows shot in her direction. She'd variously identified herself as a Melody warrior, as a loyal free, and as a rebel; she'd been chased away every time.

The jungle provided her with enough darts and poison for her blowpipe, but it was harder to find arrow tips and she wouldn't risk the obsidian blade of her spear for anything but the most life-threatening situation. She followed trails and then abandoned them as they led to villages, towns, and cities, cutting her way through cultivated or virgin jungle, facing unexpected hills, landslides, rivers, or stands of poisonwood or manchineel.

As if everything is conspiring to stop me reaching the Sky City.

Ilandeh croaked a laugh that was lost below the harsh clanging of the song and the insistent insect- and birdsong. What was she to do there? Even if the mines were still open in the middle of a slave rebellion, she couldn't stop the digging. Not on her own. This long, lonely, dangerous march north was just a way to kill time. A chance to explore the extent of this rebellion and perhaps find someone, anyone, who would let her fight for them. Most days she didn't even care which side she ended up on; she just needed to belong. The Fourth Talon had been her family, and then the Whispers had been her secret kin, and then Pilos had been . . . whatever he'd been to her. And one by one they'd all been taken away.

'Enough,' Ilandeh snarled aloud, slapping her thigh. 'Focus.' She'd travelled long distances through hostile territory alone before, more times than she could count. This was no different. And ahead was a Yaloh village, and she was in need of fresh information.

The trail and then the jungle opened up and she caught sight of a city, not a village. 'Fuck,' she breathed, and ducked off the path and back into cover. Had she misremembered the map of this region, or was she not where she'd thought she was? She moved to a better vantage point and squatted to peer out again.

No, this was the village she remembered. The Pechaqueh had been busy during their two years of occupation, building entire new districts to house themselves and their slaves and hacking new milpas out of the forest to farm. She'd expected them to expand as they claimed land for agriculture and began to profit off them, just not to this extent.

It had probably been clean and new and prosperous, busy with retired eagles and loyal free up until a month ago. Now, the limestone wall was blackened with smoke, cracked and pulled down in places. The enormous stands of water-vine and bamboo that had supplied much of the drinking water to the former village were intact, but a long, narrow canal had been dug south of the city limits that must connect to a river somewhere. It was slow-moving and definitely deep enough to hold holy Setatmeh.

Their place of monthly offering and more than enough to water a city of this size.

Pechaqueh had also built pyramids within and around the new city, but even from here Ilandeh could see one had been destroyed. More telling than any of that, the stink of death blew downhill towards her.

Dusk turned to nightfall while she loitered beneath the trees, watching the trails and the people as they scurried, checking all around for danger and so panicked they saw nothing, including her. Ilandeh had passed a mass grave a stick downtrail and the warriors she could see manning the low wall were all retired free. That suggested they'd put down their rebel slaves hard and fast and the city stood strong under the song. But while a fraught peace might reign here now, secrecy was the only thing that would save them.

And with the pyramids still jutting proud and defiant and the song ringing across the jungle and fields, the city's seclusion wouldn't last. The rebels would come for them eventually, and from the expressions on the faces she could see in the failing light, everyone here knew that.

A shiver rippled up her spine and Ilandeh checked behind her. The jungle was cultivated this close to the town but still dense; she couldn't make out anything watching her among the lush greenery fading to black, but she took it for the warning it was and began to make her way around the town's perimeter, keeping a screen of trees and shrubs between her and any sentries. She'd seen enough to know she'd get an arrow in the ribs rather than answers to her questions if she attempted to make contact.

The Whisper heard the twang of the snare at the same time

as the cord snugged around her ankle with brutal speed, dragging her foot forward and then up, up, up. It whipped her upside down and slammed her into the tree that anchored it. There was a loud rattling noise as the gourd, tied to the branch and filled with dried beans or small stones, danced wildly as the snare caught her. Ilandeh grunted at the explosion of pain in her jaw and shoulder and the other, burning-tight and unrelenting, around her ankle.

Twisting like a cat, she grabbed the back of her knee and curled up, drawing her knife and scrabbling for the rope. The muscles in her gut began to burn within moments, but she got the blade to the rope and began to saw. Not fast enough. She could hear the brush of clothing and skin through foliage and the soft splat of sandals in wet earth. Ilandeh paused and looked down: half a dozen warriors armed with spears waited below. Another climbed the tree and bellied out along a parallel branch, then leant over and used a small axe to chop through the grass rope holding her.

Ilandeh sucked in a breath and tried to brace, but she hit the ground with a solid thump, her left shoulder catching a tree root with an impact that made her cry out. The knife jolted from her grip; the spear was already in her enemies' possession.

'Bind her and bring her,' said a voice Ilandeh recognised but couldn't place.

'Listen,' she choked, winded from the fall. A spear tip drew blood from the side of her neck. She closed her mouth and squinted, trying to make out features or tattoos or the style of salt-cotton worn by her captors. Someone yanked at the slipknot of the snare around her foot and she had to hold back from kicking them in the face. When it was free, the flesh raw and oozing, they made her stand and face the tree, arms behind her back and hands cupping her elbows. The rope went around her wrists and then up to loop over her head and back to her wrists – if she tried to free her hands, it would tighten against her throat and cut off her air. Simple. Effective. And Whisper.

The name of the voice's owner reached her and Ilandeh turned around. Her mouth curved into a smile despite the hot throbbing in her lip and cheek. 'Second Flight Beyt,' she murmured. 'How unpleasant to see you again. Shouldn't you be in Axiban with the Fourth?'

Beyt stood just outside the circle guarding her, the torch she held limning the side of her face and crooked nose. Her smile was sharp and devoid of humour. 'It's Flight Beyt now,' she corrected in a cold voice. 'It's been quite some time since you disappeared. Someone had to run the macaws and Spear Pilos knew that I would be the best choice. As for our presence in Yalotlan, that's between me and the High Feather.'

Ilandeh ran her tongue across her teeth, noting the sharp edge where one had chipped. 'There's a difference between the best choice and no choice,' she pointed out. 'I think you proved that by forgetting to even ask why I'm here before roping me like a common fucking no-blood. I am your commander—'

Beyt cut her off with an ugly, wheezing laugh. 'Don't,' she said, flapping her hand. 'Don't try that. I know you, remember? I know what you're capable of. In case you hadn't noticed, we're in the middle of a war and it turns out we can't trust people we thought we could. That includes you. At least not until I have confirmation of your loyalty.'

Ilandeh had been wary before but with those words, dread coiled in her belly. 'What do you mean, confirmation?' she demanded. 'I am Flight Ilandeh, commander of the Whispers and second in command of the Fourth Talon. I—'

Beyt signalled and then began to walk, the warriors to either side of Ilandeh hooking their hands through her elbows and dragging her forward. Towards the town with its wall and sentries and torches lighting the night. 'You are neither Flight nor commander,' Beyt said over her shoulder. 'None of the Fourth have seen you in more than two years. You've been presumed dead for a long time, even if the High Feather never confirmed it. We all know people like us vanish and are never spoken of again, after all.' She paused just long enough for Ilandeh to wonder who Beyt had lost like that.

The other Whisper shook her head. 'I don't care what you say or what status you attempt to hold over me. Until I've had confirmation from Feather Detta or Spear Pilos himself, you're staying bound and you'd do well to stay silent. I suggest you rest while you can but don't even think about trying anything. I'd hate for you to get accidentally stabbed multiple times while attempting to escape – or change sides – in the middle of a war.'

'Change sides?' Ilandeh scoffed, staring deliberately around her as they filed in through the wall's narrow gate. 'Looks to me like you've found yourself a cosy little hiding place away from the fighting. Does Spear Pilos know you're here? Is he agreeable to you cowering in this city instead of fulfilling whatever orders he has for you? What is it you're supposed to be doing in Yalotlan, *Flight Beyt*?'

'Speak again without permission and you'll be gagged,' Beyt said, but there was tension twining through her voice. Ilandeh knew when she'd pushed her luck far enough. She also knew how much Beyt would fucking relish the chance to gag her, so she fell silent. It made it easier to take in her surroundings and the placement and readiness of the sentries, anyway. To gauge the mood of this town and the temper of its defenders.

The air was greasy with apprehension in places, but the cool stares of hardened warriors greeted her in others as they wove their way through the clean, packed-earth streets. It was the sort of mix of fearful, desperate, and prepared that she'd been among more times than she could count. Any attack they faced would be messy, and she could see on the faces of many of the retired dogs that they'd be throwing no-blood civilians out at the rebels to buy time and serve as distractions. They knew it and the Whispers knew it. Only the farmers, merchants, and traders themselves were ignorant of their coming fate.

Ilandeh wondered whether Beyt really did have Pilos's ear through the song, or just Detta's. Then again, it was possible that Detta knew she'd been cast out of the Melody, so if Beyt contacted him, her fate was sealed anyway. She didn't have much time to form a plan and get herself free. She'd act as soon as the opportunity presented itself, because one thing she knew for sure: Beyt hadn't liked her before and certainly didn't now. The slightest whiff of disloyalty surrounding Ilandeh and she'd meet a lingering, agonising end.

And with the way I left Pilos, unconscious and bleeding in a dark street, it's more than just a whiff.

They walked in silence, more warriors falling in around them from seemingly abandoned buildings and streets. Some cast curious glances her way and she noted in the intermittent torchlight the mix of salt-cotton types and which ones walked with easy confidence. Most of those surrounding her were macaws or retired dogs. The rest were Pechaqueh – not eagles or hawks, whether serving or retired, but merchants and artisans and possibly a few noble offspring who'd claimed territory in Yalotlan and overseen the expansion of the village into this thriving little city.

'It warms the heart to see so many Pechaqueh here, determined to fight for what's theirs against overwhelming odds. It's pretty hostile around here,' she said conversationally – and just loud enough for those following the little group to hear.

There was a burst of whispering and Beyt turned and casually punched her in the gut, hard enough to steal breath and voice but not her legs – Ilandeh stumbled, gasped, gagged, but kept walking. All the new Flight had done was prove her point. Beyt seemed to realise the same, for she dragged Ilandeh into the nearest building and signalled her Whispers to prevent anyone from following. The milling Pechaqueh began to mutter, concern and anxiety threading through their voices.

In the darkened building, Beyt punched her again, not pulling it this time, and Ilandeh went to her knees straining for air, fire flashing through her gut despite her salt-cotton. Beyt landed a third punch to her short gut that would have her pissing blood tomorrow. She grunted and then the Flight grabbed her by the throat and hauled her onto her feet, crammed her back against the wall.

'What are you doing?'

'Saving Pechaqueh lives. What are you doing?' Ilandeh

wheezed. 'You and the dogs have done well, but you're isolated and this town's defences are pitiful. You don't really think you can survive an attack, do you?'

'We already have,' Beyt snapped. 'The slaves living here—'

Ilandeh coughed out a laugh. 'Wait, you've been here since the start? How long did it take for news of the uprising to reach this town's slaves?' Ilandeh sucked in a breath at Beyt's shifting expression, shock stealing her equilibrium. 'It didn't, did it? You heard about it through the song, or the city Listener. Maybe Detta reached out to you, but either way, you knew what was happening. Did you order loyal, ignorant slaves slaughtered or was that the Pechaqueh?'

'We did what we had to,' Beyt snarled. 'We're alive and safe because of it.'

'You're alive because you're hidden,' Ilandeh told her, 'and you know it. That won't last forever. I found you easily enough and with so much cultivated jungle surrounding this place and cooking smoke drifting on the wind, either Detta and the Second will come and requisition everything you have, leaving you starving and vulnerable, or the rebels will find you and wipe you out. So I ask again, Feather Beyt: why haven't you told the Pechaqueh to leave? It's standard practice in times of—'

'Don't talk down to me. Don't you dare pretend to know better than I,' Beyt snarled, dragging Ilandeh back out into the street and shoving her to get her moving. 'If we lose this city because of your mouth,' she muttered and then halted, though there were no Pechaqueh to be seen now. Even so, Beyt was weary and wary, a part of her attention always turned outwards to her surroundings – well-trained and paranoid.

'If you lose hundreds of Pechaqueh lives because you've lied, you mean,' Ilandeh countered. 'Evacuation is according to status and you know that. They should have been gone weeks ago. What were you thinking?'

Beyt rounded on her again. 'Gone where?'

'To Detta and the Second, or whichever city they've got a firm grip on!' Ilandeh snapped. 'You—'

'No. I am Flight here, not you. One more word and it won't just be fists, Whisper. Do you understand me?'

Ilandeh nodded. The Whispers were grim, casting murderous glances at Ilandeh. The free shot panicked looks at their Flight. The retired dogs were resigned; they well remembered this from their time in the Melody.

The warriors hurried her along into another building, passed through three rooms into a tiny, windowless space smelling strongly of dried mushrooms, and forced her to sit. They tied her knees and ankles, posted a guard on the doorless exit, and left. Ilandeh shifted, testing these new bonds and trying to relieve some of the growing numbness in her hands. Her mouth was sticky with blood.

Who would her guards be? If they were retired dogs or, even better, merchants, then she had a good chance of talking her way free. The tactics, lies, and manipulations that had been part of her training as a Whisper could bend even the most mistrustful person to her will. But other Whispers would recognise what she was doing. They'd recognise every tactic she employed to win them over.

Ilandeh had no idea whether Beyt would contact anyone now to verify her claims of innocence, but she had no doubt a Pecha was already inside one of the pyramids with its Listener demanding answers about their safety here in this city. At some point soon, Pilos was going to learn that Ilandeh lived, was in Yalotlan, and was saving Pechaqueh lives. As long as Beyt didn't murder her before he summoned her to the song to explain herself, she'd probably get out of this alive.

Alive, but once more under Pilos's scrutiny. His control.

Perhaps that's why I did it. What do I care if Pechaqueh get slaughtered here?

'I can hear you thinking from here,' Beyt said and stepped past the guard and into the room. She squatted against the far wall. 'Working away, trying to decide on the best approach to save yourself. Wondering how things are going here, whether we're trusted. Where our loyalty lies.'

Ilandeh licked her lips. 'For someone with a city to defend, you can't stay away from one captive Whisper,' she countered. 'As for your loyalty, it's hard to say: you're keeping Pechaqueh here under false pretences. Perhaps you'll throw them at any rebels in the hopes of securing your lives for theirs. Or maybe you're just a touch too incompetent to have thought it through, and you're loyal to the song. Or perhaps you're planning on killing them and their allies in their sleep once you've learnt all you can from them and from Feather Detta through the song. Biding your time, as so many others did before declaring themselves traitors.'

Beyt nodded. 'Nicely done. Enough assumptions to tempt me to answer and commit myself one way or the other. But what about you, Whisper Ilandeh? Where have you been all this time? Who owns your loyalty?'

Her face was closed, remote, but there was tension cording the muscles of her neck. Despite her bravado outside, she had to be wondering whether Ilandeh was here on orders and what those orders might be. Was she to be stripped of command after all?

'You forget yourself, Second Flight,' Ilandeh said with a note of warning in her voice. 'You know we are forbidden from talking about the duties we have carried out. I can't tell you where I've been or what I've done and you shouldn't even be asking. That you are – and your refusal to escort Pechaqueh to safety, or to leave this little town that cannot possibly have any value to you as a Whisper, or to the High Feather as a strategic place of interest – says much.'

They stared at each other in silence for long, slow beats of Ilandeh's heart.

'Perhaps the Pechaqueh presence here is the very reason I and my Whispers stay,' Beyt said.

Ilandeh put her head on one side and chewed her bottom lip, contemplating the Flight. 'Or perhaps that's why you won't let them leave,' she countered. 'They're your justification for staying here, hidden and safe for as long as you can. I'm sure you, at least, have an escape route already decided upon for when you're inevitably discovered. Until then, you stay here and pretend to be in charge and risk Pechaqueh lives – and the lives of macaws and good, loyal retired dogs who could be fighting and making a difference elsewhere in Yalotlan.'

'You speak of deceit, Whisper Ilandeh, and yet isn't it funny how Spear Pilos was disgraced only a few weeks after you disappeared back then? Back during the Sky City's fall?' Beyt glanced down to inspect her fingernails as she talked. 'How he'd have lost almost everything if not for High Feather Atu. Especially with you and he being so . . . close.'

Ilandeh snorted. It became a snigger and then a laugh and suddenly she was howling with mirth, her head tipped back and tears running down her face. The shock followed by stony disapproval in the other Whisper's expression only made her laugh harder. It took a long time for her amusement to wither, taking much of her tension and remaining energy with it. She was, abruptly, exhausted.

'Ah, Beyt, my friend,' she gasped. 'You want to be Flight, it's all yours. I'm in no position to argue. You want to know where I was for the last two years? Working directly for Pilos, and indirectly for the High Feather, in the Singing City. Cut off from the Melody and hidden in plain sight, right at the heart of it all. I was their eyes and ears where they needed them. Until I was deemed too great a risk, my blood not pure enough after all. After two years, after giving them information they *never* could have got otherwise, Pilos cast me aside. When I dared to argue, he set me up and had me arrested. Then he passed judgment and tried to execute me.'

Even in the low light, she saw the shock on Beyt's face.

She bared her teeth. 'So I took him hostage just long enough to get the fuck out.' She rubbed her cheek against her knee and then heaved a sigh. 'So there you have it. If you're going to kill me now, just get on with it. I'm done with all of you. With everything.'

'Wh-where were you, in the Singing City, I mean?' Beyt breathed, quietly as if she couldn't quite believe it.

'No,' Ilandeh said. 'Pilos might have betrayed me, the Melody might be closed to me, but I was – I am – a bloody good

Whisper. I did nothing wrong then, and I won't start now. I've already said more than makes me comfortable. Get your Listener to check in with Spear Pilos if you really want to know. If he'll tell you.

'Just don't tell me what his order is for my death,' she added, surprising them both. 'Do it, but don't taunt me with it before-hand. He made it very clear just how deep his loathing for me runs; I don't need to relive it in my dying moments.' She met Beyt's eyes. 'Warrior to warrior, personal differences aside, don't tell me how he insists I die. That's all I ask.'

'You think I owe you anything after what you just did here? I'm likely to lose a third of my defenders because of your words. The Empire might lose this entire city!'

Ilandeh snorted again. 'I'm sure it will be a great loss to the mighty Empire of Songs, this ant-bitten nowhere town in the depths of Yalotlan that two years ago was a village not even worthy of having a name.'

'It has a name now. It's the Green City.'

Ilandeh stared at her, waiting for more, waiting until Beyt felt foolish for her outburst. Then she sighed. 'I don't know what you think is going to happen here, Beyt, but Detta won't send warriors to save you even if you beg him. They'd come for your Pechaqueh if they knew about them, but they don't care about the rest of you. They care about saving themselves. We are nothing but weapons, and when we are blunted or broken, we are cast aside.'

Beyt watched her in silence, her face blank. Then she stood and left without another word. And Ilandeh sat in the dark and waited to die.

XESSA

Dawn wasn't even a promise in the east when Xessa, Ossa, and Tiamoko made their way out of hiding and crept through the city towards what the Pechaqueh called the Blessed Water. Just the name was enough to make her twitch; there was nothing holy about this river or any body of water in which the Drowned swam.

Tayan of Tokoban is now an enemy of freedom.

Lilla had met with Weaver in the aftermath of Weaver's own interrogation of Xessa, via Tiamoko's translation. She'd wanted to know everything about Tayan, about what Xessa thought he was doing up there in the great pyramid. It turned out that arguing with Lilla about Tayan was far different to the uneasy feelings of betrayal she'd had to wrestle with to answer Weaver's questions. And that, of course, wasn't fair. It was Tayan who was the betrayer; everyone said so. He'd been proclaimed so.

But when Lilla had sought her out afterwards to relay Weaver's decision and what it meant for the rebellion – the capture or kill order for when they finally took the great pyramid – there'd been something hollow, something dead, in his expression. He hadn't asked her if the news made her happy because he already believed it would. She'd seen it in the tightness of his mouth, the tension in his hands as he signed. Lilla thought Xessa relished Tayan's coming execution, that her lifelong friendship with his husband was as dead as her fathers, Kime and Otek. This was how far her bitterness had brought her in the weeks since she and Tiamoko had escaped from Pilos's fighting pit into a Singing City at war with itself. They'd found Tokob, they'd found kin among those Tokob, and Xessa had destroyed it all through her unrelenting hostility.

As I destroyed Oncan and Lutek and the other Tokob I killed in the pit at Pilos's order.

If Tayan had been here – her Tayan, loyal and ambitious and curious and superior – she'd have asked him to journey with her spirit to see if it was diseased, to understand why she seemed destined to hurt her own and to bear witness to the death of all she loved.

Tiamoko touched her shoulder, startling her. 'Focus, Eja. I could see your distraction from a stick away.'

'You're not a stick away,' she signed waspishly and then grimaced in apology. 'You're right.'

'We can talk about what's bothering you after,' the big warrior signed easily, as ever brushing away her prickliness like ash from a cold fire pit. She'd never once managed to offend him, as far as she knew, not for lack of trying. 'For now, the river's not too far.'

Xessa took a deep breath and looked at Ossa, pacing easily at her right. She flexed her hand on her spear and checked the net hanging from her belt. *Focus.*

There hadn't been any nets of sufficient strength or size for her purpose, so in between battles and rescues and searching for food and medicine – and arguing with Lilla – she'd made one of her own and it was finally finished. Net, spear, dog: she was ready. And she was *hungry* for this. For her true purpose, her duty, given to her by Malel herself.

Tiamoko led the way and Ossa guarded her flank, his big

triangular ears constantly on the move. Between them, they'd get her to the river in safety – from there, it would be her keeping them safe. Well, her and Ossa. She was filled with the familiar thrum of excitement and fear; it was the first time they would have hunted Drowned together in years. There were no guarantees Ossa would remember his duty or the way they moved as one.

But she could no longer watch and do nothing while her people forgot themselves. The Tokob did not crave war, but in this there were no civilians, and the sooner the reluctant and easily swayed among them learnt that, the better.

A life under the song was no life at all and they couldn't afford for more people to choose as Tayan had chosen, giving up themselves, their ancestors and all the generations to come out of self-interest and fear. The choices people had been free to make back home didn't exist anymore. Choice required peace, and there would be no peace until the song was ended.

It wasn't just Tokob, of course: every day more people slipped out of the war party's hiding place and were never seen again, fleeing to save their lives, or giving themselves back to Pechaqueh in the hopes of forgiveness. Xessa couldn't do anything about other people, but she could do something for her own. Remind them who they were; what they were. Remind them that Malel loved them and needed them.

The eja was a creature of violence now in a way she never had been back home. She'd never craved a Drowned's death before, with the exception of those awful, grief-stricken days after her father Kime's death. She craved it now, with the same intensity with which she craved Pilos's death for what he'd done to her and Tokoban. Craved it as much as her need to get her hands on Tayan and *make him understand*. Craved—

Ossa's attitude changed between one step and the next. He no longer pranced at her side but held his head low and intent. Xessa clicked her fingers for Tiamoko and indicated the dog; the warrior nodded and brought his spear up in both hands. Moments later the smell of the river hit her nostrils and Xessa was heartened to see that Ossa understood the scent meant his time to work was coming.

She let Tiamoko continue on high alert, just to be safe, and was glad of it when they reached the end of the road and he stopped and held up a hand in her direction. Ossa moved protectively in front of her. Xessa's fingers brushed the net hanging from the back of her belt, familiar and heavy even after two sun-years in Pilos's fighting pit without one.

'Hide,' Tiamoko signed. He was already backing down the road they'd just walked. Xessa followed as he slid into the shadows at the base of an outside staircase leading up to a large flat roof. She put her hand on Ossa's face and the big dog stilled.

Xessa scanned the road ahead and behind and glanced up at the roof; she couldn't see any obvious danger, but Ossa's ears flicked rapidly back in displeasure and then forward, stiff.

Torchlight grew at the end of the road and then vanished again, passing from left to right. Xessa breathed and waited for Tiamoko and Ossa to both signal the way was clear.

Eventually, they set off again through the last of the pre-dawn shadows. The stink of the river grew as they exited the road and turned left onto a wider thoroughfare. A few dozen strides further on and Xessa reached out and grabbed Tiamoko's wrist.

'This is far enough,' she signed when he glanced back at her. 'Get up high and protect my back. If you're called by the Drowned, I should be able to get to you in time if you have to run from a distance. Malel watch over you, my friend.'

Tiamoko pulled her into a tight hug. She grinned, wide and savage, then pressed a kiss to his cheek and jerked her thumb upwards. The big warrior nodded, patted Ossa on the head once, and loped away, vanishing into the shadows. Xessa waited for Ossa's alarm signal that would indicate he'd run into trouble, but other than an ear flicked back in his direction, the dog was focused on the road ahead and, beyond it, the Blessed Water. The eja checked her weapons one last time and then sent Ossa out on a run ahead of her.

Tiamoko had a bow and quiver – he would watch for human enemies and send a red-feathered arrow into the dirt next to Xessa's feet if they were compromised. Now, though, she put all thoughts of Pechaqueh enemies out of her mind. Ahead of her lay the gleam of water and within it, the promise of teeth and claws. Her true enemy; her true purpose.

It was perhaps the most reckless thing she'd ever done, but it felt right, down in her bones and blood. The Tokob, and perhaps all the rebels, needed this, needed what only she could provide – a beacon of hope painted in green blood.

They were going to kill a Drowned.

Ossa jumped, landing back feet, front feet on the muddy bank to indicate there was no danger. Xessa let out a slow, controlled breath through her nose and ran lightly towards him, casting him out ahead of her again. The dog raced away, his head and tail high, joy and alertness in his every line. He'd always loved to work.

The ground beneath her changed from limestone to packed earth, soft under the balls of her feet and between her toes as she slowed into a walk. There was no pipe here with which to draw water uphill; the rebels were drinking from the stone cisterns that dotted the city. When they were emptied, the battle for control of the river's many tributaries, narrow and shallow and not ideal for Drowned, would begin. In other parts of the city, they probably already had begun.

Xessa wasn't here for water. She was here to remember and celebrate the Tokob way of life, to dance a prayer to Snake-Sister and to affirm her life and that of all Tokob to Malel, that she was not forgotten. It was also a promise of retribution. She was going to kill Pechaqueh gods and line them up along the riverbank. She was going to make sure they knew she was here. Knew that she was eja, and free, and *angry*.

Xessa swept her gaze along the riverbank, checking that Ossa was safe and that he had no alarms for her. It was early, the sky mostly purple and the last stars clinging to its high vault in the west. This fight would be the first in more than two sun-years that was pure and sacred. She'd killed defending the Sky City and she'd killed for entertainment in the fighting pit. She'd killed more since escaping and joining the rebellion. Those deaths were to be mourned, for they illustrated how far people could fall from Malel's grace. How far Xessa had fallen. The death that was to come – the death of a Drowned or maybe more than one – would be beautiful. And it would be celebrated.

She wore Snake-Sister's blessings of strength and speed painted on her brow and limbs, and she would honour the God-born and her gifts. The familiar tightness of the paint on her skin was a kiss, a caress, and a promise.

Movement in the corner of her eye: Ossa, again signalling there was no danger. The ground grew damp and chill as she approached the water, the fingers of her right hand looped into the net tucked in her belt and her spear warm and comfortable in the other. She rolled her head on her neck and shook her shoulders and then strode to the edge of the river. Something broke the surface, ripples spilling against the current. Xessa clicked her tongue, calling Ossa to her side.

Head, shoulders, and hands rose from the depths of the Blessed Water and a throat sac inflated, paler than the rest of the green-grey skin. Xessa's awareness flickered back towards Tiamoko up on his roof and the distance she had covered. The twitch of Ossa's ears told her the Drowned had begun to sing, and the eja lunged with her spear, her right foot coming down into the water and sending up a splash. The spear was tipped in bone and honed to a wicked point and it ripped through the Drowned's throat, piercing the sac and stealing its deadly song. It fell backwards in a splash of water and green blood, its hand scrabbling at its throat and an expression she would swear was shock in its round, black eyes.

Xessa's mouth pulled upwards in a savage grin: these Drowned were so glutted on human flesh that they had forgotten that not all people worshipped them. She took another step and thrust again, this time driving the spear through the side of its neck and back out. A killing blow.

Despite the warning in her skin and all her years of training, Xessa took a third step into the river, the water lapping up her shins, and grabbed the Drowned by its hair. Ossa was in the water next to her now, sending a bolt of alarm through her gut. The dog grabbed the makeshift padding on her forearm and dragged her out of the river. Xessa's grip in its hair in turn dragged the Drowned, and the three of them made an awkward shuffle out of the water.

Ossa herded her back from the Drowned and the riverbank alike, snarling and snapping until she complied. That had been over-hasty, overconfident, and it would get them both killed. And yet, a dying Drowned lay on the bank, and it had been *easy*.

Xessa let the dog posture, focusing on the three Drowned she could see far across the water. They were headed towards her with purpose, the lightening sky outlining their round heads draped in weedy hair. Alerted by this one's call of distress, most likely, or its suddenly ended song. Or perhaps they viewed her as their dawnmeal. She hurried along the riverbank away from the dying Drowned, wishing she had time to drive the point of her spear with slow, exquisite precision through one black eye, watch it twist and writhe and then shudder into stillness.

She did not. Three at once was two too many; the death of her father had proved that. Still, perhaps she could encourage one to follow her while the others converged on their dying kin. Ossa was signalling, alerting her to the Drowned, so she acknowledged him and sent him on another run in the direction she was moving. He bolted and she broke into an easy lope, following his pawprints in the soft mud. They'd gone no more than twenty steps when the dog skidded into a wide turn and sprinted back towards her. His ears were flat to his head and Xessa looked beyond to what might have frightened him: there was nothing there. Instinct, or perhaps a vibration in the ground that was sensed more than felt, and she spun in place, bringing up her spear, and the Greater Drowned that loomed tall over her, dripping river water, swiped with its claws. Xessa yelled and fell backwards, jabbing with the spear. The bone tip scraped across the tough hide of its chest, carving a shallow line that didn't even bleed. The tips of its claws entered her jaw and bottom lip, slicing.

Xessa landed hard, biting her tongue and cracking her right elbow into the dirt: a shard of pain flashed all the way to her fingertips. The Drowned was on her immediately, hooking its hind claws into the padding stitched to her leggings and swiping at her face again. Xessa slammed the spear across its chest and pushed it back. *Ossa. Now would be the time, dog.*

The Drowned's hands scrabbled at her salt-cotton and a claw dug another line across the soft skin of her neck; she felt the sting of flesh parting but no more. No venom. None in her face, either, by Malel's grace, though it was bleeding well enough.

She bucked her hips to throw it off, but then it grabbed her spear with both hands and wrenched it from her grip.

Ossa launched himself over her head and hit the monster in the chest, his jaws snapping at its throat. Xessa fumbled a knife out of her belt and ripped the blade across the Drowned's flank, down below its toughened hide as it arched backwards under the dog's solid weight.

He twisted away before it could close its arms around him and lunged back in from behind, low into the meat of its thigh where it still straddled the ejab waist. Xessa stabbed for its throat as the Drowned sprang off her and sideways towards the river, its movement arrested by Ossa's teeth, tearing this time at the calf. Xessa rolled in the same direction and sliced its arm with her knife, snatched up her abandoned spear and leapt to her feet. She slammed the butt into the back of the Drowned's skull and sent it face first into the mud and then punched the blade into the back of its neck. Bone spearhead grated on living bone and then sank deep. The Drowned spasmed, writhing in the mud, its claws digging deep trenches in the riverbank, and then fell still except for the wild flapping of its gills.

The eja pulled the spear free and then gave Ossa the kill

command – not that he needed the encouragement. He pounced on its back, jaws burrowing under the chin and into the side of the neck. His head jerked, big paws bracing on its shoulders. Jerked again and came away with a mouthful of pale flesh chased by a gouting green flood.

The dog dropped the meat and jumped backwards, ears flat to his skull as he put himself between it and Xessa. The eja checked him for injuries, swiping green blood from his muzzle and around his eyes, then sent him straight out again. Her motions were jittery with adrenaline but he read them easily enough and savage joy filled her, bright and sparkling as the sunlight in a jaguar's eye.

Despite their long separation, he'd settled back into his role as her protector and her ears as if they'd never been apart, as if they'd been gathering water and hunting Drowned all this time. Xessa's heart swelled with pride and love even as she checked all around herself and took several prudent steps away from the dying Drowned. The three that had been coming for her were now two, but she didn't dare assume the one that had just died was the third. That one could be anywhere, heading up- or downriver to come at her from the side.

The two she could see had paused deep in the river to watch. *Learning how I fight? Malel, I hope not.* The way they moved, their eerie synchronicity, unnerved her. It felt different to the ones she'd faced at the Swift Water so long before. Or perhaps it was just the intervening two years that had made her forget.

Xessa tongued the cut in her lip and felt the ones in her jaw and neck; still no burning or swelling. She'd been lucky. Two Drowned: one Lesser, one Greater.

Extremely lucky.

Especially as it took my spear from me.

A hard shudder of primal fear swept through her. The ease with which it had torn the weapon from her grip. The *contempt* of it. She checked in with Ossa to find him jumping; as soon as he had her attention he pointed and she swivelled to the river once more. *Oh, fuck.*

Eight or ten Drowned were watching her now, mostly Lesser,

not that that meant anything with those numbers. At least half of them were singing, a ghastly choir whose volume might be enough to draw Tiamoko to the river. Her time here was done – at least for today.

She and Tiamoko had identified five different places where the Blessed Water's banks were wide and open enough to fight, but overlooked by a distant building where the warrior could watch for human enemies, and she intended to visit each one in a random pattern the Drowned couldn't predict and kill every monster she found there. With Malel's and Snake-Sister's grace, she might drive them into the Pechaqueh-held areas of the city, making the waterways safer for the rebels and sowing fear among their enemies.

And if not, well, Pechaqueh would know the agony of the deaths of their gods in just retribution for their crimes.

Xessa summoned Ossa and then faced back into the city and circled her spear overhead three times to let Tiamoko know she was coming back. Three Drowned emerged onto the riverbank and converged on their dead as soon as she retreated, and she wondered whether they felt things such as grief or rage. She hoped so. She hoped they were frightened.

Ossa's nose led her back to Tiamoko, who was sweaty with fear. He'd stuffed cotton in his ears to dull his hearing and signed that he'd felt a compulsion to approach the river, but it had been just weak enough to resist. Now, though, he insisted they hurry away and Xessa was more than happy to comply.

She was vibrating with energy and triumph and vicious satisfaction. She had not lost sight of her true purpose; Ossa had not forgotten his training; and together they would strike fear into Pechaqueh hearts and righteousness into the spirits of those fighting for freedom. The news would reach Tayan and he'd know it was her. He'd know the message she was sending him and the ultimatum it contained.

And he'll choose. He'll choose me and Lilla. His people. He will.

He has to.

Despite her conviction, Xessa's mood soured at the thought of the friend of her heart in the heart of the city and all that he was said to be doing there. Deliberately, she recalled the feel of her spear ripping through the Drowned's throat, the image of Ossa tearing meat from the second. This. *This* was how she would serve the rebellion. While the warriors fought on the streets, her battles were the riverbanks and the creatures that haunted them.

They'd run almost a stick through the empty streets when Tiamoko took an abrupt turn down an alley. Xessa began to follow but then Ossa was snarling and leaping after the big warrior. He lunged ahead of Tiamoko, putting himself between him and three blurry figures in the shadows. The eja sprinted forwards, ready to fight, and then skidded to a halt on instinct. The three figures were taller even than Tiamoko, naked and wet and alien. Three Greater Drowned. In the city. A stick from the river.

Waiting for us. How did they know which route we'd take? How did they get ahead of us?

A Drowned could survive for an hour out of water; to have travelled so far meant they couldn't have long before they needed to return or risk death. Still, it would be long enough to kill them.

No, it fucking won't.

Xessa jerked into motion, grabbing Tiamoko's shoulder to pull him away. He slammed an elbow backwards into her chest, winding her, and she staggered into a wall, pushed off it and launched herself at him again, gasping for breath and her mind as bright and clear as the sky at highsun.

Ossa was teeth and claws and movement but so were the Drowned and Tiamoko was in Xessa's way, between her and her dog. Between her and her enemies. She pushed him hard, forcing him into the opposite wall, and slipped past. Immediately, a Drowned threw itself on her. Xessa got her spear up as it hit her, clawed hands shredding her armour and her spear haft in between its jaws. Its weight forced her back a pace, forced her into Tiamoko, who supported her only because he was trying to give himself to the rearmost Drowned, singing from a safe distance.

Ossa had caused the middle creature some real damage; it had one hand pressed to its leg, green blood spurting between its webbed fingers while the other tried feebly to push him away. He lunged in again, ripped off part of the shielding hand, and jumped back out. Tiamoko's struggles redoubled; no doubt the thing had screamed. His arm came around Xessa's throat and began to squeeze, lifting her up and backwards to expose her belly to the Drowned clinging to her front and it was over. It was all over. There was no coming back from this. All three of them would die.

Something sprouted in the angle between the Drowned's head and neck. It shuddered, right arm falling still, and then slumped. Xessa blinked and then recognised the arrow protruding from its flesh. Shot from above deep into its body cavity. A killing shot. But that was impossible.

Xessa moved even as she struggled to process what had just happened. She had to stop the rearmost Drowned from singing to free Tiamoko from its control. Her friend, perhaps sensing her intent, tightened his grip on her throat, hauling her backwards until her feet left the ground. She battered her heels into his shins and then slid her hand back and grabbed his balls and squeezed, twisting. His cry vibrated against her back and he collapsed, curling around the pain.

Xessa wriggled from his slack grip and staggered into the wall. Tiamoko's agony might be a momentary barrier between him and his need to answer the song, but it wouldn't last. She pushed herself upright and ran, leaping the shot Drowned, ripping her knife across the second's outstretched arms, and then throwing her spear. It took the third Drowned in the face, knocking it off balance and disrupting its song, she hoped. Maybe only for a few moments, but that should be long enough to break its control over Tiamoko and for Ossa to herd him away, weak-kneed or not. The dog would come back for her, but she'd be dead by then.

But they'll live. They'll both live.

Snake-Sister's settled calm fell over Xessa as she unhooked the net from her belt and tossed it underhand with a practised twist of her wrist. The pebbles tied to the edges made it flare and the net billowed open and fell to tangle the Drowned's head and shoulders. Xessa followed it in, slapping down one clawed foot that kicked at her and jamming her knife into its groin and jerking up.

She pulled out the blade and leapt away from its thrashing limbs, slipping around towards its back. The net was tough, but it wouldn't hold it for long. Its song might have already summoned more of its kin, if prowling the streets was something they did now, some terrifying new change in their behaviour.

Xessa stabbed again. The first strike went into the base of its spine, stealing its legs, and as it collapsed she followed it down. The next two blows scraped off its plated hide as its struggled, but the last found its mark, sliding from one side of its neck all the way to the middle. It toppled onto its side, the torn remains of its throat sac pulsating and its sliced gill flapping obscenely. And then it went still. Silence. Death.

There was no pride in this victory and Xessa didn't spare it a second glance, snatching up her spear and then running for Tiamoko and Ossa. The second Drowned, the one Ossa had held at bay for so long, was down, three arrows sticking from its neck and chest, shot from that impossible, high-up, angle. Xessa glanced up reflexively; nothing.

Tiamoko was kicking the first dead Drowned in the face and screaming something she couldn't read. Ossa was slumped against the wall, his eyes dull and his fur bloody – green and red. His tail thumped sluggishly and Xessa forgot Tiamoko, the mysterious archer, and the possibility of more Drowned. She threw herself onto her knees at Ossa's side, overwhelmed with guilt and panic and grief.

The dog was torn, a gaping wound in his shoulder made by teeth or claws. If the latter, he'd also be poisoned, and with so severe a wound, he'd never survive it. Xessa prayed it had been teeth. Either way, he needed stitches and rest and warm, good food. Water. Bandages. Medicine.

She couldn't lose him; she *couldn't*.

I won't.

Xessa's armour was hanging in tatters from her chest and shoulders and she ripped a strip from the bottom and turned it salt-side out and bound it as best she could around Ossa's shoulder and chest. The dog flinched and bared his teeth but allowed her to tie off the makeshift bandage. Blood seeped through too fast and she tied a second strip over the first and then, with some difficulty, got him draped across her shoulders. His wound pressed against the side of her head and she could feel moisture against her ear and cheek. Grunting, she used her spear to help her stand, cast a final glance upwards to the roof now hidden by the glare of the early sun, and knocked her spear butt against the wall to attract Tiamoko's attention. He paused in his battering of the dead Drowned, his chest heaving for air and wildness still lurking in his expression.

She leant her spear in the crook of her elbow in order to sign. 'Ossa's hurt.'

Tiamoko straightened immediately, the snarl falling from his face to be replaced with concern. She gestured him in front: she needed him focused and aware more than ever, and having him where she could see him made it easier to communicate. Besides, if there were more Drowned approaching, they'd be coming from the river – from behind.

There was no time to discuss the invisible, impossible archer who'd helped them, though now that the adrenaline was seeping from her limbs and her mind had space for thoughts other than survival, Xessa couldn't stop glancing up at the roofs. Were they an assassin who'd missed their target or a friend unwilling to reveal themself? She didn't particularly like either option.

Ossa's paws twitched in her grip and she hummed, running her thumb over his pad. She was sweating under his weight, could feel it trickling down her back. Sweat. Not blood. Definitely not her dog's blood soaking through her armour and tunic and down to the skin.

She paused behind Tiamoko as he checked the exits to a

small plaza with a squat statue in the centre. At some point since the start of the uprising, rebels had smashed off the glyphs of the Singer to who it was dedicated. Xessa hurried forward at Tiamoko's gesture and they turned down a familiar alley. Not far now.

Perhaps it was another eja. The thought came out of nowhere and sent an immediate thrill chasing down her spine. It could be an eja, someone who didn't have their dog and so couldn't patrol the riverbank with her, but who could use spirit-magic and had aided her where they could. The spots on a Drowned's body vulnerable to arrows were so few that ejab didn't bother with bows, but the join of the head and neck, if attacked from above, was one of them. And this person had known that.

A name threatened at the edges of her mind, a name beloved and unsigned, never signed, lest the familiar movements like caresses in the air turned to a grip that would crush her heart. Xessa pressed her teeth into the ragged claw-cut in her lip and focused on the pain, driving out all thoughts other than their safety and getting Ossa to a shaman. Thoughts of, of *him*, could wait. Her dog's life couldn't.

They didn't make it back. They were deep in the flesh markets and surrounded by tall storehouses and vast open spaces where bamboo cages had once held human livestock when Tiamoko signalled danger. He guided her into a long, low building and down a set of stairs into a room dug beneath the ground. It was so black she couldn't see his shape in front of her and had to cling to his shoulder as she shuffled down the steps blind.

Tiamoko used touch-sign to tell her to wait and she sensed him leave, the cooler air brushing against the sweat of her face and then stilling. With nothing else to do, she eased Ossa off her shoulders and onto the dirt floor, keeping one hand on his muzzle when she could to indicate he should remain silent. Despite the command, she felt the whine that rumbled from his throat. He was hurting; it was unfair of her to expect his silence. And yet she had no choice. The big dog leant his weight against her hip and then sagged slowly until he was lying with his head on her thigh. Xessa put her other hand over her own mouth against the threat of tears and together they waited. And they waited. In the dark and the silence and the blood, they waited.

Tiamoko didn't come back.

LILLA

Tithing barns, western edge of Singing City,
Pechacan, Empire of Songs
39th day of the Great Star at morning

'How are you?'

Lilla squinted up at Ekon. 'Thirsty. Hungry. Surviving.'

He knew that wasn't what the man meant, but since Weaver's proclamation about Tayan, he had withdrawn even further into himself. He hadn't wanted to talk about it before; he certainly wasn't going to now. Who could he speak with anyway? Who would listen to him defend a man deemed indefensible, one branded a traitor to freedom?

Ekon didn't seem inclined to press him, though. He collapsed cross-legged in the scant shadow cast by the building. The Wet would be here soon, bringing relief from the stifling humidity. Until then, they pretended the shade made a difference.

Without the sun behind him, the terrible swelling around his cheek, nose, and eye was clear and the Toko winced. Ekon noticed and smiled ruefully, his fingertips hovering just over the bruising but not daring to touch.

'It's getting better,' he said.

Lilla snorted. 'It's getting worse. Can you even see me out of that eye?' The Chitenecatl fussed with the hem of his kilt, rearranging it over his knees instead of answering. 'Thought not. How are we doing?'

Although they shared command of the war party, Ekon's familiarity with Melody structure and giving orders meant he shouldered much of the organisation and logistics. He was responsible for moving them between hideouts without being seen, for sourcing food, water, medicine, and weapons.

Lilla dealt with the civilians, both those allied with them and the others, hundreds or thousands of others, who simply hid in the city and hoped to live. He offered them protection and asked them for help as needed; he did what he could to buy their silence when they saw the war party slipping among the buildings; and he did what he could to soothe their fears. Often, those he bribed and those he comforted were the same people, and although the comfort was hollow and the bribes were triangles of stale cornbread, at least he tried.

'Well. We're doing well,' Ekon lied smoothly and Lilla snorted again and leant his head back against the warm stone behind him, closing his eyes against the sun's glare. For a man who'd successfully fooled everyone around him for more than twenty sun-years, Ekon was shit at direct lies – or maybe he was just bad at telling them to Lilla. Something warm and smug stretched and curled in his chest and he smothered it with ruthless precision.

'And how are you?' Ekon repeated.

'Worried for Xessa.'

Another evasion and they both knew it.

'Traitor-fucker,' someone murmured before the former Feather could speak again. Lilla's eyes snapped open against his will and he glared at the Tlaloxqueh retreating back.

'Ignore him,' Ekon said and patted Lilla's knee, then shifted closer in a deliberate show of support.

'People have a right to be angry with Tayan. Not everyone understands what's he's going through,' Lilla managed with an unconvincing shrug. 'I'm used to it by now.'

He wasn't used to it, not at all.

As if to prove the speaker's point, the song spiked into a

sudden crescendo of power and dominance that closed like a fist around Lilla's heart. He bowed his head against it and against the scores of hostile faces he knew would be turned in his direction. *None of us know what Tay is doing or how his enslavement by the Singer grips him. He needs someone to fight for him, and that someone is me. It will always be me. He's my husband and I love him.*

'What is it you want Xessa to do?' Ekon asked quietly. 'And I don't mean at the river, so don't deflect,' he added before Lilla could respond exactly like that. Despite the hundred other tasks he needed to resolve – they both needed to resolve – there was nothing but patience in his tone. As if this conversation was the most important thing he could be doing right now.

Lilla rolled his eyes. He hated Ekon's perception sometimes. Still, he thought about his question. No one had quite phrased it like that before and it stopped him before he could say something to cut the conversation dead. He found, to his surprise, that for the first time he wanted to answer. To explain. Everyone had listened; no one had understood. Would this be different? Malel, he hoped so.

'I don't want her to change her mind about Tayan just because I ask her to,' he said slowly and not entirely truthfully. 'I just want her, and everyone, to be open to the possibility that she's wrong. Xessa's known Tay longer than I have, they've been friends since they were infants. If anyone should have sided with me about his character it's her, but instead she's convinced he's, I don't know, evil, that he's become like the Pechaqueh and is seeking to return us to slavery. As if anyone only two sun-years under the song would forget themselves, their people and their gods like that. How could Tayan forget Malel? Forget the God-born and his spirit guides? No. Impossible.'

'To be fair, Fang, the return of all non-Pechaqueh to enslavement is exactly what he said he wanted. That's what he asked of us that day at the peace-weaving. It was the condition of that peace. And it's what the song demands every moment.'

Ekon's voice was carefully gentle, but still a familiar, burning frustration began to bubble in Lilla's chest.

'Why won't anyone listen to me? Why is he being held up as the prime example of treachery when it's not his fault? There are thousands of other people who've remained in servitude rather than side with us, but no one talks about them. Only Tayan. Only my husband is a traitor; no one else's kin. I miss him but I'm not allowed to. I'm not allowed to be sad for my husband.'

'I left my family to take on the name and destiny of Ekon of Pechacan when I was seventeen,' Ekon said quietly, staring into his lap. 'I wasn't even an adult, yet I carried a secret and what sometimes felt like the weight of the entire resistance on my back. I abandoned all thoughts of my home and family; I abandoned all thoughts of the rebellion itself. I had to if I was going to convince everyone. I could be Pecha; I could live a life of privilege and relative ease if you didn't count the wars' – he barked a laugh – 'and be respected by all, if I tried hard enough, believed hard enough. And I got that life and that privilege and respect and power. I got it all.'

'Are you saying that's what Tay is doing?' Lilla asked when he fell quiet. 'That he's pretending so thoroughly in order to stay alive that he's . . . lost sight of who he is?'

'Perhaps. When word came that the rebellion was set for the night of the Great Star's little absence, I, I felt so much. One of the biggest things was panic.'

'That's understandable,' Lilla began.

'Let me finish,' Ekon said quietly, running his thumb over one of the many Pechaqueh tattoos he bore. 'It was panic at losing everything I had. My comfortable life. My position and wealth and status. The respect and affection of important people, important Pechaqueh. I didn't want to give it up. Why should I when I'd worked so hard for it? It was mine, those were *my* achievements, *my* wealth and honour.' He swallowed and Lilla copied him, a hard ball of emotion sitting at the base of his throat.

'I had all the power and privilege I could ever want or need, and the rebellion wanted me to abandon it. Give it up. It was one of the hardest decisions I've ever made and . . . and I almost chose wrong.' Despite the bruises marring his face, his anguish was obvious. 'I thought about exposing the other rebels in the Melody so that they'd be executed and I could continue my life as a Pecha without fear of discovery. A life that would be even more honourable for having discovered a dangerous plot. I lay awake night after night imagining it, how High Feather Atu would thank me, raise me up, reward me. All it would take would be the deaths of traitors. What does that say about me?'

Lilla pushed away the sympathy welling in him and focused on the bitterness that followed it. 'I suppose you want me to say that it makes you a better man than Tay, because you gave up your power for the rebellion and he hasn't.'

Ekon stared at him. He opened his mouth and then closed it again, shaking his head. 'No,' he said wearily after a pause long enough for Lilla to feel a flicker of shame. 'That's not what I want you to say. I had status and wealth as a warrior, as a Feather. Tayan is Shadow of the Singer. He has access to, control of, a magic none of us can understand. Power and prestige we can't imagine. Maybe he doesn't want to give that up. Or maybe he can't. Maybe Xac does have complete control of him, a slave of the mind as well as the body. We can't know.'

'No, we can't. And yet everyone keeps insisting they do know. That they know my husband better than I do.'

'When our family was recruited into the resistance and I was chosen to be their eyes in the Melody—'

'Yes, yes, you were very brave and self-sacrificing,' Lilla snarled and began to get up.

'They used them to train me to be Pechaqueh.'

Lilla sat down again, his own frustration forgotten. 'What?'

'My family. They became my Chitenecah slaves and servants. I was expected to treat them . . . it doesn't matter. We all knew what the uprising could cost us – did cost us. That memory and their sacrifice was the only thing that helped me make the decision to stay true to the resistance. Nothing I could give up would ever compare with what they did to put me in the Melody. Like I said, I could have exposed the rebellion; I didn't. I could have urged Atu to put Talons in or near the Singing City itself; I didn't do that, either. I chose to let the violence come and rise with it. I chose something bigger.'

Lilla went cold. Hard as granite and as unforgiving in the face of Ekon's arrogance. 'And Tayan didn't.'

'Or maybe he did,' Ekon contradicted quietly. 'Maybe Tayan chose the magic.'

Lilla looked down at a sudden ache in his hands and found his fists clenched together. 'You don't know him the way I do,' he said quietly, but it was the last kick of a rat wrapped in a snake's coils. Instinctive. Helpless. Dying. The cold was gone, the granite with it. He was all raw, cringing flesh.

'Of course not. But I know you, at least a little. I watched you act with integrity and dignity and genuine care for the warriors around you. You wore that collar and those brands as if they were objects of pride; you never gave in to despair – or at least not where I could see you. I know you'd have chosen a good man, an ambitious man, to spend your life with. But Lilla, he had the chance to run and chose not to. He had the chance to kill the Singer and didn't. He ordered the Melody to slaughter us and they obeyed. It isn't just about the choice he made back then to save his life. It's the choices he's continuing to make every day, ones that are killing us.'

Lilla didn't want to hear this, but he was too tired to move away. He told himself that was why he stayed; why he listened.

There was no reproach in Ekon's face or voice, only a hint of urgency, a plea that he listen and understand. 'He allied with the Singer, shared his magic, and sided with him against Enet during the ritual. He chose, Lilla. Right or wrong, good or evil, Tayan of Tokoban *chose*. It's time you did the same. Fighting for freedom while defending one of the people responsible for the song that seeks to enslave us—'

No. It was too much, after all. Lilla lurched to his feet and Ekon followed him, an apology already spilling from his lips. 'Kitten, wait. I'm sor—'

'I told you not to call me that. How could—'

A warrior sprinted towards them, waving wildly. Silently. Lilla's gaze went automatically to the roofs: there were no sentries visible. They were still there, of course they were, but they'd ducked low so they were out of sight. He reached for the spear propped against the wall.

'Report,' Ekon said as soon as the man reached them, the topic of Tayan dismissed as quickly as it had been raised, to Lilla's relief and the Chitenecah clear frustration.

'Melody warriors in the streets. We're in danger of discovery.'

'How many?'

'Hard to tell among the buildings, but from the formation it looks like five pods.'

Lilla and Ekon exchanged a startled look.

'They're coming from two directions so far,' the warrior added, almost dancing in place with impatience. He gestured back the way he'd come.

Energy coursed through Lilla's body, washing away the bitterness of their argument and the lingering voices that whispered of his husband's betrayal. This was simple, uncomplicated; this was something he knew how to do.

'I'll take three hundred and go out to meet them. You hold the rest here in case they try and circle around. And send messengers over the roofs to Weaver and Xini. If their war parties remain undetected, they might have an opportunity to strike at the pyramid while we draw out such a large force. Either way, tell the messengers that we'll hold them as long as we can.' He looked up at the angle of the sun. 'If it is just five pods, tell them we can hold until dusk.

'This could be Xessa's doing,' he added. 'It might be vengeance for her victory at the river.'

'Or it might be unrelated,' Ekon said with that cold pragmatism Lilla hated – and needed. 'It doesn't matter. What matters is that they're here and they need killing.' He slid his hand beneath the fall of Lilla's hair and gripped the nape of his neck, stilling him and sending an unwelcome shiver down his spine. 'Do not be reckless, Fang Lilla.'

The Toko looked up into Ekon's face. He licked sweat from his upper lip and watched the other man follow the motion hungrily as his hand tightened on Lilla's bare skin. Deliberately, he shifted out of that grip. 'As the Feather commands,' he said. Shame chased triumph through his gut at the look on the Chitenecah face and he turned away before he did something stupid like apologise.

I reject that title.

He gestured to the warrior to lead and then, unwillingly, he hesitated. 'I'll be safe,' he murmured without looking back. 'You too . . . Ekon.'

There was no way to tell whether the estimate of numbers was correct. Melody warriors seemed to be everywhere, mostly dogs but more eagles than he'd expected. Why waste their elite if this wasn't a major offensive? Then again, perhaps Pilos and Atu were running out of loyal free and were being forced to commit Pechaqueh. Or perhaps eagles had flooded out in response to Xessa's victory – Lilla pushed the thoughts away, striving for Ekon's cold-blooded practicality.

He ducked under the humming swing of an eagle's spear and smashed the haft of his own into her face. Blood sprayed from her nose and mouth, a chip of tooth flashing white among the crimson as she grunted and swayed back a step before lashing out with her foot and kicking him in the hip hard enough to stagger him. He let out a grunt of his own and then hooked her ankle with the butt of his spear. She was fast though, and although he snatched her balance, she didn't fall. They circled like dogs, intent only on each other despite the swirl of battle that moved around them in the open square.

Lilla's war party had been forced into a scrambling retreat for half a stick until they'd reached this wide plaza, where they'd held the road mouths for an hour until they'd finally been pushed back into the open space, the Melody breaking through to form the lines that had proven so lethal in Yalotlan and Tokoban.

But most of his warriors had been in the Melody, too; they

understood now how to fight in lines and formations and the plaza was slick with blood and screams. The eagle came at him again, snorting blood and blowing a fine red mist in his direction. Their spears clacked together as they thrust and parried, circling again until the warriors behind Lilla were his own once more. The eagle was good; she was better than him, but Lilla had beaten eagles before and he would beat this one as well. He just needed good timing and good luck and Malel's blessing.

He feinted and she read it, sidestepping into him and jabbing with her spear as his own flashed harmlessly past. The flint tip tore a gaping rent in Lilla's armour and punched into his belly, scraping off his hip bone and back out.

He roared pain, grabbed her spear shaft halfway between the head and the bannerstone and pushed it wide, then stepped in and headbutted her in her bleeding face. Her legs gave way, dumping her onto the blood-spattered stone. Lilla didn't waste time adjusting his grip on his spear or hers: he kicked her in the chest and sent her crashing onto her back and then stamped on her throat with all the strength he possessed. There was an audible crunch followed by a horrible whistling, gagging sound he could hear even over the roar of battle. He ripped the spear from her hand and left her to suffocate; they had neither the time nor the weapons to put the dying out of their misery.

The Toko spun in a circle with both spears in his right hand and his left clamped to his salt-cotton and the steady leak of blood from within. The wound was hot and throbbing, a spike of nauseating pain deep in his guts and down into his groin. Carefully, he probed the wound and then inspected his hand – the blood was red and there was no hint of opened guts. A simple puncture and his innards saved by his hipbone. A few stitches and he'd probably be fine. Probably.

'Traitor! I'll fucking kill you, you treacherous fuck!'

The words were distant but clear over the cacophony of shouts, screams, and the thud of weapons into flesh and stone.

The answering roar was wordless hate, but familiar: Ekon.

Yet again an eagle, or maybe an ambitious dog, had recognised him and decided to claim glory along with his head. Lilla's three hundred had been nearly routed when Ekon had led reinforcements to their aid an hour, or two, or a year ago, and he'd been nearly dizzy with relief to see them pouring in from the side streets to attack the Melody's flanks.

Now, Lilla spun in the direction of the shout, fading out of the line so he didn't get stabbed in the back by the clamouring enemy. The fresh wound in his gut demanded he hunch over, demanded he find a quiet corner and hide, rest, writhe in pain. Sweat and tears stung his eyes as he stood tall and swept the battle for Ekon and whoever was—

There.

'Fuck,' he breathed and began to run, limping badly and half-convinced his guts were going to fall out of the hole in his belly.

The eagle and Ekon burst through the far rebel line and spun deeper into the plaza, closer to Lilla. They leapt, hacked and slashed, both of them armed only with knives. Both of them bleeding.

Ekon. *Bleeding.*

His face was a scarlet mask brighter than a parrot's wing and his left arm was clamped to his side, unbalancing him, denying him a free hand to grab at his enemy. He screamed his war cry and even from here Lilla saw the blood mist from his lips. Ekon lunged and his opponent spun around and past him, the dull of his blade flashing towards Ekon's back as he pivoted. Slashing. Cutting.

Lilla still had the eagle's spear in his hand and he slowed just long enough to breathe, synchronise his arm with his steps, and aim. The spear flew from his hand, flew long and true, only the eagle wasn't there anymore and the weapon passed behind him and skittered onto the stones. It drew his attention just long enough for Ekon to scramble back. Just long enough for Lilla to breathe again, aim again, and this time lead the man – casting his second spear at the space into which he was moving.

Lilla sprinted after it, his wound forgotten and a knife in his fist. The spear hit the Pecha high in the back, under the shoulder-blade perhaps, knocking him forward a step and standing proud in flesh and salt-cotton. A true hit. A wounding hit.

Toko and Chitenecatl surged into him from behind and one side, knives plunging in. Despite it all, despite the spear and their blades and the ending of his life, the eagle still had his own knife and Ekon gasped, low and guttural, at something he did before Lilla ripped his spear from the Pechaqueh back, leapt onto him, and tore his blade across the eagle's neck – hasty, jagged, lethal but not quickly. Not quickly enough.

He bore the man to the ground and grabbed a fistful of hair to slam his face into the stone while Ekon fell to one knee, the rich red-brown of his skin gone grey with shock and blood loss. Lilla slammed the eagle's face into the stone again, and again. Get him down and keep him down, get Ekon and get to safety. That was all that mattered.

'Ekon? Ekon! Talk to me, where are you hurt? Where?' Lilla demanded when he looked up from the Pechaqueh motionless form and found Ekon had slumped to both knees with his arms wrapped around his midriff.

He leapt off the eagle and pulled him into his arms. 'Shaman! Shaman, I need a shaman here now,' he bawled, cradling Ekon's head to his chest. 'Malel, please. Please don't. Please,' he whispered, pressing his free hand over Ekon's where it was clutching his ribs. Was that air he felt against his fingers? His lung? Had his lung torn?

'Ekon, don't you fucking dare die on me, you hear?' he begged. 'Don't you die! You can't. I'll bloody well kill you if you do.'

Ekon gasped, something that might have been a laugh if there had been strength or sound to it. 'Enough, Fang Lilla,' he managed. 'I'm not dying. I won't die from this. You . . . get up, please. Lilla, get off me, it's not as bad as it looks.'

'Shut up, you don't know what you're saying. *Shaman!*'

'Lilla. Get off me.' There was a snap of authority in it this time, enough to cut through the Tokob blind panic. He stopped his frantic search among the fighting figures for the blue of a shamanic kilt or tunic and focused on Ekon's face, still tucked tightly against his chest. He concentrated and managed to loosen his fingers; Ekon pushed himself upright with a long, low groan and swiped blood out of his eyes.

Despite Lilla's inarticulate protest, he climbed to his feet and the Toko stood too, insisting on checking Ekon's back – he'd seen the knife go in. He'd . . . the salt-cotton was ripped but no blood stained its edges. Still, there was enough dripping from the front of him. Lilla wrapped an arm around the Chitenecah ribs, hissing his own hurt and ignoring it. They just had to—

'Stop this, Lilla. Please. Stop caring about me, or whatever this is.' He paused and wiped his face again, wiped his eyes. 'I can't accept your concern in the way you mean it, so I'd rather not have it at all.' He swallowed and winced again. 'It hurts too much,' he muttered and Lilla didn't know what he meant.

Liar, he told himself as Ekon pushed free and limped away. *You know exactly what he means.* He knew, too, that this particular blade cut the one wielding it as much as the one receiving the blow.

But they were in a battle, so he wadded his feelings into a bandage and tied it around his spirit and checked their surroundings. The lines were holding and they were in a pool of relative peace at their centre, shamans busy among groups of wounded, warriors heading back to the line after treatment.

'How are your lines?' he called and hurried to catch up.

'We're holding. You?'

'Outnumbered but standing firm.'

'Aren't we always?' Ekon muttered. 'Can you fight?'

Lilla pulled a wad of material from out of his salt-cotton and passed it to Ekon, then took a second for himself and shook it out. Should have done this earlier, but Ekon's voice, Ekon's fight, had distracted him. He couldn't afford any more such distractions. He tied it around his waist, tight enough that agony lanced through him. His fingers came away bloody. 'Yes. You?'

'Yes. I've got this side of the plaza; you take that one. No mercy. We kill them all. Don't waste spear tips: once they're dying, just leave them.'

Lilla nodded. 'I know,' he said. 'Malel protect you,' he added, too quiet for the Chitenecatl to hear him.

He did, anyway. 'And you . . . kitten.'

Lilla paused, his mouth open in an automatic rebuke that didn't get past the lump in his throat, but Ekon broke into a limping run towards his warriors and Lilla had no choice but to return to his own side of the plaza. His own little slice of the Underworld.

PILOS

Pilos didn't know whether the traitors who'd sold out their kin had lied after all, or whether the rebel war parties had moved locations, but the offensive he and Atu had planned had failed. Of the ten pods who'd gone out, following starving, frightened slaves professing knowledge of the traitors' hideouts, five had come back empty-handed and five had not come back at all.

An hour later, two thousand or so traitors had come streaming towards the pyramid, seemingly intent on murdering everyone within the protective wall, and with five hundred dogs and eagles somewhere in the Singing City instead of here, the fight was harder than he liked.

Still, they weren't— Pilos howled in pain as a war club studded with obsidian shards crunched into his left ankle and tore it open.

He struck back at the Xenti before the last of the scream had left his lungs. The blow didn't connect as they dodged and, in violation of his will and good sense, his leg began to give way. If he fell here, ten paces inside the breached compound wall with the pyramid exposed at his back, it could be all over. If his eagles saw him fall . . . Pilos wasn't arrogant, but he was a realist. Those nearest would fight to defend him, leaving gaps for traitors to slip through, and if that happened, they might make it all the way to the pyramid. To the Singer.

A hoarse bellow slipped from him as he fought to stay upright, blinking blurry eyes at the Xenti coming for him again, smiling now despite the layers of bruising marring their face. Predatory. He braced his good leg and raised his club, free hand questing sideways in hopes of grabbing an eagle's salt-cotton and reuniting with the twisting, splintering line of defenders. Another wave of the enemy was cresting over the ramshackle wall and—

Feather Matla slid into the gap on his left and lunged low, so fast he saw only a blur before she rose and stabbed a knife into the Xentib armpit. Their club dragged down the outside of Pilos's arm, scoring cuts as it went, and then smashed into the stone next to him as the Xenti collapsed, bleeding from the backs of the knees – muscles torn out by Matla's knife – and deep under their arm. Dying. He tore the club from their hand and slammed it into the back of their skull with a wet crack. Dead now.

Matla grabbed him under the arm and hustled him backwards on one leg. The line closed in front of him, stitching itself back together with the traitors on the other side, and he clenched his fingers into Matla's biceps before making himself look – finally, fearfully – at his foot even as they scrambled backwards.

It was still there, and a sob of relief broke from his throat, quickly stifled. It was torn open, bleeding badly, but there were no visibly splintered bones.

Matla dragged him behind a line of reinforcements and towards the base of the pyramid, where shamans moved among the wounded. 'Stop. Stop, Feather. Let me test it.' Pilos's voice was a pained rasp, but the authority in it was unmistakable; Matla stopped. She didn't let go, though, and neither did he as he carefully – so very carefully – flexed his foot until it was flat on the stone and leant his weight onto it.

There was a spurt of blood as the torn flesh pressed back

together and a pulse of sickening pain up into his groin, but no grate of broken bones. 'Setatmeh be praised, I think I'm intact,' he gasped. Matla cocked an eyebrow in such clear disbelief that he laughed, almost dizzy with it. 'Nothing broken,' he clarified.

'Needs stitches, medicine and bandages,' Matla said.

'Take me to someone who can do the first and for the Singer's sake get me a cup of water. The rest can wait,' he said and they made their awkward way closer to the shamans. Closer; not all the way. Pilos insisted on stopping where he had a full view of the raging battle, propping himself against a defaced obelisk and then, despite his best intentions, sliding down it until he sat. He propped his bad leg up on his other knee and watched dully as the blood ran down his calf.

A shaman arrived quickly: they always did for Feathers, Spears and High Feathers. That, at least, was something to be thankful for, though he wasn't, not in the least, when the man began rotating his foot and poking at the damage. Pilos lowered his chin until he could get the top edge of his salt-cotton between his teeth. He bit down, hard, and focused past the shaman's shoulder on the fighting.

Feather Detta and the Second Talon were on the move from Xentiban, but Pilos and Atu were looking at at least another week, or more like ten days, before they arrived. It had been one of the reasons they'd attempted to flush out all three war parties at once – a calculated risk to deal a crushing blow to their enemies, who probably outnumbered them four to one, though most of their number were untrained house slaves and scribes. Still, Pilos had seen eagles cut down by house slaves and scribes more than once in the last month, and it would be happening again here. The plan had been solid; it just hadn't worked.

Pilos yowled in surprise more than pain when the shaman poured salt-water over his pulverised ankle to clear away the blood and detritus. The man leant close, peeling back the torn flesh to inspect the inside of his ankle, and then he grunted and sat back on his heels. He pulled a bone needle out of the hem of his tunic, already threaded, and poked it through the meat. Pilos yelped again, blinking hard, and then chewed his armour some more as seven stitches went in. A quick slather of medicine and a bandage tight enough to restrict the joint's movement and he was lacing up his sandal ready to go.

'Spear,' Matla began in warning.

He flapped his hand at her. 'Help me up. This isn't over and until it is, I'm needed at the wall.'

'You think we need you dead at that fucking wall?' she snarled and he blinked again, in surprise this time. 'Stay here and give us the eagle's view. Make sure we're holding on all sides, not just this one. Please, Spear.'

Pilos considered her words and then put a hand on her shoulder. 'Thank you for your concern, Feather. And your wisdom. I will do as you say – for a while.'

Matla smiled, relieved. 'As the Spear commands,' she said. 'With your permission, I will lead this section in your absence.'

'Go. And stay safe, Feather.'

She slipped away moments after the shaman left to treat another warrior staggering towards them with one arm hanging limp and bloody at his side. Pilos shifted his weight and then immediately removed it from his left leg, unable to swallow a gasp. He limped towards the great pyramid and laboriously climbed to his customary place on the grand staircase, where he could respond to a summons from the Singer within and be ready to command or coordinate the response on any of the embattled walls.

The great feathered fans used to cool the Singer had been repurposed as signal flags, one at each wall, and while Pilos couldn't see the fourth wall from his vantage, there was a watcher permanently stationed in the garden on that side of the pyramid who would sound the alarm on a bone flute, piercing enough to penetrate even the chaos of battle.

Two pods waited in permanent readiness to defend that unseen section of wall, and Atu made sure that duty was rotated among the warriors daily so that all might take a rest from skirmish and battle. The fourth wall was nestled among densely packed and mostly burnt temples and noble estates, built high and strong with broken masonry and close in to the pyramid's side so that the sentries had an excellent view of the approaches. The traitors rarely pushed at that wall, wary of being picked off without anything to show for it, but with an attack of this ferocity, he expected they'd try soon enough.

Sitting, Pilos stretched out his leg, the breath hissing through his teeth. As soon as he was settled, a wave of fatigue crashed down over his head, washing its poisons through his limbs. He let his shoulders slump and closed his eyes, allowing himself to feel the aches and the bright, gnawing pain in his leg for the space of five slow breaths. Then he straightened and examined the three visible sides of the perimeter. Any warriors looking his way needed to know he was paying attention, that he was alert and ready to fight for them, fight with them, get them the support they needed.

Directly ahead, where he'd been fighting, the eagles were holding with loyal dog warriors and civilians in support. Matla led them and he wondered, again, why she'd never been promoted to Feather prior to her retirement. She'd proven herself a hundred times since the uprising began, and he'd made her a Feather without a second thought when he needed someone to replace her fallen predecessor. Ultimately, it didn't matter; he was just grateful for her presence. To his left, High Feather Atu was holding the centre of a line and standing firm. Traitors were clambering over the walls in fits and starts, a few here, a dozen there, reinforcing those who'd already made it into the compound and who were viciously outnumbered and selling their lives as highly as they could.

Atu ordered his dog warriors forward and they threw themselves through gaps in the rebels' lines and scaled the wall until loyalists and traitors alike were straddling the top and hacking and shoving at each other.

Pilos pushed himself up to standing, ignoring the flare of pain in his leg. A few of the dogs fell to enemy arrows, but no more: the traitors were running as low on weapons as they were. The thought brought only a little comfort.

Slowly, he eased himself down onto the steps again and looked at the fighting on his right where, even after all this time, he expected to see, or at least hear, Eagle Elaq at the wall leading the loyal free. But Elaq wasn't there: his oldest friend was a month dead, slaughtered on the first night of the uprising. Decapitated, his head thrown at Pilos's feet in an act of mocking savagery that still made him snarl.

Instead of Elaq, the retired dog warrior Oteom of Axiban commanded as he had done ever since he'd arrived. Oteom had been Pilos's loyal man since the Tokoban war and in charge of his songstone mine after resigning from the Melody in protest at Pilos's demotion. An act that had endeared him to the Spear and a show of loyalty that hadn't wavered in the years since. When the rebellion began, he'd brought fifty warriors to the Singing City, fighting through Yalotlan, Xentiban and into Pechacan to pledge his spear to the cause. To Pilos.

It was a memory to stand in balance to the wet smack of Elaq's head landing at his feet, medicine to that never-closing wound, that ever-burning rage. If Pilos found out who had done that, who had—

There was a great cracking boom and part of the wall shuddered, sending warriors from both sides tumbling. It was that same weak section to his half-right, built between two gutted, slumping temples whose doors and windows were blocked with rubble. Smoke began drifting from somewhere beyond the wall as the traitors found something else precious to destroy. Smoke and blood: the twin scents always in his nose these days. The only ones left in the city.

The pitch of combat at that part of the wall changed, sharpened. Alarm skewed voices high and desperate. He leapt down the stairs two at a time, the steep angle precarious even when he wasn't injured. Pilos's battered ankle blazed with pain at each jolting step until, near the bottom, it gave way completely. He yelled and jumped, landing awkwardly on his other foot at the base of the stairs.

Pilos stared at the wall and then roared for civilian reinforcements. The word was passed quickly and he was gratified
when Pechaqueh non-combatants raced to his side, led by
Quotza, Atu's wife.

The wall shuddered some more, stone and bamboo and
even piled furniture rocking under the repeated impacts. '*Brace
that*,' he screamed and a score of Pechaqueh, some of them
wounded warriors too injured to fight unless there was no
other choice, ran heedless through the straining warriors and
slapped their hands and shoulders and hips against the barricade and tried to still its rattling. They were brave: if the wall
came down, they'd be crushed. If the traitors turned from the
fighting and went for them, they'd be cut down before the
Melody could intervene.

Pilos shouted another order, and eight warriors formed a
cordon between the rearmost slaves and the civilians shoving
at the wall and doing what they could to brace it. Paltry
protection, but all he could spare.

Quotza was one of those at the wall. Her and Atu's daughter
was hidden safely in the source with her grandmother and the
nobles who wouldn't fight or otherwise assist in the defence.
Quotza's talent lay in land and slave management, not combat,
but she hadn't hesitated to volunteer back at the very start of
the uprising.

Chorus warriors were flooding out onto the third, fourth,
and fifth levels of the pyramid, taking their places armed with
bows, blowpipes and spears: standard procedure if civilians
were called into the fray.

We need to get the Singer out of here.

It wasn't the first or even hundredth time he'd thought it
since the uprising began, and it was the one thing they all
knew couldn't happen. If Singer Xac left the source, his connection to the magic and the songstone cap would shatter. The
song would die and the Empire's way of life with it. There
would be no order to the world without the song, no reminders
of everyone's place and status. Just chaos and confusion.

The holy lord couldn't leave the source, and so the eagles

couldn't lose it. *And we won't. Please, Setatmeh, they have to break soon. They have to realise they can't win, that what they're doing is wrong.*

Please.

Pilos limped through the press of warriors awaiting their turn at the enemy and into the line behind those fighting, war club in hand and smoke thick in his nostrils. He sent another swift prayer to the holy Setatmeh, this time that the traitors hadn't set the wall ablaze. It was mostly stone, but if fire destabilised the wood and bamboo core, it might all come down.

A score of severed heads suddenly rained down among his warriors, thumping and bouncing, some trailing smoke and sparks from burning hair. They'd be eagles and Pechaqueh citizens; they always were. He didn't know what they did with the loyal free they murdered; perhaps that accounted for the smell of roasting meat that drifted daily across the city. Not just people but mercy had been burnt away – on both sides.

More heads appeared above the wall, these attached to living bodies. Pilos focused on what he could do here and now, the difference he could make to this battle, this outcome. Everything else faded, including most of the pain in his leg as adrenaline sang through his veins.

A line of warriors stepped up to either side – retired eagles, mostly, and youths who'd been preparing to take the skills tests to join the Melody and had found themselves not so much accepted as eagles as dragged into a fight for survival. For the first time in the Melody's long, proud history, he and the High Feather had accepted every single Pechaqueh who volunteered, regardless of their abilities or prowess.

For the survivors, their youth and exuberance had both quickly been worn away and now they were silent and focused, nursing aches and sprains and the hot, puffy agony of split flesh. True eagles, even if their names had never been entered into the registers and their rewards came not in jade and status but survival and second-hand salt-cotton taken from the dead. Most didn't even wear the feather in their hair – they'd run out long ago and no one would so dishonour the dead as to take a fallen warrior's feather for their own.

The wall shuddered and seemed to ripple before his eyes and Pilos shouted again at the civilians, urging them to push harder. More traitors scrambled to the top of the wall further along on his right and he roared a warning. This section was one of the most vulnerable and it was always here the attack came thickest. The rebels had tried everything short of tunnelling under the burnt temples to get into the compound.

Again they came, flowing up and over the wobbling wall in a wave so big it took his breath. Quotza was yelling at the civilians and they were holding, song bless them, holding despite what was coming for them. Because if they didn't, the wall was coming down and they'd all be dead. The Singer included.

'Pods! Triple line six paces from the wall. Don't give them momentum,' he bellowed and stepped forward to the correct range. 'You, half-pod to protect those civilians. Now!'

Those warriors not already engaged raced to obey and somewhere behind, up on the pyramid, he thought, a Melody war chant began. As one, the warriors took up the song, both to strengthen their wills and to alert the Singer and Shadow of a full attack.

The eagles who'd been fighting the previous wave died or managed to retreat into the first line, which parted to let them through to gasp a few moments of rest. There were bodies everywhere. Pilos hadn't seen an attack this big since the day of the peace-weaving. Whatever his missing five pods were up to in the city, they'd kicked over the termite mound and the bugs were swarming in response.

The song changed as the chant spread to every corner of the compound, swelling with defiance and building to match them and Pilos felt the two merge, harmonise, and lift him up. Fill him with strength and righteousness and vindication.

As ever, the traitors were led by free dog and Coyote warriors, the lethal tip of their arrowhead, the armour protecting the meat of untrained slaves who gripped sticks and homemade clubs, who wore layers and layers of ordinary cotton and maguey in the vain hope they'd offer some protection from flint, obsidian, and granite.

Still, as unarmed and unarmoured and untrained as they were, they outnumbered Pilos and his warriors. The few hundred paces that stretched from the wall to the pyramid behind yawned at their backs, giving them space to retreat into if they needed it, but giving ground and momentum to their enemy, too. Pilos promised himself they wouldn't need that space, that they'd hold them here and kill them here.

He spun the club in his hand, its heft and reach familiar, an extension of his arm. Beloved. Open space behind them was one thing, but what they couldn't do – not in this battle, not in any battle – was get pushed back all the way to the pyramid itself. Even with the Chorus supporting them from above with arrows and poisoned darts, if the enemy gathered enough fighters and forced them all the way back, they'd end up fighting fucking slaves in the source itself. Desecrating its sacred corridors, blood marring the lavishly painted murals. Unclean feet in their holiest place.

It wouldn't be the first time blood was spilt in that sanctum.

Pilos crushed that thought. The advancing rebels were nearly on them: he narrowed his eyes, deepened his stance and sang the war chant directly at them, noting how many, despite themselves, were marching to its beat. Even mouthing its words.

Fucking, *fucking* traitors.

The war drum began the new rhythm they'd devised that warned of a strong attack on the source. The enemy had yet to learn the new beats – with the luck of the holy Setatmeh they wouldn't realize Atu was calling for the pods in the city to disengage and get back here.

'We hold until the others come at them from behind and throw them into chaos,' he shouted over the chant and the first eruptions of combat. 'Song and Empire and glory! *Song and Empire and glory!*'

He thrust his club over his head and the war chant increased in volume, a driving rhythm blending with the song's strength and swelling their hearts with righteousness. He let it wash over him, scouring him clean of doubt, of exhaustion and hurts and the tinge of fear.

The enemy charged.

The reinforcements hadn't come.

Pilos, bloody and reeling with weariness, wondered whether this was the day they'd have to call the warriors back from protecting the farms outside the city that would feed them come harvest. If they did, those farms would fall to traitors and the Melody would be starving within weeks.

Highsun had come and gone and now clouds covered the sky, adding stifling humidity to the misery. He prayed for rain, for an end to the tension tightening his skin. Relief from that, at least, please Setatmeh.

The reinforcements hadn't come and the rebels were stepping over the dead and advancing, murderous determination in their tight-lipped faces. The wall behind them was smoking, shuddering, but still standing. The civilians had done their work well. He'd dragged Quotza and the others away an hour before; she'd been grimy with sweat and smoke, her eyes red-rimmed and watery and her limbs shaking with effort. Pilos had sent her back to the source, but he'd seen her since, assisting the shamans. Setatmeh, no wonder Atu was besotted with her. Pilos was more than half in love himself.

Three fortified gates provided entrances to the area inside the ramshackle wall: one led onto the grand plaza and two others into the barricaded roads between the gutted temples that had once nestled at the great pyramid's feet like chicks around a turkey. They were well-built and well-defended and it had been days since the traitors had attempted an assault on them. With the wall shaking under repeated impacts from the other side, though, it was clear enough why: there were easier ways in.

Pilos's lines were straining, beginning to bow in places and Atu had no warriors to spare to help him strengthen the defence of this part of the compound. They just had to hold. There was no other choice.

Pilos grunted and blocked an axe swinging for his head. He smashed his club into their chest and then crunched it down onto the inside of a knee. The next blow caved in their temple, fatal. He didn't have time to relish the victory, recognize their tribe or gender, or even draw a full breath before the next was on him.

An upswinging spear opened his shin, the flint head scraping against the bone and the same fucking leg as his smashed ankle. A hoarse scream tore from his throat and he batted the spear sideways and clubbed its wielder in the neck, a swiping blow that crushed throat and shoulder alike. The Chitenecatl coughed, choking on his own screams, and then gurgled and fell back. Pilos wished it was Ekon; it wasn't.

Another leapt to take his place and ran onto the point of Feather Matla's spear, and Pilos wasn't ashamed of the stab of relief that skewered his gut. How many times had she saved his life today?

He ignored the fresh patter of blood from his leg and allowed death to shelter him under its gory wings. 'Watch the sides,' he bellowed as traitors tried to squeeze past them and into the clear ground leading to the wounded, the shamans, the great pyramid.

Before he could repeat the order, a Quito leapt at him and Pilos punched the club into the warrior's face and felt the crunch of her nose, followed it up with a kick to her gut and another into her groin. She went to her knees and he punched his knife in under her jaw, grinned a savage slash of bared teeth, and shoved her aside. Reset and waited for the next. Let them come to him; don't step out of the protection of the line. His leg was shuddering; his leg would *fucking hold*.

The influx of slaves over the wall stuttered and then stopped. What were the fuckers planning? Why, when they'd got the Melody backing up from the wall, when they'd breached the wall itself, were they stopping? What trap was this?

Fresh movement to his far left caught his eye as he checked again on the High Feather's line. From beyond it, where there had been no fighting so far, streamed a crowd of warriors. They'd broken through the southern gate.

Pilos twisted to face them, his raw, parched throat forming the first warning shout and ignorant of the blaze of pain in his leg or Matla's shriek. She lunged past him, knocking into his shoulder and cutting down the warrior coming for him.

The attackers from the south were fast. Silent. Black and red paint on their faces and arms.

Black and red paint.

Eagles.

They threw themselves into Atu's line and shattered the force facing them in an instant, overwhelming the rebel slaves.

Ugly triumph revitalised Pilos and his warning became a whoop. Retreat into attack. Feint and counter. Push, push, push. '*Advance!*' he screamed, turning back to the enemy and taking a limping step forward. 'We have them on the run.'

They weren't on the run. Not yet. But his eagles trusted him and responded as if they were. The line shifted, swaying forwards and then back as the enemy wobbled, uncertainty flaring from one to the next like locusts moving in a swarm. The fastest reinforcements had already broken through the slaves and were coming to Pilos's aid. The wet smacks and snicks of flint and obsidian into flesh were loud. Grunts and curses and screams and bright scarlet out of brown skin, white bone, purple entrails.

Pilos took another step, and another, Matla on his left and his beloved eagles matching them, dogs and Coyotes backing them, civilians at the rear. The traitors faltered, halted, and the two forces splashed against each other like currents meeting at the joining of rivers, boiling into angry motion and a press for dominance.

And then, finally, the longed-for reinforcements slid in behind the traitors, cutting them off from the wall and escape. Cutting them to pieces.

Cutting their way to victory.

* * *

They wouldn't survive another battle like that. Pilos knew it and so did Atu. So did every warrior who'd seen combat before this conflict and understood the terrain and its limitations. Perhaps those idealistic young eagles might be fooled a little longer, and most of the civilians – the Shadow and Singer too – but no one else. He could see it in the faces of the dogs he passed. How long would their loyalty bind them to this place they had to hold and couldn't? Not forever.

The middle of the fucking city. Who builds the most sacred, can-never-be-abandoned-building in the middle of a Setatmeh-cursed city?

He sat halfway down the great pyramid's grand staircase, as usual. He even had a favourite step these days. Civilians scurried around the wall like leaf-cutter ants, repairing the breach and doing what they could to strengthen that whole section. Another temple backing onto the wall would be gutted to provide stone and bracing beams. Another little sacrilege to add to their tallies.

More civilians stacked bodies into three great piles – eagles, loyal free, and traitors, ready to be taken out at night and floated in the nearest stream. An offering, an apology. A way to try and avoid disease a little longer.

Gritty-eyed with fatigue, Pilos wasn't sure he'd see the waving of the feather fans signalling danger even if they were a body-length in front of him. Quotza finished the last stitch holding the front of his leg together and sat back, smearing his blood across her brow as she wiped away sweat. She didn't notice, cocking her head as she examined her work. 'Not bad. It wasn't deep.'

Pilos looked down at her handiwork. He grunted. 'Not bad at all,' he agreed, though he didn't do anything so foolish as flex his leg to see how it felt. His ankle had swollen to a truly ridiculous size during the battle and hurt far more than the slice in his shin.

'Who'd have thought stitching our daughter's first huipil would have uncovered a hidden talent for putting warriors back together again?'

Pilos snorted. 'I'm surprised you hadn't learnt such a skill long before, being married to the High Feather.' His joke fell flat; Quotza's jaw tightened and she couldn't prevent her gaze slipping past him. Atu still wasn't back from his latest round of the wall, which he'd insisted on doing himself even though there were Feathers and eagles who could have done it for him.

'Believe me, high one, we'd know if there was a problem,' Pilos reassured her. 'The whole compound would be running to his aid. For which he'd be both grateful and resentful,' he added, and this time she managed a smile, albeit small. She took his hand and laced their fingers together briefly in acknowledgment and he squeezed.

Quotza straightened and then stretched her shoulders, her spine popping and crunching. Her daughter was wrapped in a shawl and tied to her back, sleeping soundly despite the cries of the wounded and the sentries coordinating with each other as they swept the compound for enemy survivors. Chubby brown legs dangled to either side of her waist, an anklet of pearls and jet snug above one foot. They fought for the Singer and his survival, yes. They also fought so that two-year-old Pechaqueh might live to be three.

It had been an hour since the last traitors fled or were killed, and two since the five hundred eagles, now numbering fewer than three hundred, had returned from a battle of their own to throw themselves into this one. Still they searched the compound, examining dog warriors and no-blood loyalists with open suspicion while they hunted for traitors hiding in their midst.

Pilos didn't blame the eagles doing the searching, even as he winced at the angry glares following them as they manhandled and questioned the warriors. The first casualty of any situation like theirs was trust. *Just like Ilandeh and the Sky City, setting Tokob and Yaloh at odds. Only we're setting ourselves at odds with our allies.*

And what other choice do we have? he reminded himself. Still, he'd make an effort with the dogs later, swapping stories and jokes and polishing their statuses as he had in every war he'd fought during his career. Every war dedicated to peace. Under the song.

Ilandeh. Setatmeh, had it really only been this morning that a Listener in Yalotlan had contacted him and brought him to Flight Beyt's mind with news of her survival? It felt more like a week. But it gave him an opportunity, one he was sure the High Feather would agree he took.

He picked up a wet cloth and handed it to Quotza. 'For your hands – and brow,' he added as she began scrubbing at the blood. 'You should try and—'

There was a scream from below, near to the wall, not of alarm or pain, but of utter anguish. Despite his injuries, the sound had him running down the steps in an instant, grunts of agony bursting from his mouth with each stride.

'What is it?' he bellowed as he reached the bottom, anxiety tightening its fist around his gut. Atu hadn't been there, it couldn't – something was heaved over the wall from outside and then, as warriors raced ahead of him towards it, another further along. Limbs flopped as it fell. More shouts rose, fear and despair and wailing grief, and the fist tightened brutally inside Pilos until he wanted to hunch over the pain of it. Instead, he sped up into a sprint towards the closest body that had been thrown over. A councillor or noble, perhaps, who hadn't made it to the source that first night?

'*Move*,' he snarled as he reached the crowd. He had a brief glimpse of open mouths and ashen faces and then he was standing over it. A body. Small, like that of a child, but . . . green-grey and naked, with toughened hide on its torso and wide, vacant black eyes. 'No,' he breathed as his knees buckled and he fell by its side, catching himself on his hands as the world spun around him. 'No, *no, no*.'

A holy Setat, dead. A holy Setat with its throat torn out. A holy Setat with . . . teeth marks in its limbs. A cat's teeth, or maybe a dog's. Pilos's eyes roamed its sacred, lifeless flesh – ripped-out throat, mauled legs. Different wounds; different means of infliction.

A blade. And a dog.

Xessa.

It could be no one else. Only she would have the audacity to kill a god. Only she had the ability, the nerve.

Pilos breathed through nausea and spirit-terror. He stood, hauling himself up on someone's kilt and arm. 'Bring the god to the source,' he choked, his voice barely making it through the tightness in his throat.

'Spear, we can't, we shouldn't *touch it*,' a warrior whispered.

'Fetch blankets and bring it.'

'All of them?'

Pilos rocked where he stood and someone grabbed his shoulders, steadying him. *All of them? How many, what has . . . what she has done?*

'All of them,' he managed. 'With respect,' he added unnecessarily. 'And find me the High Feather.'

XESSA

They'd waited as long as they could, through the heat of the morning and the humidity of afternoon. They couldn't wait any longer; more to the point, Ossa couldn't wait any longer. His bleeding had stopped but he was weak and feverish, a fine tremor vibrating through his limbs. Xessa's own thirst was like thorns in her throat and she hadn't even lost much blood. She licked at her torn lip, seeking some hidden moisture she might have missed the previous hundred times she'd done it; nothing.

Though the thought ate at her, she had to presume Tiamoko was dead. He would have come back for her otherwise. And if he was dead then nobody knew where she was: no one was looking for her. Likely everyone thought they'd both been killed by the Drowned at the river.

No, they couldn't wait any longer. Xessa eased herself out from underneath Ossa's weight and stood. She stretched out her fingertips, but his head didn't brush them. He hadn't risen ready to follow her. The eja swallowed dryly and then showed him a flat palm anyway: stay.

If he can't walk, I'll carry him again. We go together or not at all. And seeing as staying isn't an option, we go together.

Spear in hand, Xessa climbed the stairs out of the storage room and into the building above. Her right hand trailed against the stone wall, searching for the slightest vibration that might indicate danger. The back of her neck prickled but that was sweat. She hoped. The eja moved slowly enough that her eyes adjusted to the growing light, the rich gold of mid-afternoon. Perhaps seven or eight hours since the fight at the river. More than that since Ossa had had a drink of water.

Xessa paused in the main room, bare toes spread and pressed to the dirt floor, seeking for signs she wasn't alone – the elusive tingle through her skin or barely-there scent on the breeze or a shadow that didn't match the shape that cast it.

Her heart was thumping hard and Ossa's blood, dried onto the skin of her neck and in her hair and salt-cotton, was a constant metallic reminder to hurry, hurry, *just hurry*. She didn't hurry; she surveyed her surroundings the way she'd learnt to do as a slave fighter who didn't have a dog to be her ears.

Sooner or later, though, she just had to move. Xessa took three more deep breaths, smelling the air, and then slipped to the side of the doorway and looked out; nothing. She stepped through and checked in both directions; still nothing. She could circle the building and then fetch Ossa, or she could get the dog now and move, praying the whole time.

By the time I've fetched him, someone could have arrived anyway. Better to die trying than of thirst and blood loss in a room under the ground.

She vanished back into the building, moving fast and sending four tongue-clicks ahead of her so that Ossa knew to be ready. He met her at the base of the stairs, lying so close she almost fell over him.

Xessa didn't even ask him to try and walk. She just stepped over him and then knelt facing the stairs, hands on the third step and hips low. She clicked again and Ossa clambered to his feet, his right forepaw held up to his chest and his ears and tail low. He nosed at the side of her neck but made no effort to climb onto her shoulders. He couldn't. The ejab throat closed up with grief and she swallowed viciously, forcing away the lump, and then very, very carefully she slid her head under his belly, took hold of his left rear- and foreleg, and sat back on her heels. Obediently, Ossa relaxed around her neck, but even through her salt-cotton she felt him whine as his torn shoulder stretched around her. He shook but lay still, panting hot and dry against her jaw.

Xessa's thighs protested as she stood beneath his weight, but nothing would stop her getting him to safety and medicine and drinking water. He could have hers if that was all there was, a sacrifice she wouldn't think twice about making. She retrieved her spear and climbed the stairs again. What if someone had come while she'd been down here?

I kill them and take their water and medicine for Ossa.

She paused in the doorway again, checking as best she could. Ossa was trained to gently bite her ear if he sensed danger, rather than vocalising or wriggling. He did nothing. There was only his rapid heartbeat against the back of her neck and his weight, slumped rather than alert, pushing down her shoulders. If anyone waited outside this building, he didn't – or couldn't – sense them.

There was no point wasting more time.

The eja exited the building, checking all around, and then began walking.

Xessa staggered around a corner and into a dead end, a space where two buildings were built so closely together that it had been easy to stack rubble in between and block the narrow alley. Chest heaving, sweat stinging her eyes and thirst a wild animal in her throat, still she knew she'd have to fight.

The group chasing her were armed with knives and clubs and desperation. The rebels were spread too thin to have control of all the city, so some parts, like this, were left to fend for themselves. They were peopled by those who'd decided to take no part in the fighting, or who were too old, too young, or otherwise incapable.

Still, they had the numbers and were hungry enough to

swarm a lone, exhausted warrior. Dog meat was a precious commodity as supplies dwindled and the war parties hoarded what rations they could to fuel the endless fighting.

Xessa turned back to face her pursuers and let a wave of cold deaden her heart and chill her eyes into threat.

I am eja. I am, Malel forgive me, The Mute of Pilos's fighting pit. I am a killer and I will not let them take him.

How hungry would Lilla's war party have to be to start looking at Ossa in the same way? She pushed away the thought. Tokob ate dog meat; they didn't eat ejab dogs. There was a difference.

Xessa snarled and readied her spear, letting go of Ossa's back legs and praying he'd stay still. She leant forward a touch so that his weight settled more firmly against the back of her neck and he didn't slide off, ignoring the muscles spasming in the middle of her back. She planted her feet and beckoned them on. They hesitated, jostling in the narrow space and building their nerve, and then they did as she asked.

They didn't have blowpipes, so they'd need to close with her and her spear was the longest weapon here. They'd see exactly what an eja would do for their dog. She might not need to kill them; that was for them to decide. She would make them fear her. Xessa roared and beckoned again. They'd learn—

The person closest to her stumbled and then fell, and before she could make sense of the arrow in their stomach a figure dropped from the roof above her. Xessa flinched and then lunged, but they were shooting into the crowd, not at her. The desperate little band fled like a flock of parrots.

The archer limped after them, pulling another arrow from the quiver on their belt, and Xessa caught a glimpse of a familiar tattoo: a snake winding up their forearm. They were Tokob? She let out a shuddering breath but refused to straighten out of her fighting stance. Their identity meant nothing; it certainly didn't guarantee they were friendly. Tiamoko was the only one she trusted and this person wasn't him. They were tall, but not broad enough. They were . . .

The last of her attackers vanished, dragging their wounded, and after a long moment examining the terrain outside the end of the alley, the Toko turned to face her. They were caught in shadow, as if held by it, only their hands visible in a beam of sunlight as they extended them to sign: 'Are you hurt, too, or just Ossa?'

Xessa shrank back, stumbling over a loose piece of debris. Movement in the corner of her eye: Ossa's tail was wagging, sluggish but steady. Questions rushed into her mind but she refused to relinquish her spear long enough to ask them. Instead, she reset her feet and her weapon and then beckoned the Toko forward. Out of the shadow.

They came, limping badly, with their bow in one hand and the other held far from their quiver. The snake tattoo flashed brighter as the sun hit it, and then another, not a snake but a pattern of interlocking triangles around the calf of their injured leg. Familiar. And then belly and chest passed into the light. And then face.

Xessa studied it, studied him, the cold from before a shield against emotion now. Against hope. Ossa wriggled and then whined against her neck and perhaps a similar noise came from her, but she paid it no mind. The dog wriggled again, insistent now, and she held up a hand to halt the Tokob approach. Xessa's legs wobbled as she very carefully went to her knees and then lower still so Ossa didn't have to jump. He slid from her shoulders and staggered on three legs, then made determinedly for the one who'd saved them, tail beating an increasing tempo against the dusty air of the alley.

Toxte.

Her husband.

Toxte.

His gaze didn't leave her until Ossa was within range, and then he knelt, too, and did his best to calm the joyful dog who was too torn and weary to be jumping at him like a puppy.

At Toxte. *Her husband.*

Xessa couldn't breathe. She watched, unable to move, as Toxte cupped his palm beneath a gourd and splashed water into it, letting Ossa lap it up before pouring more. And more, without hesitation or regret. And more.

A breeze blew grit into her face and she squinted, refused to blink despite the sting and the tears. If she blinked, he'd vanish. Because he couldn't be here, he couldn't be the one who'd saved her that morning. Why would he have done that and then not shown himself? So it couldn't be him, and if she blinked, or breathed, or moved, he'd disappear. Change into someone else, someone she didn't know or care about.

It couldn't be him.

Toxte was speaking to Ossa, his other hand travelling gently over the dog's head and back and flanks, looking for wounds other than the one bandaged in bloody salt-cotton. He fanned the flies away and then leant in and sniffed at it. She'd done that herself, countless times through the hours they'd lain together in the dark and the cool. She prayed it still smelt good, that her own sweat and dirt hadn't got into it and poisoned his blood. He was already hurt because of her; don't let him die because of her, too.

A dull pain in her hand finally reached her and she unclenched her fist from around the haft of her spear, not looking away. Never looking away.

Maybe . . . maybe he is here after all. Maybe this is real.

Another sound slid from her throat, crackling and grating its way out of the depths of her. Or was this a torment sent by those Tokob she'd killed in the fighting pit? Was this their vengeance? If so, it was impossibly cruel. Impossibly, crushingly obscene.

Toxte's hand was empty of water and he said something and Ossa lay down. Slowly, he stood once more and looked at her again, still kneeling in the detritus of the alley as if impaled. She almost crumbled under the weight, the intensity, the *familiarity* of that gaze. 'Xessa? Can you tell me if you're hurt?'

The movement of his hands as he shaped the signs broke

her and for one endless moment she couldn't make sense of what he was asking. How could she be hurt when Toxte was here? How could she be anything other than awake and complete and, unaccountably, terrified?

'Xessa? Are you hurt?' Toxte repeated.

He hadn't come any closer, she noticed distantly. Jerkily, she shook her head and then ignored his hands in favour of roaming her gaze across his face. He was thinner than she remembered, though she supposed they all were. Slaves didn't eat as well as free. Aside from the heavy scarring on his leg, there were other wounds marring his skin that her hands and lips and eyes had never traced. One across his brow and another disappearing down to where his ear should have been, nothing left but a flap of gristle. She lingered there, noting how the missing ear unbalanced his face, and only belatedly recognised his blush for what it was.

Toxte's hand came up and he pulled part of his hair forward, hiding the injury. Xessa was ashamed; she hadn't meant to make him uncomfortable. It was just that her hands had lost all their words and her body was as rooted as an ancient mahogany. All she had left in her to do was look.

The distance between them was only a few body lengths, but it was as vast as the Blessed Water that snaked through the city. And like that Drowned-infested stretch, she had no idea how to cross it without dying.

'Do you have somewhere safe we can go?' Toxte's patience seemed infinite, yet the question brought their predicament back to her in a rush. Ossa, a shaman, medicine. Safety.

Xessa nodded again and finally found some words, resting her spear against the side of her neck. 'Are you real?' The wrong words, it seemed, but even with Ossa lying at Toxte's feet, they were the only ones she had.

Toxte swiped the back of his hand across his cheek. 'I'm real,' he signed. 'And I'm here. But we need to get somewhere safe. We need medicine for Ossa.'

He seemed to vibrate like a hummingbird's wings with urgency, but still he didn't move towards her or stop her looking at him, instead looking back with the same hunger and, perhaps, the same fear.

'But you're in Quitoban. They said you were in Quitoban.'

'I was. I came for you. Xessa, please, please we have to move. Those people will be back. Let me . . . let me help you.'

His words penetrated and then lost all meaning, again and again. Her mind was stuck on a trail and she couldn't get off it. Had to walk it to its end. 'It was you on the roof this morning.' Not a question.

Toxte held out a hand in supplication and Xessa flinched. His face crumpled and he let it fall to his side, then raised it to sign again. 'Yes. I saw you approaching the river and knew what you were doing, so I took the spirit-magic so I could be close by if you needed me. Which you didn't, of course, not you and' – he glanced down at Ossa, grief flickering across his face – 'him. But there's no spirit-magic in me now, so I can hear.' He hardened then, like clay in a fire, so much and so fast that the next words he signed reached her when none of the others had. 'He needs you. Your dog needs you, Eja. *Please.*'

Xessa planted her spear and used it to climb to her feet, weariness poisoning her shrivelled, parched muscles. She took one step forward. Towards the alley's mouth; towards her husband. Her dog. Toxte was still, as if tempting a wild bird into a snare, and the idea was enough to make her hesitate again, but then she focused: Ossa. Safety. Medicine.

She looked around. 'It's a few sticks west. The war party. I can get him there. Will you . . . do you want to come?'

He hesitated for so long that something small and precious dried in the sudden heat of her dread.

'Do you want me to?' he asked and his question was a knife in her guts. His careful distance. The fact he hadn't called her 'wife'. He put the knife there, but she twisted it for him, unable to do otherwise. Because what if he knew of everything she'd done to survive? What if his distance, the way he'd looked after Ossa and not her, was because he was disgusted?

She'd killed Tokob. She'd said at the time she didn't deserve happiness, or to live, or Toxte. And here she was, with Ossa, alive, and with Toxte. And the promise of that, the suggestion of a future among so much despair felt like a threat.

Did she really get to have this?

Something must have changed in her face or posture, or perhaps she signed, she didn't know, but Toxte's face softened and he stepped carefully over Ossa and towards her, fully in the sun now, outlined in golden afternoon while she hid in the shadows, but he came to her, came into her shadow and warmed the chill around her.

He reached out, slowly enough that she could stop him, but the only things that stopped were her breath, her heart. And then those hands, scarred and beloved and strong and calloused, were cupping her face as gently as if she was something precious. Holding her together although she was broken. Unmindful of her sharp edges or the shattered places of her. Heedless of how she could cut him, make him bleed, make him die, too.

Toxte brought his mouth down, featherlight, on her brow, her eyelids, the bridge of her nose. Each cheek in turn, nestled among the soft heat of his fingers, and then her lips. A simple graze of skin on skin, the puff of his breath on her face, and then away.

He looked into her eyes. 'You're alive,' he said clearly. 'Xessa of the Sky City, eja of Malel and Snake-Sister, protector of Tokob and Tokoban, you're really alive.'

He stepped back before she could find words, her hands clamped to his wrists. *But not 'wife'. Still not 'wife'.*

'Safety,' he added. 'Now?' and let go. Xessa concentrated on unclenching her fingers from his arms. The loss of contact sent a shiver from her scalp down to her feet. She'd thought him a spirit; now, without his heat and the firmness of his flesh to remind her, she half-fancied him a spirit again.

'I'll carry him. You listen,' she signed and Toxte nodded, a frightening remoteness claiming his expression like a storm. Tiamoko looked like that before battle. Maybe she did, too, these days. Maybe they all did, another legacy of Pechaqueh cruelty. He returned to Ossa and knelt at his side, speaking, and the dog heaved himself to his feet. Quickly, Xessa crossed to them and knelt, twisting her back once for some relief before manoeuvring him onto her shoulders once more.

Toxte helped her stand and then retrieved his bow and put an arrow on the string. He led her out of the alley. She watched the corners and the roofs; she watched him, limping on his mangled leg but alert and swift.

Xessa clenched her jaw and checked for danger, Ossa's hind paw clutched in her sweaty fist and her spear ready in the other.

'You're alive' isn't the same as 'I love you'.

TAYAN

Xac was lying among the corpses, the *five dead gods*, and weeping. Not dramatically or loudly; quietly, like a child so afraid of the dark that they swallow their sobs for fear of being swallowed in turn.

Tayan could have done the same, with far more volume and spectacle. He didn't. He sat in silence, barely breathing through his rage and fear and disgust. None of them was *his* holy Setat, his friend and teacher, but that didn't make him feel any better. Nothing could, because he knew who'd done this. The sheer quantity of dead gods, and his years as a shaman treating knife wounds, told a compelling story. One look at Pilos's face told him he knew, too. The question was how. Not why – Xessa lived only for the spilling of green blood – but how.

Will that be what she does to me if we ever come face to face?

He didn't want to know the answer to that question. Tayan hadn't seen the eja in the crowd of enemies the day they'd rejected his peace-weaving and he'd studiously avoided wondering whether she'd made it out of Pilos's fighting pit alive ever since. Of all the ways he could have learnt she lived, this was the most bewildering. The cruellest.

This was not the time or place for the rose-cotton hanging that provided privacy and so the sickly pallor in the faces of his warriors was quite clear, that and the greasy sweat of spirit-terror that lent an ugly sheen to their skin. Tayan pointed a shaking finger at the wounds in one of the holy Setatmeh legs. 'That was not caused by spear or knife.' He didn't frame it as a question, but Pilos pressed his face to the mats in prostration and answered as if he had.

'Dog bite,' he said. 'The only explanation that makes sense is that a Tokob eja is once again killing our gods, but this time in the Blessed Water itself.'

He didn't name Xessa as the murderer, even though they both knew it had to be her; to do so would force the Shadow's hand and he'd have no choice but to order Pilos's death for it. This wasn't a slave killing a Pecha, crime though that was. It was a slave killing *gods*.

The Spear waited with surprising equanimity for Tayan to denounce him and order his execution. Perhaps shame at facilitating such a tragedy had stolen his courage; perhaps he was simply exhausted. By all accounts, the fighting had been fierce today. Xac mewled and cradled a holy Setat closer in his arms, smearing himself in dead flesh and blood. The three of them flinched and then Atu brushed the pad of his thumb beneath his eye, his breath hitching.

Xessa had done this, brought them to this. The one person who knew Tayan better than he knew himself, perhaps. *Or did, until I stepped into my greatness.* Certainly the only person who'd ever consistently opposed him, unlike Lilla. His husband had been strong and handsome, but oh so easily swayed, always guaranteed to side with him against the eja or the council of elders. Against the world.

Lilla's defiance at the peace-weaving, his broken-hearted rejection of Tayan and their marriage, had been an unexpected blow and one that bit deep. In the days afterwards, Tayan realised that he'd expected loyalty and obedience because that's what Lilla had spent their marriage giving him. His husband had never once let him down until that day, that most important day of Tayan's life.

Of all the fucking times to grow a spine.

Xessa, on the other hand . . . well, her defiance he'd expected. He'd just never thought it would take such audacious form. Even when they hadn't been aligned in their thinking, even when they'd fought bitterly over his ambition or her pride, Tayan and Xessa had always had the same ultimate goals in mind: peace, stability. Love.

And now look at what she's done. This atrocity. How can we have drifted so far apart? How can the two people who always strove to understand me, who always forgave me – eventually – not see this for the peace it can be?

Pilos was still face-down before him and Tayan wanted to give him the death he so clearly craved. But that would be too easy, a way out that the Spear didn't deserve. He'd caused this. He would put it right.

The Shadow of the Singer stared at the corpses, torn and broken and no longer holy, and his song dropped into a low, ominous rumble, promising retribution vaster than the sky and crueller than anything devised by the lords of the Underworld. *She has destroyed gods. If there is a drought, a flood, an outbreak of disease now, it will be her fault. She has caused whatever calamity comes next. She brings this upon herself and her precious rebels.*

Seven holy Setatmeh watched them from the offering pool at the other end of the source. Whether they'd been drawn here by their dead kin or had fled here for protection from Xessa, he didn't know. The Setat who had blessed him was among them and, as their eyes met, it climbed from the offering pool and approached. Atu's head made a soft thump as he prostrated; Xochi, pale and vacantly uncomprehending, knelt for one instant and then returned to her duty.

Something frightened and needy in Tayan's spirit reached, and he reached with it, holding out his hands for his god. The holy Setat bypassed him to crouch at Xac's side and survey the corpses. Softly, it crooned a lament so sweet and piercing that bruises flowered in the Shadow's spirit. The god cupped Xac's face and ran its thumb tenderly across his cheek, wiping away tears. The Singer stared up at him from puffy, bewildered eyes.

A sob caught in Tayan's throat and he tried to swallow it down; his god heard anyway, turning to look at him. Now, finally, it came to him and knelt opposite, wide black eyes staring into his. Slowly, its jaw fell open to reveal rows of wicked, pointed teeth; a clawed hand came to rest on his naked shoulder.

No song for him, no liquid language of divinity spilt from it as it leant forward and placed its mouth against his neck. Tayan shivered once, hard, and then stilled. This was not the kiss of a lover but the promise of a predator. The claws dug into his shoulder and the teeth caught a scrap of skin and pulled and the Shadow of the Singer, Tayan of Tokoban called the stargazer, waited to die.

I love you I love you I love you please don't, please, I love you. I'll make this right. I'll make it all right. Everything. I'll change the world for you. Please.

Please.

The claws retracted and the teeth parted and a cold tongue licked a broad stripe along his neck. The holy Setat sat back and looked him in the face again. Tayan was running with sweat, afraid and determined and shamefully aroused. The god grabbed his face in one wet, webbed hand and squeezed his jaw hard. Terror licked up again and this time it did sing, and for him alone.

'Ask and we shall answer, god,' Tayan mumbled. 'My life for you. My love for you. Vengeance for the dead. Only ask – and I shall answer.'

The Setatmeh hand gentled and it brought the other up to cup the Shadow's face. Acting on instinct, or some tacit permission felt rather than heard, Tayan did the same. God and man held each other's faces and stared into each other's eyes, sharing pain and love and simmering fury.

'We will find her,' he promised it. 'We will bring her here in ropes and pass judgment in this source and if you wish to be here for that, it will honour us. But if you cannot bear it, we will understand. We – I – will protect you from her.'

Yes. You will. You have promised to save us. You must do so.

Tayan startled and his hands flexed on the Setatmeh face. 'You speak?' he breathed. 'My divine love, my god, you speak?'

The holy Setat tilted its head slowly to one side. *Fix the song. Save us, or our voice will once more be lost.*

It let go and rose to its full, ominous height, towering over them all. Then it blinked and looked away and Tayan tried, as always, to cling to what he'd learnt during their communion. And he did. He could. The god had spoken and he could remember it, clear as sunlight; the gods *could speak*!

Was it grief that had broken the language barrier or something else, something that had changed in the song?

Pilos and Atu slowly sat up as the god loped back to the pool and slipped in with barely a ripple; Xac continued to ignore everyone; and Tayan sat in a daze of possibility and fascination and blessing. Absently, his hand rose to trace in a delicate circle around his eye, where the holy Setatmeh claws had marked him out months before. Marks he hadn't understood at the time, nor for weeks afterwards. Not until he'd taken the song and the Singer inside him. Not until he'd stepped into this great destiny. Gold beat in his chest and up his throat, a swell of magic that centred in his voice. He'd been blessed. He'd learnt the language of the holy Setatmeh, or—

'You will find Xessa and Ossa and bring them to me,' he said. Before the god's words and blessing, he'd intended to keep Xessa's name hidden behind his heart. There wasn't a noble Pechaqueh left alive who didn't know Tayan's past. Naming Xessa would only divide them and cause unnecessary questions when they needed strength and cohesion. Loyalty.

Now, none of that, none of them, mattered. The god had *spoken to him*.

Pilos looked up, held Tayan's eyes for a heartbeat too long considering their respective statuses, and then bowed again before finally sitting back on his heels. 'As the Shadow commands,' he murmured. Tayan wondered whether he was expecting a death sentence to follow. *Let him wonder. Let him stew in his own fears and shame. It is the least he deserves.*

'There will be no rest until that day, great Singer,' the Spear continued. 'I will lead the hunt myself should that be your order.' A promise of loyalty, a declaration of faith and commitment, but also of frantic penance. He would hunt Xessa to the ocean's edge if needs be – and beyond. He would do anything, *anything*, to find her and see her pay for her crimes.

Tayan's chest tightened but just as quickly vindication followed it. He was Shadow of the Singer; he was singlehandedly holding the Empire together while the holy lord languished in his illness, unable to wield the magic. Xessa was a traitor and a god-killer and he would not concern himself with her fate, other than to see her brought to justice. And once she was dead, he would not think about her again. Deliberately, he ran his gaze across the five dead gods and Xac in their middle. This was Xessa. This was who she was, the monster she was. She deserved nothing from him and that's exactly what she'd get.

Tayan reached for the comfort of his magic and the memory of the holy Setatmeh words in his head – words that suggested something fundamental had shifted in his song. He wasn't arrogant enough to suppose it was because he controlled it. No, there was something more to it. Something only he could learn.

If only he had time and space and peace to work out what. If only this fucking war would be fucking over and he could do the real work, the shamanic work, of healing the world.

One step at a time.

He wrapped magic around his wrists and throat and waist, draping himself in its glory and power until it steadied his heart and burnished his focus. This was truth. This was who Tayan was now. The Singer had shown him this and shared it with him, seeing in him the future. A future that was peaceful if only he could make it so.

Xessa had chosen her trail and Lilla had chosen his. Trails that led away from Tayan, that chose war over peace.

So be it. They will love me again, before their end. I demand it.

'Will the Singer grant our people the spectacle they need and deserve when these killers are caught, Shadow?' Atu asked and grief had lent a knife's sharpness to his voice. He met Tayan's eyes. Waiting for an answer.

Pilos gestured, a quelling motion, and the flick of fingers caught the Shadow's attention. The man had been friends with Ilandeh for years, had trusted her to do all the things he wouldn't, had valued her loyalty, intelligence, fierce devotion. And she had betrayed him. Tayan hadn't understood the depth of betrayal at the time, but he did now. Surrounded by corpses, he understood it all too well.

And despite those years of trust and friendship, when it came to the Empire of Songs, Pilos hadn't hesitated to order her death. Tayan should learn from that. Empire before kin. Gods before people.

Gods? Gods like Malel?

The Shadow's breath stuttered in his chest, caught on sudden thorns. Where had that thought come from? Why now? That was . . . Malel wasn't relevant to this.

'You'll get your spectacle,' he promised. 'And everyone in the Empire of Songs will know of it. I will carry it to them all, no matter the strain or the cost. I will make sure everyone knows what happens when they bring harm to the gods.'

Tayan wanted to stretch and bask in the warm sun of their approval, balm to cover the scratches left by that errant, puzzling thought. But not yet. He needed to be very clear in his instructions. In the holy Setatmeh divine commands. 'The order does not relate only to Xessa,' he said without the hint of a tremble or a whiff of hesitation. He had been chosen by the gods and he would not betray their trust. 'Any ejab discovered, with or without their dogs, are to be killed on sight,' he said, and the golden magic in his throat made his voice as cold and hard as a granite cliff. 'Bring their bodies back here to be displayed on the pyramid or the walls, whichever you think best. Or make them spectacles alongside Xessa. Or offer them to the holy Setatmeh as their playthings. But *end their threat*.'

Something shifted in Pilos's expression. For the first time, there was unmitigated respect there, tinged with surprise at his ruthlessness. Tayan put his head on one side, as the holy Setat had done before, and stared him out. *What, Spear Pilos? You think me weak? You think I, the Shadow of the Singer, will not – cannot – do what is needed?*

Pilos read the thoughts as easily as if Tayan had pressed them directly into his mind through the song. The Spear licked his lower lip and then bowed his head. Not because he had to, not because of protocol. He bowed. *To Tayan.*

'We'll have warriors searching quarter by quarter, Shadow. As many as we can spare,' Atu said, ruining the moment and the Shadow's triumph over his Spear. He and Pilos were filthy, streaked with brown smears of dried blood, dust mingling with sweat into a thick grime. The squint lines around Pilos's eyes were black with dirt.

They have their tasks, and I have mine. We each work in the ways that are suited to us.

'Offer rewards for Tokob captives. Promises of jade or land for those who bring us ejab. Set them against each other. Rewards for the dogs too, dead or alive.'

'Alive is better,' Pilos said. 'If they kill the dogs, they've got another source of food giving them strength. I will lead the search myself if you wish,' he said again. 'As the High Feather commands.'

'No. That is for the holy lord to decide,' Atu said, in the tone of one pronouncing judgment. Whatever their past, their closeness as warriors and war leaders, the High Feather knew his place. This was not his decision to make, even if it seemed like a military one on the surface.

He and Pilos looked expectantly at Xac. The Singer paid

them no heed. He was nested among the corpses, piling them close around him until he was almost hidden by cold, grey-green skin and stiffening limbs.

'Great Singer? Is it your will that Spear Pilos lead the search for the eja and her dog who have committed this great crime?'

Have I not already said so? And still they turn to him, to the man mired in corpses, and expect sense?

The last of Tayan's triumph withered. 'The holy lord's grief is as vast as the world spirit,' he snapped. 'I speak for him in this. His recovery may well be hindered by this atrocity that you have let happen. You have your orders; see that they are carried out. Immediately.'

The warriors jerked their attention away from the Singer and abased themselves. 'Look well on what your actions have wrought, Spear Pilos,' Tayan added in a softer tone. 'When this war is finally won and we have peace in all Ixachipan, you will present yourself to the source for atonement. Until then, you will find Xessa and bring her to us. You will find any and all ejab and end their threat to the gods. And you will put down this fucking rebellion before I lose the last of my patience. *Am I understood?*' The last words were pregnant with power and malice and the promise of a wretched, dishonourable death.

Pilos wilted beneath his ire, babbling promises and assurances, and Tayan let the heat of his anger burn to cold, deliberate ash. Xessa had made her choice. The killing of Pechaqueh could perhaps be forgiven, in time, once there was peace. But not this. Deliberately, he examined each of the corpses again. One Lesser Setatmeh and four Greater. Four former Singers of the Empire of Songs, torn and dead so far from the river. For this, there was no forgiveness. It was a massacre that shook the very foundations of Pechaqueh society and of the Empire of Songs itself.

Despite his discipline, his furious will and abject horror at her actions, Xessa's face danced in Shadow Tayan's memory, by turns laughing and scowling, light with mischief or dark with injured pride. Xessa and Ossa, made for each other.

They'd moved together like fire, like water. They'd moved like magic. She'd never needed words, not with Ossa. She'd barely even needed gestures. And what had they wrought together but death?

'. . . will take warriors away from the task of crushing the enemy,' Atu said and Tayan forced himself to put away the memories and concentrate once more. How quickly they dismissed the gods dead at their side. The awful, cold-hearted practicality of the warrior. And how much Tayan needed that from them so that he might focus on the higher, more important, issues. What was a war among people, really, when the fate of gods and the world dangled from the end of a fraying cord?

'Send them home.'

There was a pause. 'Shadow?' the High Feather asked, confused.

'Let it be known that Tokoban has been abandoned by the Melody and send them home.'

'The loyal free, they'll be outnumbered,' Atu protested, his concern lending wings to his words.

'They'll never reach Yalotlan, let alone Tokoban. There are two entire Talons in Xentiban, are there not? They can deal with whoever scurries through the jungle there.' Tayan felt cold and still and centred, like an obelisk. Like a pyramid. 'I will write proclamations saying that there are no Talons left in the north, that Tokoban is no longer part of the Empire of Songs – that it is my gift to them as Shadow, with the holy lord's blessing. And an offer of peace. I know my people. They'll leave the city and as they go, you can search among them for Xessa – for all the ejab.'

'You think Xessa will run?' Pilos asked, sceptical.

Tayan looked up at the ceiling for one long moment, seeking his equilibrium and his teeth savaging the inside of his cheek. 'I think, whether she does or not, the result will be fewer Tokob in the city, in which case, it should be easier to find her, should it not?'

'If she comes out to fight, yes,' Atu said.

'She'll fight.' The words belonged to both Shadow and Spear and they locked gazes for one poignant, ruthless moment. 'She'll fight,' Tayan repeated, softer this time. 'And you will find her.'

'And I will find her, Shadow,' Pilos promised.

It was as if Tayan had two hearts, one that was fragile and full of memories and was breaking under the hammer of Pilos's determination; and another that hardened like stone on the outside and yet was soft within, throbbing gently with relief that the holy Setatmeh were soon to be safe.

'Just so,' Tayan said. He felt lightheaded, not quite anchored within his body as if suffering the last effects of journey-magic. 'And there will be fewer rebels to stand against us here in the Singing City. Empire-wide, even, if I made the proclamation applicable to Tokob across Ixachipan.'

'And we know how to fight there now,' Pilos agreed. 'We know the trails and the locations of the cities. Tokoban will be brought under the song faster the second time.' He looked at Tayan with open admiration and it soothed something sharp and querulous in the Shadow's heart.

'Though there is the risk that any ejab who travel with them and manage to slip past the Melody in Xentiban return to their murderous ways once they're in their homeland,' Atu fretted.

'They could do that wherever they are in the Empire now,' Tayan pointed out with more force than intended; the warriors bowed their heads. 'It's happened here; it could already be happening elsewhere. If not ejab working with dogs, then ejab working together. It grieves me – it hurts me – to say this, but I fear there is only so much we can do. This approach, at least, draws Tokob and ejab into the open. Gives us a chance to protect the gods. If they remain hidden, who knows what evil they will commit.'

'This could work,' Pilos breathed. 'With the proper planning, I think this will work.'

Tayan stared down into his hands curled loosely in his lap. Stared at them until they flickered with whorls and vines of golden magic. Magic to strengthen; magic to soothe; magic to teach.

'Spear Pilos,' he barked and the man twitched. 'Do not grow complacent. It is Xessa and Ossa we speak of. In any other circumstances, the holy lord would demand your life alongside hers for your crimes. You have much still to atone for.' He flicked his hand at Xac and the dead gods. 'So much.'

'The Shadow is correct,' Pilos said, bowing. 'I accept full responsibility. My life is the great Singer's to do with as he will.'

Xochi twitched. The Chorus Leader had been still and silent for so long, Tayan had almost forgotten her presence. Now, though, she was agitated. She knew she'd be the one to execute Pilos if it came to it and she didn't want to.

Despite all that had happened, Tayan didn't want that outcome either. They couldn't afford it. Was the Spear's life more important than that of five holy Setatmeh? No. Of course not. But those gods were already dead and Pilos's death now would only hinder them. But that didn't mean his annihilation wasn't foretold.

'Leave,' Tayan croaked, weary and sick to his stomach. 'I have the message of Tokoban's freedom to craft. Get out and do your duty – to the Empire and the great Singer. To the memory of those holy Setatmeh dead because of your lack of forethought. Your arrogance.'

The Spear held his prostration for another few moments, his expression hidden in the mat beneath him and Atu bowing alongside, and then they rose together and fled, limping and heartsick.

Tayan reached for the soothing strength of the song and the clarity it brought. He wrapped it around his spirit and let it flick into life from his fingertips all the way up his arms and across his naked chest. His gaze roved the great oval source, from Xac on his right to the offering pool on his left. The seven holy Setatmeh still watched him like a council of elders sitting in judgement. Tayan remembered his god's teeth at his neck, its claws in his shoulder. Sweat prickled at his hairline and a delicate shiver ran through him.

If he was to step fully into his greatness, the whole Empire of Songs must know it could rely on him to make the hard decisions, to rule wisely and without fear. Everyone had to know he was a man of his word, from the holy Setatmeh to the Pechaqueh, the loyal free and even, especially, the traitors. He needed to convince them all, and then he needed to unify them all.

'For peace,' he reminded himself aloud. 'Everything I do is for that great goal.'

Including Xessa's death?

She chose that path; now she must walk it to its end. It's not my fault.

XAC

The source, Singing City, Pechacan, Empire of Songs

They are gone, dead, torn from me and from the line of my ancestors.

Torn with obsidian; torn with teeth, they say.

They think I don't listen. They think I don't understand, but I do. I do.

He did this. Him and his kind. His tribe. I gave him everything and he took it all and more. Took it from me. I must, I need, to be strong again. The song, the magic, the blood. Any of them. All of them. I must be strong. I will be strong.

I will take back my magic and—

Sweet lord? How do you feel, my love?

The holy Setatmeh . . .

Hush, great Singer, hush. It is a horror that will not go unpunished. I swear to you.

Swear? Swear on what, my death?

Y-you are distraught, holy lord. It is time you rested. Sleep now.

You can't. Don't. I don't want to sleep, I don't—no, stop!

Sleep, holy lord. *I said sleep.* You will feel better when I wake you.

Please. Don't.
Shh. Sleep, my sweet. My sweet love. Sleep.
Please . . .

XESSA

Tithing barns, western Singing City, Pechacan,
Empire of Songs
39th day of the Great Star at morning

Night had fallen early, driven by cloud and smoke, and they stole through a city unlit by torch or fire. Ossa's weight had grown steadily until the middle of Xessa's back was a solid band of agony. She kept walking, holding one hind leg for balance and reassurance both. She didn't want to think about how uncomfortable he must be, draped around her neck and torn open and hungry. Thirsty, despite the water Toxte patiently offered every time they paused to scout the next road or plaza. He'd offered Xessa some, too, and she'd accepted a single mouthful and then insisted Ossa got the rest. It was only an hour to the war party's hideout, but it felt like they'd been walking, hiding, backtracking, for days.

The stone beneath her feet was cooling and Toxte was a barely visible shape in the darkness ahead. He'd led them past sites of intense fighting and scores of corpses, free and Melody alike. Xessa had made him promise to flee and take Ossa with him if she was cornered or cut down. She'd only just got him back, even if everything felt wrong and tight between them, a badly woven bowstring that might stretch, might snap. She still made him promise not to die defending her. He and Ossa had to live; *they had to.*

Toxte had been tight-lipped and argumentative, but they weren't in any position to waste time trading words and in this she was implacable. She'd seen it in his eyes, the moment he'd remembered her stubborn streak; his frustration abruptly softened by the amused twist of his mouth. He'd agreed, reluctantly, but she would hold him to it.

Toxte had always been fast, much faster than Xessa, winning most of the foot races in the Sky City back before the war. Now, promises or not, a child could probably outrun him, the scar tissue mangling his knee and calf hidden by the night but not in her memory.

It won't come to that. We'll all three of us live, tonight and all the nights of our lives to come. Together.

And it seemed that part of that promise, at least, would come true: they would live tonight. The tithing barns were ahead, filled with shamans and medicine and safety. No light or woodsmoke gave away the thousands of warriors crammed within those walls, but she knew they were there. She prayed they were there. Tiamoko should have been here to translate for Xessa and introduce Toxte to their war party, but Tiamoko wasn't with her and she didn't know if he still lived. Her fear for him was exacerbated by a sweeping homesickness and a longing to be surrounded by people who understood her, who listened to her hands and answered with their own and reminded her, just by existing, that she wasn't a burden.

Xessa caught up to Toxte and let go of Ossa's leg long enough to lace their fingers together. He startled and then she caught the flash of teeth when he smiled. His hand tightened on hers. It was the first time she'd touched him voluntarily, she realised. The first time she'd trusted that he wasn't a spirit or an ancestor come to torment her, but a living, breathing man. Her man. Her husband. She squeezed hard and he brought her hand up to his mouth and kissed her scabby knuckles. Xessa smiled and then gently disengaged, signing that they were close.

Close to safety. Close to medicine.

Close to being able to rest, and sit, and *talk*. The need for it was bitter at the back of her tongue.

Toxte stopped abruptly and then half-turned to face her. He pointed and she just made out the shape of people, warriors she guessed, crowding the end of the alley. Xessa tapped her ear and her husband nodded; they were talking or making demands, probably that he put down weapons and identify himself.

This was why she hated being out in the city without Tiamoko, who everyone in the war party knew by sight if not by name. Big, young, painfully earnest, he'd quickly become popular, and even more so when they'd seen him fight. The bond they'd formed in the fighting pit had only strengthened in the weeks since, no matter the number of Tokob they lived among now. Perhaps, even, because of it. But now Tiamoko's absence from her side frightened her and not even Toxte's presence could mitigate her ugly, creeping vulnerability. They'd been through so much over the last two sun-years. If something had happened to him . . .

Xessa took a deep breath and sank into her focus. There was nothing she could do for Tiamoko until she knew if he lived. But she could protect Ossa and Toxte.

'Put down your weapons,' she signed and leant her own spear against the wall. She pushed gently past, angling her body so Ossa wasn't squashed and then advanced, holding out both hands and praying their hideout hadn't been compromised, that these were freedom fighters and not Melody.

An orange glow pierced the gloom, outlining a doorway, and Xessa turned to face it, letting the torchlight flicker across her face, her slashed-through brands and smeared ejab paint. Across Ossa, who was better-known than her and Tiamoko combined, the only dog in the war party. She pointed back to Toxte and nodded, patted her chest and then hooked her finger through the once-yellow marriage cord hanging there.

Two more figures approached, these stepping out of the building and bringing the torch with them. As soon as there was enough light, Xessa turned to Toxte. 'Tell them your name and that you're my husband. You know Tiamoko and Lilla. Is Tiamoko safe? He came out with me at dawn to kill Drowned and then hid me. Where is he? Is he safe? And a shaman for Ossa. Please, Toxte. A shaman and medicine.'

Her hands were a blur and Toxte was translating before she'd even finished signing, coming to stand at her side. She clutched her marriage cord again and then took Toxte's hand in hers. Anything to convince them he was who he said. Anything to hurry them up so she could get Ossa to safety and healing.

Please Malel, please Snake-Sister. Let them believe us.

'They're going to fetch someone to verify our story,' Toxte signed after an endless amount of time had passed. Xessa grimaced, but then a Quito passed Xessa her water ration. They recognised her, then. It was Toxte that was making them suspicious. She drank two mouthfuls, holding them in her mouth as long as she could and relishing the tepid liquid, then signed for Toxte to give the rest to Ossa.

The Quito looked outraged, but the ration was hers to do with as she liked and Ossa needed it more. Toxte licked his lips as he dribbled the water in small, patient amounts into his palm, but he didn't hesitate, either.

Watching his face so close to hers, so intent on his task and on her dog, sent a great crack through the wall Xessa had built around her heart, the pain of its breaking almost enough to drive her to her knees. She breathed through it, through a tight chest and throat, one hand fisted in the side seam of his filthy tunic as if he might run if she didn't hold him there. Now that she'd started touching him, she couldn't stop. The water of belief had been trickling through the limestone of her fears all afternoon, wearing them thin, and they were beginning to crack, to shatter, and she was in danger of being buried in the rubble. Exposed and reunited, crushed under a terrible, wonderful joy. She craved that crushing as much as she feared it.

Toxte's eyes strayed to her face again and again as he gave

water to her dog and they waited to be identified or killed. Sometimes wide with wonder, other times guarded, as if he expected this to end just as much as she did. He rested his cupped palm on the point of her shoulder for Ossa to drink from and its heat branded her, the contact sending further cracks through her defences.

Toxte's head whipped around, his hand clamping on her shoulder in warning. Xessa's hurts vanished in a sudden rush of adrenaline and then Toxte stepped away from her. The eja gasped, reached for him, and then over his shoulder saw Tiamoko sprinting towards them and waving his arms. The warriors guarding them stepped back at his order and gestured, allowing the ejab and Ossa to cross the invisible border into safety.

He must have seen Toxte in the torchlight, because he skidded to a halt and flung a flurry of words at the sentries too fast for her to follow. And then more at Toxte, babbling questions in that so-familiar, much-loved way. She drank in the sight of him, tall and broad and filthy. A gash held together by the decapitated heads of black ants, their jaws closing the wound, angled across his clavicle and frighteningly close to his throat, but he was otherwise alive and whole.

Tiamoko lived. And Toxte was here with her and Ossa. The warriors waved them forward, letting them in, keeping them safe. A sob broke from her chest and she didn't care enough to stifle it.

Maybe now she could rest.

Ossa was asleep, his wounds flushed and stitched and smeared with a medicine bought by four injured Tokob refusing treatment so that the dog might have it instead. Over that were bandages, and those same four Tokob – including Tiamoko, of course, and Lilla, to her surprise – had donated half of their water ration to him, too. He'd drunk his fill and now slept stretched along Xessa's thigh where she slumped in a corner against the wall, his belly ridiculously rounded with repletion.

Toxte sat on her other side, a distance between them, a space, air that shouldn't be there. She thought they'd be past that, but he'd taken up position on the other wall of the corner so they could sign and, she supposed, they needed words more than they needed anything else.

Still, her leg twitched towards him and he noticed and extended his foot to meet hers, slipping his big toe along her ankle bone. It was suddenly all she could focus on and Xessa watched, mesmerised, as Toxte's toe, bare of its shoddy, travel-worn sandal, stroked the grubby bones of her ankle and foot. The breath caught in her throat.

Toxte scraped his toenail against the skin and she gasped, gaze flying up to meet his. Despite the low light of the scattered torches, she could make out the flush darkening his cheeks.

'What are you thinking?' he signed and it was her turn to blush. He laughed but there was a hitch to it, a crooked edge to his mouth. 'I don't think your dog needs that sort of disruption.'

It was true, but it didn't make the rejection sting any less. Nor did her very real awareness of the sheer quantity of people surrounding them.

'Why didn't you come to the water this morning? You said you'd taken the spirit-magic; we could have used you. We might have been even more successful.'

She hadn't meant to ask it so bluntly, nor for it to be the first real question out of her hands, but now that she had, she needed the answer. Why had he watched and not acted? Why had he shot a Drowned in the alley to save Tiamoko's life and then, again, hidden away?

Why didn't you come to me the moment you saw me?

Toxte looked across the vast dimness of the tithing barn. It would mean nothing to him, but Xessa could tell how much emptier it was than when she'd left before dawn. Had it really only been this morning? So many people had fought and died in the battle that Tiamoko had heard and hidden her from that the building felt weird. Thronged with spirits who should have ascended the spiral path to the Realm of the Ancestors. Heavy with regret, and fear, and anguish.

Toxte's shoulders were tense, his lips pressed into a thin line. Xessa shoved his foot with hers and he startled, then stretched his neck to the side and winced in the way that meant it had cracked.

'There was a thing I noticed on the way here and I wanted to see how far it had spread,' he signed nonsensically.

'A thing?' she asked, curling her lip in sarcastic repetition. Malel, but this wasn't how this was supposed to go.

'The Drowned are different now. Different from how we've ever known them. And it's not because we're under the song here, or in Quitoban where I was. They're different as in something's happened, something's changed them. Recently. I think it was the night the uprising happened. This ritual everyone speaks of, it did something. It affected the Drowned – and not in a good way.'

Xessa's hand faltered where it was stroking Ossa's broad skull. 'What?' she signed with the other.

'They didn't just follow you from the river. You got two, and you were watched by maybe ten others. As soon as you left the water, the three you killed in the city started moving. They trailed you for a hundred steps and then slipped ahead. Parallel through the streets, outrunning you.'

'What are you trying to—'

'They anticipated where you were going to be and they ambushed you.' The words were as stark and economical as Toxte's gestures. He may as well have been signing in another language.

'That's impossible. They're monsters, animals, they can't—'

'Xessa, my wife, my love. *Eja* Xessa. Something has changed them. They're cleverer. They're . . . imaginative. As if their human minds have returned to them.'

Xessa thought about how the Drowned had moved, how they'd coordinated, how that one had sneaked up on her the moment she'd sent Ossa off ahead. And how they'd called Tiamoko into a narrow alley, with the Drowned furthest from danger – from Xessa – being the one who sang and attracted him in. If not for Toxte's presence on the roof, they'd be dead.

He was right; that was different. Different even from how they'd killed her father, Kime. She'd spent the whole day so concerned for Ossa and Tiamoko that she hadn't let herself think about it. She'd ignored the gnawing wrongness of what had happened, attributing it to the sheer number of Drowned she'd killed instead of anything deeper.

And yet, here and now . . . it wasn't the most important thing they needed to discuss, even if the rebel leadership needed to know their suspicions.

Xessa shoved at his foot again. '*I didn't know it was you.* You knew I lived, you knew exactly where I was. I knew nothing. You might have been dead or injured. You might not have come for me. I didn't know. But you'd seen me. You think that's fair?'

'You think I wanted to distract you at the edge of that fucking river with the Drowned behaving in ways we've never seen? It would have got you killed.'

Xessa wanted to argue with that, but she couldn't. 'Afterwards, then,' she insisted. 'Straight after.'

'I was following the Drowned. At first I wasn't sure if they were after you or moving somewhere else. When I suspected, I had to confirm it, and be ready to help. Afterwards, well, you needed to focus on Ossa.'

All of that was true, and yet none of it felt right.

'Tiamoko hid you when he heard the fighting and I was going to come then, but that battle swept right through the area and I couldn't slip past to reach you. Afterwards, I couldn't remember which road you'd gone down; the spirit-magic was beginning to wear off and I was, well, you know.'

Xessa did know; the shakes and nausea and disorientation would have made it almost impossible for Toxte to do anything but lie hidden and wait for the magic to leave his body. It all made perfect sense, it was all logical, and it still felt wrong.

'And?' she asked.

'And seeing you again, even though I came all this way to find you, I was scared. Tiamoko was watching over you. Maybe—'

She didn't shove him with her foot this time; she slapped his bare arm. Hard. He scowled and a horrible thought rooted in her mind, poisonous and quick-growing. 'Tiamoko is a friend. More than that, he is *a child*. But you're quick to assume, Toxte. Did you take a lover, then? Is that why it's so easy to think the same of me? If there's somewhere you'd rather be,' she signed and Toxte grabbed her by the wrists to stop the words. He let go immediately, but it was too late. How dare he hush her? How *dare he* stop her words when she had every right to ask?

'No,' he signed, hand slashing through the air. 'There is no one. There was no one and there will never be anyone other than you for me. But the way you looked, so sure and strong and focused. You knew – know – your place in this world. And it didn't include me. How could it, when I hadn't been here for the last two sun-years?' Toxte's hands were trembling and he shook them out. 'You had Tiamoko—'

'Tiamoko's a boy,' Xessa reiterated furiously. 'He's a friend. He's *not you*.'

'And you had him,' Toxte continued as if she hadn't signed. He pointed at Ossa, twitching in his sleep. 'But I, I lost Ekka.' His face crumpled. 'I lost my dog, Xessa. I let her die.'

Anything Xessa had been thinking or feeling was swept away. She didn't sign – there were no words sufficient. She just dragged him to her, chest to chest, the vicious ache in her back from carrying Ossa a poignant and stabbing reminder of what she had that he didn't.

Toxte melted into her arms, as heedless of the awkwardness of their position as she was. His breath was hot and jagged against her neck, stuttering with the intensity of his grief. A grief that, most likely, had lain festering inside him, buried beneath the wounds of losing her, his home, his tribe. A slow rot he might never have faced until today.

Xessa let the strength of her embrace speak for her, her fingers digging into his spine as she pressed kisses to his temple and behind his ear. She had lost dogs through age and sickness, but never during the duty. Never had they given their lives to save hers. Toxte hadn't specified, but he had to mean during the fall of the Sky City, in those awful hours after they'd lost sight of each other in the dark and the running and the dying.

She held him until he drew back and slumped against the wall with a thump she felt through the ground. 'Tell me,' she signed, swallowing tears. 'Tell me all of it, ever since we were separated. Tell me of the loss and the blood and I'll do the same. Because I love you, husband. I love you until the end of my life and my spirit will love yours in all the lives to come.'

Toxte smiled, small but genuine, and wiped his eyes. 'So dramatic,' he complained. 'Who's to say I won't be sick of you by then? Wife,' he added, with such profound reverence that a knot untied itself in her chest.

He took a deep, deep breath, visibly composing himself, and then he began to sign.

'We lost each other that night. Remember?' He waved away his own question, his face bitter and full of self-recrimination. Fear made its home in Xessa's gut. What had happened to him to so steal his confidence in himself? 'Of course you do. None of us will ever forget that night. I just . . . one moment you were there and then there were Melody running at us and, I don't know, I went left and you went right or something, but the next time I looked, you were gone. I'd lost you and there were people fleeing everywhere I looked, Tokob and Yaloh screaming and Melody chasing them.'

He stopped and shook out his hands again. There was sweat at his temples; his chest heaved for breath. Xessa shifted carefully so that her lower back was pressed to Ossa's long flank, maintaining that contact they both wanted and needed, and faced her husband. She took his hands in hers, squeezing his cold fingers gently and then kissing the tips of each one in turn, her eyes flickering up to meet his and then down again. The tremors in his body slowly subsided as she tugged him closer, cross-legged so they were knee to knee, and then she leant forward and drew him in and pressed their foreheads together.

Down in the small space between their bodies, she kept hold of his hands and signed 'I love you' clumsily, their fingers tangled together. She felt the puff of his laugh against her lips and chin and then he signed the same.

Xessa lifted her head and pressed a kiss to Toxte's cheek and then sat back. 'We lived. You and I are alive, here and now, together. Forget what I just said. You don't need to tell me anything if you don't want to. Not until you're ready' – she thought of some of her own secrets – 'not ever if it's too painful. It won't stop me loving you. Or needing you.'

His smile was a fragile thing, a butterfly's wing torn by the storm. Unlikely to hold him up.

'They were killing the dogs. Did you notice that? I saw three killed in the hour after I lost sight of you. Ekka . . . I kept her close, but you know how fierce she was. How protective.'

Xessa did know. She rubbed her arm theatrically. 'I remember the nip she gave me the first time I climbed into your lap,' she signed and Toxte smiled. 'Nearly put me off you.'

'No, it didn't,' he signed.

She grinned. 'No, it didn't. Put me off your lap, though.'

'You squealed, as I recall. Not very snake path of you.'

Xessa pretended affront and smiled inwardly, pleased, as a little more tension, a little more grief, slipped from Toxte's cracked expression.

'I remember what they were doing to the dogs,' she signed after a while. 'Otek died to save Ossa.'

Toxte bowed his head and she knew he was praying. 'Your father was a great man,' he signed. 'If only I'd had the chance to do the same for Ekka.'

Xessa slapped his chest this time, even harder. 'Don't ever say that. She did her duty, the way any warrior – any eja – would do. She gave you the great gift of her life, and she did so willingly. Don't cheapen her death with your guilt.'

Indignation and then self-recrimination twisted his face and he looked suddenly older, haggard in the half-light, lines at the edges of his eyes and framing his mouth she didn't remember. So much of him she knew, bone-deep, spirit-deep, and so much she'd forgotten. Or had never known at all.

'You're right, of course you're right,' he said, or something like it. She couldn't quite read it; he'd raised his hand to fiddle with the hair covering the remnants of his ear and she had to suppress a flicker of irritation.

He's my husband. He should know better than to look away when speaking.

Xessa wondered, not for the first time, what this horrible new life had made her. Quick to pass judgment and quicker to hold a grudge. She'd seen Tayan up on that pyramid, glowing with foreign magic and protected by warriors, and all her love for him had shrivelled in a heartbeat into hate. Hate that shone even brighter than her loathing for Pilos and the Singer. Hate that forbade her from speaking with Lilla; hate that drew forth poisoned words from her hands. Yet earlier, Lilla had embraced Toxte with tears and genuine delight, signing his joy for Xessa at their reunion, however much his own circumstances hurt his heart.

And now her annoyance at Toxte himself for . . . what, exactly? Grieving? Why was it easy for everyone else to be so generous with their hearts and feelings and so impossible for her? Had Pilos made her this, or had he woken something within her that had always been there, drawn it forth from the depths, to make her so cruel and unforgiving?

'I love you,' she signed, determined to be patient. 'Please tell me what happened to Ekka. I thought of her every day, along with Ossa. Even when I got him back, I didn't give up hope I might find her. And you.'

She ran her fingers over the twisted scar tissue of his damaged leg and he flushed again, this time in clear humiliation. His fingers twitched as if to make her stop and then he set his jaw and met her gaze. She ran her fingers across the knotted flesh again, letting him know it didn't matter, not this injury, not his missing ear, and not those wounds whose scars lived only on the inside. None of it mattered because he was here and he was hers.

'This,' he signed eventually, indicating his knee. 'This happened. This killed Ekka. An eagle's club smashed the bones. I couldn't walk. Couldn't breathe it felt like, though that might have just been the screaming. Ekka did her duty and protected me for as long as she could. The same club broke her back and so I, I did my duty by her.'

Xessa wiped at her tears and then seized his hands, selfishly because she didn't want to know any more but also as a point of contact, of reassurance. *I am here and so are you and we, at least, still live.*

Ossa's heat against the small of her back was a guilty joy but she couldn't – wouldn't – bring herself to regret it. Ekka's loss was a tragedy, but Ossa was a blessing all the more precious for it.

'They captured you then?' she asked when she could let go and he nodded.

'I was dragging myself away after I'd given her peace, but there was nowhere to go. Even uninjured there was nowhere we could have gone. They caught me, tied me and then splinted my leg. Stitched it shut some time the next day. I don't really know. I don't remember a lot of it. They gave me a crutch and made me walk' – even in the gloom she saw the memory of that agony and winced – 'but it healed wrong. I've spent the last two years thinking it justice for Ekka.'

Xessa shook her head in urgent denial and Toxte managed a small smile. 'I know,' he signed. 'But it's hard not to.' He scrubbed his hands over his face, weariness in the lines of his shoulders, and then grimaced and shifted, stretching out the leg and massaging the flesh around the knee. She could see now that the kneecap itself was the wrong shape, smaller than it should be and pulled sideways by the scar tissue.

Her father Kime had dislocated his knee falling down a flight of steps when she was a child; she had a vivid memory of a shaman pushing it back into place while her other father, Otek, wrestled him into stillness. Kime had often complained how it clicked in the years after and that was just a dislocation. What must this feel like?

'Can we sleep?' he signed abruptly. 'I can go—'

'Don't leave me,' she interrupted. 'Unless, unless you want to.' They paused, staring at each other in awkward discomfort. 'You could just, if you wanted, lie by my side?' It wasn't as if there was privacy for anything else, although the idea of intimacy was both unnerving and deeply alluring.

His smile was small but full of affection. 'I would like that very much,' he signed and then took her hands and kissed them, as she'd done for him.

The space was small and the majority of it was devoted to Ossa, but that just meant they had an excuse to curl closer to each other on the dirt floor. They hadn't finished their histories – Xessa hadn't even begun hers – but it didn't matter, not when his arm settled around her waist and he tugged her back into the warmth of his body. This was their truth and whatever he'd done as a slave – just like her – would not be enough to break them apart again. And she would be the person she had been before, the woman he remembered from home, the one he'd married and still, somehow, loved. She wouldn't show him the monster Pilos had made her. A small deception, but a necessary one in light of all he'd already lost.

Xessa nestled even closer, as close as she could get, and stretched out her hand to rest on Ossa's foreleg. An ear flicked, but he didn't stir.

She slept. And dreamt of Drowned.

ILANDEH

Green City, northern Yalotlan, Empire of Songs
40th day of the Great Star at morning

'I understand, Spear. Thank you. I will think about your offer.'

There was a long, pregnant pause within the small and yet infinite space of the song and the Listener's mind, and then Pilos pulsed with the richest, deepest purple of fury she'd ever seen, from him or anyone. Just a moment, but it was incandescent and unmistakable. Never had Ilandeh pushed him so close to losing control. Never had she wanted to. She wasn't sure she wanted it now, though the smallest, smuggest flicker of satisfaction curled its fingers around her guts.

And then he spoke. *No. Who is it you think you are conversing with? What choice do you think there is to make? I am giving you your life back despite everything you have done and said. And I am giving you an order, Whisper.*

'You have Beyt. She is—'

She is needed where she is. You are not. The Flight will be happy, I suspect, to put a blade in you if you refuse to obey.

Ilandeh could have pointed out she was no longer a Whisper, no longer a warrior in the Fourth Talon or any part of the Melody. No longer subject to Pilos's orders. She did not. She couldn't, because, even distant as she was from her flesh, she could feel it tingling, buzzing like a hive with adrenaline, anticipation, joy. He needed her. She was still valuable to him. She could get it all back.

Listener, I am done with the Whisper. I have instructions for you alone. Pilos's words were brusque and brutal and dismissive, and Ilandeh obeyed them without hesitation, pulling away and letting the Listener drop her back into her body like dough into a bowl.

She came slowly back to herself, the flickering candlelight leaping at the painted walls within the pyramid. She hadn't believed Beyt when the Flight had told her that Pilos wanted to speak with her. In fact, she'd been fairly certain she was being led to her death and had resolved to make it as difficult as possible for all concerned. Instead, she'd been marched to the pyramid and swept up into the Listener's mind, the song, and then Spear Pilos. Who had . . . offered to give her her life back.

Ilandeh blinked and waited until her eyes could focus on the flesh world again. Beyt and four warriors squatted between her and the passageway leading out of the pyramid. She gestured Ilandeh away from the Listener and took her place, awaiting Pilos's summons and the instructions he'd give her for Ilandeh's execution should she refuse his order. Not that she would. The moment he'd spoken she'd known it; she'd always done as he commanded with the single exception of the night she'd fled his blade and the pyramid. The chance to follow his orders again, to make him proud, was as heady and addictive as honeypot.

She shook the fine tremor from her hands and breathed deeply, centring her spirit once more within her flesh, knitting them together. Before the blinding purple of his wrath had encompassed her, Pilos had been the sickly white of fatigue, yet he'd expended the extra effort required to hold his mind aloof from hers, not even their edges touching within the Listener's consciousness and the song itself. As if the merest contact would be a violation or an infection. *Filthy fucking half-blood.* Words she'd heard a thousand times, though never from him, and yet they echoed within her in his voice.

Ilandeh watched as Beyt was drawn into the song and the Spear's presence, animation fading from her face until she was as dull and lifeless as a badly painted mural. How much of Pilos's anger and disdain, the contempt that had dripped from his every word, would still be plain to her? Would the new Flight get a glimpse of the depths of his disgust for Ilandeh?

She snorted and leant her head back against the wall. So what if she did? Despite that contempt and the fury he displayed so righteously, he hadn't been able to disguise his eagerness to once again make use of her particular skills for the good of the Empire of Songs. And the good of Spear Pilos.

She'd expected execution. She'd expected to discover that those dark, wild tales were true – that it was possible to reach through the song and stop a person's heart in their chest. She'd expected Pilos to do it himself.

What she'd got was orders. A likely impossible task. And a promise.

A promise that was everything she'd spent the last weeks wanting – and dreading. Wanting because it was safe and familiar and known, because it would give her a purpose and she was nothing without one. Dreading because it would force her into a shape she didn't think she fitted anymore, force her to do things she couldn't help but question where before she'd been stubbornly, wilfully ignorant.

And yet, when it came to it, the seductive call of obedience and the absolution of responsibility that went with it were irresistible. His voice was a leash, a whip, a reward, depending on what he needed her to be. How she loathed it, and loathed the part of herself that responded to it. Wanted it. Craved it.

Even worse – or perhaps better, she didn't know – the choice was no choice at all. None of the choices Pilos had ever given her had been. She was a half-blood and yet she had less freedom than the lowest slave warrior. She'd spent her life in ropes of her own making and Pilos had seen them and taken them into his own hands the better to control her. In coming to Yalotlan and distancing herself from him, she'd thought she might finally have cut those ropes free, and yet with a single conversation, she was bound even more tightly than before.

Beyt came out of the song. Her breath was harsh as she regained her centre and relearnt the confines of her flesh. Ilandeh had no sympathy for her. The other Whispers flanked her, weapons drawn. They expected her to run, then. Or try and fight her way free. Beyt must have primed them before they brought her here, which meant the Flight had been expecting Pilos to order Ilandeh's death.

He will have. If I don't follow his orders, I'll die on the steps of this pyramid. And if I do agree, there's a chance I die anyway. Pilos does not hoard his jade; he gambles with it.

She wondered what he would think if she named herself jade in his presence and suppressed a smile. The Listener's eyes glittered from within deeply shadowed sockets as they fixed upon her, unblinking. Her shaven scalp gleamed and Ilandeh got a stranglehold on her thoughts and throttled them into silence.

'Spear Pilos's order,' Beyt croaked after bowing to the Listener and shuffling towards the little group.

Ilandeh took a deep breath through flared nostrils. 'I am a Whisper of the macaws and former Flight of the Fourth Talon. I will do my duty.'

Of the four hundred Whispers that made up their secret, elite number within the Fourth Talon, barely twenty were in the Green City on Yalotlan's border. Of those twenty, more than half had left an hour after Beyt's communion with Pilos, escorting every Pechaqueh who wished to leave, including the Listener. They were heading for Xentiban and the safety of a Talon-held city.

The Flight had been thoroughly chastised, it seemed, and her mood was sharper than obsidian as she snapped orders at the retired free who were now responsible for the city and the empty pyramid and the preservation of the song in this part of Ixachipan.

Of the remaining Whispers, there were none that Ilandeh

knew well. So long she'd been away, first in Tokoban and then in the source, that many had died in the fighting and new blood – half-blood – had been brought in to supplement their numbers. Who knew what stories Beyt had spread about her in the years since she'd been their Flight. She'd briefly been in command again during the campaign to bring Tokoban under the song, and in those few short weeks she'd seen her predecessor Sarn disgraced and cast out of their ranks. It was no surprise Beyt had been hostile.

Ilandeh dismissed Beyt from her mind and inspected the remaining Whispers, noting the set of their shoulders and the level of curiosity they displayed. Pilos had told her to recruit two, but that was easier ordered than obeyed when faced with these strangers.

She twisted her right arm so her inner wrist was exposed, baring the chulul tattoo that named her as one of them. A few gazes flicked to it and then back to her face, wary but curious. That was a good combination. Others were contemptuous or challenging: those would be Beyt's cronies, infected by whatever poison she'd spoken during Ilandeh's long absence.

'You and you,' Ilandeh said when she'd made them wait far longer than necessary just to see what would happen. The two she indicated had been still, calm, intent. No fidgeting or sighing, no hostility or derision. 'Your Flight has orders for you from Spear Pilos, and once we're on the move, I'll have my own and will expect you to listen. I am Ilandeh. I was Flight of the Fourth, a command I relinquished in order to spend a sun-year in Tokoban's Sky City preparing it to be brought under the song. The two years after that are not for your ears. Names?'

'Olox of Pechacan and Axiban,' the younger of the warriors said eagerly, stepping forward with a bright grin. He didn't look to Beyt for permission, which Ilandeh appreciated. Perhaps it was youthful exuberance, or perhaps he didn't like his Flight.

The second Whisper, older and seasoned, Ilandeh knew by

face and reputation but had never worked with. He inclined his head. 'Pikte.'

Just that and no more.

Very well. We'll have more than enough time for small talk on our journey.

'Grab supplies and weapons, as much food as can be spared. We won't have much time to hunt, but we can lay snares on trails when we pause to rest. You're under my command now.'

'What for?' Pikte asked.

Ilandeh held up her hands. 'You see how I'm not in ropes anymore, as a result of speaking with Spear Pilos through the song? You remember me saying, just now, that I'd speak once we were moving?' She kept her tone even and pleasant and let her face be her threat. Pikte held her gaze and then looked away and nodded. 'We are Whispers. That used to mean something when I was Flight, but I accept that times have changed. What hasn't is the secrecy that shrouds us. So I won't be relaying our orders for all to hear. You'll know what you need to when you need to. Is that clear?'

Pikte lifted one shoulder in half a shrug and Ilandeh padded close to him and looked up into his face, close enough that he had to meet her eyes. 'If I'm going to have a problem with you, Pikte, best you say so now so that I can select someone else, someone whose loyalty to the Empire of Songs and the Whispers isn't quite so' – she brushed a speck of dirt from the front of his tunic and he flinched – 'shaky.'

A muscle flickered in his jaw. 'You need have no worries about my loyalty or performance, Whisper,' he said through gritted teeth.

Ilandeh stepped back. 'Of course not,' she said with a smile. 'Now, shall we get going? We've a long journey and an important task from the High Feather and the Spear. Flight? After you.'

Whatever Beyt felt about being ordered around, no matter how politely, she did a better job at hiding it in front of the other Whispers than Pikte had. She offered Ilandeh a bland smile and gestured for the three of them to follow. Ilandeh swaggered after her, shrugging on her Chorus Leader demeanour and noting how Beyt responded unconsciously to her authority.

They moved through narrow avenues and small plazas littered with debris, patches of stone still splashed with old, dried blood and stained with smoke. At least some of the slaves here had fought back before being cut down. The gardens and allotments were partially destroyed but some seedlings had begun poking their heads above the mud, taking advantage of the Wet and the rich earth. Ilandeh wondered, idly, who would control this place by the time the harvest was ready to be brought in.

'What have you heard about the Zellih at the Tokoban border, Flight?' Ilandeh spoke with the casual arrogance of a Chorus warrior, the born-and-raised expectation of obedience and response.

Beyt gave her both. 'Last I heard it had all died down some time ago. My guess is they got beaten back badly enough to not want to risk a full Talon falling on them.'

Ilandeh frowned at her back. 'Surely they know of the uprising. Whatever their reasons for those skirmishes over the border, they've got more of a chance of being successful now than they had before, yet you think they've stopped?'

The Flight turned back with a haughty glare. 'Our Listener hears from all of Tokoban's major cities, including the Sky City. If there was a Zellih war party moving through that land, we'd know about it.'

Ilandeh decided not to point out that Beyt's precious Listener was on their way to Xentiban. She'd no desire to get punched again. Besides, aside from Beyt's lack of vision and intelligence, they were no different, really. They both clung to what Pilos had given them, made them, with a desperation that was almost pathetic.

No. The Spear still finds me useful. He gave me this task, not Beyt. And in that usefulness, I can find something that's just for me. Something is always better than nothing.

She knew that voice for the obedient little animal Pilos had made her. She countered it with memories of the respect she'd earnt as Chorus Leader and swaggered ahead of Beyt, forcing the other warrior to scurry to keep up with her. Petty, but soothing to her spirit.

Ilandeh had her orders and orders always steadied her, gave her a sense of purpose and a sense of self. She clutched at them now. She was being manipulated, ordered, used, yes, but surely that only mattered if she let it?

The argument was weak and worse, it was shameful. She clung to it anyway. Clung to Pilos and his vision, as she always had.

Nallac wept, perhaps, but Ilandeh didn't. Weapons didn't need tears.

'Under the song, Flight Beyt, and may you find victory here.' The words felt foreign upon Ilandeh's tongue, their taste bitter as frog venom. They were at the low, useless wall and ready to leave, blankets filled with provisions tied across their backs and weapons clean and sharp.

Ilandeh had spent all morning interviewing as many of the remaining warriors and civilians as she could, gleaning what they knew, what they guessed, what rumours they'd heard from the few people who'd made it here and been allowed to stay long enough to talk. From the way none of the civilians could meet her eyes when they spoke of such wanderers, she knew the mass grave in the treeline contained more than just dead slaves.

The stories would all be exaggerated messes, but stories always came from somewhere, just as the giant, sprawling amate grew from a tiny seed. Ilandeh already had a few ideas about some of those seeds, but they had sticks to cover and a wide variety of people to question before she'd even begin to paint a picture of what was happening in this region.

Clearly, her easy manner and reassuring speech during her questioning had endeared her, as most of the town had come to see them off – the remaining Whispers were off to the side in a little huddle behind Beyt, while the loyal free and retired dogs and their families were grim and dry-eyed beside them.

Witnessing the departure of three more warriors who could defend them from rebel slaves but instead were walking away and taking food and supplies with them.

Ilandeh gave them a reassuring smile and then Beyt was stepping forward and grabbing her by the face, hauling her close. 'Whatever your orders are, Olox and Pikte have their own. From Pilos and from me. You don't get another chance, Ilandeh; I'm surprised and a little pissed off you even got this one. Don't fuck up again.'

Ilandeh prised her face free of Beyt's grip and ran her tongue around her gums. 'Touch me again without permission and it will be the last thing you ever do. Your threats are as meaningless and unwelcome as a dog fart, Beyt, and if you're so insecure as to find me a challenge to your position, maybe you're not fit to hold it after all.'

'You—' Beyt began.

Ilandeh leant close in turn and the other warrior flinched. 'Spear Pilos may have orders for you regarding me,' she murmured, 'but he gave me exactly none about you. So there's nothing to stop me breaking you in half if the mood strikes. Now *fuck off.*' She juggled her possessions into one hand and touched her belly and then throat, bowing her head. 'Under the song, Flight,' she added, sincerely enough that Beyt choked on it.

'Under the song,' she replied, as tradition required, voice a strangled, venomous croak. Ilandeh checked her salt-cotton and then slipped the tied blanket over her head and one arm, snugging it against her back. She slotted her blowpipe underneath and then nodded to Olox and Pikte and slipped through the wooden gate. She had food, water, weapons, and a mission from Spear Pilos.

Just like old times.

The two Whispers followed and she set off west and slightly north, towards the border with Chitenec and the vast river that marked it. It was a few days' walk; by the time they reached it, she'd know if she could trust her companions or whether their corpses needed to be dropped in a convenient ravine.

'So, Olox and Pikte, let's get to know each other. My heritage is Xentib. Olox, you said Axib. Yours, Pikte?'

'Also Axib,' Olox said when the other man refused to reply. He settled in close to her, grinning in the corner of her eye.

Ilandeh looked to her other side and then back. Pikte brought up the rear, moving easily. Alert. Wary. 'Pikte was the name of the Great Octave's son,' she said loud enough for him to hear. Best to know the temperaments of her companions now rather than be killed by ignorance later.

'The Great Octave was a traitor who murdered that son and was justly killed in turn and Pikte is not an unusual name. What is your point?' the man growled and Ilandeh got the feeling he'd answered this question several times since Enet's betrayal had become common knowledge.

'It's a Pechaqueh name. You're half-Axib.' She waited but he was silent. 'Must have made time in the Melody difficult,' she offered at last.

'No more than for any of us,' he grunted reluctantly.

Good enough for now.

'All right, let's walk this trail so we all know the route, yes? We're on the same side and working towards the same outcome so if we run into trouble, I expect you to save my life the same way I'll save yours. Understood?'

'We understand, Flight,' Olox reassured her and Pikte jerked him to a halt.

'She is no Flight. Not for years. Not ever again. Don't forget that.'

Olox stood his ground, to her surprise. Despite his youth and inexperience – he must have been recruited to the Whispers during the time she'd been in the great pyramid – he showed respect for but no fear of the older warrior. He'd probably never even heard of Ilandeh before now. She had simply vanished after leaving the siege of the Sky City, after all.

'Do we not refer to retired eagles as eagles, Feathers as Feathers?' he asked, mildly enough to take the sting from his impertinence.

'You would compare Pechaqueh who retire honourably at

the end of their service with this, *this thing?*' Pikte spat. Olox's eyes widened in shock and Ilandeh stepped in before things got out of hand. They needed to work together; they had to at least share some trust between them.

That said . . .

'Thing?' she asked, dangerously soft and even though she had to angle her chin upwards to look him in the eyes, Pikte's tongue flicked out to wet his lower lip. Unsure. 'What is it you think you know about me, warrior of Axiban and Pechacan?' He twitched at that: every member of the Fourth Talon named their Pechaqueh heritage first.

In this at least, though, Ilandeh had chosen well: the Whisper was bold. 'You betrayed Spear Pilos. You were cast out of the Melody. The whole Fourth knows it,' he accused.

She put her head on one side and gave him a coyote-sharp smile. 'Tell me, Pikte, have you ever infiltrated a town or city to carry out our work? Have you ever lived and breathed a lie and forgotten your own identity and past to gain the trust of others?' He nodded reluctantly. 'So have I. *For years at a time.* Now ask yourself whether I'd deliberately plant rumours of my disgrace – or agree to them being planted by, oh, say Spear Pilos, if I needed to create a disguise that everyone would believe without question. One that even other Whispers would believe.'

Pikte actually took a step back. 'You—' he began.

Ilandeh gave him an enigmatic smile. 'It will make sense when we get where we're going,' she said and turned to Olox. 'But Pikte is right about one thing: I am no longer Flight, so just call me Ilandeh from now on.'

She didn't wait for an answer, stepping past the silent, shocked warriors and walking on, sweeping the ground ahead and to either side for danger. Would they believe her? Her own audacity left her shaky.

'Spear Pilos says we are to discover—' Olox began, catching up to her again and chattering on as if the tension of a moment ago had never been.

'No names, no titles,' Ilandeh reminded him. 'Best get used to it now.'

'But our orders,' Olox tried and she suppressed a sigh. Was this the quality of training Beyt had passed on during her absence?

'Tell me a story, Olox,' she said with feigned patience. The young Whisper was silent, his brow creased with puzzlement.

'Don't know about you, but ten years in the Melody, the last five as a Coyote war leader, and they throw me out on some spurious charge I'm not even allowed to defend myself against,' Pikte said, venom in his voice and a squint to his eyes as he appeared on her other side. 'Ten years of loyalty. Ten years of doing their bidding, and this is what happens. Proud son of Axiban and they threw me out, wouldn't even let me prove my innocence. Well, they can fuck right off. Change is coming and I'm going to be a part of it. Find me some rebels and help them carve out a little slice of independence, that's all I want. No Melody breathing down my neck, no Pechaqueh telling me I'm shit on their sandals.'

Ilandeh saw the moment Olox understood. He opened his mouth, but she got in there first. 'We've done this a lot longer than you have and can be a little more . . . elaborate. We have the skills to weave these tales and to remember what we've said. This is your first infiltration, yes?' He nodded, embarrassed. 'Then your story needs to be simple and as close to the truth as you can make it. Easier to remember; easier to believe.'

She glanced across at Pikte, because he knew that rule too, and even if they could go deeper, it was rare that they did. She'd be unsurprised to discover whip scars on his back were she to look. 'Were you innocent of whatever crime they brought against you, though?' she asked, curious.

Pikte hawked and spat. 'What's your story then?' he demanded instead of answering.

Ilandeh smiled, sharp and toothy. 'Me? I wasn't a very good merchant, despite my ambition and half-blood status, and fell into debt. Joined the Melody and the Fourth Talon to earn out what I owed. I fought for Spear Pilos, my High Feather, and his predecessor for thirteen sun-years. Raised me up, he did, honoured and rewarded me. Two months ago he betrayed me and cast me out, said he'd kill me himself if he ever so much as heard my voice on the wind again. Thirteen years, unconditional loyalty. Killed for him and his Empire, his Melody. Would've died for him too, if he'd asked it of me. If thirteen years' loyalty isn't enough to earn me a place in the Empire of Songs, then I don't want to be in it at all.'

There was a long silence when she finished talking.

'You said simple and close to the truth,' Olox said in the end, his voice cracking with some emotion. Maybe outrage, maybe contempt. 'What's all this about being a merchant?'

She glanced back. 'We're not just gathering information for the High Feather. We need to be prepared to meet all sorts of people – rebels, warriors, civilians, eagles. There's a chance we'll meet some people who know me as Merchant Ilandeh. They know some of my story – *that* story – because we've made sure they do. They know exactly what we want them to know about me, except that last part, anyway. That's too new.

'You two, though, you're just regular Axib dog warriors defecting from the Melody. Following in my footsteps in the hopes of finding somewhere quiet to wait out the war.'

She glanced back again, just to see how they reacted to the idea that she'd be above them in blood status, at least in this subterfuge. Pikte's mouth tightened, but he lifted one shoulder in a shrug. He knew how this went. Olox still seemed lost in thought, whether about his own story or about how much truth might be in Ilandeh's.

All of it. Almost all of it's true, she wanted to hiss, spitting the venom of her hurt and hate in his face. She didn't. She was Whisper Ilandeh, who'd lied to the Singer himself for two sun-years. Who'd lied to Great Octave Enet. Who'd lied to Tayan in the Sky City and Tayan in the source. The only person she'd ever spent time with who she hadn't lied to was Pilos. Right up until the end.

'So should we know each other?' Olox asked eventually.

'I know Pikte; our paths have crossed in the last decade.

Pikte knows you. You and I had never met before we fell in together while looking for a cause to join. Over the next few days, you'll alter your appearances to prioritise your Axib heritage,' Ilandeh added, some nameless emotion, both sweet and sharp, sliding through her chest as she found the Xentib rattle in her hair and drew it out to show them, even as she forced her mouth into a sardonic smile. *Look at my disguise.*

'Work on your story and tell it me when we rest for water,' she said to Olox. The boy nodded and Ilandeh began to walk again, and then to lope, and then to run. If they wanted to test her, they'd better be able to keep up.

LILLA

Street of shamans, western Singing City,
Pechacan, Empire of Songs
42nd day of the Great Star at morning

Lilla was exhausted. He ached down to his very spirit and his body was thin, wiry, and held together, it seemed, by bandage and prayer. He eased his way across the flat roof and glanced over the edge, spear loose in his fist. The street below was clear, so he retreated, ran, and leapt the body-length onto the next roof across, rolling as he landed and the breath hissing from his teeth as his stitches pulled and flared pain across his hip. The eagle who'd stabbed him hadn't even had the courtesy to go in through his existing wound, instead opening another a finger's width below the shallow slice he'd suffered only days before. Combined, they added an edge of sickness to everything he did.

He lay on the warm stone, wincing and listening, but there was no burst of alarm or sudden pounding of feet. He was alone still; safe. He gave it a little while longer, letting the pain dull into a hot ache, until the familiar restlessness built again and forced him to his feet. He needed rest but couldn't find it. Hence his insistence on scouting the route to Weaver's new hideout himself.

Ekon had been against it, of course, and most of the war

party, too. He'd overruled them, even though it was impulsive and threatened what little trust they still had in him. His horror of enclosed spaces was growing worse despite his every effort. And every time it happened, the ringing in his head increased and an attack of crippling agony threatened that might debilitate him for days.

And so here he was, creeping across the roofs under a vast and open sky dark with massing cloud and sticky with humidity, the air so thick it clung to the insides of his lungs.

It had been three days since Xessa's victory at the Blessed Water and the day-long battle with the Melody that had happened at the same time and which had trapped her and Ossa in the city but reunited them with Toxte. They'd heard nothing from Weaver's war party since and their previous hideout was abandoned, so Lilla was visiting their next location to find out their status. He knew he might be walking into a slaughterhouse. Or a trap. He was going anyway. One more day in that echoing stone grave and he'd have lost his mind.

Crouching on a roof far from Ekon's watchful concern and Xessa and Toxte's searing affection for each other, Lilla felt the tight band around his chest loosen. He drew in an unobstructed breath for the first time in too long and relished it, tainted with smoke and death though it was. The incessant whine in his ears faded into a lower background noise he could ignore, and he stared up into the boiling clouds that promised rain before nightfall. The Wet was refilling cisterns across the city, though this early in the season it didn't give them much and that was soon gone. Still, it helped ease the water rationing problem even as it promised more danger from the Drowned, always more active during the rains.

And if Toxte and Xessa's theory about the Drowned was correct . . . Lilla shuddered.

The wind was sudden and cold and urged him to move. Jumping the roofs was noisy and tiring, but the further messengers could travel without touching ground, the better. The noise would vanish up into the sky or bounce among the buildings, making it harder for anyone to track him, and unless they were looking up at exactly the right place and time, no one would see him cross.

Lilla looked over the edge. There was a half-pod of eagles in the street below him and for one liquid thud of his heart, Lilla was so surprised he just stayed there, his head and shoulders outlined against the sky for all to see. Then he dropped flat and peered down with one eye, his fist in his hair to stop it blowing like a banner and attracting attention.

The fifty warriors were alert and heavily armed, moving fast enough to have a purpose beyond merely patrolling the area. He watched their progress down the street into a small plaza. One broke formation to tie a piece of bark-paper to the obelisk standing proud in the centre of the open space, one of only a few he'd seen that remained intact, though scrawled over in various shades of rebellious paint. They had several more sheets of paper tucked into their salt-cotton – whatever was written there, they wanted it to be known across the city.

He watched them regroup and move on, the outer warriors checking for danger. What could be so important that their enemies needed paper and paint to announce it instead of the imperatives of the song?

Tayan's song.

Lilla blinked that away – he'd selected himself as courier so he could move and run and not think in endless circles – and waited until the scuff of eagles' sandals had faded into the breeze and then waited some more. Eventually, he made his way down off the roof and to the edge of the plaza. Sweat prickled at his temples as he checked for danger, every sense straining, and then he dashed across the open space to the obelisk and tore away the paper without pausing to read it. It ripped into three and he stuffed the pieces inside his salt-cotton as he slid into the shadows at the base of the building opposite. Lilla sprinted down the street and away from Weaver's new hideout, but that was fine: he'd just circle back once he knew he'd made it out unseen. He turned a corner and his body reacted to the sound before his mind could process it: the twang of bowstrings; the thrum of arrows.

The Tokob sandals slipped as he tried to reverse and he went down hard on his hip, hard enough to knock a yelp from his chest, but the arrows drove through the air above him. He rolled as more splintered against the ground and then got his feet under him again and dashed back the way he'd come.

Lilla's hip was throbbing with each stride, but it only made him run faster: the pounding of pursuing feet echoed from the buildings to either side as he dashed past the opening of the plaza and took another side street, then immediately changed direction by running through a deserted building and out its far door. He was in an allotment heavy with mud from the night's rain, his sandals squelching deep and slowing him. He staggered on and wove through the other houses, forcing his way through the gap between a building and several lines of cotton that had been dyed and hung to dry, presumably before the uprising.

There were shouts from behind and a spear clattered to his left, bounced and clattered some more. Why chase him? He was one warrior, out on his own. No threat. He pounded across an open space strewn with abandoned and broken furniture. There was shouting up ahead and the sounds of a scuffle. Footsteps echoing behind him. *Forgive me, Malel.*

Lilla took the corner as fast as he could. A crowd of civilians was fighting over a basket of cornmeal. No warriors in sight. The Toko raced into their midst, got at least four between him and the eagles before they really started paying attention. 'Pechaqueh!' he roared. 'Melody!'

The people were starving and vicious with it, but they scattered like deer at his warning, fleeing in a dozen directions – including towards the pursuing eagles. He prayed the warriors would simply throw them aside rather than pausing to kill them but didn't dare wait around long enough to check. And there would be nothing he could do in any event. He was running because he couldn't outfight them; that wouldn't change just because a bunch of civilians got in the way.

The confusion gave him just enough time to take three corners at random and get ahead of the eagles. As soon as he was out of their direct line of sight, he climbed the stairs onto the nearest roof and then doubled back on himself, above his pursuers this time, jumping to another building moments before the warriors ran past in the opposite direction. He kept moving until the screams of the civilians were faded and torn on the wind.

Lilla crouched on the roof of a potter's shop, surrounded by smashed pitchers and clay masks and figures left to dry in the sun before firing. From the quality of the items, this had once been a high-status business and had probably catered to Pechaqueh exclusively. The thoroughness with which every item had been destroyed spoke of an orgy of violence and long-suppressed rage and he hoped it had been the slaves and servants forced to work here who'd done it.

The bark-paper tucked into his tunic scratched at the skin of Lilla's chest as he shifted to peer further down the street, hidden by the shattered masks and broken pots. It was empty, and with Malel's grace he'd make it to Weaver without further incident . . .

Malel's grace.

Malel. Tokob.

Xessa.

Lilla looked down at the triangular pattern he'd painted onto the hem of his kilt. Tokob colours; Tokob patterns. His hair was bound in Tokob fashion, too, unshaven but braided at the temples. Was that the reason for the half-pod's relentless pursuit of him; they'd recognised him as Tokob, which would only matter if they'd found the corpses of the Drowned Xessa had killed.

They knew someone was coming for their gods and there was only one people who had that ability. They were out for revenge. They were coming for Tokob.

They'd wanted to break the Melody, to sow religious fear and despair among them. Maybe they'd done so; or maybe they'd just made them reckless with hate. *Good, reckless is good. Desperate to reach those of us they see as their god-killers. If they're here for Tokob and for vengeance, we can use that against them.*

They'll have more warriors patrolling the river and the streams and ponds, too, trying to get between Xessa and the Drowned. Maybe they'll start being eaten by their so-called gods. Malel, let them be eaten.

He swallowed a manic laugh. If they were at the river they couldn't be at the great pyramid. They might be so consumed with horror for the safety of the Drowned that the freedom fighters could take the pyramid, destroy the songstone, free Tayan, and end the song.

Win the war.

It was both more and less than what they'd hoped and planned for. A distraction, yes. Despair and anger and perhaps a lessening of discipline, yes. The hunting down of any and all Tokob, no. Unless . . . unless Weaver, Xini, and even Ekon had known that such a thing was likely and had kept it from him. As they'd all kept so many secrets for so very long.

Would they betray their own allies? Would Ekon betray him? Yes and yes. For the cause, for victory, they'd do and say anything. Lilla's breathing steadied and a cold, clear focus swept over him. They were on the same side, but right now that meant nothing.

Methodically, he untied his kilt, turned it inside out, and retied it. Some of the colours were still visible, but the outlines – the pattern – was even more smeared on this side. It might be enough.

Enough to get him to Weaver and get some fucking answers.

Watchers confronted him two sticks further on and Lilla gave that week's password and then identified himself, adding that he'd seen eagles scouting the streets nearby. He didn't mention their apparent interest in Tokob; it was possible he was wrong.

I'm not wrong.

He tried not to let the anger simmer up between his ribs. Two sentries hurried him under cover while the rest stayed to check no one had trailed him. It was well done and Lilla found himself curious, once again, about Weaver's background. Either she'd led warriors in battle herself or she was a wise enough leader to relinquish control of that aspect of their defence to others more knowledgeable than she. *And yet it seems she's also willing to sacrifice an entire tribe to gain victory.*

He was handed off to a warrior with orders to be taken to Weaver and Lilla's determination to find the truth solidified. Nothing would stop him. They stepped into the long, low administration building and the Toko gasped and clapped one hand over his nose. It stank, not just with the combined odours of sweat and injury common to all the war parties' hideouts, but with the sweet, pungent scent of sickness and rot.

'What is happening here?' he asked, muffled. 'Where are your shamans?'

'We ran out of fresh bandages and medicine two days ago,' Weaver herself said as she hurried over, quick despite her bloodshot eyes and lanky, sweat-dull hair. She was bloody to the wrists. 'Don't you know that? Isn't that why you're here? I sent requests for aid.'

'No,' he said, dropping his hand from his mouth with a grimace. He looked around again. 'We haven't received any messages.'

Weaver's shoulders slumped. 'We sent four yesterday – two to you, two to Xini.'

Lilla shook his head; no one had made it to the western tithing barns.

Weaver scrubbed a palm over her cheek and eye and then grimaced and swiped ineffectually at the sticky smears of blood left behind. 'It's time to move then, all the war parties. We've about picked this section of the city clean of supplies anyway.

And the messengers were captured or killed, I suppose, like the others. Ancestors guide them to rest.'

Lilla's dying anger burnt back to flaring life. 'And who did you send, Tokob? Was it Tokob?' he asked, his voice low and dangerous. It cut through the pungent space between them, the question out of his mouth before he could stop it. 'Is that what this is, Weaver? Was this your plan? There really is no limit to what you'll do for victory, is there.'

Weaver's face was closed, unreadable. 'What nonsense do you speak? I have warriors dying from lack of medicine and you speak with all the sense of a stunned capuchin fallen from a tree?'

'Tell me which tribes the messengers came from,' he insisted, violence breathing on the back of his neck.

'One Axib, one Yaloh, two Tokob. All civilians. All volunteers. Now explain why you dare question me.'

There was a crack of authority in her voice that had nearby warriors looking up in alarm. It sent a bolt of learnt servility through Lilla; his knees tried to buckle so that he might prostrate himself and beg forgiveness. He stood tall against it.

'I was chased by a half-pod of eagles who were determined to catch me.' He gestured at his kilt, remembered it was inside out, and quickly explained his theory. 'My question to you is whether you did this knowingly, let Xessa go to the river to direct the Melody's rage onto Tokob alone. Make it easier for the rest of you to secure victory while we were the sacrifices.'

Regret and calculation flickered across her face. 'We didn't "let" your eja do anything, if you recall. Word came from your war party of her intentions and we agreed. Further word then came of the attack on your own position. I sent half our warriors to hide on the most likely routes from the pyramid to the river in case the water gods somehow called for help, and the rest to the pyramid itself along with Xini's war party. A few hours after dawn, several exceptionally brave warriors went to the riverbank to see whether she'd been successful. They brought back five corpses, two from the river and three from further into the city. A shocking, unbelievable victory we have celebrated each day since. I had the corpses thrown into the pyramid's compound to take the hearts and spines from the Melody, not to divert their rage onto your people specifically. It was to force the battle, to put them on the defensive so that we might breach—'

'They're probably taking Yaloh too,' Lilla said, the words coming from a great distance through the buzzing in his ears. 'I've seen it before: they can't tell the difference between us. They're snatching us and killing us. Shrinking your war parties, Weaver, reducing your fighting force. And exterminating us.'

Someone forced their way in between him and the tall woman and he realised he was shaking her by her tunic. The bark-paper rustled in Lilla's salt-cotton as the warrior shoved him backwards with a snarled command.

'It is unfortunate,' Weaver said, smoothing her tunic with prim composure. 'But it was not our intention. I shall think on the implications and speak with Xini and Ekon. I am sorry. For now, it might be best to keep your people under cover or in disguise.'

'Under cover? So that we might all rush out at once and draw the enemy away for the rest of you to take the pyramid?' Lilla demanded bitterly, and then barked a humourless laugh at Weaver's approving nod. As if he'd performed a trick by guessing her thoughts for the slaughter of his tribe. 'Was this why you waited for us to be brought under the song, so that you might use us in this way?'

'*No*, Fang Lilla,' she snapped. 'You think we didn't want you and the Yaloh harassing the Empire's borders while we rose within them? We did not have the people and the plans in place at the time of your defeat. If we had, you never would have been enslaved. We would have risen across the Empire and you would have fought at its edge and together we would have won. Together, we can still win. With the right strategy.'

He didn't believe her. He slid his hand into his salt-cotton instead and retrieved the pieces of bark-paper and fitted them together. His breath caught in his throat and his vision blurred as he read. It wasn't, as he'd expected, an order for all Tokob to be captured and brought for justice, with payment in the form of a pardon to those who did so.

'Fang Lilla? Fang Lilla!' Weaver's voice was alarmed.

Fingers tracing over glyphs written in a hand he knew as well as his own, he read it aloud in a strangled whisper: '"By order of the divine holy lord, the great Singer Xac, and his Shadow, Tayan called the stargazer, all Melody forces have been removed from Tokoban. That land is ceded to the control of its people in recognition of the Shadow's former allegiances. You are offered this and no more: go home and live. Raise weapons against the children of the song and not even Malel will be able to save you."'

He met Weaver's eyes, the paper clutched against his wildly beating heart as hope and homesickness and fierce love seared through him. 'It's written by my husband. I told you, *I told you*, he was with us. Is with us. Tayan's letting us go home.'

'You see?' Lilla demanded, his voice rising despite Weaver's attempts to hush him. Xini had come from his own base at Weaver's urgent summons, the lithe former estate slave to Great Octave Enet running through the shattered city to this unprecedented meeting of resistance leaders even though he was no warrior. Ekon was here, too, and Lilla finally, *finally* had his chance to make them all understand. It had been agony waiting for their arrival, but this was it. This was what he'd been praying for.

'See what, Fang?' Xini demanded in a hiss. They were deep inside the administration building, in a small room without windows where the sounds of their low-voiced argument might not carry. Not outside, anyway. Lilla knew there were warriors on the other side of the wall. Warriors who could go home!

'You've all spent the last weeks blaming Tayan for this war, for not killing the Singer, for doing – or not doing – a hundred arbitrary things. As if he's the cause of all of this, instead of another victim. But now you can see he's on our side. That's his hand, he wrote this. He's letting us—'

'Letting?' Weaver asked sharply, interrupting the eager

tumble of words. 'Who is Tayan to "let" his own people do anything?'

Lilla stopped, floundering. His gaze flicked from one to another. Only Ekon wore any sympathy, but it was tinged with pity, too, as if the Toko had misunderstood something. The anger that burnt constantly just beneath his skin returned in a flush, hotter than ever.

'He's the Shad—' he began and then cut himself off. He couldn't say that; they'd jump on it as if it justified something. 'He's saying Pechaqueh have no urge to fight us,' he tried instead, knowing it was weak.

'Why? Are they scared of you?' Weaver demanded sourly.

Lilla looked to Ekon again on instinct, a memory from the night of the uprising searing into him with a twist of fresh humiliation: *You think we have simply been waiting for you brave, noble Tokob to come and lead us to freedom?*

He winced and looked away.

'They are not giving you peace or mercy, Fang,' Xini added. He was trying for patience, but it was as thin as the hair on a Drowned's head. 'They are decimating our numbers. They are giving a significant part of the resistance no reason to stay and every reason to leave. If they are putting up notices here, they'll be doing it across all Ixachipan, in every town and city where your people live and struggle for freedom. Tayan isn't working for your benefit, Lilla. He's working to weaken us. These messages must be destroyed where they are found. We cannot permit our allies to—'

'Allies.' Lilla seized on the word and barely restrained himself from grabbing the Chitenecatl by his tunic. He needed to be calm and reasonable if he was to make them understand. Still, there was a vicious stab of pleasure through his gut at getting to use Weaver's own word play against her. 'That's what we are, your allies. Or would you use us as mindless slave warriors the way the Melody has used all of us over the generations? How dare you even contemplate taking away our choice, our consent for your fucking war. You will not permit us to leave? *Permit?*'

'*Our* war?' Weaver countered, faster than he expected. 'You call this "our war" as if you weren't planning a rebellion of your own back in the Melody fortress? I see your courage is as weak as your memory. This war is as much yours as it is ours – or it was, right up until you were given a chance to turn and run.'

'You—'

'But you *do* have that chance, and you *don't* have to fight.' These words were Ekon's, and they were quiet. Quiet enough that they sucked all the burgeoning aggression out of the atmosphere. 'We won't make you slaves to our cause. No, let me finish,' he said, holding up a hand in Weaver's face. The woman subsided, muttering. Lilla barely noticed, his eyes locked desperately on Ekon's face. Surely he understood?

'Every person in the Empire of Songs, no matter their status, chose the night of the uprising. Many stayed loyal at first and rebelled later; others rose with us and then returned to their so-called owners when it got too hard. We don't judge them for that.' He had the grace to grimace. 'We *try not* to judge them for that. But now, Tokob must likewise choose again. You can go home' – something fluttered in Lilla's throat; he was dizzy with possibility – 'and we will fight on without you. Or you can stay and bring down the Empire that will come for you again should we fail. Because they will. This is not a truce with your people; this is their way of destroying the resistance from within. When the war against us is over, if they win, they'll come for you and it will be us, those of us who survive, that are pushed into the front line to face you. The High Feather and the Spear won't have it any other way.'

They stood, a chorus of silent judgment. Lilla turned away from their anger and disdain and pity. He couldn't look at any of them. He couldn't bear to. 'You can't keep this from my people.' He clenched his fists. 'I won't let you.'

'Very well,' Ekon said and there was a flurry of whispering quickly stifled. Lilla stared sightlessly at the back wall of the little room. Their shadows moved against it like ancestors come to watch; to judge. 'We will let the news spread. But we need to know: will you stay and fight with us, you yourself, Lilla? For all who would be free?' A gentle hand came to rest on the back of his neck. 'For Tayan, who's trapped in the pyramid no matter what the rest of you do, and . . . for me? Kitten?'

The wall blurred behind a veil of tears. 'You were telling me I had to choose only a few days ago,' Lilla said, his voice ragged. 'Choose Tayan or choose a different future. A different life. Peace would be a different life.'

'Peace is for the victorious,' Weaver snarled. 'Anything else is just cowardice.'

'*Enough*.' Ekon rounded on her, the warmth of his palm slipping from Lilla's neck. He shivered at the loss of it and then pushed past them all and made his way out of the building, refusing to miss that skin on his skin.

He tilted his face up to the cloudy sun and let it scour his sight from him. Jaguar-Brother curse them, but they were right, both about Tayan's reasons and the uprising's fate if they embraced his offer.

'We didn't plan for this.' Lilla opened one eye on Weaver, mistrustful, but this time there was no antagonism in her expression, only weariness. She wore the air of someone performing an unpleasant task she thought beneath her, but a necessary one. She leant against the wall next to him, like-wise staring at the sky. 'We thought only in terms of surprise and tactics and chaos, in the swift strike and then the slow attrition. We'd expected to have Enet in the great pyramid, weakening the song and singing of a new way to live. We didn't think about love, and duty, and how the song is a disease but one that's so subtle and slow-growing that people don't even know they're sick.'

'Because if you'd ever thought about those things, you wouldn't have acted at all,' Lilla said.

Weaver fiddled with a strand of grey-shot hair. 'We had to pretend it was simple – choose slavery or choose freedom. But it wasn't simple then and it isn't now. Too many of us found freedom in service, as your Tayan himself proclaimed that day.

Is it slavery when you live in luxury and are trusted by your owners to raise their children and run their estates and increase their wealth? When you can marry and have children of your own if you desire?'

'Yes,' Lilla said quietly. 'It still is.' He wiped the back of his hand across his eyes. 'Is the freedom to go home a choice when it weakens your friends and destroys their hope for the present and the future?'

Weaver snorted. 'Yes,' she echoed him softly. 'It still is.'

He made a strangled sound, half-frustration, half-pain. Throughout everything they'd endured so far, Lilla had clung to hope and his belief in his husband. He'd insisted on Tayan's innocence, his lack of agency in everything happening to and around him. But this . . . the casual cruelty that lay beneath the surface of this seemingly generous offer took his breath. Tayan knew exactly how much pain this would cause, the fractures it would put in alliances. He'd lived through the same thing in the days before the Sky City's fall, and all he'd learnt from it was how to replicate it.

He could no longer deny that Tayan had made his choice, whether out of self-preservation or something else. It was time for Lilla to do the same.

'I – we – can't keep this a secret,' he said eventually and Weaver's lips pressed into a thin, angry line. 'You said it yourself, these messages will be going up Empire-wide, not just here, so we need to announce it, not hide from it. But when I tell my war party and the civilians with us, I'll make it clear I'm staying, that I'll fight to the end alongside my allies. Fight for freedom – for all who would be free, including them. I will tell them' – Lilla's voice hoarsened – 'that I believe it to be some trap I can't see the shape of, and that I do not believe those who flee will find safety. That I believe Tayan to have been corrupted by the song and that he, and this promise, is not to be trusted. I don't expect that will come as a shock to them, though me saying it might. And I will make sure that all peoples – all tribes – know that if they choose to believe Tayan and run, Tokoban will welcome them.

Perhaps it will lessen the divide that this proclamation seeks to widen.'

'Thank you for staying, Fang Lilla,' Weaver said quietly after a pause. 'And for speaking against this cruel lie of your husband's.'

He smiled, bitter. 'Do not thank me for convincing my people to be slaughtered alongside yours. It is Malel's forgiveness I need – and I don't think I deserve it.' He took a breath and hardened his face. 'Now go and find Ekon for news about the Drowned. I can't bear to speak to you any further.'

XESSA

Tithing barns, western Singing City,
Pechacan, Empire of Songs
42nd day of the Great Star at morning

Oncan loomed over her. Blood poured onto her face, running
into her nose and mouth and eyes, choking, blinding. Through
the blood she saw that his hands were grey-green and webbed,
fingers tipped with long black claws. The eja held her down
and pressed those claws in beneath her ribs. She couldn't
scream. Couldn't breathe.

You promised to die for us. You swore to die as soon as
Tiamoko was free. You have not – and so we will cut your
spirit from your body and punish it as it deserves. We will
leave your flesh a shell, empty and prey to any wild spirit or
cunning ancestor who can climb inside it and make it dance
until it drops.

Dull pressure, and then the sting of skin parting and more.
Flesh; muscle; liver; lung. Slow agony, the claws flexing and
burrowing in, up, under her ribs. Scraping off bone. Searching
for her heart to inject their venom. Slow. Slow. *Slow.*

Your spirit belongs to the dead. To the ancestors.
You swore.

Xessa woke with a gasp, scraping madly at the blood on
her face and clutching at her ribs. No blood; no wounds. No

dead Eja Oncan with the hands of a Drowned leering down at her. Except for every time she closed her eyes, that is.

She'd slept slumped against a wall and now her gaze danced across the expanse of the tithing barn, the fear from the dream making her twitchy and paranoid. It was mid-morning and hundreds of warriors had slipped out before dawn to scavenge for food, weapons, water, and easy kills. Still, the building was packed with hundreds more like her, snatching sleep where they could, when they could.

Toxte had left at dawn with the rest and his absence was a fierce ache. Lilla had gone to Weaver; his absence was welcome. A score of Tokob were scattered around her, stirring, sitting up as whispers passed through the barn.

Xessa snapped her fingers and then shook her forefinger from side to side. 'What?'

'Ekon and Lilla are back. They need to speak to everyone.'

Ekon was back? Where had he gone? Resentment flickered in the ejab chest. They knew Ossa was hurt. What was she supposed to do? Leave him here on his own while she attended their stupid meeting or make him limp after her?

She and Toxte were relearning how to be together during their nursing of Ossa. Caring for the dog had made it easier to care for each other. He'd seen her attitude towards Lilla and Tayan and regret smoked in her gut at his clear, if unspoken, disapproval. Now, she remembered those thin-pressed lips and unreadable eyes and hauled herself to her feet, rearranging her discarded and filthy salt-cotton for Ossa to sprawl more comfortably across.

Her arse was numb and her knees stiff; she felt like a greyhair as she staggered after the others. She hadn't fought since the river; she wouldn't until Ossa was well, but the enforced rest didn't seem to be restoring strength or suppleness to her body.

Xessa tongued at the claw-wound in her lip and glanced back at Ossa just before ducking out of the building. He was lying on his side, head raised to watch her. She signed for him to rest and smiled when his head flopped back down onto her armour. No stubbornness, for once.

Xessa passed into the brightness of the morning and squinted. There were sentries moving into position on the roofs of the barns and surrounding buildings. At least triple the usual number. They were expecting trouble, expecting loudness that might alert their enemies. And Ekon was gathering them now, while hundreds of them were out in the city. Whatever this information was, it was too urgent to wait.

Xessa slowed, seized with a childish urge to hide from bad news. Lilla would no doubt delight in her absence—she caught her first glimpse of his face and her spite withered and died. If she didn't know the shamans took good care of the war leaders, she'd have sworn by Snake-Sister that he was dying from an unseen wound. She'd never seen him look so ill, even when he had been. Lilla's shoulders were a defeated slump, his skin an awful grey instead of a rich red-brown, but it was his eyes . . . his haunted, bitter, broken eyes that stopped her. As if he'd looked into the Underworld and seen the faces of his loved ones screaming for help.

Their weeks of vicious arguments came back to her in a rush, all of them instigated by her, all of them a way to poke at him until he bled in some vain attempt to make herself feel better for betraying the oath she'd made to the ancestors. The promise she'd made that she couldn't keep: to die in penance for the lives she'd taken in Pilos's pit.

The promise that had shattered the day of Ossa's return; the promise that had been ground to dust by her husband's reappearance. She was too selfish to give them up, but staring at Lilla, she wondered whether he'd made a promise, too, and was about to keep it in the way she couldn't. Were they called to witness his death, given in sacrifice to Malel to end this war? He had the look of a man willing to do anything to make the hurting stop.

A shiver of religious awe crept up the ejab back and she pushed gently through the gathering crowd of beaten, hungry warriors towards the front. Tokob parted naturally for her; others scowled and moved only grudgingly, but Ekon had spotted her and was telling them to let her through. Lilla put his hand up to his brow and squinted and, when she stepped out into the front row of the growing audience, he flinched and took a pace sideways. Away from her.

Satisfaction tried to rise up her throat, but it was countered by trepidation. Ekon leant close and murmured to Lilla; the Toko tensed and then shook his head, and when he faced the crowd again, he'd shrugged on the salt-cotton of a war leader. Remote, impervious, ruthless. Ekon hesitated and then did the same, his own armour far more effective than Lilla's. Then again, he'd had decades of practice at pretending to be someone he wasn't. And she didn't know him the way she knew Lilla, husband of the friend of her heart.

'Notices are being put up around the city that come from the great pyramid,' Lilla began, signing as he spoke. 'Notices written by Tayan of Tokoban, Shadow of the Singer, on behalf of Singer Xac and, and himself. We presume the same information is being sent to Listeners across Ixachipan and similar notices will be displayed in all contested cities and towns.'

Lilla's gaze fell on Xessa and jerked away, desperate as an animal in a trap. Unease flickered into alarm.

'All Melody warriors are being withdrawn from Tokoban. Tayan and the Singer have said that Tokob can go home unmolested, *but it is a trap.*' Lilla's signs increased in speed as the ripple of emotion around Xessa caught her in its depths. She didn't need to examine the faces of her kin to know how the news was affecting them; she could see it in Lilla's frantic gestures even as her heart bloomed with delirious joy. *Home.*

'They are trying to break us apart, to destroy our alliances as they did in every major city before conquering it. As they did in the Sky City itself, fracturing us from the inside first. This is not a concession; it is not an acknowledgement that we are winning. If we listen to them, it will be how we lose.'

Someone jostled Xessa and she stumbled, lost sight of what Lilla said next. His words were repeating in her mind: Tayan is allowing us to go home. Tokob can go home. *We can go home.* It was hard to remember anything he'd signed after that because she was dizzy with a hope she hadn't had since before Tokoban fell. A hope for the future she hadn't even felt on her wedding day, conducted as it was under the shadow of war. But this . . . this was hope. This was home.

'—Tayan is our enemy. You all know I've spent weeks defending him but this,' Lilla was saying the next time she managed to see his hands. He gestured to a piece of torn bark-paper, 'this is written by him. I know my husband's hand. Tayan painted these glyphs himself. Tayan wants us to lose and—'

Xessa was caught again in the shoving, shouting crowd and she forced herself back to the front where she could see. Up on the roofs, at least half the sentries were facing inwards, staring down and trying to work out what was happening.

Tayan wants us to lose.

Someone stumbled into her, their elbow catching her in the ribs and shortening her breath. Lilla had signed those words with such conviction, holding himself together throughout the condemnation of his husband. *Tayan wants us to lose.*

Lilla had said that.

A dozen Yaloh broke free and moved determinedly towards the narrow alley leading out of the complex of barns and administration buildings. A knot of Tokob hurried angrily after them, pointing backwards, their intent plain. An Axi and two Tlaloxqueh were arguing with Lilla, interrupting his pronouncement. Or maybe that was where it ended, with *Tayan wants us to lose.*

Ekon hurried after the Yaloh, his gestures big as he pleaded with them, fear plain in his face. And Xessa understood. Her hope died.

This is what they want. This is exactly what they hoped for. He's right; it's the Sky City all over again.

She shoved through the crowd to Lilla's side. He flinched again when he saw her and then stiffened and his hand came up to his head, mouth twisting as if in pain. 'I don't have time,' he began. Expecting a confrontation when there were already a dozen happening around them.

The eja clenched her fists on the first retort that came to her hands and then deliberately licked her thumb and pressed it to his temple. Family. Lilla stumbled back, his fingertips hovering over his temple as if afraid to touch. 'What do you need me to do?' she signed. 'How do we make them stay? How do we make them see it's a trap?'

A few Tokob had seen her action and her words and it paused them: they all knew of her falling-out with their war leader. 'Stay?' she saw one sign from the corner of her eye. 'A trap?'

She rounded on them. 'Of course it's a trap,' she signed furiously. 'When did Pechaqueh or the Melody ever *give back* a land to its people? Are you stupid?'

Lilla tapped her shoulder and she turned away from the furious Tokob faces to find him wincing. 'Just talk to them,' Lilla signed. 'Calmly. Without insult. This isn't the gift it seems. It's a death sentence – for those of us who remain *and* for those who flee. The rebellion will fail across all Ixachipan if no one speaks against this lie, and if it does, the Melody will turn their attention on Tokoban and burn it to the ground, with everyone who's fled there in it. It's not freedom; *it's a cage.*'

Xessa's lungs hurt and she sucked in air in a dizzying rush and then surprised them both by cupping Lilla's cheek and stretching up to place a gentle kiss against the corner of his mouth. Lilla's brows drew down, a thousand emotions flickering across his face. She rubbed her fist in the centre of her chest in a profoundly inadequate apology for, for everything, and then stepped away.

The Tokob who'd seen their conversation were grim and conflicted, but they nodded when she glared at them. 'We stay,' one signed, 'and we'll help convince the rest.'

Xessa left them to it, ignoring the stiffness of her muscles and her ever-present fatigue, and scrambled halfway up an exterior staircase so she could be seen. Then she brought her hands together in a loud clap; too loud, if the wincing sentries were any indicator. Scores of faces turned to her and then many as quickly away – those who wouldn't understand her. Fine. She wasn't here to convince non-Tokob.

'Tayan did this,' she signed, her gestures bigger than normal so everyone could see. 'Tayan the Shadow. Tayan the traitor, who told us to kneel and accept our collars. Tayan who has power and prestige, who sleeps safe at night in that great pyramid, who doesn't give a single shit about his people. That's the man you want to trust with a promise of an end to violence? You think *Shadow Tayan of Pechacan* is really letting us go home?'

She blazed with scorn as she met gaze after gaze, mocking and judgemental despite Lilla's request for calm. She couldn't be calm; she was too scared and heartsick, and besides, she had too much fire in her nature for rational debate.

'Since when do Tokob take orders from anyone other than their council of elders? Tayan made his choice weeks ago and that choice was to become the enemy of all who would be free. And you now believe he is doing a good thing by letting us leave this stinking city? You think he will let us go home in peace? There is no peace while there is a song, a great pyramid, a Singer.' She looked at Lilla; she owed him that much and so much more. 'Or a Shadow.'

His face crumpled for the briefest instant, limestone cracking to reveal an abyss beneath, and then it smoothed and he turned away, hurried to a group of Yaloh who were gesticulating as they argued with Tokob. Hands were straying towards knives.

A Xenti approached the stairs where Xessa stood and stalked up them, shoving past without looking at her; none of the Tokob she'd been signing to intervened. The eja reached for the Xenti on instinct, but what could she do? They reached the roof and nearly all of the sentries on this section of the perimeter rushed towards them, eager for answers.

When Xessa turned back to the plaza and buildings below her, perhaps a third of the Tokob had vanished, too. Her stomach dropped into her feet. Was that it? After weeks of accusing Tayan of betrayal, of siding with her against Lilla, they were going to take him at his word and flee and expect to live? She wanted to scream and rage and punch them in their stupid faces. She wanted to join them in the long, hopeful race home and find it all true – Tokoban empty of human life and waiting for them. Waiting for Malel's people to return to Malel's skin.

Her eyes stung with wanting and frustration, her insides twisting with a poisonous mix of hope and betrayal. She was ashamed of the vicious pleasure she'd taken in attacking Tayan for so long, and in baiting Lilla – *very* ashamed of that.

End it then. You promised, didn't you? You promised once Tiamoko was free of the pit that you would come to the spiral path and the Realm of the Ancestors in penance for taking Tokob lives. You swore an oath to give your spirit to ours and you break it. Every day you live, you break it.

Xessa firmed her jaw. *You'll have me soon enough, spirits. But not yet.*

Almost, she fancied they howled within her, rage and impotence and betrayal, but then she was hurrying down the stairs to intercept a group of Tokob heading for the alley and away. Some of them were civilians, but not all. There were warriors of the jaguar path, too, and they needed those warriors. They needed everyone.

They had no right to force anyone to stay – they were not Pechaqueh – but that didn't mean they couldn't ask. Plead. Beg. Xessa wasn't going home, and she wasn't giving her life to the spirits. She was staying and she was fighting. And if she could do it, so could they.

Toxte, Tiamoko, and the Paws who'd gone out to scavenge, scout, and skirmish came back just after highsun. Despite everything Xessa and the rest had said, probably a third of their warriors and nearly all the civilians attached to their war party had gone. There had been a couple of nasty brawls after a group of Tokob tried to claim that they were the only ones allowed to return to Tokoban, that their land wasn't open to anyone else, and Xessa was nursing a black eye and bloody nose and a creeping sense of failure. The brawlers had still gone, arguing all the way, and fists would likely become knives the further north they got.

Doing the Pechaqueh work for them. Bending to Tayan's will and scheme. Weakening the resistance.

And so openly. Fleeing through the city without thought for who might see them, as if Tayan's words were salt-cotton and shields and Malel's benevolent hand keeping them safe. All it would take was a single clever eagle to spot them leaving and trace their origin to here and those who were committed to stay and fight would be discovered.

Despite working to a common purpose, she'd stayed as far from Lilla as she could get. As far as the splinter of spirit she'd gifted him with a licked thumb would let her, anyway. She needed to cleanse the bad blood between them, to bring medicine to their love, but she didn't have the strength for it yet, or the time during the bright horror of trying to convince warriors to stay and fight, seeking out any Tokob who looked to be wavering and using all the eloquence of her hands to remind them that the friend of her heart was a traitor and nothing he wrote or said or did could be trusted. Despite everything she'd told herself she believed over the last month, it left her feeling dirty, tainted.

Any relief she felt at seeing Toxte and then Tiamoko vanished as the cycle began again. The returning Paws learnt of Tayan's proclamation and immediately fell to arguing among themselves.

Lilla and Ekon converged on them, using the same arguments she'd seen over and over throughout the morning, and with about as much success. Within moments, Tiamoko was lending his voice and reputation to theirs, arguing that they should all stay and fight and win. That peace was for all Ixachipan, not just the north.

Toxte stepped out from behind him, scanning the little plaza for her as if the argument raging around him was nothing but a gentle morning rain that cut the humidity from the air and scattered raindrops to gleam on leaf and rock alike. A smile lightened his expression; relief and love and concern flicking one after the other across his face.

Anguish gripped Xessa as Toxte began to limp towards her, favouring his damaged leg more than usual and moving slowly.

If he stays here, he's going to die. I'm going to have to watch him die. Ossa too.

Xessa ran across the compound, grabbed Toxte's arm and dragged him away before he could sign anything. Dragged him to a quiet, empty corner and put him between her and any observers so no one would have to see his face when she did what was necessary to keep him alive.

'What's wrong?' Toxte signed as soon as she let go.

'You should go. Take Ossa and go, not to Tokoban – whatever's happening there, it isn't the peace Tayan is promising. But somewhere, anywhere safe. Go and hide and wait for this to be over. The two of you can survive in the jungle for seasons, for years if you need to. Go and do that, Toxte, go and live.'

He stilled, examining her face, lingering on the fresh bruises. 'Why are you saying this?' he signed, confused. 'What's happened? Where would we go?'

'Not me; you. You and Ossa.'

'I don't understand.'

Xessa summoned the coldness the pit had taught her, the remoteness Pilos had trained into her. 'It's been nice having you back, but your injury makes it hard for you to fight effectively and the same goes for Ossa. The best thing you can do is go somewhere safe so I don't need to worry about you. So that the real warriors can focus on winning this war.'

A muscle flickered in Toxte's jaw. 'The real warriors,' he repeated, his expression flat. She didn't let herself wince at the pain she was causing him.

'You spent the last two years as a farmer, Toxte. You haven't tested your leg in combat. You might get others killed through your slowness.' His nostrils flared. 'I wouldn't trust Ossa with anyone else, but now I don't have to. This works out best for us all.'

She didn't add the platitude – the lie – he was probably expecting, that she'd see him once the war was over. She couldn't because the ancestors were still scratching away at her spirit and they'd take their due of her one way or another.

Xessa swallowed down another mouthful of the endless sea of bitterness within her and focused on Toxte, the bewildered hurt in his eyes, the beginnings of anger thinning the mouth that had driven her to distraction for so long.

'Do not presume to tell me what I can and cannot do with a weakened leg, Eja,' he signed, cold and precise in a way he'd never been. How deep she'd cut him, to have him sign so to her. 'I've been living with it since the fall of the Sky City. I walked on it when it was still broken, across sticks of hills with a rope around my neck and my dog dead in a burning city. I well know my limits and my abilities. I can till and plant and harvest a chinampa, I can clamber through the mud of a Wet under the watchful eyes of Pechaqueh and Drowned alike. I can fight.'

Xessa held her breath, the tension in her lungs all that kept her from cracking open. 'You are a liability who will get us killed,' she signed, ignoring the shard of pain lodged in her throat. It tasted of betrayal. 'Get me killed; get Ossa killed. Go away, husband. Go and live; if you stay here, we will all die.'

Toxte recoiled as if she'd spat on him. His face closed up until it was impossible to read. Had it always been this hard to tell what he was thinking? She didn't know. It didn't matter. What mattered was that he and Ossa were safe. That they *lived*.

'I walked halfway across the Empire of Songs during a rebellion that has ended the lives of thousands and has barely even begun so that I could find you,' he signed. 'Was I wasting my time? Have the last few days just confirmed for you that our marriage was a mistake? Shall I take off my marriage cord?' His hand went to his neck.

'No!'

'Then why are you doing this?'

'I need you to be safe!' she signed, frantic. Her heart was a wild animal throwing itself against the bars of her ribs and her vision was tunnelling as if she was going to faint. Panic clawed at her. 'You have to be safe, you and Ossa, you have to be safe so that I can do what I need to!'

Toxte took her flailing hands in his own and pressed kisses to her fingertips. 'I know,' he said soothingly, 'but nowhere is safe until there is peace. And there will be no peace under the song. So we fight.'

Xessa looked instinctively for Ossa and the comfort he could provide, but he was still resting inside the barn. Resting because he was hurt, and hurt because of her. If Toxte stayed, he'd get hurt too. Better he was hurt with words than with knives. She pulled her hands from his. 'You can't fight,' she signed. 'You can barely walk.'

'*That's enough*,' he signed with sudden fury, a storm of emotions flashing in his lovely dark eyes. 'The last years have changed all of us and perhaps you've had to learn cruelty to survive, but don't be cruel to me, wife. Don't you dare. You think I haven't spent the last two years lamenting who I used to be and what I merely am now? And yet this *is* what I am, and I know what I can do – and what I can't. So if I tell you I'm capable of fighting and that I'm a warrior in my heart and body, I expect you to do me the courtesy of believing me.'

'See?' she tried, a new attack. Grief had its claws in her. 'This is why you should go. I'm poison, I'm—'

Toxte smiled then, and it had no right to be as affectionate and tender as it was; Xessa's knees trembled under her. 'No. You're not poison; you're terrified. And you lose,' he signed.

Xessa raised her forefinger and shook it side to side. *What?*

'You lose,' he repeated, smiling bigger despite everything. Despite her words. Despite *her*. 'You are not the eja in charge at the water's edge, nor are you an elder: you cannot give me orders for that is not how marriage works. You want me to die hidden away far from you? No. I'll die at your side, but until then, my love, *we'll live*. Even in this city of the Underworld, we'll live. There is nothing we can't do together.'

'I don't want you,' she lied wildly. Toxte herded her back against the wall, planting himself in front of her so she'd have to struggle to pass him.

His hands came up to sign and she closed her eyes. Fuck him, she didn't want to know. She counted to fifty in her head and still his presence tingled against her skin, the heat of his body a kiss. She slapped the wall behind her in frustration and squinted up at him, then slapped it again when a grin bloomed on his face.

'I am not Tayan,' he signed, the smile fading and something small and fierce and unbroken taking its place. The sun made her eyes hurt, but she neither blinked nor looked away. 'I will never leave you. Nor am I Lilla to be so easily turned from your side by hard words and the casting of blame. I will never choose another over you. I will lay my life at your feet and my heart in your hands and I will love all the broken parts of you, the pieces you've lost and those that together we might find again. I am your husband. I walk where you walk, live where you live. Die where you die. It doesn't matter how many times you send me away; I simply won't go.'

Xessa shook her head and he cupped it between his palms, calloused hands scraping her ears and the sharp points of her cheeks. 'I know you feel guilt and shame for the things you were forced to do as a pit-fighter. And I know you – you made some sort of promise, didn't you, some oath of atonement?'

Her breath caught as she read his lips and that seemed to be all the confirmation he needed. 'Whatever you did, you don't have to pay for it with your life. No one would ask that of you. Not even the ancestors made by your spear. *They wouldn't*,' he insisted fiercely, giving her a little shake when she tried to close her eyes again, unable to bear the tenderness in his expression.

Her hands were on his wrists, keeping his palms against her cheeks, the heartfelt, loving lie of his hands on her skin. Despite herself, she drank him in, every word and every emotion and the warm strength of his presence. How she regretted having finally told him the things she'd done in the pit and the lives she'd taken. How she regretted giving him this weapon to turn against her.

He let go and she shivered at the loss of contact. 'Oncan and the others, how likely is it that they'd learnt what it meant to fight masked long before you? Tiamoko knew, didn't he? Yes, you killed them, but they stepped into that pit knowing they were facing a Toko and they did their best to kill you first. You're the only one who didn't know. If they'd won, they'd have lived with that. So you have to live with it, too. Live on for them; don't join them out of some misplaced sense of honour.' He put his head on one side and his eyes went hard. 'How selfish you are to take the life they gifted you and throw it away. Is that how little you value them and their deaths?'

Her own words about Ekka, turned back on her. Toxte was so close she could feel his warmth, but there was a chasm between them, too. 'When . . . when I was in the pit, it was easy to be cruel,' she signed, watching her hands instead of him. 'Cruelty kept me alive – not just during the fights but every single day. I had to push away anything that would weaken me. Memories of you and Ossa, of Tayan and Lilla. Even Tiamoko. Cruelty became a habit, even when I knew Ossa was alive, even when I knew you still lived and were in Quitoban.

'So when I saw Tayan glowing gold with magic and ordering our deaths, instead of letting it hurt me, I knew cruelty would be the only thing that could keep me breathing and moving despite his betrayal. And I turned it on Lilla so I wouldn't have to grieve with him. So he couldn't make me confront how much I was hurting.'

Toxte was still for a long time and Xessa didn't dare examine his expression. She stared fixedly at their feet until she glimpsed him sigh. He lifted her chin with gentle fingers. 'And then?'

'And then, when I was so full of cruelty and self-hatred that I was sick of my own heartbeat, you came back to me. You came back and I realised I could actually hate myself even more than I did already, because your goodness shows me just how horrible I've become. And because I don't know how to stop being cruel. I don't know how to make anything better.' A sob broke from her and Toxte grimaced and tried to pull her against his chest; she held up her hands in denial of his comfort.

'We've spent more than enough time apart for one lifetime. Let's not do it again. Please.' He licked his bottom lip. 'Or will Malel and the ancestors be receiving two sacrifices today?'

She stared up at him in blank incomprehension.

'If you choose to end your life today to keep a stupid promise made in the depths of despair, then I will go with you, hand in hand up the spiral path to rebirth. We can be a sacrifice to Malel to beg for her intervention; beg her to save all Tokob and all people fighting for freedom from Pechaqueh domination and the song – whoever might be singing it. You won't go alone. I won't let you.'

Another sob burst from Xessa and she jerked forwards, hunching around the agony of her heart until the top of her head was pressed into Toxte's chest. He believed she still deserved a future full of happiness, full of him. Deserved to feel the rain on her face and the smell of the Wet on the wind; to feel stone and packed earth and mud beneath her soles; Ossa's wagging tail beating against her thigh. And that she deserved Toxte's strength and heat and compassion. He truly believed it all.

Toxte steered her onto her knees and knelt opposite. He wrapped himself around her and clung on, splayed hands touching as much of her back as he could reach, their ribs moving together with matching hitched breaths.

The sun beat down and tears stuck her hair to her cheeks and the ground was hard beneath her knees and shins and none of it mattered. They'd lost hundreds of warriors and civilians to Tayan's lies, they were starving, they were losing, and none of that mattered either, not here in this moment. Not with him. Because he loved her, cruel and unforgiving and murderous as she was.

He *loved her*.

Xessa stiffened and sat up, pulling out of Toxte's grip. She scrubbed the wetness off her cheeks and scraped back her hair. 'You left me. Back in the Sky City I, I turned around and you were *gone*.' The words surprised them both: they'd already discussed this. Xessa hadn't realised until now how much it haunted her.

Toxte flinched as if she'd punched him. 'I'm sorry,' he signed, his own eyes wet. 'I broke my promise. I won't do it again.'

'You can't say that,' she signed, the words barely legible through her whole-body trembling.

Toxte rubbed the back of his hand over his mouth and then brushed his lips against hers. 'No,' he said, his breath tickling her face. 'But I'm saying it anyway. Let me do that. Let me pretend, at least, that we can have that, have a future and a life on the other side of this war. Let me believe that, wife.'

As she'd done on their wedding day, Xessa licked her thumb and pressed it to Toxte's temple and then the hollow of his throat. *Family. Spouse.*

He shuddered out a breath, as if until this moment he hadn't been sure which choice she would make. *He always did have more faith in me than I deserved.* 'So I can stay?' he signed and the corner of his mouth ticked up. 'I mean, I'm staying anyway, but do you want me to now?'

Xessa seized his mouth with hers, dragging him to her, and his chest vibrated with a surprised noise, but then he slid a hand into her hair, the other around her waist, and his tongue into her mouth.

For the first time since their reunion, they were wholly of one mind, because the kiss went on for so long that her lips began to buzz and her neck to ache from craning up to reach his mouth. She wanted to knock him over onto his back and straddle him, sink onto him uncaring of who might see, speak with her body as well as her hands and every word a statement of love, of apology, of repentance.

Yet slowly, gradually, the intensity began to fade. Xessa clung to him still, but the kisses grew shallower, slower, fuller with love than with lust.

The next time their mouths parted, it wasn't to find a new angle but so both could breathe, and smile, and make eye contact that didn't sear with heat and want.

'Is that a yes?' Toxte signed, grinning, and for a long moment she couldn't even remember the question that had led to such passion.

'Yes, husband, you stay,' she signed, returning his smile. 'Though it makes me afraid that you are here. Ossa, too.'

'In that we are the same,' he replied. 'It might be bigger than us, bigger than anything we should ever have to live through, but someone has to be here. People lived and died under the song to bring Ixachipan to this point. Who are we to say no, it's too much, I don't want to?'

Xessa shook her head in wonderment. 'Who are you?' she asked him. 'What did I ever do to deserve someone like you, who doesn't just make me better, but makes me *want* to be better?'

Toxte flicked back his hair with a lofty shake of the head. 'I'm the best bloody thing that's ever happened to you, woman, and don't you forget it,' he signed. 'Now let's go lavish some attention on that dog of yours before he thinks we've forgotten him.'

Xessa huffed a laugh. 'Ours,' she corrected him gently. Toxte cocked his head. 'That dog *of ours*. And we can't, at least not yet. We have to convince our people not to go home.'

TAYAN

Since the holy Setatmeh bodies had been laid before him a few days before – bodies that were still in the source, at least until this afternoon when Tayan finally had permission to take them to the Blessed Water for respectful disposal – the Singer had been oblivious to all but his grief. He barely ate; barely slept; and issued no order or command unless it was in the form of a sodden cry.

Not that he'd been capable of much more beforehand. Still, the High Feather's report went unheard, at least by him.

'The response has been better than expected,' Pilos was saying, his outline wavering behind the rose-cotton hanging behind which Xac and Tayan sat.

'The pods stationed fifteen sticks uptrail towards Xentiban have intercepted more than three hundred Tokob and twice that in warriors from other tribes, and twice as many again in civilians, since the Shadow's messages went up around the city,' Atu added, approval humming through his voice. 'More may have headed into Chitenec to risk the treacherous hill country – as the Wet strengthens, they'll be forced back over the border to flatter land or killed in landslides and flash floods. For the duration of the Wet, we consider that to be an acceptable risk. And Feather Detta and the Second Talon are now only three days away. His warriors will help us bring the traitors to heel here and then we can sweep the rest of Pechacan. And with the Third and Sixth in Xentiban, they'll guard the major and minor trade trails and intercept those heading north from elsewhere in the Empire.'

'Three hundred is more than half of all the Tokob who were property in the Singing City at the time of the uprising,' Pilos finished. 'While most of our central records are lost, one of the administrators was near the great pyramid and took refuge with us when the Great Betrayal began. She was able to confirm the likely numbers we'd be facing.'

The Great Betrayal; that's what everyone was calling it now. Tayan knew the rebels would see the title as a feather of honour, claim it in ways Pechaqueh didn't intend. Not an insult, but an identity. The Betrayers. The warriors before him probably knew the same, but the title was just as important for them, confirming, every day, who and what they were fighting.

The power of words. Words like, *"the Tokob that were property"*.

Despite the tens of thousands brought from Tokoban and Yalotlan, only a fraction had been kept in the heart-city itself, their newness to the song making them unpredictable and, how had Enet put it back during the first days of Tayan's own enslavement? *"Skittish."*

'And so we have victory, do we?' he asked venomously. 'A few hundred Tokob and Yaloh and others have fled and the war is over? Have fled at my word, trusting me and my status and reputation, and what have you done? *What have you done to them, High Feather?* This is not what I ordered.'

The source descended into a ringing silence; even Chorus Leader Xochi was staring at him, her usual frown lost in the surprise widening her eyes.

Atu put his head to the mats. 'Shadow, if I have misinterpreted the great Singer's command to reduce both the traitors' numbers and their effectiveness against us, I beg his forgiveness.

What would the holy lord have us do differently? It shall be as the great Singer commands.'

All those emphases on Xac, not Tayan, as the author of the order they'd so wilfully misinterpreted. Though if it had really been Xac's, it would have been followed without deviation. Every day they undermined Tayan a little more. Refusing to admit he was the power behind the song. Refusing to see how strong the song was because of him, how it was unifying Pechaqueh and their allies. How it spoke of peace and the laying down of weapons, the restoration of society and prosperity and contentment.

How it proved Tayan's worthiness to be Singer when Xac ascended. Or died. Or was killed. Xac twitched, rousing from his stupor long enough to blink wet, puffy eyes in Tayan's direction. The Shadow patted his knee gently, sending love through the bare trickle of magic that was all he was allowed during his recovery.

Atu sat up, the shifting of his shadowy form through the cotton bringing the Tokob attention back. His mouth soured. So what if Tayan was no warrior like them, no master tactician? Neither was Xac, yet they would never have dared treat him or his orders with such disrespect. They wouldn't have dared *interpret* his very fucking clear command.

'The suggestion was masterful, Shadow,' Pilos added, paying dishonest lip service here in the very source as if Tayan couldn't taste the lies dripping from his tongue. The song – his song – swelled with anger and uncertainty and he wrestled it back under control, sweat breaking out along his hairline and dampening the back of his neck.

'You instructed us to bring Tokob out into the open, sow dissent between them and the other tribes, so that we might better locate any ejab hiding among them. We all want and need an end to the slaughter of our gods, Shadow. That is our priority. Your instruction allows us to do that.'

'My instruction was for them to be dealt with in Xentiban, not within fucking sight of the city walls.'

'What—' Pilos began and then stopped.

'What does it matter? *What does it matter?*' Tayan demanded. 'It matters that the traitors believe they can trust me! It matters to the war effort that my orders are seen to be good, that they think I am working to their benefit. Killing them on the outskirts of the fucking city? Song-damned amateurs, the pair of you!'

The silence this time was rife with offence and the slow, controlled breathing of killers holding tight to their tempers. Tayan didn't give a good fuck for their pride.

'Xentiban would allow them too much time to scatter, Shadow,' Atu said after a long pause and a final slow exhalation. 'They'd spread out, some moving faster than others, perhaps flooding into towns where our warriors are fighting to establish order. The Talons would be chasing down individuals, small family groups, stretching themselves thin when we need them ready to respond to cities and towns calling for help and monitoring the situation in Yalotlan and Tokoban. Bringing them to justice before that is simpler, cleaner, and more effective.'

Fury crackled gold up Tayan's arms, spitting and sizzling in his veins until he was incandescent with it. The Chorus Leader took a shocked pace sideways, and Pilos and Atu's outlines bowed yet again.

I should have Xochi put her spear in their backs right now.

'Pull back the hanging,' he snarled and Xochi leapt to obey. Tayan would look into Pilos's eyes and see the truth – or see the lies.

The warriors sat on their heels, eyes down and hands still in their laps. Atu's command fan was perfect, jutting from the crown of his head and adding a height and dignity it hadn't had the first few times Tayan had seen him in it. He'd grown into it, finally.

By contrast, Pilos was shrunken. His single eagle feather hung limp in the back of his hair, invisible to Tayan, while the Spear's honour-mark – the preserved and iridescent wing of a huitzilin – swept back from its place above his left ear. His eyes glittered just as brightly as he met Tayan's gaze for one inscrutable instant.

Tayan's jaw ached with tension. He was increasingly surrounded by danger, and not just from the traitors out in the city. He had his magic and Xochi and nothing else. Not even Xac and certainly not the two men kneeling opposite.

There was a splash from the offering pool. No, not just Xochi and the magic. He let knowledge of the holy Setatmeh guiding presence steady him.

'Shadow,' Atu said quietly, and with something like sympathy, 'I understand such an order was difficult for you to give. You are not a warrior, though you have seen and done much that is worthy of the very highest honour. Perhaps, if the executions had been carried out further from you, it would have been easier to, ah, to pretend you didn't know about it. Your people—'

'*They are not my people.*' The source descended into uncomfortable silence once more. 'The ruse will be discovered. Someone will survive, or flee, and word will reach the traitors here of what you're doing. I promised them they could go home and you have made a liar out of me. When the truth is known, this city will descend into violence greater than any that has gone before. Dying in Xentiban, well, that can be explained. Dying outside the city cannot. Your actions have put the holy lord at risk, this pyramid at risk. The very song itself.'

'You are correct, Shadow,' Atu said with a small shrug. 'But until then, we fulfil the Singer's order. We are at war. We weigh dozens of risks every day, make choices that hope and experience tell us will benefit us without knowing for sure we'll get that same result this time. All war is a risk. And across all Ixachipan, we are outnumbered by rebellious slaves five to one, maybe ten to one. We must reduce those numbers and we must do it fast and without mercy.'

And I will be blamed. My gift of freedom will be forgotten and all people will know is that I lured them out of hiding so they could be cut down. My name will be spat from Tokob mouths and cursed by the very shamans I once walked among. Cursed before Malel.

'And have any of these three hundred Tokob you're so proud

to have murdered been ejab?' he asked when he could master his fury long enough to form words. 'Is that threat dealt with at least?' Five holy Setatmeh crowded the offering pool today. Five who lived because they were here rather than in the Blessed Water or any of its ponds or tributaries where Xessa might hunt them.

'None so far, Shadow. Forgive my incompetence.' Pilos looked genuinely regretful.

'None so far,' Tayan mocked, 'despite all your promises. Despite . . .' *the fault being yours.* He didn't need to say the words aloud: everyone in the source heard them.

If Xessa hadn't been caught yet, she probably never would be. She'd either made it out of the city and avoided the ambushes, or she was staying. And whatever choice she made, she'd kill again, whether here or on the trail back to Tokoban. Would keep killing until she was stopped.

That knowledge cooled his rage against the twisting of his order. He saw it, suddenly, for what it was: Pilos and Atu's bone-deep fear for the gods and their reckless attempt to keep them safe from ejab. The Shadow's anger dried up as he looked again at the offering pool, at the divine spirits, *the gods*, waiting for him to help them. Trusting him to save them and fix the song. He touched the claw scars around his eye.

They need me. I want peace, yes, but they need me. *And they are gods.*

He knew it as well as he knew the golden cenote of power that streamed through his spirit and pooled in his fingertips and lungs and balls. The magic to remake the world so that all would be content.

The magic to bring learning and acceptance to all Ixachipan. Peace and stability, knowledge and medicine, trade in goods and songs and histories. Tayan could do all that; Tayan *would do* all that. He would grow a new world and he needed peace to do so. But the gods had to be safe first.

He took a deep breath. 'Be about your duties, Spear Pilos, High Feather. There must be no more threat to the holy Setatmeh.'

'As the great Singer commands,' Pilos said, but for once his eyes lingered on Tayan rather than Xac. Despite himself and everything that had happened, despite the spirits of dead Tokob that hung between them thicker than night, Tayan warmed to see respect glimmering in their depths.

The procession to the Blessed Water was ready. Atu was leading it while Pilos stayed behind to defend the pyramid and Xac. A responsibility and a punishment both, and one they were all aware of.

Tayan was going, his status as Shadow demanding it. Going to the river to restore the dead holy Setatmeh to the cradle of its waters. Fully four hundred eagles were accompanying them so that no further desecration of their bodies might be wrought and the Shadow would be kept safe. Even so, it was a risk. A glorious, reverent madness. And a duty that could not be avoided.

Tayan was afraid of venturing into the city and twitchy at leaving Xac behind, unwatched and uncontrolled. Citla would be responsible for feeding him love and strength in Tayan's absence.

The Listener swam the currents of the song so deeply that were she not crucial to their defence of the Singing City and the Empire itself, he would have found a way to eliminate her. Because of her and the other surviving Listeners, he had to maintain a constant adjustment of his spirit and Xac's within the song. He couldn't afford for anyone to question his methods of healing the Singer, which was why, within the song, Tayan's spirit appeared small, weak, and blue, a thin snake-shape clinging to the flank of the holy lord's vibrant gold immensity.

The reality was the reverse, with all that golden strength and magic being Tayan's vast and powerful spirit, connected to the capstone and all songstone, and connected to Xac through magic and necessity and . . . love. It was Xac who was small and pale and weak, that weakness hidden by Tayan's layering of his spirit over the top. He'd wondered, once, whether this had been what Enet intended to do, this or something similar. What did that make him, then?

Nothing like her. I am shaman and I know the song's magic for what it is – unifying, glorifying. Not a tool to be used and broken but a privilege and a gift. And the divine spark that gave the holy Setatmeh their second, near-eternal life.

The councillors and nobles had gathered to farewell the procession and Haapo, the useless, pretty former Spear of the Singer – who of course had survived the initial violence and fled here to safety – had tried to press a book of ritual into Tayan's hands. The Shadow had scoffed and spoken with his god and, once again, remembered everything in the aftermath. He knew how to revere the dead gods – he knew it from one who still lived. The ritual would be more beautiful because of it.

The warriors ahead of him began to move and Tayan focused on where they were going and the solemnity – and danger – of it. The shrouded litter bearing the five gods followed a pod of eagles, with Tayan walking just ahead of it. The other three pods took the flanks and rear as they exited the gate between two temples whose roofs bristled with archers to clear their path.

Despite the precautions, even because of them, they'd be a target. They all knew it. They also knew this had to be done and the eagles had vied for the honour of escorting the holy Setatmeh to their final rest. Tayan knew it had to be done, too, and he was determined to do it, but he couldn't help the shiver of fear that raised the hairs on his skin as the gate creaked shut behind them.

He squinted desperately, as if that would help him see approaching enemies, and then coughed at the sweet putre-faction of rot, the sour tang of old smoke, the sharpness of smashed stone that seemed to increase now he didn't have the illusion of the wall keeping it out. The humidity was a hand pressing down on him. The weight of judgement. The eyes of the gods.

He opened his mouth to urge the eagles to hurry when, at

some unseen, unheard signal, the warriors around him broke into a loping run. It was faster than he was expecting and he stumbled over his own sandals within the first dozen paces, the warriors hauling the litter behind him hissing and slowing so as not to run him down and barely keeping their curses behind their teeth.

Tayan flushed.

High Feather Atu appeared at his side. 'Match my stride, Shadow, and the cadence of my breathing, for as long as you can. When it becomes too much, shift to an inhale for two steps, exhale for two. You'll be able to keep going for longer.'

Resentment flared at Atu's assumption of his weakness and Tayan contemplated letting the gold burst through his skin. He refrained. It was bad enough being out here; to reveal his identity to any watching rebels would be suicide. He nodded once and concentrated on the ground ahead of him, dodging broken stone and abandoned weapons and running in time with the High Feather.

Atu was right: regulating his breathing meant he could keep going far longer. The alternative was riding in the litter with the dead gods, which seemed like both sacrilege and an admission of defeat. High Feather and Spear – and all the Melody here in Singing City, probably – thought him weak and incapable. Thought that Tayan the Shadow was nothing but Xac's mouthpiece and crutch. Well, no longer. He'd show them exactly how much inner strength it had taken to see him rise to the Conclave of the Shamans at barely thirty years old, let alone move from slave to Shadow in two sun-years. Could any of them boast such an accomplishment? No, they could not.

Tayan focused on his breath and the road beneath his sandals with renewed determination, letting the warriors take care of the rest. The wind stirred his hair and his body remembered what it was to move with urgency rather than to cringe in fear. Despite the gravity of what they were going to do, a small smile quirked one side of his panting mouth. Tayan ran.

* * *

Two new moons had risen since the start of the uprising, and Tayan couldn't imagine that a single Pechaqueh had come to the river with an offering. Perhaps a few captured warriors had been thrown in by the Melody, but even that was unlikely. What had the Singer's divine ancestors thought at being so neglected even before the horror that was Xessa?

Now, four hundred warriors, the High Feather, and the Shadow of the Singer lined the bank, facing the vast, churning brown expanse of the Blessed Water. Here to pay homage, to worship, and to grieve.

'This is why they rose just before the Wet,' Tayan said suddenly, staring at the swollen, angry river. Atu twitched and leant closer, not moving his gaze from the river. 'The traitors. Food might be running scarce but they've got rainfall to replenish cisterns in the plazas and they can dam drainage channels to collect more and then let it run away again before the gods can take up residence.'

'That is correct, Shadow,' Atu said quietly. 'And because any farms they control will ripen quickly. In another couple of months, they'll be harvesting and sharing food among themselves.'

'As will we,' Tayan reassured him and then stopped speaking. They weren't here for tactics but for solemnity.

Dozens of holy Setatmeh had fled at their approach, swimming out to the deepest part of the river as if they were afraid. Tayan had been cautioned not to show the gold in his skin outside of the pyramid, that he'd be a target, and he yearned to disobey, to show the gods who he was and so comfort them. He dared not.

It had been decades since the last recorded death of a holy Setat in the heart-city.

'Oh, Xessa. What did you do?' Tayan murmured under his breath. Atu twitched but didn't speak. 'High Feather, will you help me carry them?' he asked and the warrior, only a few sun-years younger than he, took a deep breath and dashed tears from his eyes.

'You honour me, Shadow.'

'No. We honour them. For us, this is a cruelty.'

The holy Setatmeh had been laid in the litter in some order that escaped Tayan, placed there by the few surviving shamans and Listener Citla. The first was small, only child-sized, and the Shadow could have carried it by himself. He didn't, sharing the burden with Atu as they took its wrapped form and stumbled sideways to the edge of the water.

Sweat glistened on Atu's brow and more slid down Tayan's own cheek. Despite himself and his relationship with the god – and its choosing of him – being this close to the river sparked a primal fear in his gut. He shuddered as water crept over his toes, and then clenched his teeth and waded deeper.

They stopped when they were in up to their crotches, the holy Setat floating between them. Reverently, Tayan unwrapped the cloth, revealing its grey-green flesh – greyer than before, stretched tight with the beginnings of corruption. A waft of unpleasantness accompanied its unwrapping and Tayan cursed Xac: he'd clung to them and rolled among them for so long that rot had set in. The cotton floated from their grasp, tangling around Atu before unfurling across the river's brown surface and sliding away.

'All you holy Setatmeh gathered in this and every water source in all Ixachipan, listen to me. You who make the rains fall and the rivers flow, you who bring the crops and the drought, you gods of magic and song, you ancestors of our great Singer, the holy lord Xac, hear me.'

Tayan's voice was strong and he strengthened it further with magic. No Singer could do this – no Singer could leave the source as he could – but then no Singer had had to gift five gods back to the Blessed Water. Beneath the surface, his legs flickered with gold even as their paint washed away.

'We bring you this kin of yours, its sacred life stolen by foul hands. We bring you this kin of yours, whose second life has ended. We bring you this kin of yours that it might return to the water and the magic and the song that made it. That it might find peace in you, O great world spirit—'

We cry to you, O Malel—

'That it might find succour and harmony and oneness once more. A note in the song. Eternal.'

'A note in the song, eternal,' Atu repeated, his voice cracking. Their eyes met over the corpse and Tayan nodded. Together, they pushed it sideways, deeper into the river, and released its limbs. It bobbed, dropped beneath the surface and then rose again, already passing Atu and gathering speed as the current took it.

'Be at peace,' Tayan breathed, his surroundings forgotten until something slid past his calf. He yelped and stumbled in the water, a great jolt of adrenaline making him lightheaded. He fought towards the shore, Atu sloshing in his wake. Nothing followed; nothing sang. Nothing tore his legs from under him.

The sun was falling rapidly by the time they'd committed the last body to the river. Some of the living holy Setatmeh had swum closer, pacing the dead and singing a haunting, crooning lament that nearly drove Tayan to his knees – would have if he hadn't been charged with this ritual. Their song echoed from bank to bank and the buildings lining the river, and every time they returned to shore to collect another of the dead gods, he saw grief and rage in equal measure on the warriors' faces. Most of them wept even as they stood sentry against an incursion of their enemies and suddenly, viciously, Tayan wanted them to come. Wanted an outlet for this overwhelming rush of emotion. Wanted red blood spilt in memory of green.

He followed Atu to shore for the last time, exhausted physically and emotionally but thrumming with a restless, poisoned energy. He craved violence and death. He craved retribution. His song rumbled into something dark and glorious and the eagles straightened, knuckles yellow where they gripped their spears and teeth flashing white in the growing gloom as they snarled.

This time, Tayan didn't wrestle the song back under control. Let every loyal warrior know how he felt about what had happened. Let every traitor across the whole Empire of Songs understand his wrath. And *let them tremble*.

'Kill anyone who crosses our path on the way back to the pyramid,' he growled and there was a ripple of attention and preparation among the eagles as they shook off melancholy and let sacred violence fill them. 'Leave the litter,' he said recklessly. 'I want to be in the middle of this. Keep me safe, High Feather,' he added.

'With my life, Shadow,' Atu promised. 'With my life.'

Tayan clenched his fists and took a deep breath. 'Take their heads. We'll give these traitorous snake-fuckers, these, these *frog-lickers*, a taste of *my* medicine.'

XAC

They are dead. Dead. My kin are gone.

Gone because of me? No. Gone because of him. Because of the viper nestled at my breast. Even now his anger stirs my song, his emotions control it as he controls me.

Unacceptable! I will not allow—

Hush, my sweet love. You must not tax your strength. I have sent your ancestors to their final rest with song and magic and glory, holy lord. I have done what you could not, trapped here in this pyramid. Without me, you would not have seen and felt their parting. And you did, I know you did. I felt you watching through my eyes. Wasn't that for the best? Isn't everything I do for the very best, my love?

You are—

No. I am your Shadow. Loyal and devoted to the Empire of Songs. To finding a peace. I will not let this happen again, but you must aid me, holy lord. These pointless struggles drain me. Am I not your shaman? Have I not made your medicine for two sun-years? Not since the night you failed to awaken the world spirit have you taken an offering of your own. I have done that; I have fixed you. But you are still very ill and must rest.

The world spirit . . . I failed, didn't I? Failed in my duty. Is that why you stole my song?

Hush. There has been no theft and the fault was not yours. Rest now. You are ill.

I am ill? I should be ill, punishment for failure. Punishment for letting you steal—

Sleep now. *Sleep.* There will be no more of this. No more talk. No more stories. *Sleep.*

I knew something. Before you came with your twisty words, I had, I knew what I needed to do . . .

Ssh, now. Whatever you need to do, I will do it for you. You need only let go. *And sleep.*

ILANDEH

Beyond the Great Roar, eastern Chitenec, Empire of Songs
48th day of the Great Star at morning

Eight days since she'd left the Green City and the heat of Beyt's hostility. Eight days of Pikte's grudging respect and Olox's wide-eyed admiration as they wove an aimless path north and west, stepping deeper into their disguises and gathering intelligence where they could about rebels, Melody movements, strangers moving in the land, the state of the harvest, and anything else they could glean.

Olox had proved surprisingly competent when it came to charming villagers and infiltrating loyal free, shrugging on and off the disguise of the petulant, angry warrior whenever the situation called for it. He'd been a born free farmer displaced from his home – as macaws, none of them wore slave brands and could never claim that identity with any confidence – a loyal dog warrior cut off from his pod, and a purveyor of fine carved ornaments who'd lost everything in the uprising.

His youth and good looks and wide-eyed innocence bought him more information than Pikte's gruff warrior camaraderie. Only Ilandeh was more adept than the boy, but then, no one had had quite her training over the last twenty years.

They'd walked all day today, though, and come across nothing. Not a footprint in the mud, not a discarded, burnt-out torch, not a scrap of clothing or broken stone blade or corpse. Yalotlan's western hill country had been hard going, but since crossing the Great Roar at a high waterfall mercifully free of holy Setatmeh and moving into Chitenec, the landscape had become steeper, sharper, and more treacherous. It was also significantly emptier of towns and villages of any size or importance.

'This is pointless. We've been sent to gather information on the temperament of slaves, free, and Pechaqueh. There are none in this part of the land.'

It was Pikte, of course, and his tone was more belligerent than it had been that morning. The stocky Whisper with his hair greying at the temples had run out of patience a few days before and been vocally opposed to their wandering ever since. It told Ilandeh that neither Pilos nor Beyt had divulged their real reason for being out here.

Curiosity and suspicion have kept me alive this long and they've taught me that just because something is hidden doesn't mean it isn't there. Like loyalty. Like treachery.

Pilos's words.

They echoed in her mind, spoken in the depths of the song and the Listener. Spoken with all the absolute arrogance of a full-blood Pecha, an eagle, a former High Feather. The last two words had been directed at her, and she didn't like to admit how deep they'd cut. Which was why he'd done it, to make her fret over it and swear to heal it, to heal his disappointment, his reluctance.

It was a manipulation worthy of a Whisper, and how she wished she'd thought to say that at the time. Could she have made him even more furious than he was already by implying he'd make a good Whisper – a good half-blood spy?

The idea brought a faint smirk to her lips: the outrage, the blinding heat of his abhorrence at the mere suggestion . . . what a sight that would have been.

'No orders from the Spear of the Singer are pointless,' Ilandeh said mildly. 'You know the Sixth and the Third have retreated from the north, and Chitenec itself is only under nominal Talon control now that its people have settled once more under the song. You don't think that needs monitoring? You don't think Chitenec exploding into violence again will tip the scales of this war in the rebels' favour?' She took a breath. 'I understand your frustrations, Pikte, but every time we have this conversation, we leave our disguises behind. You promised me you'd done this before, but the ease with which you drop your mask concerns me. We—'

'Are alone,' Pikte snarled, 'and I would know why we are prowling around Chitenecah hills in the middle of the fucking Wet and risking death by landslide when we could be doing real good in traitor-held cities.'

Ilandeh let him finish ranting and then let the quiet-that-wasn't-quiet of the jungle fill the tiny camp they'd made. It wasn't the middle of the Wet; the Wet had barely begun and landslides wouldn't be a concern for weeks yet. Insects and frogs and owls painted layer upon layer of music over the world and she wished, with a sudden ache as fierce as when she had her blood, that she could hear it without the song slithering over it all like a hungry snake.

The tiny fire between them heated the air, and heated the tension, until it felt as if nothing but a lightning bolt could sear them apart. The reckless, permanently angry part of Ilandeh wanted to face up to him, challenge him, demand to know whether he thought he could lead them better than her. But she knew how he'd answer that question, and once the challenge was laid out in the open, they'd have no choice but to fight over it like starving dogs. She knew she'd win, but she needed him alive. At least for now.

'Spear Pilos's orders are clear, and he does not make mistakes,' she said quietly. 'He needs us looking for patrols and war parties moving towards vulnerable towns or sources of supplies. He needs us out here, being Whispers, doing what we do best. If you would question his orders, please, the next time we come across a pyramid with a Listener within its walls, you may interrogate him yourself.'

It was a risk to say, for Pikte could accuse her of anything within the privacy and sanctity of the song, and she couldn't be sure Pilos would see through a lie, not when he was half-inclined to distrust her anyway. But the other Whisper's face tightened with an instinctive recoil at her ultimatum; Pikte had no desire to raise the Spear's wrath. Yet.

And so the steps of their dance continued, whirling them both closer to the bonfire of confrontation at its heart. So be it. Ilandeh had been instructed to take two Whispers with her, but not even Pilos would protest a death if one of them actively tried to sabotage their mission. As long as he believed that that was what had happened.

Another silence fell, this one pensive, watchful, and teeming with dislike. Again, Ilandeh let it build – she'd spent years living where she was hated; she snorted under her breath; she'd fucking grown up in a place where she was hated. Her Pecha father had never forgiven himself for taking a Xenti wife and getting a half-blood child out of his mad lust. Being hated was one of the places Ilandeh was most comfortable.

Still, she was almost relieved when, two or so hours later, Olox imitated the hunting call of a mottled owl. He'd been resting comfortably in the rubber tree above them since dusk, watching the jungle for any sign of movement under the silvery moon or the distinctive orange flicker of torchlight.

The night chorus stilled at the predator's call, and Ilandeh and Pikte heaped dirt onto the small campfire, smothering the flames and smoke alike. There was a soft thump as Olox slithered out of the tree and landed next to her. Fumbling, he found Ilandeh's arm and lifted it to point in the direction from which he'd seen movement. She used the contact to lean close in to his shoulder and brought her face to his ear.

'Enemy?' she asked and felt him shrug. 'How many?'

He turned his face, their noses brushing and mouths close enough to kiss. 'At least pod-strength if they distribute their torches as we do. Maybe more. Heading west, parallel to our trail a few hundred paces distant. No way to tell their identity.'

'Then we follow,' she breathed into his ear and felt him shiver. Silently, the three Whispers packed up their blankets and supplies and set off west, paralleling the distant group as best they could. The moonlight was intermittent under heavy cloud and the darkness was almost absolute, but they forewent torches, instead scrambling along the trail, losing it and finding it again, tripping on roots and stumbling into depressions, noisier than they'd have liked but counting on the song and the ceaseless trill of insects to mask them.

After a stick, Ilandeh swung up into a tree and searched through the night for long, slow thuds of her heart, praying for that orange glow to flicker through the darkness of the jungle. Nothing.

'No sign. Let's intercept and find the trail they're using, see if they've already passed us by,' she breathed. She felt the others nod and stepped off the path and into unbroken jungle. Joy flared in her heart. This was who she was; it was what she did; and Pilos had given it to her again. He'd made her, and now he was slipping her leash and letting her roam.

She was on the hunt.

The Whispers were filthy and exhausted when dawn broke. They'd found the trail deserted, but signs in the mud told them a large party had already passed through.

Ilandeh had no evidence other than a gut feeling to tell her she was in the right place. She hated that Pilos's hunch had matched her own. Hated that she'd already been looking for the same thing as him as she travelled north.

Pikte took the lead, moving with predatory alertness, any hint of his feelings about Ilandeh and their vague mission hidden. Olox went next, several paces between them, and then Ilandeh last. Three warriors strung out on the trail, with cover on either side to dive into should anyone signal danger, meant they should be difficult to spot and, please Setat—please Nallac, not worth shooting from a distance when they could be detained and questioned.

The sun was still far below the tree canopy, slanting in at an angle to splash leaves and vines and ferns in bright gold and luscious green and light up the flowers and insects with iridescence. The Whispers moved through the dappling, the sun cutting at their eyes every few paces and casting the shadows darker and harder to see through. A bad time to be moving when you didn't know who might be waiting for you.

Especially if you can't fully trust your companions.

The trail climbed, dipped, and climbed some more as they moved further into the morning and the hill country. No sign of habitation for sticks, but signs of people moving if you knew how to look.

After another climb, Ilandeh called a halt and sent Olox on at a run. 'Go three sticks, see what you find. Be back in an hour. Don't get caught.'

Olox's teeth flashed in a grin. She watched the words "under the song" pile up behind them before he swallowed them down. He was learning. 'I, I'll be back soon.'

'Stay safe,' she said and gave him a warm smile that made him blush. He turned and sped along the trail, leaving her and Pikte in hostile silence.

The problem was the Whisper was only going to get worse as time passed and they continued their search for information, rumours, and tales. As they drew the picture of what was happening in the north.

Ilandeh turned side-on where she squatted at the trail's edge so she could check ahead and behind in patient sweeps, and if she used each examination to make sure Pikte wasn't creeping up on her with a knife in his fist, well, that was just the natural paranoia and self-preservation of a Whisper.

The pattern they had gathered so far was that, like the rest of the Empire Ilandeh had crossed on her way north, where there were no active Melody warriors, the two sides were evenly matched. The rebels had the numbers – so many numbers – but almost half the free had spent time in the Talons. They had the discipline and the ability, and that counted for much.

They'd passed towns like the Green City where she'd found Beyt, empty of all enslaved people and secure in loyalist hands, and villages where the opposite was true. They'd met half-pods of retired free patrolling the landscape around their farms, and bands of angry rebels looking for someone to kill.

She'd be unsurprised if, deep enough in these hills, there were communities unaware there was even a rebellion happening. Some of the rebel groups knew details – the night the uprising began, that it was Empire-wide, that they were to end the song. Others had felt the wind of resistance blow across them, had seen Pechaqueh and loyal free turn against their slaves in a sudden and coordinated wave of extermination and fought back simply to survive. Ilandeh had spoken to several who'd thought it was just their own town inexplicably rioting; they'd been terrified, waiting for Pechaqueh in neighbouring regions to send warriors to kill them.

Ilandeh had told them the scale of the rebellion and urged them to keep fighting, to be free and stay free, that an end to the song was coming. Just remembering it sent a shiver of religious fear along her spine. If Pikte had heard her—

A deer coughed alarm and Ilandeh leapt off the trail and into the densely packed shadows and roots of a walking palm, wriggling into a small gap before looking out from concealment. Moments later the tramp of feet and then a flash of colour. Fifteen or so warriors were hurrying down the trail with a captive in their midst.

Olox.

And then her eyes registered the style of the warriors' kilts and the fashion of their hair and a deep well of satisfaction rose in her. She'd been right. So had Pilos, but she'd come looking first. There was a flicker of movement between her and the warriors and Ilandeh struggled out from the tree roots and scrambled onto the trail a heartbeat before Pikte.

She dropped her spear and hurried forward, pressing her palms together with her fingertips touching the point of her chin. She barged past Pikte with a muttered, 'stay still, don't speak,' and didn't acknowledge his furious, hissed question as she continued uphill towards the group. They'd come to a halt, weapons ready despite her placatory gesture, staring down with glittering, implacable eyes.

Warriors of Zellipan.

'Peace of the gods upon you during your travels,' she said in Pallatolli as she came to a halt before them.

The lead scout put their head on one side and licked their teeth before spitting into the dirt. Then they put their palms together. 'Peace of the gods upon your home,' they replied as ritual and good manners demanded. 'You speak our tongue poorly, stranger, though at least you try.'

Ilandeh nodded and let her hands fall to her sides. 'My tongue is poor, it is true. But I am no stranger to Zellipan, but rather an old friend who has not visited in far too long. When last I rested in your land beyond the salt pans, your Bird-head was Omeata. Does she still rule?'

The warrior's eyes widened and then narrowed, and they brought up a blowpipe ready to shoot. She prayed Pikte would hold still. Olox squeaked but didn't move.

'You know words and names and titles you should not. Tell me why I should not send you to your gods before the sun has moved any further.'

'My name is Merchant Ilandeh and I knew Omeata a little. When I was taken ill – this was two Star cycles ago now – she paid me a short visit when she was touring the cities nearest the border. It is an honour I have never forgotten,' she added and placed her palms beneath her chin again. 'If she no longer walks the land, I would know of it that I might remember her in my prayers.'

The warrior bared their teeth: it was bad luck to refuse to name whether a person still lived, for the speaker and the individual themselves. To risk such for the Bird-head was as good as a death sentence for the warrior. They lowered the blowpipe. 'Omeata lives, as wise as ever. I am Huenoch,' they added, for Ilandeh had offered her name easily, though the Zellih believed possession of it gave them power.

Huenoch's true name, and their claimed gender, would remain hidden from Ilandeh unless they chose to reveal it.

'What are you saying to him?' Pikte hissed. The blowpipe

came up again and Ilandeh spread her arms and stepped between it and the Whisper behind her.

'*They* did not give you permission to speak,' she snapped over her shoulder. 'I will tell you later.' She turned back to Huenoch and put her hands together, then bowed from the waist as well. 'Forgive them, warrior. They are ignorant of Zellih ways, but I will teach them so they do not anger you. Did the young one cause trouble?' she added, gesturing with her chin at Olox, who was watching the exchange with wide-eyed incomprehension.

'They were clumsy and easily spotted but committed no violence. As for our ways, you are thanked for your promise to educate your companions,' Huenoch said tightly. 'But you gendered the Bird-head. Surely you are aware of what you have done.'

Sweat trickled beneath Ilandeh's salt-cotton. Perhaps she shouldn't have taken that risk, but she'd thrown those bones now and there was nothing to do but walk the path they'd revealed. Still, Huenoch would be within their rights to kill her if they judged her words or intent were hostile.

'The Bird-head revealed her gender to all Zellih upon taking the gods' charge to rule you. But also, she gave me permission under the rules of pledged-kin on her visits to me. In return for gifts of information. I would not presume otherwise. Those permissions were never revoked, but if the revered Bird-head has no kin-claim for me now, I will respect her wishes.'

The words were coming easier now, her memory knapping them into useful shapes as she spoke with Huenoch. A few Chitenecah merchants spoke Pallatolli, and maybe some Tokob – ah, Tayan knew it, she remembered, and wondered whether he'd ever had the fortune to meet Omeata.

Would Pilos be pleased that his suspicions had been borne out? She'd sensed excitement hidden beneath his fury and disdain at communing with her, a proclaimed traitor. It had been he who sent her into Zellipan so long before. That ex-perience and her presence in Yalotlan had made her the perfect spy to infiltrate the Zellih, if they were in fact stealing through Ixachipan as he'd suspected.

Because why would they skirmish at the border during peacetime and then stop when war broke out? They had all the distraction and chaos they could possibly need to make significant gains, grabbing land and resources by the stick before anyone had the warriors to stop them. It had made no sense to her, and the thrill she'd felt when Pilos admitted they were of one mind had been undeniable. Now she just had to discover their intentions and send that information back through the song to Pilos, and she'd get her life back. Get everything she wanted.

Huenoch gestured and a warrior stepped forward. They spoke quietly and the Zellitli pressed palms together and then circled around Ilandeh and Pikte and sped away down-trail.

'May I have the youngster back, Huenoch? I vouch for the good behaviour and peaceful intent of both my companions. You may take our weapons. And, as strangers to Ixachipan, and in honour of the leader I presume is coming to meet us, I would offer you fire.' She gestured at the trail. 'There isn't much room, but we will do what we can.'

A small line appeared between Huenoch's brows – suspicion or appreciation, she couldn't tell, and then they nodded. The rope was unknotted from Olox's wrists and he was pushed out of their ranks. He rushed to her side.

'Are you well?' Ilandeh asked, gesturing at the blood smeared across his brow as she led him to Pikte.

'Scalp wound. Not serious,' he said tightly. 'What—'

'We make a fire. Quickly now. Warriors will accompany you as you collect wood and lichen, but they won't aid you. Choose well; this is important. And choose fast.'

Pikte looked ready to argue, but then he nodded once and stepped back off the trail, Olox and Zellih warriors following. Ilandeh began clearing a fire break on the path.

The Whispers brought her the dry heart of a small chay and some lichen from the underside of branches. Ilandeh added some cotton from her pack and then used a bow-drill to light the fire. It was still small and smoky when more warriors marched into view below them. When they'd intersected the trail, it seemed they'd come out between the advance scouts and the main war party.

Ilandeh's heart kicked in her chest and she arranged herself and the Whispers behind the fire to properly welcome their guests. Like the scouts, the figures who approached wore similar dress to that of all peoples of Ixachipan, save that their kilts were longer and looser, coming to mid-calf, and were adorned with birds and snakes chasing each other around the hem, while rabbits and coyotes decorated their sleeveless salt-cotton. Barazal was a high, scrubby country for the most part, and they found sanctity in different animals.

One figure stepped out from behind the others, and either Olox or Pikte gasped. Perhaps both. Ilandeh blinked, startled, and then put her hands together and bowed low. They wore a huipil of tiny, shimmering feathers rather than armour, and as they stepped into the sun, the ankle-length, square-necked robe flashed pink-purple-black with iridescence. How many hummingbirds had given their lives for this one garment? She couldn't begin to guess.

'I am told you speak our tongue and speak of the Bird-head as if you know them,' they said. 'Yet I do not know you and I have served for many rainy seasons.'

'Revered Bird-form, it is an honour to stand in your radiance,' Ilandeh said honestly if haltingly. This was more than she could have dreamt of for a first meeting. 'I had not expected to meet someone from the Bird Council here in Ixachipan. May I assist your journey that the gods smile upon you?'

The Bird-form hesitated, though whether they were taken aback at her knowledge of protocol – if it was still correct – she didn't know. They wore a thick purple paint smeared in a band across their eyes and the bridge of their nose that made their expression hard to read.

'Such assistance as you can give will be rendered at the conclusion of our meeting,' the Bird-form responded in a low, melodic voice that was distantly familiar. Had Ilandeh known them in Zellipan?

'Then may the order of events be as the gods have laid down for all right people,' Ilandeh finished. 'I was Merchant Ilandeh of Xentiban when last I walked among you. Now I am Warrior Ilandeh, of Xentiban and Pechacan. Tomorrow, perhaps I will be someone else again, living or dead, but always true to my gods and my word. Will you share water and fire with us?'

The back of her neck prickled at the lie she spoke before the Zellih shaman and the Zellih gods. Who was she true to? Which gods? Her every word was a lie in someone else's service, arising from someone else's mouth.

Nallac, preserve me from their wrath.

Ilandeh started, surprised at herself. This time, she had reached for Nallac's succour first, without thought or hesitation. She shivered in superstitious awe. From who should Nallac save her when the whole world and all its gods wanted her dead? Nallac themself included, most likely.

'I will share your water and your fire, Merchant and Warrior, child of two lives, of two tribes. Child lost, child found. Child scorned and child bound.' Each word fell from the Bird-form's lips like a curse. A prophecy. A knowing of Ilandeh that they could not know.

'It would not be the first time, after all. With the gods' permission, it will not be the last. It has been too long, my old friend.'

Ilandeh gasped, finally knowing them by their voice. 'Bird-head? Omeata? Why are—'

'No longer,' Omeata interrupted. 'Another is the Head now, and rules wisely. My new life is as Bird-form, given over to magic and our god.' She put her head on one side, amused but unsmiling. 'I thought you might have known me.'

Ilandeh laughed, giddy with relief and recognition. 'You always wore your full regalia,' she said, bowing still because the Bird-form was one of six whose authority was second only to the Head's. 'If you had the head of a quetzal and eyes of obsidian and a great gilded beak, I should have known you in an instant. Your voice was familiar, though.'

Omeata smiled. 'I should think so. We spent enough time talking during your long convalescence. Now, shall I meet your companions and hear your stories or shall we stand on the trail until the damned song-peddlers find us?'

Ilandeh's smile slipped and she dipped her chin to hide it. 'The Bird-form does us great honour,' she said and gestured. 'You are welcome at our fire. All of you,' she added.

It had taken more than two hours for all the war party to pass through the smoke from Ilandeh's fire and so be welcomed and honoured and promised assistance, and highsun was nearly upon them before the five of them – three Whispers, Omeata, and Huenoch – could sit around the flames and talk.

Ilandeh's shoulders ached from holding her hands beneath her chin for so long, and she'd lost count a few times making small talk with Omeata so she didn't have exact numbers of the war party for Pilos – but it was worth it to finally reach this moment and begin to weave the tale that would – gods willing – see the three of them embedded in the Bird-form's war party and privy to their plans.

I just pray that Pikte and Olox go along with it.

'I had suspected your spirit did not grow from a single root when you stayed in our land,' Omeata said after the Whispers had told their tales of woe at the hands of the Melody they'd served so faithfully and which had abandoned them in the aftermath of the traitorous uprising. Ilandeh had translated for them, though Omeata spoke accented, though fluent, Ixachitaan. 'You were always so volatile and conflicted.'

Ilandeh kept her face carefully blank: she'd been no such thing, she knew, but Omeata's affinity for magic had always been strong.

Or perhaps this is the first of her many tests. She wishes to see whether speaking of my heritage will provoke me.

There seemed to be no suspicion that Olox and Pikte were not full-blood Axib, at least, and neither had stumbled over claiming so despite their pride in their Pechaqueh heritage. The day they'd left Beyt's command and entered hers, they'd pushed bone jewellery through their septums and earlobes, the latter decorated with feathers and shells in Axib fashion. So far it seemed to be enough.

'It makes sense to me now,' the Zellitli continued. 'You – all you mixed people – are like the chechem and chaka, growing so closely their roots entwine. Your Pechaqueh blood is the poisonous sap of the chechem, seeking to burn and burrow and strangle the lungs. Your other blood, your true blood, is the chaka leaf, bringing relief and soothing the pains. Somehow, you have grown true despite the rifting of your spirit. It is testament to your strength.'

Ilandeh smiled and decided not to translate that for Pikte or Olox. The pair muttered occasional low-voiced comments to each other, and she wished she had a way to warn them that the Zellitli was listening, but she knew that this also was a test. Omeata had always loved her games.

'The Bird-form honours me with her wisdom,' Ilandeh said and changed the subject. She'd spent enough hours examining herself and her blood; she didn't need the Bird-form poking away at her as well. 'But it seems the Zellih have much hatred for Pechaqueh. My understanding is that you refused to aid Tokob and Yaloh when they requested it three sun-years ago. You let them fall under Pechaqueh sway. Why now seek to avenge them?'

Omeata gave her an unimpressed stare. 'Clumsily phrased, Warrior,' she said in Ixachitaan: Olox and Pikte gaped and then the former blushed while the latter shot Ilandeh a murderous glare.

'You can do better than that. And yes, you two, I hear and voice your words. Fear not, you said nothing too terrible in your assumption of my ignorance. After all, we are all warriors here and we all have our . . . beliefs about others. As for your question, old friend, what do you care whether we are here to fight the Melody or fight the traitors? You have professed a hatred for the Empire of Songs that has used you and discarded you, while those fighting against Pechaqueh rule don't want you either. So what does it matter what we do here? You hate everybody, do you not?'

'If your cause is just, we would fight for you,' Ilandeh blurted. 'That's what we want, a just cause and respect, to be honoured for our abilities and our blood not called into question.'

Omeata laughed. 'You did whatever the Melody told you. Killed whoever they wanted you to kill. For years. But now you'll only fight for a cause? Why do you assume we're here for violence?'

Ilandeh looked pointedly at the hundreds of warriors visible along the wide stretch of trail.

The Bird-form shrugged. 'As a member of the Bird Council, I must be protected,' she said blandly, giving Ilandeh nothing, no clue, no opening in which to insert so much as a fingernail.

'Surely we deserve to know who and why we're fighting—'

'Do you?' Omeata's voice was sharp and Ilandeh quickly pressed her palms together in contrition. The other Whispers imitated her, beginning to understand Zellih rules. 'Who is to say we will even allow you to break trail with us, let alone live among us? Fight for us? Why should we tell you anything? I don't know you, Warrior Ilandeh. I certainly don't know these two. If you think you can simply present yourselves to me and expect to join my warriors on our journey, you are sadly mistaken. We have no need of you. We thank you for your blessings, but our ways part here.'

The silence around the fire was taut. Huenoch watched them with the coiled tension of a jaguar waiting to pounce.

'If you will give us nothing, then there is nothing to stop us revealing your location to your enemies,' Pikte snapped. 'All your enemies, rebel and Melody alike.'

'You would need to live long enough to do so,' Omeata said amiably, 'and you would not even make it to your feet before one of my guard opened your throat.' Huenoch shifted in clear impatience and Ilandeh knew they, too, spoke Ixachitaan, and were eager to do just that.

'It has been a privilege to make your acquaintance again after so long, revered Bird-form,' Ilandeh cut in. 'It has been too long since I spoke your tongue and I apologise for my many errors and my companions' tempers. We will leave you to your journey and may the gods smile upon it. And upon you.'

She stood and gestured, and Olox scrambled to his feet. Pikte was slower to rise, engaged in a silent battle of wills with Huenoch that threatened to shatter the fragile peace. She touched his shoulder and he blinked, stood.

The three Whispers pressed their palms together and bowed. Omeata and her guards remained sitting, heads tilted up to watch them, their seated vulnerability a challenge. 'Be well, Bird-form,' Ilandeh said softly.

'Be well, Warrior.' One corner of Omeata's mouth twitched in an amused smirk. Ilandeh pressed her lips together and dipped her chin.

You win this time, she acknowledged silently. The Bird-form's smile widened in acknowledgment. In challenge.

Nallac curse her, but how she loved her fucking games.

TAYAN

The source, Singing City, Pechacan, Empire of Songs
50th day of the Great Star at morning

It was almost dawn and Tayan still hadn't slept. Since they'd sought out and killed scores of traitors in the city on their way back to the pyramid two days before, it was as if he didn't need sleep. He'd feared, at first, that it had been akin to blooding the song, but there was no lust for death in him as there had been when he was linked to the Singer.

He knew, distantly, that he was exhausted, vibrating with a manic energy that seemed to come directly from the song itself. He knew he needed to sleep; he just . . . didn't. He and his eagles had come back to the pyramid with forty-four heads of warriors, and they'd mounted them on stakes on top of the wall for the traitors to see the next time they attacked. If severed heads were the currency of this war, it was one the Melody would hoard like jade.

That same night, Tayan had scoured every wall and room and mural and staircase within the great pyramid, walking in on nobles and councillors, stepping over the few loyal, cowering slaves still within the walls. Xochi had trailed him, yawning and bleary despite her protestations to the contrary as he'd walked, wandered, inspected, and searched. The pyramid's library was vast and wonderful – and useless. He'd pawed through the shelves and opened anything that might prove instructive. None of it had been.

None of it.

Frustrated, he'd woken Pilos in the middle of the night and sent him to Enet's estate with orders not to come back without every book, scroll, painting, carved relief, and piece of bark-paper within its walls.

'The gods are different now, can you not see that?' he'd demanded. 'Though the ritual to wake the world spirit failed, it did something else, benefited them in some way. I must learn what it is. I must *save our gods.*'

And yet now, two nights later, those words echoed and bounced around his mind, *mocking him.* What had he found in those armfuls of books and items the Spear had retrieved, losing eleven eagles along the way? Nothing. Nothing of any use.

Tayan's hands clenched on the edge of the table until his fingertips paled under the pressure. 'Where did you hide it, you treacherous snake-fucking shit?' he snarled softly. Behind him on the bed, a drooling, pitiable Xac twitched. Opposite, on her small cot, Xochi's eyes opened and her hand reached for her spear. 'Hush, my friend. Sleep. All is well,' Tayan crooned. It was testament to Xochi's exhaustion that she obeyed within moments, her breathing evening out and face slackening.

He watched her, fond and distracted, and then turned back to the books again. 'What did you do with them?' he muttered, even quieter. 'Your plan wasn't just to become Singer, it was to ensure the ritual failed. That means you knew something about the song itself. Or the world spirit. Both. You knew enough to not want it to awake – why? Because it would eat the other gods as it ate the spirits in the . . .' He trailed off, staring sightlessly at the opposite wall. His eyes burnt.

'It ate the spirits in the song. I noticed that weeks ago. Every spirit trapped in the song over generations, centuries, was consumed during the ritual. Is that why the gods are more active now? Is that why I can understand them? Can others understand them? The spirits were clogging up the song somehow, like a dam in an irrigation channel, and that, what, dulled the gods' ability to communicate?'

Quickly, Tayan added it to the list of theories he'd spent the last two days compiling, focusing on it to the exclusion of all else, leaving Pilos, Atu, and Citla to oversee the war. It was by far the most compelling of the increasingly wild ideas painted across the bark-paper in an unravelling hand. And it was something he could, perhaps, get some clarity on right now.

Tayan slipped into the song, letting the fifth world rise to coat the flesh world. Easily, like stepping into his favourite sandals. It had only been weeks since the failed ritual to wake the world spirit, when the millions of spirits hanging motionless in the song had been consumed in its aborted awakening. Yet what he saw now that he was paying attention to the song rather than manipulating it gave him pause. There were more spirits, hundreds more, thousands. The spirits of everyone loyal to the Empire of Songs who had died since the uprising began.

He didn't know how he knew that, but it was the truth. *The song eats its loyal dead. Maybe all its dead? No. Surely traitors would poison it. But why eat any at all, unless the song itself has a purpose, a reason? And that reason is to wake the world spirit. We sing through its bones, so of course it wants that. The song isn't the thing itself; the world spirit is. The song is but its yearning to awake.*

And it is mine, its power gifted to humanity to further the world spirit's aims. And yet it does not care for the little spirits, the little lives, whether they are gods or people, animals or plants. The world spirit might destroy everything. And it cannot be awakened. Enet saw to that.

Yes. Yes! This was what the holy Setatmeh meant by a sickness. He'd known it before the ritual and he knew it now: there was not an infinite number of spirits in existence, and if the song captured the spirits of everyone who died worshipping it, then there were that many fewer to imbue new life. Fewer offspring born, fewer crops and medicinal plants, fewer trees and flowers, fewer waterfalls and streams. Fewer of every single thing which had a spirit until there was nothing left. Until Ixachipan was barren and dead and the holy Setatmeh moved through an empty world and empty waters, alone and grieving under a songless sky. The desolation of it almost broke him.

Tayan drifted close to a spirit hanging in the song, curious and repulsed in equal measure. It was grey and unmoving, unseeing, unlike the golden motes of every living creature who had taken the song into their hearts – a vast and glittering constellation blinding in its reminder of how he was loved, how his song was loved.

My song, not the world spirit's. Not Xac's. Mine.

The spirit of the dead human, whether Pechaqueh or not, neither knew nor cared who sang or why. He poked at it and it twitched and then thrashed away, and he recoiled in kind with a shocked squeak: he hadn't expected a reaction. Setatmeh, could it feel? Was it aware? He surged close.

Who are you? Or were you? What was the name of the last being you inhabited? What do you remember?

There was no reply and the spirit, now untouched, hung once more unresponsive. As if only contact could stimulate it, and then only to rejection, instinctive and mindless. Like no spirit Tayan had ever encountered in all his years a shaman. Where was its knowledge of itself, its past incarnations of life and its hunger, ever-present and dangerous, to live again?

If this had been the spiral path, it would be fighting him now for possession of his flesh. Here, it could not. It had not the will. Was it this apathy that blanketed and suffocated the holy Setatmeh? That had smothered them more and more with every death, adding to the layers separating them from their worshippers, from the song, from life itself?

The misery of such an existence tore at him. He *would not* allow that to happen again. No one deserved such a constricted, trapped existence.

He looked for Listener Citla's presence in the song to ask her what she knew and then hesitated. One, she was asleep, and two, he was supposed to be small and weak, the unknowing support for Singer Xac: medicine, not shaman. If he asked her about the spirits, she'd know he saw and moved within the song more than expected, and not even he had the skill to pretend to be Xac within the song world.

Then maybe she should see me for who I am. The holy Setatmeh will not wait forever. If I cannot fulfil my oath to them, they will seek out another who can and I will lose their support and love. I will lose my purpose and become, in truth, nothing but the medicine struggling to halt Xac's slow death. I have not been elevated so high only to fail. They did not choose me to watch me fall.

Decision made, Citla was easy to find; even in her sleep, her spirit nestled close to the Singer's and sparkled with red bands as bright as the pyramid's paint – the markings of a Listener. There were others scattered across the firmament of the song, though so few as to be a mockery of the Empire's former might.

Tayan curled a tendril of shamanic blue around Citla's spirit and pulled it close. The Listener jolted from sleep, resisting, before identifying him. *Shadow?*

'Tell me of the spirits that hang motionless and dead in the song, Citla. What is their purpose?'

The, the spirits, Shadow? They have no purpose; this is their reward. They rest among the song, content and loved, awaiting the awakening of the world spirit.

'There were millions of them in the song before the world spirit ate them and was forced into eternal slumber. What do you think will happen when all the spirits are so trapped? What will animate new life? How will crops grow and young be born? What will guide the Wet and fill the rivers and swell the corn? What will heat the sun or burnish the night stars if all the spirits are here?'

Citla was silent for a long time. *The world spirit*, she said eventually. *When the world spirit awakes, it will animate everything. Everything will be an extension of it; the garden it creates will be its body, its spirit. We will all exist as a part of it.*

'No. This is wrong. There is something wrong here,' Tayan

insisted. 'No one could know that for sure. The only reason to trap living spirits in the song would be for something to feed on them. That thing is the world spirit. But it will never wake and never eat again, and so we return to the question: when there are no more spirits, what will imbue new life? Citla? What happens then?

'I'm missing something,' he added before she could respond, not that there was an answer. 'What am I missing?'

Tayan let the song world fall away and sat within his flesh, thinking. He knew Citla would be staggering in and requesting an audience soon, in this deepest part of night, curious to know how he had moved and spoken and thought in the song. It didn't matter; she didn't matter. She was but hollow bamboo, a repository for reports from across the Empire of Songs, nothing more. Who would she tell and why, and what difference would it make?

'And so we come back to the books. The books that must exist that gave Enet the knowledge to do what she did. The books I cannot fucking find.'

And suddenly he remembered it: *Get the books and take Itzil and go.* Enet's words to her slave, Xini, as she lay dying in this very pyramid.

'You conniving, manipulative, beautiful, brilliant bitch,' he murmured admiringly. 'By the song, I fucking hated you while you lived and I hate you even more now you're dead. How can you still be ruining my life from the Underworld?'

Tayan pulled a fresh sheet of bark-paper towards himself and knuckled savagely at his eyes to ease the sting. He wasn't tired; he wasn't. Too much to do, too many mysteries to solve, gods to save.

'All right,' he croaked, 'let's be logical about this. What did she want? She hid her true desires behind her craving to be Singer, but being Singer was vital to everything she did. What would it bring her? What did she need?'

The Shadow stared at the wall some more and then, jerkily, he began to write.

* * *

Tayan had drooled over the edge of his notes in his sleep, his neck twisted uncomfortably on the table and paint smearing his chin.

The sun was well up and slanting in through the high, narrow window when he woke, groggy and aching and still blanketed in sleep. He pushed up from the table, wincing at the sharp pain in his neck and wiping absently at the corner of his wet mouth. He groaned, long and heartfelt and vaguely annoyed.

Something mewled and shifted and he realised Xac had come to curl around him in the night, head on his thigh and body fitted around his hips and back. Embarrassment filled him, both at his predicament and on Xac's behalf. What if someone saw . . .

'There is a dawnmeal waiting for you, Shadow.' Tayan turned his head, his neck protesting again, to find Xochi standing guard at the door. He flushed, but the Chorus Leader's face was unexpectedly soft. 'He refused to leave you to eat, Shadow. I pray to the holy Setatmeh the work you are doing will speed his healing. Listener Citla waits on the Singer's pleasure.'

'Understood,' he croaked and then reached for the cup of tepid water at the end of the table. His other hand caressed the back of Xac's skull and then gripped his shoulder and gently pushed him away. 'Sit up, my love,' he said when he'd drained the cup and washed sleep from his mouth and thoughts. Citla's gaunt visage hovered in his memory. 'There is much to do.'

The Singer whimpered and then shuffled himself to sitting, his face pressed to Tayan's chest. Tayan let none of his disgust show on his face. 'Come now, let us go and bathe and refresh ourselves. We have so much to do.'

The reality of that statement hit him with the force of a rainstorm and he let his chin sink to his chest and his eyes slip closed for just a moment. For how much longer would he be expected to bear the burden of Xac's illness, his helplessness, while holding together a fracturing Empire and working to heal the song?

Xochi cleared her throat and he startled out of his doze, blinking rapidly. 'Perhaps you should rest, Shadow,' she ventured. 'If there is anything you need to know, I will wake you.'

'No,' he muttered and forced himself to his feet, various muscles and joints in violent protest. 'No, just a bath to wake me up.'

'Shadow, there is not . . . we're running low on supplies of salt. There isn't enough treated water for a bath at this time. Forgive me.'

Tayan stretched and then grinned, suddenly sharp-toothed and awake. 'That is because you fear your gods instead of embracing them. We will bathe in the offering pool, then, where the water is fresh and clear and ever flowing. Come, my love, let us visit the holy Setatmeh and scrub the sweat from our hair.'

His eye fell on the smudged notes he'd taken. *Children's stories of Singers of old – did not ascend or die but remained in human form eternal. Truth? How?*

Ah, that would account for the dreams, then. He could well imagine how such a thing would have played to Enet's vanity, even as she was sworn to the destruction of the song. If such a person, a former Singer, did still live, would they have the answers he needed to heal the holy Setatmeh? Was that who he needed to look for, across a world full of war?

He pondered the question as he shuffled through the corridors with Xac leaning on his shoulder until they reached the source. It was crowded with administrators and councillors and scribes holding reports, suggestions, requests for aid or food or advice.

'Fuck,' he muttered, not caring if they heard him.

Tayan took his time crossing the mats, noting the few whose prostrations weren't perfect, who twitched or turned their heads slightly to the side to look at, or whisper, to their companions. They thought they could disrespect him? Disrespect Xac? Then let them see what a true worshipper of the holy Setatmeh looked like.

There were three gods in the offering pool, watching his

approach with curious tilts to their heads. Tayan knelt at the edge and pressed his face to the wet stone. 'Wise and sacred spirits of the world, your descendant Singer Xac and myself beg to join you in the water that we might cleanse ourselves. Would you permit such a thing?'

None of them was his personal god and he remembered, suddenly, why it was called an offering pool. It would be ironic if he was to be torn apart in front of the councillors and the Chorus because he wanted to scrub the grease from his hair.

Still, the gods made space for them, gliding backwards, and Tayan helped Xac out of his tunic and kilt and then removed his own. He hoped people were looking now, seeing the contrast between them, seeing Tayan lithe and healthy with skin glowing with more than just magic. The Singer was pale and weak, trembling, but he entered the water without complaint, clinging to the edge as the pool sloped downwards.

Tayan slipped in after him, gasping at the cold and then luxuriating in it. He held his breath and pushed himself fully under, his eyes open. A holy Setat followed him down, their gazes locked and its gills flicking. They watched each other and he could feel it testing him. He held his breath as long as he could and then uncurled and stood, head cleaving the water back into the air. He gasped and scraped his hair back and looked down to find the god still under the surface. He dipped his chin in acknowledgement.

Tayan reached for the cloth next to his kilt and then tenderly washed Xac, who stood pliant and obedient, watching the gods or watching the gardens through the distant colonnade, depending on how his Shadow positioned him.

Xochi appeared at the edge of the pool and knelt. 'Councillor Haapo would be honoured to oil the great Singer's skin in the absence of trusted slaves to perform that task,' she murmured.

Tayan's hands paused as he scrubbed them through his own hair. 'Does Councillor Haapo have the balls to massage the holy lord at the edge of the offering pool?' he asked with sweet malice, loud enough that the councillor himself, prostrating a dozen paces behind Xochi, twitched.

'It would be this one's honour,' he said clearly, to Tayan's surprise.

He looked to Xochi. 'Kill him if he so much as makes the holy lord wince,' he said.

'As the Shadow commands,' the Chorus Leader replied.

The light behind him dimmed and then brightened and Tayan turned to see another god had climbed the stream descending the pyramid's side; his god. Something lightened in his chest as it slipped into the water and approached him immediately.

'Divine spirit,' he breathed, 'you honour us.' It seized his face in one webbed hand, harder than he was expecting, and alarm flashed through his limbs. Did it not want them in the pool? Was it angry with him? It forced his head up and to the side, aggravating the stiffness in his neck, though he didn't dare complain, and then it pressed mouth and teeth to his throat as it had before. Reiterating its promise; its threat. Again, Tayan's stomach twisted and heat and arousal coiled within him. His hands found their way to its waist, its hips, and clutched tight.

'I am yours to command,' he promised. 'I am yours. I have . . . ideas to research, theories I want to test. Can I ask, holy Setat, is it how the song traps the spirits of the dead within it that is causing your decline, in part or in whole?'

The teeth vanished from his flesh and almost Tayan wanted them back, the threat of them as delicious as it was awful. A cold tongue licked his neck and dipped into the hollow between his clavicles and then the god let go of his face and he dared to meet its gaze.

Yes.

He quailed under the promise of its voice, its understanding, and his own comprehension. Had anyone since the first Singers ever communed like this? 'And over the centuries you have . . . lost yourselves? Lost the ability to communicate with your worshippers and descendants? Been cut off from those who love and honour you?'

Yes. Hurt. Hurts.

'Oh, my love,' Tayan breathed, anguished. 'And the spirits are to feed the world spirit as it wakens? As it did, almost, all those days ago? Because they're gone now and you have returned to us. To me. You are yourselves again.'

Yes. And no.

Tayan thought. 'And once awake, the world spirit—'

No.

Tayan's hands clutched tighter to its hips. This was who he was and what he did. This was how he showed his strength and greatness. Not in tactics and strategy. Here. Now. Because he knew what the god was telling him. 'No, it is not the spirit of the world?'

The song must soar.

He licked his lips, want and fear and magic all vying for supremacy. 'You need the song because it gives you life and magic and transformation. But the song was made to do something else, for something else. It preserves your lives, transformed, as it preserves the spirits of the loyal dead within itself. Unchanging and unable to move on. As you yourselves are.' A sudden nausea gripped him. 'Do you wish to move on, sacred spirit? Is your long, transformed life a horror to you?'

'Sh-Shadow, Councillor Haapo—' a voice began.

Tayan flapped his hand behind him. 'Take the Singer and go. Do not interrupt this most important of moments. Who do you think you are?' he hissed, the last words a venomous whisper.

Xac, shivering from the cold water and Tayan's neglect, was helped from the pool; Tayan barely registered his absence, as unremarkable as his presence had been.

'I understand. I understand what is wrong with the song now. I will dedicate my every moment to unpicking the strand of magic that holds spirits within it. I will not rest until that part of the song is unsung. I swear it.'

The holy Setat stared into his eyes for an endless, breathless moment, and then shoved him away so hard that Tayan fell, the middle of his back striking the lip of the pool hard enough to knock his breath from him and very nearly a raw cry of pain. A sheet of water flew up as he swallowed his yell and was conscious, again and suddenly, of their audience.

What would Pechaqueh think of its treatment of him? *What the fuck does it matter what they think? They've been destroying their gods' will and abilities over centuries by never once investigating the song. How could they be so dangerously ignorant?*

Showing no sign of the pain jabbing through his ribs, Tayan climbed out of the pool and prostrated himself, naked and wet, before standing. Xochi handed him a cotton sheet on which to dry himself and then a fresh kilt and his box of paints for his brow, his lip, and his chest. She knelt behind him and squeezed water from his hair and then brushed it out with a patience that reminded him of marriage.

'Thank you,' he whispered, and if his voice was choked with emotion, only she heard it.

A few paces away, the Singer lay on cushions while Councillor Haapo stroked sweet oil into his skin. It was the most relaxed Tayan had seen Xac in days. Perhaps weeks. 'Continue,' he murmured as he applied his paint with the aid of an obsidian mirror and then padded, damp and preoccupied, to his place behind the rose-cotton hanging. Not that the hanging itself mattered now – everyone had seen him naked in the arms of a god, and Xac himself was still visible – but it was the place among the cushions that was important. The symbolism. He allowed the curtain to be tied up out of the way.

Xochi, attuned to his moods so well these days, placed a low table covered with bark-paper, paint, and brush by his elbow as he seated himself. He gave her a distracted smile and wrote his thoughts in a fast and sloppy hand before he lost them.

Someone sighed very quietly. Tayan's eye twitched and he made himself keep writing for another twenty beats of his heart just to prove that he could. Making these noble Pechaqueh wait for him. Eventually, he set aside the brush and took a deep breath. 'Who is first?' he asked wearily, making no effort to hide his disinterest.

'Shadow Tayan, the nobles within the pyramid have asked me to speak—' someone began and Tayan stopped listening. The nobles were hungry. The nobles didn't have fresh cosmetics or clean clothes. The nobles didn't have enough entertainment. The nobles didn't like the stink of death.

'The nobles should be grateful we are diverting rations from the Melody protecting them and keep their maggot-plagued mouths shut.' There was a ringing silence and Tayan realised the words had been his. He didn't care. He *relished it.*

'The nobles should be on their faces thanking the holy lord for his magnanimity in not casting them out into the city for the slaves to murder. The nobles should try being of *some fucking use* in this mess the way the high one Quotza is. Do you see the Singer indulging himself in feasts and entertainment? Do I? No, we do not. We eat frugally, we sleep badly, and we work. For peace. For an end to this. To heal. What do you do? *What do you do?*'

He took a shuddering breath and strength from his Chorus Leader's presence, so close her body heat warmed his flank. A looming, and entirely genuine, warning to the councillors against replying.

'I am working ceaselessly to heal the holy lord and fix the song. You have seen the agony of the holy Setatmeh; you have heard the horrors they face in the waters and upon the riverbanks. And all you can do is think of yourselves. Your ancestors must turn away their faces in shame at your greed, your selfishness. The holy Setatmeh suffer and you whine about food and clothes and boredom. Not one of you deserves your Pechaqueh blood. Just get out, all of you. Out.'

The assembled Pechaqueh were shocked into immobility and there was unconcealed rage on several faces. He turned his shoulder to them, deliberately baring the slave brand to their eyes. Mocking them with his own supposed status and the presumed lowness of his blood. *And still I sit in greatness above you, so far above that you are but ants crawling upon my toe. I will save the gods, with or without your aid. Without would be better.*

Haapo bowed first, low to the Singer and then to Tayan without a hint of rebuke. The rest followed with varying levels of respect and humility, but they did as commanded and left. How power over them, and their recognition of it and obedience, were like honeypot. Confirming who and what he was. And what more he could be.

It drifted like feathers to rest upon his shoulders: the weight of responsibility, the acceptance of destiny. He knew as much as he could in this state, with the spider-silk thin barrier still between him and ultimate power, ultimate understanding. There was only one way he might learn more now. With a flick of command within the song, Tayan summoned Citla to the source. She would be necessary for what was to come.

Tayan's god watched him approvingly, urging him on. Even so, he felt . . . at the very edge of his control, even his sanity. The future loomed over him taller than the hill called Malel, whose top he'd never seen. Wider than the salt pans at the edge of Ixachipan. Deeper than the ocean where it darkened towards a horizon his eyes would never reach.

Tayan looked at Xac, sitting cross-legged and slack-jawed, and his heart steadied within him. The Empire of Songs needed more than that drooling idiot to lead them. It deserved more. It deserved him.

It was time to become a god.

'Did you know of my name back before you knew me, my sweet love?' Tayan whispered into Xac's ear. Citla knelt a pace away, looking like she'd died some time in the night, she was so haggard. Even so, there was calculation and suspicion in her bleary gaze.

'Shadow Tayan, your presence in the song last night was—'

'Was Tayan of Tokoban, called the stargazer, known to Singers past, my name and legacy echoing backwards through history and into prophecy? Did you know that you would be the Singer destined to meet me, and that I would be the one to save the holy Setatmeh you have so grievously hurt with your bloody, broken song? Your greed?'

The Singer moaned and drew up his knees to hug them, rocking in the cushions. Citla let out an aborted protest.

Tayan shifted closer and licked Xac's earlobe. 'Did they wonder at the strangeness of it and the indecipherable messages the bones and visions gave them about me? How eagerly they must have ascended to await my arrival and the changes to the world that I will make. My song will speak not of subjugation but of peace, for that is what I will bring to the Empire of Songs and the gods themselves. That will be my legacy while yours . . . oh, my sweet love, yours will be ignominy and oblivion. You let Enet break you. You gave up all control over yourself. How it must hurt – or perhaps it doesn't. Perhaps you don't even know that what you feel is pain.'

Tayan took a deep breath and fought back the wave of pity and sadness. Xac was a monster. Enet had been a monster. Soon he would be free of them both, and glorious in his own strength.

'You can rest very soon, my love,' he promised. 'You need not fear this burden any longer.'

'Shadow?' Citla tried again. Tayan ignored her.

'What are you doing?' the Singer murmured without warning. Tayan flinched, dread swamping his guts as heady as petrichor after a storm.

He fought it back. *No. No, my love, my sweet lord. You don't get to make me afraid anymore. None of you will ever make Tayan of Tokoban fear again.*

Liar.

Tayan jolted. *My sweet love?*

My captor, Xac acknowledged.

Another jolt, and despite his bravado it was of fear. Listener Citla's eyes closed as she sank into the currents of the song, perhaps seeking the answers Tayan refused to give her. Could she sense this unexpected lucidity in her Singer? He should not be capable of such—

Too late, Tayan realised that he'd loosened his grip on the song-magic as he'd accepted that his great destiny was manifesting, and the trickle that he allowed into Xac had deepened into a rushing stream. With the increase in magic had come an increase in awareness and, perhaps, control. He put a stranglehold on the shimmering, golden flow, but Xac had his fingers in it and was pulling it towards him, clawing at it like it was ropes of honey dripping from a broken hive.

It is making you sick! Tayan tried, squeezing tighter.

You *are making me sick*, Xac countered with savage speed and intelligence. *Are you another Enet, my sweet little Shadow? Another traitor at my side?*

There was a distant request he barely heard, perfunctory and not waiting for a response. Xochi snapped to attention, checking on Singer and Shadow before facing the approaching warriors. Atu and Pilos. Despite their casual approach, their eyes sought Xac instantly. When they turned their regard on Tayan, there was appraisal there. Suspicion.

Citla had summoned them, then. Tayan ran his thumb across the claw scars ringing his eye, steadying himself with the god's touch, its gift, its choosing of him.

'Is there cause for alarm, High Feather? I do not hear the sounds of battle nearby.' He marvelled at the steadiness of his own voice. Dribbles of gold fluttered across Xac's arms, pale but unmistakable. He tightened his hold even further and sweat gathered at his hairline as he and Xac fought for control.

'Give it to me,' the Singer said. The words were cracked and lacking any sort of melody, but they were his. 'Give back what you stole.'

Pilos leapt from his knees to his feet in a move a warrior half his age would have envied. Xochi lunged in turn, bringing her spear to bear a hand's width from his chest. 'Do not,' she commanded without hesitation.

'Great Singer?' Pilos said, trying to peer past her. She jabbed and the obsidian spear tip poked him in the chest. Pilos stepped back. 'Holy lord, are you well?'

'Give it back.'

'Allow us to aid you, holy lord,' Pilos said as he retreated further from Xochi's spear. He spoke to the Singer, but he watched Tayan without blinking. 'If you could tell us what was stolen? And by whom?'

Tayan bore down again until the trickle was little more than a thread almost severed. The merest hint of magic circulating through the Singer's veins and spirit, enough to keep him alive.

'You need to be at the wall,' he said, filling his voice with fear and sorrow. He stared into their eyes in turn. 'If what I fear comes to pass, the traitors will use it as an excuse to throw themselves at us. Your warriors will need your strength, your leadership.'

'What do you—' Atu began and Tayan let his song skip and falter.

'The books you retrieved from Enet's estate were my last hope, Spear, and they have proven useless. I am at the end of my medicine for our great Singer and, I fear, he is at the end of his time in mortal skin.'

Even Xochi looked away from Pilos in horrified realisation.

The song stumbled again and Tayan let his weariness show. 'I sent the councillors away because I fear they will tax the holy lord's remaining strength. I fear they will encourage . . .'

He snapped the threads joining Xac to the magic for an instant and the song fell into a flicker of silence and then resumed. Xac panted, the last of the animation and cruelty draining from his expression like beer from a broken pot. Atu let out an inarticulate cry and the blood left Pilos's face. Tayan put a gentle hand on Xac's shoulder, squeezing in comfort, and fed him a breath of magic again. In the quiet solemnity of that moment, he felt the brush of another's attention, their sentience. Citla. Tayan allowed the edges of the song to sharpen into a natural barrier that nudged her away and then sobbed, clutching at Xac's arm and knee.

'I fear if the councillors are here, that they will vie for a place at his side for the . . . ascension.' He let his gaze rove them again. 'That they will force it to happen somehow. I didn't know what else to do.' He spread his hands. 'I was not trained for this.'

That last was a gamble, but it also didn't matter. No one was taking Tayan's power from him. Not now; not ever.

'I don't feel well,' the holy lord said and Tayan blinked, jerking around to face him in disbelief. Dread was a cold stone in his stomach.

How is he still talking?

'Then you should rest, my love,' he soothed, distress and reassurance both limning his tone.

'Listener Citla?' Pilos murmured. 'What can you tell us?'

Tayan took a breath. They didn't believe him. So be it. He didn't need them to. All he needed was for them to sit in witness and not attempt to wrest his destiny from him. Before Citla could form a reply, Tayan released his grip on the magic, flooding Xac with so much power that the Singer gasped and reeled and his body lit up as bright as the sun. He yowled like a wounded jaguar trapped in a pit. Tayan sucked the magic back out of him just as fast, before he could cling to it. Steal it.

The Singer collapsed and Xochi scrambled forward to support him, her spear thumping to the mats. Pilos was at Xac's other side an instant later and Atu was holding Citla by the shoulders, whispering urgently to her as she writhed.

Tayan ignored them all, cradling Xac's head in his lap. Citla's face was vacant as she swam the song, looking for threats and ways to help. To heal. But he was the shaman, not her. The power lay in his hands.

Tayan seized Citla's consciousness and forced it into Xac's mind, crowding in with her until they were all blended together and it was impossible to tell one from the other. He fed Singer and Listener a bewildering, whirling series of images, calling up the blood-frenzy of offerings and the great, all-encompassing hunger that Xac still possessed, buried deep within and which Tayan had spent months suppressing. At great, exhausting cost to himself. For the Singer's own benefit; for the glory of the Empire.

No more. It is time for them to know me, and know all that I have done for them.

With barely a flicker of disquiet, the Shadow removed all the blocks and layers of muffling blanket over Xac's hunger. He drew it out of the shadows and directed it at Citla and anyone who didn't get out of the way fast enough. Not just freed it; *encouraged it.*

Xac twitched and opened his mouth. Drool slid from his teeth onto his chin, his chest blazed gold, and with a shriek – and a shrieking song – he shoved Xochi and Pilos aside and pounced on the Listener, his fingers hooked into claws and driving into her face and throat, his teeth fastened in cotton and then in flesh.

Citla screamed and fell beneath him, Atu's instincts to protect and to maintain a respectful distance warring within him so that he did nothing for one long moment, and then scrambled away. His eyes fixed on Tayan, pleading. Xochi took a halting step forwards, hand outstretched, and then stilled. She hadn't witnessed an offering before and seemed half-inclined to intervene. She'd die if she did.

Citla was thrashing, not a willing offering giving herself to the Singer, but a shrieking, clawing victim struggling to get away. The song didn't demand her willingness – Tayan couldn't, wouldn't, allow *his song* to be tarnished in such a way. This was simply an atrocity to be borne in service of a greater good. A greater glory.

And yet the bloodlust, for so long nothing but a traumatic memory and the source of many a night terror, was once again surging through his veins and muscles. Tayan's memory conjured the slaves, the offerings, he'd torn apart with knife and hands and teeth. The memory of flesh parting, of blood hot and wanted, splashing against the roof of his mouth and its grainy, flaking residue when he rubbed it in drying drifts from his hands.

He let out a shriek of his own as he tore himself from Xac's lust, away from that heady, crimson temptation. His cry drew every shocked, fearful gaze and Pilos, who was closest, took several rapid steps back, his hands up in a barrier between them. Waiting, fearing, to be summoned into his own screaming death. Citla was quiet now, her body jerking with the movement of Xac's teeth in her flesh. Her presence faded from the song.

Tayan made himself look at the scene in all its pathetic desperation. Xac would never have recovered from this madness. He flooded the Singer with magic again, raining down on him with all the force of the Wet until his skin exploded in whorls of golden light and he reared back from the wreckage of his Listener to bellow his delight. Gave him power he didn't understand and couldn't wield – and then reached through the song and ripped it from his spirit by the roots.

Silence fell in the source. Oh, there was still Xac's harsh panting as he tried to understand what was happening to him, and Atu's whispered pleas for someone to aid the holy lord, and the distant murmurs of eagles out in the gardens and the Chorus warriors holding them back from this awful, almost comedic spectacle.

But there was no song.

The song had stopped.

Silence.

Atu had his hand over his mouth. 'Holy lord,' he whispered, more breath than voice. 'Please. Please don't leave us, not like this.' He sounded very young and very frightened.

The Shadow closed his eyes and spread his arms and called on the song to find its home in his spirit. Where it was already strong and welcome, where they already worked to accomplish the holy Setatmeh will. A song that was sick and didn't know it; a song that he would heal, for he was shaman. And Shadow. And Singer.

No one else had been so trusted to restore the song and the Setatmeh to glory. No one but Tayan could lead the Empire to peace and Ixachipan to dominance.

Within the song's raging depths a thick, golden shimmer descended on Pilos, lingering, caressing around his head and neck, and then moved to Atu – dismissed him quickly – and wrapped around Xochi with a teasing, contemplative touch.

A warrior? No, my sweet song, my beautiful song, you don't need a warrior. You need a peace-weaver. You need a diplomat, a shaman, someone dedicated to healing and to harmony.

So come to me. Come to me, song, find a home in my flesh and I will bring your offspring, your holy Setatmeh, to safety. I will fix you and them and all the world. Come to me and be mine, as I am yours, loyal and true.

COME TO ME.

With a shattering wail – and the beginnings of music – the song-magic punched home. Into its new Singer.

XAC

The source, Singing City, Pechacan, Empire of Songs

Strength and power and blood, blood, blood!

How I have missed this, how I have needed it. No more will I crawl on my belly, bound to another's will, his strength my weakness. I will regain my authority, my independence, my fucking Empire of fucking Songs. My power will live forever, my heart will beat within the song and the people of Ixachipan will bow their heads in the dirt at my feet.

I will wash the Empire clean with blood. Starting with his.

The Empire of . . .

The Empire of . . .

Where is my song?

Where is it?!

What have you done, Shadow? Shaman? Traitorous fucking no-blood, god-killing, frog-licking—No. No! PLEASE, NO!

. . .

. . .

Goodbye, my sweet, tired, fading love. Rest now. Rest in the strength of my song and know peace. At last, for you, there is sleep.

Tay—

SLEEP.

PILOS

The source, Singing City, Pechacan, Empire of Songs
50th day of the Great Star at morning

This was not happening. This was *not fucking happening*. Not here and now, in the middle of an Empire-wide uprising. The Shadow was supposed to have cured—

The Shadow was kneeling on the mats with his arms outflung as if welcoming a lover. And he was glowing. It wasn't morning sunlight from the colonnade bathing him in radiance before the afternoon storms. It wasn't the flickers of magic that had graced his skin before, gifted him by the holy lord's magnanimity. No, he was pulsing with gold, a gold that swirled and roiled and tumbled beneath his skin until his hair was a sweep of black paint haloed in reflected magic and his dark eyes were, his dark eyes . . .

Weren't dark. They were amber.

The Shadow's – the slave's – eyes were amber. Rich and shiny like sap from a tree. The eyes of a Singer. And with that amber hue came the beginnings of song – a new song. The slave's song.

Tayan's eyes were streaming with tears, whether from their colour burning away or the power filling him up, Pilos couldn't tell. It wasn't grief, though, that much was clear. All this time working to save the Singer and it meant nothing when he might take power for himself, might abandon the holy lord to—

Pilos's gaze snapped back the Singer. To ascension? He would ascend? Transform into a god?

'Atu.' It came out as a whisper, easily lost beneath the wild, renewed and clamouring song. The Singer was once more occupied, lost in his hunger, but the gold that had burnt in him when he'd leapt on Citla was almost gone. Singer Xac's skin was no longer a healthy red-brown written with golden magic. The frenzy of his movements was becoming jerky, his red-stained mouth wide as he panted for breath.

'Atu.' Louder this time, but no less frightened. Pilos was a warrior, a former High Feather, a man who'd served and fought his entire adult life. But the Shadow was taking the magic and the Shadow was a no-blood, a slave, a frog-licking enemy shaman from a tribe of god-killers. The magic *couldn't* choose him. Atu tore his gaze from the Singer with a convulsive shudder and Pilos pointed, mute, at Tayan. At the bright, blazing light of him and the amber of his eyes as he knelt in the source with his face slack with desire and its fulfilment. As if the song were a lover filling him up.

Atu gasped and stumbled as if his legs had threatened to give way. He put his hand over his mouth like a child. He looked achingly young. There was a clamour from the gardens and the Chorus warriors who'd stepped up to keep back the questioning eagles redoubled their efforts, though their distraction was clear. Their Singer had lost himself again; their Shadow was rippling like the sun himself. Everyone present knew what must be happening.

Pilos's gaze was drawn inexorably back to the Shadow. *He told us to defend the walls if the holy lord ascended, but how could he know it was even a possibility unless he was its cause? Unless he was killing the holy lord and stealing his magic.*

He looked for Citla, but she was beyond helping him or being helped in turn. There was no one in the source who could Listen or venture into the song, no one who could tell him what was happening. Whether this was a murder or simply the end of Singer Xac's long struggle.

A second clamour drew his attention the other way, and Xochi and Atu flanked him to form a protective barrier between the approaching councillors and the holy lord. It didn't matter that Tayan had sent them away supposedly for the Singer's benefit; they knew what the changes in the song meant and had hurried back, their faces ravenous with desire and hope, expressions they twisted into a grief so false it made him sick as they slowed and bowed their heads.

They looked from the holy lord to his Shadow and Pilos followed their gaze, seeing what they saw as if for the first time: the slave, if possible, shone brighter than before and his eyes were even paler, unmistakable now. If he survived this, he would be Singer. It was already happening and would only be stopped if an ambitious councillor – or eagle, he glanced towards the colonnade – decided to try and take the magic for themselves.

For an instant, he thought about allowing it. Even encouraging it. If Atu became Singer, they could win the war.

And yet the magic has already chosen, even though Atu is here in the source. Atu, Xochi, scores of Melody warriors and Feathers, let alone the nobles and administrators and councillors. And the magic chose the no-blood.

He didn't add himself to the list. Pilos had never wanted to be Singer. He'd never even wanted to be one of the council who ascended alongside the holy lord. He was a man of Pechacan, of Ixachipan, and he would live and die as such.

The councillors came to a ragged, keening halt and threw themselves to their knees in a group, ugly with need.

The Singer was curled around the wreckage of Citla's body. The gold had entirely left his skin, sickly grey beneath its film of sweat and blood. His chest fluttered with quick, shallow breaths and his fingers spasmed.

'Holy lord, great Singer, you must choose your council to ascend with you,' one of them croaked. 'You must not go alone, holy lord. Who among us is worthy?'

Tayan's amber eyes snapped to the little crowd and he twisted on his knees to face the Singer. 'Ascension? You wish to go with such as him to immortality? A thousand years spent serving that? He is not ascending, Councillors. Xac is dying. He will not go to the waters. He will not transform.'

Pilos wasn't aware of striding forwards until he was standing over the Shadow with his war club raised above his head and the shadow of pain buzzing through his healing ankle and lower leg. It was still stiff, still swollen and agonising at the end of each day's battle. It was also irrelevant.

'What did you say?' he hissed. The song took him by the throat and rammed him onto his knees so hard his head jolted on his spine and the weapon fell from his hand.

The Shadow's amber eyes were as cold and alien as a holy Setatmeh. 'I said,' he began and then became aware of the wailing of the councillors. From this close, Pilos saw the tic of irritation flicker at the corner of his eye.

'The song has judged him and found him wanting,' he tried again, but quieter, for Pilos alone. 'The holy Setatmeh will not welcome another brother today, nor any family of councillors to serve him. Xac blooded the song and almost destroyed it and in so doing almost destroyed his immortal, divine kin. He let madness and avarice and cruelty guide his every action. He let the traitor Enet come within a breath of stealing his magic and using it to destroy the Empire of Songs. The only good thing to come out of that was the consumption of the spirits fouling the song and stealing the holy Setatmeh from us. Why would he be worthy of transforming into a god? He was barely even a man.' His voice had risen as he spoke, silencing the councillors again, but the final words he breathed directly at Pilos, gifting him the full measure of his contempt and disgust.

All the confusing and alarming things he'd said evaporated from Pilos's mind with those final words and, if not for the stranglehold of the song upon his limbs, he would have murdered the slave with his bare hands in the middle of the source and gone to his execution with a smile. Instead, all he could do was glare his hate into Tayan's amber eyes.

Councillor Haapo began to weep, although he had not heard that final condemnation. The others quickly followed, a chorus of performative grief with less harmony than a troop of howler monkeys. Haapo crawled across the mats and dared to lay hands on the Singer, cradling his bloody face.

'Take my strength, oh great Singer, that you might ascend to godhood among your divine ancestors. Your kin await you, holy lord. Take what you need to meet them. Please!'

Pilos gasped and looked away from the Shadow – was Haapo offering himself, his life and blood, willingly as Citla had not? And what would that do for the Singer? The song tightened on his limbs.

Another wail rose from the councillors, another noble flung themselves at the Singer and begged him to ascend. They were all of them writhing around amid Citla's gutted corpse and no matter his years as a warrior and the things he'd seen and even done in war, Pilos had to swallow his gorge.

'Can you help him ascend . . . Singer?' he croaked and Tayan's amber gaze snapped to him. For an instant there was shock there, but it was quickly subsumed by triumph. Pilos swallowed fresh nausea. 'Please help him,' he said, forcing the words out of his song-constricted throat. 'He has done so much for Ixachipan, and he has suffered for it. Please, Singer Tayan. Help him.'

Tayan – the Singer – watched him for another long moment, as if enjoying Pilos's humility, or perhaps his humiliation, and then snapped his fingers. The pressure lifted from the Spear's chest and neck. 'I can do nothing for Xac,' he said and this time at least looked like he was attempting to be sympathetic. Pilos swallowed the thought. 'It is not within my power.'

These words were conciliatory, but those he'd spoken earlier still rang in Pilos's head, words laced with the venom of spite and triumph, words ugly in their arrogance. *He was barely even a man.*

'Is it within the song's power, Sha—Singer?'

The words were Atu's and Pilos, freed of the song's compulsion, was able to shuffle sideways and look at his High Feather, taking weight from his bad leg as he did. The young warrior was kneeling halfway between Singer and, well, Singer. Tears ran unashamedly down his face and he gestured at the grotesquery of the councillors wailing and pawing at the dying holy lord. 'He does not deserve this. Can the magic not aid him one last time? It is he who made you, who raised you up and presented you as worthy to the song-magic and the holy Setatmeh.'

'You should honour him, Singer,' Pilos added. 'By doing so, you honour yourself and the long line of ancestors of which you are now a part. Honour him as you hope to be honoured in due time by your successor.'

'The long line of my ancestors? Even those who merely died, as Xac still might?' Tayan asked, mocking and glowing and wielding a magic that shouldn't be his.

'Especially those, Singer,' Pilos said evenly, refusing to be goaded. 'Even gods make mistakes, as those Singers who did not ascend prove.' *As you might*, he didn't add but Tayan understood. The corner of his mouth quirked and then he broke eye contact, rose fluidly and strode to the dead Citla and dying Singer.

The councillors, for all their supposed hysteria, scuttled out of his way instantly. He knelt in the blood and brushed the holy lord's hair back with a gentle hand. 'Put down your burdens, my sweet love, and rest with your ancestors. Ixachipan and the Empire of Songs will be safe in my care. Rest, holy lord, and be transformed.'

Magic flared and swept down his arms in a golden rush and through his palms into the dying Singer. It pooled in his throat and his belly and then spread into his chest and face and limbs, suffusing him.

'I cannot say who he will choose,' Tayan murmured, 'or whether he will have the strength to take you with him, but if I can aid him to go to the waters, then I will. My first act as your Singer will be to honour my newest ancestor.'

Pilos met Atu's neutral gaze with one of his own. Their new

Singer's first act was one of sweeping hypocrisy, and he was performing it only because they'd forced him to.

Spear and High Feather crossed to their dying Singer and knelt to one side, apart from the councillors, not wishing to be Chosen. Despite the madness of the war and the identity of their new Singer, they did not offer themselves as companions to Singer Xac in his new life.

Someone has to hold this Empire of Songs together under its new ruler. Someone has to be here to ensure Pechaqueh ways are honoured, Pechaqueh society is retained. The song may have chosen its new Singer, but that Singer must be – will be – Pechaqueh in his heart.

He will.

'Summon the Melody,' Atu murmured and Xochi hastened to the colonnade and beckoned in the eagles and Feathers, while other Chorus hurried to fetch those recuperating in the lower levels of the great pyramid. The councillors' families arrived too, and the others who'd made it to the pyramid the night the war began.

The eagles and Feathers thronging just inside the source were tanned and bloody and haggard with exhaustion, carved open with grief at the loss of their holy lord. On everyone else's face blazed ugly curiosity. They would see a Singer become a god – the most sacred transformation that none but the holy lord's closest should observe. And they would see the new Singer, could already see him, because he knelt at the holy lord's side like something from a temple painting – otherworldly.

Gold rippled and flashed and coruscated through his skin and his amber eyes were shut tight, effort and ecstasy sweeping across his features as he brought the song into his control. As he took the magic that was the foundation of Pechaqueh society and the Empire's might and tarnished it with Tokob lies, Tokob weakness.

For the first time, Pilos let himself listen to it properly, not just registering the leaps and stutters as song and Singer came together, but actually listen.

And it was . . . not dissimilar to how it had been for the last weeks. Simple and repetitive and strong. Majestic. It was, in fact, almost exactly the same as before. He grabbed Atu's shoulder and spun him away from Quotza, who'd just arrived with their daughter. 'This song is the same. This is *the same song*. For how long has the, the Shadow been manipulating the magic? How much of this is his design?'

'Pilos. We are here to honour Singer Xac,' Atu warned in a low voice instead of answering. 'We are here to keep the Melody together and fighting for victory. We are here to ensure the Empire of Songs' safety.'

'Is it still the Empire of Songs with a no-blood directing its course?'

'I wish for an end to this war as well, you know,' Tayan said before Atu could do more than gape. His voice was layered with harmonies. He opened amber eyes and looked at them, magic still passing from his hands into Singer Xac. 'I wish for peace in the Empire of Songs. I wish for all peoples in all lands to work together for harmony and prosperity. No more war; no more hate. Is it truly so hard for you to believe?'

'You want Pechaqueh to remain rightfully in charge, as it was we who built the Empire that has so blessed you?' Pilos dared to ask. Atu elbowed him and was ignored. His eyes were locked with Tayan's in a breach of protocol so enormous he wouldn't formerly have even dared contemplate it.

'I want peace and a settled world,' Tayan said, which was no answer at all as far as the Spear was concerned. What was to stop him from changing the song to one that gave primacy and strength to Tokob? What was to stop him from ordering all Pechaqueh enslaved?

'Some might say that future you fear would be justice,' the new Singer said softly and Pilos couldn't suppress a gasp.

He raised his hand instinctively to his temple. 'How are—I can't even feel you in my head. What magic is this?'

'There is no magic other than the song-magic,' Tayan said

serenely. 'My years as a shaman journeying the spiral path to Malel and rebirth were but preparation for my immersion into the song and the fifth world. They were but steps along my path to this moment, providing me with the tools I need to become your Singer and restore peace and the holy Setatmeh to health and glory. You all worried about Xac's wellbeing, but none of you stopped to wonder how those changes he suffered and the lessening of the song's power would affect his divine kin. Nobody worried about the holy Setatmeh lives as they swam through a poisoned song more lethal than salt-water. Nobody but me, a no-blood from a tribe of god-killers. You want to know why I was chosen by the song instead of you?'

'I never wanted to be Singer,' Pilos snapped, utterly failing to moderate his tone.

Atu jabbed him again, much harder this time. 'Mind your tone, Spear, or you could find yourself executed. Forgive us, holy lord,' he added to Tayan. 'He mourns your predecessor, as do we all.'

Tayan's gaze didn't even flicker to the High Feather. 'I was chosen because I put the welfare of the gods and the song and magic above even the Empire. What is the point in controlling all of Ixachipan if our gods die? What is the point in showing everyone Pechaqueh civilisation and society if they are built on the long, slow deaths of the holy Setatmeh? The war against the rebels is yours to win or lose, honoured warriors. My war is against the song's sickness and the weakening of the holy Setatmeh.

'If you wish to argue this further, at least wait until my sweet love has completed his ascent to godhood,' he added, effectively cutting off any protest or question Pilos might have. And he had many.

Tayan returned his attention to Xac, leaving Pilos shaken at the ease with which he'd entered his mind. He forced it away. In this at least, he and Atu were both correct: they were here for Singer Xac. To bear witness to his final glory.

'This should be private,' he fretted.

'No. The warriors need this. They need to see the magic and the glory for which they fight. The birth of a new god will strengthen their resolve.'

Pilos looked from Atu to Tayan and back and wondered if age and bitterness were clouding his judgement. Did these younger, brighter men have the right of it? Was he clinging to the past and traditions out of fear that the future might not hold a place for him? Singer Xac moaned then, and all thoughts fled.

Pilos joined in the Song of Ascension as the first words were sung. They harmonised with *the* song, matching its rhythm, and the two blended into something aching and bittersweet, like the glimpse of a beloved and much-missed face in the crowd, there and then gone, perhaps forever. Or perhaps never really there at all.

Singer Xac had been a god before. Now he was becoming another. His skin had been dull and sickly for months, years, but now it paled still further. Tayan stayed at his side, passing magic into his body to aid his transformation. Xac writhed gently, not as if in pain, but as if stretching out the cracks and kinks in his limbs, splaying fingers and toes repeatedly.

'Bless the song,' Atu breathed. 'Look.'

But Pilos was already looking; couldn't stop looking even if he wanted to. Even if traitors broke into the source this very moment, he'd be unable to do anything other than watch his beloved, flawed and broken Singer become the highest expression of himself.

Singer Xac's grey skin was lightened by short-lived golden flickers that faded into varying shades of green, mottling his flesh. Delicate skin was forming between his fingers and toes with every stretch and his nails were darkening and lengthening, sharpening into claws. His now-lean belly undulated, drawing his genitals up inside him even as muscle visibly grew on his slender limbs.

Pilos sang harder, pouring love and reverence and awe and humility into his voice, willing Singer Xac to become a mighty holy Setat, a glory to them all, a beacon of hope brighter than the bonfires on the great pyramid's roof.

Slits opened in the sides of his neck, gills flapping uselessly, and he writhed harder, thrashing in distress now, until his lungs remembered how to breathe. The shape of his skull was changing, eye sockets enlarging and nose flattening, jaw widening. He flipped onto all fours, dislodging Tayan's hands as if he no longer needed them. The gold was concentrated in his torso and head now, reshaping both with a rapidity that must be a sacred torment.

Singer Xac's mouth opened impossibly wide and, with a whole-body convulsion, his teeth tore free and scattered across the mat amid a spray of blood – murky blood, neither red nor green. Councillors scrabbled gracelessly to seize these treasures and clutch them tight, their voices faltering in their desire for the holy relics.

The Song of Ascension ended and the gathered Pechaqueh moved into the Song of Lost Loves, the long, long chant of names of every Singer who had gone before, all the way back to Tenaca, the first. Calling on them to welcome their newest brother and ease his ascension. Singer Xac convulsed again, pawing at his mouth as new teeth pushed through the raw gums, these wickedly barbed, row upon row. He sat back on his heels and inhaled a deep breath, gills flapping and the skin of his throat swelling. As he exhaled a high, pure note of accomplishment sang from his throat and tears pricked Pilos's eyes.

'My god,' he whispered, losing his place in the chant. 'My sweet lord.' The words were Tayan's, but in this moment they were nothing if not apt.

The last of the gold swirled through Singer Xac's chest and back, transforming the flesh there into toughened hide, armoured plates like an armadillo's to protect his organs, and then faded to green. Pilos concentrated on memorising the mottling on Singer Xac's face and shoulders so that he might recognise him among his holy kin if he was so fortunate as to meet him again.

The holy Setat Xac examined his adoring audience and Pilos trembled when his eyes rested upon him. He was privileged

– blessed – to see the final whispers of amber fade into glossy, assessing black. The last instance of his transformation.

'Will you select your council, holy Setat, my sweet love?' Tayan murmured beneath the song, so quietly that few heard him. 'Will you take any to the waters?'

The god who had been a Singer who had been a man unfurled himself to his new, full height. Tall and lean and majestic, he swept them all with that unknowable gaze, lingering on Pilos, then Atu, assessing. He sang a question.

'I would serve you as a mortal, holy spirit,' Pilos croaked, 'if that is your will. I will fight and die to protect you and your kin, and the song and the Empire you built. Ask me not to . . . Yet ask and we shall answer.'

The holy Setat stepped close and drew Pilos onto his feet and then cupped his cheek in its palm – it was still human-warm. It lowered its head until they were eye to eye. 'Fight . . . well.' The words were hard to understand, but they were *words*, not song. The Spear gasped and swayed. To be gifted with the final speech of a new holy Setat was a blessing he had not looked for nor deserved.

'I will, I swear it,' he whispered. 'And I beg you, water god, take a council if it is your will. Take companions and those who will offer you the deference and reverence that are your due. I will keep your Empire of Songs safe, but please, do not swim the waters alone. It would, it would break my heart.'

The holy Setatmeh face was no longer capable of expression, but its eyes shone with amusement and love. It pressed its cool mouth to his and then stepped away, turning to the councillors still clutching their bloody treasures, and he took them all. All fifteen. A number that should have been far beyond his strength. Had Tayan given him this gift?

Or has Tayan rid himself of the councillors he so detests?

The god rammed his claws up beneath their chins and injected so much magic into them that they transformed in a bare handful of moments, driven by his will, shrieking and cracking as their bodies withered and shrank.

'*So that's why* Pechaqueh have no medicine for the holy

Setatmeh venom. It isn't venom at all; it's *magic*. It's not a protection against attack, it's the making of kin. The making of gods.' Tayan's voice was low but wondering and utterly absorbed. Reverent and delighted. 'And they're small because, because they haven't come to the magic honestly, haven't been bathed in it, haven't worked with it. It burns them up even as it makes them gods. How did I never see this before?'

An avenue was opening in the crowd of onlookers, clearing a path to the offering pool as the new holy Setatmeh tore free of their clothing and stretched into their new shapes. Holy Setat Xac went first, loping the length of the source and slipping into the water. A rising stream of notes like bubbling laughter rose from his throat and then he ducked under the surface. His council followed, one by one, crowding into the pool until it was filled with divine forms.

The Lament of Lost Loves finally came to an end and the source descended into stillness, into silence but for the weeping of the councillors' families left behind and the furtive slide of fingers across mats for more relics – teeth, scraps of clothing, jewellery. Singer Tayan led them all in a full prostration to the pool, and then sat back on his heels before facing the assembled warriors, nobles and the families of the councillors who were no more.

He pointed over his shoulder. 'That is why we fight. That is who we fight for. For this magic and this way of life, for this glory and the unification of the song that makes gods out of people. I will do all in my power to bring this war to an end, and I need you to give of yourselves just as I will. If we lose, the song dies, and they die, and then we die.

'Do. Not. Lose.'

LILLA

Tithing barns, western Singing City,
Pechacan, Empire of Songs
50th day of the Great Star at morning

'What the fuck . . .' Lilla stood, staring blankly into the rain-streaked sky as the song began to twist in on itself, rising and falling in peaks and bright with savagery as it had been so many times before. Yet different, too. Beneath the wildness and bloodlust that had them all cowering was another thread, one he'd never heard before, a droning clangour that spoke of grief mingled with triumph.

'What's happening?' he asked, reaching without looking for Ekon. Without thinking. The Chitenecatl took his hand and squeezed hard.

'It sounds like an offering. But underneath, that's,' he paused, 'it sounds like what happens to the song during an ascension. Which means Xac is transforming, becoming the newest holy— the newest Drowned. Mictec!' He yanked on Lilla's hand, startling him. 'The pyramid will be in chaos. The song will be wild and uncontrolled when it passes to its new Singer – and that means it will not be seeking to control us. We can—'

'—take the pyramid,' Lilla said with him. They shared one grim but hopeful look and then spun apart, hissing orders to everyone around them – everyone they had left, anyway.

Weaver and Xini's remaining warriors would react the same, Lilla knew. They understood the ways of the song better than he did. All three war parties would converge on the tumble-down wall ringing the pyramid and this time they'd break it and then take the pyramid. Rescue Tayan and get some fucking answers. End the song.

Despite everything he'd said and told himself he believed since Tayan's proclamation had destroyed their fighting force and much of their hope, it was impossible to quell the butter-flies in his stomach at the prospect of freeing him from the pyramid. He'd told no one of his plan to kidnap Tayan, partly out of fear they'd kill him as soon as he was in their control, and partly fear of what they'd do to Lilla himself. Still, it had to be done. He'd learn how much of everything that had happened Tayan had been forced into. *And how much he may have chosen willingly.*

A single point of stillness amid the chaos of the milling warriors caught his eye: Xessa, Ossa, Toxte. Toxte was signing rapidly and snapping questions to anyone close enough to answer. Lilla whistled and Ossa's head came up and then his tail wagged furiously. Whatever bad blood remained between Xessa and Lilla, the dog didn't care.

Toxte stopped signing and gestured and Xessa's intense, wary gaze snagged on Lilla.

'We're going for the great pyramid, to take it while the new Singer wrestles with the magic,' he signed as he approached. 'Xac's going to be the newest Greater Drowned and at some point he'll leave the source for the river. If you want it, we'll clear you a path to the stream running down the pyramid's side. When he comes out, he's yours for the killing.'

Xessa lit up and then just as quickly her fire guttered. Her fingers brushed Ossa's skull and the dog's tail wagged again as he leant against her side.

'Two ejab, one dog. Toxte can compensate for Ossa's injury,' Lilla signed quickly. 'Or you can say no. It's not an order, it's not even a request. It's an offer. If you want Singer Xac on the point of your spear, he's yours. For everything he did to

Tay that made him what he is,' he added without quite meaning to. Xessa hesitated, looking at Ossa and then Toxte, who nodded.

'For me,' Lilla added, quietly but aloud. Toxte looked at him for a long, impenetrable moment, and then blinked and turned to his wife. Lilla held his breath, but Toxte didn't sign his words, didn't betray him or seek to influence Xessa.

The slow smile that spread over the ejab face was cruel and lascivious, and then she looked down at Ossa again, her indecision clear.

'Toxte,' Lilla called. 'We'll need to know before we take down the wall. Either way, I'll respect your choice.'

Toxte nodded and Lilla let the purposeful movement of arming warriors sweep the ejab from his sight and told himself he wouldn't think about it again, think about Xessa's spear ripping into the monster that had made Tayan into his own image. Allegedly.

They were formed up into their pods – so few now – and almost ready to leave when the wildness of the offering melody faded and the ascension music increased in tempo. Its wailing grief jarred against the triumph beginning to bleed into its notes. An uneasy mix that left Lilla faintly nauseous.

And then the song stopped, cut off mid-note to leave them all in breathless, unexpected silence. Everyone stilled. Only Xessa was unaffected, but she took one look at the warriors surrounding her and signed no questions, for once patient with something she didn't understand.

A weight lifted from Lilla's skin that he had forgotten was there. As it had been when they'd sawed through the thick leather of their slave collars, so it was now. Something so familiar as to have become unremarkable was missing, and its absence became the most important thing about it. He drew in a breath so deep that every sore muscle, every bruise in flesh and bone, and every stitch in his belly pulled and protested – and he relished them all. He spread his arms and turned his face up to the rain and closed his eyes, a smile tugging at his mouth for the first time in weeks.

Silence. Perfect and beautiful and reminding him of who and what he was.

And fleeting.

No more than five or six breaths and the song returned. Lilla flinched, a whole-body rejection of the haunting, sourceless music that once more insinuated its way through his skin and muscles, infecting every part of him, worming its way closer to his spirit and then claiming it, staining it like blood in linen.

'It doesn't matter,' he roared, heedless of maintaining the quiet that kept them hidden. They wouldn't need it after today. After they ended it. 'It doesn't matter,' he repeated, 'we go anyway. Their new Singer will be struggling to command—'

'It's the same.'

'—the magic as they learn its limits and their own. The Pechaqueh will—'

'The song's the same. It's the same as before.'

'—be reeling from the loss of Xac and—'

'*Enough! It's the same song, Fang.*' Gentler, now. 'Lilla, it's the same.'

Lilla's voice died in his throat. It was Tiamoko speaking, the young warrior's face earnest and sympathetic. He pushed gently through the crowd until he reached his side. 'Lilla,' he murmured, gripping the Tokob wrist. 'It's the same. Listen to it. If Xac is dead, and Tayan was his Shadow and his support within the song, and this is the same as it was before, then it must be him controlling it. Lilla, I'm sorry, but surely that means Tayan is, is the new Singer of the Empire of Songs.' His hand tightened and then slid up to grip Lilla's bicep. 'And you know it. So what do we do now?'

Lilla couldn't breathe. Couldn't blink, his eyes fixed on Tiamoko. Couldn't move, his limbs granite, mahogany.

Xessa appeared. 'Breathe in,' she signed and put one hand on his sternum and the other on the back of his neck. She nodded and inhaled, exaggerated, pressing on his chest as she did. Lilla's lungs stuttered and the air he breathed was as raw and tainted as if it was heavy with smoke, but it filled him and then gusted out on a sound he was glad Xessa couldn't hear, even if Tiamoko and several others close by could.

When his lungs were a howling void, Xessa tapped his chest again and more air found its way into him. Toxte was standing just behind her, a blur in Lilla's stinging eyes as he focused on Xessa's face. They cycled through another seven breaths before the world returned to him in fits and starts – sound first, unfortunately, because that meant he could hear the song again. Tayan's song with its bitter load of condemnation and its imperative to surrender to Pechaqueh dominion. And then his awareness of the warriors around him; fidgety, frightened, eager to run, whether towards or away from danger.

Xessa. Toxte. Tiamoko.

His family.

Ossa was next, pressing his broad, blunt head to Lilla's thigh with the acceptance and love that only a dog could give, and then two more stuttered breaths later, Ekon's hand skimmed up his arm and around his shoulders and drew him against his chest, solid and warm and alive and unconditional.

'Kitten. I'm here. Whatever you need.'

The words and the hands and the concern steadied him. Xessa's bleak guilt and fierce love that he'd missed for so long; Tiamoko's cold ruthlessness so at odds with the laughing boy he'd been; Ekon's quiet strength and unfailing support no matter how many times Lilla pushed him away.

He took another shaky breath and let Ekon's arm support him for one more glorious, undeserved moment, and then he straightened. 'We go anyway,' he croaked. 'We take the pyramid and end the song, no matter the identity of its Singer. I won't listen to its lies anymore. We go.'

Hello, Lilla.

Lilla's fingers spasmed and he fumbled the knot tying his armour closed. Looked around, but the small square was silent even as it was packed with grim-faced warriors. Thunder rumbled a warning overhead.

What are you doing, husband? Oh, there's no need to be afraid.

The Tokob knife was in his hand and he spun in a circle, seeking. 'What is this?' he snarled. Amusement bubbled through him – not his amusement. 'Are you, are you a spirit?'

'Lilla?'

More amusement, tinged with mockery. *A spirit? You wish me dead, husband? Was proclaiming yourself a widower for all the world to see not enough? Now you wish it were true? You wish for my death?*

Something twisted in him then and a spike of hurt shivered through Lilla's whole body. He gasped and staggered, hunching over.

'Lilla!'

I have taken control of the greatest magic the world has ever seen, husband. And with it, I will make a peace for all peoples. Will you help me? Will you help me weave a peace that will last forever?

More pain ripped through Lilla, this time concentrated in his head, behind his eye. His knife fell from his hand and he cried out. 'Stop it,' he begged, even now unwilling to name the voice that couldn't possibly be coming from within. It was a trick, some trick of his broken head, a new torment he was conjuring himself. It couldn't be him.

Interesting. It is me, Lilla. Your husband; your Singer. I am Listening through my song. Your lover can tell you what that means if you care to learn more.

'You . . . you betrayed us,' Lilla gasped. There were people crowding around him, too many and too close, and he tried to twist away from them, but they were everywhere and the pain in his head was growing and Tayan was *inside him* and gleeful, uncaring of Lilla's hurts. 'Betrayed Tokoban. Betrayed Malel.'

Another wrench inside him and he might have screamed; he did collapse to his hands and knees. Someone had their arm around his back. Someone else had his face cradled in their palms. He shrank from all of it.

Malel betrayed me! My spirit guides betrayed me! I am the one bereft and abandoned. I am the one alone surrounded by enemies.

Each word rocked him with the force of an axe blow. A pause.

You betrayed me. Didn't you, Lilla? Refused to claim me. Abandoned me. And yet here I am, despite it all. Singer Tayan, ruler of the Empire of Songs, which I will bring to peace. And I will be your husband again, Lilla, despite your betrayal. If you acknowledge what I have become. Together we can end the war. Think about it, you and me, ruling this Empire together, securing its legacy of peace and tolerance. We can do that. Just come to me, Lilla. Come to me and pledge your-self and you will be welcomed.

He sounded sincere. He sounded reasonable. He sounded insane.

'Get out of my head.' Above, a hissed conversation and finally, blessedly, space opening around him. It didn't ease the tightness in his chest, but it was a start. It did nothing for the pain, either, building with every thud of his heart until it was something unstoppable.

Give yourself to me and my song, husband. Together we can be glorious. Powerful. Loved by all.

'I don't want to be powerful,' Lilla muttered, swallowing sour spit. 'That's your dream. I only ever wanted to protect those I love.'

And you think being the Singer's consort wouldn't let you do that? Or is it that those you love no longer includes me? This is your last chance, Lilla. Surrender to me and live in power and glory and luxury, husband to the Singer of the Empire of Songs. Tayan and Lilla, together again. Us against the world.

'If that's what you think our marriage was, then you never understood it at all. Or me. The only part of me you held was my heart, and that was willingly given. Now you would put a collar on me yourself. You are not the man I married. Get out of my head.'

Tayan went, vanishing as silently as he'd arrived. The pain didn't lessen.

Lilla retched and spat bile onto the stone between his hands and then carefully, slowly, sat back on his heels. Feeling twice his years and as empty as if his spirit had fled his flesh, he pulled his salt-cotton over his head and handed it to Ekon, kneeling opposite looking stricken.

'There is no transition from one Singer to the next we can exploit. No confusion or difficulty in wielding the magic. Tayan is in perfect control. He . . . Listened? To me?'

Ekon nodded, troubled. 'Though how he has the skill of it, being Tokob, I don't understand. Enet could do it, not well, but she could. But she was half-Pecha. We assumed . . .' he trailed off.

'We should send messengers to Xini and Weaver; if we attack now, we'll be up against a Melody mad with grief and maybe even disgust at a Tokob Singer, but that will just make them fight harder. They'll have to prove to themselves and to us that everything is fine.' That was Tiamoko, and again Ekon nodded.

'And they'll fight to honour their new god, Xac,' he added. 'I agree. The turmoil won't be enough to give us the advantage. But after a few days of a Toko slave giving them orders and wielding their precious song, that might be enough for discontent to set in.'

Ekon stood. 'Tiamoko, send messengers to our allies and ensure they understand Tayan is Singer and his apparent strength and mastery of the song. Everyone else, give the Fang some privacy.'

'Take that inside so it stays dry,' Lilla said softly to Ekon, gesturing at his salt-cotton as the crowd reluctantly moved away. Thunder cracked, perfectly timed to the flick of his fingers, and he jumped. The rain got harder, colder. 'I'm going to rain bathe.'

He didn't dare look at the emptying plaza, warriors hurrying into shelter now there was no battle to prepare for. Didn't dare blink too hard for fear of the agony washing through his head. If he could just stay calm and not think of everything his husband had just said and done, he might be spared the worst of the attack.

'Are you—' Ekon tried.

'Please don't. Please.' Ekon hesitated again, and Lilla made himself stand, swallowing against nausea and the unbearable brightness of the storm-dark sky. 'Privacy,' he croaked. Ekon's face was lined with concern, but he made himself step back, clutching Lilla's salt-cotton to his chest as if it was the man himself.

'You need food and rest, kitten. Don't stay out here too long.'

Lilla raised a hand in acknowledgment before easing out of his tunic and untying his kilt, his fingers thick and clumsy. Didn't have the energy or any need to take off his sandals. Cold rain, cool wind, quiet. It might be enough. He prayed it was enough. He draped his clothes over a low wall and turned his face up to the roiling black clouds, opening his arms and letting the droplets hammer his skin, flow over his face and chest, his belly and back, run down his legs. Lifted his dampening hair and pulled it forward over one shoulder for the rain to run through the grooves and lines of scar marring his back.

Stood motionless except for the minute rocking of his heart thudding, breathing through the pain in his head and the roiling of his gut, carefully not remembering the way it had felt to have Tayan inside him, speaking directly to him, spirit to spirit. Begging him for the second time to betray everyone in return for some imagined power and a chance for them to be together again. What did that mean, that he'd asked again? Did it mean love? Or did he just want someone he thought would love him no matter what?

He'd sworn back during his life in the Melody to betray everything to save everything. How many times did that have to include Tayan?

No. He's the one betraying me.

So why does it feel like I've just committed the greatest evil of my life?

Someone clicked their fingers and he startled and then slowly opened his eyes. Xessa. She was holding out his kilt and looking determinedly over his left shoulder. He let his arms fall to his sides and then took the wet cotton and turned his back to wrap it around his hips, cold material clinging to wet flesh. Not even enough time to scrub sweat and dirt and blood from his skin before it began again. The judging. The relentless need to be strong. He took a careful breath and then faced her again, to find Xessa's face creased with pity. A bolt of pain and shame seared through Lilla's head and he snatched up his tunic and fought his way into it to hide the ruin of his back.

Toxte was a few paces behind Xessa, clearly ready to step in if she needed him. As if Xessa was ever the one who came out of these confrontations bleeding.

'I haven't the stomach for another argument,' he signed as soon as he was dressed. Pain pulsed warning behind his eyes and Toxte made some small, stifled noise of protest; Lilla ignored both. 'You're right. There: satisfied?' He made to step around her and she grabbed his wrist.

'What do you mean, I'm right?' she signed. 'I didn't want to—'

Lilla's face twisted and the momentary calm under the rain was gone. 'You want me to paint the glyphs of it so that you can read its truth or are my words good enough? I said, you're right. You've won. Tayan chose them, and chose power, instead of us. He betrayed you, me, the Tokob, the rebellion, Malel herself. Is that what you want me to say? Does it make you happy to see me admit it?'

Xessa clenched her jaw and reached for him again and Lilla slapped her hand away, then shut his eyes as pain flared bright as lightning across the inside of his skull. Skewering his brain. He let it be the tinder to his anger and glared at Toxte over her shoulder, warning him not to interfere. The other eja was thin-lipped but silent.

'Lilla,' Xessa signed and he slashed his hand through the air.

'No. You wanted this; now you'll stand there and read it.

Tay was captured in Malel's womb along with the Drowned
you got for him. Who knows what the Pechaqueh did to him
in punishment for that: perhaps it broke his mind. Perhaps he
wants to kill us all for losing the war and leaving him to be
captured in the first place. Or perhaps he really has exchanged
every good thing in him for power and status. Whatever the
truth of it is, you've been using it as a whip to lash me and
I don't know why. And as you saw, I've already got enough
of those types of scars. I don't know what cruelty it feeds in
you to hurt me, Xessa, but it ends now. Don't,' he added when
Toxte stepped forward to protest as Xessa recoiled.

'I am not in a position to change Tayan's mind. He was just
in my head and I couldn't convince him not to make war on
us. Neither of us have *ever* been able to stop him when he
sets his mind to something. But I'm done with these arguments.
With you. You stayed when he offered Tokob a way out and
I'm grateful for that, but I can't – I won't – keep doing this
with you. I don't know what you want and I don't care
anymore. All I do know is that twice now he's asked me to
put on a marriage cord shaped like a slave collar and twice
I've said no. If that's not good enough for you—'

'She's trying to apologise, you judgemental fuck,' Toxte
snarled as his patience snapped and he stepped up to Xessa's
side. 'Give her a chance.' Lilla barely heard him. A thick wave
of nausea rolled from his belly up into his throat and he sucked
in a breath through his nose, sour spit flooding his mouth
again. 'Lilla?'

'Are you hurt?' Xessa signed, reaching for him.

Lilla flinched. 'Don't touch me,' he spat and even if she
didn't catch the words, the intent was clear enough. 'Get back,'
he added, barely able to see them through the agony and the
rain. Instead, Toxte stepped in and grabbed him by the shoulders. With a snarl, Lilla broke free and swung a slow, clumsy
punch that the eja evaded with ease. 'Just leave me alone.' His
voice broke and he spat more bile and the pain was monstrous,
every raindrop hitting his skull with the force of a landslide.
And then Ekon was there.

'She wants to know what's wrong with him,' Lilla heard as Ekon pulled a swatch of cloth from his belt and bound it quickly over the Tokob eyes. The darkness helped a little. Ekon's arm slid around his waist and he put his own over the Chitenecah shoulders. Slowly, they began to walk.

'When he was captured below the Sky City, the Melody broke his skull. Moments of intense emotional stress trigger blinding headaches that can last for hours. By Mictec's grace, combat isn't one of the causes, or the Melody would have thrown him to the holy—the Drowned years ago.'

There was a long silence, then: 'We didn't know.'

Ekon's back tensed under Lilla's arm. 'That's because you didn't ask, isn't it? Because all you've done since our arrival is spit venom at him. He's asked you to leave him alone and you're still here. But I'm not asking. I'm telling. Go away, ejab. Now.'

The rain vanished from Lilla's head and shoulders and the darkness of the blindfold increased as Ekon led him carefully inside and around the seated and lying warriors. The material soaked up his tears, and those that escaped would just look like rainwater. And then he couldn't even care about that: there was stone and salt-cotton under him, a shawl or blanket covering him, and Ekon's warm thigh under his cheek. Lilla turned his head into the darkness of the Chitenecah belly and wrapped his arms around his waist, curling up as small as he could before the pain crested. He sucked in a breath and Ekon shoved a wad of material into his mouth, then curled over him to stifle the sounds of his agony. His screaming.

'Lilla? Lilla, kitten. I'm sorry, but we have to go.'

Lilla was curled on his side in a corner of the barn, facing into the wall with his salt-cotton wrapped around his head. Some time after the first wave of agony had receded and he was bracing for the next, Ekon had bullied him out of his wet kilt into a dry pair of leggings, too short in the leg and tight enough that under any other circumstances he'd have been blushing and, possibly, preening, and then found a second shawl to patiently, carefully squeeze the water out of his hair for him. Hours before, perhaps. Days. Time lost all meaning when his entire world was reduced to nothing but the high, incessant ringing and the pain searing through his head. He'd vomited twice. Ekon had been here to clear up the first time, but not the second. The thin, congealed pool of mostly water and bile sat by his face. Lilla couldn't bring himself to care.

Someone ran their hands across his back and up to the base of his neck, massaging lightly. 'Lilla, the Melody's found us. We have to leave now. We have to run.'

The words made no sense, but then the salt-cotton was pulled from around his head and Lilla mewled and curled tighter on the stone. Lips pressed to his temple and cheekbone. 'Come on, kitten, you have to get up. I can't carry you.'

Outside the sphere of his agony, the Toko was aware of hurrying feet, people rushing – not quietly – and the injured being hoisted in blanket slings or hobbling with spears as crutches. Everyone moving, fast and loud, the colours of their paint and clothes too bright, the movements too jerky. Nausea clenched his gut and he turned his face away and groaned.

Ekon was relentless. He pulled Lilla over onto his back and then grabbed the shawl wrapping him and hauled him up to sitting. The Tokob head swam and the pain rammed into him and he cried out and clutched at it, tearing at his hair and scalp, desperate to dig it out. To crack open his skull and pull out the sliver of obsidian that was surely lodged within it.

'Get up, Fang Lilla. The enemy has found us and they are going to kill us. You are endangering your pod, your Paw. Me. Stand the fuck up.'

Ekon shifted on the balls of his feet, his knees spread wide around Lilla's torso, and got his arms around him and then stood with a grunt, dragging Lilla up with him. The dim interior of the tithing barn tilted and swooped and he cried out again, but then he was standing, wobbling and sickened and with tears of pain streaking his cheeks. Ekon's arms were the only thing keeping him upright. He opened his eyes to slits.

The Chitenecah face was very close, and the closest to panic he'd ever seen, his lower lip pinned between his teeth.

'Please, kitten. Please, my love. You have to walk. You have to *try*. I can't leave you here.'

My love. You have to try. My love.

Lilla didn't dare nod in case his head fell off. He let the shawl fall from around his shoulders. Ekon exhaled in relief and dressed Lilla carefully in his armour with one hand, the other steadying him, and then tied the laces for him. He passed him a spear, draped the shawl over his head, and then hooked the Tokob other arm around his shoulders.

'I'm sorry, kitten, but we need to move fast. It's going to be bright out there. I just need you to move when I move, all right? I'll keep us safe.' Ekon kissed his cheek again. 'I'll keep you safe, I swear it. Trust me.'

He didn't give Lilla time to answer, if he could even have found words within the grinding shards of agony. One moment he was standing, nauseous with pain, and the next Ekon was walking him through the barn towards the nearest exit.

Daylight was knives through his eyes and Lilla cried out, flinching and trying to turn back. Ekon was babbling something but he didn't falter, didn't let Lilla falter either, dragging him forwards.

'Please. Ekon, I can't.'

'You can. I know you can. Walk with me, love. *Please*. We can't die here.'

'Leave me.'

Ekon's arm tightened painfully around his ribs. 'Never,' he snarled with such passion that it cleared a little of the haze from the Tokob mind. 'You hear me? *I will never leave you.*'

Lilla tightened his grip on his spear and on Ekon. He gritted his teeth and swallowed his whimpers and walked into agonising daylight – and war.

Ekon shoved Lilla against a wall and lunged past him to take a woman through the throat with his spear. They were little more than blurry outlines against the incandescent day and the blessed shadow of the shawl; still, the Toko clutched his spear in both hands and slitted his eyes, doing what he could to focus. To help.

'On the left,' he croaked and somehow Ekon heard him and spun into the new threat. 'Behind you,' he added but the Chitenecatl was already in motion, leaping high over a foot sweep and deflecting a strike at the same time.

The eagle behind him glided closer, out of Ekon's eyeline, and Lilla lurched into his path and struck, too slow and weak. The warrior cracked his club down on the spear and knocked it from the Tokob weakened grip. Lilla threw himself onto the eagle, grabbing him around the chest. The club slammed into his back but without force, winding rather than shattering a rib or breaking his back. They crashed onto the stone, Lilla on top and struggling not for the club but to contain the warrior's limbs, wrap him up in his arms and legs and just cling on until Ekon could rescue him.

Adrenaline and the nearness of death cleared some of the pain-fog from his mind. He was weak and uncoordinated, but not entirely helpless. The warrior tried to roll them and Lilla dug his teeth into the man's neck and bit down as hard as he could, shaking his head like Ossa with a rat or a lizard. The man screamed and the pain in Lilla's head screamed with him, and then someone fell over them both.

A sandal connected with Lilla's arse, spearing pain down his leg, and then somebody landed on him. Wetness spread over his legs. The weight slithered away and a spear stabbed down with expert precision, past Lilla's face and into the wound he'd bitten in the eagle's throat. Lilla stared at the obsidian blade, so close it was hard to focus, and then it vanished.

'Lilla? Are you hurt?' Hands slid under his armpits and pulled him up onto his knees, and then, when he was steady, to his feet. The liquid that had run over his legs was blood, hot and sticky as it soaked through his leggings.

'Not hurt. You?'

Ekon was grim and slathered in blood, but he shook his head. He grabbed his spear and Lilla's, and then the dead warrior's club, too. He passed spear and club to Lilla, pulled him in against his hip with his free hand, and got his bearings. They were in a bubble of quiet, the running battle having moved on without them, and Lilla could have sunk back to the stone and wept.

Instead, he put his arm around Ekon's neck, the club dangling from his fist, and just waited, his head down in paltry protection against the cloudy sky.

Ekon squeezed his waist. Lilla took a fortifying breath. They ran.

THE LISTENER

Empire of Songs
50th day of the Great Star at morning

*There is a lamentation within the song that cries for the holy
Setatmeh. That—*

What?

*—cries for what is lost and does not know how to find it.
There is a lamentation without a question. Where is the
question?*

What the fuck? Who are you? Who dares confront me in my
own song? I am the Singer; this is my domain and power. Speak!

That is not the question you should be asking, Singer.

Tell me your name.

Is that more important than the sickening of the gods?

... What do you know of the song and the holy Setatmeh?
They are my ancestors, my divine kin. Who are you to claim
knowledge of them?

... Very well. You seek to play games, to hide your identity
as if you can match me in status. But what makes you think
they are sick?

*A better question. You weep for them within the song. I
hear it; I hear you. You would not weep if there was no need.
You would not search for knowledge.*

This is a nonsense. You speak in riddles and expect me to answer when I don't even know who you are. Be gone from me.

Feed the world spirit.

What? What did you say? Who are you? . . . Stranger, I order you to speak. Come back! If you have knowledge, you will give it to me. I am your Singer; how dare you disrespect me? Stranger!

ILANDEH

Outskirts of City of Glass, Chitenec,
Empire of Songs
55th day of the Great Star at morning

There was a new Singer. A new song, powerful and demanding. Familiar.

Tayan's song.

As she walked, Ilandeh listened to its dips and swirls, its indomitable will and ambition. Everything it represented was what she had a chance to regain: peace and status and future. Perhaps more, even, because their Singer *was not of Pechacan.*

Maybe once there was peace, Singer Tayan would rebalance Ixachipan, removing ideas of blood purity and prioritising ability as the true determiner of status. Ilandeh had ability. She'd been Chorus Leader once; she could be so again, but proudly, with a Xentib charm in her hair and Nallac's name on her tongue. She could rekindle her friendship with Tayan and make it true, not based on a lie this time, the way her every friendship had been throughout her adult life.

Can I?

The question was smoke from a burning manchineel tree, strangling her lungs in a slow attrition of poison. Could she rekindle their friendship when Tayan appeared to be repeating all the lessons he'd learnt in the last few years as a slave to Enet and the Singer. Their cruelty, their selfishness.

Of all she'd expected from him, it hadn't been a song that was so very Pechaqueh: *surrender. Live at the mercy of your betters. Bow your necks to us.*

Tayan of Tokoban, shaman and slave, had taken the greatest magic ever to move through Ixachipan and made it his own. And then he'd turned his back on Malel and her God-born. He'd turned his back on his people to clutch at the magic that had broken them.

Ilandeh knew the depths of her hypocrisy in judging him. Not just because of the way she'd lived her life under the song's lies, but because she'd acquiesced to Pilos's demand, his order, the very instant she'd heard it. She hadn't just been relieved; she'd been *completed.*

And I wasn't even offered the greatest power and magic ever to exist; all he's giving me is a chance at my former life. A chance to serve and grovel and lick shit from the sandals of people who believe they're better than me.

Deliberately, Ilandeh visualised exactly that and then swallowed convulsively as her gorge rose. Pilos didn't want her and neither did the Melody. So it was a good job that she'd rejected both, that she would – if they'd let her – pledge herself to the Zellih cause instead. Whatever that might be.

She, Olox, and Pikte were marching with Omeata's war party again. This was the third time they'd intercepted the Bird-form's warriors in the last week, each time providing vital information about their route, whether that was the presence of rebels, a fiercely contested city, or a landslide that had washed out the trail.

Omeata had been suspicious, of course, sending her own scouts to verify their information. That verification had bought them a little more trust each time until yesterday, when the Bird-form had stated she would take them into her war party if they proved they could be trusted within view and not just, as she'd put it, "while skulking around in the jungle".

They had a place at the rear of the war party, under constant watch but involved. The first step. The second would be earning that trust Omeata had spoken of. The third would be to find out the extent of their purpose in Ixachipan.

During the days they'd been shadowing the Zellih and skipping ahead of them to break trail and provide advance warning, Ilandeh had finally divulged the extent of their mission to Olox and Pikte, of Pilos's suspicion that the Zellih had never returned over the border, of the need to find them and then find out their intentions. The boy, predictably, was excited and eager; this was real Whisper work, something that would make a tangible difference to the outcome of the war. Pikte's response was also predictable: tight-lipped disapproval.

They'd found a pyramid half a day out from their second encounter with the Zellih and Ilandeh had relayed their location and the war party's to Pilos, slipping out of her disguise for just long enough to beg a Listener to intercede on her behalf.

Pilos had been utterly blank within the song, giving her neither praise nor censure despite her news. Instead, he'd reminded her to find out exactly what the Zellih planned and then cut the connection. A dismissal; a slap in the face.

Ilandeh put it out of her mind. Tomorrow, the Whispers and the Zellih would conquer the City of Glass. It stood ten sticks away on a flat plateau above terraced farms, and beyond it obsidian fields were scattered at the base of mountains. None of that mattered to Ilandeh as much as the knowledge that the city lay a mere week's walk from the border with Pechacan. Like the rest of Chitenec, the region was firmly under Pechaqueh control.

We're going to attack a peaceful city.

No. A city in which a small number of the population controls and owns the rest is not peaceful. It is monstrous.

Ilandeh held that conviction close to her heart as the war party slipped through the jungle edging the farmland in the last hour before dusk, the insistent downpour muting sound even as it set every leaf and slender branch to movement. Before the next dawn had clambered over the edge of the world, they'd have exited the trees and slipped through the terraces and up the winding path to the city. When it awoke, they'd already be at its walls. And Ilandeh would be killing again. Pechaqueh, loyalists, rebels, civilians. Anyone who stood against the Zellih.

Ilandeh was intimately familiar with the greasy anticipation of battle. The hours that slowed and smeared and never ended – and yet were gone too soon. The random kicks of anxiety that made her heart race. The compulsive repetition of the plan and her part in it – where to move and when, which approach to take, who she was responsible for and to, cycling through her mind like the wheel of the stars, the seasons, the sun. An endless, unstoppable rotation that stole any hope of rest.

A commotion up ahead snapped her out of the spiral of her thoughts. She hurried forwards and, between one step and the next, the song failed. Fell away as if it had never been, leaving a silence ringing and profound in its wake. The Zellih were milling excitedly and muttering among themselves.

'It isn't what you think,' she said in Pallatolli, gesturing back the way they'd come. 'The song hasn't ended, it's just . . . broken here.'

'How?' Huenoch demanded.

'The pyramids must have been torn down in this area, weakening and then snapping the song. It's a pocket of silence; no more. If you were careful, you'd be able to find the exact edges of it, the invisible line between magic and no magic. Step back that way, and you'll be under the song again.'

Some of the Zellih listened; most ignored her, speculating on what the silence might mean. Ilandeh might be native to Ixachipan and know the song intimately, but the Zellih had no reason to trust her words. Their doubt meant nothing; she'd tried, and she'd been seen to try. That would get back to Omeata, which was all she wanted.

More Zellih were crowding into the quiet space in the air or stepping back and forth across the border, morbidly curious. The first time Ilandeh had come across a place of silence, she'd been terrified, thinking the Singer must be dead, perhaps murdered by rebels or even by Tayan.

She'd jumped backwards on the trail, an instinctive shying away from danger, and immediately been back under the song. Two days of diligent, queasy investigation had led her to a dozen destroyed pyramids, all of them deep within the jungle. Another symptom both of the scale of the uprising and of how thin the Melody was stretched that it couldn't even protect the pyramids that carried the song.

Ilandeh had hurried through that first pocket of silence, her skin crawling at the emptiness in her bones, so very different from how suffused with song and magic she'd been in the source itself.

By the fourth instance, she was forcing herself to linger, to sit inside the quiet. The year she'd spent in the Sky City before the conquest hadn't been the first time Ilandeh had lived outside the song. Still, while she'd hated the silence of Tokoban, she'd had her duty and her orders and her lies to occupy her. All the messy business of survival and deception to counter the emptiness. But in those still places within the jungle on her lonely trek north, where it was just the trees moving and birds calling, monkeys and insects and the million other noises of life, so many of which were dampened beneath the song, she'd learnt to relish the quiet.

There was a peace in the song's absence that she'd never felt before, a settling that allowed her spirit to be exactly what it was, complete and perfect in its blending. She felt it again now, among the wondering, awestruck Zellih; a gentle reiteration that she was good and whole just as she was. Or at least that she could be, one day. Without the constant reminder of her inferiority, Ilandeh was free to be exactly what her nature dictated – strong and decisive, ruthless and compassionate, fierce and tender. She wasn't a macaw or a Whisper or a half-blood. She wasn't Pilos's dog or Pilos's weapon. She was Ilandeh of Xentiban and Pechacan.

She was Ilandeh.

And Ilandeh had sworn to destroy the City of Glass in the name of Zellih gods and Zellih superiority.

Despite that gnawing, ever-present knowledge, the absence of the song drained the tension from her as the life of the jungle rushed to fill its absence. Birds and insects trilled and chirred; the wind blew green and laughing through the canopy so that branches rubbed together in familial affection; leaves rustled; and the Zellih fell silent one by one as they came into the quiet.

Pikte was scowling and Olox was wide-eyed and pale, sweat on his upper lip. She moved to stand beside him.

'Is this your first time out from under the song?' she murmured. He nodded, jerky and frightened.

'I know you have not felt this before, but it is what we are fighting for,' she told him, intent until he nodded again, with a little more composure this time.

'It is . . . strange but glorious. Not to be commanded, controlled, told I am worthless.' Ilandeh squeezed his shoulder. This was where the danger lay. This was why no-bloods could not be trusted out from under the song. The Pechaqueh in Whispers yearned to go home and hear it again, and that yearning was believed to cancel out any errant ideas from the weaker half of their blood. It was why Whispers could be trusted to act independently while even career dog warriors were not.

'Stay strong,' she murmured, more breath than voice. Olox let out a giggle tinged with hysteria and her grip tightened until she was likely to leave bruises in his flesh. 'You are a proud son of Axiban and this is everything you want,' she reminded him. 'This silence, this lack of song, is the great gift we will bring to Ixachipan. Enjoy the first taste of freedom you have ever had, my friend.'

Her gaze was as fierce as a hawk's as she willed him to play his part. Their position was far too tenuous for doubts about blood or loyalty now.

'It is overwhelming,' Olox choked. 'It is more than I ever thought it would be.'

Ilandeh nodded and raised her voice. 'Though you have cast aside your oath to the Melody, I know how hard the silence is. I know the doubt that creeps in at the edges when the song isn't there to blunt them. There is no shame in stepping back inside it if it will help you sleep. I ask only that you spend as much time outside it as you can first, to fully understand the import of what we are trying to do. What we *will* do.'

Olox took a deep breath and nodded, and this time she knew he understood. She let go of his shoulder and he tapped his forefinger to the long, delicate bone piercing his septum, grounding himself in his Axib heritage. 'Thank you for your wisdom, Ilandeh,' he managed, and then Omeata was striding into their midst. Her advance checked as the silence engulfed her, and Ilandeh clearly saw her eyes flutter closed for the briefest instant.

'We camp here tonight, in this place where people have destroyed the song to free themselves,' the Bird-form said and no one disagreed. 'Tomorrow, we take the City of Glass.'

'Revered Bird-form, is there a reason for this act? This attack? May we understand our purpose here?' Ilandeh asked when the cheering had subsided. Pikte came to stand at her shoulder and Olox flanked her other side. She and Omeata locked eyes for an endless moment.

'If you live, if you prove yourselves loyal, I may tell you. If that isn't good enough for you, take the trail.'

The Whisper licked her lips and pressed her palms together beneath her chin. 'You need not doubt us, Bird-form,' she promised.

Omeata spread her arms in the silence of the song. 'Perhaps. Your actions will mean more than your lies—I mean words.' She smiled apologetically and then beckoned a warrior to her side.

Ilandeh's gaze flicked to Olox. He'd taken a few paces sideways until he was back under the song, bathing in it. How likely was he to kill eagles or Pechaqueh nobles, if that was the order they were given for the morrow?

She looked back to where Omeata was whispering in the

tall warrior's ear. They nodded, pressed their palms together in acknowledgment, and then vanished into the jungle.

Something cold and hard formed in the pit of Ilandeh's stomach. She wouldn't be surprised to learn in the coming weeks that Zellih war parties were destroying every pyramid they came across after she'd so loudly proclaimed that to be the cause of this silence. Rebels were already doing it – this very place was testament to that – but if the Zellih did the same, it could tip the scales into entire swathes, even whole lands, emerging from under the song's sway.

Next to her, Pikte shifted and there was a sudden hot sting across Ilandeh's forearm. She jerked away. There was a thin red line in her skin and a few beads of blood. Ilandeh glared at him, but he'd already made the knife vanish again. A warning; a promise. He, too, knew what Omeata had likely told the warrior.

Instead of helping Ilandeh to gain the Bird-form's trust, Pikte was warning her against any further revelations that might harm the Melody. As if this wasn't what Whispers did, how they were so effective at cultivating trust and infiltrating communities. This balancing of risks, the push-pull of what to reveal and what to hide, what information could be sacrificed to further their ultimate aim, was the backbone of a Whisper's method.

Ilandeh was walking the edge of an obsidian blade with no option but to keep putting one foot in front of the other. Never before had she had to work so hard or hold so many different stories, lies, truths together. Enough to fool Omeata and the Zellih on one side, and her fellow Whispers on the other, into each thinking her loyalty lay only with them.

'Where in the war party do you want us, Bird-form?' she asked, slipping her scratched arm behind her back.

'Why, warriors, I want you in the front line,' Omeata said. 'You have much to prove, do you not?'

Ilandeh swallowed. 'You honour us.'

The Bird-form cocked her head. 'I do,' she agreed and then swaggered away, her guards falling in around her.

As soon as they weren't being watched, the Whisper grabbed Pikte's arm and dug her thumb hard into the pressure point inside his elbow. He hissed and jerked, but she held on. 'Threaten me again and you won't live to carry out whatever instructions Beyt gave you,' she said in a low voice, and then clapped him on the back and offered him a warm smile. She didn't wait for a response, didn't bother to explain to a confused Olox; she turned back into the silence and examined the ground beneath the trees for a likely resting place.

By the time she finally glanced back at them, the pair were cutting palm and ferns to build a rain shelter big enough only for two. Every move Pikte made served only to show the Zellih the cracks forming between them. Ilandeh needed to fix their relationship – or end it permanently.

Leaving them to it, Ilandeh built her own shelter while all around them, the war party settled and night – who was also Nallac – cast their blanket over them.

The Whisper crawled into the small, low space she'd built and lay on her side looking up and out. Through a shifting gap in the canopy, she could see the stars, put there by the mischievous black-handed spider monkey, who'd poked his fingers through Nallac's blanket of night to expose the eternal light beyond. In punishment, his hands, and those of all his descendants, were stained with darkness.

The story came back to her with the force of the Wet and Ilandeh found herself smiling as she curled under her shelter's green-scented roof, remembering her mother telling her that he'd done it to deny night a place in the world, for darkness meant danger for all small, soft creatures such as himself. His courage made him beloved of all like beings, and even Nallac couldn't help but admire his ingenuity – it was why they had allowed the holes to remain and become the stars, guides for those who knew how to read them, and faint light for all else by which to see and run and hide.

Her mother's voice, hazy with time and deliberate distance, returned too, along with the admonition for the young Ilandeh, the impressionable Ilandeh, to never forget the black-handed spider monkey's lesson. Do wrong, but only if it accomplishes a greater right.

That memory had been lost to her for most of her life, and Ilandeh hated that it haunted her now. Hated that of all the legends she'd learnt, it was the black-handed spider monkey who stole darkness from the night that had remained unremembered all this time, waiting to pounce.

Do wrong if it accomplishes a greater right. Is this what you meant, Mother? Am I finally living the lesson you tried to teach me?

Ilandeh stared up at the canopy some more, unseeing now, unsmiling. Again, she mourned the loss of her beautiful, narrow, blind obedience.

She rolled over and shut her eyes. Gods, but she hated this. Hated all of it. She clutched her spear to her chest.

Hated everyone.

'If they're Pechaqueh, kill them. If they raise weapons against us, kill them. If they run, kill them.' Ilandeh translated the Pallatolli for her companions. Olox murmured a shocked protest and she trod heavily on his foot.

Omeata looked at them and switched to Ixachitaan. 'We don't know where they're running. Could be to reinforcements, could be to a cache of weapons. If they surrender, they live. Anything else, and they do not.'

'But,' Olox tried and Ilandeh stamped again, even harder. He cut off with a pained grunt.

'They stand with us, they stand aside, or they die. We have neither time nor inclination for mercy,' Omeata added. 'You were Melody warriors, were you not? You should be used to slaughtering innocents.' She smiled at Ilandeh's flinch.

'Are these the same orders all your war parties have been given?' Ilandeh struck back. Her palms were damp and not only at the prospect of what was to come.

'All our flocks?' Omeata asked in Pallatolli with wide-eyed innocence. 'Whatever do you mean?'

Flocks, yes, she remembered suddenly. *That's what they call their war parties. Because of how they move, seemingly without discipline.*

That didn't help her now, though, so the Whisper backed down. Now wasn't the time to push the Bird-form. 'Do we three still have the honour of being in your front line?' she asked instead, copying the change in language.

'You certainly do,' Omeata replied with a smirk. 'In fact, Huenoch has requested the honour of fighting beside you. They are keen to see your skills and determine how much of a loss to the Melody you are.'

Ilandeh pressed her palms together and nodded at the tall warrior. 'The honour is great,' she said as if unaware that Huenoch was more a threat to the Whispers than to the enemy. She knew Pikte and Olox would understand that when she told them.

'In fact, you may move to the front now,' the Bird-form added, flicking her fingers. She still wore her huipil of humming-bird feathers, and the purple paint across her eyes was fresh and vibrant. Everyone in the war party – the flock – had painted themselves. The Whispers had done likewise, and all three bore representations of Nallac on their arms. The god of Xentib and Axib alike.

Ilandeh suspected Pikte, at least, would have painted something else, some devotion to the Singer or the song, even the world spirit, on his belly or chest where it couldn't be seen. His hand had drifted to the tattoo of the chulul on his shoulder more than once; he did it again now as they wove through the ranks and she used the narrowness of the path to step close and slap lightly at his fingers.

He jerked and met her eyes; she frowned at his tattoo and was gratified to see understanding and embarrassment flicker over his features. He was a Whisper; he should have better control of himself than this. His hand fell from his shoulder and he straightened his back and walked faster, sliding between the Zellih. Ilandeh, Olox, and Huenoch followed until there were only two lines of warriors between them and the trail.

The City of Glass crouched above them as they marched up the long road winding about the plateau. They'd be spotted soon and their intentions couldn't be mistaken for anything other than hostile. There would be Pechaqueh up there, civilians and retired warriors. Children and old folk. Omeata hadn't said kill those Pechaqueh who fight back. She'd said, "If they're Pechaqueh, kill them." That was more than just a test for the strangers who'd requested to join the Zellih cause; it was an order for all the warriors of her flock.

But also a test.

Huenoch walked in intent silence and Ilandeh breathed and wondered if she would need to kill them and her companions during the coming slaughter. And if she could. Only the most experienced Whispers were ever tasked with taking Pechqueh life, nearly always as political assassination rather than in combat. And this wouldn't even be that – this would be their disguises rendered in blood, the proof and truth of their stories given physical, violent form. What would Olox do when confronted with the requirement to cut down the people he believed were chosen by the gods to rule the Empire of Songs?

Ilandeh had killed Pechaqueh, not just in self-defence since the start of the Great Betrayal but on Pilos's orders over the years and in defence of Tayan when he'd been Shadow. Her concern wasn't whether she could kill a Pecha, even an unarmed one; it was whether she could stop once she began.

Her own wilful murder of Pechaqueh wouldn't be enough if Olox and Pikte faltered, though. If Huenoch saw anything suspicious, they'd either attack the Whispers immediately or inform Omeata. And of course, being in the front line was yet another of Omeata's tests. *Prove your loyalty. Prove the truth of your words and promises, your tales of woe and abandonment, your desire for vengeance.*

Make me believe it.

Making Omeata believe it would come down to more than just killing Pechaqueh, if there was a "just" to be found in any of this. It would be down to what Ilandeh did if her companions refused the Bird-form's order. Omeata didn't care about them; she cared about Ilandeh and what she'd do. All this was her test. Whether Olox and Pikte survived meant nothing to the Zellitli. Ilandeh wondered how much it truly meant to her.

The front ranks of the flock rounded a corner and the City of Glass appeared, outlined against the multi-hued grey of the sky. Already Nallac was muttering their discontent, the storm god's warnings going unheeded by all but Ilandeh.

'We hear you, god of storm and sky, star and sea. Whether lightning strike or fire spark, you kindle with us and for us. Your body holds the seed and gives the seed; you grow the plant and water the plant. Bring; take; give; steal. We fight now for balance. We ask that you grant it to help all who walk beneath your sky.'

Ilandeh spoke the prayer in time with her stride and tried not to think of the other times she'd heard it, chanted with a fearful desperation as the Melody drew closer and Xentib lives were threatened – a Melody that had contained Ilandeh, marching to the song's beat and the High Feather's orders. A half-Xenti born well before that people had been brought under the song, because her mother had foreseen what was to come and acted on it. Given herself to a Pecha and Ilandeh had never asked why.

Ilandeh the half-blood. The murderer. The coward.

Why was she marching up this hill to a peaceful city in order to destroy it at the whim of a Zellitli and under the orders of the Spear of the Singer, who'd betrayed and almost murdered her?

And yet even as she asked herself those questions, Ilandeh marched. Climbed. Checked her weapons and her armour. Because where she was going now aligned with both Omeata's and Pilos's designs for her, and possibly her own, insofar as she had any, and so she let them push her onward. Once again, it was easier to give in to the whims of others.

Above them, the warning drum sounded and the City of Glass's gates slammed shut.

An answering rumble, from thousands of warriors' throats and Ilandeh's own, and the war party broke into a run up the last bend in the trail.

The Zellih had come to Ixachipan, and they had no mercy in their hearts.

THE LISTENER

Empire of Songs
56th day of the Great Star at morning

There is a lamentation within the song. A slow grinding of—
   No. You will not do this. You will not appear in my mind and simply begin speaking, preaching, mocking. Who do you think you are? You will tell me your name or I will crush you in this life and all the lives to come. I will destroy you. I will *make you irrelevant.* Now, you will identify yourself.
   Those are not the right questions. The holy Setatmeh are running out of time. Every time another spirit—
   Stop talking. Stop. I will not be disrespected like this.
   Holy lord, you must feed—
   GET. OUT!

THE SINGER

*The source, Singing City, Pechacan, Empire of Songs
56th day of the Great Star at morning*

'*I want to know who they are*,' Tayan shouted, flinging a plate towards the colonnade. It shattered against stone and Chorus warriors ducked flying shards of pottery. From the gardens came distant shouts of alarm and running figures; a Chorus stepped out to reassure them there was no danger.

Tayan ignored them.

'Who the fuck thinks to come into *my song* and speak to me as if they know me? And refuse to identify themself? They must be discovered and destroyed! I will not be violated like this!'

'Holy lord, I cannot advise on this matter,' Xochi said. 'The song-magic is not something I have any experience in. Perhaps the Listeners across Ixachipan can—'

Tayan threw his cup, water arcing from its lip to splatter the cushions, the mats, and the Chorus Leader's salt-cotton as she dodged. 'There is a spy within the song,' he yelled. 'Don't you understand what that means? The danger it presents? Twice now someone has simply appeared to mock me, refusing to name themself or state their purpose, speaking in riddles *to me*. To *their Singer*. Is there anyone in this fucking pyramid who understands what this means?'

He looked to the offering pool, because his god would see the danger, but the water was empty, churning gently as the waterwheel in the pyramid's foundations forced it up and into the pool and out and down the building's side. Over and over.

There were no cushions arrayed beyond the hanging where the Singer's council would sit; Tayan had no councillors. Xac had taken all of them to the waters with him, song be praised, and his successor had no desire to be plagued with more. Now, though . . . now he wished for someone, one single person, who understood the pressures he was facing.

'High Feather Atu and Feather Pilos, Spear—'

Tayan let out a scream of pure frustration, one clearly misinterpreted by the two warriors, for they sprinted into the source with their weapons at the ready.

'Peace, warriors, peace,' Xochi cried, waving her arms. 'There is no danger here.'

The Singer rounded on her, fists clenched by his cheeks. 'No danger? I've just fucking told you of the danger we are all in.' Atu and Pilos exchanged alarmed looks. 'There is a spy within my song. Someone who came to me, Listened to me while concealing their identity. Someone who knows things they shouldn't about the magic and who claims to know what ails the holy Setatmeh, yet will not tell me who they are or how they can possibly have such knowledge when I, as Singer, do not!'

He stared at the three warriors facing him, dread slicking his gut. 'What do you know of this? What do you know of the holy Setatmeh? You are Pechaqueh – was it one of you, seeking to destroy my authority?'

'*Holy lord*,' Atu said so forcefully that Tayan took a step back. 'You are overwrought and we have much to discuss about the war. Please—'

'Aren't you listening?' he screamed, stamping his foot and looking for something else to throw, the flesh of his arms and hands coiling with gold. 'There is a spy in my song and you pester me with the war? That is yours to command, yours to win. Are you incapable of making a single decision on your own? Why don't you bend over so I can wipe your arses for you while you whinge about the fucking war?'

Atu's jaw bulged as he clenched his teeth, but his voice was calm. 'The Zellih have launched attacks across the north. They have shown themselves, and they are numerous and merciless.'

'Setatmeh have mercy,' Xochi breathed into the echoing silence.

Tayan sucked in a breath to shout some more when the High Feather's words sank into his consciousness. 'You, you said they'd disappeared back into Zellipan, that we didn't need to worry,' he said, flabbergasted. 'You said we could abandon the north because it wouldn't be a threat. That it was under control.'

Atu bowed his head. 'I did, holy lord.'

'Where did they attack?' he managed, retreating to the safety of his cushions and pointing opposite. The High Feather looked sick; Pilos looked haunted. He was carrying a roll of bark-paper and spread it on the mats between them, angled to face his Singer. The map of Ixachipan.

'Here,' he said, pointing. 'And here. And here.'

Tayan watched his finger as if it was a poisonous snake as it traced across three locations in Chitenec. 'But that's . . .' he began, with no idea what he was going to say next.

'Three cities, all peaceful under the song,' Pilos continued, voice neutral but relentless. 'All peopled with Pechaqueh, loyal free, and loyal slaves, and all a week's march from the border with Pechacan. Each had a Listener who relayed word of the attack before they were killed. None had a significant Melody presence. With the Listeners dead, we have no way to tell what the Zellih wanted or who won, how many citizens still live, whether the Zellih have retained control of the cities, or what happened to any survivors. We do know they appeared to show no mercy to Pechaqueh, warriors or not.'

The Singer frowned. 'I don't understand. They were seen in Tokoban, not Chitenec. When did these attacks happen? How did they get from one city to the next without word of the battle or their movement reaching us?'

Pilos coughed. 'Holy lord, the attacks all happened today.

At dawn.' Tayan just stared at him, waiting for it to make sense. 'There are three confirmed Zellih war parties in Chitenec, holy lord, each large enough to take a city in a single day.'

The Singer laughed, shrill. 'That's not possible. They must be traitors pretending to be Zellih. There can't be Zellih in the Empire of Songs. Not in Chitenec. How could they get to Chitenec? How, Spear?'

His temper, already frayed from the stranger's presence in his song, was ready to snap. He shuffled up onto his knees and grabbed Pilos's forearm, digging in his fingernails. '*Tell me how,*' he hissed.

The muscles in the Spear's arm tensed, standing out in cords under his Singer's grip, and then relaxed again. 'We didn't have enough people with the right skills in place in the north to discover them sooner, holy lord. Some Whispers scattered across the three lands, but we were relying on hearsay and rumour from the Listeners, much of it filtered through frightened gossip. Shadows under the trees, evidence of people passing, a glimpse of warriors moving on an exposed ridge bare of vegetation. It was never enough for us to hunt them down and confirm their presence. But then Ilandeh turned up in Yalotlan near the Chitenec border and I gave her the location of an unidentified war party that might have been Zellih. She went to track it. She and two others are with the warriors that took the City of Glass under the Zellih Bird-form, if they survived, and—'

'Ilandeh? Former Chorus Leader Ilandeh? What do you mean, she's with the Bird-form's war party? You said Whispers.' He didn't wait for another mumbled, inane explanation; he tore into Pilos's mind and found it himself. It took only a moment, Pilos's defences as able to withstand his Singer's advance as the foam on a cup of beer.

Ilandeh was a half-blood? Gods and ancestors, that was your plan? That was her secret? he asked within Pilos's mind. He paused just long enough to marvel at how effortless she'd made it seem, here in this very source. *I suppose, in light of my own unique experiences of the last months, I understand your position, Spear. I also understand – and appreciate – hers. Your contempt of Chorus Leader Ilandeh, despite all she did for you, is quite astonishing. And, dare I say it, its bite is familiar. Yet your sense of superiority was so fragile that when she dared to question you, you betrayed her.*

Tayan snorted at the rich purple flood of fury that Pilos was utterly unable to quell.

'You trusted her more than any eagle under your command, until she stepped out of the place you'd made for her,' he said aloud. 'The cage you'd built around her. Which of you was in the wrong, Spear? Isn't it truer to say that she was a daily reminder of competence and you couldn't bear it, the idea that maybe the people you rule and disdain are actually your equals?'

They are not, Pilos replied immediately, bursting with the bright sunset-orange of conviction. *They would not reject the song if they were. They would not struggle to understand all we do for them, the good we bring to their small lives. They—*

'Ilandeh never rejected the song.' Tayan spoke over him. 'She knew intimately the benefits of this Empire; why else dedicate her life to its expansion and stable government?' There was a long pause. 'What, no more words?' he mocked. He slipped from Pilos's mind before the Spear could babble an answer, then sat back on his heels with a ragged exhalation and let his mockery fade as the full import of Ilandeh's abilities and the risk she was taking settled on him. 'She's doing to the Zellih what she did to—in the Sky City.'

'Eventually, yes, Singer,' Atu said for Pilos, who was breathing deeply and wiping the sweat from his brow from Tayan's intrusion. 'But for now she's learning what she can and informing us when she can. She cannot Listen of her own accord, so if she has information for us, she must find a way to escape Zellih notice without arousing suspicion and then locate a pyramid with a Listener. It makes communication difficult.'

Tayan waved his hand, cutting him off. He closed his eyes and slipped into his song again, but this time he thought of Ilandeh, the shape and taste of her spirit. There.

'—traumatic communion will destroy her disguise,' Atu was fretting.

'Quiet.'

Tayan slid to the edge of Ilandeh's consciousness and then in, soft as moonlight shadowing the face of a beloved. The Whisper was in what must be the City of Glass and she was dragging a corpse by its arms, shuffling backwards. He could feel her exhaustion, not just from the physical labour of moving the dead but from the hours of fighting that had created those dead. Fatigue was a poison and she was full to the brim with it, her hands and arms sticky with blood, more spattering her legs when she glanced down to check her step. Ilandeh dragged the body to a pile of others and heaved it into place, then straightened and stretched, fists pressed against her spine and back arched so she was looking up into the sky. The sun was falling behind the clouds, but it wasn't raining where she was.

'Mixed-blood. The Bird-form requires your presence,' a voice shouted in Pallatolli and Ilandeh's head whipped around.

'Ilandeh, go and speak with the Bird-form and know that I hear their words as well. Get me something I can use, their next target, their ultimate goal. Anything.'

The Whisper had stilled when he spoke inside her, her breathing rough. *Tayan?* she ventured, disbelieving.

'Your Singer,' he confirmed. 'Now go.'

She took another couple of breaths and then did as ordered, sweeping him into the Bird-form's presence.

'You are lucky I speak the tongue of Barazal. Ilandeh, Olox, and Pikte survived the City of Glass's destruction. They slaughtered civilian Pechaqueh as well as any who stood against the Zellih. Bird-form Omeata is pleased with them and they have a place in her flock; her war party.'

Tayan's eyes opened. Pilos and Atu were intent. 'Omeata has told them nothing about any other attacks. Nothing about why they are fighting, though they have promised that will come. Zellih killed Pechaqueh without mercy but allowed no-bloods who surrendered to live. Like the rebels, they are coming for Pechaqueh society. They are coming for me.'

He scrubbed his hands over his face. 'The traitors are ignorant and they are angry. Their treatment has been less than kind and I understand them rising against us even if I do not condone it. They are children breaking what they're not allowed to share. But the Zellih; their grievance was historic and with the Tokob, disputes over land and salt rights mostly, despite the plenitude of it sitting on the pans between us. Regardless, if Omeata won't talk to Ilandeh, we won't know what they want and we can't weave a peace.'

'She'll get the Bird-form to talk,' Pilos promised, 'but I don't know how long it will take. As for the other war parties, we have Whispers within a few days' run of each. If you could contact them, holy lord, or the closest Listener, to relay orders to infiltrate or ally, we may learn more. At the least, we'll get updates on their movements and likely next targets.'

'We should also think about moving a Talon back to Chitenec,' Atu added and Tayan barked a laugh.

'Didn't we just move them out because Chitenec is peaceful? Don't we need them elsewhere?'

'We did and we do, holy lord, yet we also need to evaluate the threat level.'

Tayan flopped onto his back among the cushions and stared up at the lavishly painted mural above him. 'I just want some good news. Just one fucking day where everything goes right, where there is no new catastrophe to manage,' he grumbled. There was nothing but embarrassed silence from the warriors. 'Xochi, tell me what we've accomplished so far,' he said, needing the now-familiar litany to soothe his spirits.

Xochi's sandals whispered across the mats as she stepped closer. 'Chitenec and Tlalotlan are both back in Pechaqueh hands, great Singer, the last of the rebels dying or surrendering. The storms on the Quitoban coast have flooded the chinampas and tidal marshes, causing widespread devastation and effectively ending any cohesive rebellion in that part of the land. They're more concerned with saving their crops where they can; High Feather Atu has sent the Fifth Talon to maintain order. They'll claim the harvest and then ration it out to those who surrender or provide information on the locations of rebel strongholds. In the south, only Axiban continues to fight hard, but they're being squeezed from three sides. They can't hold out much longer. And Feather Detta and the Second Talon marched into the Singing City yesterday.'

The relief in her voice at that last was profound, yet her words didn't soothe the way they used to.

'The Fourth and Sixth Talons are in Xentiban to protect us from any northern unrest, only the unrest is in the west, in Chitenec, and it's Zellih,' he said sourly, 'while the actual north appears to be . . . what? A major city hasn't fallen to the rebels in a week; I get reports from Listeners daily and they seem to be holding. What of Xentiban?'

'The rebels are struggling against the numbers of two full Talons,' Atu said. 'Resistance is crumbling; we're gaining ground.'

'So despite everything, we're winning everywhere. And as soon as we are, these Zellih appear to upset the balance again. Forgive me if it feels deliberate.'

It wasn't a question and he waved away the need for anyone to answer, sitting up again with a grunt. It also stopped them contradicting his assertion of imminent victory. Tayan knew his view was simplistic; he also didn't care. He needed the illusion, just for now, that something was under his control and moving towards the desired outcome. He *needed it*.

Because despite his own words, they weren't winning everywhere. At best they were fighting to a standstill in Yalotlan and Tokoban. Chitenec was no longer peaceful. Axiban seemed determined to drown itself in blood. And they weren't even restoring peace here, in Pechacan, birthplace of the song-magic. They couldn't restore it in the heart-city where it was most needed.

Because of Xessa. Because of Lilla.

'Ilandeh doesn't know what the Zellih want. Did any of the Listeners who reached you during the attacks have theories?

And Xochi, you've been a faithful adviser to me these last weeks; sit with us,' the Singer said. 'Let's talk this through face to face, without formality.'

Despite his seeming concentration, a large splinter of Tayan's consciousness was prowling the song, searching for the stranger who had dared to confront him. Another, smaller sliver was lodged in Ilandeh's consciousness. It was uncomfortable and disorienting, but the Whisper was a crucial pair of eyes on the situation in Chitenec and he couldn't afford to miss anything she experienced.

When the four of them were seated on cushions with cups of water at their elbows, Tayan spread his hands. 'Talk to me. What are our options? All of our options, big, small, stupid, impossible. What do we need to end this?'

'More warriors,' Pilos said.

'Fewer enemies,' Atu said at the same time. They glanced at each other and shared a grim, familiar smile.

'Both would be preferable,' the Spear acknowledged with such dry humour that he startled Tayan into a laugh.

'Make an alliance.' Three sets of eyes swivelled to Xochi and the Chorus Leader blushed and then raised her chin. 'Make an alliance and we get more warriors and fewer enemies. Just because the Zellih with Ilandeh killed Pechaqueh and let no-bloods live doesn't prove they're here to end the Empire. It could just be a show of strength to put themselves in a position to make demands. If we find out what those demands are, we may be able to reach an agreement. And if we can, that's three confirmed Zellih war parties to reinforce us – more allies, fewer enemies.' She offered a small smile to Pilos.

Tayan pursed his lips and then gestured. 'Well? Ilandeh had no best guesses for me; what secrets did she tell you? Is this just an opportunistic land grab while the Empire of Songs eats itself, or is there more to it? Can we buy them?'

'It depends on their price, Singer,' Pilos said eventually. 'Ilandeh will need to propose it in a way that doesn't reveal her to be our agent, which will be difficult as long as she is not fully trusted. If we wish her to maintain her disguise, we must be patient. If we wish for the offer to be made now, any growing trust on the Bird-form's part will be lost and Ilandeh will be once more on the outside of any decision-making. We will lose any possible knowledge of the other war parties' movements, at least until we can get other Whispers infiltrating or shadowing them.'

'And before any offer of alliance is made, we need to agree on the concessions Ilandeh has the authority to offer. What can we give them in return for their aid against the traitors? Forgive me, holy lord, but they have been Tokob ancestral enemies for generations. What if their demand is Tokoban?'

Tayan looked blankly at Atu. 'What do you mean?'

'What if they wish to extend the border of Zellipan over the salt pans and into Tokoban, to claim it for their own? Is the Singer prepared to concede possession of an entire land in Ixachipan to the Zellih to end this uprising?'

'I . . .' He didn't know what to say. The thought of giving Tokoban to the Zellih made him sick. It was his land, his birthplace, and he was Singer. He should be able to defend it. But one land in return for all the rest? Perhaps it wasn't so much to ask. And the Tokob were the god-killers – the only true god-killers. They needed to face justice for that.

Against his will, memories of a lifetime in the Sky City battered at him: his childhood with Xessa, his decision to walk the spiral path of a shaman, his initiation, meeting Lilla, the first time he communed with Malel, his wedding day . . .

Xochi spoke, shattering the bright shining whirl of images before the silence could become embarrassing. 'Forgive this one for speaking in such company, but it is Chitenec they are conquering. It may be that land they wish to claim. As for an alliance, they may already have sided with the traitors, and that is why they let no-bloods live but not Pechaqueh. The Zellih began moving at our borders a few scant months before the uprising. I find it hard to believe it is mere coincidence that they travelled across the salt pans on a whim and within months Ixachipan is ablaze.' She looked apologetic despite that her words had the ring of truth to them.

'No such alliance was made with Tokob elders before they were brought under the song. I was a member of the shamanic conclave; nothing happened without our knowledge. So if not Tokob, then who? The Chitenecah? Then why are they destroying cities there?'

'Perhaps the agreement was made after the fall of Tokoban and that is why you do not know of it. Some of the free who settled that land may have been traitors who travelled into Zellipan to buy reinforcements at the very time we thought we'd finally made a peace,' Xochi said quietly.

'We cannot know for sure,' Tayan snapped and Xochi bowed under the rebuke. 'Not until they either declare it openly or Ilandeh discovers it. You,' he added, turning on Atu. 'You said it was safe to abandon the north. You have yet to give me an explanation for this.'

'In light of this new intelligence, it's clear that executing Tokob and all who fled north was a mistake,' the High Feather said slowly, 'because if they'd run into Zellih war parties trying to claim their land, they'd absolutely have resisted. And yet, although we are fighting a war, not every decision can be made purely from a military point of view. We could not – *will not* – risk our holy Setatmeh by allowing maddened Tokob and their frog-licking god-killers to roam the north unchecked. We had to choose between the possibility of losing the north and doing all we could to preserve our gods. Only history will tell whether we chose right, great Singer. But choose we did, and it cannot be unchosen now.'

Tayan's heart was beating in his throat and he knew his every emotion was flickering across his face like cloud shadows. The source was quiet, oppressive with humidity and not enough breeze. 'So. We come back to Ilandeh,' he managed at last. He cut his eyes at Pilos. 'Perhaps the fate of the Empire of Songs rests on her shoulders. Try not to kill her this time.'

'As the holy lord commands,' Pilos said tightly. 'If I may be permitted to make a suggestion?' Tayan nodded. 'We should start a rumour among the rebels that there are Zellih war parties ravaging the north. That they are there at the rebels' own invitation, and that any lands they capture they can keep as a reward for allying. Make it clear that the traitors waited to rise until Tokob and Yaloh were enslaved and removed from their lands so that the Zellih could claim territory more easily.'

'And when Chitenecah, Tokob and Yaloh abandon the fight here to go home, you execute them again?' Tayan asked sourly.

'Or not,' Pilos replied. 'Maybe we do let them go home. Maybe we let them flood Chitenec and sweep the Zellih before them. Even if there is an alliance, it may not survive such a rumour because the ordinary traitors, those not in command, they didn't agree to any such thing. They're fighting to regain their ancestral lands and there is no victory without them. We could let the traitors and the Zellih kill each other while we restore order in the rest of the Empire. It isn't perfect, holy lord, but it may buy us one of those things we wanted: it may buy us fewer enemies.'

There was a long silence and Tayan let it stretch as he imagined it, the north in flames again, each side getting weaker as they fought and killed and died until the Melody could sweep up their broken pieces and dispose of them.

But—

'What of the holy Setatmeh in the north?'

Pilos's shoulders slumped and he spread his hands. 'That is beyond my area of expertise, Singer. All I can say is that we acted once in an effort to preserve the gods and it contributed, in some way, to the current situation. Can we afford to do the same again? That is not a question I can answer. I know what my heart tells me, but hearts are often liars in war.'

'It is a risk, holy lord, but if it worked, if the rumour started in such a way that no one could trace it back to us, it could change the outcome of this war in our favour,' Atu added.

Tayan took a deep breath and curled song and magic within his lungs to strengthen his voice. 'Do it,' he said and his words glittered as they fell from his lips. 'I will find a way to protect my divine ancestors; I swear it.'

LILLA

Pilos's fighting pit, entertainment district, Singing City,
Pechacan, Empire of Songs
60th day of the Great Star at morning

Lilla startled awake, a cry of recognition and longing trapped behind his teeth. The tatters of the dream faded, the image of Tayan walking away from him – leaving him – saying "kill them all" – once again the only thing he could remember and the very last thing he wanted to.

Or perhaps not a dream. Perhaps Tayan had invaded his sleeping mind as he periodically did his waking one, searching for answers, for their location, for their next move or decision. Perhaps he'd put that memory there as a torment. Was this what they were to each other now? Were the only gifts from nearly a decade of marriage weapons with which to cut at each other?

Lilla rolled over carefully, not just because the cage was crowded – *too crowded, too many people* – but in case his head split open and his brains fell out. Tayan had Listened to him three times in the last ten days, each invasion triggering another of his headaches as he'd fought to prevent his husband from scrabbling through his every thought and memory and to keep their location a secret.

Not even the primitive defence of closing his eyes and stopping his ears could prevent Tayan's intrusion as he searched for clues to better destroy those who rejected his call. Lilla had tried asking what had made him like this, had tried begging, had thrown memories at him, both sweet and bitter. Tayan – the Singer – had swept all of it aside and dug into his head like a ripe mango.

Because of it, Lilla was no longer joint war leader with Ekon. He had no role in the decision-making anymore, nor did he know the numbers of their wounded or the state of their rations. Anything that Tayan might learn and use against them, he couldn't know. He'd offered to go it alone, separating himself from the war party to keep them safe.

To his surprise, it had been Xessa who disagreed, pointing out that if Tayan could find him, he could find her and Tiamoko and Toxte, probably any Toko he wanted to. If Lilla left the war party, Tayan would just find someone else to Listen to. At least this way, they knew who he would target and could feed the Melody false information.

He heard muted conversation and the shift of bodies and opened his eyes to cautious, wincing slits, but there was no pain. Hadn't been for two days, but still the fear of it lingered like vomit at the back of his tongue. He focused and found Ekon's face close enough to kiss, his eyes closed and lips parted.

Against his will, Lilla's face softened out of the expectation of pain and he studied the man curled on the dirt next to him. Fatigue, and the rigours of both battle and command were carved deep, and there was tension around Ekon's mouth even as he slept. One hand was fisted very gently in Lilla's salt-cotton, keeping him close. *Keeping me safe.* The other was cushioning his cheek from the hard floor, little finger curled softly against the fading bruise around his eye. He'd shaved the sides of his head above his ears in Chitenecah fashion, and Lilla brushed his fingertip against the fine fuzz of regrowing stubble, so gentle as to almost not be contact at all.

Ekon's eyes opened anyway, alert and wary with no

transition from sleep. Lilla flattened his palm over the man's cheek and grimaced. 'Sorry,' he mouthed. The edges of Ekon's eyes crinkled in the smallest smile.

His gaze drifted sideways and then he smiled again, a little bigger. 'Everyone's gone,' he murmured. 'We must have slept late.' Lilla looked over his shoulder and found the cell empty; that must have been what woke him. Though they had more than enough space to spread out now, he didn't move.

The Melody hadn't found them yet and Lilla wondered if the rebels had decided to stay and just rest for a few days. He wanted to ask and couldn't. Wanted to help Ekon bear the burden of command and couldn't. Were the other war parties in the entertainment district? He had no idea.

It was on the tip of his tongue to apologise, but he didn't do that, either. Ekon didn't need the burden of his guilt on top of everything else. Ekon needed . . . a lessening of his burdens. Or something else to focus on. Lilla concentrated on sweeping his thumb across the Chitenecah cheekbone, not quite meeting his eyes.

'I'd like you to do something for me,' he murmured. Ekon made an inquisitive noise. 'I'd like you to take the marriage cord off my ankle and dispose of it.'

Ekon stilled, even his chest, his breath. Lilla licked his lips and made himself look into his eyes. 'I don't know how you feel—' He cut himself off, fingers tightening on Ekon's face. 'That's not true. I do know – or I think I know. I . . . hope I know.'

The Chitenecah hand tightened in Lilla's salt-cotton, hope and caution warring for dominance. 'You do know,' he whispered. 'But I don't understand what you're asking.'

'It is a practice among my people. When the mourning of a dead spouse is done, or when a new start in life is sought, we take off the marriage cord. Many widowed people keep it as a symbol of a love lost but not forgotten, while those whose marriages end in heartache or failure sometimes choose to destroy it. Others simply bury it.' He took a very deep breath. 'And some people ask a new loved one to dispose of it for them.'

The noise Ekon made this time was wounded, as if Lilla had stabbed him. 'Are you—'

'I'm sure. Yes, I'm sure. Until recently, I clung to the belief there might be something to salvage between Tay and me. I no longer believe that. The things he's done . . . That is not the man I married. It—'

'You don't need to tell me this, kitten,' Ekon murmured, shifting on the stone so their legs tangled together. He still hadn't let go of Lilla's salt-cotton. 'You've never needed to justify yourself.'

Lilla slid his hand from Ekon's cheek back into his hair and scratched gently at his scalp until he shivered, a full-body reflex. 'Liar,' he said affectionately, his heart suddenly easing at the sight of Ekon relaxing like a cat in a sunbeam under his touch. 'You've done nothing but make me justify everything I've ever said or thought or done since we met.' He tightened his hand into a fist, Ekon's hair wrapped in it, and watched the man's pupils dilate. The noise he made was small but eloquent and Lilla shivered again. 'And I've done nothing but reject and hurt you, over and over. I didn't know myself, my mind, or what I wanted, and I know it caused – I caused – you pain.'

'Please don't,' Ekon murmured with seeming difficulty. 'We both said and did things we regret, but we're both here now. Alive, just about. Faithful to our gods if nothing else. Can we—'

'Kiss me,' Lilla whispered.

There was a jerk on his salt-cotton and then Ekon surged against him and seized his mouth with his own. He'd expected something soft, chaste, perhaps even hesitant, but it was as though his words had broken the barrier keeping a landslide at bay.

Ekon's breath punched out of him as their mouths met, a moan part-desperation and mostly feral, a growl of need and relief that sent a bolt of arousal from Lilla's chest to his cock and on into his toes. Their mouths were sour with sleep and it didn't matter when Ekon's tongue pushed past his lips and teeth, carried on another moan, and then his hand was on Lilla's hip, pushing him flat against the stone so he could roll half on top of him. Lilla gasped into the kiss and found his own hands clutching at filthy salt-cotton and seeking beneath it for hot, grimy skin, his hips shifting with little needy twitches he couldn't control and didn't want to. He wasn't even hard, though it wouldn't take long; he just wanted, needed, closeness. As close as they could get in daylight, in public, while dressed.

Only we're not in public. We're alone. Lilla had traded his too-tight leggings for a kilt and was glad of it now when Ekon grabbed his thigh and pulled it up around his hip. The Toko wrapped his other leg around him too and the noises they made were obscene and echoed loud in the stone room and out through the bamboo gate. Neither cared. It was as good a warning as any other to anyone in this part of the fighting pit to leave them undisturbed and so Lilla felt neither shame nor hesitation in seizing Ekon's tunic and dragging it over his head.

He got his mouth on a nipple when Ekon stretched up to pull his hair free and sucked hard; Ekon squirmed and mewled but didn't stop him, long fingers wrapping around the back of his head to hold it there. His other hand was braced by Lilla's head and he used the leverage to roll his hips down and forward and the Toko had to break off his assault to gasp a half-formed, heartfelt '*yes*'.

Ekon flattened him to the stone again and seemed intent on devouring him, on stripping him and fucking him despite the lack of privacy or oil and Lilla had half a mind to let him. To beg him to do it. He bucked upwards as Ekon's hand slid beneath his armour and tunic, fingers hot and calloused and strong as they gripped his flank, just missing the mostly healed wound along his hip. Gods, but he wanted him, wanted him to fuck the last of the hurt – all his hurts – right out of him. No more pain, no more doubt, no more being torn between two loves. Just a good man, and a good fucking, and the deep, world-shattering pleasure of being filled up. Lilla moaned and it was loud and unashamed, more eloquent than any words he could ever say.

Ekon tore his mouth away. His eyes were wild in the gloom, his lips bruised from kissing, his chest heaving. 'Sorry, I'm sorry, is this too much?' he gasped, not looking sorry at all but leaning back anyway.

Perhaps not so eloquent as all that, then. Lilla tightened his legs around the Chitenecah waist, hauling his weight back onto him. Stitches pulled and wounds flared, but Ekon ground helplessly down again and a strangled gasp of pleasure bounced and slithered across the wall. 'Not too much,' Lilla managed. 'Not enough. *Not enough.*'

Ekon stilled again, and then pulled himself from Lilla's grip and collapsed onto his side next to him. Lilla reached for him and the Chitenecatl pinned him easily to the floor with a hand on the centre of his chest, sending another bolt of pleasure through him. He started to wriggle, to test the strength of that hold, but Ekon's expression distracted him.

'You just want to forget Tayan?' he asked, his voice as wrecked as he looked. There was a thread of sadness winding through his words and he stared intently at his hand on Lilla's chest, refusing to meet his eyes. It was clear he'd take whatever the Toko offered, and it was equally clear that he'd misunderstood everything that was happening here.

'What? No! Ekon, do you not understand? I'm sorry, of course you're not familiar with Tokob customs. Asking you to get rid of my marriage cord, it's not just a favour. It's a statement. I'm asking you to help me shed the skin of my old life and grow a new one, brighter and more vibrant. I'm asking you to share that new life. To . . . be with me.'

Ekon took a breath and Lilla put his fingers against his mouth, hushing him. 'Let me say this. Please? You deserve my words, Ekon. You deserve the truth, finally, after all this time.'

Lilla took a moment to compose himself. He couldn't mess this up, but there were so many things to say. Where to start? 'I didn't lie when I said to Xessa she'd won. A lot of people in the last weeks have told me to let Tay go, or at least to have the courage to examine his actions without bias. I didn't want to, because why should I? Who were all these people telling me my husband was a bad man when they don't even know him, when they can't know him the way I do?'

He put his hand on Ekon's cheek and tilted his head so they were eye to eye.

'You never once used what happened between us to try and convince me to let him go. You were the only one who had something to lose – or something to gain, maybe – by convincing me to give him up. Everyone else wants me to hate Tayan, wants me to admit I'm wrong and they're right. You were the only one who wanted me to protect myself from being hurt. By him, by myself, by the people I thought were friends. Even by you, maybe.'

He pressed a gentle kiss to Ekon's lips. 'I don't just want to forget Tayan and lose myself in you. I *can't* forget him; he was a part of my life and heart and spirit. But the man I remember and the man he is now, they're not the same person. I spent two years praying he was alive while fearing he was dead, but I never stopped to think how those years would change him. Or change me.'

He stopped again, seeking for the right words and finding them elusive, clumsy in his mouth. 'I didn't become your lover so I could kill you. I told myself that was the reason, that there wasn't anything I wouldn't do to build a rebellion, and I told you that, too, in the aftermath. It was a lie. The truth is, when we came together . . . that was all me. I kept insisting it was part of the plan – get close enough to kill you – but even before the first time we had sex, I knew I'd messed up, that everything I was trying to build was in jeopardy. Because I wanted you. And I wanted to be wanted by you. And I was going to have to kill you.'

Ekon swallowed thickly, his throat clicking and his eyes damp. His breath was rapid, shallow, and his fingers had tightened on Lilla's arm until it hurt.

'It was me, Ekon. It was all me,' he whispered and took a deep, shuddering breath, already wincing at the incandescent hope flaring in the Chitenecah eyes. 'And although he's done all the things he has, and although that part of my life is dead and gone and I want that marriage cord off my leg, I love Tayan. I always will. He was the love of my life.'

The betrayal, the agony, lasted only a moment before the gates slammed shut in Ekon's expression. That moment was an eternity too long for Lilla and he seized Ekon's face and dragged him close, urgency in his belly. 'But that doesn't mean *I don't love you, too.*'

'W-what?' There was confusion, wariness, and such naked need in Ekon's face that something calm and warm settled in Lilla's heart and gave a contented sigh. The words had been only half-thought before they burst from him, and it wasn't until he heard their faint echo from the stone wall that he knew how true they were.

'I love you,' he repeated, softer this time. 'I'm sorry it took so long, and I'm sorry it's so messy and complicated, because I do still love Tay and I hate that I love him. You deserve better, Ekon. Better than a man who planned to kill you when he was – he is – in love with you. And better than a man who still loves someone else. But everything that I can give, I do. I give it to you. *I love you.*'

Ekon kissed him again, none of the passion of before in it this time, but a tenderness so aching that it blossomed a bruise on Lilla's heart. 'I'll take what I can get,' he croaked. 'It's more than I deserve.'

Again, Lilla caught a glimpse into the depths of Ekon's self-loathing, carved patiently out of his spirit through a lifetime of deception, murder, and the denial of his people, tribe, and god. Would the half of his heart he had left to give away be medicine enough to heal that wound? He had no idea. All he did know was that he had to try.

'You deserve the world, Ekon, and you deserve it to be peaceful and free. You deserve to hear your people's rituals and your god's teachings. You deserve to be loved.'

There was denial in the set of Ekon's mouth, but he didn't voice it.

'You haven't said it back, you know,' Lilla said abruptly, sensing that of all the emotional blows he'd dealt this morning, that one was a step too far. Perhaps this would be easier. He hoped it would be easier. He hoped, selfishly, that it would be reciprocated. He sat up, away from the temptation that came from being horizontal in proximity to Ekon, and pulled him up, too.

'You have to ask?' Ekon murmured, folding one leg beneath him and pressing the other to the Tokob thigh.

'I want to hear it,' he said and hoped it didn't sound too much like begging. 'If you want to say it.'

Ekon blew out a breath. 'Kitten, of course I love you. It's physically impossible for me not to. But we made a fucking mess of it last time around, and you've just said you're still in love with Tayan, so I doubt it'll be any easier this time. And I don't—I understand that. You were torn away from each other; neither of you chose to separate. Why wouldn't you still love him? Just because your marriage is over doesn't mean it wasn't sweet, you know.

'It doesn't mean it wasn't good or that you weren't good together. Who Tayan is now doesn't alter how you felt about each other then. Don't let anything spoil that. If memories are all you're to have, then cherish them. I'll, I'm here. In whatever capacity you want me, I'm here.'

Lilla winced again and Ekon stilled, his face closing off. Waiting for the axe to fall. He drew his knee up, breaking contact with Lilla's hip, and rested his arm casually on it to hide part of his face.

'Ekon . . . If we're starting again, we have to start *honest* this time. So this is my honesty: I need – *I want* – to save Tayan if I can and if it's possible. I need to know the truth for my own peace of mind, what he wants, or wanted. And then I can love you as you deserve.'

Ekon looked away. 'And if he offers you everything? If he is the man you married after all and he still loves you, too?'

'That's not going to happen,' Lilla said, but he couldn't be sure. What if Tayan did come back to him? What if he gave up being Singer? *No. He threw his marriage cord on the ground and ordered the Melody to slaughter us – and he was looking into my eyes when he did it. There's no way back from that.*

'Even if he still loves me, what we had is broken beyond fixing. I don't want him; I want answers. I want to know what happened to my husband, what obsession or ambition the song-magic uncovered to turn him from the man I loved into the Singer telling us this.' He waved at the air.

The Chitenecatl laughed, low and strangled and bitter. Then he nodded, as if reaching some decision, and Lilla grabbed his hands on instinct, swamped with selfish fear. 'I'll help you find out,' Ekon said, strained, staring at their linked hands as if they held a shared future and not one filled with doubt and blood and betrayal. Lilla made a confused noise and Ekon finally looked up, fierce. 'I'll help you,' he insisted. 'Whatever happens afterwards, you deserve the answers only he can give you. And I . . . won't stop you if you choose him.'

'You won't fight for us?' Lilla burst out.

Ekon's smile was bleak as he gently extricated his hands from the Tokob grip and then raised them to kiss Lilla's fingers. Then he stood. 'I've been fighting for us every day since the uprising began. Before, even, when the eagles said your status stained my own and I refused to let it.' He took a step away as Lilla reached for him.

'Maybe I just know when I'm beaten. Or maybe I think it's time you fought for us instead.' He crossed to the gate in the bamboo bars and hesitated. 'I just don't know if you will,' he said softly, and left.

Lilla had stayed in the cage for a long time, alone with his thoughts and Ekon's last words. Then, determined, he went after him.

It took him almost an hour to find him, only to discover he was busy with reports of numbers and rations and the latest sightings of the Melody. All things Lilla wasn't allowed to know about in case Tayan read them from his mind. He couldn't intrude on that, and he had no idea whether that was Ekon's intention.

He haunted the edges of the room until, eventually, Toxte proposed they gather for duskmeal and herded them both into

Xessa's old cage, where Xessa and Tiamoko already sat. Ekon sat by his side as they formed a small, intimate circle, but wouldn't look at him, maintaining a brittle formality sharper than the blade of his spear. *We said we love each other, and now he can't look at me. Because I told him I still love Tay. What a fucking mess I've made. Again.*

While Lilla's side of the conversation had been a disaster, he felt like he'd finally glimpsed some of Ekon's truth and it was self-destructive and festering, an infected wound that wouldn't heal without tenderness and time. Neither of which were easy to find in the middle of a war.

Once, that would have been excuse enough not to try, because Ekon was right: Lilla hadn't fought for them. It was time that changed. He shifted close and slid his arm around the man's waist, offering him a small, questioning smile when the Chitenecatl glanced at him. Ekon's face was blank for a long moment and then he exhaled very quietly and relaxed into it, pushing their shoulders together as he listened to Tiamoko tell a tale of Tokoban before the war.

Hope, small and bruised, fluttered in Lilla's chest, and he relished Ekon's warmth and the long, thin lines of him under his hand. Despite the company and all the broken words and dreams that had passed between them, arousal sat deep in his belly. His thumb slid under Ekon's tunic and stroked slowly at the skin of his flank. A question; a promise. A plea.

Xessa, who had spent weeks railing at his loyalty to Tayan, was now staring at him in open outrage as if this was somehow worse, and Lilla let his face and eyes go cold as he stared her down; she blinked, grimaced, and turned back to Tiamoko's story.

'Don't antagonise her,' Ekon breathed.

Lilla squeezed him briefly. 'Fighting for us,' he replied just as quietly. The body under his arm tensed and then melted, and Ekon slid his own arm around Lilla's back and then leant his head on his shoulder. The Toko exhaled, giddy with relief and with promise. He and Xessa still loved each other fiercely, but they weren't tied together by Tayan anymore, only by their shared memories of him. It would change the dynamic of their friendship and he'd let it, no longer the peace-weaver between his husband and the eja. They could be friends now on their own terms, and that included Xessa accepting Ekon as part of Lilla's life. And if she wouldn't, well, he'd lived without her for the last two years. He could do it again.

Lilla's attention wandered from Tiamoko's story and fell on Toxte. He, too, was barely listening. His gaze roved the cage and his shoulders were rigid as he sat with his bad leg stretched out into the middle of their circle for Ossa to lounge against. Their eyes met and Lilla quirked his mouth in sympathy. Being in the place where Xessa had suffered so much was hard for him, the smallness of these cages and the fact that even if fighters had shouted conversations, questions and insults among themselves during the long evenings, she wouldn't have known. She'd have been utterly isolated whenever she wasn't dragged out to train or fight. Even then, unless Tiamoko was with her, she'd been alone.

'Ekon, you must have some stories,' Tiamoko said when they'd laughed dutifully at the conclusion of his. 'You were at the heart of the Melody and Pechaqueh society. What can you tell us about them? It doesn't need to be funny, but it would be good if it was,' he added hopefully. Lilla snorted. There was still so much boy in the enormous, muscular warrior in front of them.

Ekon hesitated, uncomfortable, and Lilla gave his waist a comforting squeeze. 'Please?' he murmured.

'I . . . I'm sorry, I can't. I shouldn't be here; this is your time together. Tokob time.' There was misery and guilt hidden in the corners of his eyes that probably only Lilla could recognise.

'Please stay. We want you here. *I* want you here,' he said as Ekon began to stand. 'Or let me come with you.'

'Stay,' Toxte added. 'You are welcome in our family,' he added, signing for his wife, and Xessa twitched and then gave a single stiff nod.

The Chitenecatl hesitated and then slowly relaxed, though he shifted out of Lilla's embrace. Ossa whined and flopped onto his side, pawing at Ekon's knee. He leant forward and hesitantly scratched the dog's chest and Lilla waited for a flurry of words from the eja, but what she signed surprised him: 'A little further down, between his front legs.'

Quietly, Lilla translated. Startled, Ekon looked at her. She wasn't smiling, but she pointed, and he did as he was told. Ossa's tail thumped and he lifted his foreleg for better access, his tongue lolling in a canine grin.

Ekon gave him a few more chest rubs and then sat back, smiling until Ossa's explosive whine of complaint made him jump. A big paw batted at his knee and Xessa huffed a laugh. 'Don't stop, Feather Ekon,' she signed. Tiamoko translated but didn't add the honorific; the eja didn't notice.

Ekon leant in and scratched the dog for a few more moments before straightening. Again, the whine, the raking paw, the demand. Toxte sniggered and even Xessa had a small smile lightening her features.

'Have I just become a slave to this dog?' Ekon asked good-naturedly as he shifted closer on the stone and resumed petting yet again. It took him a moment to register the sudden, uncomfortable silence and then he stilled, mortified. 'Fuck, I'm sorry, I'm so sorry. My words were ill-thought, not thought at all. I beg your forgiveness.' He scrambled onto his knees and then prostrated, palms and brow pressed to the stone. Every human present recoiled instinctively, but Ossa hauled himself up, still limping, and went to investigate, shoving his nose against the side of Ekon's face and then burrowing under his chest to discover whatever smell had caused him to press so close to the ground.

Lilla's face was hot with second-hand embarrassment and again he awaited the explosion of venom and derision. He stared at the three Tokob, fully prepared to defend his lover, when Tiamoko snorted and then whooped. Toxte cracked next and eventually even Xessa, and Lilla allowed himself to turn to the commotion next to him. Ossa was jumping on the Chitenecah back, licking his ear and face and worming under his belly in a delirium of play.

'You can sit up,' Toxte said with studied innocence and something relaxed in Lilla. Ekon complied, only to be bowled over onto his back and crushed beneath the big dog's paws and wriggling weight. 'Wrestle him, but mind his shoulder,' the eja added.

'I suspect – ah! – I suspect I'm going to regret – ow – I'm going to regret taking your advice,' Ekon managed, carefully wrapping his arms around Ossa's ribs and pushing. The frenzy increased and the dog's back paw came down on his balls and he grunted but gamely got a handful of ear and tugged. Ossa seized his wrist between his jaws and slobbered, mouthing at his arm without doing any damage.

Xessa let it continue a little longer and then clicked; Ossa let go of Ekon and looked at her, tail wagging. A long string of saliva dripped from his lolling pink tongue onto the Chitenecah neck and Ekon exclaimed in disgust. The eja clicked again and Ossa padded over to her side and flopped down, his head in her lap and tail still thumping. She smiled, full of tenderness, and stroked from between his ears along his spine.

'Is it safe to get up?' Ekon murmured and Lilla laughed and hauled him upright and into his arms. And then he noticed the blood. Ekon's hand closed on his as he began to investigate. 'It's just a scratch, I promise. Those claws are tough. I promise, kitten,' he insisted, pulling the neck of his tunic back into place.

There was another long silence. 'I'm sorry, did you say "kitten"?' Tiamoko's voice was polite over barely suppressed laughter, and of course he was translating that, of course he fucking was. 'Fang Lilla of the Sky City, notorious hunter and warrior, hero of the Great Betrayal, is privately known as *kitten*?'

Lilla closed his eyes and exhaled for a long time. When he opened them again, Ekon had pressed his lips together in silent, anxious, amused apology. He summoned his dignity and fixed Tiamoko with a haughty stare. 'And what of it?'

Tiamoko was grinning, but he spread his hands wide. 'Absolutely nothing, Fang Kitt—Lilla. Not a word will pass these lips,' he promised, and Lilla knew he was in for trouble for the next month. He relished it. Ossa's acceptance of Ekon had broken the scar tissue that bound them all together, revealing raw tender flesh beneath. But a rawness they could work with, a tenderness they needed if they were to once more, truly, become kin.

Even Xessa seemed softer. 'And what do you call him?' she signed.

Lilla looked at Ekon and the corner of his mouth turned up. 'I call him lover,' he murmured and then smiled wider as the Tokob all made puking noises.

'Tell us about Enet,' Xessa signed. Toxte and Tiamoko both spoke her words at the same time and Lilla didn't miss the flicker of jealousy in Toxte's face.

'Sorry,' the big Toko said quickly. 'Being back here, old habits. I was Xessa's voice . . . Sorry.'

'And I thank you for that,' Toxte said. 'Truly, as Malel is my witness. Don't mind me. In fact, please sign. I'd rather cuddle.' Xessa turned a puzzled face on him and then rolled her eyes when he slotted behind her and wrapped his arms and legs around her. Rolled her eyes but leant back into his embrace with a sigh, tangling their fingers together across her belly.

'She was the rebellion's greatest weapon, and she nearly accomplished everything she'd set out to achieve. Ultimately, ah—' Ekon broke off and turned a questioning glance on Lilla.

'You can tell them,' he confirmed, 'though we all already know at least some of it.' The versions of the story of Enet's death that had gone through the war parties were garbled.

'You know it was a, a Drowned that killed Enet? Well, it was that same Drowned that you captured in Tokoban, Eja,' he said, pointing. Xessa's mouth dropped open and she glanced up at Toxte as if for confirmation. He looked equally bewildered.

'How is that possible?' he asked.

'It killed Enet to save Tayan's life. It had followed him to

the Singing City, along the rivers that merge into the Blessed
Water. No one knows why. But according to Xini and Itzil,
Tayan and the Drowned became friends of a sort. It marked
him – he bears claw scars around his eye – and often sought
him out. When Enet attempted to seize the song-magic for
herself, Tayan and the Drowned killed her and destroyed the
rebellion's greatest hope and strategy, not that Tayan knew
that at the time.' He paused, but no one had questions.
Tiamoko was rapt, his hands moving automatically as he
translated.

'Enet died hated and will be remembered that way forever,
and she deserves it, but her strength of will, her ability to
remain almost uncorrupted by the magic, is remarkable. All
the things she did, all those terrible choices she made while
bearing the weight of so many deaths to give us this chance
at peace is . . . But those deaths cannot be discounted. Should
not be. Not just the people she offered every new moon but
those she procured for the Singer. Hundreds of them. And her
own son, of course, offered up to Xac's blood-madness to keep
our hopes alive. That's how dedicated she was. But still, she
was perhaps even more a monster than the Singer. He was lost
to the world while she knew exactly what she was doing every
moment of her life. It's hard to reconcile all that with someone
on our side.'

No one moved or spoke. Were they all wondering whether
they'd have that same strength of will? Lilla's own attempt at
subterfuge had been largely bloodless and even so it haunted
him. The manipulations and coercion of good people. The
unclaimed kin who'd never know why or what had happened
to their loved ones. His own sisters and mother. He shivered
and pressed a kiss to Ekon's cheek and pulled him close in
against his side again.

'She would have become Singer?' Xessa asked, her gestures
choppy.

Ekon waited for Tiamoko's translation. 'Yes. An Empire-
wide rebellion coupled with a song that spoke of peace on
equal terms and a slow lessening of its power until we could

force a truce before, ultimately, she ended the song forever. Mictec decided otherwise.'

'How did Enet resist the song?' Toxte asked.

Ekon exhaled. 'Enet and I, and the few others like us, we trained for years to take on the appearance and, and *conviction* of loyalty. We made it our way of life long before we were forced to move in Pechaqueh circles, though in Enet's case, of course, she was half-Pecha. As Pechaqueh will have told you, over and over again, you must become like them in your heart. Well, we really did. I gave up my tribe and land, my family, even my name. I—'

'Your name?' Tiamoko interrupted. 'It isn't Ekon, then? What is it really?'

'That name is no longer spoken or thought,' Ekon said sharply and then held up his hand in apology when Tiamoko blanched. 'I am sorry. That name . . . and the boy who was given it, both died long ago. Only Mictec knows it now.'

'And your family?' Toxte pressed, though gently.

Ekon bowed his head, that self-loathing Lilla so hated and feared clear in his expression. 'Remember what I told you, that as a boy I was trained in the ways of the Pechaqueh by taking my own family as slaves? And that the Pecha boy Ekon was found alive among his dead kin and dead traitors?'

Lilla nodded and then sucked in a breath. *Malel, no.*

'The slaves who slaughtered the Pechaqueh to put me in the son's place were my family. I didn't know that was how it would happen until it was too late. I thought they'd . . . I don't know what I thought. I don't know where I expected them to get the bodies from and it never occurred to me to ask. For all my training, I was painfully naïve.'

'What do you mean?' Tiamoko asked for Xessa.

'To become Ekon the Pecha there had to be no survivors of my Pechaqueh family who could expose me as an imposter. But there couldn't be any Chitenecah survivors, either. We staged a small slave rebellion – my Chitenecah family ambushed Pechaqueh on their way to take their son for the Melody trials in Tlalotlan. Everyone died. Ekon, I, was the only survivor. If they were all dead, I wouldn't be tempted to look for them or risk my place as an eagle by freeing them or taking too much of an interest in a slave family. And so that there was nothing to hold over me if anyone found out who I really was. Can't threaten someone's family if they don't have one.'

His smile was a slash of pain and it widened into a ghastly grin at the horror on the Tokob faces around him. Lilla could see him welcome their loathing, practically drinking it in to add to the poisoned lake already in him.

This is why he was so determined to sacrifice his life on the way to the Singing City. This is why he said he was destined to die at the Melody fortress. He wanted – still wants – to reunite with the kin who died to put him there.

'Did your family know that was to be their fate?' Toxte asked gently.

'Yes. I know that now. I had warrior training – I was a Pecha about to join the Melody after all – and I saw they were leaving themselves open after they'd struck a killing blow so they were killed in turn. Enough to make it look real, that no one suspected it was a suicide. A sacrifice in the old way, to Mictec – to die fighting so that others, me, all of you, might live. It was glorious.'

'And you hate it.' Xessa's gestures were gentle, as was Tiamoko's voice as he translated. Ekon flinched as if she'd struck him and gave a single, short nod.

'We will pray for them,' Toxte said.

Ekon swallowed hard. 'It was long ago.' The dismissal in his tone couldn't mask the remembered pain but it told them he wouldn't speak more about his past.

'As for Enet, her situation was different,' the Chitenecatl continued in a hoarse rasp and a ripple went through the room, as if the spirits of Ekon's family had been drawn close by his tale and now retreated once more. 'Itzil was her birth-mother, a Chitenecah surrogate for the Pecha woman unable to conceive. They kept the circumstances of her birth secret – when Itzil became pregnant, the family moved to a remote estate so no one would discover the truth. They returned to the Singing

City when Enet was a month old, the perfect, beautiful little Pecha baby. Itzil nursed her but had no other contact. Despite that, as soon as Enet was old enough to understand, Itzil told her the truth and raised her in the conspiracy.'

Lilla sucked in a breath. 'How old was she?'

'One Star cycle.'

Tiamoko puffed out his cheeks. 'That's a big secret for someone so young to keep.'

Ekon held up his hands. 'Of that I cannot speak. I don't know why Itzil chose to tell her then. Four sun-years later, suspicion fell on Enet's parentage and they planned to kill Itzil. Enet suggested the removal of her tongue instead: Itzil couldn't read or write, so she wouldn't be able to betray them.'

Again, Ekon appeared to revel in their disgust, as if hoping to drive them away. Toxte noticed and his mouth turned down. He squeezed Xessa tighter. 'There is nothing we were not trained to do for the cause. It was likely Itzil put the idea in her head, but even so, for a twelve-year-old girl to suggest . . . it is a horrific thing.' He sighed and rubbed his hands over his face. 'As soon as it was done, Enet secretly taught Itzil to write. The old woman has a phenomenal memory and could record almost word for word the private conversations that she, a tongueless, invisible slave, was party to. She was never suspected – could never be suspected. She was nothing, less memorable than a damaged plate at duskmeal.'

Xessa clicked her teeth together several times, a sure sign of agitation. 'Tell me Itzil got her revenge,' she signed.

Ekon smiled sharp as a coyote. 'That she did. A slow, lingering poison that seemed like a wasting illness for Enet's Pecha mother, and a heart seizure caused by overwork and grief for her father. He was well-known for over-indulgence in honeypot and Tlaloxqueh vision herbs. In reality another poison. Enet took over the running of the estates, farms and businesses at fourteen, and over the years took a succession of influential lovers, including a young and besotted Xac. When he became Singer, she entered the source as one of his courtesans.'

'A pity she failed at the end,' Xessa signed and Tiamoko flicked a glance at Lilla before translating. Lilla slid his hand from Ekon's waist up to his chest and felt the way his lover sucked in a breath.

'She did more than the rest of us,' he said tightly. 'She took the world spirit and cast it so deep into the earth and its sleep that it will never wake again. It will never steal the gods from us. Your Malel is safe and alive because of what she did. My Mictec also, the god I haven't been allowed to worship for more than twenty years. The god I had to *disdain*. And she wouldn't have failed at all if not for—' He cut himself off with an effort.

Tayan. If not for Tayan.

He could see Xessa understood, too, and braced himself for a renewal of hostility. She breathed out through tight lips – and then looked down at her lap. How much of her anger was actually grief, he wondered. One day he'd ask, but not now. Not tonight.

'How did you all cope, knowing she was one of you and killing all those people? Your people, our people? The hundreds she fed to the Singer like honey-roasted fig?'

That was Toxte.

Lilla wanted to step in and protect Ekon from all these questions. He didn't. It wasn't his place and this wasn't his story. And they had a right to ask.

'We didn't know. Until the night of the uprising, no one but Xini, Itzil, and perhaps three of the rebellion's leaders knew Enet was one of us. The risk of exposure was too great. If I'd been compromised and tortured and given her name to save myself, everything would've fallen apart.' Ekon's voice and shoulders were tight, but he answered readily enough.

'So that's how it worked,' Tiamoko mused. 'You had one contact – Weaver – and Weaver probably had one contact higher up, and maybe she knew about Enet and maybe not. And Enet would never have known about any of you because of the danger of her position. She had to trust that the rebellion existed and she was acting in its best interests, but she couldn't know for sure.'

'Correct. Itzil was her go-between when it came to orders: an old slave resting in the shade on the way back from market could overhear all sorts of whispered instructions or coded language. And it's a good thing Enet knew so little – despite her strength of will, she'd begun to lose control, especially in her latter years. Her proximity to the song, to the power she was actively cultivating and drawing into her body, meant that she'd have done anything to save herself. We were taught to preserve our lives and our mission no matter what.' Lilla could *feel* the shame rising from him like smoke. 'If we had to let others die to save ourselves, to preserve our secrets, then that's what we did.'

Lilla couldn't sit in silence anymore. He drew Ekon's face to his and kissed him on the mouth, then swept the others with a glare.

'We've all been subject to the song's manipulations. To an extent we still are. We've all done and said things because it was easier to give in, just this once, than fight for something small and trivial. And it's how the song gets us, how the Pechaqueh get us. We allow the small indignities and ignore them when they're perpetrated upon others. And then, when we're used to the small ones, we start ignoring the bigger ones. And bigger and bigger, until we've been sold a fine jade mask and got home to discover it's painted clay.'

'Now imagine you're Tayan,' Ekon added before he could say anything else, before anyone could respond to his outburst. 'He was enslaved like the rest of you, subject to humiliations and fear, and then he was granted huge power, not just magic but authority, power over the lives of others. He went from nothing to everything, from slave to Shadow. From afraid to making others fear. He had the Singer's ear and the Singer's magic. Would you have done better if it were you?'

Lilla's breath caught in his throat.

'Enet would have fallen long since if not for Xini and Itzil. As it was, even they almost weren't enough to stop her. Enet used Tayan as a barrier to retain the last of her humanity, but she did it to bring us to this point. She couldn't afford to worry, or to care, about what happened to him because of it.'

Ekon stared at them each in turn, gaze lingering on Xessa. 'And so as for what he's become now, none of you are qualified to judge him.'

Xessa was on her feet before Tiamoko had finished translating, and Lilla lunged to meet her, putting himself between her and Ekon.

'Hey you, Feather Ekon. You've got some fucking explaining to do.'

'Just gut him like he deserves. Him and the rest of the lying, traitorous leadership.'

The voices came from the cage entrance and Lilla looked that way to find warriors crowding against the bamboo bars and pushing in through the gate. They were armed. He pivoted on instinct to protect Ekon from this new, bigger threat. His hand went to his belt; his knife.

'What is—' Ekon began.

'Tell us what you know of the Zellih stealing the north, you snake-fucker. Tell us how you betrayed us and tricked us into joining your rebellion. And then you better start praying to Mictec for forgiveness, for you'll get none from us.'

XESSA

Pilos's fighting pit, entertainment district, Singing City,
Pechacan, Empire of Songs
60th day of the Great Star at morning

Xessa clapped once, hard, making everyone jump, and Ossa leapt in front of her with his ears pinned back and threat in his stance. The Tokob at the entrance grimaced when she tapped her ear twice, knowing full well that anger was twisting her features. *Has everyone fucking forgotten how to sign?*

Toxte was speaking and signing, asking what was going on, and she focused on that – for now. She could have it out with the Feather afterwards. Ekon couldn't go anywhere, after all, not with warriors blocking the only exit. Xessa smiled, bitter. She well knew how it felt to be trapped in this cage with death waiting on the other side.

'The Zellih have invaded Tokoban and Chitenec. They're on their way here as allies,' Toxte translated. He'd turned his body and hands towards Xessa while he watched the speaker at the gate and she couldn't quite read his expression. It made everything awkward and she felt a flicker of irritation that he wouldn't face her.

'But Tokoban was the trade,' he continued and the ejab annoyance was arrested with the suddenness of a trip snare. 'The Zellih give Weaver, Ekon, and Xini warriors and they get our homeland in return. They get all the north, some say. Why else did the rebels wait until we'd been defeated and stolen from our land to rise? Because they knew we'd have fought the fucking Zellih who came to steal our homes and bury Malel under the wings of their so-called Sacred Bird and its sacred shit! They're saying that the Zellih demanded our removal before they'd fight and the rebels agreed. They're saying this was all planned – our defeat, our enslavement – to secure aid from Barazal. And on top of all that, they trick us into fighting their war. What's your answer to that, Feather fucking Ekon?'

Xessa's fingertips were numb, her head light, her skin too tight. She didn't see what reply Ekon made.

Tayan. Tayan told us to go home. He put proclamations up all across the city, the whole Empire of Songs, telling Tokob and Yaloh to go home. What if he wasn't trying to weaken the rebellion but instead warn us that our land had been traded away?

Malel, what if he's on our side after all?

Xessa backed to the far corner of the cell, bringing Ossa with her. Toxte limped after them. She'd cursed Lilla's loyalty to Tayan and rejoiced when he'd finally seen sense. Had he been right all along?

'Wait. No. Is he helping? He says Tokob and Yaloh can go home and hundreds do, and they'll be fighting the good fight against the fucking Zellih, but isn't the outcome still that the rebellion is weakened? No, that it's weakened even more! Tokob aren't in the cities to fight the Melody, and the Zellih can't advance out of the north because our people are fighting back. We're preventing them from aiding the rebellion.'

Toxte watched her flurry of words and she saw the moment he caught on. He swore, long and vicious, and then stopped and shook himself. 'Xessa. My love. What does it matter anymore?' She sucked in an outraged breath. 'I'm serious. What does it matter whose side he's on when our side is falling apart? Doesn't this remind you of the Sky City? Isn't it Tokob against Yaloh against Xentib all over again, and all the while the Melody get closer? We need—'

His head whipped around, hands stuttering, and then he was limping fast across the cage. Xessa followed; of course she followed. She already knew she wouldn't like the reason, but she went. Anger simmered in her belly, against who she didn't know. The whole world, probably. Malel herself, and Snake-Sister and Jaguar-Brother too. Tayan; Lilla; Toxte. Herself.

Lilla had a knife in his hand and the warriors were no longer at the gate – they were pushing into the cage, edging closer to Ekon who was shouting and empty-handed. Toxte stood alongside Lilla, facing his people and allies with the Feather behind them.

'—is Chitenecah,' she caught him sign as he shouted. She missed the rest.

Tiamoko was off to one side, conflicted, that shaky, sick look in his eyes he only got when the world had lurched out of true for him. She'd seen it only a few times in the last few years and remembered, with a flash of grief, how he'd worn it after his first masked bout. She understood now, all too well.

She waved and he looked up, startled. She tapped her ear again.

'—swear on Mictec I don't know what you're talking about,' he began translating, jerking his head at Ekon. 'Xini and I are both Chitenecah; Enet was Chitenecah. We would never agree to the loss of our homeland as the price for freedom and wouldn't expect others to pay it either. The rebellion's leaders have made the hardest and most heart-breaking decisions over decades, over generations, but I don't believe they would sanction your enslavement and then the theft of your lands, our lands, to further their cause. You are valued and honoured allies. We cannot win without you. You keep saying "they said", but who are "they"?'

'I spoke to Weaver about this very thing,' Lilla added as soon as Ekon fell silent. Tiamoko was frowning as he signed and Xessa understood: he'd spoken to Weaver about what, exactly? 'I asked her outright whether she'd waited until Tokob and Yaloh were under the song so that she could use us as extra allies. It was after Xessa's great victory at the river, and Toxte's Malel-blessed return. I asked her whether we were to be sacrifices to her war so that she might breach the great pyramid and kill the Singer. She scoffed at the idea. I have no reason to disbelieve her.'

'We're leaving,' Tiamoko signed next, indicating the group at the gate. As if Lilla's words were smoke, not voice. 'Give us Ekon and the rest of you can make your own choices. But he's ours, and then we leave. We're going home. We're going to take back Tokoban, Yalotlan, and Chitenec.'

'The Melody had word of Zellih raiding parties crossing the border into Tokoban in the last weeks before the uprising began,' Ekon said and Tiamoko's shock as he translated was obvious. Xessa's stomach dropped into her feet. 'But ask yourselves why it has taken three moons for news of a Zellih presence in the north to reach us? Because despite the Second Talon's arrival in this city, *we are winning*. We are winning and so they turn to subterfuge, as they did before, to weaken us and sow division. This is the same lie as the lie that Tokoban was free and open to us. It's just wearing different paint. We—'

'You just said the Zellih were raiding Tokoban,' yelled a Toko at the front of the crowd. It was Anoq, young but usually level-headed. He was from the south of Tokoban and he'd been training to become eja when the Melody came. When Tayan had made his proclamation that Tokob could go home, Anoq had abandoned his fight in Axiban and come here, intending to pass through the Singing City on his way north. Xessa had convinced him to stay; from the depth of anger on his face, she wouldn't be able to do it again.

'Raiding, exactly! How does that make them our allies?' Ekon began and Xessa stopped watching Tiamoko. She strode to Ekon. Lilla turned to her in alarm and she glared at him, then put her hand on the Chitenecah shoulder and gave Ossa the protect command. It was different to the guard command that forced song-claimed civilians away from the water. "Protect" meant exactly that. No one harmed Ekon unless they got past the dog's teeth first. It was the most obvious show of support she could make and coming on the heels of his revelation of Zellih raiding parties – when exactly had he been going to tell Tokob that? – it made a powerful statement. She hoped.

There was shock on Tokob faces when she took her place at Lilla's side, a barrier between the aggressors and Ekon. Toxte flanked her immediately and Tiamoko completed the little line, trusting her to have chosen right.

'Go back to Tokoban and free it from Zellih control?' Xessa signed with as much contempt as she could muster, knowing one of the others would translate for the non-Tokob. 'We couldn't even save it from falling under Pechaqueh control. What makes you think you'll do better this time?'

'They've traded it to Zellih in return for aid!' Anoq shouted, signing with it. 'Even if we win here, we can't go home, while the rebel leaders, whoever they are, get everything they want. But if we kill the war leaders, they'll have to rethink.'

'And if we go home now, we walk from one war straight into another and most likely lose both. If we're too busy fighting each other, the Melody wins. We wipe each other out and they crush what's left. Nothing changes. Nobody wins but the fucking Pechaqueh. The song wins.'

Anoq was still furious, too fiery to have made a good eja, she could tell, but a few people further back were looking thoughtful.

'If they did it – *if* – then there will be time enough to murder the allies who sold our land once we've won. Time enough to work out a strategy for reclaiming any territory sold or traded away. But for now, we need to know whose side the Zellih are on. If it's ours, then . . .' Her hands faltered. Then what? By not opposing them they were giving implicit permission for Tokoban to be stolen from them – again.

That's why the Zellih rejected Tayan's peace-weaving. They'd already made an agreement to ally with the rebels. They'd

already been promised our land and others', and they needed
us to lose so they could take it during the unrest they knew
was coming.

Nausea sat bitter at the base of her throat.

'"If it's ours, then" what, Eja?' Anoq demanded and around
him the faces of their allies, their war party, were angry, disbelieving, craving violence. 'What do we do if they've been
promised our homes for aid?'

Xessa lifted her chin and glared at him as she signed. 'One
fight at a time. Drawing water is always more important than
drawing green blood.' It was an old ejab saying and she saw
it strike home. 'We end the song. Then we go home and see
what awaits us.'

Xessa's words weren't as convincing as she'd hoped.

Ekon had had a dozen more altercations as the evening
deepened into night, each more fractious than the last, until
Anoq had drawn a blade and demanded the Chitenecatl step
aside or draw one of his own. He'd stepped aside and the
young eja had led more than a hundred Tokob out into the
darkness, equal numbers of Yaloh and Chitenecah following.

When Xessa had gone to chase after them, Lilla had stopped
her. 'We are not Pechaqueh. If we force them to stay, we may
as well put collars on their necks.'

'But—'

'I know.'

'But without them, we're going to lose.'

'. . . I know.'

Strangely, the admission had strengthened them both, as if
knowing it was pointless took away a fear so huge and looming
that they couldn't even see it. They'd fight and die and the
Empire would win – but it would be bloody and weak and it
would never, ever forget what the people it considered less
than human could do.

It would be a fine legacy, for as long as the memory lasted.
They exchanged a bleak smile and she reached out, tentative.
Lilla dragged her into a brief embrace, quickly over and much

missed as he stepped back. Still, it was a start. An apology. A healing.

Many of the Chitenecah who'd gone with Anoq had done so after accusing Ekon of a lack of connection to his home and people. He'd paled under the torrent of invective, as if the words were a dart that struck true, its poisoned tip sinking deep. Even so, there was no vulnerability in his stance or eyes; the mask of Feather Ekon was firmly in place. It served only to prove the Chitenecah point for them.

'Do you think it's true?' Xessa signed when Anoq's group had vanished into the night and the remains of the war party had retreated in silence and trepidation back into the fighting pit.

They were standing at the entrance to the row of cages where Xessa had been held. Toxte and Tiamoko were flanking Ekon. Protecting him.

'Which part?' Lilla asked. 'The Zellih invasion, or that the rebellion's high command really did offer them the north to fight? Your husband's translating this conversation for Ekon, by the way, so be nice.'

Xessa's hands itched to sign "I'm always nice," her standard response whenever Lilla had teased her or railed against her fiery temper back home. She refrained. Despite their earlier embrace, there was a long road ahead of them before they reached banter. 'All of it. Any of it. I don't know.'

'I don't know, either. I don't want to think it's true. I don't want to face that possibility. We've been divided enough, first by Tayan, and now . . .' Lilla laughed and then coughed. 'And now again, maybe, by Tayan. It feels similar to his last betrayal, but this carries more weight of truth.'

'But we don't know the last time was a betrayal,' Xessa signed reluctantly. Malel knew she didn't want to defend Tayan's actions, but Lilla had faced stark truths, eventually, and done so without flinching. She owed him this. 'Those who left after that first proclamation, they could be in Tokoban by now. Maybe living free and peaceful, maybe fighting Zellih or thousands of loyalists. Or maybe they never got there.'

'There's no way to know short of going there ourselves,' Lilla said with voice and hands as Ekon and the others crowded close. 'But we know the shadowy, secret high command will apparently do anything and sacrifice anyone to gain their victory.'

Ekon winced and then raised his chin. 'Their victory? Or our victory? The victory of all Ixachipan?'

'All Ixachipan except the north,' Xessa signed, leaping to Lilla's defence with a speed that surprised them both. 'Where were our promises in return for aid, Feather Ekon? Where are our riches and lands and wealth?'

'And that is why this rumour cannot be true,' Ekon said clearly when Toxte had translated. 'The leadership would never make such an alliance, knowing the rift it would cause.'

'Not unless you planned on it never being discovered,' Lilla signed and said and Xessa blinked. She hadn't been sure whether their relationship would be a barrier between Lilla's fury and his lover.

Ekon's nostrils flared and a muscle jumped beneath his eye. Angry. Straining for calm. Yet aware enough to keep his face turned towards her. 'And how would we accomplish that? How would our great climactic battle of this uprising go, us and the Zellih bringing down the Melody and destroying the great pyramid, tearing down the capstone and killing the Singer and then . . . what? Thanking them for their aid and saying oh, sorry, we made a mistake. Tokoban isn't yours after all. Nor Yalotlan or Chitenec. Off you go back to Barazal and take your dead with you. Or do you believe we're planning on exterminating everyone of Tokob, Yaloh, and Chitenecah heritage on the Zellih behalf?'

Xessa looked to Toxte, who raised an eyebrow. The man made a good point. More than one, in fact.

'Swear it,' she signed, jerking her chin for her husband to translate.

Ekon twitched, looking at Toxte and then back to Xessa. 'Swear on what? What will make you believe me?'

She sucked her bottom lip into her mouth and chewed on

it. 'Swear on Mictec. Swear on the song. Swear on your hope for an easy death. And swear on Lilla's spirit.'

Ekon's eyebrows rose with each statement, but he didn't protest. There was no hesitation, even as Lilla began to sign in the corner of her eye, no doubt telling her she had no right to ask such a thing.

The former Feather dropped to his knees and pulled his knife from his belt. 'Mictec, goddess of death from who comes all life, the circle eternal who claims and steals and kills, who grows and offers and births, hear my vow. I know nothing of a scheme to offer Tokoban or any land to the Zellih in return for military aid. Bind my words to my life and take both if I should lie. Know that I give them willingly if ever I speak an untruth while invoking your name.'

He dug the tip of the knife into the back of his wrist, drawing a bead of blood. Lilla winced.

Ekon's nostrils flared as he inhaled, suddenly looking sick. 'Song of Ixachipan, magic of the world spirit and voice of the Singer of the Empire of Songs, hear my prayer. I—'

Xessa stepped forward, waving her hands. 'No. No, don't. Not that one, please. I'm sorry, that was cruel. You've spent enough of your life loving the song. I won't make you swear on it.'

Ekon's shoulders slumped and he nodded a thanks so heartfelt that a lump formed in her throat. Malel, but she was a malicious spirit sometimes.

The Chitenecatl ran through the other two vows, drawing a little blood each time. Visibly upset at swearing on Lilla's spirit, as she'd expected. As she'd hoped. She could feel Lilla's barely controlled anger where he stood rigid next to her, and as soon as the last vow was made, he dragged Ekon onto his feet and inspected the cuts in his arm, bringing it to his mouth and licking away the blood, encouraging the wounds to scab.

'Satisfied?' he signed.

'Yes. Are you?' she countered, unable to stop herself. Toxte and Tiamoko made almost identical grimaces and she forced her hands to her sides before she added anything else.

'Yes. An hour before midnight, I'd like you to set out for Xini's hideout, Xessa, and you to Weaver's, Toxte. We need to establish communication and I can trust both of you not to become parrot-headed if the situation there is volatile. Can't I?'

'Yes, Fang,' Toxte signed before Xessa could form a reply.

'Go in the dark, be safe, and do what you can to get Tokob sentries set up, and pray to Malel there are enough of us left to do it. I want line of sight so we can all sign to each other without setting foot in the streets. Now more than ever we need to communicate.' He grimaced. 'Ekon will handle it. I can't be any more involved than this or . . .' He waved his hand towards his head and Xessa had a horrible memory of his face twisted with agony, with incomprehension and violation as Tayan scrabbled through his mind and brought with him a pain that had driven the warrior puking to his knees.

'You're assuming we can trust Xini and Weaver.'

Lilla and Ekon exchanged a long look. 'What other choice do we have?'

They had three hours. Xessa pointed to the end of the row of cages. 'The end cage is empty. Leave us be,' she signed and then grabbed Toxte's hand and dragged him away before anyone could respond or protest. She planned on making the most of the time they had.

He'd promised that where she went, he'd go too, yet just a day – was it a day? – later, they were separating, even if only for a few hours. Still, Xessa would take the smell and taste and feel of him with her. And no one was going to deny her that. Not even Toxte.

Not that her husband appeared reluctant. They ducked through the bamboo gate and Xessa put Ossa into a down and stay on the other side, blocking the cage entrance. Almost before she'd finished the command, Toxte was pulling her to him and she went gladly, spinning them and pressing him back against the stone wall to kiss him, and kiss him, and kiss him.

Toxte's arms were wrapped around her back, hot and strong

and as well-remembered as they were missed, and he was letting the wall and his good leg take his weight. His pulse was hammering against her chest as she stretched up to his mouth and pressed herself against him as if she wanted to climb inside his skin. She did.

Toxte twisted and pinned her to the wall and Xessa pushed forward, putting space behind her, unable to be trapped in this place of all places, not even by him. He hesitated, mouth leaving hers long enough to check her expression and seeing something that had him letting her go in an instant.

Xessa sucked in a deep breath and, for the first time in this fucking pit, she had no qualms about showing her true feelings. 'Don't cage me.'

He understood immediately, as she'd known he would. 'Never,' he signed. 'You lead.'

Xessa's belly flared hot and wanting at that and she steered him towards the narrow cot and pushed him onto it. He fell with a laugh and held out his arms and she slid into them and then flung her leg over his hip. He pulled her half onto his chest and kissed her again, squirming beneath her, his face beloved and scarred and drugged with her. Intoxicated. Intoxicating. Honeypot given form.

Xessa took one of his hands and slid it beneath her kilt until he could grip her thigh and arse. Toxte's pupils dilated as he grabbed and then pressed her down against his groin and she threw back her head to gasp, then kissed him again, shifting all the while. Toxte worked his hand around and in between them until he could slide his fingers into her and Xessa shuddered and clenched as he bit kisses into the side of her neck, grinding against his palm and shoving her arms beneath him to haul him closer, *closer.*

His other hand cupped the back of her skull as if it was the most precious jade, at odds with the relentless motion and his rampant, desperate kisses. Xessa experienced both equally – the love and the lust – and they swirled and combined and neither was more precious than the other. Both brought her to tears. She was lost in him and the pleasure he wrought.

She made some sort of noise that he tongued out of her mouth and swallowed, encouraging more and louder and harder and oh, oh, oh.

She needed. She *needed*. His fingers were relentless, his mouth hypnotic, and his other hand abruptly left her head to wrap around her waist, helping her move. His face was slack with pleasure at her pleasure and his eyes narrowed in concentration as she tensed, joyful and determined. How she'd missed that expression, the desperate arousal that was nevertheless leashed and under tight control, the ecstasy that was doubled, tripled, by the knowledge of her own.

Toxte panted and bit the line of her jaw and crooked his fingers and pressed the heel of his hand *just there* and Xessa climaxed faster than she had in her life, clinging to him with all her strength as ecstasy and shivers rippled through her and tightened her body like a strung bow, her forehead thudding down onto his chest as she clenched and curled and came.

Came forever, came for an eternity.

When the intensity finally released her muscles, Xessa slumped against him and just breathed, twitching as the shocks jolted through her. The air was sweet and tinged with gold and she could have stayed like that for hours, sated and unthinking. Only she wasn't sated. Grunting, she wrapped Toxte tighter and rolled them. She misjudged the width of the cot and the impact with the hard-packed earth hurt, but she didn't care. *She needed.*

She grabbed Toxte's hand and sucked his fingers, then kissed her taste into his mouth as she wrapped her legs around his hips. Panting, Toxte fumbled their kilts out of the way and then slid into her, slow but relentless, forcing a long exhalation of sound from her throat. Her neck arched as his face contorted with agonised ecstasy. Tears gathered on his lashes. She held him close and matched him thrust for thrust, saying with her body what her hands were too busy to chant: *I love you; I love you; I love you.*

Xessa put her palm against the side of his neck and felt his noises as he drove into her, stealing as many from his mouth as she could in between the need to breathe, to hold him, to dot every available piece of skin with kisses. Toxte reached back and hooked her knee with his elbow and hauled it up to her shoulder; she tightened around him and grinned as he visibly fought for control – and lost, desperation and denial and then overwhelming pleasure chasing each other across his beloved, much-missed, never-forgotten face.

Her husband muffled his cries against the filthy salt-cotton she hadn't had time to remove. She still felt them and the quick, panting breaths that carried them. Xessa locked her ankles together, unwilling to let him go even when he eventually stilled, and when he finally lifted his head he was smiling, albeit dazed. She kissed that smile, and then each cheek and the tip of his nose. Then she bit it, because it was there and she could, and his laughter vibrated through her ribs.

'You're as bad as Ossa,' he said. One side of Xessa's mouth turned up and she squeezed deliberately, making him gasp. 'I take it back, I take it back. You're much better.'

She nodded, satisfied and self-satisfied and belatedly becoming aware of how uncomfortable she was, her lower back scraped raw. She didn't move, just guided Toxte's head down to her chest and breathed slowly as he let his full weight down on her. They stayed that way for a long time, unmoving, just resting, and despite her discomfort, Xessa's eyes were closing towards sleep when Toxte's head jerked up from her chest. He turned it towards the gate and spoke, then gently slapped her leg when she instinctively held him close in the grip of her thighs.

She pouted but he reared back, his face serious, and she released him. He stood, flipping down the front of his kilt as he did, and then dragged her to her feet. 'Lilla wants us. There's something wrong.'

'For fuck's sake,' she signed, very deliberately, 'it has not been three hours.' She pulled off the decorative strip of material bound around her bicep and wiped quickly between her legs, then looked for somewhere to dispose of it. Toxte held out his hand and she passed it to him absently, wondering what could be so wrong that Lilla would disturb their very obvious alone time.

'I had plans,' she added, trying to cling to the moment for as long as she could.

Toxte stopped and grabbed her and pulled her against his chest and kissed her, filthy and hard until she was dizzy from lack of air and lack of blood in her brain. 'So did I,' he said, his hand ghosting from her breast down the front of her tunic, her kilt, and between her thighs. He stepped back. 'And yet.'

Xessa stared at him, slack-jawed and then furious at the tease, which only made him grin and arch an eyebrow. Effortfully, she composed herself, brushing back her hair and refusing to rub her thighs together against the throbbing deep between them. *Malel, I could eat you alive and you'd fucking thank me for it*, she thought.

'And yet we answer to the kitten,' she signed eventually and was rewarded with Toxte throwing back his head to laugh. It was almost worth it.

Almost.

He set off down the corridor, tucking the strip of fabric inside his armour as he went. 'Are you keeping that?' she asked, scandalised and blushing.

He winked and patted his chest where it rested. 'Might even sniff it later,' he signed and laughed, ducking when she slapped at him.

And then they came out into the open air of the pit itself and smelt the smoke.

PILOS

The sudden movement of traitors heading north through the early part of the night had been the signal to get ready, confirmed an hour later by one of the spies seeded in the rebels' ranks.

As hoped, the rumour had spread like fire through a dry milpa, carried in the mouths of dog warriors pretending to be hungry, frightened civilians. They'd spoken openly of the Zellih attacks in the north, naming Chitenec and speculating hard on Tokoban and Yalotlan; simply mentioning those lands would twist the rumour to accommodate them. A few brave, true Chitenecah dogs had even pretended to be rebels abandoning the fight to go home and free Chitenec from the Zellih, loudly proclaiming their disgust at the rebel leadership as they hurried through the night-time streets.

Some had been confronted; not all had made it back. Atu had praised and honoured them equally, polishing their statuses and reaffirming the no-bloods as vital allies and honoured members of the Melody.

This time, the traitors who'd fled were to be given safe passage north. They were going to stop the Zellih, after all.

It all worked in Pechaqueh favour – so long as the holy Setatmeh were safe.

Pilos still didn't know what Tayan planned to do about any ejab who might be heading north, but for the first time since the holy lord Xac's ascension, the Spear trusted his Singer. Tayan's willingness to abandon his homeland and his ruthless decision to rupture the alliances among the rebels was an act worthy of an elite Whisper. Worthy of Ilandeh at her best.

Now, though, he put it all from his mind and squinted into the orange and yellow glows marring the night. Smoke caught at his nostrils, tickled his throat. Stung his eyes. The song had blessed them, stopping the rain barely an hour before they began burning.

They'd been scavenging anything flammable for the last few days and storing it in the abandoned temples flanking the great pyramid, keeping it dry. As soon as their informant told them of the traitors' new hideouts, they'd begun stacking it inside specific buildings and storage pits running under roads. Safe from the rain and lethal to their enemies.

Now the necklace of fires was burning, a great half-moon surrounding the war parties on three sides and driving them south towards the slaughter district and the waiting Melody. The burning storage pits collapsed roads and buildings, cutting off entire avenues and leaving no way through for the panicking traitors. Song willing, this would be the last, great push and the Singing City rebellion would be crushed. They'd restore order and the Singer would proclaim peace here and the Melody and loyal free throughout the Empire would take heart.

We win here, tonight, and it's the beginning of the end of the war.

The fires roared high, the rain had stopped – and the heat dried the timbers of adjacent buildings just enough for the flames to leap. And spread. And consume. Pilos's fighting pit would be gone now. The source of wealth and the reputation he'd built on the fighters he produced there likewise gone. He mourned its loss, but he didn't regret it. He wouldn't.

He stood in the slaughter district at the head of seven pods, facing the wall of black and orange smoke and squinting into the hot wind as they waited to go to war. Over and through the growing fires and the whump and crash of collapsing buildings, Singer Tayan's song soared and twisted like a bird in flight. A song which was strong and imperious and *achingly, devastatingly beautiful.* A song of such purity that it was incredible to realise it wasn't made by a Pecha. That this was a no-blood's song; a slave's song.

The realisation baffled him every time he encountered it, and it twisted something in his chest, something sharp and flaying and resentful. Singer Xac's song hadn't been beautiful for years, had instead been a warbling, stuttering wail that made no sense and spawned violence in all who heard it. Yet his slave's song was this, was everything Xac's could and should have been and Pilos couldn't help what he felt even as he strove not to feel it. Even as it was dangerous to harbour such thoughts. It was *unfair* for his successor's song to be so majestic in comparison to Xac's. It was a childish, selfish response, beneath the man and the warrior and the politician Pilos thought himself to be. And yet it was there.

Because Tayan was a foreigner who'd ascended higher than any Pecha and what he brought to the song was . . . strength. Beauty. Belief.

'Spear! They come,' a warrior hissed. Pilos narrowed his eyes against the glare and embraced the impending violence. People were hurrying out of the smoke and the buildings marking the edge of the entertainment district. The flames chased them, only a few rows of streets behind. Siting the slaughter district at the back of the entertainment district was practical: the animals killed in the pits were often sold here for meat and magic afterwards.

Those fleeing so far were civilians, red-eyed and smoke-stained and fearful. Seeing the warriors of the Melody arrayed against them did nothing to help that. They halted, milling around as the fire roared closer, the strong, song-blessed wind fanning it so that it jumped from building to building,

leaping across roads. Many ducked back into the maze of
avenues, preferring to face the fire – at least for now. Pilos
expected they'd be driven back out soon enough. It would
take more courage than these no-bloods possessed to stand
in the path of a fire rather than flee the arrows and darts
of their betters.

Others edged around the big open space and ducked into
side streets – where they would encounter more Melody pods
waiting for them. Pilos grinned. It wasn't going to be that
simple. The civilians who'd emerged so far were thin and
skittish, with a half-starved feral dog wariness in their flinching
forms that spoke of people who wanted only to be safe and
filling their bellies.

They'd chosen not to fight, and therefore they'd obey the
orders of anyone who had control of them – or a supply of
food. When the Melody won, these slaves would throw themselves on Pechaqueh mercy and swear they hadn't raised
weapons against their betters. They'd bend their necks for
their collars without hesitation and be glad of that familiar
weight when it settled once more upon their skins.

Possibly the only good outcome of the war dragging on this
long was that the fires of hate burning in the rebels' bellies
were beginning to dampen, while those in the guts of the
civilians were already long dead. All they wanted was an end
to this, one way or the other. They no longer cared who won,
so long as they could be safe and fed and their children out
of danger.

More figures came slinking out of the fires. People in blood-
stained salt-cotton, armed with bows and blowpipes, spears
and knives.

Warriors. They showed no hesitation, nor even surprise, to
find the Melody waiting for them. Pilos smiled, grim and
self-satisfied, as they were forced to push gently through the
milling crowd, many of whom grabbed at them desperately,
babbling questions and begging to be saved. It slowed their
advance and hindered their formation, exactly as planned.

A warrior concerned for the people cowering behind is a

warrior not paying attention to the eagle ahead. And that's a warrior a few breaths from death.

Pen them back against the flames and press them from both sides. Not daring to push forward across the open space ahead. Their backs burning, and death in front of them. And mixed in with them, children screaming and greyhairs cowering.

Yes.

'*Advance*,' Pilos bawled and thrust his spear into the air. He didn't wait to see if they'd go with him; he knew they would.

The civilians were panicking, yanking at the warriors' saltcotton to make of them human shields.

'No mercy!' Pilos screamed, limping faster. 'Song and Singer and Empire!'

'*Song and Singer and Empire*,' his pods roared back and then they were within arrow range. The enemy only had a few bows, and the smattering of shafts that fell among them did nothing to slow their advance. The four pods hidden in the side streets had scores of bows each and Pilos's war cry had alerted them. Arrows slammed into the edges of the traitors' straggling lines, dropping dozens. Screams rose over the crackle of fire and the civilians broke first, bunching together away from the archers on either side. The warriors followed, an inexorable contraction as everyone shied away from the lethal rain.

Perfect.

'For the Singer!' Pilos howled and again his pods repeated it back to him in a driving roar so loud his eardrums fluttered. The second signal. It brought the pods out of the side streets to squeeze the enemy even tighter until they lost all cohesion. Fire and death behind. Warriors to the sides. Pilos and his fury in front.

They came together in fire and blood and death.

The trained rebel warriors were outnumbered and outfought, spending their lives exactly as Pilos had predicted to protect cowering non-combatants. They were starting to panic, not

just the civilians, but warriors too. Some threw themselves
back into the burning streets; a few knelt, hands empty and
raised.

The heat beat against his skin and sucked the moisture from
his mouth and eyeballs, whipping away his sweat as fast as
it appeared until thirst combined with smoke to close up his
throat. Every inhalation was accompanied by a high-pitched
whistle. Heat exhaustion, fatigue, and thirst were as lethal in
a fight like this as a blade in the eye.

It was worth it. They were winning. The enemy was falling
faster as they tried to concentrate on too many things at once:
protecting themselves, staying in formation, protecting the
non-fighters, evading the flames. All as they'd planned.

The pods that had come in from the sides had little to do
other than avoid the heat and keep them penned in. The fires
had begun to curl into the streets where they'd been concealed,
cutting off their retreat now as well. Dangerous, but as those
last escape routes were closed by fire and eagles, the traitors
had nowhere to go but directly at Pilos in an attempt to break
past his pods and reach the sweet promise of freedom and
open air beyond.

Pilos stepped back out of the front line, and then through
the second and third, eagles taking his place as naturally as
breathing. He grabbed a couple of warriors resting at the rear.
'Go for the flanks and pull twenty archers from each side. I
want them set up back here, shooting over our heads into the
mass. Remaining archers on each side to do the same. Let's
end this before we all get cooked.'

'As the Spear commands,' they croaked, their voices as
cracked as his. They touched bellies and throats and loped off
in opposite directions.

The air was a little cleaner here and Pilos paused to suck
in deep, dry lungfuls and then cough them back out. He had
a vicious headache brewing in an ever-tightening band around
the top of his head and his eyes were as dry as dust. The
muscles in his spear arm were stiff and slow and he forced
his hand to relax, flexing his fingers and rotating his wrist.

His beloved war club, abandoned and found and abandoned again over months of battle, was finally lost for good and he held a replacement, ugly and unfamiliar, weighted wrongly. He dropped that, too, and shook out his arms and then rotated his damaged ankle carefully, casting his gaze across the melee as he did. It would be over soon.

There was a shout over the clash and screams and rumble of fire, a warning shout. Nothing unusual in that, except for how far back Pilos was from the fighting for the shout to sound close by. He snatched up his weapons and turned, checking the open plaza behind him.

'Shitting *fuck.*'

More traitors, warriors all from their armour, weapons, and movements, were streaming towards their rear. They were bloody and smoke-stained; they must have fought their way through both the fires and the warriors setting them. A counter-ambush, and cunningly sprung. Instead of trapping their enemies against the flames, they were about to be surrounded themselves.

He checked left and right and saw the archers from the flanks converging. Those eagles who were resting before another push at the traitors were also moving, not needing orders, forming up into a triple line facing out into the massive plaza.

Pilos beckoned the closest. 'Send word forward to crush them. No rest; no reinforcements. Drive them into the flames, but break them. And you,' he added, grabbing another, 'get me two pods from the western flank to secure a retreat. I don't expect we'll need it, but I'm not losing every warrior here to these no-blood shit-eaters.'

'As the Spear commands,' she said and raced off west.

Pilos took a few more breaths and shook out his limbs again as his warriors stepped into line to either side. He braced his spear against the ground and beat a rhythm against it with his club. Others copied him, stamping or cracking weapons into those held by their neighbours, building up volume, stirring their blood for battle – and alerting the engaged pods to a threat at their rear.

The advancing rebels were organising into pods and others into Paws, muddling the order in a way that made Pilos wince at its ineffectiveness. Or would be, if there weren't quite so many of them. It looked like this might be every rebel warrior left in the Singing City gathered to face him.

Good. Then I can end this, here and now.

His own line was three deep and strong, without gaps. Effective; lethal; proven.

It was hard to tell in the dark, but they looked to be massing by tribe. It wasn't something they did often, but he realised the purpose of it when he spotted the small, fierce band of Tokob at the front, jeering and posturing. They wanted him to know they were still here, that they hadn't hurried north with their kin. They wanted the Melody – or perhaps the Singer – to see that they still lived and still fought.

Was Xessa among them? Was Ekon, who Tayan's former husband seemed to have adopted like a pet? The husband himself? If he could take their heads, he might break this rebellion for good, not to mention removing one of the greatest threats faced by his gods.

The front rows loped forward like coyotes, moving with the easy familiarity of trained warriors. Those behind were stiff with tension, their weapons gripped tight, but unlike the civilians crying and fleeing and dying behind him, these were determined to fight for what they thought was freedom instead of recognising it as the ropes and bonds of superstition and savagery.

War cries rose up – old cries, calling on false gods and spirits instead of the holy Setatmeh and the Singer.

'For the song,' Pilos screamed in reply, the rest of the line echoing him. The beat of their weapons against each other and against the ground increased in tempo, though they made no move to advance. It would be a mistake they wouldn't survive.

'Ready!' he shouted as the enemy got closer. The Chitenecah led, the first tribe to be brought under the song. The most loyal – or so every Pecha had thought. They'd become so integrated into society that half-bloods of Chitenecah heritage were occasionally accepted as heirs or trusted to manage estates in distant corners of the Empire. Now a few hundred of them were screaming the name "Mictec" and racing towards Pilos and his line.

Ah. And there he was. Feather Ekon. Not with his adopted tribe after all, then.

He stands against his friends, who he betrayed.

He stands against me. Who he betrayed.

'I want him alive!' Pilos screamed, pointing. Even those eagles who'd never met Ekon were aware of his face and name by now. All of them knew of the sheer scale of his treachery and, while every Pecha wanted to be the one to slay him, even more did they crave to see him brought low, brought before Pilos and their High Feather bound in ropes and ready to be flayed alive.

Atu had let it be known that that was to be the fate of any rebel leader taken alive. The slow and expert peeling of flesh from their still-living bodies. Pilos would look into Ekon's skinless, lidless face and staring eyes before he was staked out for the heat and blood loss to kill while every Melody warrior who wished to pissed on his raw flesh.

Energy and righteousness flooded him and washed away the fatigue, made him forget his raging thirst and sick headache and heavy limbs. He raised his war club and pointed it at Ekon. The former Feather saw and angled towards him, raising a club of his own in acceptance of the challenge. No, not a club of his own: Pilos's club. A grin split the Chitenecah face when Pilos recognised it, only widening as the Spear howled his fury and beckoned, desperate to sprint across the slaughter district and tear his beloved weapon from his enemy's dead hands; with an effort of will that left him trembling, he remained in the line. Let Ekon come to him. Let him come and taste Pilos's vengeance.

Behind the Chitenecah, the rest of the tribes were advancing, Tokob mingling their edges with Yaloh, who blended into Xentib, each bolstering the others' strength. As easily as that, Pilos's pods were outnumbered.

Another familiar face among them, and another reputation to match. And a title he wore in mockery: *the Singer's husband. Lilla.*

Pilos gestured at him, too. 'Alive,' he shouted and got another roar of assent. Axib came next; Quitob; Tlaloxqueh. All of them, every tribe Pechaqueh had brought into glory and who now rejected it. Whose lives had been steeped in greatness because of the Singer and who, despite Pechaqueh best efforts, were too uneducated, too uncivilised, to realise the gifts they'd been given. In other circumstances, he would mourn for their incomprehension. Now, he wanted only to end them and restore peace to his beleaguered, beloved Empire of Songs and spare his Melody more death.

'Draw the attack,' he called. 'Archers hold until they're committed.'

The front ranks braced, Pilos in their midst, and the attackers moved within range, yet no arrows fell, no stones were whirred to snake-strike speed in their slings and then sent flying with lethal accuracy. The enemy was out of long-range missiles. A grim smile devoid of humour split Pilos's face. *Come on, traitors. A little closer.*

A little closer.

They did so, faster and nearer with every beat of his heart.

And then, as he was raising his club to signal his archers, the front rows of running warriors dropped and rolled over their shoulders to steal the momentum from their legs, and those running behind them skidded to a halt and raised bows and slings and let fly, and Pilos realised they'd both used the same tactic.

'*Loose!*' he screamed as enemy arrows drove into his warriors. A flight arced overhead and screams rose on both sides. A second and then a third volley and Pechaqueh were flinching backwards despite their training, the small, brightly painted shields strapped to their forearms more suited to deflecting spear strikes than protecting against missiles falling unseen from the smoky sky.

The front rows of the enemy bounced back onto their feet

and began to run again. Run at them, ignoring the arrows, intent on only one thing.

'*Brace!*'

They came together with a muted roar that devolved into screams and grunts and voices raised in mercy ungiven. And Ekon threw himself at Pilos with murder in his eyes. Murder, and shame. Perhaps even regret.

'Slave. Son of a fucking slave,' Pilos grunted as their clubs thudded together. 'I'm going to cook your heart for dogs to eat.'

Ekon disengaged and then swept the club at his face, other hand stabbing with a flint-bladed knife out of nowhere. 'Dogs?' he panted. 'You mean Ossa? The dog you gave to the eja so that she could kill five fucking Drowned?' His voice rose into a shout and even though the screams of battle thundered around them, a wash of cold fear slid down Pilos's spine.

It was one thing to confess before the Singer and High Feather; it was quite another for his own eagles to know he was complicit – more – in the slaughter of the holy Setatmeh.

His lips writhed back from his teeth and he attacked with renewed vigour. 'Fucking no-blood,' he grunted, kicking at Ekon's stomach. The other man twisted, taking the blow on his hip and letting it spin him in a circle and drive the momentum of the club as it cut humming though the smoke and the night towards Pilos's ribs.

Pilos deflected.

'No-blood? I'm a full-blood fucking Chitenecatl. And yes, I am the son of a slave, but I'm not – ah! – ashamed of that.' He ducked and weaved, making a half-moon step to strike at Pilos's elbow. 'Where do you think my strength comes from if not my family?'

'You squawk like a fucking turkey. Shut up and fight. Let's see if your blood can bear the lessons I taught you.'

It was an empty gibe and they both knew it. Pilos would never have elevated Ekon to Feather if he was incapable. Grinning, Ekon adjusted his grip on his club – on Pilos's club – and spun the knife in his other hand so the blade lay along his forearm.

Pilos's own second weapon was a spear, and it was lost somewhere on the stone behind him. He grinned, too, and pulled his third weapon, a short-handled axe, from the back of his belt. A little of Ekon's confidence wisped away like smoke and he readjusted his grip.

'Come on,' Pilos grunted. 'You pathetic, snivelling dog, come on.'

Ekon did, sliding beneath the Spear's next attack and flowing into one of his own, lashing the club diagonally for Pilos's injured ankle while swiping at his face with the knife. Pilos jumped backwards, avoiding both weapons and trying to entice Ekon to follow him, to step in among the line of eagles. He didn't, staying securely among his own – or as close to them as it was possible to get in the shoving, swaying, flame-lit night.

It began to rain.

Around them, the traitors fought well and hard, using Melody tactics against Melody eagles, each side's movements and traps cancelling out their enemies'. Victory would come down to discipline, strength, numbers, and will.

It would come down to small, intimate little battles like this. Pilos stepped forward again, both for his own status and honour and because he weakened his line otherwise. Ekon spun the war club in his hand and then deliberately brought the smooth polished head down on the paving stones at his feet. The crack of stone hitting stone was as loud as a thunderclap and Pilos yelled and jumped forward, realised too late he was being goaded. Ekon wouldn't risk destroying his weapon in the middle of a battle.

Still, he'd already moved, and Ekon let the club bounce back up from the ground and then whipped it higher, flicking his wrist at the last moment so that the head clipped Pilos under the chin, smashing his teeth together with the tip of his tongue caught between them.

Pilos's head snapped back so hard his neck bones crunched and pain exploded through his mouth, jaw, and neck. He flailed on instinct, trying to retain his balance before something thudded into his chest and took him the rest of the way off his feet.

The back of his skull bounced off the stone as he fell and his teeth clicked together again. His mouth was full of blood and a scrap of flesh that was probably the severed tip of his tongue, and something else sharp and hard – part of a tooth. Lights were flashing behind his eyes and he was dizzy, unsure which way was up.

Ekon was on him a heartbeat later, and a heartbeat after that screaming as Pilos's hand-axe chopped into the side of his calf. Ekon dug his knife into Pilos's forearm, gouging a deep slice. Pilos spat blood, tongue, and tooth at him, let go of the axe and grabbed his shoulder, dragging him off balance.

They rolled, thrashing and roaring, through the blood and across the rain-wet stone. The storm was heavy enough that puddles were already forming. The Spear's knee dropped into a carved blood-gutter and nearly dislocated when Ekon wrenched him over and tried to pin him. Pilos was unarmed, fighting for possession of the traitor's knife: straining, clawing, snarling. Bloody saliva drooled from his mouth, smearing them both as they rolled yet again, and warriors were stumbling over them, kicking them out of the way, stabbing blindly downwards. He didn't know whose line they were in anymore, whether the spears were aiming for him or Ekon.

Ekon was on top when a sandal kicked him in the side of his head. He arced off Pilos and landed hard, casting up a spray of water and making no effort to break his fall – stunned by the blow. The knife skittered from his hand and Pilos snatched it, bellowing triumph.

He surged up and over, renewed energy tingling through his limbs and pulsing in his bloody mouth, shoving Ekon onto his back on the rain-slick stone and straddling his waist as the light from the fires began to dim under the relentless downpour. He felt a momentary twinge of disappointment that he wouldn't get to see the life fade from the traitor's face as he bled to death, but it only lasted an instant before discipline reasserted control. He couldn't kill Ekon like this. He had to be taken alive. Skinned. Tormented.

Pilos grabbed him by the face to slam his skull into the ground but something hurled itself at him and knocked him sprawling off the traitor's prostrate form. Agony flashed through his forearm and hand, and he rolled away, bellowing. A club? A long knife? The pain was monstrous and he couldn't tell what had caused it as he rolled a second time, seeking distance to get his bearings and his feet under him. A long, low rumble of threat that wasn't thunder made every hair on his body stand on end and he paused, the primal terror of the jungle stilling him.

'Hello, Ossa,' he gasped, lurching onto his feet and pressing his bitten arm against his armour. He still had Ekon's knife but wasn't stupid enough to raise it. 'Who's a good dog? Remember me? Remember the turkey and lizard I fed you twice a day for two years? Yes?' The words were slurred through his broken tooth, his mangled tongue, barely comprehensible, and did nothing to stop the growl drifting like smoke from between Ossa's jaws. Fires danced, reflected in his eyes.

Like one of the torments of the Underworld.

He risked breaking eye contact with the dog to find Xessa closing in on them, her favoured weapon of a spear firm and lethal in her hands. She'd sent the dog to save Ekon's life. As if he needed further proof of the man's utter unworthiness.

Ekon scrambled to his feet. 'One wrong move and he'll kill you.'

'Maybe. But I think it would kill Xessa if I hurt her dog, no?' Pilos threatened.

'You can fucking try,' Ekon said, but it was a touch too breathy to be convincing. Ossa's long, protracted rumble of threat, though, oh yes. *That* was convincing.

The dog was planted in front of him, shoulders big and hackles raised, barely visible but for the orange points in his eyes and reflecting off his bared teeth. Rainwater trickled down Pilos's back like the fingers of a lascivious spirit. He shuddered.

And then his eagles flanked him and he saw, just, wariness come into Ossa's stance. At the same time, Xessa made a complicated series of sounds and the dog slunk backwards, staring at Pilos the whole time. Snarling. Ekon backed away with him, limping.

There was a rumble of thunder, then a long series of lightning flashes followed by cracks so loud that the ground shook beneath their feet. Ossa flinched and Pilos looked while he could, the battle revealed and hidden in snatches. Desperate. Messy. Even the eagles' lines had fallen apart as the rain battered them and stole their vision and cohesion.

When he was at a safe distance, Ekon raised his club – Pilos's club. 'I'll see you soon, Spear Pilos. Don't die before I get to crush your skull.'

Pilos spat bloody saliva onto the stone. 'It won't be you who takes my life, traitor. I swear by the holy Setatmeh.'

Ekon's teeth flashed in a grin. 'We'll see,' he said and then they were gone, running through the storm, and their rebels, their traitors, melting away like salt in water.

'Spear? Do we give chase?' croaked an exhausted, sodden eagle.

Pilos watched for a few more heartbeats. 'No,' he said eventually. 'They're trying to lead us into an ambush. Let's not give them the fucking satisfaction. We've bled them this night. We've killed more than they can afford to lose, and hundreds of northerners have abandoned them. Back to the pyramid to rest and plan the final stage of bringing this city back under control.'

There was a ragged cheer from the Melody; Pilos didn't join in. Ossa's growl, Xessa's implacability, and Ekon's "I'll see you soon" all mingled in his head.

They'd won this night, as near as anyone could come to winning a fucking mess like this. So why did he feel uneasy, like a trained monkey had performed a clever trick he couldn't quite understand?

'You.' He grabbed an eagle by her soaking salt-cotton. 'We lose no one to attacks from behind, do you hear me? A single warrior falls to a rearguard action and I'll feed you to the holy Setatmeh myself.'

The eagle cowered, touching belly and throat repeatedly, and then scrambled away into the darkness as soon as he released her. He gestured to some others. 'Flanks and front,' he snapped. 'It's your heads if we run into trouble.'

ILANDEH

Sky Jaguar Hill, Chitenec border with Pechacan,
Empire of Songs
66th day of the Great Star at morning

The City of Glass was a shattered ruin six days behind them. The defenders had fought well and hard, but as she'd expected, they hadn't had enough warriors to do much more than delay the Zellih entry into the city.

Two full days of fighting and it had fallen to their control. Hundreds of slaves took one look at the war party marching to conquest and rose against their Pechaqueh owners, rebelling for the second time in three months and doing the Zellih work for them. Many had subsequently joined Omeata's cause, presuming them to be friends.

Olox and Pikte had both survived despite the looming presence of Huenoch and Ilandeh herself. Both had fought and killed, following Omeata's orders about who to slaughter, spare, and capture seemingly without hesitation. Ilandeh had been surprised – and a little impressed. As for her own perform-ance, after the first Pechaqueh fell choking on her own blood, she'd killed easily and without qualm or concern. They died like everyone else and their blood was red like everyone else's. Like her own. She'd assassinated more than a few during her time as Pilos's top Whisper, but that had been political and she'd believed in Pilos and her orders back then. This was different and it had felt different. Had felt like justice.

Everyone you ever killed felt like justice because it was Pilos telling you they needed to die. Don't make this something it isn't. It's just another mission.

Another mission for which she'd fought and killed and destroyed a city for an invading force. Not because they were cruel or evil or greedy, though many of the inhabitants were all those things. No. For a reason she wasn't important enough to learn. Exactly as it had been with Pilos. Just because it was Pechaqueh being punished this time didn't make it better.

Not only Pechaqueh. Anyone who stood against us.

And now they were going to take Sky Jaguar Hill, sitting on the border with Pechacan and only five days from the Singing City. So close. They were so close to the heart of everything. The end of everything.

The hill was a place sacred to Chitenecah. Or it had been, before they'd been brought under the song and replaced Mictec with the world spirit and the holy Setatmeh and the Singer. It had been the source of much fighting during the rebellion, changing hands four times before the Pechaqueh finally asserted dominance, and Ilandeh didn't like that it was the Bird-form's next target. It was too open a provocation. And it would almost certainly have a Melody presence.

It was as if she wanted to do battle – or wanted everyone to know exactly where she was. Drawing eyes and attention to allow other, smaller forces to move unseen, perhaps.

Holy lord? Tayan? If you're watching, I hope you understand the implications of this.

Ilandeh slowed her steps until she was near to Omeata's honour guard, and then put her hands together. 'Peace of the gods upon you during your travels. I wonder if the Bird-form would bless me with an audience?' she asked in Pallatolli, walking just off the trail beside the lead warriors.

'Peace of the gods upon your home,' one answered stiffly. They turned to look at Omeata, who jerked her chin in acceptance. The warriors broke formation to allow Ilandeh into their square and she let the Bird-form pass her and then took up a position one pace behind, moving in step.

'May the Sacred Bird guide your steps and thoughts, Bird-form,' Ilandeh said after a few moments. 'I wonder if I have disappointed you?'

'Hmm?' Omeata asked, not turning to look.

'We have not spoken since the fall of the City of Glass. Did my performance not meet your expectations?'

The Bird-form barked a laugh. 'No, no, by all accounts you're quite the talented murderer, Warrior Ilandeh. I've merely been waiting to see what you would do next.'

'Do next, Bird-form? I pledged you my allegiance in return for a place in your flock to bring down the Pechaqueh who spent their lives disdaining me. To end the Melody that used me and then cast me aside. You said you would give that to me, and so I do only what you order. You have not given me further instructions since the city's fall and so I have done nothing next but march and eat and shit and sleep.'

'How eloquent,' Omeata said with a snort. 'But as you say, you wanted a place in our flock and you have it. What more need is there for communication between us? You are no longer the only foreigners among our number. I'm sure there are some of your own kind you can find to walk with.'

There was a long silence but for the thud of feet and quiet conversation among the warriors surrounding them.

'Oh,' Ilandeh said eventually. 'Then I am disturbing you. Forgive me; this warrior troubled you for no reason.'

Omeata twitched and looked back. 'Do not speak in the language of the enslaved,' she growled. 'It does not suit our tongue.'

Ilandeh gasped. 'I do not! I am no slave. I have never been a slave. I simply offer you respect and apologise for interrupting.'

One of the honour guard stepped in close, a short stabbing spear threatening. 'Do not answer back,' they said calmly.

'But I did not,' Ilandeh insisted, outraged.

'They made you their slave the day they said they were

better than you,' the Bird-form said, relentless. 'And the day you believed it, you became one.' She cocked her head in that eerie, birdlike gesture so precise it had to be deliberate, and then turned and walked ahead again. Ilandeh very deliberately didn't grind her teeth.

'Any warrior in our flock may request an audience with me, whether to speak of war or home, family or loved ones. Talk may be inconsequential or of the utmost importance. When I challenged you, you backed down, became humble and full of doubt. That is not the warrior's way among my people.'

The look she spared for the Whisper this time was almost pitying. 'As for your actions and what you are expected to do now, nothing. I expect nothing. I suppose I had thought you might begin teaching your companions Pallatolli, or at least ensuring they are well-versed in Zellih customs. Our new allies, too. But you have not. Are our ways unimportant?'

'Not at all, Bird-form. As someone finally able to embrace a part of their heritage previously denied me, I would never disdain someone else's beliefs or culture.'

Did she lie? Was that a lie? Ilandeh had no idea.

'I have not spoken of Zellih customs because Olox, especially, felt some, how can I put it, some spirit-fear in the aftermath of the City of Glass's fall. He killed Pechaqueh for the first time. As a Melody dog warrior, an Axib, he was taught – we've all been taught – that Pechaqueh life is worth more than ours. It is one thing to refuse to be a weapon anymore; it is quite another to choose to be that same weapon against the very people who once wielded you. I did not want to use Zellih sacred customs as a distraction; that would not give them the reverence they deserve. As for the others, they have already rebelled once. They are too full of joy and bloodlust at this renewed chance to pay due attention to my teachings.'

'In that you are correct,' Omeata said and then beckoned. 'You may walk beside me.'

'I am honoured.'

'In that you are correct,' she repeated and grinned. Ilandeh snorted. 'And do you share the youngster's opinions? Did you find killing Pechaqueh difficult? Huenoch tells me they do not think so. They feel you enjoyed it.'

Ilandeh licked her lips. 'Enjoy is perhaps too strong a word, Bird-form. As you know, I was forced to join the Melody when I could no longer pay my trading debts to Pechaqueh suppliers. My half-blood status meant nothing to them. They cared only for jade. I was treated better than no-bloods, I mean non-Pechaqueh, but—'

'People of Ixachipan.'

'What?'

'The term "non-Pechaqueh" still gives Pechaqueh primacy in your language, in your mind. You hold them up as the standard and refer to everyone else by how they relate to that standard. "Non-Pechaqueh" are people with the pure blood of their own tribes in their bodies. You should name them with respect.'

Ilandeh walked in silence for a time. 'You are right,' she said and meant it. 'I thank the Bird-form for the lesson.'

'Words have power among my people, as I think you know. Names have power. That includes the names of tribes and lands, not just individuals. We have our public names and our private names, as we have our public and private genders. When you use a name with respect, it changes your perception of that person or people.'

A companionable silence fell between them. Highsun was approaching and clouds with it. It would rain soon, but for now the ground around them steamed and the humidity was heavy enough to bead on their hair and skin, a million tiny jewels glistening. They made Omeata's feathered huipil shimmer even more until she glowed with every step.

The fields to either side were thick with mud and green with life. Chitenec, at least, had returned to peace quickly enough that crops could be sown, albeit late. They'd have slim pickings, but they'd be better off than most of the other lands.

No, they won't. The Singing City and the Melody will claim most if not all of this. Those Pechaqueh who own the fields will take the rest and share a little with their slaves. Everyone else will go hungry.

'It must be difficult for you,' Ilandeh said at last.

'What must?' the Bird-form asked without much interest.

'Well, your place on the Bird Council forbids you from taking active part in these battles you order, does it not?'

'Of course. I would never risk the efficacy of the Council by putting myself in unnecessary jeopardy.'

'So you are reliant on others' descriptions of threats, others' expertise in scouting, on the march and the hunt, and in battle.'

'And why is that difficult?' Omeata asked, suspicion coating her words.

'Well, you can't truly know how much of a threat your flock faces without being in the thick of the fighting. You have not confronted an eagle warrior or a dog warrior. Not even a slave warrior pushed into the front line because it's fight you or be killed by their own side. You have come here, put yourself in danger here, are leading warriors through Ixachipan, yet you can't really understand what they are going through.'

'You think I do not face danger?' Omeata asked a beat too quickly. 'I am the Bird-form and my strength is magic, yet I am attacked by this song and its lies every moment of the day and night. How do you suppose I access my magic and the Sacred Bird in such a situation? There are more threats to life than just spears and knives, warrior.'

'Ah, you are right, of course. I hadn't seen it that way until you spoke.' Ilandeh pressed her palms together. 'Forgive me, I had forgotten the quickness of your mind and the sharpness of your intellect.'

'You flatter,' Omeata said, eyes narrow.

Ilandeh laughed. 'Maybe a little. It doesn't mean it isn't true. It just struck me that you share some small similarities with the Singer. They, too, are forbidden from certain forms of interaction for their safety and the safety of our Empire. Forgive me, their Empire. Not that that stopped Singer Xac, though the results of his lack of restraint were clear to all. Certainly to you, being subjected to this song that is so unfamiliar and hard to bear.'

Omeata halted and turned to face her. 'Hard to bear?'

Ilandeh stopped, too, and automatically touched belly and throat, her knees softening ready to prostrate. She forced herself to stand tall and put her hands together instead. 'I have offended you.'

'You have,' the Bird-form said and the honour guard moved with that perfect, eerie synchronicity to aim their spears at Ilandeh, flowing where necessary so that no point came near Omeata and yet she was still protected. It was beautiful and it was lethal and it was very much not for show.

'You liken my care for my people to the Singer's imprisonment in their pyramid? You think me so weak that the song is a struggle for me? Yes, you have offended me. There is nothing I would not do for Zellipan and the Sacred Bird. There is no one I would not kill if it ended the threat against my people and my god. I think you and your Axib companions should walk at the rear. Not with our new allies from the City of Glass. The very rear. Make sure no one sneaks up on us from behind. It will be your lives if they do.'

'I thank the Bird-form for the opportunity to make amends,' Ilandeh said. 'I will not betray their trust.' In the circumstances, it was wise not to gender Omeata. The Whisper wasn't sure she still had that privilege.

Omeata's eyes were narrow within the band of purple paint. 'See that you do not. Now leave my sight.'

There was something wrong with Omeata's tale. Something that grated, like sand in the eye, tiny and invisible but impossible to ignore. A constant irritant.

She was lying.

Those tiny, almost-missed hesitations in her responses, as if she was reminding herself of the facts of her story. She said I appeared conflicted back then in Zellipan. She said my mixed heritage is obvious and my struggle to reconcile it has blunted my edge. And so, by making me doubt my own abilities, she hides any slips in hers.

But I'm the liar. I'm the spy and the storyteller, not her. I'm better at this than she is, and something about her story stinks worse than an infected wound. Why else would she still hide their true purpose in Ixachipan? The allies she took from the City of Glass, are they true, or are they a mural painted bright and bold to hide the real message written beneath?

And the timing is too convenient. You were attacking at the Tokoban border before the uprising. You destroyed pyramids. And then you vanished into the north and did nothing for three months. Or seemed to do nothing.

So no, Bird-form Omeata, I don't believe you're being truthful about—

'I've done it.'

Olox's voice was low and casual and as he spoke he pointed at a particularly verdant section of the field they were passing. Perhaps someone had dropped a whole basket of seeds there. Perhaps they'd been fleeing Melody warriors at the time. Or rebel warriors. Who knew anymore where the violence came from or who was innocent? Whether it had been watered with blood or rain, the field was green and lush, bright even in the dullness of the afternoon.

'Done what?' Ilandeh asked as she nodded, smiling.

'Got word to High Feather Atu about the fall of the City of Glass, our next destination, the execution of Pechaqueh and allying with slaves. All of it.'

Ilandeh's stomach dropped into her sandals. 'What? How?'

'There was an Axib girl playing at the side of the road a few sticks back. I got chatting to her, played catch as we walked along, and eventually asked her to pass a message to the Listener in the pyramid back there.'

'And you believe she did?' Ilandeh asked. 'Why would she do that?'

'I gave her the greenstone beads out of my plait,' Olox said, fingertip touching the braid that began behind his right ear. 'She can buy two weeks' worth of cornmeal with that. She told me. And she didn't get the beads until she returned with confirmation the message had been received.' Olox tossed something into the air and caught it again. A small, polished stone. Ilandeh recognised it as a river-stone, worn smooth by ever-flowing water. Supplicants often brought one with them to a pyramid when begging for a Listener's aid, retrieving the stone from running water as proof of their dedication – or desperation.

'So the High Feather and Spear Pilos know . . .'

'Everything,' Olox confirmed with a grin, tossing the stone up and catching it again.

Ilandeh swallowed hard. 'That we killed Pechaqueh?'

The Whisper almost fumbled his next catch; the stone skittered and bounced out of his hand twice before he caught it on the third attempt. 'Everything. It's our duty to keep the High Feather informed and the opportunity was too good to pass up.'

She hadn't told them that Tayan could visit her whenever he wanted and this was the result. Information passing to the Melody without her knowledge or permission. Information that changed everything. 'When are we going to strike, Ilandeh?' he murmured, tossing the stone again and catching it.

'Strike?' she asked, even though she knew what he meant. She snatched the stone out of the air and laughed, skipping sideways and taunting him. Deflecting attention.

'We know everything we need to. More than enough. It's time to put an end to the threat,' he insisted as he made a grab for her.

'We do not, and you might have just destroyed our disguises,' Ilandeh hissed, throwing the stone directly at his face. He caught it with a teasing jeer, but he understood the gesture. 'You will do nothing else without my direct order, is that clear? Nothing.'

'I understand,' he said, but she could hear the undercurrent of defiance in his tone. He was angry, pouting that she hadn't praised him, and petulant. She remembered she'd once planned on using his infatuation to bind him to her; that moment had passed. Olox was being driven by Beyt's orders and possibly encouraged by Pikte. He couldn't see the bigger picture and didn't realise that sometimes the best thing you could do was to withhold information until you fully understood what was happening and all the implications.

And whether you've been lied to or not.

She could have told him that, taught him that, if she'd had the chance. This mission was the perfect proving ground. She could have crafted him into a Whisper undetectable to anyone other than his High Feather and other Whispers. Instead, and with Omeata's disapproval sitting heavy on her, it might be that Olox had to die to preserve Ilandeh's place in the flock and the trust of the Bird-form.

But if Olox died, Pikte would follow. She couldn't trust either of them, or Omeata, or a single person around her.

Ilandeh snorted. But then, when had she ever been able to do that?

Hello, Whisper Ilandeh. You have some fucking explaining to do.

The words were a knife blade to her brain. One moment she was walking in the rain and the next she was on her knees in a puddle and screaming. Dimly, maybe, she thought she heard Olox shouting, but her head was full of Tayan and today he didn't care about subtlety or precision. Didn't care about her disguise or the fragile trust she was trying to build.

And then, between one shriek and the next, he was still. Present, but quiet. Vigilant, but not actively seeking to harm.

Ilandeh took a shuddering breath, half air and half bloody saliva, and coughed it back out. She spat and blinked away tears. The outside world was a cacophony of faces, moving figures, brightly dyed clothes, and cold rain. Too much of everything, too much of all of it. She closed her eyes. Sought the still place inside herself. Brushed delicate mind-fingers against Tayan, uninvited and unannounced and crouched like a jaguar on a branch, awaiting the deer.

Only Ilandeh was no prey animal. 'Hello, my old friend. Do we have the chance to talk this time? It was nothing but orders before. I didn't even get to congratulate you on your ascension. How does it feel, choosing power over your people?'

Tayan scoffed. *A little ironic coming from you, Whisper. You who destroyed cities and entire societies out of what? Love for your precious Pilos? Loyalty to people who saw you as nothing more than a tool? And now, it seems, you fight for our enemies. And not just our enemies, but the enemies of the holy Setatmeh, too. Why was it that Atu had to hear of your movements and intentions from your subordinate? I think you're a traitor.*

'*Our* enemies, Tayan of Tokoban?' she thought savagely. 'Which of us is the traitor? And what is it you think Pechaqueh see you as? You don't honestly believe they want you as their Singer?' She told herself she didn't regret the question as he twisted inside her, tearing into her mind, ripping open her hopes and shitting on them. She didn't, she wouldn't regret it – up until she did. Up until she was screaming again.

Ask me to stop. Beg me.

'Please. Please, I'm sorry. It is the deception. It isn't me, it's what I do as a Whisper. It's why I'm so good at it. I disappear into the story I've created so deeply that I cease to think in any way other than how that person would think. In this case, a traitor to the Melody and the song. Please, Tayan, ask Pilos if you don't believe me. He communed with me when I was in Tokoban and—'

There was no song in Tokoban. You lie.

'Do you not remember the journeys I made to the edge of Xentiban, looking for lost kin? You don't really think I was there hoping to meet my mother, do you?'

Ilandeh gripped her mind like a strangler fig around a pom. Allowing no hint of anything other than what she wanted him to know to filter through.

Tayan's mind tinged purple, just the merest hint of anger. At her, or at himself, because he couldn't decide whether to trust her? It didn't matter, as long as she got through this intact.

Be careful, little Whisper. Even I don't know the limits of what the song can do, and while you are under it, you are under my control.

Ilandeh choked a laugh. 'Control? You're a shaman, Tayan. Devoted to medicine and to healing. Devoted to Malel. Who are you to control me or anyone?'

Who am I? I am the fucking Singer, and you will do as you are told.

The laughter came easier and with more mockery. How mad did she look, she wondered briefly, kneeling in the rain and giggling and screeching? 'Do as I'm told? I'm forty-three sun-years old, Tayan. Older than you by far. You don't get to tell me off as if you're my parent. Or as if you're Pecha, even. Don't forget, it's only because you have the magic that you can talk to me like this, and it's only because of my Pechaqueh father that I can hear you. You—'

Tayan was the one laughing this time, and it was tinged with a malice more suited to Xac – or Enet. *That is where you're wrong, Ilandeh. Don't you remember me going into the song day after day to strengthen Xac? How do you think I did that?*

Ilandeh hesitated, blue with caution within the song-space. 'Listener Chotek or Shaman Kapal guided you.'

He laughed again, slick and ugly inside her and blooming pink with triumphant pleasure, and the Whisper's stomach flipped over. No. Impossible.

Believe me, Whisper, anyone with the knowledge and skill can Listen. Anyone can move through the song. Anyone. Even strangers. He was pensive, suddenly, as if he'd remembered something. *Your ability to hear me has nothing to do with your Pechaqueh heritage; that is simply another lie they tell you. Tell everyone. Listening is a skill, not a blood-borne gift. I have spoken to Lilla with as much ease as I speak to you. Never forget that.*

Omeata, learned in magic.

Ilandeh recoiled both physically and spiritually. No. Absolutely the fuck not. It didn't bear thinking about. It wasn't real, it couldn't be done. She didn't believe it. Besides, what of the rebels? If it was possible, they'd be coordinating better; they'd be winning. There was no way there wouldn't be someone somewhere who'd learnt to Listen. Yet everything she'd heard on her journey through Ixachipan since the night of the uprising affirmed that the rebel forces were isolated, fighting their own bitter little wars in their own corners of the Empire. They didn't have that sort of communication. So Tayan had to be lying.

'I don't believe you,' Ilandeh thought flatly. 'You realise the Pechaqueh in the source and all the warriors of all bloods gathered to protect the pyramid have no respect for you? They'll be looking for ways to assassinate you and ensure the song-magic goes to someone more suitable as soon as they can.' She pulsed orange with conviction, projecting her belief into the link he'd forced into her.

'If I'd still been Chorus Leader, I'd probably have been the one they tasked with doing it, ending your life. A full-blood Pecha wouldn't want to get their hands bloody, after all, not if they were intending on becoming Singer immediately afterwards.'

She didn't give him a chance to reply, breathing through the spikes of pain as he latched claw after claw into her mind and spirit, cutting, prying. 'I'd have found it hard, you know, killing you. I was glad you were out of the Sky City when we were pushed to act. You might have been the closest thing to a real friend I ever had while working for the High Feather.'

A friendship based on a lie! Tayan roared. She cowered, unable to do anything else, and then curled her lip despite the pain when he rippled pink with pleasure at having hurt her. So, this was what power did to him. This was direct proof of how the song corrupted.

Ilandeh had lost sight of who she was lying to and why. Everyone; no one; herself. Only that last was irrefutable. Her body was kneeling in Chitenec, which was peaceful, and yet she was surrounded by Zellih bent on destruction. Her mind was invaded by a man she'd respected, even loved as a friend, as he sought to break her to his will.

'You realise you're destroying my disguise?' she asked. 'No Zellitli will trust me now. You've lost your spy in the flock. You've done this, not me.'

Ilandeh shrieked and clawed at her skull again, fingernails digging trenches in her temples, drawing blood to the surface of the delicate skin as Tayan, apparently, decided to make sure there was no way back for her with Omeata. Perhaps hoping the Bird-form would slaughter her.

'Our friendship did begin out of expediency, yes. But tell me then, great Singer of Ixachipan, how many friends do you have now? Why are you talking to me instead of to them? And don't say you're looking for answers to Olox's report, because you haven't asked a single question. That was an excuse to come to me. Because you know, deep down and despite everything, that somehow, within the lies I was living, I was the only one who's ever been honest with you. And you need a friend now, don't you? You need someone to trust and there's no one, not a single person in that great pyramid, who doesn't want you dead.'

Tayan laughed but it was unconvincing, so he made up for it by twisting through Ilandeh's mind until she was nauseous with pain. *You want to be my friend, half-blood? You think you're qualified?*

'You're the no-blood,' she struck back, gasping. 'You tell me.' She braced, a whimper sliding from her throat, but nothing happened. There was a long pause, winding her nerves tighter and tighter until she thought her spine would snap under the tension.

Are you a traitor, Whisper Ilandeh? Tayan asked eventually, his emotions so tightly held that she had no idea what he was thinking.

'Rest assured, holy lord. I know my place,' Ilandeh replied, though she couldn't keep her lack of respect from bleeding through. 'I'm on my knees in the mud, am I not? I will do all that the song and the High Feather requires of me.'

What about what your Singer requires of you?

'That too, holy lord. Once you know what it is you want.'

Ilandeh thought about adding that he clearly didn't want her as a spy among the Zellih if this was how he behaved; she resisted, but the shape of the thought was clear in her mind and she knew he saw it.

Shut up. What is your next target? What are the targets of the other flocks? What are their numbers?

'Ah. So it is more than just Omeata. To answer your question, Singer, I have no idea. Omeata doesn't trust me enough yet to tell me her plans; I was unaware of the existence of other flocks, though I suspected they were here. You speak Pallatolli; you have learnt about their culture. So you know about the Bird Aspects, the seven members that make up their ruling council. The Bird-form is one. If you'd given me time, I could have discovered how many Aspects, how many flocks and warriors you were facing, but you didn't. I suspect the Bird-wings at least, and possibly the Bird-tail, but what if it is all seven? The seven flocks of Zellipan? You think you can defeat that?'

Impossible, Tayan breathed and the inside of Ilandeh's mind was coated with his thick, sticky black fear. *They would never send so many. You will discover their purpose, their numbers, their plans.*

'I have just told you, you have destroyed my disguise with this communion. I will be able to discover nothing.'

You will do as your Singer commands.

Tayan loosened his hold just a little, as if that would change anything, but it was enough that Ilandeh came back to her body for the first time in what might have been hours. She was panting, crying, snivelling, her complete lack of dignity only combated by the agony he'd put in her. A shimmer in the corner of her eye had her screwing up her face, but she didn't turn away. She knew those colours and that ripple of movement. Omeata.

'Bird-form,' she croaked aloud. 'The Singer . . . invades me. I beg forgiveness. If you have a message for him—'

Don't speak to them when I am here, Whisper. Don't disrespect me like that.

Ilandeh giggled, unable to stop the bubble of hysteria from rising and bursting. 'Disrespect? You want to know disrespect? The Zellih will not stop until they have control of the song. They are coming for you, Tayan. We are all coming for you.'

Kill the Bird-form, the Singer gasped and it wasn't pain but plea this time. *Fucking kill them.*

Ilandeh laughed again, making no effort to hold back her emotions, her contempt. She mocked him with every laugh, with every breath, with every strangled sob. She didn't reply, just let him feel what she felt. Let him see how much she'd cared for him back in Tokoban, despite herself and her orders. And how she'd watched over him in the great pyramid while appearing to disdain him.

And exactly what she thought of him now.

You . . . you fucking half-blood fucking nobody. His rage shone so bright it blinded her, lit her up purple and burnt her to dust. *Who do you think you are, you conniving, manipulative little shit. You think to question me? To insult me? I'll peel your fucking face off for this. I'll rip your guts out and make you eat them.* Filthy *fucking half-blood!*

'Goodbye, great Singer. I hope you sleep easy,' Ilandeh said aloud. She didn't know if it would work, expected to be punished for it, but to her surprise there was no answer, just the slow, sickening slide of a mind leaving hers like a blade exiting flesh. Sucking, pulling, harming.

Gone.

She toppled off her knees onto her side and curled up. Above her, the Zellih aimed their spears at her shivering flesh.

XESSA

Choosers' offices, western district, Singing City,
Pechacan, Empire of Songs
68th day of the Great Star at morning

Toxte unwrapped the nameless, shapeless lump of meat and put it down in front of a drooling Ossa. He didn't meet Xessa's eyes and she was glad; better to pretend neither of them knew where it had come from. Who it had once been.

Of all the myriad, numberless things Xessa could choose to have nightmares about, that trek through the flame and the smoke to Weaver's hideout to coordinate the counter-ambush was the worst. She'd lost Ossa for nearly an hour, sending him out on a run from which he just didn't return, and in the night and the smoke and the panic, his black hide had been invisible. She'd roamed the streets, clicking and whistling from a parched and burning throat, peering through burning eyes and unable to stifle her coughing.

Almost, she'd believed him gone. Lost forever. Dead from smoke or thirst or flames or spear. Dead. She'd blamed everyone – Lilla for sending her to Weaver, Pilos for setting the fires, Ekon for making her go alone. Herself. Always, endlessly, herself, as she roamed the streets with no idea where she was or where she was supposed to go, her message for Weaver's war party forgotten, abandoned inside her salt-cotton.

Until she'd smelt water, in the hour before the rain came. If the storm had broken sooner . . . but it hadn't, and she'd followed that wet, welcome, and worrying scent to a small stone cistern and found her poor, poor dog lying at its base. So desperate and lost and alone that he'd ventured to the water that he knew to be a threat. Looking for her? Or simply looking for relief from the heat and smoke and flame?

She'd doused him in great sweeping splashes of water and helped him drink, washed his face and eyes and paws, weeping and heedless of the prickle of fear for the first time in her life. Focused instead on the water's life-giving blessing. If a Drowned had leapt out of it at that moment, she'd have torn it apart with her bare hands to save her dog. She'd carried him to Weaver and passed on the message. They'd still managed to spring the counter-attack in time to avoid complete defeat.

And Xessa hadn't let Ossa out of her sight since.

She told herself it was just a memory now, and it would fade with the others. She hoped. For now, she grounded herself in this place and this moment, her calf pressed to Ossa's flank and her shoulder against Toxte as they watched the dog tear into the meat that they knew – and would not admit – was human.

Meat and rest and water had done much to restore Ossa to his former strength and mischief, though the humans were still tight-chested from breathing in so much smoke, even four days later.

'Refugees arrived today,' Toxte signed eventually as Ossa tore meat from splintered bone. 'From the north.' Xessa frowned. 'Hundreds who left that night, and hundreds more. Nearly all Chitenecah, Tokob, and Yaloh.'

Xessa straightened up. 'Why? What made them come back?'

'There are mass graves ringing the Singing City to the north and west, fifteen, twenty sticks out. Open pits filled with corpses, most unrecognisable from the humidity and the rain, but . . . their clothing, some tattoos, still identifiable. It's,' he paused and swallowed, rubbing his thumbs against his fingertips as if to ground himself. 'People are saying it's all those thousands who went north after Tayan's proclamation of a free Tokoban.'

Xessa inhaled and immediately coughed. Ossa looked up from his meal and then continued gnawing on the bone.

'What,' she began and then just stopped. What could she ask? She already knew the answer. 'Even back then he was luring Tokob to their deaths? Luring everyone, anyone? Does Lilla know?'

'Ekon says to leave him be. It would just let Tayan know that we know, and that some among us were prepared to flee. Anoq's here, too. Led them out; led them back.'

Xessa curled her lip and her husband slapped her shoulder gently. 'He's guilty and frightened, but mostly he's shaken by what he saw. The implications of it. He's questioning things now, but he's fragile too. One wrong move could send him away again. And we need him, Xessa. We need all of them.'

Xessa's stomach threatened to reject its meagre contents. 'There were elders and civilians among those who fled,' she signed, her gestures choppy with emotion. 'There were children. How could Tayan do such a thing?'

Toxte just shook his head; he had no answers. 'Anoq brought others, people who'd bypassed the city on their way north only to come across the graves and realise the truth. They'd been hiding between the pits and here ever since, too frightened to move. Some hundreds and mostly civilians. We might convince some to fight, at least.'

'I don't suppose any ejab?' Xessa asked casually.

'Two plus Anoq, but you're the only one with a dog,' Toxte said.

She licked her teeth and watched Ossa eat for a while. 'We don't need dogs,' she signed eventually and slanted him a look from beneath her lashes.

Toxte shifted closer. 'Xessa, my love, I know that look. You've got a horrible idea and you know I won't like it. It's the sort of idea you'd have shared with Tayan, who would have been all for it, which is how I know I won't like it.' He pointed at the dog. 'You've got until that meat's gone to convince me.'

Xessa looked at the fragments of bone and muscle and swallowed hard. It was still obvious what it was. *And it's what will happen to all of us if we lose.*

She nodded, once, and began to sign.

It didn't take long for Toxte's face to change, alarm to fear to denial to grief. He cut her off with raised hands. 'You can't mean this. It's moon-mad. It's worse than that: it's stupid. It won't work. I won't let you.'

Xessa breathed through her instinctive indignation. He was allowed to feel that; he was allowed to tell her that. He was her husband and it was his love talking. Still, no one had ever told Xessa what she could and couldn't do since she'd been a girl still learning to walk the snake path.

'My love, my heart,' she signed gently. 'I do not need your permission. I need your help.'

That stopped him. 'My help?'

A tear slipped down Xessa's cheek to the corner of her mouth; she licked it away. 'I know what I'm asking. I know how dangerous it is. And I know I cannot do this alone. But if anyone can – if *anyone* has the ability – surely it is ejab.'

'You want me to come with you?'

She rubbed her mouth. 'No, I really don't. I want you to take Ossa home and live. I asked you to do that once, and you refused. And then you said you'd be at my side forever. I don't want you at my side for this, Toxte, despite that promise, but I do need you there. Will you stand with me? Will you risk death to—'

'I walk where you walk. You're not the only one to remember that promise or hold it true.' He pointed. 'But not him.'

'Malel no, not him. Never Ossa. He's seen too much of war; I won't put him through this, too.'

'Good,' he signed fiercely. 'He shouldn't be a part of it.' His hands fell to grip her leg, just holding on, just making contact.

'Do you think Anoq and the other ejab will join us?'

'All we can do is ask. Do you think the spirit-magic will work?' Toxte countered.

'You're the expert on that. You took it that day at the riverbank. Did it stop you hearing the song?'

Toxte was about to answer when he looked over her shoulder and then pointed. She twisted to see Ekon, Lilla, and Weaver approaching. Their numbers had been so reduced by the rumours and fighting that they were sharing the building with the old woman's war party. The three of them stared with varying levels of disgust at the meat Ossa was eating and then looked away. They understood, too.

'Eleven hundred,' Ekon said as soon as they'd sat, the ejab shuffling sideways so Xessa could see everyone's faces and hands. 'That's how many warriors and civilians have swelled our numbers. That replenishes our war party and more.'

'Does it outnumber Feather Detta and the Second Talon?' Weaver demanded and it was obvious from the strain that this was an argument that had been going for some time.

'We've already bled the Second,' Ekon began.

'Does it matter?' Xessa signed bluntly and Weaver scowled when Toxte translated. 'We're always going to be outnumbered. Do you have some grand plan if we reach a certain magical number of warriors or fall below a different number? Will you sell someone else's land, for instance?' She didn't need to be able to hear to know that the silence was awkward. 'Toxte and I have something to discuss with our friend,' she continued before Weaver could respond.

Ekon's face fell, but he began to stand again.

'Stay,' she signed. 'Weaver, go away and take Lilla with you. Ekon will tell you our plan later. Sorry, Lilla.'

Toxte was openly thinking of a way to translate that wasn't so peremptory, so Xessa blew air through her lips and flapped her hands at Weaver in agitated dismissal, then pointed at Ekon and the floor. The old woman began to splutter and Lilla was scowling but he rose and helped her to stand, talking earnestly as he led her away from their tiny refuge among the hundreds of warriors crammed in this building.

Ekon watched them go in open disbelief and something like worry, and if she felt like a hypocrite for naming him a friend after how she'd treated him and Lilla the last weeks, well, she probably deserved it.

'Snake-Sister's tits, Xessa, do you ever think before you sign?' Toxte asked.

'Snakes don't have tits. They lay eggs,' she responded primly and grinned when he actually clenched his fists in exasperation. She adored driving him to the edge of his sanity. 'Oh, shut up. You love it. You love me.'

Ekon shook his head, having no idea what they'd just said, and then mimicked Xessa's dismissal of Weaver and jerked his head in the direction she'd gone. Then he blew out his cheeks and looked to Toxte. 'You married an insane creature,' he said, expression awestruck. 'Mictec and Malel, you are a braver man than I am.'

'That's true, I am,' Toxte said and signed without hesitation and Xessa laughed. Even though it was Ekon, the teasing tasted like home. It tasted like Lilla and she understood, perhaps for the first time, what he saw in this tall, lean, scarred Chitenecatl who'd lied to the world for the length of his life. 'You two were deep in conversation when we got here. What are you cooking and why can't Weaver know about it?'

The ejab looked at each other. 'Shall I tell him?' Toxte signed.

Xessa took a deep breath. 'Sign as you speak, so I can track the conversation.' She made eye contact with Ekon. 'You'll understand why Lilla can't know this when he tells you,' she added, trusting Toxte to translate. 'And you'll understand what it's going to do to him when he does learn the extent of our – my – plan.'

The former Feather began to speak and then cut himself off, gnawing on the inside of his cheek instead. 'Tell me,' he said.

Toxte took a deep breath and then gestured at Xessa and himself. 'We are ejab. Deaf to the songs of the Drowned. Well, I'm not deaf to the song itself, but its influence is lessened when I have the spirit-magic in me. We are ejab,' he repeated, 'and our duty is to kill those who sing.'

'I'm coming with you, and Lilla will insist on coming too.'

Of everything she'd expected Ekon to say, that wasn't it. 'Lilla's body can't stand the spirit-magic, and you have no idea how you'd react to it, either. You wouldn't be able to help us.'

'We won't take the spirit-magic. We'll take the offer of a peace-weaving to Tayan. I can't imagine he'll be surprised by that. We've been fighting for three months, losing more than we win, and now supposedly our own rebel leaders have betrayed us. A peace-weaving isn't an unlikely outcome in the circumstances.'

'And then what?' Toxte signed and said.

'That will be between Lilla and his husband, but I imagine he'll ask him why he's doing all this. What he's trying to achieve. Make him see he's hurting more people than he's helping.'

Despite his words, Ekon's face was the sort of blank that spoke of carefully hidden pain. Xessa felt a stab of empathy and took his hand in hers on instinct, then pressed a kiss to his knuckles. Ekon startled and then managed a wan smile and a squeeze of her fingers.

'Tayan has had the chance to walk away from everything before now and he hasn't,' she signed. 'He's got more power – real power – now than he had even as a member of the shamanic conclave or as our peace-weaver. He won't give that up for love and if Lilla thinks he will—'

'I don't think Lilla expects that, or at least, not consciously. But I promised to help him get answers and he deserves the chance to ask them. I just want to be there to pick him back up afterwards. But that means we have to tell him.'

Xessa shook her head. 'We tell him part of it, not all of it. He can't know about us,' she signed, gesturing at herself and Toxte. 'As soon as he arrives at the pyramid, Tayan's going to do that thing to his mind. He might even do it to you,' she added, panic threatening.

Ekon grimaced. 'Unlikely. Lilla will be too tempting a target. But if he does, well, I've had twenty years pretending to be something I'm not. I've got some defences in place to deflect his attention away from where I don't want him to go. If that doesn't work, at least we're already in the pyramid. In his presence. We can do what we need to.'

Xessa's heart gave a single great lurch of betrayal and then began pounding on the cage of her ribs like a drum calling to Malel. Perhaps it was. She realised as she swallowed bitter bile that she'd expected – no, she'd hoped – Ekon would talk her out of it. When he'd appeared with Lilla and Weaver and she'd known she had to tell him, that strange twist in her belly had been relief. She'd *wanted him* to talk her out of it. Instead, he'd not only agreed to her plan but bettered it.

They stared at each other for a long time, perhaps each willing the other to back down, or perhaps each needing the other to tell them they were right, this was right, it was the right decision and it didn't make them monsters because the doing of it would save countless lives and bring about a lasting peace.

And destroy Lilla.

No, she realised. *We're monsters anyway. But even the monstrous can do the right thing.*

She took a deep breath and it was like the air flowed over her heart, cold and piercing. She curled in around her chest and ordered herself not to cry.

Ekon said something Xessa didn't catch.

'We need to decide what we tell Lilla,' Toxte signed.

'And Weaver,' the Chitenecatl added when she glanced his way. 'We can't keep this from her.'

'They both get the same story,' Toxte said. 'We three know the truth, and the peace-weavers and other ejab know as much as necessary to be convincing. No one else.'

On that, they were in agreement.

'He'll know we're not telling him everything,' Ekon had said before he'd left to find Lilla and Weaver. 'He'll have his suspicions and his fears, and I won't be able to soothe them. He's going to know I'm lying, and then he's going to agree to come with us, and he's going to expect us to, to . . .' He'd trailed off, but if he was hoping the ejab might have an answer for him, he was disappointed. Things still weren't right between Xessa and Lilla, and with what they were planning, it was likely they never would be.

When Ekon was gone, Toxte leant forward to scratch Ossa's rump. He shifted to sit opposite her again so he could keep his signs small and just between them. Private despite the Tokob nearby. 'That's a good man. And a broken one. I'm glad it's not us having to decide how much truth to tell their lover, or how much suspicion to have for what they're told. This is far more complicated for them.'

Xessa looked at Ossa lying in front of her, his strong white teeth cracking the last of the bone. 'Is it?' she signed gently. She took a breath. 'Don't worry, dog. We'll come back. I promise we'll come back to you.'

Toxte seized Xessa and dragged her into a fierce embrace, pressing a dozen desperate kisses across her face she had no hope of keeping up with, before shoving her away almost violently. She rocked where she sat and Ossa gave Toxte the sort of hard stare that had both dogs and humans showing him their bellies.

'I love you, Eja Xessa. Wife. Lover. Passionate, crazy, beautiful idiot. I love you like the sun loves the earth and the moon loves the night. But you're so fucking stupid sometimes. *We are ejab.* If this fails and Tayan has become what we believe he has, he won't let us walk free from his pyramid. Lilla, yes, perhaps, for the sake of a dead love if nothing else, but us? We don't get a happy ending, my love. You're asking me to walk beside you to my death. And I will, you know I will. I've said I will and I mean it. But you need to understand what this is, the finality of it. So you say your goodbyes to Ossa when the time comes, and make sure you know in your heart that it is a goodbye, but don't you dare let him see your grief, you hear me? He goes and lives with someone who will love and honour what he is, who gives him all the meat and all the cuddles he wants. But he doesn't get to scent your fear when we say goodbye to him. Do you understand?'

Xessa's heart was choking her, but she nodded and blinked away the stinging. Toxte was right, as he was right about so much. She and Ossa had been separated for two years under the worst circumstances; the separation that was to come needed to happen gently, with love and not anguish.

'Tiamoko will take him until Lilla can get back here,' she signed. 'I'll make them both promise to live and go home together, live next door to each other. He'll rule their every day until the end of his life. And I'll be waiting on the spiral path when he comes home to me.' It was hard to breathe.

'And I'll be waiting with you,' Toxte promised, and it freed her lungs to inhale. The air tasted of grief.

'And so will Ekka,' Xessa signed. 'We'll be a family again.' She leant forwards and buried her face in Ossa's neck, felt his contented rumble and then the grind of teeth on bone. *A family in death.*

Tiamoko accepted Ossa willingly, confused that Xessa was going somewhere without him but trusting enough not to question her. She had to resist the urge to grab him and press herself against his solidity. She'd told him before, in the pit, that it was like hugging a tree, but one that could hug back, and she had a sudden craving to be enveloped in his safety again.

She resisted; the boy was too astute these days and Xessa didn't have another farewell in her. To Ekon's rage and Xessa's surprise, everyone's surprise, Weaver had forbidden the Chitenecatl from attending the peace-weaving at the pyramid. Ekon was war leader: they couldn't risk losing him on this foolish quest.

And despite the ferocity with which Ekon had embraced Mictec, his freedom, and his Chitenecah heritage, the habit of obedience was still embedded in him. He'd raged and threatened and grieved and even begged – but he'd allowed Weaver to dictate her will.

As for Lilla, Xessa knew him well enough to see the relief hidden in his heart. She'd been an unwilling witness to their hasty, unprepared-for parting, and it had almost destroyed her, but the truth was Lilla was glad Ekon was staying behind. Now she had to say goodbye to her dog.

Ossa sat by Tiamoko and shoved backwards until he was leaning against the warrior's hip, his tongue lolling in a doggy smile.

'He's just eaten, but there's a cache of, of meat on a high shelf in the main building, left of the door. I don't think anyone else will want it.' Her hands were clumsy and she didn't much care if Tiamoko understood her implication. That meat was for Ossa; he'd see the dog got it.

Xessa knelt and buried her face in his ruff, smothering her fear and hurt and the snarling, howling longing to stay here with him, where there was at least the illusion of safety. She prayed she didn't stink of fear as she made herself let go and sat up. 'Tiamoko. This is my dog. My heart. Don't react.'

He tensed anyway and she glared at him until he flicked back his hair and nodded.

'If I don't come back, they'll try to bring my body so he can say goodbye. If they don't manage that, you need to keep him close; sooner or later he'll try and look for me.' Tiamoko started to sign and she shook her head, needing to get the words out now before she lost her courage. 'If I don't come back, you have to take him home. You and Lilla. He'll be yours, both of yours so you both need to live. Promise me you'll take him back to Tokoban. *Promise me.*'

'Xessa—'

'Is that a promise, boy?' she demanded, brittle and fragile and breaking and shattered.

Tiamoko straightened up. 'I promise, Eja. I swear on our ancestors and Malel. I will protect him and love him and see him back home until you can rescue me from him.'

She couldn't help but smile at that last and signed her thanks that it was the last expression Ossa saw cross her face. 'Don't you dare be good for him,' she signed to the dog, kissing his muzzle and getting a tongue in the eye for her trouble. 'Be the worst you can be. And don't ever be sad.'

Ossa wagged his tail and licked her face again and Xessa nodded once, jerkily, and stood. Ossa stood, too, and she showed him a flat palm. He sat again. She clicked her approval and walked away.

I'll see you soon, my friend. I'll see you soon. I'll see you soon. I'll see you soon.

The chant was just enough for her to keep her composure until she exited the building and was lost to his sight. Then she burst into tears. Toxte found her in the next instant and wrapped her up in his arms; his own farewell with Ossa had been bittersweet but brief and she knew he'd been thinking of his own lost Ekka in the moments he'd murmured in the big, twitching triangular ear before walking away.

Ekon, Weaver, and Lilla were waiting, as well as the peace-weavers from the other tribes and Eja Anoq, the only one who'd agreed to come with them. Perhaps he had a point to prove. Weaver, as usual, had the sort of face more normally found carved on a temple's side – implacable, uncaring, other-worldly. Ekon looked like he was going to vomit up his own entrails; Lilla had the glassy stare of one who'd glimpsed the Underworld.

Not a happy little party, are we?

Guilt tried its best to swamp Xessa; she gripped Toxte's hand hard enough to make him wince and faced them all with a defiant chin. Everyone had agreed to this. It was her plan, but they'd said yes.

Ekon took a pace forward and the eja had to fight to hold her place. 'There is a custom among Tokob,' he said slowly and clearly, 'that I believe is kin to one among my own people. A custom I have never before had the opportunity to enact.' A small, private smile lightened his features. 'It is a claiming. Of family.' He stepped forward again and then, clearly signalling his intentions, he took Xessa's face between his palms and kissed her brow and each eyelid. 'Come home safe, sister.'

It was very hard to breathe, but Xessa found a smile for him, licked her thumb and pressed it to his temple. She watched as Ekon claimed her husband, and was claimed in turn, then snapped her fingers for Toxte to translate. She kept her signs small and Ekon between her and Lilla so he couldn't see, even as she knew how that would annoy him.

'I'll do all I can to send him back to you, but if I do, you don't ever leave him. What happens – what we do – is going to shatter who he is and I see that same breaking in you. I know you're a, a shell, a shadow. I know you've given everything to this, that you've given us this chance through a sacrifice we will never understand. And I know people have asked things of you your entire life. I don't have the right to ask, Ekon of the Chitenecah, kin of mine, but I will – no, I will demand.'

She stepped so close that Toxte could barely see the signs that flickered between her chest and the Chitenecah. 'Lilla gets to be happy.' Ekon jerked as if she'd stabbed him, a shine coming to his eyes and one hand rising to press against his mouth. 'He also gets my dog, and my dog will bite your cock off if you make Lilla unhappy. Am I clear?'

'You are understood,' Ekon said formally. 'And despite your threats of genital torture, I expect you to come back, too. You're not the only one who can make demands, you know. Bring him back to me.' He hesitated and took a breath. 'Bring yourselves back. Please.'

Xessa stretched up on her toes and kissed the Chitenecatl on his cheek, and then turned away as she'd done with Ossa. She was done with goodbyes. Done with emotions. The only thing she had left was the need to understand – and the need to end this. One way or another, once and for all.

Xessa was the sort of calm and focused she only got when approaching the water to perform her duty. She walked with

Toxte and Lilla in the centre of a Paw of peace-weavers. That they were all also talented warriors, who knew the danger they were walking into, was part of the plan. A few paces behind was Anoq, the young eja twitchy but determined to make up for his earlier blunder. She took strength from their strength and tried not to think too much.

The city was a stinking ruin. Grimy and empty and its colours faded to mud and ash. So many dead; so many fled. More spirits than living people now. More angry ancestors.

When she'd been taken to fight in other pits during previous Wets, she'd seen slaves scrubbing the splattered mud from the base of prestigious buildings so the limestone and murals remained vibrant. Now that mud was knee-high and growing by the day. The stone roads were likewise filthy, and soft, silky mud slid between her toes and flicked up the insides of her calves as she walked. She grinned down at her feet – she was going to trample this through their most sacred building soon. She should roll in it just so she could smear herself across the walls when she got there.

A flock of birds, purple-blue-black and small, shimmered overhead from a nearby garden, and Xessa wondered what they thought of the madness of the humans who shared this city with them.

'Do you think Weaver's superiors did make an alliance with the Zellih and offer them Tokoban in return?' she asked Toxte in a pointless attempt to distract herself from what they were attempting.

Lilla caught her gestures as well. 'Ekon thinks so, though he swears on Mictec that he wasn't part of that, and I believe him.'

'He didn't even know about Enet; they wouldn't have told him something like that,' Xessa signed and saw Lilla's surprise. Had she been so awful for so long that he was expecting an argument here, now, with what they were about to attempt looming over them? Regret was bitter on her tongue and she jumped forward to grab his hand and pull him to a halt. He looked down at her, but she couldn't meet his eye. She simply threw herself against his chest and prayed he'd catch her.

He did, caught her so tight that for one long, glorious moment she couldn't breathe, crushed in his embrace with all the fierce love they'd both poured into Tayan. Once. When he let her go – too soon – she made herself step back. 'I love you,' she signed. 'And I'm sorry for all of it. So sorry. I didn't—'

'We are living in unprecedented times. None of us could predict how that would change us. I know you . . . have your plans,' he signed and Xessa went cold. Toxte came and pressed himself against her flank. 'Don't, just don't be hasty, that's all I ask. Don't act without giving him a chance to talk. Please, Xessa. I know he's a talker, I know he can convince a jaguar to put its head in the snare, but please. We owe him that.'

Do we? Do we owe him anything— Xessa cut herself off and, hating herself in a way she rarely had even in the last two sun-years, she hushed him. 'We are here to weave a peace. And I am—'

Lilla's face twisted with disbelief and a flash of hate so strong and beautiful it stole the strength from her spine and the words from her hands. She staggered and Toxte's arm snaked around her waist. How was it that only heartbeats ago they'd been embracing like the kin she hoped they still were?

'Let's just get this done,' he signed and it was cold and it was lethal. He caught up with the rest of the party, leaving them behind.

Xessa took a moment to straighten her salt-cotton and adjust the turkey feather over her right ear, and then she began walking again. Toxte limped at her side, beloved and brooding. The space on her other side was empty of the big, pacing black dog who was her shadow and her spirit and Xessa's heart ached at his absence.

Lilla was stalking ahead, separate from both the peace-weavers and the ejab, and she wanted to try and fix things one last time, because they weren't going to get another chance. She rubbed her kilt between her fingers, preparing some words, but then their scouts threw up their arms in warning and the group stopped, wary and tense.

Lilla looked back at her once, expression neutral, eyes empty, and then he shook himself and pushed through to the front of the group to confront the Melody warriors facing them.

Toxte squeezed Xessa's hand and brought it to his mouth. The kiss stuttered across her knuckles as a series of violent twitches rippled through his muscular frame. His pupils had contracted – the spirit-magic was beginning to work.

She nodded once and made herself smile, then held out the rope and presented her wrists so he could tie them. Rika, the peace-weaver from Quitoban, stepped forward with pots of powdered charcoal and white ash to paint her face in stripes. In offering to Malel.

Xessa caught a glimpse of Lilla. He'd been talking to the eagles confronting him, but now he stood slack-jawed and silent as Xessa and Anoq, ejab and so-called god-killers, prepared themselves to die.

THE SINGER

Tayan prowled the currents of his song like a hungry holy Setat patrolling a riverbank. His newest ancestor, the Setat who had been Xac, had visited him along with his own personal god, and he'd communed with the latter and then, with some trepidation, the former. Would it have any memory of its last moments before ascension? Did it carry any anger towards him?

It did not, and a weight had lifted from Tayan's chest. Its approval was the final confirmation he'd needed that he was the Singer chosen by the magic and the gods, by destiny and prophecy, despite the stranger within the song and their occasional taunting visits.

Tayan had told the gods that traitors were heading north to push back the invading Zellih and that ejab might be among them. He'd spoken of his fears for the safety of all holy Setatmeh and begged them for their aid, even though they too would be at risk if they agreed.

The newest Setat volunteered its services, expressing a vast desire to see the world after so long trapped in the great pyramid. It wanted to stretch its newly strong limbs and feel sun and rain and the depths of rivers upon its skin. It wanted sensation and to glut on offerings and for the first time in years, Tayan was content for it to do so.

The former Xac would travel north through the waterways to warn its kin that not everyone they sang for would come to them willingly, that some would come with nets and spears and the sharp teeth of dogs. That if that happened, they should flee, god or no. Their existence was more important than their pride.

Such a communion between Tayan and the gods would not have been possible before the holy Setatmeh awakening. He suspected, too, that communication among themselves had been likewise stunted by the spirits polluting the song. Those holy Setatmeh living in Tokoban would surely have fled or taught each other caution if they could have; for an instant, Tayan had a vision of what life in the Sky City might have been like if all the holy Setatmeh in the Swift Water were as vital and intelligent as they were now. A delicate shiver crept across his scalp.

He focused back on his song, examining various golden motes and the strength of their love and devotion to the Empire, their connection to him.

The stranger haunting me knows something. Perhaps my anger and condemnation of them have been hasty. Perhaps they, too, want the holy Setatmeh to be healed and freed.

And they had told him how to accomplish that.

Feed the world spirit.

Tayan's own spirit kicked petulantly. *I cannot feed the world spirit, because it sleeps deep in the earth where Enet put it. And the god, my god, told me that it is not in fact the world spirit at all, but something else. I cannot wake something whose name I do not know. Whose intentions and powers are unknown.*

But the stranger had not told him to wake it; they'd told him to feed it. Had seemed sure he'd be able to, despite its slumber. Supposing it slumbered.

There was so much that he did not understand, so much that could change even the most careful experiment to catastrophe.

Tayan approached the nearest spirit, hanging grey and motion-less and unaware. He poked it and it twitched and then tried to thrash away, jerking and flailing like a fawn in a snare. Tayan got a firm grip on it and it turned on him, hooks growing on its form and sinking into his golden vastness. It was savage, desperate, but mindless. A series of reactions and instincts unmoderated by a consciousness. Less aware than even the oldest and most faded ancestor on the spiral path.

Tayan ripped free of its barbs with contemptuous ease and closed his magic around it and crushed it into splinters. He paused, suddenly uneasy – did this count as blooding the song? Was he going to be overcome with lust as Xac had been before him? Was this why the nameless Listener had told him to feed the world spirit instead of disposing of these pallid, pathetic spectres himself?

Panicked, he pulled away, out of the song and back into his flesh. He was in the source – obviously – and his body was relaxed. Hungry, but for normal food, not anything . . . sinister. His song was powerful and beautiful, a sonorous soaring promise of peace if only the traitors would lay down their weapons. Tayan checked his surroundings: no bodies, no blood. He was safe. This time.

'Holy lord!'

Tayan startled and scrambled to his feet, his heart thumping. He staggered, the blood rushing from his head too fast.

'What is it?' he demanded of the warrior dropping to their knees before him. Xochi had appeared at Tayan's side, armed and alert.

'Delegation from the traitors, holy lord,' the warrior mumbled into the mats. 'The offer of a peace-weaving and a, a surrender.'

'A peace-weaving and a surrender? What nonsense are you speaking? How can it be both?'

'The peace-weavers wear the patterns of all tribes under the song, and they are accompanied by two people professing to be ejab. They say they are willing to give themselves up to you and to death to prove the sincerity of the peace-weaving.

A sacrifice to their god, they say, that you might hear their words.' The warrior lifted his head against all protocol; he was grinning. 'The war is over!'

'Hold your tongue,' Xochi snapped, but there was a blaze of hope in her face, too. 'Would ejab really sacrifice themselves like this, holy lord?' she asked and then stammered an apology for speaking out of turn.

'Yes. They're ejab. Though they do not seek death, they'd give their lives if they had to so that others might live.'

It worked. The rumour of the Zellih has split them. They've lost too many warriors and now they'll take peace on any terms.

I've won.

'Where's Pilos? You, go and find him and get him here. Xochi, get me some turkey feathers and my medicine chest and then have food and water brought out.' He hesitated. 'And close the curtain, at least to begin with. Hurry.'

'You shouldn't be left alone, holy lord,' she fretted as the messenger ran out to find Pilos, decorum forgotten. Tayan knew how he felt.

'They're not here yet, are they? And they'll be escorted in under guard. Be quick now.'

Xochi hesitated again and then touched belly and throat and strode from the source. Tayan heard her low-voiced bark of command and three Chorus warriors stepped in. He ignored them, pacing from the hanging to the offering pool and back. It was mercifully empty: what would he have done if the delegation really had brought ejab to surrender and the pool was full of holy Setatmeh?

I would put myself between my enemies and my gods and shield them with my flesh. My life.

'What if it's Xessa?' he asked himself and his heart twisted in his chest; it would be. There was no doubt about it. Not Ossa though. She wouldn't risk her dog, not even for peace.

Tayan stalked back to the cushions piled behind the rose-cotton, finger-combing his hair. Was his paint vibrant? There was more in his medicine chest; he could touch up if he needed to. He had to look his best, wearing Tokob and Pechaqueh sacred markings – heritage and destiny. Who else would they send? That axe-faced old woman, probably. What had they called her? Digger or Painter, some sort of trade. He hadn't paid too much attention at the time.

'Holy lord,' Xochi said, returned with his chest and a clutch of turkey feathers. 'They have reached the compound wall under guard. What are your orders?'

Tayan swallowed and held out his hand; she passed him the box and then tied the turkey feather above his right ear. 'They are to wait until I'm ready. I will view their approach from the top of the grand staircase. I want to see who they've sent and I will have them see me. From a distance.'

'As the holy lord commands,' the Chorus Leader said and snapped her fingers at one of the warriors by the wall. 'Peace-weavers are to hold outside the wall. Triple the sentries on all sides. Maintain discipline: this could be a distraction.'

'As the Chorus Leader commands.' The warrior hurried out.

'Spear Pilos requests—'

'Get in here,' Tayan bawled and Pilos rounded the corner, dropped to his knees and pressed his brow to the mats for a single heartbeat before rising – before Tayan gave him permission to rise. He didn't care. 'A peace-weaving, Pilos. The rumours, the battles, the fires, the arrival of the Second Talon. Have we done it? Are they capitulating? Where's Atu?'

Pilos pursed his lips. 'It's possible,' he conceded and Tayan clapped his hands. The corner of the Spear's bruised mouth twitched. He'd lost the very tip of his tongue in the recent fighting and had a pronounced lisp now; the urge to laugh every time the man spoke was unbearable. 'If I may advise the great Singer to hold on to his caution? There's a long way to go yet; we haven't even met them. And . . . surrendering ejab? This could be difficult for you – and they might be counting on that. As for the High Feather, he is with the wounded in the healing temple. Shall I send for him?'

Tayan's mirth dried up. 'No, get him on the wall in case this is a trap,' he said as he dropped into the cushions and held up the polished obsidian mirror. As he'd suspected, the blue line on his chin had faded and he quietened long enough to replenish it. 'As for Xessa, if it is her, she should know better than to try and outwit me. I may not be a warrior or an eja, but I have seen and done things she will never understand. Things that would have her pissing her kilt. I will do what the song requires, Pilos. I will bring justice to my divine kin killed by her and her sort.'

Pilos nodded his approval and fastened a turkey feather over his ear. 'Xochi, a feather for you and every Chorus within the source. None for those guarding the corridor and gardens.'

'I understand, Spear.'

Tayan examined himself in the mirror for a long time and then laid out the ingredients for the journey-magic on the low table, before standing and adjusting his kilt. 'Spear Pilos, Chorus Leader, will you accompany me to the grand staircase? And signal the wall – our guests can come in.'

Tayan stood halfway up the grand staircase, surrounded by warriors and shining gold with magic and power beneath his salt-cotton armour. And no one was looking at him.

'What is this?' Pilos breathed and then hurried down six or seven steep steps to squint at the wall. 'They're attacking before they've even got assassins through the fucking gate? Amateurs.'

Xochi was shading her eyes. 'I think they're fighting each other? No, they're trying to stop the peace-weavers. Have they split into factions, those who want to surrender and those who are in it to the end?'

Pilos nodded. 'If so, whatever happens here, we won't get a full surrender. But we may well get enough of them to lay down weapons that those who are left become ineffective and easily broken. That's good enough for me.'

The fighting at the gate was a blur to Tayan, so he slipped into Xochi's mind and directed her gaze towards the unrest. She grunted at his lack of subtlety, but apart from an initial and instinctive recoil, she no longer fought his intrusions.

The world around him leapt into focus and Tayan sucked

in a shocked breath, taken aback as always at the sharpness and shapes and colours of the world. With ruthless discipline, he didn't gawk as he wanted, but focused on the commotion at the gate. The peace-weavers were under armed escort and the whole party was embattled. The Singer could see eagles and traitors fighting side by side as they lunged for the gate. On the wall, warriors were beginning to loose arrows and darts down into the struggling mass, and then the gate opened and dog warriors poured out in a lethal wave, taking the fight to the attacking faction. The peace-weavers and their escort broke for the gate; not all of them made it through alive.

Tayan watched until the group – smaller now – was approaching the base of the staircase. It wasn't the old woman leading them. He withdrew from Xochi's mind, recoiling on instinct and absurdly grateful when the sharpness of his vision dimmed. The Chorus Leader hissed in pain but still caught his elbow when he stumbled. 'Holy lord?'

'We'll . . . I've changed my mind. Standing here waiting to receive them does them honour they do not deserve. They can come to me.' He didn't wait for their response, just spun on his heel and headed swiftly back inside, where it was cooler and the stone cut some of the humidity. That was the only reason for his sudden shiver.

Tayan forced himself not to run, but he couldn't stop his fists clenching and unclenching by his sides. He breathed slowly through his nose, timing it to his footsteps, and by the time they reached the source, he was outwardly calm again. He sat on the lush blue cushions and fiddled with the rose-coloured cotton until it hung perfectly, obscuring him from sight.

'Xochi. Stand closer to me.'

'As the holy lord commands.'

They waited. And waited.

'. . . bigger than I expected, but not as lush. Still, I suppose that's war for you.'

Tayan bared his teeth, caught Xochi looking, and smoothed his features again. On the other side of the hanging, between

Singer and so-called peace-weavers, Pilos was motionless, a big, comforting presence.

'You will enter on your hands and knees as all slaves must when moving into the great Singer's presence.'

There was a long, tense silence, and then: 'I think not. For one, we are not enslaved. For another, that's Tayan. Of Tokoban. And my days of crawling to him are long gone.'

His voice was different. Deeper, more assured, or perhaps it was just hoarseness from months of shouting across battle-fields. He was using the mild, bland tone that had always driven Tayan out of his mind with frustration. The one that refused to be provoked, no matter how much he pushed.

'Xochi? Stand closer to me.'

'I . . . as the great Singer commands,' she said and her use of his title sent another shiver through him, this one of deter-mination.

'Let them in.'

The source was silent but for the scrape of sandals on the mats, and then someone laughed, low and muffled; someone else coughed unconvincingly. Did they really think they'd won something by being allowed to walk into his presence?

'The peace delegation is here, great Singer,' a warrior said and Tayan heard someone hawk and then spit.

The Chorus warriors in the source shifted and looked towards their Singer, but all wore the peace feathers. Their anger was clear, though.

'Hello, Tayan. I presume that's you hiding behind the curtain. Any chance of you showing your face so we can talk this through like adults?'

The Singer hesitated, but he needed to see. He signalled and Xochi drew back the curtain and tied it up out of the way. 'Husband.' Despite himself, he drank in Lilla's face and form like honeypot. He was thin, much thinner than he'd ever been, his body seamed with scars and knotted with muscle unsoft-ened by fat. His cheekbones were blades, unbalancing his face, and there were lines carved deep around his mouth. 'You look old, husband.'

'Former husband,' Lilla said mildly. 'You look . . . well. Sleek. Easy living suits you.' He smiled to take the sting from it and it was his old smile, half-forgotten and beloved. 'I see your slave brands are still intact,' he added and it was as if he'd thrown a nest of biting ants in Tayan's face.

His hand slapped against his upper arm without conscious input. It was true. In the chaos of becoming Singer and everything that had happened since, he'd forgotten to score them through. Singer and slave. A slave to the song, to the holy Setatmeh? To Pechaqueh prejudice and arrogance?

None of that.

He didn't explain or excuse; he simply made a performance of running his fingertips over the raised lines of the brand. Someone shoved through the grouped traitors in their stinking, filthy kilts and salt-cotton. The cleanest thing about them were their tatty, ragged turkey feathers.

Even though he'd expected to see her, even though he'd braced for it, Lilla's presence had upended his equanimity and Xessa's scornful contempt as she dragged her eyes over him where he sat in luxury made him flush.

She'd painted her face in the black and white stripes of a life offered to Malel for the good of the tribe, the good of the land. A black stripe ran through one eye; a white stripe highlighted the other. Neither could mask the scornful glitter of her eyes.

'Eja,' he croaked, not sure if he'd manage to say her name. Then his breath caught and he turned back to Lilla. 'You bound her hands?' he demanded, genuinely shocked.

'Hers and Eja Anoq's.' He gestured to a squat, powerfully built man towards the rear of the delegation. He was similarly painted. 'We wanted to prove the sincerity of this peace-weaving and we weren't sure you'd let them in here otherwise. Besides, you might have had guests,' he added and gestured with a grimace at the offering pool.

'But she—'

'She's as angry a kicked hornet's nest, yes, even though she chose this fate willingly. At this point, I'm honestly not sure which of us she'd try to kill first if we released her.'

Tayan grinned at the thought, inviting Lilla to share in that horrified contemplation of their shared fate – and then blinked and looked away. 'Anoq? I don't know you,' he said, signing automatically. Anoq's lip curled but he didn't speak, raising his arms to show off the rope binding them from wrist almost to elbow. Tayan wasn't surprised he was so thoroughly restrained; he looked strong enough to break lesser bonds.

'He hails from the corn town at the foot of Malel,' Lilla said for him, turning side-on and signing. Anoq nodded. 'He and Xessa worked together for victory at the river recently.'

Tayan's gaze returned to Xessa and whatever he'd been feeling at seeing her again – also thin and lined and baked hard by privation – withered and died, like a holy Setat under her spear. *She deserves nothing but my hatred.*

She wasn't even looking at him. Wasn't even offering him the basic respect of acknowledging his presence. She was glaring at Pilos as if she could burn him to death with just the hatred in her eyes. For his part, the Spear of the Singer wore an uneasy mix of relief and suspicion.

'Your pit-fighter, Spear Pilos,' Tayan said with forced cheer. 'Are you glad to have her back?'

'Not really, holy lord,' Pilos said. 'She killed five of our gods.'

Xessa read that from his lips and a slow smile spread across her face. She shrugged elaborately and then tried to sign something. 'I'd wager she's saying she's killed far more than five during her years, Spear,' Lilla said calmly.

'Wager? Wager what?' Tayan demanded. 'Your freedom?'

Lilla's mild gaze rested on him again, a long, slow perusal that filled, moment by moment, with contempt. 'No,' he said, and only that. Tayan flushed and chased the redness automatically with gold to cover it. His former husband was even more adept at getting under his skin than Xessa had been.

'The ejab recognise that Pechaqueh – and I hope only Pechaqueh, Tayan – will want blood and vengeance for those deaths and so they are here as sacrifices to Malel to carry the hopes of all peoples to her ears that peace may be woven and it may be strong.'

Lilla met Tayan's eyes. He took a step forward and then halted obediently at Pilos's snarled command. 'You and me, Tay. Can we fix things the way we always used to? Can we make it right?'

The song soared, triumphant and self-satisfied and slick with gloating, and with the exception of the ejab, everyone in the peace delegation flinched. Tayan's heart was thumping in his ears and his breath whistling high in his chest, but he met Lilla's calm gaze again, cleared his throat roughly and gave a jerky nod of his head. 'We can try,' he said and throughout the source, Pechaqueh and traitors alike breathed out.

Tayan insisted the ejab hands remained bound. He had no need to see Xessa's spite and ignorance, her blind refusal to understand, flailing away in the corner of his eye.

Instead, he was forced to endure her unblinking, judgemental scrutiny, and when he couldn't bear the weight of it any longer, he had four Chorus warriors take her and Anoq to the other end of the source next to the offering pool, and if that was an expression of his own spite, well, he'd learnt it from her.

Now he'd have to turn his head if he wanted to see her and it was easier not to. Easier to concentrate on Lilla. Xochi had repositioned herself between the ejab and her Singer, leaving Pilos the only warrior between him and the peace delegation. There were Chorus along the walls, though, and despite their peace feathers, they'd react in an instant if violence broke out.

Idly, Tayan wondered how badly this would have gone if Ilandeh was still his Chorus Leader. He hadn't been in the Sky City when she'd committed her murders and fled, but Xessa had. Oh, Xessa would have had some signs for the Whisper if she'd still been here. Likely the peace-weaving would have died without even taking its first breath.

'Tayan? Shall we begin?' Lilla was still using that fucking voice, but was that a hint of warmth in it, too? A hint of familiarity?

Don't be drawn in by it. He's no diplomat, no orator with a tongue blessed by the gods, but he'll use his earnestness and his knowledge of me to wring every concession he can from this peace-weaving.

Don't let him.

Tayan didn't look at his former husband, instead studying those who'd accompanied him. He didn't recognise any of them. Their hair, patterns and paint told him they hailed from every tribe except Pechaqueh. All Ixachipan had sent a representative to weave this peace.

Much of what was to come would be tedious and pointless. Almost, he wished for the axe-faced old woman to be here. Warriors at peace-weavings thought their presence equalled a voice in the discussion when they were simply there for appearances. Lilla he could weave with, but he didn't know these others and it would devolve into bickering over concessions soon enough. Each tribe would want something just for themselves; each would want something they thought precious, or to make sure their ancestral enemies got a worse outcome than they did. Yaloh would want more favourable trade terms than Xentib; Xentib would want greater access to obsidian than Yaloh. Soon enough they'd be arguing over numbers and painted lines on a map, arguing with each other as much as with him.

Tayan would be reluctant witness to all of it. And afterwards, he would have to decide how to send the ejab to their deaths in a way that seemed like justice to Pechaqueh but didn't destroy the peace-weaving in its infancy. Xessa. He was going to send Xessa to her death.

She committed atrocities and she will have relished them. I can't pretend I don't know that. Just because she's standing over there, contemptuous and beloved and painted for death, doesn't mean I can change her fate. I can't; I won't.

'What happened to Ossa?' he asked. Lilla looked down at his lap and Tayan turned to Xessa. 'What happened to Ossa?' he asked, this time in sign.

Xessa clenched her jaw and looked away, blinking so the

tears filling her eyes didn't spill and mar her sacrificial paint. The room became very still, not just the delegation but the Chorus lining the walls. In that stillness, with every eye on the eja with her bound hands hovering at the bridge of her nose but not quite touching her face, the sounds of the battle at the wall were quite clear.

'He was a good dog,' Pilos said quietly, 'even though he never really liked me much.'

Lilla jolted like the Spear had punched him. He swallowed. 'He was,' he breathed. 'He did his duty well.'

Without meaning to, Tayan lowered the clangorous triumph of his song into something a little gentler, a little sadder. It was blasphemy, because of who and what Ossa had been, but Pilos was right: he was a good dog. It wasn't his fault he'd been trained to kill gods.

'Let us weave a peace,' the Singer croaked, 'before we are all lost in sentimentality.' *Peace first, and then Xessa and Anoq die.*

The hypocrisy of it was ludicrous.

There was the merest flicker in Lilla's expression and he brought his hand up to the turkey feather to conceal it, stroking his forefinger along the vanes. 'No enslavement,' he said.

Tayan licked his teeth and stared at Lilla before letting his gaze roam the source again before finally falling on the ingredients of the journey-magic laid out on the table. With a lurch, he realised he should have mixed it and he and Lilla drunk it before they began their discussions, but with that opening demand, it was too late.

It didn't matter, though. The journey-magic was to connect him with his gods, but Tayan had his song – *the* song – to do that for him. Every moment of every day, sleeping and waking, he sang with the holy Setatmeh and crafted the magic through which they swam. He did not need to, to *lick frogs* to visit his gods. He was practically a god himself.

'No enslavement?' he asked, tossing back his hair and leaning forward to pin Lilla with his gaze. 'You ask much, Fang.'

Like a mirror, Lilla leant backwards, a small but symbolic

shift in body weight. 'I ask much? I don't think so. No one owns another's life; they cannot. It's impossible. Xessa did not own Ossa,' he said, signing it for her benefit. 'She asked him to walk by her side and fight and live with her, and he did. He stayed out of love and he fought for her out of love, whether the blood he spilt was green or red. If a dog can do that and be a friend, a companion, but never a possession, then how can a person be one? Even though you still wear your slave brands, Tay, no one ever owned you. No one ever owned me or any of us. Pilos never owned Xessa. And no one will ever own another person again. That is one of the conditions of this peace. Is this thread woven?'

Tayan's eyebrows shot up, but his Spear got there first.

'And yet she was. She was my possession,' Pilos snarled and flicked an unguarded glare at Tayan that he understood and chose to allow. He twisted to face Xessa and began to sign. 'I owned the Mute. I made the Mute. I trained her and I fed her and I patted her on the head when she killed for me. Four Tokob she slaughtered at my command. Oh, I owned her, body and spirit. And why? Because she wasn't strong enough to stop me. None of you were; that's why you were brought under the song. And then we gave you everything, civilised you and embraced you and raised you up out of the dirt to be so much more than you were before.'

'You speak so in a peace-weaving?' Lilla demanded.

'This is your custom, not ours,' Pilos said. 'You call it a peace-weaving and yet your people are at our wall this very moment trying to swarm in here and slaughter us all. Slaughter the Singer!'

'They are not ours,' Lilla said quickly. 'They are people who have become enamoured with the fight and with vengeance, with death. If you offered them peace or the chance to kill Pechaqueh, they'd choose the latter every time. But they are few and desperate. That's why they tried to stop us. They're fanatics working directly for whichever leader decided to sell the north to the Zellih. There's no negotiating with them, no stopping them.' Bitterness twisted his mouth. 'Believe me, I've tried. But we're here to represent the majority of freedom fighters within the Singing City and, we believe, all Ixachipan. We want peace, Tay. Please. We just want peace.'

'You lie,' Pilos snarled.

'Tayan, there is no room for impulsiveness here,' Lilla signed and Tayan stopped translating. Because he agreed. Pilos wasn't helping; his presence was a distraction.

'Thank you, Spear, for the reminder of what occurs at our walls,' Tayan said aloud. 'Go and assist the High Feather in the defence. This is a peace-weaving and I am choosing to believe the weft to my warp is here with honest intent. Besides, I am quite safe with Xochi and the Chorus watching over me. And my former husband would never break the sanctity of the turkey feathers.'

Pilos twisted to face him and then looked quickly down. 'Forgive me, Singer, but are you sure of that?'

'I'm sure, my friend,' Tayan said. 'Please, protect the pyramid. Our warriors need you, never more so than if those facing them are fanatics as the peace-weaver suggests.' He smiled gently and Lilla returned it, tension sliding from his face and shoulders, and Tayan let him bask in it for a moment before hardening like resin in the sun. 'And I'd prefer to have your eyes on the battle. We've only got their promise that this isn't some wild, half-formed plan to distract us while they attempt to take the wall or something equally doomed to failure.'

Lilla flinched, contempt tightening the muscles around his eyes. 'We are not Pechaqueh. We have no need of lies.'

'Spear Pilos, the wall and our defence, if you please. I need you there more than I need you here, for now. I will summon you back if that changes,' he added at Pilos's stricken look.

The Spear took a breath and then spun on his knees to press his brow to the mats. 'As the great Singer commands,' he said as he sat back up, the picture of dignity. Juxtaposed with Lilla's open-mouthed shock, it was all Tayan could do not to laugh. He nodded, formal and appreciative, and Pilos left them.

There was a definite lessening of tension when he was gone,

and the heat of Xessa's death glare reduced a little. Tayan wondered how much she'd understood of what was happening and felt a pang of belated shame that he hadn't facilitated her comprehension.

Prisoner. Eja. Going to die soon. You don't owe her anything. The reminder didn't soothe him as much as he'd expected.

'All right, Lilla, let's get this done. What do you and your traitors want?'

Less than diplomatic, but it would serve. Lilla, of course, retained his dignity; not so much as his eyebrow twitched. Like the tone of voice, it was a provocation that Tayan couldn't voice and couldn't ignore. How would it sound? *My former husband is being too diplomatic at this peace-weaving. My former husband is being too understanding. My former husband is being too fucking nice!*

'No enslavement,' he began again and Tayan flapped his hand, urging him to his next demand. 'Very well, though we will come back to that point before this weaving is done.' He took a breath and glanced reflexively at the rest of his party; they were silent and mostly scowling. 'Although it has caused much argument among our number, I can tell you now that what we don't want is an end to the song of the Pechaqueh.'

Tayan's heart leapt and he leant forward eagerly. 'You don't?'

'No. It is Pechaqueh and it belongs in Pechacan. We would not steal Pechaqueh culture from them – or from those who have come to love and embrace that culture.' He looked like he'd eaten something rotten when he said that, but at least he didn't hesitate. 'We just don't want it in our lands. Pechaqueh culture in Pechacan, Tokob culture in Tokoban and so on. No slavery and no forcing of one people's laws and customs onto another. We don't demand the end of Pechaqueh culture, and you don't steal ours from us – or us from our land.' He spread his hands. 'That's pretty much it.'

Tayan blinked and looked to Xochi for support. Beyond her, Xessa was watching him again.

'Chorus Leader. Your thoughts.' He didn't phrase it as a question.

'You honour me, holy lord. My thoughts are that the request is for no slaves and no song, however prettily phrased. The peace-weaver says in one breath that he does not wish to destroy our culture and yet his twin demands do that very thing. It is impossible.'

'Is it?' Tayan asked softly, turning back to Lilla. 'What if we agreed?' His former husband was all the way there now, engaged, straining forward and alight with hope. Beautiful. Flawed. Broken. 'Of course, we would have a couple of requirements of our own if we were to grant such concessions.'

'Naturally. This is a peace-weaving.' He paused and then grinned, that old irrepressible grin that had been the thing that first attracted Tayan to him. The smile that said anything was possible if you tried hard enough, believed hard enough. It was a shame that smile had been a lie. Marriage to Lilla hadn't been quite that exciting and "no" more often than "yes" had been the answer to Tayan's questions about what was possible and his plans to discover the same.

He smiled without mirth. 'No ejab. If our gods choose to live in your waters, they will do so unmolested. If they—'

'Our gods?' Lilla interrupted sharply. 'Tay, power is one thing, even this power. But the Drowned are not gods. They are—'

'I watched my predecessor transform upon the moment of his ascension. I watched Xac become a god. You have no idea who or what the holy Setatmeh are. We will stop taking slaves from the rest of Ixachipan and you will disband the ejab and forbid them from ever taking a holy Setatmeh life. Is this thread woven?'

'How will we source water?' Lilla demanded. 'How will we irrigate our crops and wash our children and elders? What will we drink?'

'Every other land manages,' Tayan pointed out patiently. 'Everyone here with you today as part of this peace-weaving has managed for generations. Only Tokob met the gods with violence.'

'No. No, these people don't manage. *Pechaqueh who have*

stolen their lands manage by sending people like these, enslaved people, to fetch their water for them and they don't particularly care if those slaves came back, because they're infected with your fucking song and think it's normal to hold a person's life so cheaply.'

'You hold the lives of gods cheaply. How is this different? In the majority of cities and towns, the people and the holy Setatmeh have a close relationship. The gods are honoured at new moon and in return they are peaceful and quiet the rest of the month, allowing as many people to visit their domain as need to.'

That last wasn't entirely accurate: Tayan was sure that Pechaqueh only went near water during offerings or when there was no other choice. Still, it sounded good.

'Please stop,' Lilla said quietly. 'This is a question of simple mathematics and you know it. You're a clever man. One person sacrificed to every Drowned every month? How many Drowned are in this city? A hundred? That's a hundred deaths a month, every month, forever. Even a major city like this could be emptied of life within a generation at that rate of attrition. You'd be permanently engaged in population management just to survive. You'd be forcing people to bear children. Children who might grow up without parents because they in turn had been sacrificed. A disproportionate burden put on those – and only those – who can give birth. And how do you choose who's torn apart each month? How long before the wealthy begin bribing their way out of being selected and it's the poor, the friendless, the weak, who get chosen over and over? The very system of slavery and sacrifice we're here to end would reassert itself within a Star cycle, probably less.'

The mildness had finally left his voice and now it rang with passion – and with disdain. As if Tayan was a precocious but unworldly child failing to see the nuances of life as it was.

'This very reason is why the Empire of Songs had to keep expanding. The longer it went on, the more Drowned were made, who needed sacrifices, and the more slaves were needed to feed them, so the more lands were taken, over years and years during which more Drowned were made. The cycle needs to be broken or it will eventually consume the world.'

Tayan sipped some water, taking his time. 'And so we come back to it – you want your cultures to remain the same, but that of Pechacan must change. We must either trap our gods in Pechaqueh waters or allow you to kill them. Where is the peace in this? We must give up our Empire and the song's glory in your lands. Give up our system of society and way of living and worship, while you get your lands, freedom and all back. What exactly are you conceding to weave this peace? Neither of us is starting from anything the other might consider to be common ground. That makes things difficult.'

Lilla scrubbed his hands through his hair, scratching at his scalp and almost dislodging the peace feather. 'It does, Tay. But we've done difficult things before, made hard decisions but correct ones. I believe we can do this, too. We just—'

Tayan coughed and drank some more water, dizziness washing over him. He blinked and focused. *Must be more tired than I'd thought.*

'—keep your gods in Pechacan?'

The Singer snorted. 'They are gods, Lilla. Would you tell Jaguar-Brother he could not roam the sky and jungle, fields and hills, as he chose?'

'Jaguar-Brother doesn't sing innocents to their deaths and tear people apart for sport,' the Toko snapped and Tayan was weirdly pleased to see the crack in his smooth exterior. Lilla must have recognised it; he forced himself back to mildness. It didn't matter. Tayan had seen through it now and he knew the passions that churned beneath.

'Jaguar-Brother takes only what he needs and, when he is needed in turn, we take him. He gives us his life in mortal form and we make magic with his skin and bones. Sometimes we do it to protect a town or city, and we do it with regret and reverence. You may not have walked the jaguar path, but you know this, Tay. You even took part in making that magic. You say Pechaqueh gods should not be killed; did you learn nothing from ours before you came here?'

Again, a hint of frustration in the Tokob voice, and Tayan smirked before another rush of dizziness spun his head on his shoulders. 'Xochi, a small meal, please. And some honeyed water.'

Xochi touched belly and throat and then flicked her fingers at one of the Chorus warriors, who disappeared out of the source and was immediately replaced by another. Lilla watched the exchange with a sort of mildly impressed contempt. *All this protection just from me? You flatter.*

Tayan bit his lip so as not to snort laughter. Over-tired and possibly ill. He'd been doing too much for too long and it was catching up with him. And what had Lilla said? *Easy living suits you.* If only he knew the real rigours of his Singer's life.

He and Xessa being here didn't help, either; Tayan's heartbeat was erratic as memories conflicted with the requirements of the world now. But if he could get through this, if they could weave this peace, then he could rest. Yes. Peace.

'Let's try again,' he said, concentrating on the buzzing in his fingertips and smoothing the agitated waves of his song into something gentler and more in control. 'Criminals,' he said brightly. 'Those convicted of crimes are sent to Pechacan to be dealt with as we see fit. A deterrent in your lands and a solution to the, ah, numbers problem in ours.'

Lilla's eyebrows drew down into stubbornness and Tayan sighed. This thread probably wouldn't weave either. The Chorus returned with food and water, but the sight of it made him nauseous. He left it untouched on the table with the ingredients for the journey-magic. Oh, he was supposed to have taken that. Never mind.

'Well?' he asked. *Weave the peace and rest. You have a duty to everyone in Ixachipan to bring this to an end. Focus.*

'Holy lord? Holy lord, I believe you are overtired.'

Tayan roused and realised his chin had sunk to his chest. 'What? Outside, the fight. How goes the fight?'

'We are receiving regular updates, holy lord. There is no

need for alarm. The Spear and High Feather have it under control.'

'We should come back. We'll get nowhere now,' a Quitob woman leant forward to say in Lilla's ear. 'I think he's drunk.'

Tayan shoved Xochi's hand off his shoulder. 'What's next on your list?' he slurred and giggled. 'What's the next thing we cannot agree on?'

Movement in the corner of his eye and he turned too late. Xessa's hands had already stopped moving and two of the Chorus warriors guarding her and Anoq were clutching their necks and stumbling. He blinked, slow. Xessa's hands. There was something important, something he needed to remember. Why was he so tired?

More movement, this time big and loud and from several directions at once. High-pitched shouts and someone in a yellow kilt tumbling to the mats in front of him, and then a peace-weaver, covered in crimson. More yellow-kilted warriors lunged in from the walls and the peace delegation rose up and met them. Warriors with spears, those in turkey feathers open-handed, or so it seemed, and yet almost as many warriors fell as traitors. And the traitors were seizing those dropped weapons and fighting back.

Tayan blinked but his head was stuffed with cotton; this illness was aggressive but he had his medicine box right here. He just needed—

The Chorus warrior who'd fallen nearby flopped onto her side and he saw the feathered dart sticking out just below her jaw. Her movements seized with frightening swiftness, her eyes bulging with fear, and the Singer had nothing in his medicine box to treat something that fast acting. The image of a tiny golden frog hopped through his mind and he smiled before remembering how lethal it was, before understanding what was happening in his pyramid.

Lilla had leapt to his feet and ripped the turkey feather from his hair. He stabbed the quill into the hand of a grasping, weaponless Chorus warrior. Within moments, the warrior was clutching her chest. Poisoned darts tied to peace feathers.

Clever. Despicable. And so very, very Lilla. No. Xessa. One of them.

Xochi loomed over him. 'Move, move, move,' she bawled into his face and got her hand in his armpit and dragged him up to standing. Got a handful of hair too and twisted and tore it out.

Tayan squealed and found himself in his body again. 'What the fuck?'

'Move,' Xochi insisted instead of replying. 'And contact the fucking Spear and get him back here.'

Tayan couldn't. The pain had restored some clarity – he still didn't know what was wrong but it was bad, a slow sucking away of his will and emotions – but his grip on the magic was wandering and weak. If he tried to Listen now, it could do irreparable damage to both him and the song.

'Get me out,' he gasped. 'Xochi, get me out. It's your job, your duty. You have to die for me.' There was a noise behind him and he flailed, twisting around. The space before the offering pool was peopled with Chorus warriors slumped, fallen, paralysed, but no ejab. Just coils of abandoned rope.

Rope up to his elbows almost. How many darts could you hide under there? Praise Setatmeh they didn't throw any at me. Something in them recognises me as their Singer, even if they cannot hear my song. They recognise me as their ruler, their god, even if they will not admit it.

Tayan wasn't helpless, even if he was sick, and he wasn't unarmed. He pulled the stone knife from the back of his belt and clutched it in a sweaty fist, squinting desperately at the chaotic motion all around him. 'Xochi?'

'I'm here. I have you. Contact the fucking Spear.'

Someone lunged at her and she responded on instinct, spear clacking against stolen spear, stepping into range, parry and strike and defend and stay alive.

A moment later someone else grabbed Tayan by the back of his salt-cotton and twisted the knife out of his hand, wrenching brutally at his wrist. They began dragging him away before he'd even registered the knife's loss over the pain. He twisted and kicked, scrabbling back over his own shoulder, and managed to turn far enough to see who had him in their implacable grip. 'Lilla?'

His husband gave no sign that he'd heard. Tayan slapped backwards at him, digging in his heels but unable to prevent himself from being dragged away as Lilla tightened his grip and bent him backwards, off-balance, and it was move or fall.

'Help! Xochi, help me!' He heard her roar of affirmation, her screeched commands to "protect the Singer!" Despite the danger and his fear, something swelled in his chest at the swiftness of her response and the edge of panic in her voice. Running feet and a thump and thud, the mats shivering as a body impacted with the ground. 'Xoc—'

Lilla wrenched again and Tayan's feet went from under him; he fell with a yelp but didn't hit the mats. Somehow, his husband – *former, former fucking husband* – swung him around and up and threw him over his shoulder. And then he broke into a run.

Each step drove the breath from Tayan's lungs, his sternum slamming into Lilla's shoulder over and over until the pain was dizzying and he could do little more than sip at the air and grunt it back out. He wriggled and tried to kick again, tried to summon his song even though he was tired and hazy amid the fear. Agony blazed white-hot on the inside of his thigh and Tayan screamed. His song skewed wild and warbling like a troop of monkeys in flight. He tried to reach back to his leg – had Lilla stabbed him? – but he was jostled too much to find the source of the pain.

'Help,' he shouted again – or tried to. Only a thin wheeze emerged from his throat, a stuttering croak as the next stride drove the air out of him again. 'Lil—Lilla.'

'We break the song, we get you out, you get better. Recover. Understand?' The words were staccato and wild and made no sense. Out of where? Recover from what?

'I'm . . . fuck, your Singer,' he wheezed and tried kicking again. There was another burst of pain on his inner thigh – he felt fingers on his skin and realised Lilla was pinching him. He howled and slammed his fists on the Tokob back but couldn't twist free. The mats under them changed colour – they were no longer in the source. They were leaving. Fleeing. And if Tayan left the pyramid, he'd lose the magic.

'No. No! You don't, ah, you don't know what you're doing. No, I won't go. I won't go!'

Heedless of his pleas, Lilla ran down a set of stairs to the next level and the sounds of combat fell away. Tayan was clawing and thrashing his legs, twisting to try and get his knee into Lilla's head, when the man came to an abrupt halt.

'Put him down.'

Tayan twitched and tried to see past Lilla's flank. 'Spear? Pilos, you have to help me.'

'Put him down,' Pilos warned again.

Lilla spun and twisted at the same time, bringing Tayan down off his shoulder to form a barrier between them, his face crushed to Lilla's chest, and less than a heartbeat later something hit him between the shoulder blades and drove air from his lungs. Pilos had shot him. He'd shot him!

He dropped to his knees, face pressed to Lilla's hip. His husband cupped the back of his skull and Tayan had to fight years of habit that wanted him to nose into Lilla's groin. He giggled and then bit it back.

'Am I bleeding?' he asked, voice muffled.

'No, love. It was a club, not an arrow. Now hush.' And he pressed Tayan's own stone-bladed knife beneath his ear.

Kneeling at Lilla's feet and facing back the way they'd come, he had a clear view of Xessa sprinting towards them.

'Spear?'

'I see her,' Pilos said grimly. 'Are you hurt?'

There was no time to answer. Lilla jerked his head hard against his hip and pressed the knife in beneath his ear until skin parted and stung. Pilos swore, Tayan whimpered, and then Xessa caught up with them. He had a glimpse of her strong legs and bare feet driving her forwards and then all was motion and confusion and Tayan wasn't on his knees anymore but spinning towards her. He stumbled, arms flailing, and Xessa caught him.

'Take him and go,' Lilla said and lunged away before either of them could respond, striking at Pilos low, high, high, *high*, low in a bewildering flurry Tayan couldn't follow. Pilos was defending frantically with just a knife.

Tayan wanted to tell them to be careful, that that was the stone knife, it was sacred, but again a hand grabbed his armour and Xessa was moving, dragging him, dragging her Singer, and trusting Lilla to keep Pilos penned back.

'Spear!' he screamed, writhing in the ejab grip as he was pulled past.

'*Chorus! Protect the Singer! To me, to*—' Lilla attacked again and the Spear's words were lost in the grunt and flow of combat.

Tayan dug in his heels, writhed, and punched Xessa wildly in the back of her head and then gasped at the pain shooting through his knuckles. Fear and adrenaline had already cleared some of the unnatural apathy from his mind and the pain focused him a little more. He just needed to make her stop so they could talk. If he could just sign with her—

The eja flinched under his blow, turned and punched him in return, a single devastating strike that broke his nose, blood gushing and his eyes tearing as he choked and then wailed, his knees going soft. Blood splattered his salt-cotton armour and fine kilt, pattering onto the mats. She didn't allow him to rest or come to terms with the pain; her grip was unrelenting as she dragged him along the corridor, checking behind every few paces.

They reached another set of stairs. Another flight closer to an exit. Xessa was taking him from his power, from the song that had made him and raised him up when everyone and everything had said he was less. He was the fucking Singer of the fucking Empire of fucking Songs and he clung to the corner of the wall with the last of his strength, resisting the ejab pull. She pivoted back towards him, her mouth a twisted snarl of hate and panic amid her sacrificial paint. She raised her fist again.

'Why are you doing this?' he signed in a flurry. 'Just let me explain!'

Xessa checked their surroundings for danger and then rested her stolen spear so she could communicate. Before she'd even formed a word, Tayan shoved her in the chest with both hands and every shred of pain-fuelled strength he had.

Xessa flailed, her mouth opened in a guttural scream, and she went over backwards down the stairs.

LILLA

The source, Singing City, Pechacan, Empire of Songs
68th day of the Great Star at morning

Lilla still didn't know the full extent of the plan. Weaver had promised a distraction at the wall that would get them in, which he presumed was the sudden attack by freedom fighters determined to murder him. If that had been fake, someone should have told the warriors, because they'd killed Toxte.

Lilla hadn't seen the eja fall. Just a gasped wheeze, as if his breath had been stolen, and he fell beneath the churning warriors only steps inside the wall. With her hands bound, Xessa couldn't ask what had happened or even fight back, and Lilla had been so intent on preserving her life that he hadn't been able to do anything for her husband.

And then they were in the source, confronted with Tayan, and there was no time even to tell Xessa how sorry he was. Sorry for Toxte; sorry for her. Because no one would let her leave now that they had her. Not Tayan; certainly not Pilos. Lilla hadn't understood what her sacrifice and Anoq's was supposed to accomplish, or why it was Anoq instead of Toxte who'd been painted and bound to be a messenger to Malel.

Tayan had sat before him sparkling with gold and with Pechaqueh sigils painted in shamanic blue on his hands and brow. Beautiful. Luminous. The most perfect thing Lilla had ever seen – and the most obscene. The words that fell from his mouth were the reasonable, measured speech of a lunatic. Yet as the peace-weaving progressed, he grew more and more distracted, vacant or perhaps absent. Controlling his song, no doubt. Lost in his stolen magic. The disrespect of it had grated on Lilla, though not as much as the casual mockery and disdain for Malel and Tokob way of life. He'd spoken as if Lilla and the others were children slow to understand, as if their demands were laughable, pathetic.

Lilla had no idea what signal Xessa had been awaiting, or who among the peace-weavers had given it, but when she'd slipped her bonds and revealed the poison-tipped darts tucked against her wrists, and Anoq had done likewise, the other members of the peace-weaving had risen as one.

Lilla had risen, too. Even he knew the peace-weaving was dead by then, and it was obvious there would never be an agreement between them. Besides, it gave him the chance he'd wanted.

The darts tied to the turkey feathers had been Ekon's idea, a way to arm them invisibly, and it had worked better than they'd hoped. And now Xessa had Tayan and was getting him out and Lilla had a Spear of the Singer to kill. With Malel's grace, he'd live and get out, too, and then he and Tayan could finally talk. Properly talk.

'Is your plan to die here in some futile declaration of love?' Pilos snarled as he backed away a step to readjust his grip on his knife.

'Has he named a Shadow yet or is your plan to let us take him and then seize the song for yourself? Because you're not doing much to stop us,' Lilla countered, pressing forward, harrying him. Pilos took another pace back. And then another. Towards the source. The big, open room full of Chorus warriors, if any were still alive from their battle with the peace-weavers. And each step took him – and so Lilla – farther from Tayan and Xessa.

He stopped and the Spear grinned. 'An eagle would have realised sooner.' They faced each other, chests heaving, waiting to see who'd move first. 'This only ends one way. You're trapped in here, inside the pyramid, which is inside a wall defended by thousands. Your only way out is death. What exactly was your plan?'

'Honestly? Not a clue. I just wanted to ask Tay why he betrayed us. Why he went over to the enemy and abandoned his gods for monsters.'

Pilos put his head on one side, studying him. 'No,' he said softly. 'I think there's more to it than that. Despite your many flaws, you're a decent leader and I don't believe you'd throw away the lives of your warriors for something so petty and unimportant as one man's betrayal. You certainly wouldn't risk Xessa.'

'Did he summon you back?' Lilla asked. 'I heard his bodyguard, Xochi, is it, tell him to call you back. How does it work?'

'You want a lesson in song-magic?' Pilos asked and laughed. 'I think you're trying to distract me. I'm older than you. I'm better than you. And I've been fighting a lot longer than— Singer? Stay back!'

Lilla leapt, twisting in mid-air like a cat to see behind him. It wasn't a ruse. Tayan was approaching, dazed and bleeding with his nose mashed sideways. And he was alone.

'Where's Xessa?' he roared, sprinting for him.

Tayan came to an uncertain, wavering halt. 'My song. What are you doing to my song? It hurts.' He seemed bewildered. 'Why are you hurting me?'

'Singer, move,' Pilos shouted, but it was too late. Lilla reached him first and dragged his body before him as a shield. Again. He put the knife against Tayan's neck. Again. Pilos halted two steps away, his breathing ragged.

'Back off,' Lilla gasped. 'I said back off.'

The Spear didn't move. 'I don't think you're going to hurt him. I don't think you can. He's had you by the balls since the day you met, hasn't he? You've never been able to deny him anything.'

Lilla wrenched Tayan's head back by the hair and pressed the knife harder against his skin. 'Back. Off.'

'No.'

The song lurched and slowed and then veered off into bouncing disharmony. Its call to surrender was fading and Tayan was limp in his grip, breathing harsh through his mouth and whimpering with every exhalation. 'My song,' he moaned.

A line appeared between Pilos's brows. 'Singer?' His gaze snapped to Lilla. 'What is your plan?' he demanded again, urgent now.

'No closer. I won't warn you again.' Pilos ignored him and took a soft step forward, knife out to the side so he could arc it around Tayan and into Lilla's flank.

'What are you up to, slave?'

'Don't.'

'Oh, but I must. It is my duty as Spear of the Singer, as Feather of the Singing City. As former High Feather. As Pecha. I have all the rights and permissions in the world to do what I'm about to do, and. You. Won't. Hurt him.' He struck.

Lilla jerked Tayan's body into the weapon's path; it ripped into his armour even as Pilos gasped and pulled his strike. Tayan screamed, high and shrill, and Lilla shoved him into the wall, lunged and drove his own knife into Pilos's shoulder, twisted, and wrenched it free.

Tayan fell and Pilos grunted, blood blossoming on his salt-cotton. Lilla stepped past his former husband and punched the Spear in the temple, kicked him hard in the face as he slumped, confiscated his knife, and then hauled Tayan back to his feet. There was no blood on his armour. Pilos's reflexes had halted the strike.

Not that that had been Lilla's expectation: he'd thrown Tayan in the way of that weapon purely on instinct. And he didn't feel bad about it, either.

He needed to get his back to a wall and he needed a spear the better to hold off enemies while he waited for the rest of the plan to unfold. Whatever it was.

'I don't feel well,' Tayan said suddenly. 'Did you poison me? How did you get poison in my cup? Did you bribe Pilos? He doesn't like me very much. Where's my medicine box?'

'Where's Xessa? What did you do to her?' Lilla demanded, dragging Tayan back along the corridor.

Tayan pouted and struggled futilely in his grip. 'She's a god-killer. She deserved it,' he said and cold washed through Lilla's spine. 'I need . . . what are you doing to me? It's so hard to hear my song. I *don't feel well.*' He was whining and petulant and Lilla gritted his teeth and hurried him down a cross-corridor and through a door, praying the room beyond would be empty. It was.

It was also luxurious and clean despite the small but obvious signs of neglect and disrepair everywhere else. Tayan giggled and slapped playfully at Lilla's arm. 'This is my room and I don't recall inviting you. Are you trying to seduce me, husband? After all this time? Think I'm' – he coughed and swayed and smeared blood from his nose across his cheek – 'ow, think I'm that easy for you?' He pulled his arm from Lilla's grip and stumbled to a basin standing next to a pitcher, poured some water, and washed his face, cursing and whimpering.

'Tay, do you want to come with me?' Lilla whispered, both hoping and dreading that he'd hear him. 'Do you want to go home?'

'I want,' he said and turned back with damp, bloody face and swelling nose and eyes and paint smeared across his chin, 'I want you to kiss me.'

'I—'

'I fucked Enet, you know. Hundreds of times. When I belonged to her, before I belonged to Xac and the holy Setatmeh and the song. Before I became the song. I fucked her. I promised I'd tell you when I saw you again, so that there wouldn't be any secrets between us.'

Lilla couldn't look away from him, from the mesmerising ochre of his eyes.

'I fucked her and I liked it. And you fucked Ekon and you liked it. Didn't you? Don't you?' He nodded. 'Tell me about it, and about him,' Tayan said and there was a snap of command in his voice that Lilla responded to.

'You're so beautiful,' he whispered, stepping forward.

'Tell me about Ekon.' Gold whorls danced up his tattooed throat as he spoke.

'He's good. Kind and fierce and loyal. Ruthless when he needs to be; tender even when he shouldn't be. He's got dimples,' he added and smiled. 'I love his dimples. I love him. I love you.'

'Of course you do,' Tayan said, golden light spilling down his arms. 'Come here.'

Lilla crossed the space separating them with relief. His need for Tayan was overwhelming, painful in its intensity. The song was in his heart, in his heartbeat, and it was Tayan's song, strong and driving and irresistible and Lilla bent his head and pressed his mouth to his husband's, a sharp inhale through the nose as need swamped him. He seized Tayan around his slender shoulders and grappled him to his chest, tongue probing his mouth and desperate, animal noises coming from him.

'Tay. Tayan, please,' he gasped. 'Please, my love, my heart. I need you.'

Tayan had one arm around Lilla's waist, clinging on as Lilla bent him backwards and pressed hot, devouring kisses to his face and throat. 'I know you do,' he gasped and pulled something out of the back of Lilla's belt. His knife. Why did Tayan need a knife? 'What if I asked you to give me all that you are?' he whispered and then shoved his tongue in Lilla's mouth. Something cold and smooth pressed beneath his eye and Tayan bit him hard enough to draw blood.

Lilla yelped and pulled away, licking at his lower lip. Tayan's chest was heaving and his knife hand was shaking. 'You would, wouldn't you? If I asked, if I *ordered*, you'd give me everything – give me your life. I could' – he shuddered and swallowed heavily – 'I could end you and you wouldn't even put up a fight. But that would blood the song.'

'Tayan,' Lilla whispered, leaning in helplessly for another kiss. Tayan slashed the knife at his face, the pale stone blade gashing his cheek.

'Get out,' Tayan said. 'You don't have the strength to end my song. No one does; *no one*. Get out of this room and out of this pyramid. You have for as long as it takes me to change my mind, and we all know that's not very long. *Leave,*' he commanded and the force of the word propelled Lilla backwards across the room. Love and lust and the overwhelming desire to crawl inside Tayan's skin, to bare himself to his hands and mouth, his teeth and nails and knife, began to evaporate like water on hot stone.

'What did you do?' Lilla whispered, loathing creeping in at his edges. His fingers came up to brush against his stinging mouth. 'What did you just do to me?'

The Singer held the stone-bladed knife in both shaking hands, refusing to meet Lilla's eyes. 'I just saved your life. Now go.'

Lilla pulled open the door and made himself leave even though his heart and body yearned to go back to Tayan. And then he shut the door behind him and . . . it all stopped. Dropped away. Like walking from blistering cloudless highsun into the cool of a shadowed temple.

The song was surging like the ocean during a storm, powerful, unstoppable, all its earlier weakness vanished. Had that been what stopped Tayan from killing him, this sudden restoration of the song to its former state? Lilla was strung taut, muscles clenched as if he had been fighting Tayan's command, fighting his mind's complicity, its surrender. He hadn't even noticed it happening, the moment when it had all changed and he'd lost control.

When it had been Tayan controlling him. If he went back in that room, Tay could give him that knife and tell him to kill himself and he'd do it without hesitating. He knew it in his bones. The Singer could make anyone do anything if they were in his presence. And the Singer was Tayan.

How much of that kiss had been real? How much had been Lilla wanting Tayan, and how much had been Tayan telling him that that was what he wanted? It wasn't just coercion. It was violation. He scrubbed his hand against his mouth, telling himself he couldn't still taste his husband's mouth.

If Xessa confronted him, she wouldn't be controlled by his song. Anoq wouldn't be if the spirit-magic works the way they hope it does. They can do what I can't. They can . . . end this.

And I understand now. I understand him. And it does need to end, the song, his power. Him.

Lilla shuddered, skin crawling with the memory of Tayan's control, and began to run.

The source was strewn with bodies, dead or dying, paralysed Chorus warriors and sliced-open freedom fighters.

Rika of Quitoban was still up and fighting, and Lilla recognised her opponent as Xochi, the Chorus Leader.

He sidestepped them, found a short spear that would serve for now and was looking for an opening to finish the Chorus Leader when someone croaked his name. He spun, searching the wreckage of broken bodies.

'Anoq! Anoq, I'm here, where are you hurt?' Lilla dropped to his knees at the ejab side, signing in a flurry.

'Roof. Steps in the gardens. Toxte.' Anoq's signs were slow and there was a great scarlet puddle soaking into the mats beneath him.

'Toxte? Anoq, Toxte fell,' Lilla signed gently.

'No. Roof. Finish it.'

He had no idea what Anoq meant, but there wasn't time for clarification: the eja convulsed and his eyes rolled back in his head. Lilla held him as he died, and then cut the jade bead from the ejab hair and put it in his mouth. 'Find the spiral path to rebirth, my friend,' he murmured.

He snatched up his spear and slipped between the columns into the garden, leaving Xochi to Rika's spear. If Toxte really was up here, doing Malel knew what, then he could get to Tayan and either kill him or drag him out of this fucking pyramid by the hair. Either would end the song, at least temporarily.

Lilla found the steps leading up from the uppermost garden to the pyramid's summit. To the platform on which stood the four columns supporting the songstone cap. The single immense block of stone that took Tayan's song and spread it across all Ixachipan like a disease.

Lilla pushed through giant ferns and squelched through mud that held nothing but tangled roots and the chopped remains of shrubs or trees. Burnt for cooking or turned into darts, blowpipes, arrows, perhaps even clubs or spears. He paused at the bottom of the steps to listen. It was quiet.

Stealthily he began to climb, spear to stab, free hand to grab.

The capstone seemed to glow against the dull grey clouds promising rain racing overhead. There was a dead warrior face down on the steps, the back of their skull smashed open. He continued on, feet soft and focus steady, breath steady. No fear or doubt, just movement and reaction. As patient and lethal as Jaguar-Brother.

Two more corpses on the platform beneath the songstone, and beyond them Toxte, sitting splay-legged against one of the columns.

The eja jerked when Lilla came into his field of view, a hammer clenched in his hand raised to threaten. His other was pressed to his salt-cotton and the red leaking from beneath it. Lilla checked behind him one last time and then knelt by his side.

A hammer? And then he looked up and saw the damage to the songstone. He didn't know much about song-magic, but Tayan's distraction, his weakness and debilitation, suddenly made sense. And his sudden return to clarity must have been when Toxte was discovered and injured.

It was all a distraction. The peace-weaving, the sacrifice of the ejab. It was all just to get Toxte up here.

He'd wondered why it was Anoq painted for sacrifice and not Toxte; he'd wondered how the man could stand by and watch his wife be slaughtered, but he'd known he couldn't ask. Now it made sense.

'My friend. How bad?' he signed.

'Bad enough that I'll be shitting blood for a week,' Toxte replied shakily, and the rich red-brown of his skin was grey. 'Xessa?'

'She took Tayan while I was fighting, but then he came back

without her. The main corridor from the source, left of the colonnade. I'm sure she's made it back out by now. Can I ask? The songstone?'

'Chisel broke,' Toxte signed and then laughed, a ghastly, breathy wheeze that contorted his face with agony. 'Got some chips out of it, but no more. Tried to smash one of the columns then, see if I could tip it off the roof. Then they came for me.'

'All right, you sit there and rest and I'll see what I can do,' Lilla signed. He straightened and stood beneath the capstone, staring up at it. The chips and scratches were clearly visible. He stretched up to brush his fingertips across them and Toxte grabbed his ankle. He looked down.

'Don't. Even through the spirit-magic I can hear it; feel what it's telling me. It dulls it, but it's still there. Without that barrier, I don't think you'd be able to touch it at all. I don't think you'd survive.'

Lilla blinked and let his hand fall back to his side. He nodded his thanks.

'Got to find my wife,' Toxte signed suddenly. 'Help me up.'

'Toxte, no. You need to rest,' he protested, eyeing the quantity of blood that had already leaked from the ejab gut.

Toxte shook his head, stubborn. As stubborn as Xessa. 'Got to find her. You found Tayan, didn't you? And said what you needed to? There you go, then. Help me up. Besides, you gave me directions for a reason. You know how this goes.' He was implacable and so Lilla did as he asked, supporting the ejab weight as they returned to the gardens.

'The offering pool stream flows out of the pyramid just down there,' Toxte signed and pointed. 'It was unguarded when I climbed it. That's the way I'll bring Xessa when I find her.' Lilla nodded. 'Take it and leave, Fang. It'll be a risk, but I haven't seen a single Drowned since we arrived. It's ironic, but I don't think they like the violence – or they fear it. It's probably the safest way down to ground level and from there, pretend to be a dog warrior and try and get out. Malel bless you, my friend. We'll see you out there.'

Lilla clenched his jaw and nodded once, then licked his

thumb and pressed it to Toxte's temple – twice. 'One for you and one for Xessa. No, not now,' he signed as Toxte began to return the gesture. 'Later. When we're all together again. Don't forget.'

The eja grimaced but then nodded. 'You might be waiting a while,' he signed slowly. 'We are ejab and we have our duty when it comes to monsters who threaten the safety of our world.'

He waited, still and sympathetic. Lilla inhaled so deeply that his ribs creaked and his salt-cotton tightened across his back. 'I did find him, but it's funny: when it came to it, there was nothing at all worth saying to Tayan of Pechacan. He made it very clear where his loyalties lie. And yet. If you can, if you have that much mercy in you despite everything . . .' His hands faltered.

'I swear to you that we do,' Toxte signed and grief was another scar on his face. 'Look after Ossa, Fang. And take these.' He pulled two charms out of his salt-cotton, thick plaits of hair adorned with beads and feathers and, in the case of one, the green-dyed bones of a frog. Xessa's hair. Toxte's hair. 'They might ease his pain a little if he can still smell her.'

Toxte smiled and then winced, his hand fluttering to his gut. Then he straightened. 'Go, Lilla. Malel and the ancestors guide you. Go back to that good man who's waiting for you.' He choked. 'Go back to your dog.' He turned away before Lilla could reply – before he could even begin to think what to sign. He didn't look back.

Lilla watched his slumped and limping form vanish into the ragged gardens and then stayed there for a long time alone, the charms clutched in his fist. Knowing what they were going to try and do. Knowing that whether they succeeded or failed, he'd never see either of them again.

It didn't feel like the sort of tragedy that occurred every day, every hour, in a war. It felt personal, and huge, and unfair. And he couldn't stop it. No, he *wouldn't* stop it. It was no longer his fight and Tayan was no longer his husband. He'd chosen Drowned over ejab and that wasn't an argument Lilla would get in the middle of.

Eventually, he turned away, his heart burning within him, and went to look at the capstone again. He stabbed at it with his spear until it splintered and only chipped a single piece of stone free. He hammered at the nearest supporting pillar until his arm burnt with fatigue. It was granite, immoveable.

If he'd known the plan, he might have suggested something else, but that was a regret for the small hours of the night when he couldn't sleep, not for now at the very summit of the great pyramid.

He went to examine the stream. Of all the ways to die today, this hadn't been one he'd considered.

What if there's one there? What if it sings for me?

His hand slipped on his headless spear, greased with sweat.

So what if it does? Could it be worse than what Tayan did to me?

He already knew how it felt for a Drowned to sing and to be helpless in obedience, because despite their difference of appearance, that was exactly what his former husband had become. A Drowned.

Crouching low, Lilla slipped down the red-painted limestone wall to the level of the source and its offering pool. The sound of rushing water was loud and his scalp tightened. *Steady like Jaguar-Brother*, he told himself, *soft and focused and ready to move.*

He could see the stream's length all the way to the bottom of the pyramid, widening into shallow pools at each level before dropping down again. The trench the water was in had steep sides; he wouldn't be able to see much while he was in it, but then no one would be able to see him, either.

Lilla slid onto his belly and crawled to the opening into the source. He could see part of the room and the bodies, the blood. Rika had vanished, and the few surviving Chorus warriors were spearing the fallen peace delegation to ensure they were dead. No sign of Xochi, Tayan, or Pilos.

No sign of Xessa and Toxte.

Tayan had let him live; Toxte had told him to leave. He stared into the source and then down the stream again. The water was a steady flow, endlessly powered, Xini had told him, by slaves walking in the waterwheel in the pyramid's lowest level. Slaves who spent their lives in the wheel or in a cage beside it, never seeing the sun.

'Ah, fuck,' Lilla muttered. Praise Malel for Itzil and her maps: the waterwheel room was very near the slave entrance to the pyramid, and the slave entrance was right next to where the stream reached ground level and flowed away to rejoin a tributary of the so-called Blessed Water.

It was practically on his way out. Lilla could do nothing for the ejab lost somewhere in the great pyramid, but he'd free those people from their bonds and destroy that fucking wheel before he left. It wasn't much, but to those people enslaved down there, it would be everything. It would be freedom. He couldn't leave them there. *The way I'm leaving Xessa and Toxte.*

He swallowed bile and held the talismans up as he slid into the trench, consumed with the need to keep them safe and dry and protected. He bit back a scream as water flowed over his legs and belly and back, almost up to his chest before his legs, weak with fear, slipped from under him and he lost his grip on the edge. He fell down and away.

Away from the pyramid.

Away from Tayan.

XESSA

Xessa woke to pain and confusion and a wild, lurching moment when she had no idea where she was or why. She was lying at the bottom of a set of stairs in a corridor painted in swirling blues like water. A river flowing along the walls. Within its depths, here and there, were round-eyed faces and clawed hands.

Xessa shuddered and pain wracked her, in her lower leg and her chest and the side of her head. Had she fallen? She was lying on her side with her face stuck to the mat with saliva, blood, or some sticky mixture of both. Holding her breath, she eased over onto her back, cataloguing the spikes of hurt driving into her. Something in her right shoulder or clavicle, possibly her ribs, and her right ankle or foot. Right side of her face and the back of her head. She'd fallen badly, then.

Tayan.

Xessa panted shallowly as it came back to her. He'd hit her and she'd hit him, and then he'd signed he wanted to explain and instead he'd pushed her. Shoved her so hard that her feet had left the top step and—she remembered with vivid clarity his face, twisted up into a rictus of terror and self-obsession and triumph.

She'd seen nothing of her Tayan – of Lilla's Tayan – left in him. Just the grasping, greedy fingers of power and control and domination closing around emptiness where her friend had once been.

Despite her anger and contempt over the last months, grief lodged in her throat like a bone, a singular and all-consuming pain among the myriad hurts of her body. She let it wash over her like the Wet and scour her clean of doubt.

She was eja and, as she had said to Toxte, their duty was to kill those who sing. Besides, it was getting hard to breathe, and she remembered from – a bitter snort sprayed blood from her nose – Tayan's medicine lessons that you shouldn't lie on your back with broken ribs.

She pushed herself up, injuries screaming, and spotted her spear. Relief cascaded through her and Xessa grabbed it – *thank you, Malel, for sparing my left side* – and used it to take some of her weight as she stood. The world spun and dipped around her and she clung on and breathed, but it was no good. She hunched over and vomited, the spasms jerking her ribs and shoulder until her head swam again, this time with pain.

There was blood on her face and puke on her salt-cotton, but she had her spear and poisoned darts on her wrist and her duty burning clear like a flame lit in Malel's womb to honour her God-born. She limped to the bottom of the stairs and looked up. There was a bright splash of blood about halfway down. Hers. Grimly, she put her bad foot on the bottom step, gritted her teeth, and stepped up.

Climbing those stairs was the most painful thing she'd ever done, and that included every battle against Drowned and Melody she'd fought, every wound, every time Drowned venom had entered her body and made her want to claw her own skin off.

Didn't matter. She had to get to the roof and find Toxte, make sure he was safe and help him finish breaking the song-stone. In the chaos that would follow, they'd find Lilla and

Anoq, Rika and all the rest who were still alive, and make their escape.

As for Tayan, he could come with them if he'd finally woken up from his lust for power and control, or she could put a knife in his eye. She no longer cared. Something that wasn't a broken bone twisted in her chest but she ignored it. She didn't care. *She didn't.*

The corridor was long and straight but also, somehow, swaying gently as she hopped along it, foot-spear, foot-spear, lean against the wall to breathe, foot-spear, blink away sweat or maybe blood, foot-spear. The source didn't seem to be getting any closer, and she needed to get through it and into the gardens and up more Malel-cursed steps to Toxte.

She'd do it. She'd do that and more. They could still win this, still change everything. They just had to break that fucking songstone. Whatever Xessa thought of Enet and the things she'd done to become who she had, and to reach so high and almost, almost grasp a destiny far beyond the ejab imaginings, her knowledge of songstone had been unparalleled. And, therefore, so was Xini's and Itzil's. The sanctity of the great pyramid was due to its songstone cap, the original piece of worked stone that had channelled – or perhaps released – the very first song. It was immense compared with the capstones of all other pyramids and had survived centuries of sun and storm, rain and wind, with only minimal degradation. Its power was undimmed even after so long, but it could be broken.

Enet herself had carved and then cracked a songstone cap and the magic had failed in it on the instant. If they could crack the great pyramid's capstone, the song would return to where it came from. Perhaps the sleeping world spirit, perhaps something else. It didn't matter. The song would stop. There would be silence. And in that silence, the chance for a new beginning.

Had Lilla been honest during the peace-weaving when he'd said the song could stay but only within Pechacan? If Tayan had agreed, to that and their other demands and the Drowned being likewise confined to this land, would they have actually woven those threads? Lilla had been desperate to, and while she had missed much of what they were saying, his earnestness had been painfully clear.

Imagine if they'd actually woven it. I'd have had to interrupt to send someone to the roof to stop Toxte destroying the songstone. 'Sorry, Tayan, my mistake, we never thought you'd agree.'

Xessa huffed a laugh and hopped another few paces before leaning against the wall again. The corridor didn't appear any shorter, but when she looked back the way she'd come, the stairs were out of sight.

Tayan had always had her and Lilla to remind him he was just a man, a talented shaman and a good friend and husband, but a man. Nothing remarkable. There were things he'd never do and places he'd never see. Secrets he'd never solve no matter how hard he worked at them because they were Malel's secrets. The Drowned were one such and he bore the scars and the weight of a dead ejab spirit on his conscience to remind him of that. Whatever had happened during his time here, it had changed him in ways she couldn't understand. Removed his recognition of those limits until he seemed to think he was invincible, that he could do anything he wanted or make others do it for him.

Tayan, her Tayan, was still in there, but he'd been subsumed beneath a version of himself that she didn't recognise. Was this always going to be his fate, even in the Sky City? Had she done this by capturing that Drowned? He'd become obsessed with it almost immediately. He'd spoken of how it told him things.

Xessa slumped against the wall again. Was this her fault? Her eyes closed without her permission and she concentrated on breathing and the pain. Perhaps she had. Perhaps she'd pushed him onto this trail somehow, even though she'd never meant to. Did it matter that she hadn't meant to? Yes, actually, but that didn't change the outcome. Just because she'd showed him the path didn't make her responsible for him walking it. That was his choice. His mistake.

But if they broke the song, then he might . . . get better. They could take him home and fix him, her and Toxte and Lilla and Tiamoko and – she choked – Ossa.

Not so long ago I was going to stab him on my way past and forget him in the next moment.

That was then. I've changed my mind. He always said I was contrary.

She sobbed another laugh that made pain pool in her chest and pushed off the wall, wobbled and hissed at the hurt thrumming not just through her right side now, but everywhere. It was growing fast, stretching tendrils of sparkling pain along her veins and muscles and nerve endings until she was lit up like the night sky in a wash of debilitating agony.

Xessa gritted her teeth and one of her upper molars grated and shifted, sending its own starburst of pain through her jaw and cheek. She kept moving, head down, just hopping and breathing and leaning against the wall. Occasionally remembering to check behind her for danger, and ahead for—

Xessa toppled against the wall, trying to make sense of the scene in front of her. Toxte. Her husband. Had he broken the capstone?

Is it over?

Toxte had Tayan pinned against the opposite wall thirty or so strides ahead. Tayan was signing frantically, but the gestures were lost between their bodies and she couldn't work out what he was saying. Or maybe he was wild with the song's absence and Toxte was restraining him until the madness left him.

Or maybe – movement in the corner of her eye – maybe Tayan was distracting him. Xessa's head jerked around and there he was: Pilos. Coming from the other end of the corridor in a fast, unstoppable rush, and Toxte hadn't seen him. She screamed and Tayan flinched, his gaze jerking to her for an instant before he redoubled his struggles, keeping Toxte's attention firmly fixed on him.

The spirit-magic. Toxte couldn't hear her. And he couldn't hear Pilos.

Xessa clicked on instinct, but Ossa wasn't there to leap to

her husband's aid. She staggered away from the wall, hefted her spear, and threw it with all her strength. Her right leg buckled as it left her hand and the weapon flew wide, missing Pilos by a good margin.

Missing Pilos but clattering into the wall beyond Toxte and Tayan. Her husband saw it and ducked, pulling Tayan away from the wall and spinning them both to face Xessa, thinking she was the enemy. He had his knife at Tayan's neck and there was blood staining his armour and a great red sweep of it down the front of his kilt.

She could see it because he was facing her. Because he had his back to Pilos.

'Behind,' she signed, but it was too late.

The spear went in low, all the momentum of Pilos's run and Pilos's bulk and belief and hate driving it through Toxte's armour, through his back, and out of his belly in a spray of torn cotton and crimson. Toxte stiffened and his eyes met Xessa's. His mouth, stretched wide in agony, curled up at one corner when he recognised her and then he sliced the knife into Tayan's neck and spun again, tearing the spear from Pilos's hand and driving his blade deep into the man's shoulder. The salt-cotton there was already bloody and the Pecha staggered under the blow, one leg buckling.

Xessa began to run. Agony blazed through her leg every time she put weight on it, but she didn't stop. Didn't slow. Screams vibrated in her chest and throat but they were all of them for Toxte's pain, not her own. He saw her coming.

'No,' he signed. She ignored him, her gaze going to Pilos. Almost casually, he took hold of the spear sticking out of her husband's belly and tugged on it, twisting him around so they were side-on in the corridor and she could see them both.

'She's my wife,' Toxte said, signing it too. 'You hurt my wife.' He reached a bloody hand for Pilos's face.

'The Singer hurt your wife,' Pilos said, twisting his head away from the touch but making sure he – and Xessa – could read his lips. Despite herself, or perhaps because of what was coming, Xessa slowed to an agonised hobble once more. 'I made her great. Be proud of what I made her. She'd have been nothing if not for me.'

He twisted the spear and Toxte arched and screamed; blood poured from his mouth and took his strength with it. Pilos let him drop to his knees and slowly – almost reverently – twisted him again, this time to face Xessa. Then he braced one foot on Toxte's lower back and pulled the spear out of his body. Toxte slumped over his knees, red hand pressed to the red wound pumping blood onto the fine mats beneath him.

Pilos stepped past him and collected Tayan, wrapping a hand wet with Xessa's husband's blood around his upper arm. 'Leave them,' she saw Pilos say. 'They're no threat now.'

She was only a handful of hobbling steps from Toxte, and Pilos and Tayan were backing away at the same speed, maintaining the distance between them. Pilos, the man who'd tormented her and moulded her and made her kill Tokob. The man she'd sworn to murder for all he'd done to Tokoban, to Ixachipan, and to her.

The man who'd given Ossa back to her, and with him her chance at life. Her *desire* for life. *No. No, I owe him nothing but a slow fucking death. Nothing more!*

But when it came to it, she let them go. Without hesitation.

Toxte was kneeling in a seeping pool of blood, more of it splashed and smeared across the mats and walls. Kneeling and bleeding – and breathing. Still breathing.

Xessa looked up one last time, in anger or goodbye, she didn't know. Pilos was watching her with the wariness of the warrior, but Tayan watched with something she didn't understand. Tayan the stargazer, Tayan the eternally curious, watched her reach Toxte with an utter lack of interest. As if it – they – meant nothing to him. His hand was pressed to the gash in his neck and he let Pilos move him, and he watched as if they were nothing, ants playing out their lives on a twig.

'Was this what you chose instead of us? Instead of your people, your gods, your land? Is this stone cage worth the price you've paid with your humanity?' she signed.

Something flickered in Tayan's expression, a rawness like a hand reaching out of a dark place begging for help. Then he licked blood from his lips and straightened his shoulders with a haughty flick. The man she knew, the boy she'd grown up with, vanished behind a painted version of a Pecha. A false Singer.

Xessa spat blood in his direction and dismissed him and Pilos both and focused on her husband. She and Toxte had had a plan, a private plan not even Ekon had known about. They'd sworn that the death of one wouldn't stop the other doing what needed to be done. *For all who would be free.*

But now that moment was here and it was the wrong way around. It was Xessa, the confessed eja, who was supposed to die, cut down for her so-called crimes. It was Toxte who was supposed to find the strength to keep going, not her. She couldn't; she didn't have it in her to step around her husband and take on Pilos for the chance to get at Tayan – and yet. And yet they'd promised.

They'd sworn before Malel that what was important was accomplishing their goal and that they wouldn't prioritise anything over that. Not each other; not their allies. Nothing. Who they were, what they were, wouldn't stand in the way of victory. Xessa had sworn to let Toxte die if it meant ending the song. Now she was confronted with the truth of that promise.

Blood drooled from the side of Toxte's mouth as his head came up slow as sunset to meet her gaze. 'Hello, beautiful. You look like shit.'

Xessa's heart shattered. 'Hello, you shit. You look beautiful.'

Toxte grinned and nodded once in apparent satisfaction. 'Finish it then. For all who would be free. I couldn't stop the song—' He coughed, his face cracking and twisting in agony, and then bubbled in a breath and continued before she could protest. 'But you can stop him. I know you can. I know . . . you.'

'I know you, too. And I love you,' she signed, her right hand clumsy and her left empty of any weapon. 'I won't be long. Wait for me.'

His eyelids fluttered as if on a long-suffering sigh: *of course I'll wait*, she could imagine his hands telling her, though they didn't. *When have I done anything other than wait for you, live for you? Why would now be any different?*

Xessa swallowed hard against grief and pain and then lifted her eyes to Tayan's and let everything fall away but her last surviving duty.

'I am Eja Xessa, daughter of Kime and Otek. Wife to Eja Toxte, companion to Ossa. I am eja and I bring water and life to my people. And *I kill the monsters that sing*.'

These signs were no prettier than the last ones, but they were clear enough. Tayan's arrogance vanished like meat in front of a hungry dog. He paled and tugged at Pilos's arm, urging them away, but the pit-master didn't move. He said something she didn't bother to read. Laboriously but with growing speed, she set off towards them again.

She passed Toxte and his fingers grazed her calf, leaving a bloody smear. Almost she stopped at that momentary, maybe final, press of skin to skin. Instead she pushed on and didn't even glance down at him, knowing it would take the last of her will if she did. Xessa's left hand pressed against the wall, doing what she could to take some of the weight from her right leg, but it wasn't the pain she feared so much as the limb collapsing beneath her. She needed to be close for this.

Very close.

Not long now, ancestors. Lutek and Oncan and you nameless, faceless Tokob who died at my hand and Pilos's order in his pit, I thank you for your patience.

Not long now, my fathers.

Not long, Malel. Snake-Sister. Jaguar-Brother.

Not very long at all.

Xessa was mere strides from Tayan when Pilos stepped past him and raised his spear. She laughed, adrenaline sparkling bright in her blood and broken bones, a manic energy that dared him to come at her. Five hobbling strides and she grabbed the short blowpipe from where it hung beneath her salt-cotton and ripped it free, tore the dart out of its holder on her wrist with her teeth, and spat it into the tube.

Brought the blowpipe up to her mouth. Blew.

The arrow took Xessa in the shoulder and spun her sideways so that the dart flew wide. She flailed on her bad leg and spat another dart into the blowpipe, twisted back around – and a second arrow hit her, low in the gut and through her armour.

The archer was running along the corridor from the source, a woman. A peace-weaver. The Quitob Rika.

Informant. Traitor.

Xessa didn't waste time wondering why or how long. She lunged, blowpipe to her mouth, and blew with as much strength as her battered ribs would allow. The dart flew but it was too weak, dipping and hitting the mats a body length in front of Tayan.

Rika's third arrow went in close to the second, central in her belly and driving deep. Xessa coughed and her fingers spasmed; her hand fell to her side.

She met Pilos's eyes and bared bloody teeth, took a few more wobbling steps in his direction. 'I taught you better than that,' he said, or something like it.

Her blurry gaze slid to Tayan. He was remote, a veil between him and his emotions, or perhaps simply uncaring.

Another arrow, though this one hummed past her. Xessa turned to follow its trajectory. It had hit Toxte in the side, under his arm; he'd been trying to stand.

No. Absolutely not. I will not allow him to be hurt.

She loaded another dart – Rika was advancing, shouting something she didn't bother reading. She faced Pilos and raised the blowpipe. He narrowed his eyes and stepped in front of Tayan and, over his shoulder, she could just make out the ugly triumph on the Singer's face.

Xessa wrapped calmness around her spirit and took a deep breath and held it. Rika loosed her arrow and Xessa let her right leg collapse beneath her – and blew. The arrow took her in the throat; her dart took Rika in the leg. She'd never have reached Pilos, let alone Tayan, but Rika could pay for her betrayal. For the arrow she'd put in Toxte.

There was very little pain now. She could still breathe, though not for long: blood was filling her lungs. She could still walk, though not far. *Just far enough.*

She dragged herself to her feet and put her back to the Singer and the slaves to his song, his lies, and slid along the wall to Toxte. It didn't matter what they did. Only he was important.

Only him.

Toxte was slumped on his knees, but he twitched and reached a wavering hand for her, then saw the arrows. Despair washed across his face and a grief so terrible it was as if she was already dead.

'Hello, beautiful,' she signed as she eased onto her knees, fighting not to choke. Still fighting. Always fighting.

Toxte's shoulders hitched. 'Hello, you shit. What are you still doing here? Go. Go and live, my love.'

'I think I'll stay,' she signed and smiled, swallowing blood. *Not long, Malel. We come to you, and we beg you welcome us and forgive the wrongs we have done.*

Toxte closed his eyes and a tear slid down his cheek. Then he shook his head. 'No. You said you wanted to go home. You need—'

Xessa leant forward and the arrows in her gut buried themselves deeper, but she couldn't scream because she could no longer breathe, and it didn't matter. Her hands had always been the most eloquent part of her, whether raised in violence or soft with love.

She kissed his bloody mouth and the feathers fletching the arrow in her neck brushed against his chest. They pressed their brows together and looked down into the small space between their bodies, where her hands were moving.

'Toxte, my love. I am home.' He rolled his head in wordless denial, blood stringing from his lips to spatter the clumsy, stuttering movements of her hands. 'I am home,' she insisted. 'You are my home. You always have been.'

Dull thuds in Xessa's back, three, four, five. Arrows rocking her where she knelt. Rika's petty vengeance before the venom paralysed her. None reached Toxte, which was as it should be.

All the hurts were far away now, and her body starting to follow. Toxte shifted off his knees and onto one hip, curling in against her chest, avoiding the arrows sticking from her body. He leant his head against her shoulder and rolled it until he could look up at her, his arm wrapped around her waist.

'I love you,' he told her.

He smiled, and there was blood on his teeth and a deep, abiding joy in his eyes, as if there was nowhere he'd rather be.

Never had he looked more beautiful. More alive at the end of life. More hers.

It was a sight that would sing her spirit to Malel – and Xessa would walk the spiral path with him, hand in hand into death.

Into rebirth.

Into the light.

THE LISTENER

Empire of Songs
68th day of the Great Star at morning

How goes the good fight, holy lord? How goes the saving of the Setatmeh?

Begone. I have no interest in your riddles and your posturing. Leave me.

. . . That's it? No insults today, great Singer? No demands? Truly, something momentous must have happened. Or are you unwell?

I am well. I am bruised and bloody, but I am still here. Still Singer. I killed my friends today, you arrogant, condescending nobody who thinks to bait me and herd me in a direction of your choosing. I've had enough. I am too—I can't sleep. I watched them die and it felt, I felt . . .

Nothing?

Nothing.

Why did you kill your friends, great Singer?

Because they were going to kill me.

Then they were never your friends to begin with, not if they could turn against you so completely. They were vipers at your breast, waiting to strike.

. . . Interesting. And are you my friend?

No, Singer, but I am an ally. My life is given to magic and the truth of the song. You must feed the spirits in the song to the world spirit. You can do it in such a way that it will not awake. I can tell you how.

The world spirit? Really? I am weary, Listener, of your intrusions and of this day. And you have suggested this before, which shows only your ignorance of the spirit world and how it lives in partnership with the flesh world. They give life to us. Destroying spirits will destroy the world. Whether they're trapped in the song or annihilated altogether, they cannot inhabit new life. They cannot become people or animals or plants or waterfalls or clouds or stone or the Wet. If I kill the spirits, Ixachipan will die, and everything that moves upon and within it will also die.

Not so. You are gifting the spirits back to the world spirit. Where do you think they come from in the first place? Malel? I had thought you'd moved past superstitions of old. The world spirit may sleep, but it gifts splinters of itself to the earth even as it dreams. New spirits for old. It is a cycle – or it would be, if they weren't being trapped in the song. If you do not do this, the holy Setatmeh will slow and stiffen and lose their voices. Their intelligence. They will become as they were before the ritual – helpless, voiceless killers, able only to sing and eat. Will you see their divinity stripped from them? Will you condemn them all to silence and base instinct? Or will you set them free and be the great Singer who changed Ixachipan?

There are corpses around me, Listener. My friends are dead. I don't know you and I don't trust you, but you will tell me how to do this and I will listen, and I will decide for myself. Speak and then leave me.

Ah. There he is. The great Singer Tayan. As you command, holy lord. Listen well.

LILLA

Choosers' offices, western district, Singing City,
Pechacan, Empire of Songs
68th day of the Great Star at morning

Lilla sat on the roof and stared out into the night. He was on watch, allegedly, but all ten Talons might have been marching towards him with flaming torches and great feathered flags and he wouldn't have seen them.

Over and over, he relived the day, and over and over he saw what Tayan had shown him through the song. Shown all of them, every last one, whether freedom fighter, traitor, or Pecha. It had struck them all in the same instant, a wave of warriors falling to the ground as the vision stole everyone from awareness of their surroundings and into Tayan's maddened, mocking triumph.

Xessa and Toxte, him curled around a massive gut wound and nestled against her chest, her back spined like a lizard's with arrows. Their weight holding them upright against each other in a perfect, awful tableau. Clothed in blood. He could see it now, could see it from every angle as Tayan had walked around them in a slow circle, inspecting them and projecting that image with slick, malicious glee.

Lilla wanted to believe that there was grief in there some-where, too, but he hadn't sensed it. Nothing but triumph and self-righteousness. The image haunted him. If he'd killed Tayan, it wouldn't have happened. Maybe.

But I didn't kill him. I kissed him and then I ran away. I let Toxte go to Xessa. I left them behind.

The sweeping power of the vision had ended the battle at the wall in a heartbeat; the freedom fighters had no taste for blood, and the loyalists were grappling with the implications of Tayan's display of magic and control. Each side had drifted away from the other, moving into the city or behind the wall in a numb, almost drunken daze.

Next to Lilla on the roof, Ossa sat on his haunches, two long charms made from ropes of hair and rattling bones and beads resting around his neck, dark against the darkness of his coat. He lifted his nose to the sky and howled, a low, mournful note that went on for far too long and blended uneasily with the battering vainglorious song.

Where had this joy in death come from in Tayan? This joy in the deaths of friends, loved ones? When had Tayan so lost himself?

'What does it matter? It doesn't matter. He doesn't matter. He's a monster. A *monster*.' Lilla whispered the words with the fierce urgency of a prayer, because it was. A prayer to still the whirlpool of his thoughts, to soothe his guilt and revulsion. A prayer to excise the roots of love from his spirit and burn them on the pyre of his marriage.

A sob, raw and grating, choked from his throat and Lilla pressed one aching, scabby hand over his mouth to muffle it. Not because they might be discovered. Not to minimise the chances of disturbing the wounded and defeated and despairing warriors huddled in the building below, listening to Ossa's grief soar through the night.

No. Because if he allowed himself to cry, he wouldn't stop. He'd rage and scream and maybe throw himself from this roof just to put an end to it. He'd—

Ossa shoved his nose against Lilla's hand and then under his elbow, wriggling in until his arm encircled the dog. He put his head on the Tokob shoulder, facing away from him, and a long, pitiful whine eased out of his shaking ribs.

Lilla could feel human hair under his forearm, braided tightly and scratchy with charms – including, he'd discovered with a pang of grief so intense it stole his breath, the jade beads every warrior wore in their hair that were to be placed in their mouths to see them safe to the Realm of the Ancestors. They'd known no one would do that for them if they fell in the source, and they'd chosen to give them to Ossa so that, if they couldn't find their way onto the spiral path, they might stay near him instead.

Hundreds were dying across Ixachipan every day, maybe thousands, and Lilla knew most of them wouldn't get the ritual of the beads performed for them, either, if they had it or something similar among their people. In that moment, he didn't care about anyone else. Just Xessa and Toxte, curled together in death in the heart of the source, the place where the magic that created the Drowned was born.

Lilla shuddered in a breath and Ossa wriggled as far into his lap as he could, another grief-stricken whine breaking from him. He tucked his head under Lilla's chin, a shivering ball of misery, and every part of Lilla responded in kind, for the loss of the ejab and the loss of Tayan and the monster he'd become. He choked on another sob and then, when he couldn't hold it back any longer, he wrapped his arms and legs around the dog, buried his face in his neck, and cried like a babe.

Ekon came to him when dawn was bringing the softest blush of colour to the east, having respected Lilla's broken-hearted plea for a night of privacy. He sat a pace away and stared out over the building's edge and they watched until the world coalesced into shape and a hundred different blues and greys before other colours began to bleed into the world.

Finally, the Chitenecatl shifted his gaze to somewhere near Lilla's left ear. 'How can I help?'

Lilla had thought the tears were all used up, but his burning eyes filled with more at the simple, low-voiced offer. These weren't of grief, though. These were of rage. He turned to look at Ekon. 'Give me something I can still believe in. Anything.' He reached out and Ekon seized his hand. 'Please.'

'Me, ki—Lilla. You can believe in me. And Ossa. You have Tiamoko and every member of this war party, everyone from the Eighth Talon who rose with us and stayed with us. You have Malel and her God-born. And you have two of the fiercest and most loyal ancestors looking down on you, blessing you, urging you to keep fighting.'

'I should have gone back for them.' His voice was very small.

'Lilla, even if Tayan wasn't in your head stealing your secrets, they weren't going to tell you the extent of their plan. They knew how much it would hurt you to learn that if they couldn't end the song or get Tayan out, they'd kill him. Even though part of you must have known that, for them to look you in the face and tell you would have been too much. They loved you enough to take that burden onto themselves so that you didn't have to do it. That was their true sacrifice, and they did it for you.'

Lilla's chest collapsed in on itself and he dragged in air with a wheeze.

'And if you'd gone back for them, you'd be dead, too. What would Ossa do then? Or Tiamoko, who worshipped Xessa? Or me? Those four men you saved from the waterwheel were more than just four lives saved. You've destroyed the ease of their water supply. It's still there, but you broke the wheel. That means they need to carry every gourd and pitcher from the bowels of the pyramid to every single person who needs it. And if there's no water in the offering pool then the Drowned won't visit. How long before it looks like the gods have turned their faces from the Singer and his Melody?'

Lilla nodded miserably. He'd told himself the same when he'd been leading those four men out of the pyramid to rejoin the battle at the wall any way they could. Ekon's words did nothing to ease his grief or his guilt.

'So. How can I help?' Ekon asked again.

'Is everyone here, all the leaders?' Lilla asked and his voice was a rasp. Ekon's lips thinned but he nodded without hesitation. 'Then we need to know. One way or the other, we have to know exactly who it is we're allied with.'

Ekon stood and held out his hand. Lilla eased Ossa's head off his lap and then took it, let the Chitenecatl pull him to his feet. 'Kitten,' Lilla whispered. 'Say it. Say my name.'

'Kitten.' Ekon said it like it was the name of his god, with reverence and solemnity, and kissed Lilla's knuckles and then his mouth. Ossa rose and pressed his flank to the Tokob thigh, head on his hip as he stared up at him. Lilla shuddered in a breath at the contact, the need, and let go of Ekon's hand to rest his palm on the dog's neck. He ached everywhere, from scalp to soles and spirit to bones.

'And if they sold Tokoban to the Zellih?' Ekon asked, taking his other hand instead. Lilla stared at their entwined fingers and wished it meant more than it did, but everything was too raw. Perhaps that would change in a day or two. Or perhaps this was the last time he'd hold Ekon's hand. Perhaps Weaver would gut him like a snake before the sun had cleared the horizon.

No. Because then Ossa would be alone.

Lilla raised Ekon's hand to his lips in turn and kissed his calloused palm. It felt like goodbye. He let go and willed all the cool impassivity of a stone carving into his face.

'Then we have a decision to make,' he said and Ekon swallowed visibly and rocked his weight back into his heels, a retreat without moving a step.

Ossa was pressed to the Tokob right hip, where he'd always stood beside Xessa, leaving her spear arm unencumbered. Lilla was right-handed, though. Perhaps he'd retrain him to—no. No, Ossa didn't deserve that. He deserved to stand where he'd stood for her.

The dog's ears and tail were low and there was no readiness, no eagerness in the lithe lines of his body. Lilla ran his forefinger down to the charms. 'You owe me a licked thumb, remember,' he murmured to Toxte. 'You and Xessa both. Save it for when I see you in the Realm of the Ancestors, though.

Go gently and find your peace; you've earnt it, both of you. I'll take care of this one.'

He was exhausted and haggard, his eyes burning from crying and lack of sleep, but he straightened his shoulders. 'Where's Weaver?'

'I'll take you to her,' Ekon said. 'And I'll stand at your side.'

'Against her?'

A dimple flashed, there and gone in the bare dawn. 'Against the world, kitten.'

Ekon led him off the roof and the warriors waiting at the bottom of the stairs to take over the watch nodded and then inclined their heads when Ossa trailed past them. They weren't Tokob, but they did the ejab honour through him and Lilla had to press his thumb and forefinger to the sore, delicate skin beneath his eyes to hold back the sting. He couldn't be emotional for what was to come, despite that his whole being felt like a single raw and exposed nerve. Too many were depending on him.

Tiamoko found them a few paces further on. 'You're going to get answers from Weaver?' he demanded in a grating growl Lilla had never heard from him before. 'I'll come with you.'

'No, boy, I need you to stay here and keep everyone back,' Lilla said. 'There's too much anger. We won't get the truth if we threaten her. Weaver would rather die than bend, even to her so-called allies.' The venom in his voice surprised him; he'd thought himself calmer than this.

'Xessa—'

'*Is dead*,' Lilla snarled. 'And she would have my fucking hide if I let anything happen to you, or if I let you lose your temper and take it out on an elder, even a snake-fucking one like Weaver.' He softened his tone and gripped Tiamoko's shoulder. 'I'll get us answers, 'Moko. I swear.'

Tiamoko stilled and then snorted gently. 'You haven't called me that in years.'

Lilla startled and realised he was right. 'I've been thinking about the past a lot,' he murmured and Tiamoko choked. 'Keep everyone calm for me, all right? And make sure everyone knows Ekon had nothing to do with this. He didn't know. He—'

'I'll make sure. I believe it, too,' he added and then met the Chitenecah gaze. He dipped his head. 'I believe you.'

'Thank you, warrior. That means more than you know.'

'Ossa, do you want to stay with Tiamoko?' Lilla asked.

'Ah, don't worry about that. I know Xessa told you we were to share him, but I think that was more for my sake than his. As long as I still get to spend time with him, I'll be happy, but you two are meant for each other. You need someone other than this one to worry about,' he said, punching Ekon's shoulder.

Lilla thought about arguing and instead let it go. They were all grieving in their own way, and if being around the big dog was too much, well, he wouldn't force that on Tiamoko. Instead, he reached out and cupped the back of the boy's head and drew their brows together, then licked his thumb and pressed it to his temple.

Tiamoko made a wounded sound but he returned the promise in an instant, and then pressed his thumb to the side of Ossa's head, too. Lilla coughed an approximation of a laugh, but then he nodded and claimed the dog as family, too. 'Just remember, next time he licks your face he's reciprocating,' he said.

Tiamoko watched the dog sadly for a moment. 'I look forward to it,' he said eventually. 'If it comes.'

Lilla stared up at the sky and breathed deep, and then he squeezed Tiamoko's shoulder once more and gestured for Ekon to precede him. The Chitenecatl didn't ask permission as he ducked into the building and Lilla followed, Ossa slinking at his side. Wanting only closeness. No. Wanting Xessa.

'Fang Lilla has questions about Tokoban,' Ekon said loudly into the gloom. Weaver, Itzil, and Xini jerked and looked up. 'And I have questions about Chitenec, and questions on behalf of all the free peoples of Ixachipan. Fang?'

'Is it—'

'True?' Weaver interrupted, pushing past Itzil and folding

her arms across her chest to glare at them down the blade of her nose. 'What will you do if it is? Abandon us like the rest of your people?'

'Most of them came back, if you recall, and I think the time for arrogance is long past, don't you?' Lilla said with as much mildness as he could manage. The same mildness that he'd used with Tayan the day before. Malel, had it only been yesterday? He'd aged a decade. A century.

The image Tayan had shown him came to him again, coated in that same hateful glee as before. Inviting him to share in it, to revel in cruelty and force it upon others. Upon Weaver. He blinked and took a steadying breath.

'Is it true?' he asked again. Weaver was silent, doing her best to stare him into submission. 'This isn't a test, Weaver. It isn't the spring planting games to honour the gods; we're not all going to have a good laugh over beer afterwards regardless of winners and losers. This is about the very foundations of our alliance. It's about our home, and it's about Ixachipan.' *Mild and neutral and infuriating. Push her into recklessness.* 'Is it true?'

'What does it matter?' she snapped. 'We're losing, aren't we? You stand and whine about the loss of your lands when none of us have owned ours in generations. Chitenec has been poisoned by the song for so long that we may never get the bad magic out of it. We'll be growing godless crops forever. And you want to cry about losing Tokoban? You don't even know what that feels like. You—'

'Don't change the subject,' Ekon said tightly. 'Don't deflect us away from the point. Lilla asked you a very simple question, and it's one that more than just Tokob want the answer to. Did you sell Tokoban *or anywhere in the north* to the Zellih in return for aid?'

'*I* didn't,' Weaver said and Lilla felt a wash of relief before he understood her emphasis.

'Let me guess, it was these mysterious leaders who send you your orders?' he asked before he could stop himself, the sarcasm dripping thick as honey from his tongue because mildness could go and fuck itself. 'The leaders no one's ever seen. The ones who are somehow still surviving out there in the city, and not only surviving but keeping track of our location to tell you what to do every day, even though no one ever sees messengers. Those leaders?'

'You have no understanding of what's really happening here,' Weaver said stiffly.

'And you strive for freedom without ever counting the cost in human life. There's really nothing you wouldn't do, is there?'

The old woman drew herself up, as if it was something to be proud of. 'No. There really isn't. I have given my life to the cause. I have sacrificed and lost and done things that haunt me. I have struck deals and sold information and betrayed people before they could betray us. All to bring us to the point of victory.'

Ekon laughed, high and wild. 'The point of victory? Where is that? Are we standing on it now? Are we close enough to victory that we can reach out and touch it? Because you just admitted we're losing and your barbaric, heartless, idiotic decision to *sell out the Tokob to their ancestral enemies* only hastens that defeat. Have you ever wondered whether your secret rebel leaders, your *fucking owners*, are actually on our side? Is there anything more guaranteed to fracture an alliance than a betrayal of this size? And you thought you could keep it a secret? How?'

He flung out an arm in his passion, almost catching Lilla in the face. 'Where are they supposed to go? Where are the Tokob supposed to live once Tokoban belongs to the Zellih? Will your shadowy masters provide a place for them? Do you honestly believe Tokob will stand idly by and let their land be stolen so that everyone else gets theirs back? What—'

'What if we agree?'

Ekon's mouth closed with an audible click of teeth and he turned on the balls of his feet to face him. 'What did you say?' he squeaked.

Lilla didn't look at him. 'Weaver. What if we agree?'

'Then we can win,' she said promptly. 'All the calculations

point to it. If we retain rebel loyalty and gain Zellih warriors, we crush the Melody and destroy the song. We sacrifice one land to save all the others. And . . . of course we'll look after you. There will be a place for you in every land, any land where you wanted to settle.' She gestured at Ekon. 'Chitenec, with your lover.'

It was an admission. It was the closest they'd get to her saying *yes, we gave away your home because we need the warriors and you don't matter.*

Lilla wished he was angrier. 'And what if we wanted to *settle* Tokoban?' he asked, the mildness back in his voice. He could see from the suspicion and confusion in Weaver's face that she was as helpless to pierce it as Tayan had been.

Her nostrils flared. 'That . . . is not something I have authority over. It would be for Zellih to decide.'

Lilla laughed and it was harsh and grating and it made Ossa pin back his ears and step protectively in front of him. The dog's lips peeled back from his teeth. *You just need an excuse, huh, boy? Me too. Me fucking too.*

'Control that—' Weaver began.

'One more word and I'll command him to kill you,' Lilla interrupted with lethal softness. The woman closed her mouth. 'There are things I will not tolerate in this conversation, and you speaking to, or even looking at, this animal is one of them. Am I entirely understood?'

Xini and Itzil had been silent witnesses, but at that, Xini put his hand on Weaver's forearm and squeezed. 'We understand,' he said. 'As for what was done to your land, it wasn't Weaver's fault. The alliance with the Zellih was struck by those who give us our orders. Those who see all.'

'No,' Lilla said with complete confidence as it all suddenly tumbled into place. 'No. Malel, but we've been stupid.' His tone was almost, *almost* admiring. 'There is no other tier of leadership above you three. Is there? You told us the very night we met you. Call me Weaver, you said. And Ekon, you said that people high up in the hierarchy were known by their trades, not their real names, so that if you were tortured, you couldn't identify them. But you, Xini, Itzil, even Enet, none of your identities were hidden behind your trades. Why weren't you known only as the Warrior? Why wasn't Enet the Politician or perhaps the Trader if that was too risky? Why did everyone know who you were? Why is it only Weaver whose identity is secret?'

'Is this true?' Xini demanded. 'Are you the real head of the rebellion? Are you it? There's no one else? It's been you all along deciding what we do, who we kill, who dies, who lives? You were commanding Enet and pushing her to become Singer? You chose to give away Tokoban without consulting anyone?'

'Nonsense,' Weaver snapped. 'Everyone is very tired. We are in the middle of a war and you especially, Toko, are grieving. Because of that, I will forgive your behaviour.'

'Forgive?' Ekon choked. Lilla stilled him and together they watched as a series of complicated emotions flickered across Xini's face. Itzil wore only one: grief. Grief for her daughter, Enet, and her grandson, Pikte. Both lost to an uprising that, while just, appeared to have been built on a lie.

Xini took her arm and led her over to the corner of the room and helped her to sit, leaving Weaver alone in front of Toko, Chitenecatl, and dog.

'It's not what you think,' Weaver snarled suddenly. 'You have no idea what you're—'

'Mictec be merciful,' Ekon breathed and Lilla felt a surge of triumph and another of love, almost overwhelming in its unexpected intensity; he'd worked it out, too.

'Weaver,' Lilla said. 'Interesting choice of name. Weaving all of us together into a pattern that benefits . . . who, I wonder? What's your real name, Weaver?' He took a step forward, Ossa pacing him, Ekon at his other side.

'Perhaps it was your trade,' Ekon added with a soft malice that made Lilla wary and uncomfortably aware of the other man's presence. 'But that trade itself was a disguise. Wasn't it? We accepted your explanation that it was too dangerous to know your name. But why would that be when, as Lilla says, I knew Xini's and he knew mine? Why would a simple enslaved weaver have to be anonymous but the estate manager of the Great Octave herself could be known?'

He looked at Lilla. 'You're right, kitten. We've been so fucking stupid. But I think I know now why she chose it. It's a reference to the Moctezuma bird, isn't it, *traitor*? All those great woven nests made by the females while one single male protects them within his territory. One bird that brings together all the others and dominates them. Rules them, even.'

Lilla found Ekon's hand and squeezed it, then held on to it. 'Bird, you say?' he asked conversationally as they stepped forward again and Weaver stepped back. 'There's something about the Zellih, isn't there, and their worship of a sacred bird?'

'It is not the Moctezuma,' Weaver said hurriedly, 'and you are speaking out of turn. How dare you accuse me. I have brought us this far and I can bring us all the way to victory. You cannot do it without me.'

'And all it will cost us is thousands of lives and the loss of Tokoban and perhaps all the north. Who wins, ultimately?'

'The Zellih,' Ekon said. 'The Zellih win. Oh, they lose warriors too, but far fewer than us. And perhaps they gain territory, or perhaps something entirely different. Who can say, when we're fed so very many lies.'

'Have you lived in Ixachipan all your life, *Zellitli*?' Lilla asked. 'Did you willingly give yourself up to slavery to better ingratiate your way into the rebellion and come to head it, or is your story even more complicated than that?'

'I don't know what—' Weaver started and Ossa began to growl. A long, low rumble that made Lilla's hackles rise, let alone the dog's own. Ossa had had enough of the tension in the room, it seemed. The Toko didn't blame him.

'Ossa can smell liars,' he said, though he had no idea if such a thing was possible. 'Maybe he can also smell Zellih. Or traitors. Or mass murderers. I think you're all four, which puts you in a difficult position. Where are your people?'

'Everywhere,' she snarled and then closed her eyes and raised her hands in supplication, but the words she spoke made no sense. 'Omeata Bird-form, hear my words. Strike for the heart and the head, do not hesitate—'

Lilla didn't hesitate either. He clicked a particular pattern of sounds. And Ossa tore the old woman's throat out.

'We didn't know,' Xini said before Weaver had even stopped bleeding out onto the floor. 'Kill me if you want to, but I swear on Mictec, I swear on Enet's spirit and the spirit of her boy Pikte. We didn't know. For all who would be free.' Itzil was nodding along frantically.

'For all who would be free? That's what she said,' Lilla growled, but Ekon touched his arm.

'A child's spirit is sacred to Mictec. Xini would not risk the boy with a false oath. I promise.'

'I was born in Pechacan and bought by Enet's Pechaqueh parents when I was four years old to be her playmate and so that she might learn to govern slaves from a young age. I have never been further north than Chitenec, never set foot in Barazal—' Xini babbled, and if he feared for his life, Lilla didn't blame him. There was very fucking little stopping him from taking it.

Itzil was writing on the wall with a stick of charcoal. She snapped her fingers and Xini cut himself off to read it and then swore, long and low. '"Listener",' he read. 'Shit, you're right. Those last words Weaver spoke, they weren't directed at us. She was communing through the song.'

'Omeata Bird-form,' Lilla repeated, because it had struck him as familiar at the time. He sucked in a breath. 'Malel, of course. The Bird Council of Zellipan. I don't know their names but I'm sure Bird-form is the title of one of their leaders.'

'And we know there are Zellih in Ixachipan. If Weaver somehow learnt to communicate through the song, they might have been talking to each other all this time,' Ekon said, appalled.

'Enet could Listen once she was Chosen,' Xini said. 'Tayan can Listen. Weaver obviously could. Does that mean anyone can learn the skill of it? Think what that would mean for the resistance!' His gaze went to the old woman. 'For those without the ability to speak.'

'Xini, focus,' Lilla said and Enet's confidant and former slave jerked and then grimaced, raising his hand in apology. 'I agree, and Itzil, I am not dismissing this as an option, though any Toko will teach you and your kin to sign should you wish it. I know you've already picked up a few words.'

Itzil gestured and Lilla barked a short laugh. 'I'm afraid I'm spoken for already, though I appreciate the offer.' He sobered again. 'If you want to know who was giving Weaver her orders, I'd say the answer is this Bird-form. The Zellih have been manipulating us from the start, pushing us into conflicts and battles that weakened us and the Melody both. Every warrior left in the Singing City, whichever side they're on, is close to breaking. And now, assuming her message got through the song, the Zellih are coming. How do we stand against them and the Melody both?'

'I think this is premature,' Ekon said slowly. 'When word of the Zellih presence and the loss of Tokoban spread, Weaver was wary. More than that, she was furious. She didn't start that rumour. Which means she may well have summoned them ahead of time. No doubt we and the Melody were supposed to hack at each other some more before they arrived to slaughter us all and claim the city, or whatever it is they want. But they're coming, and we have to face them. And the Melody.'

'Then the rumour came from the pyramid,' Lilla said. 'Tayan received word the Zellih are coming and he knows he doesn't have an alliance with them. He wants to make sure we don't form one either, so he says our leaders have given away Tokoban to our enemies. And it worked,' he added bitterly.

Ekon touched his hand, incongruously gentle considering they were standing over a cooling corpse and discussing all the ways both Weaver and Tayan had betrayed them. 'And most of them came back,' he reminded him, though of course, the reason for their return was no less appalling.

Ossa was pacing around the body and licking the floor at the edge of the blood pool that had formed beneath it, drooling.

Lilla glanced to Xini and Itzil. 'I'm sorry, but he's been injured and he's hungry. And she was a traitor.'

Itzil turned her back immediately, but Xini grimaced and then nodded. 'What is it you Tokob say?'

Lilla grunted. 'We sustain what sustains us, in the endless circle. And Xessa will be laughing her arse off at this, that I can promise.' He pursed his lips and kissed. Ossa looked up, vibrating and his eyes brighter than they'd been since Lilla had come back bearing only locks of hair instead of people. He clicked and the dog pounced, muzzle burrowing between kilt and tunic into the soft, hollow belly. It was a relief; he'd been worried Ossa's grief would be so great he'd simply wither away.

'So what do we do next?' Xini asked, a little too loud over the sound of tearing flesh.

Lilla recoiled. 'I have no idea,' he said. 'The rumour that parts of our leadership have given away parts of Ixachipan has taken on a life of its own and I don't think we could stop it even if we could prove it's a lie. So can we use it?'

Ekon paced between him and Xini. 'You want to find the Zellih and pretend we agree to the alliance? Pretend we agree . . . what exactly?'

'Did Weaver say anything that might tell us where the Zellih are now?' Lilla said instead, dodging the question for now. 'She said to strike at the head and the heart both. That's here, surely. Do we think they're coming here?'

Xini glanced at Itzil. 'She spoke of Chitenec a lot,' he said slowly. 'We thought it was just because we are Chitenecah. But perhaps that's where they're coming from. So then why does the rumour say Tokoban is the prize?'

'The speed with which it spread could mean the Pechaqueh were panicking,' Ekon said slowly. 'To me, that says Chitenec. Tokoban is three weeks away. If the Melody had news of them in Chitenec eight days ago when the story first reached us, they could be here in days. They could be here tomorrow. They want to ensure that we meet the Zellih with violence, rather than an offer of friendship, so they spread the rumour just days before their arrival to ensure our anger is still hot. As for why Tokoban,' he added when Lilla muttered a curse, 'perhaps simply because it worked so well last time. Or perhaps to deflect our attention from the trade-road between Sky Jaguar Hill and the Singing City, which is the most direct route they can take.'

'I say we intercept them,' Lilla said and everyone turned to stare at him. 'We take that trade-road, we find them, and we tell them the alliance stands. They can have Tokoban, Chitenec, whatever was agreed. We bring them back here and together we end the song.'

'But there is no alliance?' Xini said, baffled.

Lilla looked at Ekon, needing to see something, anything, that would tell him he was making the right choice. And Ekon nodded, his eyes hard as flint. 'No, but we'll tell them there is and present them with thousands of warriors to help them end the song. Weaver lied to us; we lie to them.'

Something vicious and primal in Lilla's spirit yowled its approval. 'Those are *our lands*. We use the Zellih to gain victory. And then we cut them down where they stand. For all who would be free.'

ILANDEH

Something was wrong. Something had struck the Bird-form not long after dawn the day before, some sort of vision or message from her god, but it had been cut short and Omeata had been in a brutal mood ever since.

Ilandeh's own situation was precarious enough without Omeata stalking through their camp looking for people to impale. Ever since the Singer's invasion of her mind at Sky Jaguar Hill, she'd been so far outside the circle of trust that she had no idea what had happened to put the Bird-form in such a foul mood. Only Omeata's curiosity about the song and communing through it had spared the Whisper's life, though Ilandeh suspected there was another reason. Especially as she was half-convinced the Bird-form herself could do something similar. The strange vision she'd had the day before practically proved it.

The flock had taken four Chitenecah cities including Sky Jaguar Hill now, killing all who stood against them and all Pechaqueh. Only the carrion feeders flocking to the feast had moved in the still and silent city as the Zellih left it and crossed into Pechacan. If there were survivors, they were hiding until their killers were long gone. *If* there were survivors. It had been bloody and brutal and without remorse. It had been more Melody than anything, and the Whisper didn't like it. To preserve her life and place on the periphery of the flock, she had no choice but to follow every order Omeata or Huenoch gave her.

Pikte and Olox had distanced themselves from her, too, though they watched relentlessly from a distance. Tayan's communion with her had confused them; the Singer himself stooping to question a Whisper? They didn't know what to make of it and so far that had been enough to prevent them murdering her. No matter what Beyt had ordered them to do, the Singer had chosen to speak with Ilandeh and leave her alive. Who were they to act against her in light of that?

Ilandeh looked at the vast flock stretching ahead of her on the road, the thousands of their number milling and mingling like bats gathering to roost. They were taking the direct road to the Singing City, and she marvelled at Omeata's knowledge of the route. No longer did they ask the Whispers or any of their new allies for directions; they knew exactly where they were going and, she guessed, they always had.

She turned and walked backwards, looking over the heads of the stragglers to the next flock. And the next. It wasn't often Ilandeh was surprised, but in this, the Bird-form had outwitted her. Two Zellih flocks had appeared out of the surrounding farmland as if summoned by magic, one from the north, the other waiting for them to catch up on the road to the Singing City. They were six, maybe seven thousand warriors strong now, led by the Bird-form and both Bird-wings. Three of the seven Aspects were in Ixachipan and they were intent, focused, and hungry.

The war was reaching its climax and it was likely the Melody didn't even know it. If nobody Listened to her, nobody could learn what she knew, the numbers among whom she marched, their location. Their destination.

Perhaps there was no right and just resolution to this war. Perhaps there was only whatever caused the least amount of wrong, the least amount of pain. She listened to those around her, or as many as would talk in her presence, anyway. That was the thing about being a Whisper. You didn't just pay attention to the people in charge. In fact, they were usually the people you spoke to last. Instead, you listened to the common folk at the sharp end of poverty, the ones with the least power and privilege. It was what they talked about that most often introduced you to the important parts of their lives, the things the leaders wouldn't even know about, let alone concern themselves with.

And what the common Zellih warrior wanted, needed, was determined to get, wasn't land or riches or prestige in Ixachipan. It was the ending of the song. But why would a native of Barazal, where the song did not exist, care about its destruction? Especially if Omeata was using it to communicate?

If only Tayan hadn't burnt her fragile trust with the Bird-form to char. Ilandeh had no way to learn Omeata's full intentions or who she was talking to through the song, though the seamless arrival of the flocks of the Bird-wings pointed to their involvement. How so many Zellih could manipulate Pechaqueh magic, though, was beyond her. *If I'd still been trusted by Omeata, perhaps I could have discovered that. What a gift that could have been to the rebels.*

Perhaps it still could be. She already had Tayan's ear; if she could regain Omeata's trust, she might be in a position to understand the status of the war and its likely outcome. Perhaps even change that outcome. The time for playing nice was over.

Ilandeh wandered close to Olox; he and Pikte walked at the rear, though not close by. The boy glanced from the corner of his eye but said nothing, so she didn't waste time with niceties. 'Target. Bird-wing left. Tonight.'

She didn't wait for a response, because doing so would suggest she doubted her own orders or that he'd obey them. Instead, she lengthened her stride and caught up to a trio of Xentib who'd allied with them after the fall of the City of Glass. Most of these new allies didn't know she'd been ousted from Omeata's presence, and they easily invited her into their conversation.

Ilandeh agreed with a shy smile and a flutter of hands that spoke of nerves and the Xentib urged her to relax and told her she was among kin. She showed them the rattle tied in her hair and they smiled indulgently, well remembering how such things had been laughed at before the uprising. They understood her pride in her heritage.

Ilandeh lost herself in the rhythms of their speech and it was some time later that she looked over and found Huenoch walking a few paces away. They were watching her silently and she raised an eyebrow in question. They looked away but kept pace.

All day.

Olox's knife was hungry. Ilandeh could feel the boy watching her, always watching, the stars in his eyes faded to cold, grim points like the eyeshine of a jaguar just before the kill. As for Pikte, he watched with her open hostility in private, and treated her as if she was already dead when they were in Zellih company. These were the warriors who would help her kill the Bird-wing.

They were camped in an open, muddy milpa a stick from a river. Closer than Ilandeh liked but far enough that they shouldn't be troubled by holy Setatmeh. And if they were, well, she'd made sure there were a few people closer to that river than she was. If they were careless enough to not pay attention to their surroundings when they made camp, that wasn't her fault. And if Omeata wasn't going to ask her to route-find anymore, she was going to have to accept the dangers inherent in travel through Ixachipan during the Wet.

There were enough puddles from the day's rain that drinking water was plentiful, and the three Bird Aspects had their own rubber-coated rain shelters to rest beneath. Everyone else made do as best they could.

Pikte had gone to forage while Olox and Ilandeh unfolded the heavy maguey that made up their packs and tied it between two spears embedded deep in the rich earth, a lone rubber tree the third anchor for their shelter. The material gave them a low sloping roof against the rain and the third unfolded pack material provided something that was only damp for them to sit on. And by using their spears to support the shelter, they showed themselves mostly unarmed and so less of a threat.

At least until they'd killed Bird-wing left. After that, it wouldn't matter.

'Five days from the Singing City,' Ilandeh said as she sat under the shelter. Olox was as far from her as he could get without it being obvious. 'We'll be getting real vengeance soon. Bringing an end to this.' She waved her hand above her head, indicating the song. The song that had done something it had never done before in all Ilandeh's life – showed her a vision.

It had struck them all at the same instant, even the Zellih, but alone out of everyone in the combined flocks of three Bird Aspects, she had known both the location of what she was seeing and the identities. She'd let herself feel everything those images conjured in her. Sacrilege at the blood spilt in the great pyramid; grief for Xessa, who hadn't liked her, and Toxte, who'd seemed far too nice to have anything in common with his wife; and disbelief that it was Tayan himself showing her what he'd done. Gloating, and triumphant, and crowing, and hurt. His pain was as much on display as the corpses, whether he'd intended it or not.

'The new Singer's power is great indeed to have done what he did and shared a vision with everyone under his song. To show us that he'd survived an assassination attempt. That is too much power for one person to have. But not for much longer,' she added, both for those who were no doubt listening and to dig at Olox and his disguise. Test him. Remind him who he was and why they were here. Something both he and Pikte seemed to have forgotten.

We are Whispers, and you jeopardise our very lives with your questioning, your disloyalty. Is this what Beyt taught you while I was gone? Is this the quality of a Whisper in Atu's Melody? Pathetic.

Pikte returned empty-handed, propping his spear against the tree and squeezing rainwater from his hair and kilt before creeping into the shelter with them. They sat in silence but for the growling of their empty bellies and watched the shadows lengthen beneath the clouds. Like so much else, Ilandeh didn't know why they'd made camp so early. Perhaps they were waiting for yet another Bird Aspect and their flock. If so, their numbers would crush the Melody when they reached the Singing City.

It was too wet for a fire and they had nothing to cook anyway, and so the approaching torches in the dusk were both obvious and ominous. Huenoch, of course, carried one, and the rest of Omeata's honour guard walked with them. In the centre of the torchlight, the Bird-form's feathered huipil shimmered with every step. Flanking her, left and right, came the Bird-wings. Their attire was closer to that of the warriors', long, loose kilts and salt-cotton, but each wore a harness across their chest that supported a frame of thin bamboo rods standing up from their shoulders. From the frame arced a wing in flight, one sweeping left and the other right.

Ilandeh had to admit that as they approached, with the darkness falling around them, the three did resemble the body and wings of a bird. It was eerie, beautiful, and the perfect opportunity.

'Fuck it, take all three,' she breathed to the Whispers and then pressed her palms together beneath her chin and bowed. Olox and Pikte copied her.

'Peace of the gods upon you during your travels, revered Bird Aspects. We are humbled that such as we may stand in your radiance. May we assist your journey that the gods smile upon you? We have neither fire nor food to honour you, but you are welcome in our shelter.' She stepped to one side, Olox moving with her and Pikte the other way, opening a path into the small, damp space.

'The revered Bird-wings were curious about our allies,' Omeata said smoothly, without moving. Ilandeh bowed again. *Allies? You're just waiting for a reason to kill me. Not that you need a reason. So what are you waiting for, then, my old friend? I'm curious.*

'I told them how you have proved your loyalty in our battles so far, taking Pechaqueh life and that of anyone who stands against us. Bird-wing right, in particular, was most keen to meet you.'

Bird-wing right was on Ilandeh's left, opposite Pikte who'd stepped under the branches of the rubber tree and now snatched up the spear he'd leant against it. He didn't bother fighting his way past Huenoch and the rest: he simply cast it, hard and true, and punched the Aspect off their feet.

Ilandeh began moving as Olox's short blowpipe, dart already loaded, came up and he took aim at the other Wing. She kicked him hard in the ribs, timing it for after he'd already blown the dart, and then she threw herself on Omeata, shielding her with her body and crying out for Huenoch to do something.

Pikte had already fled and now Olox did likewise, streaking across the fields. Ilandeh scrambled to her feet and set off after the boy. She knew this road and this part of Pechacan. She knew exactly where he was headed.

Pikte, on the other hand, had been clever. He was going for the river. As dangerous as that was, one person throwing themselves into the water while babbling prayers might survive any holy Setatmeh living in it but if the Zellih attempted to follow, they would absolutely attract a god's attention. And the Zellih had never had holy Setatmeh to fear. Their waters were safe and so they were swimmers; in the heat of the chase, it was likely they'd forget where they were and jump into the river in pursuit. No Setat would allow such sacrilege to pass unpunished.

Ilandeh had only her knife and the blowpipe bouncing on her back. It would be enough, if she could catch him in time, though Olox was younger than her. Fast, too.

The pyramid loomed over the fields with the faint blush of sunset staining its milky capstone a delicate orange. 'Don't,' she yelled as she pounded over a raised stone road and down into the mud and crops of the next field. Olox neither slowed nor acknowledged her and the chase went on, both of them labouring through thick mud and weaving among the waist-high corn.

Olox fell with a gasp and a grunt, but he was up and running again before Ilandeh had gained more than a few strides. She tried to see where he'd fallen and look for tangled roots or a stone, but it was impossible as the cloud cover and dusk combined. She had to slow rather than risk a broken ankle and the boy reached the pyramid a good thirty strides ahead of her.

Ilandeh ran after him, praying that whichever Zellih were following had lost them in the dusk. If not, they were both about to die. She threw herself up the steps into the pyramid and then onto her knees to crawl the long internal passage leading to the chamber where the Listener resided – if there was a Listener. There hadn't been warriors guarding the pyramid, so they might be lucky and find it empty.

A flicker of orange light quashed that hope: if there were candles, there was life. It vanished and then reappeared as Olox reached the end of the passageway and dropped down into the chamber.

Ilandeh scrabbled the last length and tumbled out herself. Olox and the Listener had already joined hands. She crossed the space and flung herself down, slapping both hands on theirs and forcing them apart, forming a third point of contact. The Listener's mind swept her up and sent her to Pilos and she burst in to find him blue with caution and Olox orange with conviction.

'Olox and Pikte killed the Bird-wings and destroyed any last chance at getting close to Omeata. I'll do what I can, but it's likely I'm irrevocably compromised, tainted by association, and after the Singer's visit to me, I don't know if I can fix this. The Bird-form lives and she'll absorb the Wings' flocks. Seven thousand warriors, five days from the Singing City. We've just left Sky Jaguar Hill.' Ilandeh barked the words at Pilos, ignoring Olox, and didn't wait for a response, pulling her hands free of theirs and then retching at the agony as her mind snapped back into her body without the Listener to guide it safely back to her flesh. She shook her head and then dragged out her knife and stabbed Olox in the side of the neck where there was no surviving it, and then the Listener in the chest.

Pilos would know what she'd done; he'd experience it as if it was his own body she'd slashed. She just had to hope he'd understand. Ilandeh dragged the choking, writhing Whisper across the small chamber to the passageway, which was loud with the scuffle of people approaching. Zellih. Turning him around and evading the weak pawing of his hands, she stabbed him again in the calves and the back of one thigh, then let him slump against the wall, smearing it with blood as he collapsed. She took his knife and, before she could think too hard about it, reversed it in her grip and slashed it upwards, scoring her salt-cotton and then biting deep into her exposed clavicle and the side of her neck.

She gave a hoarse, keening cry and shoved the knife into Olox's hand, then staggered back to where the Listener was lying in a pool of his own blood. She collapsed. Heartbeats later, Huenoch fell into the chamber and immediately whipped up their spear, looking for threats. Olox was at their feet, almost dead. Should be dead. *Why isn't he dead yet?* The Whisper pointed a bloody finger in Ilandeh's direction and tried to speak.

'I stopped him, Huenoch, before he could reach the Listener,' she gasped, her hand clamped to the cut on her neck. 'No message was passed through the song, I swear it.'

They stared at her and then kicked Olox over onto his face, saw the wounds in the backs of his legs, and looked speculatively at the low passageway through which they'd just crawled. 'Perhaps,' they said. 'That is a Listener?'

'Yes.'

'Are they communicating through the song now?'

Ilandeh made a show of forcing herself onto her knees and one hand to crawl across to him. 'I can't tell. He's near death. I don't think so.'

He was though, and it was likely he was still linked to Pilos.

Could the Spear see this, see the scale of the deception she had created to regain her place among their enemies? Could he see the lengths she went to for him, for her High Feather in all but name?

Can he see it's all a lie?

The Zellitli approached, stepped past her, and stabbed the Listener in the eye. 'They aren't communicating now,' they said dispassionately.

'Bird-form approaches,' called a voice and moments later Omeata slithered out of the passageway, paused to check the feathers on her huipil for damage, and then examined the room with a sceptical tilt to her eyebrows.

'A pretty little scene,' she observed mildly. 'Show me your wound.'

Ilandeh didn't have to fake her wince when she unpeeled her hand from the slice in her neck. She'd come dangerously close to hitting the big vein that would have killed her as surely as it had killed Olox. The irony wasn't lost on her.

Omeata crouched opposite her and Huenoch held Ilandeh by the hair; they'd already kicked her knife away. 'Convincing,' the Bird-form added, still in that tone of mild amusement. 'Bring her. And have some warriors destroy this pyramid so no one else gets the wrong idea. It is just the structure that needs pulling down, correct?'

'No, Bird-form. You must smash the pale capstone at its summit. The pyramid itself can stay intact – only the songstone needs cracking and then the magic will run out.'

She knew Omeata knew this; she knew why Omeata was testing her.

'See it done,' she added to Huenoch. 'Up you get, Warrior Ilandeh. Someone should see to that wound for you.'

'I can stitch it myself, thank you. Your shamans should see to the Bird-wings. Do they live?'

'They do not.'

Ilandeh put her bloody palm against her clean palm and bowed her head. 'I grieve their loss, even as I thank Nallac and the Sacred Bird that you are safe. I hope I did not hurt you.'

Omeata licked her teeth and then put her head on one side. 'I shall have a bruised arse for a week and my elbow clicks when I straighten it,' she said and lifted her left arm to show the lump swelling the joint.

'I beg the revered Bird-form's forgiveness. I reacted without thought.'

'You reacted faster than my honour guard, who let two Aspects lose their lives,' she said and Huenoch blanched and bowed over their joined palms. 'The bruises to my body and dignity are a small price to pay for my continued existence.'

She stared around the pyramid's interior. 'And did your treacherous friend make contact through the song?' she asked and Ilandeh almost turned the question back on the Bird-form, hungry to know who it was she'd been speaking with in the same way.

'He did not, Bird-form.'

Omeata looked to Huenoch. 'I can't say with certainty, Bird-form, but it seems unlikely. We were close behind them.'

'The traitor Pikte?' Ilandeh asked.

'We have him,' the Bird-form confirmed. 'He will be dealt with in the way of our people.'

The Whisper bowed again to hide her grimace. Pikte would have his arms broken and bound behind him, and then be staked face-down in a puddle or shallow pond. He would live for as long as he could keep his head out of the water, and then he would drown. Or he would live until a holy Setat came to investigate the splashing, though that would be a new addition to the Zellih traditional method of execution. 'The Bird-form's wisdom is great,' she muttered.

Ilandeh got to the crawling passage to leave the pyramid before her knees buckled from the pain and blood loss. It seemed like a good time to pass out, and a good addition to her disguise, so she didn't fight it.

The last thing she saw was Omeata's eyeroll as she collapsed.

PILOS

The Singer had two black eyes, a crooked nose, and a temper to match.

He was also drunk, though not on beer or honeypot. Rather, he was drunk on his own song and the heady taste of relief and triumph and mostly on the news that Atu and Pilos had brought from the city. As best they could tell after two days and nights of searching, quartering street by street and plaza after plaza, the traitors had fled. Gone. Given up the fight.

The peace-weaving had been their final roll of the bones. What they thought they were going to accomplish, though, was a mystery. Lilla, at least, had seemed to believe the nego-tiation was genuine.

Xochi had told Pilos of Tayan's increasingly strange behav-iour as the peace-weaving had progressed, and he'd seen his confusion for himself during the fighting, but if the Singer had an explanation for it, he wasn't sharing it.

In the end, though Tayan had been wounded, they'd failed. The Singer's former husband escaped, and the slaves who kept the waterwheel turning were likewise gone – but the rest of the peace-weavers were dead, as was the Mute, her husband,

and the other eja. The threat to the holy Setatmeh in the Singing City was over.

The threat to the great pyramid, the Singer, and the song itself was not over, however. Ilandeh's latest intelligence was that the Zellih war party, the flock, was only five days away, had tripled in size, and had every intention of accomplishing what the traitors had so spectacularly failed to do. While Ilandeh had contrived the deaths of both Bird-wings, at the justifiable loss of two Whispers, there was nothing she could do about the sheer number of warriors marching on the Singing City.

Which was why it was so hard to understand the Singer's giddy pleasure.

The First and Second Talons, the Melody's pride, were shattered beyond recall, as well as the Singing City detachment. Horrific losses. Appalling, ludicrous losses that on paper, from history, would have had Pilos and Atu scoffing at the incompetence of the leaders who had suffered such reduction.

And yet no Feather or High Feather since the beginning of the Empire of Songs had ever faced what they'd faced.

And they're all we've got to face the Zellih. Not even the Talons in Xentiban can get here in time.

'Holy lord, the revelations of Whisper Ilandeh should—'

'Do you see, Pilos? Do you see what my song has done? What my actions, my faith, and purity of purpose have done? Two deaths and the traitors ran away. That's all it took; two deaths! I have brought us victory!'

Pilos's expression must have been a very particular type of politely neutral because Xochi took one look at him and winced, rocking on her heels as if she wanted to step away. Pilos didn't blame her. He felt like a pot of cooking rubber and Tayan had come along and thrown a hot coal in just to see what would happen.

'The Singing City is safe, Pilos. I'm safe! The song is safe. Can I do it now? I'm going to do it now. It's been long enough. I'll send the announcement through the song that the Singing City is secure and the traitors defeated. It will hearten the rest of our warriors and brave civilians, won't it?'

Despite the manic edge to his voice and manner, Tayan's earnestness and unrestrained joy were infectious. A smile quirked the corner of Pilos's mouth until his automatic sweep of the room for danger showed him the other source of Tayan's mania. His smile died. 'I can see no reason why not, Singer,' he said woodenly, 'though you understand, of course, that this is only a temporary reprieve. We have only days to rest and prepare, Singer, before the next attack.'

Tayan waved away his concern. 'We'll beat them as we beat the traitors. I will purge the song of spirits before that day, to enlighten and embolden our gods, and they will give us their blessing in return. We'll have the victory, Pilos, I know it.'

'This one is honoured by your trust,' the Spear said flatly. 'Your Melody has accomplished great things in this city over the last weeks. If I might beg that you acknowledge their effort and sacrifice in your announcement, it will not only honour them but it will bring heart to all warriors fighting in the rest of Ixachipan. It will remind them that victory can be theirs and that we acknowledge all they've done so far. To know their Singer is proud of them will do much for morale.'

'I will,' the Singer said eagerly. 'I will do that. I'll do it right now. Everyone needs to know of our victory. That the song and its Singer are safe, that the heart-city still beats. They need to *see*.' He laughed, high and boyish, and Pilos twitched.

Tayan dropped to the mats where he stood, closing his eyes, and then just as quickly opened them and jumped up. He took several rapid paces away from the colonnade, his colour suddenly sickly. 'They . . . I will wait until they're done,' he croaked. 'Xochi, stand closer to me.'

'Of course, holy lord. Forgive me,' the Chorus Leader said, crossing the grubby mats to take her place close enough to the Singer that they had to be able to smell each other's sweat. She snapped her fingers and the Chorus warriors guarding the line lashed out with the butts of their spears, hard enough to bruise, not to break.

Their targets were the few dozen slaves who'd come to

surrender in the previous week, hungry enough and scared enough that they'd remembered that a life of service in return for food, clothing, medicine, and education wasn't a fucking hardship but a privilege. They were roped to each other by their necks and the ends of the central line were tied to columns on opposite sides of the source. They moved to and from the massive pile of rubble scattered across the once-pristine mats inside the source, bricking up the colonnade that led to the gardens and had flooded this holiest of spaces with light and scent and birdsong. It was the holy lord's latest obsession, and Pilos approved.

'Holy lord, Whisper Ilandeh's—'

'Faster!' Tayan snapped, kicking out at a Tlaloxqueh who was struggling to lift a sharp-edged rock, his hands already cut and abraded from the broken-edged stone. The man yelped and gripped it again, pressing it to a similarly raw chest and staggering upright, his mouth a stretched rictus.

'When it's finished,' the Singer added to Xochi in a lower voice, 'take them somewhere and kill them. Toss them in with the corpses from the latest battle and make sure the others don't see you do it.'

The Chorus Leader touched belly and throat. 'As the holy lord commands.'

'I must be safe,' he added yet again, gripping Xochi's wrist. 'You have to keep me safe or everything is lost. We can sacrifice anything else, everything else, but *you have to keep me safe.*'

'We will, great Singer. We will do everything and anything to protect you and your song.' Whatever Xochi's private thoughts, she kept them well-hidden as she politely but easily twisted her wrist free of the holy lord's grip and stepped back, putting herself between him and the slaves.

Already, the wall was waist-high and the light in the source fading. Despite its scarcity, the Singer had ordered part of their stock of firewood burnt to make mortar so that the wall would set strong and immoveable. The slaves' and warriors' entrances had been likewise closed off. Even the stream leading from the offering pool was bricked up. With the waterwheel destroyed and the slaves who walked it vanished, the pool itself was empty but for a puddle of stagnating water in its centre.

No fresh water; no gods.

Fingers of superstitious dread trailed along Pilos's spine. Tayan was sealing himself inside the pyramid, leaving only the grand staircase – wide, open, easily defensible – as a way in and out. The silent gloom of the source and the evidence of everything that had occurred here set his nerves jangling. Like this, the Melody could concentrate all its strength on defending a single entrance. An enemy would have to throw thousands of warriors at the grand staircase to make progress against a determined enemy with nowhere to go and everything to lose.

Unfortunately for us, the Zellih have those numbers. And according to Ilandeh and Olox, they're less than a week's march from the Singing City.

It didn't make a difference to Pilos who he was fighting, not by now: they were enemies and they had to be stopped. The song must be preserved. All else could crack and shatter and burn and rot, but as long as there was a song, there would be an Empire to rise from the bones and ashes. He probably wouldn't be alive to see it, but that didn't matter. His legacy didn't matter. The Empire of Songs, which he loved, mattered.

And for the Empire of Songs to survive, the source and the Singer needed to survive. Hence the brickwork. Hence five pods from the Second Talon busy in the city streets creating killing fields and ambushes, pit-traps and dead ends and shooting platforms. Whether it was Zellih or rebel slaves who came for them next, they wouldn't find things so easy.

The Singer fidgeted and fretted, darting in to push at the rubble wall when the slaves were sufficiently far from it, checking it was solid. He was thin and nervous, the skin around his fingernails chewed raw and his lower lip in a similar state. Dark circles shadowed feverish eyes and his paint, blue and vibrant against the dullness of his red-brown skin, was wavering and crooked.

The Singer was a man on the edge of collapse, either mental or emotional. When he broke, would his song break with him? Would they be subjected to another madman wielding the Empire of Songs' ultimate power? And what would that mean for the war to restore order, peace, and harmony across Ixachipan? Pilos refused to look towards the rose-coloured cotton hanging, where the Singer was supposed to sit in state and no longer did.

His fingers curled into his palms as he stood, armed and impassive, while his holy lord darted and fretted and pulled his Chorus Leader around by her armour to keep her close. Only time would tell, and it was moving faster and faster with every passing day.

'Holy lord, please, may we discuss Whisper Ilandeh's report of a Zellih advance?' Pilos asked for the third time. He could hear the strain in his own voice, the thread that would soon enough become impatience. Irritation. 'We have lost more warriors than in any campaign in the Melody's history. How will we—'

The Singer scowled. 'The numbers matter not, only the victory. No one has ever fought in a war like this. Every Melody warrior, serving or retired, is honoured and revered. Every civilian who took up weapons, or grew food, or applied medicine to our warriors, is honoured and revered. Together we will restore peace, for none can stand against us.'

The Singer was bright gold as he spoke these words and the truth of them harmonised through the song, lifting everyone loyal to its music, regardless of the part they'd played – or not – in the war so far. Yet Pilos flinched; everyone in the source did. They weren't just hearing the Singer speak these words. They were feeling them, each one reverberating in their spirits as the song itself did. Was he . . . doing that thing again? Listening to all Ixachipan at once, bringing his words to millions, no matter their allegiance?

How does he do that? What Tokob magic does he bring to the song to accomplish such . . . awful beauty?

And then the gold faded from the Singer's skin and his voice from their minds and Tayan slumped, running with sweat. He heaved for breath and wiped a trembling hand across his brow, smearing sacred paint into so much nonsense.

The words lingered, were the slow beating of a drum in his chest, and the susurration of awe and determination that swept through the corridors of the source proved that all had heard them, felt them, and been raised up by them.

One thing you had to admit about Singer Tayan was that he understood diplomacy. As long as his own life and safety were secure, he was prepared, even eager, to recognise and thank those who served and fought for him. As long as they recognised his contributions in turn.

It was a phenomenon in a Singer Pilos hadn't previously encountered and one to which he was not immune. These flashes of greatness, of unity, that Singer Tayan showed at the most unexpected moments—

'Though they can all die if doing so keeps me safe,' the Singer added when he had his breath back.

And there it is. The flaw in the songstone that causes it to crack.

Xochi turned towards Pilos and then away before her eyes could meet his.

'Gods, but I'm tired. Tired of these conversations, of having to nurse warriors' fragile egos day and night just so they'll do their song-damned duty to me. I've half a mind to go into isolation, cut myself off from the song and everyone entirely until this is done. Sometimes it's better just not to know, don't you think?'

'I – ah, forgive me, holy lord, but in my experience, no, it's never best not to know. I am a warrior and knowledge is what has always allowed me to find victory, whether swiftly or at the end of a long and arduous campaign. I—'

'I need knowledge too,' the Singer interrupted, his mood changing lightning-fast to one of earnest agreement. 'I am a shaman and a member of the shamanic conclave, the youngest to ever be elevated so. I have walked the spiral path and communed with Malel herself. I am friends and kin with the holy Setatmeh. I alone out of everyone knew what Enet was doing here in this very pyramid and defeated her, saving this Empire from a Singer who was a traitor. You think I don't need knowledge? You think I don't understand how knowledge is power? I am the one saving the holy Setatmeh.'

Pilos put his head to the mats and didn't answer. There was nothing to say. The Singer would bring them to victory and peace, and Pilos would be his Spear and Atu his High Feather and between them, Ixachipan would be a peaceful Empire of Songs and the Zellih would be either back over their border or dead.

The thoughts were childish wish-fulfilment, unbefitting a warrior, a Spear, and former High Feather. Pilos clung to them anyway, precious candlelight against the dark and the monsters pressing at the door.

'We must speak of Whisper Ilandeh's information,' Tayan said abruptly, as if that wasn't what Pilos had been trying to do all day. 'We should decide how to deal with whatever happens next, should we not?'

It was a phrase which Pilos had long ago translated as the Singer's way of inviting others to speak in his hearing on matters which he didn't understand, but on which he would nonetheless then give orders.

As a warrior, Pilos recoiled from it: the Singer's ignorance was dangerous, especially if he became wedded to a course of action that would lead to disaster. On the other hand, as a politician he was well-used to dealing with people with more power than education. He didn't like it, but he'd spent fifteen years sweetening his talk and asking the opinions of people who weren't clever enough to have one. He didn't like having to play this game during a war, and especially not with the Zellih only days from the city's outskirts, but at least he was experienced enough to do it with some grace.

He plastered a reassuring smile on his face and, with the Singer's permission, invited Xochi to join them. Atu would attend, too, when he returned from overseeing the preparation of the city's defences.

In the darkening source, against a backdrop of grinding stone and the promise of a small, intimate little massacre of slaves, Spear Pilos set out to explain the finer points of military strategy to the Singer of the Empire of Songs.

Again.

'How went the day?' Pilos asked. He was sharing a duskmeal of stale cornbread and shrivelled palm hearts with Atu and Quotza.

'Good. We've removed wall supports in buildings on all the major avenues east and west now. They're basically held up with spit and prayer. When the Zellih come, we'll collapse everything and drive them in the direction we want them to go. By the time they make their way through our ambushes and traps, their numbers will be closer to ours and they'll be scared and fucking furious.'

'Exactly as we want them to be,' Pilos said with grim satisfaction. 'Though I could wish we had another six months to prepare, not a few days. We weren't built for this,' he added quietly and Atu tilted his head in silent question. 'The Melody. We were made to expand one land at a time. We were made to bring people to civilisation and peace under the song, not to be fighting on all fronts in every land at the same time. That's no way to win a war, but it's a bloody good way to lose one. A new enemy appearing now is just rubbing salt in our many wounds and I'm tired. I'm so fucking tired.'

'And yet we do our duty,' Atu said softly and Pilos looked up from the last of his food at the strange tone in his voice to see despair painted across the High Feather's thin face.

'Forgive me, my friend,' he said hastily, lurching forward to grip Atu's knee. 'Of course we do our duty. Of course we fight. Our Empire needs us.'

The High Feather gripped his hand in turn. 'What if we can't win?' he asked and Pilos's stomach sank. 'Spear Pilos,

Feather and former High Feather, my great and true friend, I am asking you: what if we can't win? What's your contingency plan?'

'Ah, fuck, it's that time, is it?' Pilos muttered. He pulled his hand from Atu's, rose, and crossed to a shelf. He took down his painted map of Ixachipan and unrolled it on the floor between them, the others moving the remains of duskmeal to one side. He was filled with a bright calm, like the sun sparkling on a still green cenote. Bottomless. Cold. Deadly.

'We must hold the great pyramid, which means we have to hold the Singing City. But we don't have to hold Pechacan.'

'We can't be surrounded,' Atu said, taken aback.

Pilos quirked a mirthless smile. 'We're in the middle of Ixachipan, Atu. We're already surrounded; we always have been. We can survive if we hold a corridor to the sea,' he said and traced his finger west through Chitenec to the ocean.

'Why do we need a coastline?' Quotza asked.

'To resupply and launch attacks at random points in other lands. Not now but in the future, when we begin to expand again. We can lose everything else, but we are the heartland, the heart-city, *the heart of Ixachipan*. We need access to the ocean. So. We've already pulled out of Tokoban and Yalotlan. If it comes to it, we do the same everywhere except Chitenec. We hold as much of Pechacan and Chitenec as we can, but we absolutely hold the Singing City and a corridor to the sea. We bring in all our forces, we use our civilians and children as sentries if nothing else, and we hold that corridor.'

Pilos used the tip of his knife to trace the painted borders of Pechacan and Chitenec, and then scratched his own, much smaller border – a narrow strip of land leading to the ocean. 'We want this' – he indicated the two lands – 'but we'll settle for this if we must. And within whichever border we can hold, we kill everyone who doesn't pledge instant allegiance to the song. It becomes a sanctuary for all Pechaqueh and all the loyal free who've stood and fought with us so far, and are standing and fighting across Ixachipan. Think of those numbers in a small area. Difficult to feed and arm, though this corridor does go through an obsidian field, as well as farmland, but the sheer number of people we'd have would make it easier to defend it. Then we murder anyone who crosses our border until they learn not to.'

He sat back and met Atu's assessing gaze. 'We have our coastline. We can choose to strike along it or to expand what we already hold. Or both. But that, I think, will be a task for a future Spear of the Singer.'

'The holy lord would not appreciate his song being curbed,' Quotza said into the thoughtful silence. 'Every land we abandon, they'll destroy the pyramids there and cut themselves off from it. Didn't each new land acquired lend strength to the song?' Atu nodded. 'Then surely the reverse is also true. The Singer's song will weaken. From what I know of our holy lord, that will anger him.'

'At least he will be alive to be angry,' Pilos said, which was milder than the others had been expecting, judging from their expressions. He quirked another smile. 'And that is our main and only concern. You asked for the contingency plan, High Feather, but I believe and pray we are a long way from that yet.'

'Do you truly?' Atu asked.

'I do. The Zellih are coming and they outnumber us. They've merged their flocks into a truly frightening size, but we've heard nothing else – yet – of any others. The Bird Council of Zellipan numbers seven, yet they've sent only three Aspects. Are the other four still governing their land, or holding the line of retreat that gives Omeata a way out? It's a bold move to come into Ixachipan without a secure exit and judging by who they're killing in each town and city they take, if there is an alliance, they don't seem to be doing much to preserve it. Almost as many no-bloods as Pechaqueh fall to their spears. There's no real way to know unless Ilandeh can get the Bird-form to reveal all, and I don't think she has enough time to build the necessary amount of trust for such intimacy.'

'You've got other Whispers in the north?' Atu asked.

'And the west, yes, as many as could move there. Combing

jungles and visiting towns and cities, looking for word and rumour. If the other Aspects are in the Empire, we might yet learn their locations, though what we'll be able to do with that knowledge with our forces concentrated in the south . . .' He let the words die and Atu didn't fill the silence with false hope.

Pilos wondered, yet again, why he'd chosen a Whisper whose loyalty was in doubt.

He answered himself, as he always did, with the truth: that despite everything that had passed between them and all the things she'd said, she was the best he had. The best he'd ever trained. *And because I want to believe she can be saved.*

'Even if she can't discover the extent of their plans, Ilandeh's gifted us the deaths of two Bird Aspects. That will count for much in what comes.'

'It makes it harder to defeat them when we don't fully know their motivations,' Atu said, again studying the map.

'Presume the destruction of the song, the Singer, the source, and plan our strategy to prevent it accordingly,' Pilos said. He'd been aiming for humour but it came out flat. Quotza winced and then began collecting the plates, squeezing Pilos's wrist as he handed his over with a nod of thanks.

Atu's moment of despair seemed to have passed. When he met Pilos's eyes this time, his own were bright with conviction. 'Wait for a Listener to contact you, Spear, then use them to contact all our Feathers across the Empire. Tell them to be ready to move on Pechacan. Let's get them in place to secure that corridor to the sea. We can suggest it to the holy lord afterwards.'

'There is no need,' said a voice and the Singer stepped around the corner and into the room. Atu blanched and threw himself onto his face. How long he had been standing there listening, Pilos didn't know. His paranoia was growing worse by the day. At least this time all he'd heard had been true and to his own benefit.

Quotza woke their daughter and Tenaca grumbled as she was gently pressed into a prostration. Pilos bowed likewise.

'Forgive me, great Singer—' Atu began.

'I have heard all your plans. My heart grieves at the potential loss of life and land to come, and my song cries out at the thought of being diminished. That said, you understand who the heart of our Empire of Songs truly is. You understand what must be sacrificed for victory – and what, who, can never be sacrificed. I will relay this information to the Feathers and Listeners myself. High Feather, you will accompany me in the song. Whoever we need to contact, whenever, I will do so. We can no longer afford to wait to be contacted in turn,' he added severely, as if the fault of that was somehow theirs.

'As the holy lord commands,' Atu said.

'If I may add, Singer?' Pilos asked and Tayan grunted. 'The Talons are still doing what they can to protect enclaves of innocent Pechaqueh in distant lands. May we—'

'As long as they can keep up, but the Talons are not to wait for them. Loyal free too, if they have proved themselves our friends.'

'Your wisdom is as great as your song, holy lord.'

The Singer snorted. 'It is a preparation only, is it not? We have Zellih to kill first. We have broken the rebels in the Singing City. Next we will break the invaders. This plan is our last resort and I do not expect we will need it. Am I understood?'

The words were more threat than question. The warriors bowed beneath them.

LILLA

Road to Sky Jaguar Hill, northwest Pechacan,
Empire of Songs
73rd day of the Great Star at morning

'Warriors up ahead. And there's a fuck of a lot of them.'

Ekon cut himself off in the midst of a long monologue about the freshness of the earth and the purity of the wind untainted by death, all his dramatic whimsy – something Lilla had never seen in him before and couldn't help but be charmed by – drying up like a frog on a hot coal. Although he was slightly taller, he put one hand on Lilla's shoulder and pushed himself up onto his toes, shading his eyes and staring along the pale limestone road into the distance. Warriors and civilians around them were stopping, too, murmuring, pointing. Several began to look around, left and right, for somewhere to hide.

Yes, the open farmland smelt better than the Singing City, but that's exactly what it was: open farmland. Aside from a small strip of forest to their left and a distant estate with a tall wooden fence surrounding it on their right, there was nothing but muddy fields and half-grown crops for sticks in every direction.

'Is it them?' Ekon murmured. 'I think it's them. They're not walking with Melody precision and they number too many anyway.' His squeezed Lilla's shoulder. 'I think we found them. Mictec be praised for putting us on the right path.'

He put his back to the advancing Zellih and gripped the Toko by his salt-cotton. 'Are you ready?' he demanded.

'I'm ready. It's too late now for everyone to pretend they don't know about the rumour and it won't be particularly hard for me to play the grieving, broken warrior who just wants a fucking end to this war. If I have to lose my home to get it, I'm just about ready to do it.'

Ekon winced. 'I'm so sorry.'

Lilla found a smile for him. 'It's a lie, remember? Draw them in, throw them at the Melody, win, and then betray them.'

'I know. And I know you, kitten. Can you stand there and offer the hand of friendship, knowing we're going slaughter them once they bring us victory? Is that who we are now?'

Lilla sighed and then pressed an impulsive kiss to Ekon's jaw. Since the great pyramid, since Tayan and Xessa and Toxte – since the vision of them dead and Ossa's unrelenting grief and his own conviction that if he'd killed Tayan or kidnapped him, they'd still be alive – he'd done what he could to honour them by grasping for hope and affection where he could. By daring to love in spite of Tayan, and the war, and the killing.

It felt transgressive, this seizing of joy amid despair, and it was both unfamiliar and alluring. It felt like something their enemies would hate, and so he revelled in it all the more. After years of enslavement and months of fighting and days of grief, transgression was both dangerous and vitally, unstoppably necessary. And it was freedom.

Ekon's lips grazed his cheek in return but then they were both squinting into the distance at the mass of humanity flowing towards them, unable to look away for long from what might save them; or what might end them.

'It's not who we are, but it's what we've been made, I suppose,' Lilla said quietly, eventually. 'Whether we like it or not, this war has changed us. The Melody are using any and all tactics; Tayan is, well, you know what Tayan is doing; and the Zellih have manipulated the course of this uprising from the start. Whatever it is they want out of it, all Ixachipan or something completely different, I don't know, but I'm beginning to learn that the only way to survive is to be as ruthless as those around us. I'd never have considered such a thing before, but Ekon, look at their numbers. You can't tell me that wouldn't change everything for us. And they're coming anyway. We might as well take advantage of them.'

They shared another brief, chaste kiss, and then broke left and right, shouting orders. There were too many civilians with them, at least twice the number of warriors they commanded. There were *children* with them, and Lilla had grown up on stories of Zellih wars with his ancestors and their savagery and lack of mercy.

'If you're not fighters, get moving towards the trees,' he bellowed and pointed. 'We have common cause with the Zellih, but there are no guarantees. If they attack, we'll give you all the time we can. Exit the trees on the far side and keep going. Stay out of the cities and towns; stay off the main trails. Gods and ancestors go with you. And maintain discipline!' he added as the shouts and screams began. The noise cut off quickly: they were used to that, to moving silently and stifling the children's cries against their chests or with their hands.

Lilla's heart was thudding with adrenaline and nerves. What if this didn't work? It was a huge risk they were taking. *It's no bigger than staying in the Singing City and slowly losing*, he reminded himself. Something pressed against his leg and he looked down, then dropped to one knee and reached for Ossa. The dog shied away, whining and his ears flat, then nosed back in for a moment and a single lick against the Tokob cheek. 'Go with the others,' he said and pointed at those fleeing. 'Ossa, go.'

He tried to remember the correct click-whistle and couldn't. The dog whined, understanding anyway – perhaps – and all of a sudden he wasn't aloof anymore. He burrowed into the small, rank space between Lilla's thighs and elbows, pressing his face to his ribs. He was shaking.

'Oh, you good boy. You good boy, Ossa. Good dog.' Lilla kissed his head and neck and stroked his ribs. The "good" phrasing came back to him and he clicked it and Ossa's ears pricked and his tongue came out again, swiped with a little more fervour against his neck.

The Tokob chest heaved once and he bit back the sound of his grief with such savagery that he chewed the inside of his cheek to ribbons. Blood burst against his tongue, sharp and salty and metal, and he swallowed it down.

'Hey, boy. Hey, Ossa. You need to go with them, yes? You need to go—' He flailed for a moment and then saw a Tokob family. He didn't know them, but Tokob was Tokob. He called out and one of them turned back. 'Please take him. His name's Ossa. Please, please he's an ejab dog. He needs—'

'Of course. Of course! Hey, Ossa. Come on, boy, come with us.'

The dog whimpered and burrowed deeper into Lilla's embrace and he choked and clutched him tight. 'Hey,' he whispered eventually. 'I've got to fight, maybe, though I hope not. I've got to go and you can't, you shouldn't, come with me. You've done enough of that for a whole lifetime, good boy. It's time for you to rest.' The family approached. 'Don't force him,' Lilla said desperately, everything he had left of his life and home bound up in that one sleek, scarred, and trembling form. 'Please don't force him. But he shouldn't be here for this. Just in case.' *In case they cut me down for being Tokob. In case they start a war out here in the milpas. In case it turns out I can't say the words that will give them Tokoban. If that's what they want.*

'We understand,' the woman said.

'Lilla! I need you.'

It was Ekon and the Toko groaned and made himself stand. Ossa pressed against his legs but the woman coaxed him away, leading him with her three children. Lilla wondered if that was the last time he'd see the dog – or that the dog would see him.

'No,' he whispered vehemently. 'Malel, no. No!' He looked

back one last time and then ran to Ekon, pretending he didn't hear the high-pitched yip. 'Where do you need me?' he rasped, dashing tears from his eyes.

Ekon grabbed the back of his neck and gave it a squeeze. 'By my side,' he said softly. 'For as long as you can.'

The warriors under Lilla and Ekon's command, even bolstered by those who'd fled to the city over the last weeks, numbered just over three thousand. A conservative estimate of the Zellih put them at more than twice that number.

'We've faced worse odds in nastier situations,' Ekon said confidently. Lilla turned very slowly to look at him and the Chitenecah cheeks darkened in a flush, but he didn't retract his statement.

Lilla snorted softly. 'That's not as reassuring as you think it is,' he replied, not entirely truthfully. Just having Ekon there was a reassurance. His confidence a warm blanket. 'All right, let's see what they have to say.'

Ekon untied the two tatty turkey feathers from the head of his spear. 'Let me,' he said and leant close to tie the feather into Lilla's hair above his right ear. His eyes were intent but his fingers were gentle and the Tokob breath hitched and adrenaline moved his mouth without his conscious input.

'I love you,' he whispered. Ekon jerked and his gaze snapped from his hands to Lilla's face. 'I haven't said it since the pyramid. I wanted you to know, in case . . . You don't have to say it back.'

'I love you too, kitten,' Ekon said, his smile going crooked. He pressed a soft kiss to the Tokob mouth and finished tying the feather in place before running his fingertips along the vanes, straightening them.

'Let me do you,' Lilla said, aware of the double meaning and smiling again at Ekon's sharp inhale. He blinked innocently and held out his hand. 'Your feather, lover?'

The Chitenecatl shook his head but handed it over. 'Don't make promises you can't keep,' he threatened very softly.

'Oh, believe me. If we get out of today alive, I'm keeping

it,' Lilla said and was delighted by the blush staining Ekon's cheeks.

He put the feather in his hair and kissed him in turn, knowing the sudden direction of his thoughts was a response to stress. The years since his capture had taught him the limits of his mind's ability to cope before it needed to think about something pleasurable for a while. To create and maintain the illusion of control. Besides, he did want Ekon writhing under him and begging for more. He wanted it very much.

'Ready?' he breathed.

Ekon shook out his shoulders and touched the turkey feather set high in his hair above the section where it was shaved in Chitenecah fashion. 'Absolutely not. Let's go.'

'If they don't respect the sanctity of the peace feathers,' Lilla began.

'Stab their leaders in their fucking faces and pray it gives us a head start,' Ekon confirmed. 'Don't wait for my say so.'

Behind them, Xini cleared his throat. 'Itzil is with the civilians. At Weaver's insistence, I did nothing but oversee my war party and mourn the dead, and now I have to wonder why she did that. So with your permission, I'd like to accompany you,' he said and indicated the feather in his hair and the knife in his hand.

'You're a war leader, Xini. You don't need our permission,' Lilla said and saw something in him cringe. 'But if it helps, you have it.'

Xini's smile was wan. 'Thank you, Fang,' he said with brittle dignity, making no excuses for the habits ingrained by a lifetime of servitude. 'And thank you for what you are about to do.'

The enormous war party had come to a halt and now a small group broke from the front and advanced towards them. Eight or nine, it looked like. Lilla and Ekon glanced at their warriors and then beckoned the first six to join them. None were Tokob. 'Stay easy. Stay alert.'

The group walked in silence for a few dozen steps until

Lilla came to an abrupt, disbelieving halt. 'That's Ilandeh,' he croaked. *'That's fucking Ilandeh.'*

'Stay easy,' Ekon reminded him, but the Toko barely heard him over the sudden high-pitched whine in his head. He made to rip the turkey feather from his hair and Ekon grabbed his hand in a crushing grip. *'Easy,'* he repeated, this time with the snap of command, and it cut through the madness. Lilla didn't even realise he'd been holding his breath until the air punched out of him. He dragged in another and held it, then exhaled with tight control.

'I'm all right. It's all right, love, I'm here,' he said. He was lying and they both knew it, but Ekon just gave him a long, assessing look and then sighed and let go of his hand. 'I can't believe she'd be here to make this even harder,' he muttered. 'To see me hand over Tokoban like it's a, a possession.'

'You're not handing over anything,' Xini said quietly. 'You are a child of Tokoban, not its owner. You can't give it away. Remember that.'

'I still have to look her in her fucking face when I do it, though,' he muttered, knowing he sounded like a child and too incensed to care. 'She's going to stand there and smirk at me the whole time. What is she even doing with the Zellih? I should demand her life in exchange.'

'Are you innocent then, Fang Lilla?' Xini demanded in a deceptively mild tone. 'Before the Melody came for you, did you ever skirmish with your Yaloh neighbours, your Yaloh enemies?'

Lilla blinked and focused on the slender man beside him. 'What?'

'The Yaloh. Are they your friends or your enemies? Your neighbours and allies, or thieves of game and land and forage?' Lilla set his jaw, refusing to answer, and Xini snorted and folded his arms across his chest. 'They are both, are they not? Friends when it suits you, enemies when it doesn't. You see nothing wrong in that, in your people's attitude to their neighbours. Who am I, a Chitenecatl, to tell you how you should think about Yaloh? Who am I to tell you you're wrong?'

'And so the lesson I'm supposed to learn is who am I to say Ilandeh was wrong? When she walked into my city, befriended us, and then murdered our elders and ejab before fleeing and leading the Melody to our destruction? That's a little more than some stolen fucking game along our border.'

Xini nodded, sympathy softening his mouth. 'She did all those things and more, I've no doubt. She also spent two years keeping Tayan safe. She bled and nearly died more than once to protect him. She was a friend to him, I believe. Within the limits of her ability and her role, anyway. And she did all that while living a lie so great that I cannot even imagine the strength of will it took. And I served Enet, who lived a similar one.'

Lilla took a breath. 'After what I saw in that fucking source, do you think I care that she was a friend to that man? Ilandeh may as well have been his teacher in murder and betrayal. He certainly learnt to emulate her quickly enough. Whoever she is, whoever's side she was, or is, on, she should have put her knife in his eye.'

'Should she?'

'No.'

'Did you?'

'. . . No.' Lilla choked on the word as he forced it out. *I kissed him instead.*

Beside them, Ekon was vibrating with anxiety. Every moment they stood here was a moment in which the Zellih might choose to walk away – or walk over them.

'None of us are innocent. None of our hands are clean. Ilandeh may be trying to make amends in the only way she knows how,' Xini said.

'Or perhaps she's the spy she's always been,' Lilla grated.

'Perhaps,' Ekon said quietly. 'Or maybe she's as lost and broken as the rest of us.'

'My heart bleeds,' he snarled, and tried to mean it. He growled and then deliberately touched his thumb and forefinger to the turkey feather, wishing this one had a poisoned dart tied to its end, too. 'Let's just get this fucking done.'

They walked the rest of the way in silence, anger withering to awe and eventually dread. The sheer number of warriors ranged against them was almost impossible to comprehend. Lilla had never seen more than his own Eighth Talon drawn up in formation during his imprisonment in the Melody fortress; even that had been a shockingly large number.

'Jaguar-Brother, lend me your patience in the hunt, that I might not stab that dog-humping bitch in the face if she so much as breathes near me.'

They stopped five or six body lengths distant. 'Ah, does anyone speak Pallatolli?' Lilla asked belatedly. Ekon and Xini both shook their heads. 'Balls. All right, do what I do, and pray I remember it correctly. I learnt it from Tayan,' he added bitterly.

He pressed his palms together under his chin then bowed from the waist. 'Peace of your gods upon you,' he said. 'Forgive us that we don't speak your language. I, ah,' he floundered, trying to remember Tayan's lessons back when he'd been going to try and weave a peace. 'Fang, war leader and estate . . . manager,' he said in the end, indicating each in turn, and Xini made a surprised and then thoughtful sound. There was something about names and the giving of them, but he couldn't remember what and the whine in his head was steady and distracting. *Not now. Please, Malel, not now.* Sweating, he refused to look at Ilandeh.

'Peace of the gods upon your home,' a woman in a striking feathered dress and purple paint said in accented but understandable Ixachitaan. 'You tried, at least. That is more than many of your tribe would do. I am the Bird-form; this is my honour guard. And this one is Warrior Ilandeh. Mixed-blood. Pledged-kin. Treat her as you would treat me.'

The tips of Lilla's fingers paled from the force with which he pressed them together. 'It is an honour to meet the Bird-form of Zellipan. We have heard that you are allies of the freedom fighters of Ixachipan and are marching to our aid, so we have come to welcome you.'

Lilla straightened up and dared to examine the party before

him. The honour guard were tall and muscular and intimidating. The Bird-form was slight, slender, and enigmatic within her feathers and paint. And Ilandeh was . . . thin. Haunted. Brittle. He lifted his chin and gave her a dead-eyed stare. A small smirk touched her lips as she matched his glare with one of her own, but then it faded into something vulnerable and she looked down. Lilla didn't trust that vulnerability any more than he trusted anything else she did or might say.

'Allies, is it?' the Bird-form asked. She cocked her head to one side just like a curious parrot. 'And who told you that?'

Xini spoke before Lilla could. 'Everyone knows it, across all Ixachipan. The Melody know it, Pechaqueh and loyal free know it, and we know it. You're here for us, to fight with us. The agreement was made with our resistance leader, the woman known as Weaver. She offered you Tokoban in return for military aid and here you are. She knew a civil war was coming – she even helped plan it – so of course she did all she could to ensure a victory by any means necessary. But she also meant for your agreement to remain a secret, particularly from our Tokob allies' – he gestured at Lilla, who didn't need to try very hard to look disgusted and bitter and defeated – 'in the hope that in the aftermath of victory, we'd be too weary and grateful to contest the annexation. That was a grave oversight and an insult to our intelligence. Would the revered Bird-form please enlighten us as to their understanding of our alliance?'

Lilla fought to stop his mouth from falling open. It was easy to forget that the slender figure beside him had been Enet's closest adviser and was every bit the politician she'd been.

The Bird-form sniffed. 'If all we wanted was the land south of our border, why have we come all this way?'

Xini spread his hands. 'Why? Because you have allied with us, Bird-form, and as such you owe us warriors and weapons. You owe us battles and victories or you make of Weaver a liar. And because you can't destroy the song from Tokoban.'

Ilandeh was thoughtful, watching the exchange with bright, interested eyes. Cataloguing responses, looking for lies – *she'd fucking know how to sniff them out if anyone would.* And very carefully not looking at Lilla.

'And where is Weaver now?' the Bird-form demanded.

'Dead, I'm afraid,' Xini said calmly. 'Enemies found her.'

It was hard to read the Zellih expression beneath the wide band of purple paint, but then the Bird-form's attention flickered to him and her gaze had weight and challenge and aggression. 'And what do the Tokob have to say?'

'To Weaver being dead? Personally, I rejoice in it. I'd have sought her death for such a betrayal myself if she'd still lived.'

'Don't play with me, boy. There is too much at stake. What say you about Tokoban?'

Lilla narrowed his eyes and stepped forward, stiff-legged like Ossa squaring up to a threat. He summoned a memory of the dog's courage, his raised-hackle warning, his fierce loyalty. 'We say fuck you,' he grated and behind him Ekon swore under his breath. 'We say take your fucking stupid bird god and leave before it shits all over us. We say Tokoban is ours, and you don't deserve to even speak the name of our land. Malel curses you.'

Xini cursed too, very quietly, but then Ekon stepped up to Lilla's side, silent support even though his words were destroying the plan he himself had devised. Ilandeh's mouth was a perfect O of disbelief. That alone almost made it worth it.

Lilla sucked in a breath laced with knives. He licked his lips and his hand found Ekon's and he clung with all the strength of his arm. 'And we say . . . we say the song must end, not just for us but for all peoples. We say every tribe has been cast out of its land, some for generations, while we have suffered for only a few years. Perhaps it is only fair that we know what it means to be dispossessed. Perhaps we must acknowledge that victory is more important.'

The Bird-form cocked her head the other way. 'Interesting,' she said.

Lilla let go of Ekon and took four rapid paces forwards. The honour guard surged to meet him. 'And perhaps you need to know that if you ruin my land I will pull your lungs out of your chest for my dog to eat while you watch. And choke. And die.'

Ilandeh spoke in a low voice to the Bird-form, the Pallatolli rolling from her tongue like pebbles thrown down a temple steps. Of course she fucking spoke the language. Of course she fucking did. Lilla swallowed the saliva his heart told him to spit in her face.

Ekon pulled him back to their little group. 'Hate to say this, but I think what happens next is down to whatever that trai-tor's saying. Pray to your gods and get ready.'

'Actually, the mixed-blood was telling me that the Fang is someone she trusts,' the Bird-form said, holding up a hand and cutting off Ilandeh's words. Lilla blinked. 'She says you hold your honour highly and your people even higher, that your own personal status meant nothing in comparison with your family's safety. She says that if you say Tokoban belongs to us, then we can trust that.'

The Zellitli watched him with complete focus, the sort of intent more common to a predator on the hunt. Lilla was pinned under her gaze like a rat in a constrictor's coils. His mouth went dry while his palms dampened.

He licked his lips again, unsure if words or dust would emerge when next he spoke, and did what he could to ignore the increasing pitch and volume of the whine in his head. *Please don't*, he thought desperately. *Let me get through this at least.*

He put his shaking hands together beneath his chin and the Bird-form, Ilandeh, and then the honour guard did likewise. A beat later and Ekon and Xini copied him. 'In return for your aid to end the song in Ixachipan, it . . . Malel forgive me. Ancestors and loved ones and all Tokob who still live, I'm sorry.' Grief tightened his throat, despite that the words were untrue. Would never, could never, be true. 'It is yours. Tokoban belongs to the Zellih.'

* * *

'The mining operations on Malel have stopped.'

Lilla straightened and wiped the back of his hand over his mouth as his sandal pressed mud over the vomit-filled hole. The pain had levelled out at a pitch and intensity that allowed him to just about continue functioning, though it brought waves of nausea he couldn't ignore.

Ossa had already turned to face the speaker and wrinkled his lips in a silent snarl. Ilandeh halted, her hands open and empty and her attention fixed on the dog.

The Zellih had insisted on a welcome feast, inviting the civilians travelling with the freedom fighters out of their hiding places, and then shared their supplies with them all with a generosity that had made Lilla both suspicious and envious.

Everyone else, it seemed, whether warrior, civilian, shaman, or child, had looked on the food with awe and then fallen on it with the single-minded ravening intensity of a swarm of locusts. Only Tokob had held themselves aloof, sharing their own meagre rations among themselves rather than join in with the people who supposedly now owned their land. Lilla had been seated with Omeata and Ilandeh, partly a courtesy and partly as protection: watching him give away their land had made the Tokob murderous.

Even though he knew the extent of the plan and the necessity of this deception, Lilla's words had carried the weight and shape and grief of truth even to his own ears.

'What?' he asked now, blankly. He put his hand on Ossa's head but didn't try to calm him.

Ilandeh stepped closer and Lilla drew his knife. Didn't even try and make it casual or hide what he was doing. The Whisper stopped again and once more held up her hands. 'You told me to go to Tokoban and end the mining operations digging into Malel. They are ended.' Her mouth quirked. 'Though it had nothing to do with me. I never even got as far north as Tokoban before I ran into my old friend the Bird-form. But I have it on good authority that the rebellion put a stop to it. I thought you might want to know. It was important to you, back then.'

'Many things were. Promises. People. Places. It turns out the worse things get, the fewer things you need. The fewer things are important.' He hesitated. 'Though that one remains so. I am glad it is finished.'

Ilandeh stepped forward, hunger consuming her features. 'And what is it you need now, Fang Lilla? What else is important?'

He laughed, and it was as bitter as Tayan's journey-magic. 'I need the world to be still and quiet. Everything is so loud these days. I need the pain and the noise in my head to go away. And I need Ossa's grief to leave him before it breaks us both.' He breathed out hurt like it was smoke. 'I just gave away my land to people who will not respect it, so that they will help me destroy the people who stole it and did not respect it. Where is the sense in that?'

'Quiet and still,' Ilandeh repeated, as if to herself. As if she'd heard nothing after that. A small, tired smile flitted across her mouth and was gone. 'Wouldn't that be nice.' Then she looked up and grinned, sharp as a cat. 'Do you own Ossa now, then?'

Lilla shook his head. 'No. He was . . . her dog. I won't say her name in his presence. I'm just living beside him now, doing what I can to ease his way.'

'You won't claim to own a dog, but you believe you just gave away an entire land? My, my, Lilla, and here was me thinking Tayan was the arrogant one. You really think you're important enough that you get to decide the fate of Tokoban?' Ilandeh tutted and shook her head. 'The land knows its people. It will wait for you; it will welcome you. I pray to Nallac you'll be restored to each other sooner than you think.'

'What—'

'Ah, the revered Bird-form is beckoning me. I must go.' Ilandeh hesitated and then glanced back. 'She talks through the song. Listens. She's coordinating with the rest of the Bird council. But the wings are dead and the head is missing. I don't know what that means yet. Oh, and your former husband likes to come and talk to me sometimes. I'll try not to be around you next time he does in case he looks through my eyes and sees your warriors. It should be a surprise, don't you think, when you fall on his city?'

Lilla could have told her about Tayan's visits to him, but what would that achieve? Did she think herself better than him, believing the Singer visited her alone? Since . . . the pyramid, since Xessa and Toxte – *since the kiss* – Tayan had stayed away. Lilla wouldn't survive another violation, would die if faced with his former husband's gloating malice one more time. Did Tayan know that? Was it mercy that prevented him from tearing into Lilla's mind, or had he grown bored of the torment?

Maybe he's afraid to see what I think of him now. Maybe he's ashamed.

Ilandeh smiled then, and it was one of the saddest things Lilla had ever seen. 'The Bird-form of Zellipan, the Singer of the Empire of Songs, and his Spear. Never have I been so rich in my friends.'

'Sounds to me like you deserve every one of them,' Lilla bit back and Ilandeh's smile sagged as if he'd punched her. Then she took a deep breath and examined the sky. 'Rain soon. We camp here tonight. Tomorrow we march for the Singing City. And I'll have to decide what the fuck I do next,' she added in a murmur, and he could tell the words weren't meant for him. 'Quiet and still. Huh. Wouldn't that be nice.'

ILANDEH

Road to Singing City, central Pechacan,
Empire of Songs
74th day of the Great Star at morning

Ilandeh slipped through the night, walking to the edge of the camp and behind a stand of chay to squat and relieve herself. Others had used the bushes for the same purpose and the ground was sharp with the scent of urine.

She didn't linger, and not only because of the stink, feeling her way back through the darkness – what with the proximity of the Singing City, Omeata had forbidden the making of fires or burning of torches, and thick cloud cover blotted out the moon. She stumbled over a warrior and hissed apologies as she tried to find her former sleeping place, where she'd left her rations and blanket and spear. Her sandal connected with someone else's head and there was a muffled curse, a scuffle and harsh threats; she danced sideways and trod on a hand, causing another squawk of outrage.

Ilandeh crept on, disturbing more warriors and increasingly lost, until finally she stumbled into a clear space, muttering more apologies, and sank down onto her haunches. Slowly, the night quietened around her and she looked up at the expanse of cloud. 'Nallac, god of storms and choices, bad and otherwise. Tell me what to do,' she murmured. What would the world be like by the time this Wet was over? Who would rule and who would be dead? What would freedom look like and who would it belong to?

'Well?' asked a quiet voice some time later and Ilandeh jumped. Omeata Bird-form was watching her and snorted at Ilandeh's expression as she took in the fact the area was clear because she'd stumbled through the Bird-form's ring of guards. And Omeata had allowed it.

'Forgive me for waking you,' she gasped in Pallatolli, pressing her hands together hastily. 'I, ah, it's dark. I didn't mean to intrude. I will leave the revered Bird-form to rest.' She stood.

The Bird-form waved her back down. 'Oh, sit. Tomorrow we go to war, something with which you are so intimately acquainted. But I would know your god's answer.'

Ilandeh lowered herself back to the dirt and gave her a blank look. Omeata sighed. '"Nallac, tell me what to do",' she repeated. 'Well? What did your god have to say?'

The Whisper pressed her palms together again and then scrubbed them over her face and back through her hair, wincing as a finger caught in a tangle. 'Nothing, Bird-form. Nallac said nothing to me. I'm not sure they ever have. I'm not sure they want to.'

Omeata sat up. 'So dramatic,' she said with low mockery. 'You think gods are so petty? If you are sincere in your prayer and your devotion, Nallac will listen. Whether they intervene is another matter, but they will listen, and that is what is important, is it not?'

Ilandeh wasn't so sure. Surely intervention was the point? 'Do you believe so?' she asked instead, settling herself more comfortably. 'You who were Bird-head the first time we met and are now Bird-form. Did your god tell you to do that or was it your choice? Is it . . . a demotion?'

Omeata's guards squatted a few paces away, watching the Whisper with unwavering focus even in the darkness. She could feel their gazes, the weight and texture of them. Assessing. Disdaining.

'Do not presume to question the Bird-form,' Huenoch

threatened in a low growl. Omeata raised her hand and cut them off.

'It is not,' she said. 'It is merely a change, a different path. A choice like the one you made, former merchant. But as to your earlier question, yes. I know it listens. As one of the Sacred Bird's representatives, I am a river carrying its words to my people.'

'I envy you,' Ilandeh said and was surprised by the depth of truth in her words. 'To believe so unwaveringly must be a comfort.'

'And a burden,' the Bird-form said very quietly. 'Its dreams are great.'

'Yes. And a burden.' Ilandeh took a breath. 'And it was the Sacred Bird's requirement that you conquer Ixachipan under the pretext of ending the song? It's not just Tokoban you're here for, is it?'

'I believe you are in disgrace, Warrior Ilandeh,' Omeata said mildly. 'And yet you think to question me?'

'I think I will be dead tomorrow, one way or the other,' Ilandeh replied with complete honesty. 'Whether by the hand of Huenoch, or Lilla, or Pilos, or you, or the Singer himself, or any of a thousand others. I would hate to die curious when I could die satisfied. But if it is too much, Huenoch is right here with their knife, while mine is, well, wherever my blanket and pack are. I have no idea.'

Omeata huffed a laugh. 'You have never lacked for courage, mixed-blood, I will give you that. To answer your impertinence, the song is a justification for the few who don't understand it to possess the many who reject it, whether consciously or not. You were one of those people possessed not long ago. Why question my motives when you have come to see the truth yourself? You were cast out by your beloved Melody and abandoned by your Spear Pilos, were you not? It is why you have given us your allegiance, because we are set on doing what you cannot. Or will not.'

Ilandeh barked a laugh, too loud in the stillness of the night. 'Believe me, Bird-form, I had more than enough chances to end the life of the Singer.' She picked at a flat tangle of jicama that sprawled by her feet.

'Why didn't you?'

The Whisper sighed from the depths of her spirit. 'The magic would simply pass to another. That's what the song does, that's how it sustains itself. It wouldn't have made a difference.'

Omeata hummed. 'It would have made a difference to you.'

She nodded; she couldn't deny that. 'And yet I am but what they made me,' she murmured, 'and Pilos told me to keep him safe.' It didn't soothe as it once had.

'So we need to do more than just kill the Singer tomorrow if we are to have victory.'

Ilandeh's gut gave an unhappy little lurch. The Singer. Tayan. 'Yes, Bird-form. To destroy the song forever you must break the capstone at the great pyramid's summit. If you fight your way into the source and kill Tayan but the songstone remains active, it will find another Singer. Anyone within the pyramid will be a possibility.'

'Including me?'

'It, it is possible, Bird-form,' she said haltingly. 'Though—'

Omeata laughed, low and mocking and a little bit cruel. 'I jest, Ilandeh. You always used to be able to tell when I was teasing you. Not now, though.'

The Whisper forced a chuckle. 'Not now, no. The years have changed us both, I think.'

'You more than me, I'd say.'

Ilandeh sighed again. 'Of that there is no doubt. Ah, forgive my mood, Bird-form. It is one thing to liberate slaves in Chitenec at your side and quite another to face Spear Pilos across a battlefield. The promise of tomorrow fills me with dread.'

'And yet you will fight? Even though I haven't told you our full plans?'

'You said yourself that Pilos never used to tell me his reasons; why should you? And,' she paused and gazed up at the sky for a moment, embarrassed, 'you call me a mixed-blood, but it doesn't feel cruel coming from you. You say it as a statement of fact, not an insult. Or at least, if it is, it's too subtle for me to notice.'

'And that's enough to make you pledge yourself to me?'

Ilandeh spread her hands. 'Being treated as a person, whole and complete, instead of a mistake or a stain on my father's honour? Proof of his weakness? *Yes, Omeata.* A thousand times yes.'

She coughed and then gave a little bow. 'Forgive me, that was emotional and inappropriate and I should not have used your name. I wish you a restful sleep, Bird-form.'

Ilandeh pushed up onto her feet and stumbled in the jicama vines, her ankle twisting. She yelped and lurched, collapsing back onto one knee, and Omeata's hand shot out to grab her forearm, jerking her further off-balance. Flailing, she grabbed the Bird-form's elbow in turn and then immediately let go, gasping at the breach of protocol. Saving Omeata's life had been one thing, but touching her without permission during peace was another. She scrambled wincing onto her feet.

'Bird-form, forgive me,' she hissed, putting her hands together and hobbling on her twisted ankle. 'Ow, fuck, I—' Huenoch and three others hauled her away, blades against her skin. 'I'm sorry, it was an accident. Bird-form, did I hurt you?'

Huenoch growled, tightening their grip on Ilandeh's upper arm until she gasped. Omeata was rubbing the inside of her elbow where the Whisper had seized her. 'I am not hurt,' she said softly and the guards stopped dragging Ilandeh's hands behind her back to bind them. 'Have you broken anything?'

Ilandeh rotated her ankle carefully, leaning on the guards who restrained her. 'No, thank Nallac. It will be sore for a few days, but it won't impact my ability to fight, Bird-form. I swear.'

The commotion had stirred a swathe of the Zellih and they watched her with open hostility as the Bird-form signalled the guards to let her go. The Whisper pressed her palms together and bowed again. 'Forgive me,' she repeated. 'I have disturbed you all. With your leave, I will try and find my sleeping place. Unless you wish me to take the watch until dawn?'

The Bird-form waved her away. 'Go and sleep,' she said. 'I will have need of your skills tomorrow.'

Three of the honour guard released her; Huenoch did not. 'Are you helping an injured warrior to her rest, Huenoch?' Ilandeh asked sweetly, 'or do you wish to share my blanket?' They recoiled and shoved her. She stumbled again and choked on another cry.

'Huenoch!' Omeata snapped. 'Have some grace.' The warrior stiffened at the rebuke and bowed their head, then grimacing offered her their arm. Ilandeh matched their expression of disdain but her ankle was throbbing, so she leant her weight against them and together they limped slowly away from the Bird-form's resting place.

As soon as they were out of sight, Huenoch wrenched their arm away and scowled as her nails scored their flesh and she wobbled and then hissed in pain. 'Get off me,' they threatened. 'Whatever that was, you won't get away with it.'

'Peace, Huenoch. I have no ill intent here,' Ilandeh said. 'You listened to our conversation. Was there anything in it that was a threat to Zellipan or the Bird Council?' There was no answer and she looked back, a questioning tilt to her head. 'I pledged the Bird-form my allegiance. My life. Tomorrow I'm going to risk it for her, perhaps even lose it. If we both survive and you're still' – she gestured up and down at them – 'suspicious of me, we can have a fight about it afterwards. For now, I'm going to – oh, sorry, did I tread on you? Sorry – I'm going to try and find my blanket and get some sleep.'

Ilandeh spent the rest of the night alone in the open. Zellih had got tired of her stumbling and limping among them and directed her to the edge of camp. Her belongings had probably been stolen by now. As long as she found a replacement weapon before they reached the Singing City, she didn't care. She had nothing of sentimental value left and she'd spent countless nights sleeping curled up without a blanket. One more would make little difference.

Hello, Ilandeh.

Ilandeh rolled onto her back and stared up at the night. The rain had stopped and the clouds parted just enough that she could see a few stars. Probably she should have expected this, but his presence still took her by surprise. 'Hello, Tayan,' she said softly. 'What can I do for you?'

You will address me correctly.

'Will I? And what will you do if I don't?' She conjured up pictures of the fall of the City of Glass, of the massacre at Sky Jaguar Hill, Pechaqueh cut down as they fled, lit by flames and painted with blood and screams. She thrust it at Tayan, along with memories of the great gaping hole in the hill above the Sky City where the womb had been. Where she'd discovered the songstone and found Tayan himself with a captive holy Setat.

The Singer flinched away from the images and then, deliberately, immersed himself in them and in her, drawing forth more memories of slaughter and death, these ones at her own hands. People she'd killed – Pechaqueh civilians, Xentib warriors. The people of her blood. And Tokob, and Yaloh, and on and on into infinity. An endless parade of the dead, victims of Ilandeh's blade and Pilos's order. Olox and Pikte came last and it was the Whisper's turn to flinch, but although she tried to keep control of her mind and memories, both were at the Singer's mercy. And it seemed he had none left.

You think to hurt me with these pretty pictures, little half-blood? You think to frighten me? he asked and danger threaded through his voice and his song like poisoned honey. The song that was imperious and arrogant and pounded against her nerves and spirit and flesh, screeching of surrender and forgiveness. The next image was of Xessa and Toxte, the same that he'd shown her and everyone under the song six days before. She'd seen it in Lilla's face, as wild and broken as a spirit-haunted eja. She carefully didn't think about him now, or any of the rebels sleeping fifty or so strides away.

You think anything you show me can hurt after this? After I ordered this?

'And you feel nothing, Tayan? You, of all people, feel

nothing? She was your friend. More than that; she was, she was the other part of you.'

The song is the other part of me now, and I will always do what is right for the song. I did what I had to then and I will again and again, as many times as it takes until we have peace. I already know how to fix the holy Setatmeh. I know to feed—

He cut himself off, turning over the image of the dead instead and poking at it, as if trying to feel something, anything, and then pawed through the contents of her mind again – and paused over a new memory: the tiniest sliver of wood, its wickedly sharp tip dark with viscous fluid, tied alongside her fingernail.

What is this?

'Tell Pilos and Atu that the Bird-form will be dead by highsun tomorrow. It will throw the Zellih into disarray. If they are deep into the Singing City when she falls, their cohesion will shatter and they'll be vulnerable despite their numbers. Highsun, remember. Tell the Spear I did my duty,' she added in a whisper, her thumb tracing over the tattoo on the inside of her wrist. 'I did all that he required.'

Tayan flickered green with interest and enthusiasm. *That was well done*, he said approvingly and Ilandeh shivered under the praise. *You could have done it earlier, but yes, I can see how losing their leader in the middle of a battle will cause panic, which my warriors can exploit. It seems Pilos was right to trust you after all. I always did, you know*, he added conversationally, flickering orange with truth, a tiny distant lick of flame in the darkness. Ilandeh couldn't help her own pink bloom of pleasure in response.

'You must be very lonely,' Ilandeh thought abruptly. She wasn't sure where the words were coming from unless Tayan's own emotions were bleeding into her mind. She braced for pain, gritting her teeth in the hopes that she might swallow down her screams. The last thing she needed now was to attract any more attention. She needed to keep as far from Omeata as she could before the poison did its work. Incredibly rare and incredibly dangerous, she'd carried it in a hollow hair bead for more than two years. The weapon of last resort, and a method of suicide should she need it.

Tayan didn't bring her pain. He sat quiet and small in her mind and didn't refute her suggestion.

'The last time we spoke I offered you friendship,' she added. 'You rejected it but here you are again, another night, another conversation with me.'

Yes. Here we are again.

Ilandeh waited, but he said no more. 'Are you then? Lonely?'

I have . . . people to talk with. Visitors. Old friends. I have all the song and all the spirits to comfort me. I have the holy Setatmeh, who I will save and heal. I have Xochi and Pilos, Atu and even Quotza and little Tenaca.

'And you haven't answered my question,' Ilandeh whispered when Tayan fell silent within her. 'Are you lonely, great Singer?'

You should come back to me, he said abruptly, infusing the words with the startling bright orange of a chel's breast plumage. Conviction, belief. Truth. *Come back to me, Ilandeh. Come home.*

Home. The word was a spear to the heart, carrying so much meaning for them both she sagged beneath its weight, her bones sinking into the mud under her back. 'Home? My home was the Fourth Talon. The Melody fortress. My home was wherever Pilos sent me.'

Your home is the source. With me. Ilandeh, come home to me. Be my Chorus Leader again. My protector. My friend.

'Pechaqueh,' she tried.

You think I cannot deal with Pechaqueh petty anger? No one will touch you or harm you. I will not permit it.

Come home, Ilandeh, and together we can bring peace to Ixachipan and a new form of order to the Empire of Songs. A Tokob Singer, a half-Xenti Chorus Leader. Think what we can do. No one would stand against us. We can take this Empire and improve it. You can have everything Pilos promised and so much more. Real respect and honour and status for being exactly who you are. No need to hide your heritage.

No need to feel shame. You think I feel shame? I'm the fucking Singer and a Toko and I am proud of it.

You can be, too, if you just come to me. Because yes, I am lonely. I need you, Ilandeh. I need a friend.

She breathed out, long and slow, staring up at the few stars scattered among the clouds, Nallac's shroud of night pierced by the black-handed spider monkey. *Do what is right.*

'Yes,' she said quietly to the stars and her god. 'I would like that. I would like to come home.'

Tomorrow, then. I will see you tomorrow.

'Tomorrow, Tayan.'

He left her then, and Ilandeh lay sleepless until dawn, weaving the threads of all she'd learnt that night into the tapestry of everything else she knew. All those half-finished sentences, those careless intimations and murmured nonsenses. The promise of an alliance in return for Tokoban. Finally, she thought she understood what the Zellih wanted.

THE LISTENER

Empire of Songs
75th day of the Great Star at morning

Setatmeh bless you, great Singer. I sense many spirits hanging within the song again. Does it begin to affect the gods?

There's going to be a battle today, they say. The last great battle of this war. And we have to win.

Do not let it distract you, great Singer. Cleansing the song will only strengthen your warriors and make your victory that much swifter. It will strengthen and heal your holy Setatmeh, who in turn may sing for your enemies. The gods must be preserved. Woken.

The gods must be woken, yes. Yes. My song will strengthen my warriors and steal strength from my enemies, and as I cleanse it of the poison of the spirits, the holy Setatmeh will lend their magic and voices to the battle to come. I will bring us victory; I will do this. And then Ilandeh will come home to me.

Ilandeh?

My friend. You told me you are not my friend, only my ally, and in this endeavour to save the holy Setatmeh I will work with you. But I will have friends around me again afterwards. Human and holy both. Once Ixachipan is at peace again and you are free to travel, come to the great pyramid and introduce yourself. It would be good to meet you face to face. Until then, I will have my Ilandeh at my side. A friendship begun with a lie may continue in honesty, she told me. But you seem troubled, my secretive stranger. Did you think you were my only ally, my only support? Such arrogance!

... *I, it is nothing, great Singer. For now, it is time to begin.*

Yes. It is time. Time to cleanse the song. Time to keep my promise to my gods.

And me, mine. That is all any of us can do, holy lord.

PILOS

The source, Singing City, Pechacan, Empire of Songs
75th day of the Great Star at morning

'They've been seen on the road. They'll be entering the city in an hour.'

Pilos paused in the cool darkness of pre-dawn and then deliberately drained his cup of water. 'Numbers?'

'About what we were told,' Atu said, his voice steady. 'Seven thousand by estimate.' The barest hesitation. 'Plus three thousand or so rebel slaves. Ekon leads them.'

Pilos breathed very quietly and put down his cup. 'So that's where they went.'

'It looks like the alliance is fact,' Atu said and Pilos finally looked up and met his gaze. 'Our attempt to twist it to our advantage has failed. We are badly outnumbered.'

'You believe we'll lose?'

The High Feather drew himself up. Here, in privacy, where they could be honest, he straightened his shoulders, his eyes flashing in the gloom. 'No. Traitors and uncivilised foreigners? Never.'

Pilos smiled at his fervour, rich with affection, with love. 'You are a great High Feather, my friend. For what it's worth, you have done remarkable things in this war. If it is not too self-indulgent to say, I am very proud of you.'

Atu's face softened and he inclined his head. 'I learnt from a great teacher,' he replied softly.

Pilos's instinct was to bat away the compliment; instead he held Atu's eyes and felt everything that had brought them to this moment, the years and wars, the peace and politics, the betrayals and deaths. And every bittersweet glance they'd let slip away unremarked.

He'd spent the days since Xessa's death expecting his Singer to order his execution, to finally face judgement and justice for the part, however unknowing, he'd played in her massacre of the holy Setatmeh. And every day his Singer had let him live. He was deeply, achingly grateful to have been allowed this moment.

Pilos had given his life to his Melody and his Empire. He understood, now, that Tayan had withheld his execution so that he might give his life in truth this day. Give it to save everything he loved.

I will. I will do that. I will do all that is required of me. I am Pilos. I was High Feather and I am still Spear of the Singer. I am a warrior and a man of honour. No one takes my status from me. I will die as I have lived – protecting my Melody and the Empire of Songs, which I love.

Pilos stood and touched belly and throat. 'Whatever they want, they're not going to get it. We're going to bring them to their fucking knees and send them back to Zellipan in pieces for their so-called Sacred Bird to peck at.'

Atu nodded, grim and hard. 'Song be praised.'

'Song be praised,' Pilos agreed. 'What are your orders, High Feather?'

'As we planned. Get them into the city. Lure them in if we have to, and then spring our traps. Setatmeh willing, the traitors will be leading them, thinking they know which areas were safe last time they were here. It'll take them hours to navigate the city and, if your Whisper can be trusted, their Bird-form will be dead or dying before they face us.'

'The Singer himself took it from her mind, High Feather. Whatever else she might be, we can trust Ilandeh in this.'

'Once it's formations and tactics rather than ambushes and pits, it'll be down to discipline and will. It'll be down to us,' Atu said.

'It always is, High Feather. Atu. All our lives, it's been down to us. You and me.'

Atu stepped forward and grabbed Pilos by the back of the neck, drawing their brows together. 'Singer, song, and Setatmeh,' he murmured, and then kissed him hard and long on the mouth. 'Stay alive.' Kissed him again, softer this time, lingering, thumb caressing his cheek. 'Stay alive.'

Pilos watched him walk away, fingertips hovering over his lips but not quite touching and his heart beating somewhere in his throat. 'You also,' he croaked, a plea and a prayer. Atu didn't look back.

Lips buzzing, Pilos tied a small shield to his right forearm and then grabbed two spears from where they leant against the wall. In his belt was a hand-axe and a knife. No war club this time; he wanted the longer reach of the spears, and his own beloved club was still in the traitor Ekon's possession anyway.

Pilos ran his hand over his salt-cotton and checked his paint in an obsidian mirror, and then followed his High Feather out of the source and down into the compound, to join the thousands of grim-faced warriors awaiting their orders. The Singer had invited him and Atu to stand with him at the grand entrance to address the warriors; both had declined. It was the fighters they needed to be among now, not the rulers. Atu stood on the bottom step of the staircase, his full crown of feathers adding to his height and dignity, while Pilos stood on level ground just before him. His own command fan was stiff and proud and jesting with a playful wind.

They were unmistakable as the Melody's leaders – and that was as it should be.

Quotza had spent the previous day painstakingly washing and oiling the feathers of both their headdresses until they were as clean and pristine as possible considering the circumstances. It was a labour of love Pilos didn't deserve, and one she had pleaded with him to perform.

He gazed up the steep staircase to where Singer Tayan stood in the mouth of the grand entrance, holding so much magic in his skin that he blazed like a second sun, his features impossible to distinguish. Murmurs of awe and adoration rose from the thousands staring up at them. Pilos shared their reverence. Whatever and whoever Tayan had been before, and despite his recent paranoia and increasing . . . unpredictability, in this moment he was a Singer worthy of the name.

The song was a swelling majesty of strength and belief. Everyone who fought with it in their heart was right and good and true, their weapons sharp and their minds clear. This was the gift of the song; this was the gift of the Singer. To fight for him was to know glory. To fight for the song was to build a victory that would herald a new world and they would be pre-eminent within it. Pilos breathed in music and felt it fill him like sunlight, like invincibility.

This song was like honeypot. He wanted to drink deep of its promises but needed a clear head.

Understood, Spear. There. Is that better?

Pilos twitched; he hadn't even known the holy lord was in his mind. But the song lessened just a little and he saw a ripple go through the gathered warriors, as if awaking from a shared dream. Clarity returned to their faces, calculation and deter-mination replacing glazed devotion.

'Thank you, holy lord,' Pilos said and looked up the steps towards his blinding golden Singer. Tayan nodded.

'We have defeated the traitors who rose against the song and civilisation and driven them from the heart-city,' Atu bellowed. 'Be proud of that, my fine warriors, and know that when they write the songs of this time, you who fought here will be foremost in their thoughts.

'But we do not yet have peace. Traitors and invaders from a foreign land march on our city. Barazal has sent its locusts to swarm upon us. Like the ungrateful slaves and treacherous free, they have no love of the song or its Singer in their hearts. What they love is conquest and death and tyranny. As we have stood for the last months, we must stand again. As we have fought, so must we fight again. Spear Pilos and I will be fighting by your sides, in the line with you. We achieve victory today and I believe the war will be over,' he roared and lifted his spear into the air. 'So we stand! And we hold! And the Singer lifts us up and treads down our enemies and we *fucking win the day.*'

Pilos joined in the roar of affirmation that split the dawn and rent the sky, raising his weapons and screaming his belief and his joy in the coming conflict.

The song took on a driving rhythm, a particular cadence and melody that conjured words he hadn't heard in years and never thought to hear again. Pilos spun and stared up at the Singer in disbelief as, from three and a half thousand throats including the High Feather's, they sang the war chant commemorating the fall of Tokoban and the unification of all Ixachipan under Singer Xac and High Feather Pilos.

The holy lord was singing with the rest. Singing of the fall of Tokoban. Of Pilos's last and greatest victory.

This next one will be even greater, my Spear. I believe in you.

Pilos swallowed and touched belly and then throat, bowing to the singing Singer in acknowledgment of this message. This affirmation. This restoration of status in his holy lord's eyes. Then he stood and listened, the hairs standing up on his arms and the back of his neck as his Melody sang of his triumph.

When it was over, he looked helplessly at Atu, overcome. 'Well,' he croaked. 'Let's go and win, shall we?'

The High Feather grinned and gestured for him to go first, to give the order.

I love you, he wanted to say. Instead, he faced the warriors who would fight and die for them. 'Feathers and Coyotes, eagles and dogs. To your positions. Remember, we want them all in the city before we trap them, and that means we need to give them something to chase and something to fight. Just because you look like you're running away doesn't mean you're defeated! We are the Melody and this is the Singing City. The heart-city! And we are the blood that pumps through its veins. We march to war – and to victory!'

Pilos was glad they were filtering the Zellih into the city through several different paths, because it meant no one, including himself, could see their numbers in their entirety. A thousand warriors might march past their position, but the eagles and dogs numbered almost four times that, and so victory was assured. It was illogical, but it was also the only way to keep fear locked in its cage. If they acknowledged that they were actually outnumbered more than two to one with no way out except by winning, they'd lose before a single blow was struck.

Far to the north, a drum beat a loud, swift rattle. The full strength of the enemy was within the city bounds. It was time to begin. Another drum, this time to his right and beating a deeper, slower rhythm. The war party passing them was twitchy, hearing the drums but not knowing what they meant. Suspicious, but unable to do anything about it. Atu had set other drum rhythms, meaningless ones that stuttered across the sky at random moments so the invaders might not learn which were important and which merely distractions. They'd been listening to drum rolls echo across the city for an hour now, and nothing had happened to any of them.

Until now.

From the edge of the city came a slow, rushing rumble, echoing from the walls until it seemed to surround them, and then a chorus of thin screams drifting from the west. Thick dust plumed up; the distant tail of the war party had been crushed by falling buildings, their line of retreat sealed. They were trapped in the city now, and the only way they could move was where the Melody pushed them.

Some of the invaders bolted towards Pilos's hiding place, while others spun and stared wildly backwards, hissing questions in Pallatolli and bunching together. Splitting their ragged line into two groups. Perfect. He lifted the bone whistle and blew it once. Arrows and darts swarmed into the groups, forcing them further apart as screams and shouts rose. Those trapped at the back sprinted for the nearest wall to get out from under the withering rain; at a second blast of the whistle, warriors in the roofless building pulled away the supports and fled. The wall teetered and bulged outwards, then slumped into the street taking Zellih down beneath it. Rubble filled the road, cutting off the very rear of the war party from those who were left and now fleeing madly forward, deeper into the city.

Pilos leant out from his hiding place and watched them go, then blew the whistle twice when he judged them deep enough into the next ambush. Buildings on both sides fell this time, a landslide of stone that buried the enemy. More screams, mingling with the song into a glorious, righteous music until they faded into whimpers and into silence under the shifting stone. Into death.

It hadn't got all of them. But it had got enough. Perhaps three hundred dead or crushed by the two collapses just at this site. Those left were split into groups, shying at shadows, with nowhere to go but to clamber over the rubble and the corpses and continue on a road littered with traps and ambush sites.

'Fall back to our next position,' Pilos murmured, and his pod slipped backwards and away. From the north, another rumble of falling masonry, this one so distant he felt it only through the bones of his ears and ribs. Too distant to make out the screams. He smiled anyway, grim and pleased, and hurried after his pod to the next street, the next ambush. The next little victory.

The atmosphere among the Zellih had changed. First doubt and then fear crept among them like jaguars stalking prey, soft as shadows, inevitable as night. They bunched tighter, moving in fearful stops and stutters, slamming their spear butts against walls and then cringing back in case they fell. A couple of false collapses had them skittering into the centre of the street, where a pit opened up beneath the feet of the lead warriors, casting them down onto the stakes lining the bottom.

Those who hadn't fallen leapt sideways, their attention on the ground, and Pilos collapsed the next pair of buildings, taking even more Zellih into the Underworld. Every side street had been blocked off except for the ones they wanted their enemies to take, and now the survivors, panicked and ill-disciplined, were presented with a choice – continue on straight, or break left down an open avenue. He could see their fear and indecision.

Best hurry them along, then.

He blew the whistle again and the Zellih panicked immediately. This wasn't armed warriors they could stand and face; this was the city eating them handfuls at a time.

The whistle was the signal for dog warriors to race out of hiding behind the war party and throw clay pitchers into the street. The pitchers smashed, spraying boiling rubber across the stone and against heaps of debris – heaps of furniture and cloth.

The dogs fled as quickly as they'd come, and Pilos waved and flaming arrows arced over their retreating heads and thudded into the mess. Fire rippled up, great clouds of acrid black smoke following, and the stench of burning rubber and linen made Pilos wrinkle his nose and stifle a sneeze into his elbow.

The Zellih were gaping at the ragged curtain of flame instead of running, and so another signal sent archers on both sides of the road loosing into their midst. Yet again, they broke and fled – and this time half took one road, and half another.

Perfect.

The next ambush was face to face, and the Spear hadn't wanted to be fighting so many. Now, he didn't have to. He led his pod at a run down the stairs and forwards, parallel to the fleeing Zellih but one street over. They'd discover the dead end they'd fled into soon enough and double back, at which point the Melody would have filtered through the only building not lethal with snares and pits to come out behind them and cut off their retreat. Meanwhile, those who'd taken the other road would come into the territory of the next pod in this part of the city. And that pod had its own basket full of surprises for them.

And so it proved.

Once the enemy realised they were trapped, they fell into a formation with their spear-fighters at the front. Pilos and his eagles matched them, flowing down the street while archers paced them on the buildings above.

'For the Empire!' Pilos screamed and his eagles echoed him and they surged against the Zellih like waves battering the Chitenec coastline. It was a chaos of fast spears and screamed threats and the slip and slice of obsidian, stone, and bone into salt-cotton and flesh.

Shouts became screams, insults became pleas, and the Zellih line dissolved into shoving towards and away from the Melody. Blood, saliva, and sweat flew and the symbols painted on Pechaqueh hands and faces smeared and warped, while salt-cotton absorbed some blows and was torn by others.

A Zellitli stabbed for Pilos's groin. They were short and stocky, with arms wider than the Spear's thighs and a nose many times broken. They were also fast and as sure-footed as a spotted cat, and it was spear against spear.

Pilos kicked out, not high or obvious, just enough that the ball of his foot cracked into the Zellih shin. They stumbled and he drove his spear into the path they were taking, ripping open salt-cotton. The warrior snarled and battered Pilos's spear down, his many injuries and the months he'd spent fighting already protesting the exertion, and then jumped forward until they were almost chest to chest. Their fist caught him a glancing blow to the cheek that snapped his head sideways and Pilos stumbled on his bad ankle but kept his footing. Swung his spear unsighted and the shaft hit something – someone – and ricocheted back in his hands even as he blinked away stars and tears.

Feather Matla stepped past him and jabbed her spear tip into the Zellih howling mouth and punched it out through the back of their head, then ripped the spear from their hands. Pilos got a face full of spraying blood as the warrior collapsed and wiped it off along with sweat as he nodded at Matla.

The Feather grinned and slid into place on his left as if she'd fought there for years, not months. Her presence gave him a few moments to rest and take stock. The enemy had fought hard and well, trying to break their line, but the pods held firm and penned them back, drove them back, and the street behind his eagles was littered with corpses and splashed with blood.

His warriors were ruthless, precise, and lethal; they were grim, but they were joyous. Two hours into the battle not just for the heart-city, but for the lifeblood of the Empire of Songs itself, and everything was going their way.

'Finish them,' Pilos roared, and his warriors surged to obey.

THE LISTENER

Empire of Songs
75th day of the Great Star at morning

There. Did you feel that? That great upsurge in power? That is—

Yes, I feel it. I feel the song – my song – lightening. The magic growing. All these dead Pechaqueh and loyal free, all of them thinking they were going on to glory and instead their spirits becoming the ash that chokes a fire of air until it dies.

You are welcome for the teaching, Singer. Thousands more will die in this very city today. You would do well to continue—

This city? What do you mean? How can you know what's happening in my city? Are you here? You are, aren't you? You're here in the Singing City. You treacherous fuck!

I—no! Let go of me. Let me go!

I have been more patient than you deserve, but I will have my answers now, Listener. Who are you? And where are you? I've crushed spirits to extinction inside my song. Do you want to see if I can do it to you? Hmm?

. . . no. No! My name is Zama, but I am known in life as Omeata. Do you remember?

It cannot be.

Oh, but it is, gentle peace-weaver. I had thought you might have recognised my thoughts and shape from when you came to Zellipan, but now, just as then, you are too caught up in yourself, glorying in your feathers and paint and authority.

Impossible. You are not she!

I travel with your precious Ilandeh, you know. And she's going to bring me to you and then you will learn the truth about so many things. So many, many things. Actions have consequences, Singer. You should make your peace with Malel.

I—You won't get in. You'll never get in, I'm protected, I've got thousands—

We'll see you soon. Tayan.

ILANDEH

Omeata was slowing. It was barely noticeable in the stop-start, run and fight, sidestep that pit, duck that arrow, flow of the running battle, but it was noticeable to Ilandeh.

She'd been watching for it, after all. She needed to know the poison was working before she made her next move. There was perhaps an hour until highsun, when Pilos and Atu would launch a final, all-out attack at the expected time of Omeata's death, capitalising on the Zellih fear and confusion, their milling lack of leadership.

She'd been grimly impressed with the tactics the High Feather and Spear had employed so far. The whole city had been turned into a weapon against them, the detailed knowledge the rebels had brought to the alliance proving useless now that not a single street or plaza could be trusted to be safe. Pits and snares, collapsing walls, and dead ends that looked open only to trap you in a killing field to be cut down. They were the sort of dishonourable tricks favoured by Whispers who needed to cause the maximum damage and disruption with the least number of warriors. Even with the Second Talon now in the city, the rebels must have bled them hard to force them to take such steps.

She could guess, roughly, where Lilla and the rebels would be. The invading war parties had been split into at least four groups by the availability of open roads down which to advance, and the rebels had taken the nearest without a backward glance. An alliance, yes, but not an easy one. They needed the Zellih; they just didn't want to fight alongside them.

Ilandeh knew the city; knew, too, where they were being herded and how long it would take to get there. If the freedom fighters were moving at about the same pace as Omeata's flock, then Ilandeh just needed to get away, take a few side streets and roofs, cross a couple of plazas, and she could find them.

Of course, to do so she'd run the risk of tripping any number of traps or ambushes or being found and killed as a traitor. It didn't matter that Tayan had summoned her or that she was going to him. What mattered was that she was Whisper Ilandeh, traitor to the Melody, and she could be damn sure that Pilos wouldn't have bothered rescinding that order the day before what was probably – possibly, hopefully – the final battle of this long, Empire-wide war.

Whoever won here today would win across all Ixachipan.

The Bird-form crouched behind the remaining warriors of her honour guard. Her gorgeous feathered huipil was folded neatly and wrapped in a blanket and tied harness-like around her chest and back. Enough layers that it was probably effective against darts and even arrows shot from a distance. She still had the purple paint across her eyes, and more streaking her arms and legs, but other than that she was dressed the same as her flock.

As Ilandeh watched from behind a corpse – the Zellitli moaned and leaked blood; not a corpse, then, or not yet – Omeata pressed her hand to her heart and then stifled a cough. Palpitations. A growing coldness in the chest. Blurred vision. Slowly enough that she might not notice for a while, but the symptoms would increase, with loss of muscle control in her hands next, making it harder to wield weapons. Then loss of balance, tunnel vision, chest pains, and finally paralysis. She'd live inside her unresponsive body, possibly for hours, while the poison shut down her organs. Unless someone killed her first.

Unable to move, to speak, even to blink. For now, though, all her symptoms could be explained away by fear and adrenaline.

Huenoch might work it out earlier, because the blurred vision and clumsy hands would be more noticeable in the warrior than the Bird-form. Either way, once it became clear that they were both suffering from the same affliction, it wouldn't take long to realise who'd done it to them.

Yes. Definitely time for Ilandeh to leave.

The road ahead narrowed again and someone was suggesting they go back the way they'd come when there was another of those awful rumbling crashes and a wall behind and to Ilandeh's right slumped into the road. She was already moving, because if there were Melody warriors behind that wall, they'd be scrambling over the rubble and as soon as the dust cleared, they'd be right there, in the street with them. Omeata might not even live long enough to die of Ilandeh's poison.

The warriors in front fell, stuck with arrows, and got back up and kept going where possible, their bodies shields for the Bird-form scurrying behind them. Got up and fell again and this time stayed down.

The wall beside her bulged and for one mad instant the Whisper tried to push it back upright, but then she spun and charged directly at the wall opposite and with a strength born more of hope than expectation, she sprinted, leapt, and somehow scaled the wall like a cat, her fingers hooking over the top and her spear lost below. She rolled over and onto the roof, slid back to her feet, and pounded away. With luck and Nallac's intervention, no one would have seen her go. Not the Melody; not Omeata.

Now to find Lilla.

And then go home.

* * *

As expected, the Singing City freedom fighters were doing far better than the Zellih. They'd stayed as one group numbering a few thousand, bigger by far than any of the ambush parties that were trying to pick them off and splinter them into smaller bands.

And they were counter-striking. They'd caught a pod and torn them apart, then sprung the ambush meant for them on the reinforcements that came to the pod's aid. They were crouched in the aftermath of that ambush, corpses and rubble and spent arrows and darts littering the ground, when Ilandeh found them.

The Whisper let out a low whistle then ducked a shower of stones, yelping when one thudded into her thigh with a solid thwack. She slid over the rubble and staggered down the other side, then dropped to her knees and gasped for breath. 'Don't think I was followed, but get some lookouts on my backtrail, will you?' she panted, pointing with a wavering finger over her shoulder.

Lilla slithered over corpses and broken stone to put his knife at her neck. 'Why are you here, murderer?' he snarled, pretending he didn't see as Tiamoko gestured for four warriors to keep watch as she'd suggested.

'Omeata's poisoned. Dying.' She glanced around without moving her head in case she slit her own throat. 'You didn't bring Ossa?'

'Ossa is outside the city with the civilians. Safe. Not that it's any of your business. How do you know Omeata's poisoned?' he demanded, keeping his voice low with an effort. Ekon scrambled over just in time to hear that last. He swore beneath his breath and then leant close, intent on her answer.

Ilandeh gave them both an unimpressed stare. 'I'm a fucking assassin, Lilla, and you want to know how I know she's been poisoned? Why do you think Pilos put me with them?' She held up her hands before he could do more than choke on everything he wanted to say to her. 'Listen, the Sing—Tayan contacted me last night and I told him what I'd done. *I said listen!* I told him that Omeata would be dead by highsun and that they needed to have all the Zellih in their chosen killing field beforehand so that when it happens, they can take advantage of the chaos.'

Lilla looked like he wanted to beat her to death and she rolled her eyes. 'She is poisoned, and she is going to die. But not until tonight. Midnight, maybe a little earlier depending on how much water she drinks, how much adrenaline . . . it doesn't matter. What matters is Pilos and Atu think they're going to win at highsun. They're expecting the Zellih to fall apart. When they don't, they'll be the ones in chaos.'

There was a long pause. 'And they trust the information you gave them?' Ekon asked with tightly controlled excitement.

'I didn't give it to them. I gave it to the Singer. Everyone knows you can't lie to the Singer.' She painted an innocent expression onto her face and blinked.

Ekon swore again, long and excited this time. His eyes were dancing. Lilla was less enthused. 'Whose side are you actually on, assassin?' he asked in a cold voice.

Ilandeh smirked and spread her hands, innocence vanishing. 'I'm just trying to end the war. All the wars. Zellih defeat Melody, then the Bird-form dies. The Bird-wings are already dead. And I'd lay jade on the fact that your Weaver was actually their Bird-head. If I'm right, that's four Aspects dead. That automatically triggers a council election; the surviving Aspects and every warrior of good standing, whether they're in Ixachipan or Zellipan, must assemble at Bird Mountain to elect replacements. It's an inviolable law of their people. You won't have to betray your alliance.'

She smirked again, unable to hide her satisfaction. 'Melody's defeated, Zellih go home. You've won.'

'That simple?' Lilla demanded sourly, but she could see reluctant interest in his face.

She gave him an unimpressed glare. 'No. Weaver might not have been the Bird-head. But now you know what you need to do to make them leave: find another of their flocks and kill its leader. I imagine you'd find one in Tokoban soon enough. And don't give me anything about honouring the alliance, because I know you didn't make it in good faith. For now, though, stay alive, fight, and don't back down at highsun. Omeata will still be alive. The Melody will panic, and you can win. Understand?' They both nodded. 'Good. Mictec and Malel bless you, and Nallac bless me. Maybe I'll see you again.'

'Where are you going?' Ekon asked as she began to crawl away again, partially hidden by a fallen wall.

Ilandeh looked back and winked, her disguise so perfect they saw only what she wanted them to. 'Places to go. People to kill. Whoever gets Pilos buys the beers.' She looked away and the humour fell from her face. There was nothing else to say, whether of truth or of lie, so she ignored the soft call of her name and scrambled away. Victory was in the hands of the gods and the hands of the warriors. It was down to who wanted it more, and who had the numbers and ruthlessness to see it done. And this time, she honestly couldn't tell which way it was going to go.

There was a small gap where a collapsing building had hit one still standing and the rubble hadn't completely filled the roadway. She crawled into it and along, her own body blocking out the ambient light until she was slithering through the darkness and wondering if there was a way out at the other end after all, or if she'd inadvertently found a path leading down to the Underworld.

Just when she was about to lose her mind, light began filtering back in and she let out a shaky exhalation. She was, as she'd hoped, a few streets away from a series of three interlinking plazas with a narrow road leading from the middle one that would, Nallac willing, take her all the way to the great pyramid.

Ilandeh flitted from road to roof to building to road again as somewhere nearby masonry crumpled and scattered. There were high-pitched yells of alarm and warning, and then screams of pain and of rage, and a vast dust cloud billowed up not far ahead. The first of the linked plazas was only a few dozen strides away, but as she got closer a pod of Melody warriors staggered into it. They were bloody and sweaty, dust in their hair and caked in the lines around their eyes. They collapsed in the open space, heaving for clear air, while others deposited the injured and then hurried back into the dust for more.

Someone's wall collapsed the wrong way.

She wasn't wrong: the warriors who'd gone looking for their wounded burst back out of the dust cloud with a group of Zellih chasing them. Ilandeh crouched out of sight and watched them massacre each other. It didn't take long; the pod slotted into formation and fought as one, the healthy supporting the injured or cutting them out of the line if they weren't of use. The Zellih couldn't hope to match them.

When it was over, the reduced pod checked their surroundings and then headed off west. It seemed everyone had some sort of fall-back position to retreat into that would either lure their enemies deeper into the city or allow them to set up another ambush. Ilandeh waited a little longer and then slid out of concealment. Wary, she scuttled across the road towards the corpses and then picked her way over and around them. She found a spear with a sharpened bone head and claimed it. Someone grabbed her ankle; the Whisper looked down into a woman's face, pulled her leg free, and used her knife to open her throat.

'Sorry,' she muttered, and hurried on her way.

The second plaza narrowed into the expected road and, at its end and looming over the buildings bounding it and the roads leading from it, was the rear of the great pyramid. Blood-red and ominous, its white shining songstone cap glittering at its summit. And cutting through the middle of this quiet, empty, undamaged plaza ran a swift, deep stream.

Ilandeh's heart kicked in her chest and she studied the water in both directions. 'This is the stupidest fucking thing I've ever done,' she murmured as she approached the stream and followed it as it wove between tall, wide, windowless buildings whose entrances were all on the far side of the structures. She left the plaza behind, left the distant roars of combat behind, and slipped between stone walls with only the sound of her own laboured breathing and the gurgle of water to accompany her.

The stream bent to the right and she followed it into another long, narrow plaza. At the far end, the temples slumping in the great pyramid's shadow were hollow ruins, while between them stretched a ramshackle perimeter wall.

'Hello, Ilandeh.'

The Whisper whipped around, spear snapping into guard and her legs coiled beneath her ready to lunge – or run. She gaped. 'Bird-form?' she managed, utterly confused. 'But how?'

'Is that our way in?' Omeata asked, pointing at the stream. 'Risky.'

'Our way in to what?' she tried, flailing for equilibrium and failing to find it.

Omeata tutted and folded her arms across her chest. 'You don't really think we came here to fight a war over land, do you? I'm here for the song – at least in a way. So, I'll ask one more time: is that our way in?'

'How did you find me? You didn't follow me.'

'Didn't I?' A pause. 'You're right; I didn't. But I knew you'd be going to the great pyramid, and I knew you wouldn't be able to just stroll in through the front door. This is the only other way.'

'Weaver told you the city's layout.' Omeata blinked, silent. Neither confirming nor denying Ilandeh's guess, and then she coughed and rubbed the heel of her hand between her breasts, grimacing. Suspicion twisted into guilt. 'Don't you need to be with the flock? It's nearly highsun. There are hours of fighting still to come.'

'They have their orders. They know what they're here to do. And what I'm here to do. So, how exactly do we get in?'

Ilandeh glanced at the water again and repressed a shudder. 'Play dead; we're just corpses in the water.'

'That's it? What if there are song-twisted monsters in there?'

Ilandeh shrugged. 'Then we'll be corpses in the water.' The stream led towards the left-hand temple and vanished inside. She looked at Omeata, who sniffed.

'After you, mixed-blood. Just in case there's something nasty waiting for us.'

Omeata carried no visible weapons, but Ilandeh was helpless to resist. Didn't want to. This wasn't at all what she'd planned, but the Bird-form was dying and Tayan had never been a physical threat to anyone. And the Whisper in her, who collected and catalogued and analysed information, wanted to know how right she was. How many theories were going to prove fact.

She took a deep breath and stepped into the stream, lay on her back with her spear propped across her chest, and let herself be washed away. Omeata followed her in, cursing quietly at the cold.

The stream carried them into the building and Ilandeh let her face relax, her mouth open, her body float as it would. She was a corpse, nothing more. Just a dead warrior who'd fallen and was being carried away by the water. Unfortunate but unremarkable.

Despite her precautions, there was no one in the temple to see her pass by, neither mortal nor divine.

There was a square of perfect blackness ahead of them.

'Ilandeh? What's tha—'

The stream sucked them down underneath the pyramid and into the dark.

Ilandeh had been afraid more times than she cared to remember, but she'd never felt anything like the clinging, viscous fear that enveloped her as she bobbed along the underground stream with her face barely able to break the surface before it scraped across a rock ceiling above her. How many times did she think she'd drown before the smallest glimmer of light gave her hope?

More times than she wanted to admit. But there *was* light and then her flailing hand broke the surface and there was open air above her. Ilandeh gasped and sobbed out relief and gasped some more, then fought her feet down onto the stream bed and pushed up to standing. Her head smacked into something hard and rattling and she winced, cold panic clawing at her. The stream was hip-deep and she hurled herself out, rolling over once and then scrambling onto her feet with her spear clenched so tightly in her fists that the muscles in her forearms throbbed.

She was breathing too fast, her heart beating hummingbird wings in her throat, and what the fuck was that sound? Ilandeh turned, a shriek lodged in her chest. A Chorus warrior was staring at her, wide-eyed and frozen halfway into a prostration. They'd thought her a holy Setat, then.

Omeata rose behind them with a knife in her hand. She plunged it into the warrior's back and they twisted on instinct, tearing the hilt from her hand. The Whisper's reflexes kicked in even as her mind was still a hot white panic, and she threw her spear and punched the warrior off their feet, the tip buried deep in their belly. She followed at a run and was in time to slap her hand over their mouth after they'd crashed to the stone. She ripped her knife across the warrior's throat before they could do more than wheeze.

Thanking Nallac for the gift, she stripped out of her sodden useless armour and clothes and changed into the yellow tunic and kilt of a Chorus warrior.

The salt-cotton was wet with blood front and back, and the waistband of the kilt was bloody, too, but they'd do what she needed them to. Ilandeh pushed the corpse into the stream. It bobbed once and vanished beneath the pyramid. The thing she'd headbutted when she stood up was the waterwheel, its structure broken and the slaves who walked it missing.

Taking deep, deliberate breaths, Ilandeh concentrated on the small, mundane details of their surroundings until she'd controlled her panic. She'd survived the stream and she'd offered another in her place just in case. She remained undetected and she was inside the pyramid; she was, as she'd promised Tayan, home. Now she just had to find him and explain that she'd brought a guest.

Ilandeh glanced at Omeata. The Bird-form was likewise undressing; in her case, shrugging into the feathered huipil. The bottom half dripped water, but the garment obviously gave the woman some sort of comfort and, Ilandeh couldn't deny, added an authority and mystique that made her other-worldly and unknowable.

She was also far more relaxed than the Whisper. But of course, water didn't hold quite so many terrors for a Zellitli as it did for her.

Retrieving her spear and putting her knife back in her belt, Ilandeh felt her way to the dimly lit stairs and began to climb. Off to her right, the slave entrance had been bricked up, but that wasn't the only reason for the dark. There were no torches or candles. And there was no life. Where were the councillors and nobles and administrators who'd have fled here when the uprising began? A lack of slaves was understandable, but the pyramid felt deserted. Echoing. Ominous.

Ilandeh climbed to the next level, where the slave quarters and storerooms were located. Empty. The next, with its administrators' offices, Choosers' records, and the library. Empty. Water trickled from her hair to soak into her new salt-cotton and dribble into her eyes. She blinked it away and kept moving, Omeata a rustling shadow a pace behind.

She should have been fighting her way through crowds of people, using the dead warrior's armour to convince everyone that she was Chorus bringing an important captive for the holy lord's personal questioning. That she wasn't doing that was not a relief. It was unnerving.

Outside it was almost highsun, yet no light filtered in. Every level of the great pyramid had exits onto gardens; there should have been *something*. Instead there was the gloom and the smell. It was almost as rank as the city without and Ilandeh couldn't help the shudder of superstitious dread that prickled her skin as she walked these so-familiar halls, made monstrous by shadows and echoing silence. Silence except for the song.

Tayan's song, heard from within the pyramid, with all the strength and magic that afforded it, crowed of victory, a song that bled her heart and uplifted it at once. A song of Empire's might and Pechaqueh right. What of everything he'd spoken of just the night before when he'd visited her, of blood being second to skill and wit, of an Empire that was peaceful and equal and just?

'Tayan!'

Ilandeh screamed his name in sudden fury when she was on the penultimate level of the pyramid and Omeata jumped and let out a little shriek of her own and then smacked the back of the Whisper's head, hissing at her to be quiet. Ilandeh ignored her. 'Tayan of fucking Tokoban, I'm home just like you asked. Like you ordered. Where are you hiding? Where is everyone and what is it that your song is saying? What about your promises to me? *What about your promises?*'

Her voice echoed along the darkened corridor and into silence. No response. Not from him; not from anyone. Not even a Chorus warrior. Ilandeh halted and put her back to the wall. Her empty hand stilled Omeata and then pressed her against the stone – she needed to be able to see beyond the Bird-form to anything, anyone, creeping up behind them. Maybe Chorus; maybe Drowned. Maybe Tayan himself.

What if there was no one here but the Singer because he'd broken as Xac had broken? What if he'd slaughtered them all, everyone who'd taken refuge here? She'd seen him and Xac kill people, had been witness to that brutality more times than she cared to remember.

'Ilandeh?'

The voice was quiet with distance and tentative, at odds with the surging triumph of the song, but she recognised it. Recognised him. 'Fuck,' she breathed as a chill ran through her.

A long corridor, a staircase, another long corridor, and the source. And Tayan. She looked at Omeata, almost invisible in her paint and feathers, and then forward into the dark. 'Stay close,' she breathed. 'We're nearly there.'

'Sacred Bird be praised,' Omeata whispered. 'Soon.'

LILLA

Less than an hour before highsun they'd entered the grand plaza, pushed, lured, and driven there, to discover the Melody – or what was left of it in this part of Ixachipan – lined up waiting for them. Their backs to their own ramshackle wall. Grim and giddy and ready for slaughter.

Lilla hated the burst of gratitude he felt towards Ilandeh for warning them almost as much as he hated her. Behind the crumbling, poorly-built barricade rose the pyramid, its walls as vibrant as fresh blood and the vast carvings of spirits and Drowned and Singers almost alive with colour despite the clouds piling up tall enough to obscure the sun, who hid his face in shame at what his children did.

Ekon had held the rebels aloof until the Zellih and the Melody were fully engaged before he threw them in at the side. They fought conservatively, saving their strength, and they watched. They'd come through the city with far fewer losses than the Zellih, who looked to have lost a third, perhaps even half, of their number. They were evenly matched with the surviving Melody, and now it was the freedom fighters whose numbers tipped the scale. Still, that meant nothing. The Melody was fighting for its own survival, and the survival of the song and the Empire of Songs. They had to win, and it made them savage. More merciless than Lilla had ever seen them.

He fought defensively, watching over Ekon and trying not to think about how close he was to the pyramid. How close to Tayan. An axe flashed through a gap towards his lover's flank and Lilla leapt in the way, sweeping his spear up to deflect it. The axe thunked into the wooden shaft and something flew off into the press of shoving, screaming humanity. The bannerstone, unbalancing the spearhead from the shaft? It didn't matter, he'd compensate.

Lilla twisted the spear, kicked the warrior in the crotch and stabbed him in the face, a great sweeping slice that opened him from upper lip to hairline and took out an eye. The eagle's shriek was so loud and terrible it rang clear over the battle and then he fell back, clawing at his face.

The Toko lunged to grab up his fallen axe before the tide of battle kicked it away but it slipped from his grip. He tried again; dropped it again. Someone jostled him and he shoved backwards out of the front line, his warriors taking his place, and held up his hand with distant curiosity. His first two fingers were missing and the third ended at the middle knuckle. Blood flowed steadily from the stumps and Lilla's incomprehension vanished under a sudden wave of sickness, cold and slimy, that rose from the soles of his feet all the way up to his head. He wobbled and then the pain was there, as if it had been waiting for him to see and understand before leaping from the shadows with claws and fangs extended.

He sucked in a breath and yelled.

Tiamoko appeared and pressed a wad of linen down onto the stumps and squashed it around the remains of the fingers, emotionless and practical as Lilla wheezed and bellowed. He wound the linen over and around and then down over his hand and wrist and back up to squeeze over the stumps again. Lilla strained, but he couldn't pull his hand from Tiamoko's implacable grip.

The boy tied the ragged ends of the linen in a perfect little bow on the back of Lilla's wrist, patted him on the cheek, and closed his injured hand back around his spear shaft so that he hissed and spat like an angry chulul. Then he turned him and pushed him back into their lines without uttering a word. Stunned and stumbling and sick with pain, Lilla went.

Not long after – or perhaps a thousand Star cycles of pain and distraction and disbelief later – it happened exactly as Ilandeh had predicted. When the sun stood at its highest point, the Melody began an eager, over-confident push – and were met with firmness. They regrouped and pushed again, harder and faster and expecting the enemy to crumble, and this time were met and more. Met and pushed back. And then more than pushed back; the Zellih formed into an arrow tip and counter-attacked, each driving step opening a gap for another warrior to move into from behind, lengthening their line so they outnumbered the Melody's front. Slowly, inexorably, they began to cleave them in two.

The High Feather threw in the reserves to strengthen the failing centre but it was too late; overconfidence had already had its way with them. Between one breath and the next, the Melody was fully committed, with nowhere to run except behind their wall and no more reinforcements coming – and the Bird-form still alive. Allegedly. The Zellih still fighting under her command.

Allegedly.

Lilla hadn't seen her since before dawn when they'd begun their approach to the Singing City. He'd scoured the grand plaza and hadn't seen her. Maybe she was hiding, or it had all been a lie, or a hundred other reasons, but that woman in her purple paint and huipil of a million shimmering feathers had either radically changed her appearance or was dead.

In the end, it didn't matter; the Zellih fought on while the Melody had expected them to fall apart.

The panic Ilandeh had told Tayan to expect manifested, but in the Melody, not their enemies. Both sides, in the end, had gambled everything on the word of a self-confessed liar and assassin. Lilla could almost admire the sheer audacity she had

had to lie, within the song, to its Singer and be found truthful. *Almost* admire.

And then that song veered and faltered. The song that had brayed of superiority and demanded surrender, that demanded love and worship and adulation, lost cohesion, lost power, and lost itself.

Lilla pretended that it didn't matter, that he didn't care because he was here, crushed among his own warriors and facing down maddened Melody eagles and dogs, his fingers trampled somewhere beneath their sandals. And because they were going to win. His people, all those who would be free, were going to win. The Zellih and the Melody were going to slaughter each other and somehow, in the aftermath and the silence of no song, they would negotiate, trade or kill their way to freedom.

The song dipped again and a corresponding roar went up from the Zellih and the rebels alike and they pressed forward, herding the Melody against its own wall and trapping them. This time the rebels moved even before Ekon had given the order, flowing as one like a flock of birds banking in the sunset, pressing in from the side and crowding the Melody, restricting their ability to form their preferred lines and squares.

Lilla moved as his warriors did, the hot awful throbbing in his hand impossible to ignore, though less frightening than the weakness of his grip on the spear shaft.

It was just a couple of fingers, not my hand. Not my head. Thank you, Malel, for small mercies.

He tried to mean it even as the agony conjured a greasy sweat that stung his eyes and slicked his armpits.

The flow of battle shifted him back into the front line and there was no more time to count fingers or wonder who was winning; there was only the fight, the latest in an endless string of fights, and as Lilla had reminded himself a thousand times before, he was good in a fight. Prepared. Ruthless.

Deadly.

He ducked a club and shoved his spear through a gap between two dogs and into the armpit of the eagle behind them, then ripped it out and caught the right-hand warrior's arm with the spear tip as he pulled it back, a long slice just above his elbow. His mouth opened in a howl and a second spear went in under his chin and snapped his jaw shut. Ekon.

Ekon again.

Ekon always. Forever. If he'll let me. If he'll have me.

Despite the pain in his hand and the nearness of the pyramid and its Singer, an unexpected but welcome little lurch of joy and hope shook his guts. Ekon. And then he saw what his lover was seeing.

'We can't let them through the gate,' the Chitenecatl said, just as Lilla stabbed the dog warrior lunging at him and shouted: 'We have to keep them out of the source!'

Ekon grinned at him, wild, exuberant, and also strangely joyful. As if there was nowhere he'd rather be than fighting at Lilla's side. The Toko smiled back, helpless not to, and again they moved as one, plunging into the line of eagles and screaming at their warriors to follow.

The freedom fighters understood what was needed and went with them, forming into an arrow tip with Lilla and Ekon at the front. Months of effort, little sleep and less food, endless days of pain and exhaustion and the constant grinding churn of fear, all fell away and Lilla fought on in a brittle, glowing bubble of focused determination. He and Ekon moved together like water, like magic, like an eja and her dog, deflecting strikes the other didn't see, leaving attacks for each other to counter, not needing to communicate in any way anyone else could understand. Just needing to move, and so moving, and breathing, and killing, and living.

It was probably an awful way to fall in love, but that didn't make it any less real, and the sudden recognition of it, despite having already told Ekon he loved him, almost got Lilla killed. Because he had loved him before, but not like this. Malel, never like this. This was unconscious synchronicity, it was one spirit in two bodies, and one purpose in a shared life. A common goal and a common enemy and someone to stand beside and face it all.

It was beautiful.

Lilla's hand was clumsy with pain and lack of grip, but he slipped the stab of a spear, jinked left and then dodged right; the eagle's next thrust followed his feint, leaving him exposed and looking in the wrong direction.

The Toko drove up out of his squat with all the power of his thighs, his spear stabbing straight and true for his enemy's gut. Somehow the eagle intercepted, parrying with such force that it jarred the spear out of his weakened hand to clatter to the stone. He was unarmed. *He was unarmed.*

The world slowed in its focus and movements, every person and object surrounding Lilla sharpening into exquisite detail. The ricochet of his spear hitting the ground and bouncing back up, not high enough to snatch. The cruel smile beginning to twist the eagle's panting mouth. The bright beads of blood arcing between them from another fight, another warrior being opened up to the sky and rain and the judgement of the gods.

Jaguar-Brother's paws landed softly to either side of the one who walked his path and Lilla felt the warm, rank breeze of his breath against the back of his neck. The nudge that set him moving.

He threw himself into his enemy's legs. The eagle's spear ripped open the back of his salt-cotton, the tunic beneath and the skin below that, cutting through scar and muscle alike, but he fell under Lilla's tackle and Lilla followed, catching a knee beneath his chin so that he bit his tongue. He scrabbled for his knife and tore the point up the outside of the Pechaqueh thigh. Skin and muscle parted from knee to hip and the eagle screamed, high and terrible.

Lilla snatched at the spear and even in his agony the warrior tried to hold on to it, so he punched the knife in again, this time higher towards the groin and on the inside of the leg. Searching for the killing place and not finding it. Not caring, because the eagle was down and bawling and not a threat and Lilla had wrestled the spear from his grip.

Blood rushed hot down his back as he scrambled back to his feet, his salt-cotton hanging loose and crooked from his shoulders. How many more wounds could he sustain before the sheer number of them killed him? An aggregation of injuries, like cracks in a wall multiplying until the whole building crashed down.

But no. He would live for Ekon, and for Ossa, and for himself. And for those ancestors watching him with narrow-eyed mockery and a challenging arch to their brows.

Lilla drove the spear down through the eagle's salt-cotton and into his belly, and then wrenched it back out in a spray of blood. The world began to move at a normal speed once more.

'Thank you,' he gasped to Jaguar-Brother. 'And you can shut up,' he added to Xessa and heard her laugh.

Another eagle came for him with lips pulled back and a surfeit of hate in their face. Lilla grinned like a cat, heedless of his missing fingers or the blood leaking down his back, consumed with the need to kill and kill until there was no one left to face him. No one who'd dare raise their head, let alone a weapon, in his presence.

Jaguar-Brother rumbled his approval, or maybe it was just thunder, because in the next moment Lilla's maimed hand slipped on his spear, the linen bandage slick with blood, and a sickening pulse of pain weakened his grip yet again. Ekon, as always, knew and understood; he spun in from his flank and tore through Lilla's opponent with lethal grace, slicing and stabbing four, five, six times until the woman's salt-cotton was as ragged as an unfinished shawl.

She collapsed to her knees and toppled onto her side and they stepped over her, maintaining contact with the steadily retreating eagles. Retreating towards the wall; towards the gate in the wall.

Among them Pilos, the Spear of the Singer and the architect of the fall of Tokoban, the holder of Ilandeh's leash and the man who'd done all he could to break Xessa, who was one of the bravest people Lilla had ever met. Pilos, surrounded by eagles and wearing murder in the paint on his face and with blood sliming him to the elbows.

'You!' Lilla roared and somehow Pilos heard him and met his eyes, his own narrow. There was no recognition in them. Lilla could have been anyone, but mostly, he was no one. Not a Fang from Tokoban; not a Pod-leader of the Eighth Talon; and not even the Singer's former husband. No one. He bit down on the flare of resentment and pushed on, Ekon at his side. Him at least, Pilos recognised.

Bad luck. It's not his hands that are going to kill you; it's mine. It's me, Spear, it's me. You destroyed my land and people and society; you enslaved us and got Xessa and Toxte killed; you made Ekon shrink and cower and fear himself. Hate himself.

How dare you think that now you get to hurt him. He is mine.

And I say no.

The thoughts tumbled through his head and he wished, with everything in him, that he could say these things to the man's face, that he had time and space to enunciate, brutally and coldly, exactly how much Lilla detested him and how little the world would miss him when he was a cooling corpse lying on rain-slick, blood-slick stone.

Pilos thrust at Ekon, ignoring Lilla and determined, it seemed, to finally kill the Feather who had betrayed him and the Melody. Lilla batted the spear sideways before Ekon could intercept, shoving the Chitenecatl behind him and stepping into Pilos's space, close enough to taunt. Close enough to kill.

'*No!*' Ekon shouted.

Now, finally, Pilos's attention was on him and there was that recognition Lilla's ego demanded. That his skill and ability demanded. Recognition – and respect.

''Moko! Get him out of here!' Lilla bawled and didn't wait to see if the big warrior did as he ordered. He just threw himself on Pilos and forced him to respond, their spears clacking together and every impact sending splinters of agony through the stumps of his fingers and up through the bones of his wrist. And then Pilos slammed his spear shaft down with exquisite precision, mashing Lilla's maimed hand and making him howl. He hurled himself backwards without conscious thought, trying only to get away.

Pilos followed.

His eagles did not, as if there was some unspoken agreement among them to let their Spear fight one on one. Like this was an exhibition, or a bout in his fighting pit. Putting on a show as he'd forced Xessa and Tiamoko and countless others to do – spilling blood for Pechaqueh greed.

As if the fate of Ixachipan didn't hang on the outcome of the day.

As if they know he'll win.

There was no such agreement among the rebels, who didn't care for battle honour and the false status bestowed by a Melody they didn't belong to and a society they disdained. And Lilla, blinking away involuntary tears, didn't care for a fair fight. He cared for victory, and he'd squander every shred of dignity and even the chance to kill this man to get it.

His ego had demanded respect; it hadn't demanded a spectacle. It didn't get it.

A Tlalox of the Eighth Talon used Pilos's focus on Lilla to slip in at the side and attack the Spear's flank; a tall eagle intercepted him, fury twisting her features. As quickly as that, the space Pilos and Lilla had had for their duel was gone. The lines crowded in around them again, hacking at each other in a frenzy, and the Toko found his spear arm crowded by that same Tlalox, though this time he was choking and falling backwards, weapon clattering underfoot as his hands went to his chest and the rapid spread of scarlet through his armour.

Lilla ducked behind him for an instant, an eye blink, and then he shoved the wounded man with all his strength. The Spear leapt away from the seeming attack, forcing space for himself, and in that moment Lilla moved.

Pilos's gaze went from Tlalox to Toko, realisation dawning. He brought his spear to bear and Lilla grabbed it in his wounded hand, his weak and bloody and bandaged hand. The hand that wasn't strong enough to stop it.

It wasn't meant to.

Pilos had braced for resistance that wasn't there. His balance tipped into his toes as Lilla let the haft slide through his hand until the bannerstone at its middle arrested its motion, slamming into raw and severed flesh so he screamed despite himself. Pilos jerked to a halt, mouth opening perhaps in surprise at his cry, perhaps in understanding – it didn't matter. Lilla rammed his own spear up under the man's chin even as he began to rock backwards and away.

It wasn't a clean strike, there was too much pain and movement and adrenaline in him for that. Too much shoving on him and on Pilos, both of them swaying and stumbling to the rhythm of the struggle. The spearhead caught on existing scar tissue patterning Pilos's lower jaw and tore free, raking up the outside of his face.

He wrenched backwards, mouth open in the beginnings of a scream, and a war club broke his shoulder and crushed his upper chest. Ekon. Despite Lilla's every plea and wish. Despite it all. *Ekon.* And didn't he have the right, more than the right, for what he'd been forced to do? Pilos's spine curved under the impact and he gasped a broken, wet sound, and his spear fell from his hand.

Lilla stabbed him in the belly. 'For Xessa,' he grunted. 'For Toxte.'

'*For my family*,' Ekon screamed and clubbed him again.

Pilos went to one knee, clutching at the spear inside him with the hand that still worked and his shoulder crushed almost into his chest. The eagles around him roared their distress and freedom fighters surged in a joyful mass to meet them, snatches of a dozen tribal songs cast to the air.

The fighting increased in frenzy.

And Pilos stood. Against the pain, and despite his impalement, he stood. 'We gave you everything, laws and prosperity and something greater to which to aspire,' he croaked, the fire in his eyes undimmed. He pushed closer, forcing the spear deeper into himself. 'Perhaps our failure was in believing you capable of appreciating our gifts. You savage, unruly children. You will never know who you might have been.'

'Shut up. *Shut up!*' Lilla paused to master himself, the high whine of impending agony ringing in his ears. 'It is you who does not understand,' he raged as the battle shoved at him. 'You could have kept your song and your gods if only Tayan had agreed. We'd have done it and walked away. No more death; no more violence. Pechaqueh in Pechacan with their songs and their gods. And the rest of us in our lands with our gods. Alive and free. *Free*. That's all we wanted.'

'And so to get your way of life back, you'd destroy ours. You speak of your traditions and your nobility and then you do to us what you say we did to you.' Pilos coughed and Lilla felt it jerk on the weapon that joined them, sending jolts of pain through his hand. The Spear of the Singer was shaking, only standing against the agony by a strength of will that Lilla hated as much as he admired. Next to him, Ekon was unmoving, perhaps appalled at what he'd done, perhaps as hungry for Pilos's last words as Lilla himself, poison though he knew they'd be.

'Hurry up and kill me. Your self-righteous, self-pitying prattling is an agony no one deserves. Not even me.'

The song jerked again and Lilla saw Pilos flinch, as if that hurt more than the spear driven into his belly or the shoulder and ribs crushed beyond repair. For an instant, a heartbeat, he knew that making him listen to the death of the song, if that's what this was, would be the cruellest thing he could ever do – and that Pilos would deserve every excruciating moment of it. Instead, he twisted the spear and ripped it sucking out of Pilos's belly.

Pilos didn't even have time to scream before Ekon's war club – his own war club – crushed his temple. He fell.

There was no hot wash of pleasure or vindication or triumph in Lilla's belly. Instead, there was a moment of stillness, of shock and disbelief, and with it a wild veering of the song as its usual sordid arrogance and mocking superiority faltered. As if the song knew its Spear was no more.

As if it wept.

Lilla stood motionless, Pilos's blood on his spear. Next to him, Ekon. There were strands of hair in the blood caked to the war club's head. They didn't – couldn't – look at each other. Of all the things he'd never expected to feel, it was shame that coiled, uneasy and gently writhing, within the Tokob belly.

No. No, that is not me. That is Tayan. That is the song. I have done nothing wrong.

He looked at Pilos, jerking on the stone, one eye a red starburst and half-protruding from his skull, and wondered if he lied, told himself he didn't, and wondered again.

Tiamoko shoved between him and Ekon and stamped his heel into the depression clubbed into Pilos's head, caving it in. Spat into his twitching face. Screamed his war cry. And charged.

Ekon bellowed Mictec's name and Lilla's own throat shredded under the force of his shout. Together, the three of them formed the tip of a new arrow and the rebels responded, storming forwards in an unstoppable, implacable tide that the Melody couldn't counter. Pilos's body was lost under their driving feet.

Step and kill; step and kill; *step and fucking kill.*

Above them, around them, inside them, the song veered again. Twisted high and frightened and unsure, any imperative it had once contained fled like a mortal from a Drowned. Or a Drowned from an eja. Lilla grinned and there was the thrill he thought he'd feel, tingling from his soles to his scalp and buzzing in his missing fingers.

Step.

And kill.

ILANDEH

'That's far enough.'

Ilandeh stopped a few steps inside the source, Omeata clutching a fistful of her kilt in an unexpected show of timidity that did nothing for the Whisper's state of mind. The colonnade was inexpertly bricked up, like all the others, and gaps let in dozens of chinks of light, enough that she could see the expanse of mats, the cotton hanging, and the distant, empty offering pool.

She could also just about see the outlines of two figures seated behind the hanging and began to kneel.

'What are you doing?' Tayan asked and Ilandeh whipped around, gasping. He was standing on the other side of the source with Xochi beside him.

She glanced back at the hanging; the figures hadn't moved. She inclined her head briefly in their direction just in case and then prostrated herself before Tayan. 'Holy lord. I present to you the revered Bird-form of Zellipan, known as Omeata. They have . . . I don't really know. Something to say, an offer to make. They've been less than forthcoming, so I'm not sure. They're not why I'm here, though. I was coming anyway. Coming home, like you said.'

The Singer ignored her. 'Zama,' he said and Omeata came to stand at Ilandeh's side.

'Tayan.'

Ilandeh lifted her eyes to the ceiling murals and sighed, somehow simultaneously astonished and unsurprised. Tayan hadn't wanted her; he'd wanted a guide for Omeata. 'Zama? You tell him your heart-name and not me?' she muttered. 'I presume he's who you've been talking to, not just Weaver—'

'I purged the spirits from the song.' Tayan spoke over her. 'I did that because you told me to and I thought you were Pechaqueh, or at least a true believer. Because the holy Setatmeh were suffering. You will tell me the truth of what I've done or Xochi here will cut your head off and I will wear it as a fucking hat.' His tone was entirely reasonable considering the words pouring from his mouth.

He pushed away from the wall and the Chorus Leader came with him. She was intent and focused and Ilandeh knew she couldn't beat her. No, that wasn't true. She *didn't want* to beat her. And she didn't want to have to try.

She didn't want to kill anyone else today, no matter whose side they were on. No matter if her own life was at stake. She sighed again and let her spear fall from her hand to thwack into the mats. Tayan jumped; no one else did.

She held up her empty hands. 'I'm done. Finished. I'm just going to stand over here and listen. It would be nice if one of you told me the truth about something, anything. Pick a fucking topic, I don't care. Just treat me like I'm a person worth talking to, worth confiding in. Just once.'

The words tumbled to a halt. Omeata and Tayan were staring at her with identical expressions of contempt. As if she'd walked into their presence, squatted, and pissed on the floor.

Omeata put her back to her as if she were an insect. Ilandeh's fingers twitched; with an effort of will, she did not reach for her spear.

'We don't want Tokoban. We don't want Chitenec or Yalotlan or any of your pathetic little lands. We want our god back.'

Tayan opened his mouth in automatic rebuke and then closed it again, frowning.

Ilandeh smirked, her frustration forgotten. *One. Let's see what else I got right.*

Weeks of casual conversation, intent observation, and patient deduction had given her a list of possibilities for the Zellih motives. Now that they were all here and it had begun, she wasn't leaving – none of them were leaving – until she had some answers, even if only for her own peace of mind.

'I don't understand.' Tayan looked to Xochi; the Chorus Leader twitched her head to the side, her eyes on Omeata.

'Of course you don't,' the Bird-form said, 'and for once it's not because you're not Pechaqueh. They don't understand, either. No one does, because you don't understand your own history. You steal magic and twist it to your own ends. You make it something it's not and then you worship the lie that it looks like.' Tayan reached and Xochi caught his hand and held it tightly, then shifted in front of him, an armed and armoured warning.

'Speak plainly,' he barked from the safety of her shadow.

Omeata smoothed her palms down her huipil and pressed them together for an instant of silent prayer. Not totally unaffected then. Cognisant of the fact she could be slaughtered at any moment, especially as Ilandeh had stepped away from her spear. 'The world spirit who generates the song with which you control your Empire is no such thing. It is no world spirit, though it is a god.'

'I know this,' Tayan began.

'It is our god; Zellih god. It is the Sacred Bird stolen from us almost nine hundred years ago and imprisoned beneath the soil of Ixachipan. Trapped and unable to free itself, it can do nothing but sing of its agony and its loss, its yearning for the sky and those who loved it.'

This time when she paused, Tayan had nothing to say.

Two, Ilandeh thought smugly, and settled herself more comfortably against the wall.

'For centuries, we had no idea where its cage was hidden. And then Pechaqueh discovered the song and the power within it. For us, it was our first step towards reunification with our god; for Pechaqueh, it was the promise of dominion. Empire. Instead of listening to it and helping it, learning who it was and where it came from and why it sang, Pechaqueh took its magic and used it to make themselves feel important.'

'It is the world spirit. It is our—' Xochi burst out, unable to contain herself.

'Oh, shit,' Ilandeh breathed.

Omeata glanced at her. 'You at least begin to understand. The world spirit that could only be awakened when all Ixachipan was under the song's control? That world spirit? Who do you think planted that rumour within Pechaqueh lore and legend? We have been driving you to this moment for generations.'

'Impossible,' Tayan croaked. And again, louder: '*Impossible!* If all you've ever wanted is to free your god, why wait? Why did the Empire need to cover all Ixachipan?'

'Pechaqueh have manipulated the Sacred Bird's pain for centuries. Every year that passed increased its anguish, but it also increased your Empire's reach and the number of spirits under the song who would feed it when the time came. The power of its prison was that it starves it of contact and of life, and without interaction, the Sacred Bird is nothing. That is why we embedded the legend of the waking of the world spirit into your religion. It needed to be able to glut itself on life to help it regain freedom. Xac fed it with the ritual to wake the world spirit. And you, Tayan, you fed it just today.'

The Singer clapped his hands over his mouth, stricken.

'I have heard you, lamenting within the song how Pechaqueh never looked deeper, how they never understood the magic they manipulated. And what did you do? Exactly the same as them. How clever you thought yourself, Peace-weaver. Shaman. How very clever. And yet you yourself looked no further than they had. You saw only what you wanted to see: Power. Glory. Legacy.'

This one I did not expect, Ilandeh admitted with manic

cheer, rapt at the unfolding of a scheme vaster and more audacious than she could have imagined.

'You took the song as it wept and claimed its pain as power. Took grief and said it was strength. Took sadness and twisted it into control. None of you tried to visit the being, the god, that was singing. None of you looked deeper. You made a lament for what was lost into greed for what you'd never had, and you've been chasing it ever since. Every Singer has been consumed by the Sacred Bird's pain, has been twisted by its despair into a monster – and you called it divinity. Something to aspire to.'

Omeata's chest heaved with the passion of her words and she swayed and had to put a hand against the wall to steady herself.

'You want to know why you can't understand the so-called holy Setatmeh? Because they have lost the facility for language. It is burnt out of them by the Sacred Bird's magic that they steal and eat to try and live and which ravages them into fractured, tormented versions of themselves. You think they are gods? They are demented spirits living out the only punishment the Sacred Bird can manage from within its cage. They are nothing but extensions of its pain and its desperation.'

'Liar. You lie! I speak with my Setat daily,' Tayan shrieked, lurching forwards and blazing with so much gold that Ilandeh had to throw up a hand to shield her eyes. Xochi hauled him back. 'It communicates and I listen and I comprehend. The gods tell me to fix the song, to heal them.'

'That is not the voice of a mindless remnant of a Singer past,' Omeata said, her voice hoarse. She paused to cough and then rubbed at her brow. Dizziness. Loss of sensation in her hands, if the clumsy gesture was anything to go by. She'd need to sit soon. She wouldn't be able to deny she was ill, even if she didn't know just how ill.

'It is the voice of the Sacred Bird,' she continued doggedly, 'asking to be freed. And that is what I am here to do. Finally, after centuries, we have the magic and opportunity to restore our god to us.'

'Xochi, do something!' Tayan squeaked. The Chorus Leader raised her spear. Omeata glanced at Ilandeh; she stared back, bland and unmoving. The Bird-form's eyes narrowed in the gloom and the shadows of her paint, but she didn't insist.

Instead, she sniffed and nodded once, and then stepped forward with a terrible sympathy twisting her features. Xochi growled a warning that she ignored. 'It is not your song, Tayan. It was never yours, and never the Pechaqueh either. It is not even native to Ixachipan. The song belongs only to one being: the Sacred Bird itself. Nine hundred years ago Zellipan went to war. It forgot itself and the teachings of its god. In its arrogance it took on all of Barazal – and it lost. We lost. In retribution for our crimes, every shaman of Barazal came together and worked a great magic, *a mighty, world-changing magic*, and between them they took our god from us and cast it out. Cast it into Ixachipan and thrust it deep beneath the earth. We have spent almost a millennium existing without our god, paying for what our ancestors did and nudging you to this very moment, this very truth.'

Omeata turned from Tayan's slack, disbelieving face to Ilandeh. 'The rebels are so very proud of themselves, you know. They've been planning this uprising for three generations. Three generations!' She barked a laugh and then coughed hard, inspected her palm and turned it so no one could see it.

'Three generations,' she muttered again. 'They should try being patient for three times three centuries. *That's* dedication. *That's* loyalty.'

'Pain is not a contest,' Ilandeh murmured softly, pushing away from the wall and standing tall. It felt disrespectful, somehow, to slouch as she said the words. 'And no matter the outcome of today's fight, there are no winners. Not for something like this.'

'Oh, we'll win,' Omeata whispered. 'Nine centuries, Ilandeh. To feel the brush of our god's feathers against our cheeks after so long. After generations of ancestors have lived and died without that succour . . .'

'Like the Chitenecah? Like my own people, the Xentib?'

Omeata scoffed – and coughed. 'That is nothing. You do not understand loss.'

Ilandeh seized the Bird-form's hands. The slickness of blood coated one palm. '*Pain*,' she reiterated, '*is not a contest. We are all wounded.* And what you propose to do here today will wound a million more.' She took a breath. 'And perhaps that is as it should be, though nearly all of them are innocent. Just people who believe in the song and its Singer.'

'This is nonsense,' Tayan interrupted and Ilandeh flinched, having almost forgotten his presence. He seemed so unimportant in this; it was the telling of the history that mattered. The recognition of a nation's pain and the repatriation of its god. 'My song is mine. *Mine.* It owes nothing to you or anyone. Certainly not some mythical fucking bird. I have had enough of mad ravings and disloyalty. Xochi, kill them.'

'*Stand. Down.*' The Chorus Leader halted mid-step at Ilandeh's dead-voiced command. 'You can end this, Tayan. Free a god from its cage and restore the hearts of an entire people. You just have to let go.' She stretched out her empty hands. 'You just have to stop. Please. Please, Tayan. Just stop. Be my friend again.'

He drew himself up, amber eyes flashing with contempt. 'I am your Singer. I would not stoop to friendship with a creature such as you. Xochi, I ordered you to kill them.'

Xochi was pale and sweaty, wildness in the corners of her eyes. She made no move to advance.

'You're losing out there,' Ilandeh said. 'I can tell by the tenor of the screaming. I'd say you're not long from losing the wall, and when that happens, your enemies will be taking the grand staircase and then they'll be taking your head. Instead, why not help Omeata create one of the greatest and most important pieces of magic Ixachipan has ever seen? You can end the war by ending the so—'

'Shut up. *Shut up!*' Ilandeh shut up. 'You will never have my song. Neither of you.'

Omeata took a deep rattling breath. 'It is not within your power to stop me. I will wake my god and free it. I will send it back to Zellipan so that when I return there, I can feel its feet gripping the bones of the earth and know that every breeze and wind and storm comes from the beating of its wings above us. I don't care what happens here. I don't care about you. I will free the Sacred Bird and we will leave, every flock in Ixachipan. The Zellih will be gone and we will cause no trouble on our way. We never wanted conquest, or land, or death; we just wanted connection.'

Ilandeh swallowed against the sudden growth of thorns in her throat as the Bird-form coughed, thick and wet. What had she done?

'Are you saying the war is over?' the Singer asked and Ilandeh wanted to claw out her own eyes. *What had she done?*

'Against us, yes,' Omeata said and then coughed again, harsh and prolonged, red speckling on her chin and around her mouth. She swallowed a thick mouthful and Ilandeh's own throat moved with convulsive self-loathing. 'My people want nothing from you, no land or slaves or tithes of crops. Nothing but our god's freedom.'

Tayan paced across the darkened source and then back to Xochi. Out, and then back. And once more. 'No,' he said in the end.

Ilandeh blinked, astounded. 'Holy lord, you can end the war,' she began. The song skewed high and ominous and seized her by the throat, cutting off words, thoughts, and breath. She choked. Beside her, Omeata did likewise. The song slammed them both onto their knees yet again.

'This is my power, do you understand? Do you have any idea what I have given for this? The lives sacrificed for this? Are you *so fucking ignorant that you don't understand what you are asking*? How dare you try and steal my magic from me? Do you know what happened to the last person who did that? And who she was to me? Do you want to see?'

The Singer flashed with a gold that Ilandeh had always thought was stolen but now realised was *stolen*.

'*Do you want to see?*' he roared again and strode across the source, ignoring Xochi's inarticulate cry of protest, to tear down the hanging concealing the two figures who'd sat so very still throughout all these revelations.

Three, Ilandeh thought, sickened. *Nallac forgive me, but that's three.*

'They're not to be disturbed,' Tayan threatened as the song released its grip and Omeata made a choked sound of disgust. 'You're to *leave them alone.*'

His voice was rich with the song's harmonics and power, but there was weariness, too, and an undercurrent of grief that had the potential to drag them all into its claw-tipped depths. A grief that could manifest in violence or hate. And yet he'd released them from the song's compulsion, almost as if he wanted them – or perhaps just Ilandeh – to push against that order. As if a part of him needed to be made to face what he had done.

Ilandeh walked across the source, ignoring Xochi's tired protest. Tayan watched her approach with a demented, brittle righteousness, his chin raised as he dared her to pass judgment. She did not. She cupped his face in her palms and kissed his brow. 'It's all right, my friend,' she murmured. 'I won't interfere with them.' She drew him against her chest and wrapped her arms around him and stared at the bodies.

At Xessa and Toxte.

They'd been arranged in a similar pose to that which was seared into her mind from Tayan's projection of it. Toxte curled against Xessa's chest, and her head tilted down to rest against his. The half-dozen arrows that had pierced her were gone, and someone had washed them both – Ilandeh glanced reflexively back at the dark, scummy water in the bottom of the offering pool. Her stomach heaved and she swallowed sour spit.

No amount of washing could prevent the swelling of their bodies as rot set in, nor the sickly-sweet odour of corruption that hung around them. Tayan's arms came around Ilandeh's waist and he clung, tight enough to squeeze the breath from her on a long exhalation of hurt. She was bruised and torn and aching everywhere; she'd pushed herself beyond her limits for days, weeks, months now. It didn't matter. She stared at the bodies and was glad she couldn't see their faces. She didn't want to know what Xessa and Toxte looked like seven days dead in this silent, humid tomb.

'We should let them rest,' she whispered hoarsely. 'You're right, Tayan, they shouldn't be disturbed.'

He snuggled tighter against her. 'You understand,' he whimpered. 'You understand me, don't you, Ilandeh?'

She took one more look and then kissed the side of the Singer's head. 'Yes,' she murmured. 'I understand you now. I understand that you, a Tokob shaman and the youngest to ever be elevated to the shamanic conclave, had aspirations and ambitions that could never be fulfilled without this sort of power.'

'Yes,' he said, drawing away to look into her face. 'You see? You see, I knew it would be you. I knew out of everyone you would see the breadth of my vision, the scale and rightness of my ambition. That's why I brought you here; it's why I need you. Together, we can do such wonderful things.'

Ilandeh nodded and even found a smile for him. 'Believe me, I see your ambition. And I see that when you could no longer bend to accommodate the beliefs of those who hate you, that it became easier to break and then break them in turn.'

'What?'

'Warrior,' Xochi threatened without heat. 'Don't. Please.'

'Step back, Chorus Leader. This isn't between you and me. Omeata, do what you need to do.'

The Chorus Leader inhaled, sharp as obsidian. She began to protest and then cut herself off. Stepped backwards into the shadows until she was nothing but a whisper of a shape.

Tayan shoved out of Ilandeh's embrace, betrayal twisting his features, and stumbled into the tableau of corpses. Xessa's body toppled sideways and landed with a wet smack and a wave of stink rolled up strong enough that they both retched and covered their mouths and noses, backing away.

Ilandeh had a single glimpse of Toxte's face, his eyes sunken and his teeth and gums exposed in a bloated face. She gagged and grabbed Tayan by the wrist and dragged him away, towards the blocked-up colonnade where there might be a little fresh air wafting through the gaps.

Behind them, Omeata began a strange, warbling chant in a language neither Pallatolli nor Ixachitaan. A sacred language, probably, one Ilandeh had never heard. 'You can't!' Tayan tried. 'You mustn't harm the song. Leave it alone!'

The Whisper kept tugging on his arm and the closer they got to the meagre light, the more she could see his pallor and glittering eyes. A fine tremor ran through his hands; his fingernails and lips were bitten raw and the paint on his lip and chest was smeared and faded.

Ilandeh closed one nostril and then the other and blew to clear the stink of rot from her lungs. It seemed she blew the last of her restraint with it. Yes, he was broken, and yes, he was pitiful, but both those things just made him dangerous.

But she was dangerous, too, and not just with weapons. She grabbed the Singer's shoulders and shook him. 'What foulness is this, Tayan? What evil are you committing here? *You are a shaman*, dedicated to medicine and healing, and you keep rotting corpses in your home? *You are the Singer*, wielding a power that you were not born to and do not understand and which does not belong to any in Ixachipan, and what do you use it for? You twist its greatness and promise to your selfish purposes and then blame others when things go wrong.' She shook him again. 'You should be ashamed of yourself.'

Tayan lashed out with the song and Ilandeh screamed and collapsed to her bruised and aching knees yet again.

'*The magic chose me!*' he shouted, bending to yell it in her face, saliva dotting her cheeks. 'I am the Singer, the one true ruler of the Empire of Songs, of all Ixachipan. It chose me and I chose it and I will use it as I see fit. I will make Ixachipan worship me.' His voice dropped to a whisper, low and sultry and edged in malice. 'I will make the whole world love me, whether they will or no. I will spread my song into Zellipan and they will be fucking grateful for it, worshipping me instead of some dead fucking bird. But I will start with you.'

The song wrapped its fingers around Ilandeh and drew her up onto her feet again, stumbling helplessly forward. 'Look at them,' she tried while Omeata continued to sing and power, a different sort of power, began to press down on the source. Magic that wasn't song and yet contained a voice. A great, straining, yearning voice that wanted to cleave to the sky and stretch vast wings and return home at last. That wanted only to be free. It lifted Ilandeh too, countering the song's clenching greed. 'Look at Xessa's rotting body and tell me that is love,' she insisted.

'It is,' Tayan said. 'It is proof of my devotion. As you will be devoted to me. My devoted little Whisper.'

Ilandeh tensed every muscle and still took another step forward, reluctant, inevitable. 'What are you doing?' she gasped as he took her jaw in his hand and smiled again. Revulsion filled her. 'Get off me. Let me *go*.'

'You will love me,' Tayan growled, his fingers clenching as he manipulated the song. Gold burst in his face and arms, so bright that it lit up the room, brighter even than the spears of sunlight through the wall. 'You will love me because I say you will. Because if I can feel the truth of it from someone like you, someone whose every breath is a lie and whose very purpose is to be bent and broken to the will of others, then I can *make everyone love me.*'

'Holy lord, that's enough. You shouldn't over-exert yourself,' Xochi said and crossed the room to touch his shoulder. Tayan twitched and his song flickered, just enough for Ilandeh to wrestle her way free. Her stomach clenched on emptiness, bile souring her throat and the back of her tongue.

'Everyone who was important to you already did love you, Tayan,' she said with effort, her tremors lending a vibration, a vulnerability, to her voice. 'Lilla, Xessa, Toxte, Tiamoko. Malel and her God-born. You were so loved. So very loved. Why could that not be enough for you?'

'Because they left me,' he said and the gold in his skin dimmed and then faded completely. He sounded very young, and very alone. 'They left me in that cave in the hill with a fucking Drowned. They didn't come for me when the Melody appeared. I was no one; I was unimportant because I'm not a fighter. And then I came here and was still nothing.'

He blinked and vulnerability twisted into malevolence. 'My spirit guides abandoned me. Malel refused me. And Lilla didn't claim me. Everything that has happened is his fault.' He flung out an arm to point at the corpses. 'And their fault. They did this. They did all of it. I meant nothing to anyone. *But I refuse to be nothing any longer.*'

'Oh, Tayan,' Ilandeh breathed.

He grabbed her arms, his mood switching again. 'I can still fix it,' he babbled. 'I can fix everything. I'll heal the song and join it with Malel and Nallac and Mictec and we'll all be together. Malel will respond to me again, I'll visit the Realm of the Ancestors and Xessa will forgive me, and—'

'The song does not belong to you. You are the last Singer of the Empire of Songs, Tayan. It's time to let it go. Let the Zellih god return to Zellipan. Let there be quiet for a while. Wouldn't that be nice? To sit in the silence? To be quiet and still?'

'Silence?' Tayan choked. 'Do you know what happens when there is nothing but silence? Do you know who visits you? The dead. The dead visit you.'

'Yes,' Ilandeh agreed heavily, 'that they do. And so they should.'

'No. I will not see the dead except on my terms. I will not lose the song. And I will not be manipulated by a fucking half-blood with a lying tongue. Xochi, kill her.' Tayan shoved Ilandeh and she staggered backwards and then gasped as the Chorus Leader's spear rammed up under her salt-cotton and into her back. The obsidian spearhead scraped over her lower ribs and then bit deep.

'Tay—' she croaked. Her fingers spasmed for the Singer, but for all his madness, he had the reflexes of a paranoid Tlaloxqueh vision dancer who hadn't slept in three days. He was already halfway across the source, backing rapidly from Ilandeh and Omeata and from the corpse of the friend of his heart.

Xochi pulled her spear out with a shocked gasp, as if she hadn't meant to do it – or as if she'd been commanded by the song. Ilandeh grunted and rocked on her feet, tasting blood. And then Xochi was stepping around to face her and the Whisper let her, refusing to draw the knife in her belt even now.

There was anguish on the warrior's face as she shoved her spear into Ilandeh's hands. 'Finish it,' she breathed. 'End the lie. I can't do it. He's my *Singer*.'

He was mine before he was yours, she wanted to say, but didn't. She concentrated on tightening her hands on the spear instead.

'Where is everyone? Why is the pyramid empty?' she demanded, woozy enough that this seemed like the perfect moment to ask.

'High Feather Atu sent everyone away yesterday. They're heading for the coast of Chitenec.'

Ilandeh grunted and then coughed. 'Corridor to the sea,' she mumbled and Xochi nodded. 'Chorus Leader,' she managed, inclining her head.

Xochi touched belly and throat. 'Chorus Leader,' she answered.

One side of the Whisper's mouth turned up in a bloody grin and then she followed Tayan across the source, trying her best to ignore the blood, hot and sticky, that ran down her back and thigh.

'You told me to come home, Tayan,' she managed as Omeata's singing grew more frantic, more raucous, and the pressure in the source continued to rise. The song was squirming and thrashing, searching for a way out. Or maybe that was the Sacred Bird. Or Tayan. Or Ilandeh herself. 'You were going to *be* my home, as I would have been yours.'

'Back off, half-blood scum. You think to class yourself as my equal? You are nothing but a tool. Your arrogance is your downfall. Remember your modesty and the truth of your blood. Remember—'

Tayan's foot came down on nothing and he squeaked, an absurd sound part-surprise, part-anticipation of pain, and tumbled backwards into the offering pool, sending up a splash of stinking, scummy water. Ilandeh stepped into the pool after him and left the spear on the edge, drawing her knife.

'No. No! Get away from me, you don't understand, you don't see what I see. *We can have it all.*'

'You're the only one who wants it all, Tayan, and not even that would make you happy. The rest of us, we just wanted to be free. To be accepted. Acknowledged as people with thoughts and feelings and abilities. You could have given us all that; you could have remade the world so that it included us. Instead you chose to perpetuate a lie. You chose, Tayan of Tokoban.' Grief choked her, or maybe it was death. 'You chose this.'

She knelt, straddling his waist in the filthy water.

'*You keep telling yourself that,*' he screamed, and then, incomprehensibly, 'Only a Pecha can end the Pechaqueh.'

Despite herself, she hesitated, her thoughts slow. Lightheaded. 'What is that supposed to mean?'

'That's what they said, that's what the ancestors told me back in Tokoban. When I looked for a way forward, a way of peace. They said, "only a Pecha can end the Pechaqueh". But you're not a Pecha, so you can't kill me. You can't destroy everything I've accomplished. I won't let you.'

He pushed against her, song and hands both and one far more effective than the other. Once again, Ilandeh fell still and obedient under his magic.

'You won't hurt me. You can't hurt me,' Tayan babbled, thrashing in the stinking water. 'I am your Singer. *I own you.*'

She twitched and then jerked, filling with a hot, seeping anger. 'Omeata?' she called and glanced over to see the Bird-form flail a hand. She didn't know what that meant unless it was a plea for more time, so she put the Zellitli from her mind. Despite his words, Tayan deserved the deepest depth of her compassion. Surprisingly, it wasn't hard to give.

'Hush, my friend,' she breathed. 'Neither of us is Pechaqueh, except, perhaps, in our hearts. Despite it all, at least for me. But it doesn't matter. Whatever that prophecy meant, we're not the ones to fulfil it. Leave that to future generations.' She cupped his cheek and leant down. 'But in one thing you're right. I am a liar. I have lied my entire life, and I have been lied to. I have tried to forget one half of my blood in favour of the other. I believed I was worthy, or at least that I could become worthy, and worth something, if I just worked hard enough. That was a Pechaqueh lie, and one that you perpetuated. You have forgotten Malel, Shaman Tayan. You have forgotten your home, Tokob Tayan. You have forgotten those who love you, husband and friend Tayan.'

'No. Don't! It is my song, mine! I can do anything, be anyone, save everyone! You have to let me—'

'And I lied to myself, here in this very source not so long ago. I told myself I wouldn't kill anyone else today. Remember Malel now, Tayan, and ask her forgiveness, as I will ask mine of Nallac for what I am about to do.'

'Ilandeh? Ilandeh, there's a holy Setat. Ilandeh?' There was no reverence in Xochi's voice, only terror. 'What do I do?'

'Enough,' Tayan yelled, gold rushing through his skin for the last time. 'You will love me, you have to love me. I order you to love me! *I order you*—'

The obsidian slid into the hollow of his neck with obscene ease and stole the words, the lies, and the breath with which to speak them. 'I'm sorry it has to be this way,' Ilandeh said as the magic thrashed and beat at her, the song shrieking and whirling and rising into a horrified scream of denial, its Singer too panicked to use it against her. Another song rose, too, a shrieking song within the very source and the thud of running feet getting closer.

Ilandeh waited as long as she could, until those thuds fell silent because whoever made them had leapt from the edge of the offering pool towards her, and then she threw herself off Tayan's body and, twisting, thrust upwards. A move she'd watched once, and abhorred, when Eja Xessa had performed it at the Swift Water in Tokoban. A move that had torn at her spirit at the time.

One that saved her now.

The Drowned bore her down into the water and everyone, it seemed, was screaming: Tayan's a hoarse, wheezing denial; Ilandeh's and Xochi's both piercing and full of spirit-terror; and the holy Setatmeh own, a choking, song-laden screech. Her knife had taken it low in the belly and on, downwards to the groin, a rip from which its guts fell as it thrashed on top of her, limbs battering and gills flapping madly.

She had her hand under its chin, forcing its teeth away from her flesh, stabbing and hacking with her knife. Almost, Ilandeh thought she heard Xessa's strange, huffing laughter echoing through the source. Almost, she saw the glint of approval in those haughty eyes.

And then the song stopped. Its raging clangour cut off mid-note, leaving a taut silence like the air after a thunderclap. Tense with waiting. But not because the Singer was dead. Not yet.

Ilandeh kicked the Drowned off her. Tayan was breathing in little bubbling gasps, pawing at the wound and trying to stuff his blood back in. The Setatmeh claws raked her arm; she cut its wrist and hand with her knife until it curled away from her.

'The song is over, Tayan, for you and for the Empire. The Zellih Sacred Bird is being freed. You could have lived to see the world change in truth. You could have understood the wonder of it, been a part of it. I bet you'd have been so curious about the possibilities if you hadn't become all this. If you hadn't lost yourself.'

Tayan reached for her face and despite herself Ilandeh let him, his hand slick and hot and sticky with blood.

'I think you tried to hold it all together,' she murmured when it was clear he couldn't speak. Next to them, the holy Setatmeh flailing lessened. Green blood added its own viscous mess to the slime of water around them. 'But in the end, your fear overcame your judgement. Those with disproportionate power are always the most afraid; they know they'll face justice at the hands of the oppressed eventually.' She took a breath and sat back on her heels, Tayan's hand falling from her cheek to splash into the water. Omeata's voice was a skirling wail, small in the endless silence of the song.

Ilandeh laughed without humour. 'Ah, Tayan, ignore me. Who am I to tell you where you went wrong? Even if my past was blameless, who the fuck am I to speak to your life? We all make our own choices and live with our own mistakes. That's what living is. At least now everyone will get an equal chance at that.'

She brushed his hair back from his cheek. 'I am what others have made me. If I cannot be of one blood or accepted as a whole person, I must serve the needs of both. As for you, my old friend, may Nallac guide you to safety. You seem tired, Tayan. Perhaps you should rest.'

She stood then and climbed back out of the pool. He'd live a little longer, and she didn't want to have to leave him to die alone, but she knew what came next. Xochi was looking down at Singer and Setat with the air of someone who'd been kicked in the head.

'It's so quiet,' she breathed. 'It's . . . it's so quiet.'

'It is quiet, which means what? Which means what, Chorus Leader?'

'That Pechaqueh will be coming to take the magic,' Xochi said slowly. She looked at Ilandeh and away, looked at Omeata shimmering and sweating and screeching her divine words.

'Stand with me until it's done,' the Whisper pleaded. 'Stand against them. For all who would be free. For the truth you learnt here today. Please, Xochi. Stand with me.'

The Chorus Leader wavered and for one heady instant, Ilandeh thought she'd convinced her. And then she shook her head, wide-eyed. 'I can't. I can't let this— I'm Pechaqueh. I'm sorry, it's too much, I can't let you,' she started. Ilandeh nodded weary acceptance and drove her knife into the woman's belly, doubling her over, then flipped it in her hand and swiped it across her throat on the upstroke.

'Forgive me, Chorus Leader. Your dedication was exceptional.'

Xochi flailed and Ilandeh stepped out of range, dizzy with silence and loss of blood and as many shimmering regrets as there were feathers on the Bird-form's huipil.

'Hurry up, Zellitli,' she shouted as she reclaimed Xochi's spear from the pool's edge. 'I'll buy you as much time as I can, but it may not be long.' She contemplated telling Omeata she was dying, but what was the point? Why tarnish her triumph? Why admit she was the one to have stolen her life? Though it was a lie, like so much else, maybe Omeata would die thinking Ilandeh had helped her.

She spent a moment in silent contemplation of the dead ejab, holding her breath as she bent and rummaged, and then she left the source and limped along corridors and down steps to where the first hint of daylight stretched from the distant doorway. Then she waited. She waited for the Pechaqueh to come, first to aid the Singer, and then to fight each other for the magic to take his place.

Obedient and expendable, Ilandeh waited, armed with a spear, a knife, and a wrist-guard full of poisoned darts and blowpipe gifted her by Xessa and Toxte. And as expected, one by one they came, and one by one she fought them and killed them, both yearning for and dreading the arrival of a particular, well-beloved form.

It wasn't Pilos who came to kill her in the end. It was High Feather Atu. Nallac knew how he'd managed to extricate himself from the frenzy before the wall – the sounds of combat were at a shrill pitch she'd never heard before – but suddenly there he was, command fan lending him height and monstrousness in the half-light of the pyramid.

'No closer,' Ilandeh rasped, moving into clear space away from the corpses she'd made. So many corpses, despite her promise. 'It's over. The song is over. Let there be peace, High Feather. Let's all just stop.'

'I never trusted you,' Atu spat. 'I trusted Pilos, and he vouched for you time and again. I should never have listened to him.' He rushed her then, armed with a splintered, headless spear that would still kill her if it reached her flesh.

Ilandeh backed up, let the darkness swallow her and the distant sunlight outline him. She was still bleeding and she was so very, very tired, but far behind her Omeata was still fucking singing and the pressure was still fucking building and the godsdamned Sacred Bird still hadn't clawed its way free. And until it did, she couldn't let anyone into the source.

'Please don't,' she tried and he lunged. Ilandeh parried on instinct, a little slow but effective – just – and struck back. Slow again, easily deflected. With the light behind him she couldn't see the glint of teeth as he grinned, but she heard the sharp exhalation of triumph. A single exchange and he knew he'd won.

I killed Tayan. I killed Xochi. I killed a fucking holy Setat. I can kill him.

She could; she just didn't want to.

'Atu—' He attacked again, moving with a speed born of terror. Not of her: his world was shattering around him and someone, anyone – him? – needed to take the magic so that it might continue. The splintered spear ripped open Ilandeh's upper arm, an ugly raking gouge more blunt force than sharp point.

The Whisper wheezed out a breathy shriek, smashed the spear up and to the side, and stabbed High Feather Atu high in the chest. Her spear caught in salt-cotton, punching him off his feet but not penetrating the armour. He crumpled with a pained grunt, hit the wall, and pushed himself upright again.

Ilandeh took the opportunity to scurry backwards, tripping over corpses and moving farther into the dark. It couldn't be much longer. *It couldn't.*

Atu slumped against the wall a second time and she wondered whether he was carrying a concealed wound. She prayed he'd stay down. He didn't.

I just need to keep him out of the source.

She kept moving, only fighting when he charged her and forced an exchange, backing up as slowly as she could.

'It's over,' she tried again when they were three corridors and one flight of stairs from the source. 'Just stop.' She scored a puncture wound to his cheek that scraped off teeth; his return strike sliced a rent in her kilt and shaved hair and flesh from the outside of her thigh.

In the end, with the pressure building to an overwhelming force in her ears and on her skin, Ilandeh turned and ran for the source. Ran from the pain and the promise of more. Lightheaded and dizzy, she fled the High Feather and left his outraged bellow to stir the air behind her.

Xochi had made it into the corridor before succumbing and Ilandeh slumped opposite her, steps from the source's entrance with blood painting her skin and nothing to see in the gloom but death and crimson. Bright as the tail feather of a macaw.

Her heart was stuttering in her ears as she blinked owlishly into the light-speckled source and saw Omeata, arms outflung and back arched into an impossible curve, shimmering and sweating and screaming her words. Tayan, to her surprise, had dragged himself from the pool and sprawled on his belly, hand outstretched towards the Bird-form as if to stop her.

Ilandeh faced back into the darkness of the corridor and saw Atu's slow, gliding approach. She sobbed out a breath and gripped her spear and then slid down the wall as her legs gave out.

It didn't matter.

With a ringing cry loud enough to shake spiderwebs and plaster dust from the walls, the Sacred Bird of Zellipan burst from its cage and rose into the sky. Ilandeh's ears popped and then popped again as the pressure that had been building over the great pyramid suddenly lifted. A door opened; a god released. Its presence vanished from earth and air and sky and blood, taking its magic with it. The world shifted and settled, everything the same; everything different.

Atu halted and then went to his knees, head bowed under the impossible weight of feathers.

It was over. The distant roar of battle stuttered and then failed as the Zellih, presumably, felt the freeing of their god and did as Omeata had promised: stepped back from killing. As they gave the Pechaqueh a victory that meant nothing in the absence of the song. The silence was profound. A silence unheard in Pechacan in centuries. Until somewhere up on the pyramid's summit, a quetzal sang its high-low, high-low song.

And in the darkness and in the blood – her darkness, her blood – Ilandeh grinned.

THE SINGER

I am the song. I am the Singer and the song. I am the Empire and its ruler. I am Tayan and I will bring peace. I will bring the holy Setatmeh back to health and strength. I will bring all the world under my song.

The song is no more, Tayan. It is over.

Zama, or Omeata, or whatever your name is? You've stolen it, haven't you? You've stolen my song? You will GIVE. IT. BACK.

Have I? It was already stolen, along with the god who sang it. I have simply returned both to my people. It is a restoration of Zellih religion to Zellipan. And I do not have the power or the magic to give you a god, even if I wanted to.

We'll hunt it down. We'll hunt it and catch it and harness its magic. Its song will be my song.

Then we will be waiting. But not for you, I think. I think you should make peace with yourself, your past, and any gods who still listen.

You'd be wise to do the same! You're dying, you know. Ilandeh killed you. You'll never see your home again and your Sacred fucking Bird will never thank you.

It is a god, Tayan. It doesn't need to thank me. And I know. I knew the moment she did it and I am grateful only that she chose a poison that allowed me to live long enough to see the

Sacred Bird free. It is only fair; she has been treated poorly, and we have ravaged Ixachipan to reach this moment. I am only sad she did the same to Huenoch. They were my child and they will die afraid, if they have not already fallen. But what about you? What about Malel?

Malel? I am the Singer. I rule Ixachipan. I brought us to victory and . . . and Malel is. Malel is . . . do you think she listens still, even now? If, if I said I want to go home, do you think she'd listen?

I think all you can do is ask, Tayan of Tokoban, called the stargazer. But she is a god. Her mercy is as vast as her wrath, I expect. Pray she listens with the former. And for what it's worth, and though I am no doubt alone among my people in this, I forgive you. And I think Ilandeh did, too.

I . . . truly?

Truly. Ah, do not weep, shaman. Pray.

Malel? Malel, I want to go home.

Malel?

Light glowed in the darkness, a golden shimmering form appearing, and at their feet spread a winding, spiral path. Tayan raced towards the figure, his hands outstretched, moving so fast he didn't even feel the snap of his spirit as the last of its frayed threads broke free of his flesh.

'Xessa? *Xessa!*'

The eja was waiting for him, a familiar smile and a familiar challenge in her narrowed eyes. She held up her palm and slowed his advance. 'You have much to atone for,' she signed and he halted, bewildered. Behind her on the path were the spirits of dogs gone before, who had waited and were now reunited. Not Ossa, though; not yet.

'Atone?' he asked. Beneath the path on which they stood curled another, and it led downwards. Tayan's eyes followed it until it vanished far below and then he turned back to her and reached out; she stepped away.

'Xessa?' His signing of her name was small, vulnerable. Her eyes narrowed still further.

'Don't pretend ignorance or play on my emotions. You must face what you've done. You must make amends. I'll be waiting afterwards, but you have to do this now. Go and be brave, Tay. Be strong as you never managed to be in life.'

'Go where?'

She pointed to the downwards path. The path to the Underworld.

'How long?'

She pursed her lips and then shrugged. 'As long as it takes to atone,' she signed slowly.

'I don't understand. I tried to help everyone. I want to come with you. Please let me come with you.'

'Not yet.'

Tayan clenched his fists. 'I said, *I'll come with you*,' he growled.

The eja took a step forward, facing his threat with one of her own, and her dogs came with her. And then so did Toxte and his beloved Ekka, appearing as if from nowhere. 'And that is why you cannot come yet,' she signed with more patience than he'd ever seen from her. 'You must learn why what you did was wrong.'

Xessa put her head on one side and there was little of mercy or forgiveness in her expression. But there was love. There'd always been love and there always would be, perhaps, if he tried hard enough to deserve it. She nodded as if coming to a decision. 'You'll be gone a long time, I think, Tay. But I'll be waiting for you to come back.'

He hesitated, hope blooming. 'You'll wait; you promise?' She nodded. 'Why?'

Her smile, beloved and familiar and forgotten, went crooked. 'Because they made us both into monsters. And you shouldn't have to suffer that alone.'

EPILOGUE

'There's someone at water-temple one asking for you. Wouldn't leave a name. Said they'd wait as long as it took.'

Lilla looked up from the basket he was very badly weaving and frowned, glad of the excuse to put it to one side. He was learning to compensate for his maimed hand, but he'd little enjoyed weaving when he had ten fingers, let alone now.

He collected his spear and made his slow way downhill through the city, Ossa pacing at his side with his head and his tail raised. Tokob, Yaloh, and Axib waved from the market as he passed by and Lilla waved back.

The pyramids had been the first structures to come down, but there weren't enough people yet to build anything in their place, even with the daily arrival of more. Mostly Tokob, even after all this time, but not all. Too many people had no memories, or awful memories, of the lands they were born in – if they had even been that lucky. Thousands were of mixed heritage or could claim a tribe only by virtue of their parents having been born in their ancestral land. And thousands more simply wanted a fresh start far from any place they'd ever known. A lot of them ended up in Tokoban.

The rubble from the destroyed pyramids had been stacked,

and each day a stream of people carried loads of it uphill and dropped it into the abandoned mine pits. He skirted one of the piles now, Chitenecah and Tlaloxqueh and Xentib filling their baskets and chattering and laughing as they did. It would take more Star cycles than he had left to fill those caverns, and doing so would never repair the womb of Malel or its magic. They did it anyway. It had become a new type of prayer, one common to all peoples and all gods. Lilla's hand rose to his temple, where a ghost had just licked her thumb and pressed it – or perhaps it was just a strand of hair tickling his skin.

The corner of his mouth quirked up anyway, but then Ossa's demeanour changed: they were approaching the Swift Water. The wag dropped from his tail and his head came up higher, ears ever-moving and sensitive nose twitching.

'Easy, boy,' Lilla said and then clicked him into rest. A dozen ejab had arrived over the last half-year and they'd taught Lilla all the correct commands, including those that were only ever used at the river – and only so that he knew how to calm the dog, not use him.

Thanks to Ossa's prowess in other areas, there were three litters of puppies within the limits of the city and the ejab who'd returned were beginning to train them, borrowing Ossa to show them how it was done, though never at the water's edge.

That was an inviolable rule and Lilla was willing to enforce it, with violence if necessary. Ossa had done more than his share of fighting. He'd never risk his life again.

Yet that threat, too, was growing weaker by the day. Even though there had been Drowned in Tokoban before it came under the song, they'd still somehow been connected to its magic. But now that there was no song at all, many had died. Nearly all the Lesser Drowned, as far as they could tell. The rest were thin and weak, sickly. The ejab and shamans estimated they'd die out before the end of the next Star cycle. Until then, life went on as it had before the wars, with water rationing, and water-temples, and people risking their lives with only spirit-magic and dogs, spears, and nets to protect them.

Lilla walked past the water-temple's entrance to the figure sitting in its shade, who scrambled to their feet at his approach.

And halted, the grain of the spear shaft suddenly pressing into his palm. The thumb of his other hand rubbed over the stumps of his missing fingers, a nervous habit, and Ossa rumbled a growl and stepped between him and the shadowy figure.

Ilandeh stepped into the light. 'Fang Lilla. I have heard that Tokoban takes in all strays and refugees as long as they're not Pechaqueh. I—'

'You are Pechaqueh.'

'Half-Pechaqueh. Half-Xentib. I thought you might find a place for me. I can hunt and trade and speak Pallatolli, and I believe the Zellih are your friends now, more or less. I can fight and kill. I can lie and manipulate. I can cook and I can teach young warriors a thousand dirty tricks. I cannot build a wall or a house, and I cannot weave material or make pots. I can promise to learn to do those things if you need me to. I would like to help you rebuild the Sky City in any way that I can.'

Her voice was quiet and she met his eyes without flinching. He didn't know if what he saw was sincere; he didn't know how to trust her.

'And if you don't want me here, I will leave.'

'I don't want you here.'

She jerked as if he'd punched her. She was thin and scarred, pale as if she'd lain sick or injured out of the sun for months. There was a wildness around her mouth and eyes more usually seen in spirit-haunted ejab. 'I understand. Malel bless you, Fang Lilla.'

High above the city, above the great scar in the hill where songstone had been dug and a Drowned had once been held captive, an eagle screamed. Ilandeh flinched and turned away.

A muscle flickered in the Tokob jaw. 'It's nice, isn't it?' he said abruptly.

She halted, facing away. 'What is?'

'The silence of the song.' Ilandeh turned and nodded cautiously. 'Do you know how that silence came to be that day in the Singing City?' Another nod, even more cautious, and a single step out of range. Lilla rubbed over the ache in his heart with the heel of his hand. 'Yes. I thought you might. But when we took the pyramid after, I looked for you and you weren't there.' He scratched behind Ossa's ear when the dog pressed against his thigh, rolling his eyes to look up at him.

'I think that's a story I need to hear, whether or not I wish to.'

'I will trade it for the story of Spear Pilos and High Feather Atu, if I may make such a request,' Ilandeh murmured, her voice rough. 'The latter I left alive, in the end. The former . . . well, as I said, a trade.'

'You were in love with Pilos, weren't you?' Lilla asked, perhaps a little cruelly.

'I loved him. I was not in love. . . He died well?'

Lilla sighed and looked uphill to where, to no one's surprise and least of all his, Ekon was watching and waiting. Spear in hand. Still as a jaguar on the path amid the bustle of the market.

'Is all well, kitten?' the Chitenecatl signed.

'All is well,' he signed back. 'Don't go anywhere, though.'

Ekon's shoulders relaxed. 'I love you. I'm here. Whatever you need.'

Lilla breathed and scratched again between Ossa's big, triangular ears and then looked back at Ilandeh and gave a single nod. 'He died well,' he said eventually. 'He died with conviction.'

The Whisper made a noise he pretended not to hear. 'Come on then,' he said quietly, looking at his dog and then his lover, but not at her. 'Let's go home.'

ACKNOWLEDGEMENTS

This book was a beast that fought back more than once, and two people deserve a special mention for helping me draft, plot, and wrestle it into shape: Harry Illingworth, who doesn't just agent like an absolute boss, but read and provided feedback when I was convinced I'd messed up the structure and reveals; and Leife Shallcross, who helped me hammer out the characterisation and plot twists and controlled my wilder impulses to melodrama. *The Dark Feather* is a much better novel because of you both.

Thanks as always to the writers of the Bunker, and also to Illers' Killers, the chat group made up of many of my agency sibs. We're pretty sure Harry's either mortified or deeply concerned we're unionising, but somehow he keeps on advocating for us anyway.

Big thanks to the HarperVoyager team new and old: editorial – Elizabeth, Chloe and Laura; publicity – Emily and Maud; and art design – Stephen Mulcahey.

A note of gratitude to David Bowles, whose ongoing cultural expertise has been invaluable in the crafting of this trilogy and its myth and societies, and to the Fantasy Hive and all the other book bloggers/grammers/tokers/tubers who championed *The Songs of the Drowned*.

My great and heartfelt thanks to Joseph Balderrama, who narrated this trilogy with his whole heart and guts, despite the sex scenes, and who brought my beloved characters to life in ways I couldn't imagine. It's truly wonderful to hear their voices.

All my love and gratitude to Mark, Mum and Dad, Sam, Rhys and Morgan, Lisa and Simon, and all my extended family and friends, for dragging me away from the laptop when I needed a break, and pushing me back to it when my procrastination got out of hand.

And to Bailey the miniature poodle. We didn't have a dog when I first wrote Ossa and so I didn't really understand how richly rewarding – and endlessly exasperating – having an animal companion could be. I do now. Thanks, buddy. You're a monster.

And to the readers: I hope you enjoyed reading this series as much as I loved writing it. I'll see you again soon for another adventure.